# O F

# L O V E

# A N D

# L I F E

Three novels selected and condensed
by Reader's Digest

# OF
# LOVE
# AND
# LIFE

The Reader's Digest Association Limited
LONDON

The Reader's Digest Association Limited
11 Westferry Circus, Canary Wharf, London E14 4HE

**www.readersdigest.co.uk**

For information as to ownership of copyright in the material of
this book, and acknowledgments, see last page.

Printed in France

# CONTENTS

# SARAH HARRISON
## flowers Won't fax

Isla and Jen have someone in common—Richard. Richard is Isla's husband and Jen's lover. The two women could not be more different. Isla is a popular and elegant actress while Jen is an artistic and scatty single parent. When a chance meeting brings the two women together, there begins an unlikely friendship that is to survive beyond a tragedy worse than either can imagine.

# chapter one

'**B**ASTARDS!'

'I'm sorry?' asked Isla politely.

'Bastards!' repeated the cab driver, his neck reddening.

This time Isla confined herself to a small, sympathetic sigh. She sensed that the driver's outburst was due as much to a well-mulched misanthropy as to any immediate exterior stimulus, and didn't want to attract or aggravate it in any way. All through the 'Where There's a Will' lunch at the Café Royal, during which a doughty Labour baroness had given out awards to disabled high-achievers, she had smiled and reacted and listened with focused thoughtfulness to a series of moist-eyed carers, neighbours and family members. It had been a cause of almost hysterical relief when one of the award-winners, a wheelchair athlete with hair extensions, had placed a hand on her knee.

'This is just triffic,' the cabbie announced, and switched off the engine.

The northbound traffic in Regent Street was stationary. The midsummer heat, rancid with fumes, vibrated thickly around the cab, which was inauspiciously positioned between a bus and a coach full of tourists.

The cabbie wound down his window to its fullest extent and leaned out. 'Oi!' He bellowed at some unseen figure further down the street. 'What the fuck's up, mate?'

As a drama student in the early seventies, Isla had had a brief relationship with a Mancunian Buddhist, the legacy of which was a knowledge of relaxation techniques. Now she settled the length of her spine evenly against the back of the seat, uncrossed her legs and allowed her

9

hands to rest loosely on her thighs. She took a deep breath and closed her eyes as she slowly exhaled.

But the Mancunian's long-ago lessons were no match for a London cabbie with a serious beef. The loud exchange through the open window continued for the best part of a minute, followed by a more muted but equally intrusive burble of complaint which Isla was too polite to ignore.

'. . . don't give a monkey's that the rest of us got homes to go to and livings to earn.'

Isla opened her eyes, and caught the choleric glance of the driver in the rearview mirror.

'It's too bad,' she agreed.

'I mean, you're going to Hampstead. I live in Stockwell. That lot'—he indicated the coach to their right—'to *Phantom*, *Saigon* and all points west, and what are our chances?' He made a gesture to indicate she shouldn't dream of answering. 'Don't get me started.'

Isla crossed her legs and laced her fingers together. It was stifling in the cab. She gazed out through the glass, transferring her attention to the neighbouring bus. Some passengers were cutting their losses and getting off to walk. One woman on the long seat near the door sat slewed round, her chin resting on her crossed arms, eyes narrowed, cat-like, in the glare of the sun. She had a square jaw, a wide mouth, and the sort of thick, coarse blonde hair that positively flourishes on inexpert chopping. Lucky thing . . . Isla adjusted her gaze to her reflection and touched her own sleek black bob, every delicately snipped and chemically enhanced inch of which set her back several pounds.

'Here we go,' said the driver, with grim relish. 'Here come the excuses.'

Two policemen in short-sleeved shirts and fluorescent waistcoats, and carrying walkie-talkies, were advancing between the rows of traffic, stooping to talk to drivers as they went. The approach of hard information seemed to cheer the cabbie. He wound the window down again and welcomed one of them, a young man in his twenties, with a smile.

'Go on, surprise me. Lights at the Circus up the spout?'

'I'm afraid not,' said the policeman with scrupulous, bland politeness. 'I'm afraid we have a security alert. We've cordoned off the area.'

The cabbie mopped his face and neck. 'So what's the choice between getting blown to bits and dying of heat stroke, officer?'

'We're organising a diversion right now, mate, we'll get you moving again any minute.'

'Is that a minute as in a couple of hours, or as in this time tomorrow?'

The policeman smiled at Isla and she saw the split second of recognition. 'As in pretty soon.'

'Oh dear,' she said. 'Do you think we're in for a summer of this?'

'Let's hope not. Doesn't do anything for the tourist industry.' He tapped the roof of the cab and moved off.

'Bugger the tourists,' growled the cabbie. 'What about the workers?' As the traffic inched forward with an optimistic revving of engines, he added for good measure a final explosive: 'Bastards!'

When Jen saw the police approaching, she disembarked from the bus. It could only mean one thing. She wasn't about to join the rush back to Piccadilly Circus for the tube, but neither did she want to be stuck in a traffic jam. With no particularly clear plan she set off through the Burlington Arcade into Piccadilly, and then up past the Royal Academy to Green Park. A dense wedge of hot, agitated, would-be travellers packed the entrance to the tube, so she went into the park and sat down in the shade beneath a tree. She got out her bottle of Evian water—now slightly warm—undid the cap and took a long swig. She was going to be late back, but that might be no bad thing.

Jen had spent the day recharging her batteries at the pictures—first the Tate and then the Odeon Leicester Square. That was the one true perk about being self-employed—one had no need of terminally ill aunts or pressing root-canal work to provide a pretext for bunking off. In fact a person in the artistic line of business positively owed it to herself to play hooky from time to time.

She screwed the top back on the Evian and hiked down to lie flat on her back on the grass. The afternoon sun glittered between the leaves, and the irritable drone and blast of jammed traffic increased her sense of having escaped, for a second time in one day.

With which happy thought, Jen slept.

Richard Wakefield arrived in Selwyn Street only five minutes after his usual time of five o'clock, the Jag having made light work of the back roads between chambers and Crouch End. He was therefore not in the least surprised to find the house empty. Even when he was late, which was often (and with ample justification), Jen could be relied upon to be later, or to have forgotten that he was coming at all.

He had his key, of course, but decided to stay in the air-conditioned comfort of the Jag for a few more minutes before braving Number 65. There was a clarinet concerto on Radio 3, and the notes tumbled forth cool, liquid and civilised as chilled Pimms . . .

Richard gazed across the street at the house. He'd known at once that she wasn't there—the cats, Cain and Abel, were loitering outside, a sure sign that their mistress was not at home. As he sat with the engine running, the cats moved to the gate and stood there with their snakelike tails aloft, staring at him. Richard was more at home with dogs. Cats unsettled him, and these two treated him with a casual contempt which familiarity had done nothing to improve. Not, he observed, that this prevented them from materialising at his arrival in the expectation of access to the house. Richard took evil pleasure in keeping them waiting. In this his professional experience was of great assistance. He had met many Cains and Abels in his time, both in and out of the courtroom, and fancied he could outcool any of them, particularly when he held all the cards—and the key.

He loosened his tie just enough, and undid his collar button, surveying the long rows of terraced houses with a sort of guilty fondness. More happy hours than he could remember had been spent in Selwyn Street, but he was awfully glad he didn't have to live here. As with first-class air travel, it was space that made the difference. Especially undedicated, seldom-used space. In his own house, overlooking the heath in Hampstead, it was the acreage of lawn shaded by mature trees . . . the great, high-ceilinged hall with its leisurely curving staircase . . . the galleried landing with its many tributaries . . . the cool, leafy orangery . . . the library . . . all those tranquil, largely undisturbed expanses that enabled each occupant, even when the boys were there, to be unaware of the presence of others.

The last movement of the clarinet concerto rippled, swirled and crescendoed to its conclusion. A little reluctantly, Richard switched off the radio. He was already out on the pavement, car locked and tie straightened, when Keith Burgess rounded the corner on his push-bike. For a split second Richard considered making a fast getaway, but unfortunately Keith had already spotted him.

'Who-a!' cried Keith, putting a foot down on the kerb outside Number 65. 'If it isn't Rumple of the Bailey!'

'Good evening to you.' Richard crossed the road with long, unhurried strides and an air of urbane geniality. 'It looks awfully as if she's out.'

'She expecting you?'

'Probably not, but that doesn't mean anything.'

'Ah, our Jen . . .' Her lodger shook his head. 'A stranger to the diary.'

He nudged open the gate and pushed his bike up to the front door, propping it against the chipped windowsill, and fished his key out of his breast pocket. Richard watched him with scientific interest. Keith was a primary-school teacher who wore a nylon short-sleeved shirt, knitted tie and cycle helmet (a cagoule, Richard knew, would be neatly rolled in his saddlebag), and kept tropical fish in a tank on his chest of drawers. He was hopelessly naff and incorrigibly nice. Keith could only have been in his early thirties and yet he appeared to Richard to be sexless. However, this lack of any overt sexuality made him extremely safe, which was another reason why Richard was never less than civil to him.

'There we go,' said Keith, pushing the door and standing back with one arm extended in an exaggerated display of deference. 'Age before beauty.'

The cats trotted ahead, tails aloft, almost tripping Richard up. There were two bills and a circular on the mat. He picked them up and put them on the corner of the stairs as Keith followed, removing his helmet.

'Now then, who's for a cuppa?'

'No thanks.'

'I trust you'll forgive me if I do,' said Keith.

'Please . . .' Richard made a graceful, don't-mind-me gesture, and went into the living room, where he drew back the overlong calico curtains on their rattling wooden rings to their full extent. The room, now bathed in full sunlight, was like its owner—indifferently maintained, tousled to just this side of slatternly, but uniquely seductive. A room to sink down into, a room in which to remove one's shoes, loosen one's tie, and to let it all, as the slang had it, hang out.

Keith appeared in the doorway, a Garfield mug in one hand.

'I hate to leave you like this, but I must away upstairs.'

'Please,' said Richard again. 'You carry on.'

From an ingrained habit of caution Richard waited till he heard the door of the bedroom close before sinking down on the multicoloured sofa bed, his head at one end, his crossed ankles on the other. Jen's throws, shawls and cushions smelt faintly spicy, a mixture of joss sticks . . . a hint of vegetable korma . . . Morning Mist Body Splash . . . essence of Jen. He closed his eyes, cradled in the room's special atmosphere. He didn't have to look to see it in all its familiar detail, from the peonies in the white jug in the hearth to the brutal female nude on the wall to his left. The fireplace at this time of year was filled with giant pine cones from woods in southern France and flanked by the natural sculptures of silver-grey driftwood. On the chimney breast were a collection of masks, a dozen leering, slant-eyed faces in wood, ceramic, papier-mâché and metal, genial or malign according to one's mood. The wooden floor was painted cobalt blue and stencilled with creamy, lilylike flowers, but there were tufts of dusty cat hair drifting near the skirting board. The door, painted with a trompe-l'oeil second door that stood permanently ajar, was dappled with fingerprints, and the windows were smeary. The round beechwood table, the only furniture of any real value in the room, was home to a drawing board, piles of books, and a wicker basket overflowing with mail, opened and unopened. Brushes, sticks of pencil and charcoal stood in a bamboo vase. A plain calico screen was covered with photographs—mostly of Jen's daughter, Claudia, some of Cain and Abel, and a small group of Other People's Pets, the raw material of Jen's livelihood. An easel bearing an oil painting of a golden retriever stood near the window.

He lay on the sofa for about ten minutes and then went in search of the bottle of Bell's with which he made a point of supplying this plonk-swilling household. In the kitchen the cats were sitting on the gas boiler, facing each other but gazing his way, like ornaments on a dresser. Richard took the Bell's from its place between the chickpeas and the Italian rice, poured himself a generous shot and added a finger of cold water from the tap, splashing his jacket in the process. Tutting, he removed the jacket and hung it carefully over the back of Jen's prized Shaker chair, the only one in an otherwise undistinguished and unmatched junk-shop sextet.

Richard sat patiently, legs crossed, gazing out of the back door at the tangle of dog roses and rampant pelargoniums that overhung the turf in Jen's back garden. Generally speaking Richard disliked being kept waiting, and hated the arrogance implicit in unpunctuality. But with Jen it was different. Here, in the familiar snug seclusion of 65 Selwyn Street, he was perfectly content to wait.

The hall floor was made up of big black and white tiles, like a chessboard. Isla removed her shoes the moment she'd closed the door behind her and felt the coolness strike up through her tired feet and ankles. Was there, she wondered, any bliss to compare with that of taking off one's high heels at the end of a long, hot day . . . ?

She went into the library and pressed the button on the answering machine. The first voice was that of Marjory Dix in Bradenham.

'Hello . . . hello? Am I there? Sometimes your little tune plays and sometimes it doesn't, but I hope you can hear me now. I do hope your journey down won't be too atrocious, what with these beastly people up to their old tricks in London, but perhaps things will have cleared by then. Anyway, all the stuff you asked for is there, except for the aubergines which were simply *not* to be found. The entire country must be making ratatouille. The sweet peas are simply rioting. I've put a posy in the drawing room but left you to pick more if you want to. The Fylers told me to tell you—'

At this point Marjory was cut off, and called back. 'Sorry, my fault, butterfingers! The Fylers have confirmed for Saturday night, presumably you know what for. Not much else to report. See you tomorrow. Cheers to both.'

The second message was from her husband. 'Darling, this is me on the mobile, in the Tottenham Court Road. We seem to be caught up in the backwash from this infernal bomb scare. If it turns out I'm too late we'd better cut our losses and make an early start tomorrow. OK? See you soon.'

Isla stood quietly in the library, digesting this message as the tape whirred back on itself. The noble, rather sad eyes of her grandfather, General Henry William Munro, gazed down from his frame. She tried to assemble the calm dignity befitting the general's granddaughter and the colonel's daughter . . . But Tottenham Court Road? The machine reset itself with a beep, and she didn't bother to turn it off. She decided not to think too hard about the Tottenham Court Road.

Jen remembered the arrangement with Richard as she hopped off the bus in Crouch Hill at a quarter past seven. Remorsefully, she quickened her pace over the Broadway towards Selwyn Street. Her chronic unpunctuality, which she was the first to acknowledge, had the unfortunate side effect of invalidating genuine reasons for lateness.

She saw the Jag at once, parked in its usual place opposite her gate, though at this time of day it was surrounded by the more modest vehicles of Selwyn Street's other residents, home from work. It was funny the way people's cars began to look like them. Parked patiently at the kerb opposite Number 65, hemmed in by lesser vehicles, the Jag seemed, like its owner, a model of handsome, intelligently confined power and understated wealth.

Jen was practically running by the time she reached the gate, and cannoned into Richard coming the other way.

'Whoops!' He caught her shoulders, bracing them both.

'Sorry!'

'No need to be.'

'There was a bomb scare in the West End.'

'I know.'

Jen pushed open the gate. 'Have you had a drink?'

'I fear so. Look—' She stopped, looking over her shoulder. 'I really must go.' He tapped his watch, pulled a face. 'I'm awfully sorry.'

'Don't be, it's my fault. As usual.'

'Even you can't be blamed for the activities of the IRA. I'll be in touch one day next week.'

'OK.'

He pulled the gate to and kissed his hand to her. '*Au revoir* then.'

'See you.'

He walked away from her across the road, pointing his key briefly at the Jag to unlock it. She turned in the doorway to watch him drive away. He didn't look at her, but lifted his forefinger from the wheel as the Jag purred down Selwyn Street and away.

The ground floor of the house was full of the gravelly moan of Billie Holliday. Richard put down his briefcase and walked across the hall towards the back of the house. His wife was in the orangery, sitting in one Lloyd-loom chair with her stockinged feet up on another. The length and beauty of her legs still brought his heart into his mouth. Her elbows were on the arms of the chair, her fingers laced loosely round a misty glass of white wine. She turned towards him as he entered, her eyes dreamy with the music.

'Hello, you.'

'Hello. Sorry I'm late.'

'It doesn't matter. We'll go in the morning.' She took his hand and held it to her cheek. 'You did warn me.'

Richard went to the kitchen and came back with ice cubes in a tumbler, and a bottle of ginger beer. Isla watched him as he took the first few luxurious gulps, leaving a moustache of creamy bubbles on his upper lip. He was carrying a few extra pounds round the middle these days, but it quite suited him. The weight gave added physical presence to his great height. Here was a man of substance, in every respect. His bespoke suit—a dark grey with the faintest stripe—was rather creased, and he appeared to have tightened his tie carelessly, causing a slight tuck in one corner of his collar.

'You must be whacked,' she said.

'I wouldn't say that.' He bent to kiss her, his lips cool and damp from the ginger beer, then sat down heavily on the cane sofa, carelessly crunching the disarrayed cushions, and gave her his hot, secretive grin. He represented all that Isla liked in Englishmen—the solid confidence, the overgrown schoolboyishness which could be insufferable but which, when combined with intellect and charm, was irresistible.

'So tell me,' he said, 'how were the saintly sufferers?'

She laughed. 'Not all that saintly, you'll be disappointed to learn. One of them massaged my knee during the main course. Very uplifting.'

'For him, certainly.'

'Did I say it was a man?' For a split second she caught his shock. 'Your face is a study.'

'It was, though, wasn't it?'

'Of course.'

'Phew . . .' He took a swig. 'Only one never knows these days.'

**I**sla and Richard had bought the cottage in Bradenham five years earlier when Giles had first started at Hawtrey's, the exclusive and eccentric public school favoured by Richard. It had seemed a good idea to have a country bolt hole within easy reach of the school, and also of Richard's father's retirement home.

They referred to Brook End as a cottage but it was actually two cottages knocked through, by some enterprising and far-sighted former owner, to create a spacious house. Its long, low, amiable frontage overlooked a lane with only a minimum of through traffic, on the far side of which were the stately acres of The Bury, the property of Bill and Barbara Fyler. At the back of Brook End the garden was bordered on one side by the stream and on the other by a lovingly husbanded bank and hedge, full of wild flowers and birds' nests.

Beyond the end of the garden, as if to remind arriviste townies of the realities of rural life, could be glimpsed the steel turrets and angular overhead walkways of Norman Brake's grain silos. Norman was a noted misanthrope who, in common with thousands of others, had a soft spot for Isla. The lane circled Brook End, snuggled affectionately against the hedge, before widening past Norman's dilapidated farm buildings and climbing the gentle hill into Silver Street, Bradenham's main drag.

This was where Marjory Dix lived. At Number 41, Heron's Halt. She was someone who could truly be called 'a good woman'. She was in her early sixties, unmarried, house- and garden-proud, an upholder of family values with no family of her own, but surprisingly tolerant of 'the young', as she called them. Wherever community endeavour was, there was Marjory to be found, toiling cheerfully in her dirndl and Hush Puppies, seeking neither praise nor reward. She believed in neighbourliness in its broadest sense. When the Wakefields spent their first weekend at Brook End it was Marjory who had befriended them at once. She continued to play the part of *ex officio* caretaker and housekeeper to the extent that Isla had given her a key to the cottage and their London number. She wouldn't hear of payment, but they did their best to thank her with theatre tickets and bottles of wine. A few of the locals, the Fylers and Richard among them, laughed, not unkindly, at Marjory behind her back, but Isla refused to join in.

'She's a thoroughly nice person and I don't know what we'd do without her.'

'Employ someone we could dish out orders to without feeling guilty about it?' Richard would suggest, putting his arm round her shoulders to show he didn't mean to be cruel.

'Speak for yourself,' said Isla. 'I don't have any problem asking her to do things, and I honestly believe she considers it a pleasure.'

'And I, my darling,' said Richard, 'honestly believe that you underestimate the effect you have on people.'

This, Isla conceded, was probably true. She at all times resisted the idea of her own starriness, those qualities attributed to her by the press and public which ensured her a place in the hearts of both. She wasn't falsely modest, but there was a streak of canny Scots realism in her which told her that that way madness lay. She'd been a quite successful model, then moved into acting, and played toffish young women in assorted made-for-TV films and commercials. Her big break was as Sophie St George, the well-bred heroine of the long-running action series *Lady In Charge*. The part could not have been called demanding. Its chief prerequisites were A1 legs, unspoilt top-drawer looks, and perfect, rounded vowels, all of which Isla possessed. What she brought to the part in addition to these attributes was a humorous warmth and a sympathetic intelligence in her eyes as she warded off the half-serious advances of her partner, the lecherous rough diamond Jake Sparrow, played by Ned Braden. Ned was a ruggedly handsome bachelor, whose sexual ambivalence was a well-kept secret. Isla on the other hand had no secrets. Where other actresses complained that viewers were unable to distinguish between them and the parts they played, Isla happily admitted that, martial arts aside, she and Sophie St George were one and the same thing. Her adoring fans discovered this to be true as she opened fun days and fêtes, and supported a variety of good causes, all without losing her easy, diffident charm. She was that rare and priceless thing, a class act with the common touch.

Isla's modesty was genuine, for she felt she had much to be modest about. She was too much of a professional not to know by now what her assets were, but she also knew she had them by luck rather than skill or application. What she had learned to do was 'be herself' in the way that her mother had always advised. And if the self that was available on a particular occasion was not up to scratch she could effortlessly switch on the more appropriate one and put it through its paces.

It was this talent—or charm, in its magical sense—which had helped her forge a harmonious relationship with both her husband's former wives, and with the sons of the second, who even at six and eight had seemed to look down their noses at her and regarded her small store of celebrity as suspect. She persevered. She was never less than kind, but also withdrawn. As she went about her life with Richard she watched his mutinous offspring from the corner of her eye. Her instinct told her that small boys were like wild animals, shy and unpredictable, their aggression sparked by fear rather than hostility. So it made sense to move smoothly, avoid direct eye contact and raised voices: to do nothing, in fact, to activate the fight or flight mechanism. It worked. Slowly, they came round.

Now Giles and Marcus were both at Hawtrey's, completing their A-level and GCSE years respectively. Giles was smooth, lazy and ambitious. Marcus was clever and off the wall and didn't give a shit. Neither of the boys was expected to do particularly well in their exams, but this was not a source of great concern, either at home or at school. Richard had chosen Hawtrey's for the 'progressive' reputation gained by the founder, Quentin Hawtrey, in the late 1920s. Richard himself had been ruthlessly directed through Winchester and Cambridge to the Bar by his own father, with outstanding success and commensurate material rewards. But Richard was typically ungrateful, and was determined, via his own sons, to make some perverse point about personal fulfilment. Isla, as a childless third wife plucked from the domestically unstable ranks of show business, kept her counsel. Isla Munro was good at keeping quiet, and pondering things in her heart.

**D**inner at The Bury was considered locally to be something of an honour, but Bill and Barbara's style of hospitality did nothing to convey a sense of privilege. Drink was strong and free-flowing, food plain, plentiful and filling, and chairs capacious and comfy. The Fylers had several dogs. Bill kept springer spaniels as gun dogs, who were housed in kennels and a pen adjoining the barn. In a separate kennel, nearer the house, was an unpredictable Rhodesian ridgeback, Janus, an animal just waiting for some unsuspecting villain to trespass and make his day. But in fact neither the springers nor Janus were the problem, which lay with the two indoor dogs. Portia was an ancient Rottweiler with sagging upholstery and halitosis that could have halted a cruise missile. To be befriended by Portia over the pre-dinner drinks was to be exposed to slow torture by proximity. Pepe, Barbara's Jack Russell, was fighting fit, and made his typical entrance through the air at lap height, teeth bared, skimming from chair to knee at lightning speed, and coming to rest on whoever had the most expensive clothes.

'Thought you were coming down last night?' Bill said, pressing navy-strength gin on Isla and a large Bell's on Richard.

'There was a bomb scare in town and it made us both late, so we decided to cut our losses,' said Isla.

'Where was this bomb?'

'Suspected, only. In Oxford Street.'

Barbara entered from the kitchen. She wore a long Indian cotton dress in shades of brown, teamed with a cashmere cardigan. Pepe circled her legs intently as she shook peanuts inaccurately into a Limoges sugar basin.

'It was some bloody bomb scare held these two up,' announced Bill.

'What so-and-sos they are,' agreed Barbara. 'Pepe, no! Nut, anyone?'

Pepe's beady, sharklike eyes remained fixed on the nuts as they were dispersed. Isla declined. Richard took a handful but remained standing. Bill, Scotch in hand, hove alongside his guest for the usual bullish inquisition on the legal profession. Barbara sat down on the sofa by Isla.

'Poor old Portia's got the gutsache.'

'Poor love, what have you done with her?' asked Isla, looking deeply concerned to disguise her relief.

'She's in the washhouse, looking very sorry for herself, but best place for her. If she chucks up in there it's nothing a wodge of newspaper and a damp cloth can't handle.'

'I don't envy either of you.'

'That's dogs for you.' Barbara proffered the nuts again, restraining the quivering Pepe with her free arm.

'I won't, thanks. I'm saving myself for dinner. Now tell me,' went on Isla, touching Barbara's wrist lightly with her forefinger. 'How is Nell?'

Petronella was the Fylers' twenty-six-year-old daughter, a tall, raw-boned young woman who when put in a frock looked, as Richard succinctly put it, like an Aunt Sally, but on horseback became a Valkyrie.

'Nell's going great guns, I'm happy to say. She's got a flat in Swiss Cottage with Robert Scott-Chatham. Did you ever meet James and Angela?'

'I don't think so . . .' mused Isla.

'Nothing in it, she assures me,' Barbara went on doubtfully. 'This mixed sharing goes on all the time. Not that it's any business of mine any more what she gets up to. What about your two, Richard's two?'

'We're going over to the school tomorrow, and taking them out.'

'Do use the tennis court if you want to—it's only standing idle.'

'Thanks, that's very kind, we may well.'

'I'm going to slip away and check my greens,' said Barbara. To wish for an *al dente* vegetable at The Bury was to court certain disappointment. 'Don't let Pepe take any liberties.'

Bill replenished drinks all round. 'She told you about Nell sharing with the Scott-Chatham pillock?'

'Oh yes, she did. It sounds like a good arrangement.'

'That's just where you're wrong!' Bill jabbed an unlit cigarette in her direction. 'He's a prize toe rag. I don't want him sniffing round my daughter with his eye on the main chance.'

Richard covered his eyes in despair. 'Steady on, Bill—this is the nineteen nineties, mixed sharing isn't even new. And anyway, Nell's free and over twenty-one. What's your problem, for God's sake?'

Bill rounded on Isla. 'You know what I'm getting at, don't you?'

She shook her head. 'I hate to let you down, but I think you're overreacting, I really do. Barbara seems to be taking it perfectly in her stride.'

'Traitor!' Bill made a wild gesture which slopped Scotch on the priceless but already heavily stained Persian rug. 'You take their side against me? Me, your ever-genial and eternally lustful host?' Thoroughly wound-up by this tirade, Pepe barked noisily.

'Shut up, William.' Barbara appeared in the doorway. 'You're upsetting the dog.'

Bill swallowed the remaining Scotch and bore down on Isla. 'Come on, I vote we revive the old tradition of escorting the ladies to the table.' He proffered an arm the size of a well-upholstered sofa-back. 'Will you take this withered limb, my dear?'

Conversation over dinner, fuelled by a full-blooded supermarket claret, was typically noisy and contentious and led to more of the Nell question.

'I don't just think, I *know* that frightful Lothario is after her,' declared Bill, stabbing savagely at the heart of some Stilton cheese.

'So what if he is?' asked Barbara. 'Cupid's dart and all that.'

'Stuff Cupid. The thought of that brainless, gutless oaf as a son-in-law fills me with complete and utter gloom.'

'You're leaping ahead a bit here, surely,' said Richard. 'A bit of nooky in Swiss Cottage's one thing, wedding bells quite another.'

'There's no telling him,' Barbara said. 'He's a dinosaur. We both are, but he's a helluva lot more of a one than I am.'

'A dinosaur—and that from my own wife!'

'How do you think they died out?' asked Isla. 'Not enough mixed flats.'

'Ah. Ah. Ah. Now we have jokes!'

'I was never more serious in my life.'

'OK, all right, have it your way.' Bill dusted his huge palms together, releasing a shower of crumbs to be hoovered up by Pepe. 'But I still don't want that Nth-rater getting his clammy paws on the Fyler fortune.'

Barbara let out a piglike snort, and Pepe immediately leapt onto her lap and thrust his face into hers.

'I beg your pardon, my heart?' asked Bill.

'Fortune, my eye!'

'Not at all. Compared to the SCs we constitute bloated plutocrats, and as such Nell's a bloody good catch.'

'Forgive my saying so, but you're talking about your daughter as if she were a brood mare,' commented Richard.

'If you ask me, Nell could do with a bit of sex life, and she's not so daft that she's going to marry some chap just because he bonks her,' said Barbara.

'Language, dearest!' barked Bill absent-mindedly. It was just as well he said something, because Richard and Isla were helpless with laughter.

As they paid a good-night call on the ailing Portia before leaving, Bill placed a hand on Isla's shoulder.

'Do this poor old man a favour. Go and pay Nell a visit when you're back in the smog. Have a womanly word. Report any developments.'

'Don't be such a fathead,' said Barbara, making kissy faces at the dog. 'What possible excuse could poor Isla find for dragging across town to see Nell? And why the hell should she anyway?'

'Absolutely,' said Richard. 'Why should you?'

Isla cuffed him. 'Of course I will. It'll be a pleasure.'

'Good God 'n' stuff,' cried Bill. 'That was easier than I thought.'

You thought I was joking, didn't you?' said Richard in bed.

'About what?'

'About Nell.' He stroked her hair. 'I wasn't—why should you?'

'No reason, except that it would amuse me.' Isla knew that self-interest was the reasoning most likely to appeal to her husband.

'Oh well, in that case. There's no accounting for taste . . .'

Isla felt Richard's hand cupping and pressing on her cheek, and rolled her head to face him.

'You're too good,' he said.

'Oh Lord,' she said, appalled. 'Please. I do hope not.'

'You are . . .' He was amorous.

'Too good for what . . . ?' She turned on her side, into his arms.

'For all of us. Definitely too good for me.'

'That's true.' She smiled, kissed, settled. 'But then, who isn't?'

# FLOWERS WON'T FAX

Richard had gone after Isla with a single-minded passion which had surprised even his colleagues and his closest friends. Already divorced from the boys' mother, Caroline, after eight years, and with a youthful mismatch to a fellow lawyer, Donatella, haunting his past, they'd all thought he would concentrate on being single and sought-after.

But once he'd met Isla, at a show-business party to which he'd been invited by a grateful client, that was it. He had to have her. He called, he wrote, he sent flowers. Part of her charm, people considered privately, was her unavailability. But when the breakthrough came, in the form of dinner at Claridge's, Richard was, if anything, even more smitten.

'She's quite, quite the best thing on two legs,' he told Archie Stainforth, a slightly younger colleague and friend of many summers' standing. 'I simply adore her.'

'But you're not exactly alone in that, are you?' Archie pointed out. 'I mean, half the male population of England's infatuated with her, so she must be awfully used to it.'

'She's not in the least actressy, if that's what you mean,' said Richard. 'She's one of the nicest, warmest, funniest women I've met, and as for the packaging . . .'

Archie looked understanding. 'Yes, yes. Quite. But then—well—that is her job, isn't it? I mean, being funny, warm and beautiful is how she makes her living. A pretty handsome one, I should imagine.'

'That's an extremely unworthy observation.' Richard looked aggrieved, and Archie, a famously soft-hearted soul, even more so.

'I'm sorry, no offence intended. Maybe I'm just jealous.'

'You've no need to be. I'm probably making a fool of myself in the most public way possible.'

'No, no, no,' said Archie, who actually could not have borne to see his friend humiliated. 'No, no, not at all.'

Richard knew that he meant it. When Isla agreed to marry him, Archie was quite moist-eyed with delight. His happiness consisted of the happiness of those he cared for. When Richard visited Archie and Alison in their large, shambolic house in Camden, he always came away feeling two things—first, that they were a profoundly happy couple and, second, that whatever the vagaries of his own emotional life he was awfully glad he wasn't Archie. At some point around his late thirties, Richard had at last acquired enough self-knowledge to realise that he was not cut out for the long domestic haul. Seeing the selfless tolerance and cheerfulness of Archie and Alison made him realise how wretchedly inept he himself had been in the dark days of his union with Caroline.

His marriage to Isla was as near as possible the perfect relationship of which he'd always dreamed. He could not find it in himself to harbour any regret about their lack of children, though he suspected it might in the past have been a source of sadness to Isla. If she had raised the subject of adoption, or—God forbid—fertility treatment, he would of course have seriously considered the options. But she never had.

She seemed, now, to be asleep. He gazed into the dark, close secrecy of her face. A woman with a public persona was owned, in some strange way, by everyone who knew her name. But Richard knew that much as he himself might like to do so, Isla could never be owned.

They arrived at Hawtrey's the following morning at eleven. The order of the day was that there were various exhibitions of the students' work, and teachers were available for consultation. Neither exhibitions nor consultations were compulsory and Marcus was hanging about at the school gate hoping for a swift getaway.

'You don't want to waste time in there,' he complained through the open car window. 'It'll be the same old bollocks.'

'Why not let us be the judge of that?' said Richard. 'Hop in.'

From Marcus's look it was clear that this suggestion was on a par with tea with the Queen Mother. He withdrew from the side of the car as if electrocuted. Richard smiled coolly.

'We'll see you back here then . . .' The Jag slid forward. 'Good grief, what does he look like?'

'Memorable?'

'OK, OK, let's leave it at that.' Richard parked outside the school's main entrance.

Giles, suave in a black polo shirt and jeans, was in the front hall, sitting sideways on the edge of a table covered in leaflets.

'Hi there,' he said. 'You're looking at the man in charge.'

Isla kissed him, and he claimed a second cheek as well. She wondered what he said to his friends about her.

'In charge of what?' asked Richard, taking in the milling throng of big shirts, rugged boots, nose-studs and rumpled jackets, which could contain students, staff or parents, it was so hard to tell . . .

'Today's events. Have a leaflet.'

Richard stared at it and passed it to Isla. 'How come you're doing this?' asked Richard, unable to keep the suspicion out of his voice.

'Just got lucky I guess. Plus, I'm the oldest inhabitant.'

There was no prefect system at Hawtrey's, responsibility being handed out as a cure for delinquency or a concomitant of long service. Richard suspected that if his older son qualified on the latter grounds, his younger would soon make it on the former.

Over coffee in the refectory they were approached by the headmaster, Bruce Aldred. He was a burly, open-faced man in his early forties, who had once been a monk. His style of leadership was shirt-sleeved and democratic, with a muscular plain-spokenness which had helped to set the tone of Hawtrey's in the 1990s.

'Good morning, good morning.' He proffered a hand like a shovel to each of them in turn, and pulled a third spindly green refectory chair well out from the table in order to sit down, which he did with arms folded on chest and thighs well apart. 'So how do you find them?'

'Pretty true to type,' said Richard. 'Marcus saturnine and hankering to be away, Giles in the thick of it.'

'That's your boys.' Bruce clicked his teeth, and then added, 'Playing against the role as usual.'

Richard grew wary. 'How do you mean?'

'Marcus is a thorn in the side of everyone over twenty in this establishment, but he's actually doing rather well in spite of himself. Giles of course is affability itself, but puts the pleasure principle before all else.'

'Oh dear,' said Isla, 'what has he been up to?'

'Pursuing a vibrant social life. Nothing wrong with that, but there's a limit to what can be tolerated in a school even as broad-minded as this.'

'We're talking sex, here, are we?' enquired Richard in a robust tone, which Isla recognised as covering a certain amount of embarrassment. 'Was it another pupil?'

Bruce nodded once, lips pursed. 'That's the problem we have with it. A non-close-encounter policy is key to this operation.'

'So you're keeping him busy,' said Isla.

'Well, yes, and putting him on the spot a bit. Being singled out puts him in a more exposed position, makes it harder to get up to all sorts.'

'What about the girl?'

'A very together young lady in Marcus's year, her people are out in—'

'Hang on a second.' Richard looked stricken. 'She must be underage!'

'Strictly speaking, yes, she is. Was. She's had a birthday since.'

'What other way is there of speaking? It's illegal.'

'Yes, it is. But if anyone chose to enforce that particular law half the teenagers in the country would be clapped in irons.'

Richard shook his head, massaging his temples vigorously. 'God . . .'

'Do her parents know?' asked Isla.

'Not at the moment. It may have been technically illegal, Richard, but we're not about to criminalise it. These are two healthy young adults and the evidence is that they were taking precautions'—Richard groaned—'so as far as we're concerned the matter ends there.'

'But the implications are horrendous. I mean this girl's in your care—it doesn't bear thinking about in today's climate.'

Bruce made a facial shrug. 'We take our responsibilities extremely seriously, but we try to live in the real world.'

'I'll talk to him, naturally, I'll talk to him today . . .'

On the drive back to Bradenham Giles was in high good humour, while Marcus put on headphones and closed his eyes.

'You know,' remarked Giles, leaning on the back of Isla's seat, 'this may come as a surprise to you, but I can't wait to be shot of that place.'

'Is that so?' said Richard. 'You do surprise me.'

'No, honestly, Bruce and co think they're the dog's bollocks with their liberal regime, but when it comes down to it they're no different to anyone else.'

'Glad to hear it,' said Richard grimly, peering frostily in the rearview mirror. 'Had any thoughts about what you're going to do when you leave?'

'Certainly have. Chris Beales and me are going to start up as party organisers. There's serious money in it.'

'If it was as easy as that, everyone would be doing it.'

'Chris has got contacts,' said Giles, and fell back in his seat with a smile as though that closed the matter.

Much to Isla's surprise, when Richard suggested a singles after lunch, Giles acquiesced.

'Sure, if you want to get thrashed. Best of three, right?'

Isla, left alone with Marcus in the garden, broke the silence.

'So,' she said. 'How were the exams?'

'All right.'

'And what about everything else?'

'Bit of a global question. What would you like to know?'

'I don't know . . . Tell me something.'

'No,' said Marcus. 'Not in the mood.' He stretched his arms in the air, rolled forward and stood up. His shrunken T-shirt revealed a frighteningly thin torso. 'Think I'll take a walk.'

Isla forebore to offer company. She was relieved rather than offended. She and Marcus understood one another. She sat in the sun with the last of her wine. It was very still and she could hear the irregular plop of the tennis ball, Giles's voice raised from time to time in glee or despair. When Richard returned, he looked damp and dishevelled, with a dangerously high colour.

'Who won?'

'Don't ask. I have all the technique, but he has youth on his side.'

Isla lowered her voice slightly. 'Did you manage to . . . ?'

'I did.'

'And how did it go down?'

'It sank in. I think. It's a bit hard to tell, he's so bloody affable.'

Isla held out her hand to him. 'Well done. What line did you take?'

After a split second's hesitation he took the hand. 'Trust,' he said. 'I played the trust card. Our relationship with him depends on trust, Hawtrey's is run on a basis of trust. And that has to be a two-way thing. Would you agree?'

'Yes,' said Isla. 'I would.'

# *chapter two*

CLAUDIA DELANEY descended from the passenger cab of a Dutch container lorry on the Oxford ring road. The driver leaned across to bid her farewell.

'You have my address and number. Don't forget to visit if you're in Holland. I live just outside Amsterdam.'

'I will, thanks.' Claudia picked up her khaki canvas fishing-bag, swung it over her shoulder, took a couple of backward steps, hand raised, and began to walk determinedly away. She knew the driver was gazing after her because it was a full thirty seconds before the lorry's engine started up. As it roared past her she didn't look up.

Claudia was a seasoned hitcher of lifts, and on a sex-pest scale of one to ten the Dutch driver had scarcely made the cut. Far too nice: earnest, interested, persistent. She was glad to see the back of him. She paused, dumped the fishing-bag on the ground and studied the road map. Kersney Court, she estimated, was about two miles from here as the crow flew, more like four as a loaded pedestrian. She glanced at her watch. Time, at least, was on her side. She'd left Paris at eight that morning and it was now three. Taking into consideration the hour's leeway she always allowed herself, and the hour's lateness which was a given factor with her mother, she'd stroll in with time to spare.

Claudia was twenty-one, six foot, and barely ten stone, with dark red hair and bronze eyes interestingly flecked with black. Because of her exceptional height and striking looks men had been coming on to her since she was in her early teens. They were generally rebuffed. She was not so much picky as uninterested. Her own mother was an object lesson, in Claudia's view, on the unwisdom of being too susceptible to the male of the species.

She dressed specifically to counteract what she saw as her own natural disadvantages. She used no make-up and her hair at this moment was barely an inch long all over. Today she wore a brown-and-pink-printed cotton dress that drooped unevenly to mid-calf, a pair of plimsolls grey with use, and a spinach-coloured cardigan tied round her waist. As well as the fishing satchel she carried a shoulder bag, both of them slung diagonally across her torso like cartridge belts.

Unfortunately for her, Claudia's looks were more than up to the challenge, and her determined efforts to repel only had the effect of throwing her eccentric beauty into sharp relief.

Claudia took her responsibilities seriously, especially those towards her mother. She loved Jen with a stern, protective passion, and despaired of her almost as passionately. How could someone who Claudia allowed was a wonderful parent be such a lousy judge of character? And why on earth couldn't she get a grip? Because what got Claudia's goat most of all was her mother's apparent lack of concern about the mire of muddle and make-do that was her life. Her father, Mo, was now married to a tympanist with the Bournemouth Symphony Orchestra and had a brood of legitimate children of his own. She and Jen enjoyed a friendly relationship with all of them, but Claudia would have liked a little more order. For ages now, since she was a child, there had been Richard, who appeared to be what passed for a fixture with Jen. A fixture, but not a fitting. In the early days she'd been at primary school and it had been impossible to avoid coming into contact with him from time to time. To do him justice, he'd always maintained a polite, benign distance with her which was unthreatening. But it had just gone on and on. What, she wondered, could possibly be in it for her mother? How could she be satisfied with something so patently unsatisfactory? These days Claudia made damn sure she didn't run into the fat cat, with his cigars and his big swanky motor . . .

She paused to consult the map again. She had long since turned off the ring road, and now turned up a lane, homing in steadily on her destination. Claudia had been spending the weekend with her friend Ben who was studying at the Sorbonne in Paris. It had been fun. Elke, his

Danish girlfriend, played tenor sax with an all-girl group in a bar in Bastille, and they'd gone there in the evening and hung out with wonderful-looking gay women in the sort of relaxed, intelligent atmosphere that she found completely *sympathique*.

Surprisingly it had been at this bar that a man had come up to her and told her she should be a model. It had been such an unlikely setting for this approach, and such a hackneyed line, that she'd actually laughed in his face. But he'd been completely unperturbed and handed her a card with the address at which she would be able to contact him or his colleagues. At the time she hadn't even bothered to look at it. But over peppermint tea at three thirty in the morning in the flat, Ben and Elke had made her do so and they'd all three shrieked with pleasurable disbelief to see the name of a designer of whom even Claudia had heard.

She still had the card in her bag, but she doubted she'd do anything. She had a combined studies degree at London to complete next year.

The hedge to her left had given way to a high wall, and now she came to two immense griffin-topped stone pillars flanking a gravel entrance. Halfway down the right-hand pillar the words 'Kersney Court' were discreetly engraved. Claudia put the map away and turned in.

Twenty or so yards past the entrance the drive became a recently macadamised cart track, with cattle grids at regular intervals. Fat white Charollais cows dotted the park on either side. Their presence deterred Claudia from striking out across the grass towards the house, whose tall chimneys she could see sticking up beyond the trees to her left.

She had agreed to come here, rather than hitch a lift straight back into town, to give her mother an excuse to escape, and map-reading support. She should, of course, have said no—a woman of Jen's age ought to have been able to depart and find her way home without assistance—but had, as usual, weakened and come miles out of her way to provide the necessary.

She heard a vehicle turn in off the road and come bumping down behind her. Claudia moved aside onto the grass without breaking stride or altering her speed.

To her annoyance a filthy Land-Rover with two labradors lolling in the back pulled up alongside. The driver, middle-aged and wearing a checked Viyella shirt, hung an arm over the side and raised his voice to counter the amiable barking of the dogs.

'Like a lift?'

'No, thanks.'

'Are you sure? It's a helluva hike if you don't like cows.'

Claudia gave him a cool stare. 'I don't mind cows, and I like walking.'

'Tremendous.' She couldn't tell if he was being sarcastic or not. 'I'll leave you to it then.'

The man bumped away, the labradors still barking in the back.

It was a further fifteen minutes before she reached the house and she slightly regretted not having accepted the lift. Plimsolls were not designed for serious walking, and she had a blister. She yanked irritably on the iron bell pull and stood back to survey the house. Long windows, tall chimneys, a slate roof with parapets, an impressive pillared entrance and loads of ivy. Nice. The only jarring note was her mother's white Renault Diane parked bang in the middle of the forecourt.

Distant barking accompanied the opening of the door.

'You made it then,' said the man from the Land-Rover. 'Come in.'

'Thanks.' Smarting with embarrassment Claudia stepped over the threshold and into a big hall. The man was in his stockinged feet.

'I live here, you see,' he said, catching her glance. She nodded. 'So please—what can we do for you?'

'I'm meeting my mother here—Jen Delaney.'

'Ah.' He clicked his fingers. 'Is she the pooch-lady?'

'She's an artist,' replied Claudia crisply.

'Sorry, didn't mean to sound flippant.' She gave him a look which acknowledged the lapse but did not absolve him from it. 'She's with my mother, I believe.'

She followed him across the hall, her plimsolls slapping on shining oak floorboards, his feet moving soundlessly in rumpled wool socks.

'Sorry to interrupt the sitting,' said the man cheerily, 'but I've got a visitor for the artist.'

The room was a library rather larger than the whole downstairs of 65 Selwyn Street, and a great deal grander. A state-of-the-art television stood on one side of the fireplace. An old, very thin woman sat in a wing-back chair on the other. At her feet lay a comatose basset hound, which lifted its head glumly as they entered. Claudia's mother was kneeling on the floor a few feet from the dog, camera in hand. As the dog's head rose she cried, 'Oh, thank you, God! Good boy! Stay—!'

Everyone waited obediently as she took a Polaroid. And then again as the photo came into focus.

'Magic!' Jen pronounced, displaying the developed article. The old lady smiled, patted the dog with a gnarled hand alight with diamonds, and turned her tortoiselike head to look at Claudia as Jen came over to embrace her. 'This,' said Jen, 'is my daughter Claudia.'

'And over there,' said the man to Claudia, 'is my mother, Lady Olivia Saxby. Which only leaves me and I'm Anthony Saxby. How do you do?'

He held out his hand, first to Jen, then to Claudia. The basset hauled itself onto its feet and waddled over. 'Hang on,' Claudia said, crouching to pet it. 'Who's this?'

Three voices answered at once. 'That's Horace.'

Claudia made a fuss of Horace, who stood staring wretchedly into her face as though this were his very last fuss before facing a firing squad.

'What about some tea?' asked Lady Olivia.

'I'm gone,' replied her son. The door closed behind him.

Claudia rose and lifted an eyebrow at her mother.

'Well, actually, we should be going,' said Jen.

'In a minute, in a minute.' Lady Olivia peered at the cherub-encrusted clock on the mantelpiece and jerked bent fingers at the sofa. 'It's ages till my nice chef comes on the box. Sit down.'

They sat. Horace, after a moment's tragic indecision, waddled back to his mistress. Lady Olivia stared at Claudia with the unabashed appraisal of a two-year-old then asked, 'Now where do you get your looks from?'

Jen laughed. 'Not from me!'

'I can see that. Your father?'

'My father's very tall,' replied Claudia.

Lady Olivia scratched and scratched at Horace's loose neck, sending him into a trance. 'Are you an artist too?'

'No. I'm at university.'

'Anywhere I might know?'

'London.'

'Ah yes, I dimly remember. And what are you studying? It's all a mystery to me. I had no education myself.'

'I'm taking combined studies.'

They both looked at her, Jen fondly, Lady Olivia with a frown. 'What's that, a bit of everything?'

'Pretty much.'

'Sounds just the ticket.'

The door swung open and Anthony Saxby came in carrying a high-sided butler's tray with tea things. As he put it down on a table in the window, Lady Olivia asked, 'Couldn't you be a rock star?'

Jen snorted with laughter. Anthony said, 'I hope you're not addressing me.'

'I'm talking to Cleo—'

'Claudia.'

'Don't you think that's what she should do?'

'Yes,' said Anthony, handing an unmatched porcelain cup and saucer to Jen. 'Good idea. Sugar?'

'I've been telling her for years,' said Jen, 'but she won't listen.'

Claudia smiled thinly. What was she doing here? She tried to conjure up an image of Ben and Elke and the bar in Bastille, but they seemed like memories of another life. Except, of course, for the designer's card.

'Perhaps,' she said, 'I'll be a supermodel instead.'

They all laughed, glad she'd taken the joke on board.

'So, Mrs Delaney,' said Anthony, sitting on a chair near Claudia. 'Tell me, I'm interested—is doing dog portraits profitable?'

'I don't only do dogs. And that's a bit of a leading question under the circumstances . . .' Jen smiled at Lady Olivia, who was applying a Crown Derby table lighter to a cigarette.

'Ah . . .!' Lady Olivia exhaled luxuriously. 'I don't see why. I'm paying her two hundred pounds plus expenses. Cheap at the price.'

'I'd have thought so,' agreed Anthony. 'I imagine you need danger money with some sitters.'

Claudia, embarrassed by money talk, looked down at her knees. Her mother gave her rich, meat-and-potatoes chuckle.

'*That's* true. And, by the way, I hate to be picky but I'm not Mrs.'

Oh please, thought Claudia. Oh no. Gimme a break.

'Who is these days?' commented Anthony with what even Claudia conceded was a deft touch, giving Jen the opportunity to leave it there. Which of course she didn't.

'Not many, it's true. But I never was. I was before my time.'

Claudia smarted, but the Saxbys laughed. Anthony said smoothly, 'By middle-class standards, perhaps, but you'd have to be up early to beat us. The Saxby escutcheon is so besmirched it's barely legible.'

'Cleo—' rasped the old lady.

'Claudia . . .'

'Don't let it embarrass you. Our family tree,' Lady Olivia continued, 'is absolutely littered with bastards.' She jabbed her cigarette at Anthony. 'Him over there, he's one.'

Claudia couldn't look up, let alone catch his eye. Her teeth were gritted. She heard him say smoothly, 'So you tell me, Ma, so you tell me.' He leaned towards Claudia. 'But we don't talk about it.'

Jen was apologising before the Renault had rattled over the first cattle grid. 'Oh, Red . . . what can I say?'

'Nothing.'

Jen put an arm round her daughter's shoulders, causing the car to make a detour through the cow pats. 'Oops! I'm so terribly sorry. I can be so crass . . . I don't know what comes over me.'

'It's OK. Forget it.'

'I would, except that I know you won't. I just hate it when people make assumptions.'

'I know.'

'Can you forgive me?' An anxious, pleading glance, another bone-shaking swerve.

'Watch out! Yes!'

Between the final cattle grid and the right-hand turn into the road, Claudia realised that her mother's assessment was exactly right: Jen had put the matter behind her, but she herself couldn't, quite. She was an honest young woman, and had to admit that the reason for this was Anthony Saxby, her fellow bastard.

That evening they ate Jen's special macaroni cheese, deliciously mixed up with bits of crispy bacon and fried onion, in the living room. Keith was out. Not, as Jen conceded, that he ever intruded, but his excruciating self-effacement—creeping down the stairs, running taps at half-strength, closing kitchen cupboards so slowly that they clicked twice—created a kind of uneasy backdrop to evenings in.

'Where is Norbert?' asked Claudia.

'What day is it?' Jen glanced abstractedly at her empty wrist. 'Tuesday? It's karate.'

Claudia stayed her fork, lowered it to the plate. 'You're telling me he teaches martial arts? That we have Karate Keith?'

'No, I think he's got a more peripheral connection with it—opens up the school hall, makes the orange squash, that kind of thing.'

'Well, it's nice he's not around. I don't know how you put up with it, it'd drive me crackers. It does drive me crackers.'

'Now come on, Red. He's no trouble and his money is as good as the next man's and always on time. A dream lodger in fact.' Jen used her knife to pick up what remained of her cheese sauce and licked the blade with long, catlike strokes. 'Now then. Who cares about him? What about you? What happened in Paris?'

Jen was a good listener, because she was genuinely curious. Now that Claudia felt more relaxed it was a pleasure to talk about her weekend to someone who was so absolutely on her wavelength. She talked and Jen sat curled up on the sofa, a model of attentiveness. Claudia knew she'd remember every word because she was a clever woman with a selectively retentive memory—much too bright to be turning out idealised pictures of overindulged animals.

'Ben sounds nice,' Jen said at one point. 'He's *simpatico*.'

'Yes, he is,' agreed Claudia, adding just in case, 'and he seems to be very happy with Elke.'

'Oh, I wasn't suggesting anything.'

'Perish the thought.'

They exchanged sidelong smiles of understanding. Claudia felt indulgent towards her mother. 'There is one funny thing I haven't told you yet,' she said. 'Hang on, let me show you.' She bent down to get the designer's card from her bag. As she did so, the phone rang.

'Don't go away, I'll be back in two ticks.'

In the hall, her mother lifted the receiver.

'Hello?' She never said the number. 'Oh, *hello*.' She never said the name of the caller, either. But Claudia had a pretty fair idea who this might be. When Jen came back into the room there was a subtle but unmistakable change in her manner that confirmed her suspicions.

'Richard?'

'How did you guess?' Jen sounded unabashed, but didn't catch her daughter's eye. 'So, come on then—what were you going to show me?'

'It doesn't matter,' said Claudia. 'It was nothing exciting.'

Isla didn't in the least mind visiting Nell Fyler. She enjoyed such projects, and was flattered to be asked to undertake them. She'd engineered the meeting by ringing Nell and saying she was going to be in her area for a dinner one evening the following week and could she drop in beforehand?

Nell had reacted in her rather offhand way. 'I don't see why not. I think I'll be around.'

'Well obviously,' said Isla gently, 'I shouldn't bother if you weren't going to be there.'

'No, I suppose not. Anyway, I should be.'

Isla drove down to Swiss Cottage. She did, in fact, have a dinner to attend, but it was a private one with the Stainforths, at whose house she was meeting Richard at eight fifteen. In consequence of this she was not dressed up, but wearing loose khaki trousers and a cream silk shirt. This casual ensemble was not missed by Nell.

'Come on in. Not a black tie affair, then.'

'No, not this one . . .' Isla bumped cheeks. 'Just friends, at their house.' She followed her into the living room.

'Grab a pew,' said Nell. Isla lowered herself onto a sagging hammock of a sofa. Nell's home was packed with overspill from The Bury: frayed Persian rugs, chintz covers, threadbare tapestry cushions, hunting prints and thin-lipped family portraits.

'I just got in,' said Nell. 'What can I get you?'

'No really, I'm fine.'

'I usually have a g and t.'

'Go ahead.'

'Suit yourself,' said Nell bluntly, and went into the kitchen. Isla watched her through the open door. Her carroty shoulder-length hair was cut straight and sensible and no mascara enhanced her sandy-lashed pale blue eyes. For work, at an adventurous but expensive gallery in Belgravia, she wore a navy suit, scuffed navy court shoes and a black velvet hairband; no rings, but a string of mumsy pearls and pearl studs, all undoubtedly real. Isla liked Nell, but it was difficult to see her as the innocent victim of a predatory gold-digger. She did not come over as a young woman one would choose to cross.

'Are you sure you won't change your mind? Orange juice?'

'No thanks.'

'Salt and vinegar crisps?'

'Now you're talking.'

Nell came back into the room holding two packets of crisps, one of which she tossed unceremoniously to Isla. ''Scuse fingers, simplest way.'

'Where's your flatmate?' Isla asked, tweaking at the packet. 'Still at work?'

'Still at the office. I'm not sure he goes in for anything as taxing as work.'

'Really? What sort of office is it?'

'Public relations.' Nell sucked her teeth. 'I ask you. Look, it is nice to see you. Sorry if I was a bit brusque when you arrived.'

'Were you?'

'Have you seen the Aged Ps recently?'

'Yes, as a matter of fact we were in Bradenham for the boys' open day last weekend, and we went round there for dinner. That was what made me think of you when I realised I was coming down this way.'

'How did they seem?'

'Very bullish, except that Portia's not well and your mama's obviously worried about her.'

Nell sighed. 'Mummy will have to get over it. The old bitch is on her last legs.' For a split second Isla misunderstood this observation, and it must have showed. 'Portia, I mean. She's fourteen—that's a colossal age for a Rottweiler. It's no use breaking one's heart over animals,' said Nell. 'They have a shorter life span than us and that's all there is to it. One simply has to move on. But I've got a super idea for Mummy's birthday present this year.'

'Now look,' said Isla, realising that time was limited and the more straightforward she was the less suspicion she would arouse. 'I didn't come here to talk dogs. How are *you*?'

'Fine. In rude health as always.'

'Still fancy-free?'

'Yes.' Nell shot her a piercing look, very like her father's, from beneath ginger eyebrows. 'Who wants to know?'

'I do. You know me, I like gossip and romance and affairs . . .'

'Then you came to the wrong place. No, I have one or two jolly girl-friends who give nice dinner parties and in the autumn Scotch and I plan to push the boat out if we're spared and do a lunchtime drinks.'

'Scotch being Robert?'

'That's right.' There was the sound of the front door opening. 'Anyway, you can see for yourself.' She raised her voice. 'In here, you! I want to introduce you to an old friend of my mother's!'

As she shook hands, Isla realised that whatever she had been expecting this was not it. Robert Scott-Chatham was tall and toned with a sculpted bad-boy face, almost black eyes and fetchingly scrubby hair: blue suit, open-necked white shirt, highly coloured tie protruding from jacket pocket; must-have Gucci belt and black lace-ups. Isla, accustomed by experience to assessing the success or otherwise of image-promotion, recognised an adept and witty practitioner when she saw one.

Still beaming delightedly, he flopped down in a chair and professed himself gobsmacked.

'No disrespect to Nell's esteemed parent, but when she said an old friend of her mother's I didn't picture anything like'—he swept a hand up and down—'you.' He continued to gaze at her through narrowed eyes. 'Am I allowed to say that you're even more stunning in real life?'

'You're definitely allowed to say it. In fact, as the decades roll by, you're positively required to say it! Thank you.'

'Are you working on anything special at the moment?'

'I mainly do rent-a-face these days.'

'She's far too modest,' said Nell. 'You do all this charity stuff now, don't you? She's working on her OBE.'

'Oh yes, I'm Our Lady of the Good Causes,' agreed Isla, laughing. 'I eat a lot of mediocre food, have my photo taken with the bravest and the best and make a few undemanding speeches, that's all. I'm not required to dirty my hands with any real work.'

Scotch frowned. 'Why do you run yourself down?'

'I wouldn't want to overstate my usefulness.'

'You couldn't, I'm sure. You must be one of the best-loved actresses of your generation.'

'Even if you're right, which I doubt, serious actresses want to be best-respected, not best-loved.'

'Maybe you never were a serious actress—'

'Scotch!' barked Nell. 'Give over.'

'No, I meant no offence. What I meant was that perhaps this—what you do now—is your real vocation. And just because you're not emptying bedpans or swabbing pus doesn't mean it's not useful.'

'That's a jolly good way of looking at it,' conceded Isla.

'Tell me something,' asked Scotch. 'Who does your PR?'

**S**upper with the Stainforths had been taken in the kitchen for as long as anyone could recall. Archie was upstairs officiating at a bedtime that sounded like a student uprising, while his wife prepared vegetables.

The house in Camden, though not as large as the Wakefields' in Hampstead, was a substantial residence which had suffered the ravages that decades of Stainforth family life had wrought. It was a source of wonder to Richard that Archie managed to appear in chambers each day looking halfway decent and able to represent his clients perfectly creditably. How, out of all this chaos and clamour, was it done?

Having arrived first, Richard sat on the wheelback chair with the wonky leg, drinking a gut-wrenching Bulgarian red (his own bottles of pleasing claret would accompany supper) and submitting to Alison's interrogation as she chopped carrots to accompany her 'special' chicken chasseur.

'So how are your brood?' asked Alison. To her, children were always a brood. 'All well?'

'Yes, we saw them the other day—'

'My goodness, Richard, you don't know you're born! Think of us, seeing all of ours every blessed day!'

'Believe me,' said Richard humbly, 'I do.' Archie was several years younger than him, and Alison younger than that, but she had the knack of making him feel like a schoolboy.

'But they were in good fettle?'

'Marcus always looks terrible, but appearances are deceptive. Giles'— Richard paused fractionally before deciding not to spill the beans— 'Giles plans a career as a party organiser.'

'Really?' said Alison brightly, scraping carrot chunks into a saucepan, and beginning on potatoes. 'Still, all jolly fun,' she said vaguely, adding, 'We wouldn't be without them, would we?' There was a tremendous thud from above, followed by roars and shrieks and a thunder of footsteps. 'I wonder if Archie needs a hand—will you excuse me for a mo?'

'Please, of course.'

Alison beetled into the hall and up the stairs, calling as she went, 'Archie, *Archee*! What's going on up there?'

Richard sipped his fiery red with pursed lips. The front doorbell made its distinctive sound, like a football rattle being swung slowly. From the hurly-burly of the upper reaches Alison's voice came faintly. 'Richard—! Be a dear and get that . . . !'

Richard rose and went to open the door.

Isla stepped in and kissed him. 'Where is everyone?'

'Upstairs, mostly, doing bedtime.'

'Oh good, in that case I'll tell you about Nell and her flatmate.'

They went into the kitchen. Richard lifted his glass. 'Rocket fuel?'

'I'll wait. Listen.' Isla sat down opposite him at the table. 'He's an absolute sweetie, handsome and charming and altogether delightful.'

Richard raised his eyebrows. 'Do you realise, my darling, that you have just described Bill Fyler's worst nightmare?'

'No, no, no.' She shook her head impatiently. 'You don't understand. How can I describe it? He's actually very, very *nice*.'

'Holy cow.'

'Be serious. You know me, I'm not particularly gullible, I'm a pretty shrewd judge of character and'—she stroked his hand—'I'm a connoisseur of male beauty.'

They laughed quietly to one another, their faces drawing closer together, and kissed. Archie pounded across the hall.

'Sorry—oh! We needn't have worried about leaving you two alone for five minutes!'

Isla got up and hugged him. 'What have you done with Alison?'

'I handed her the baton. Twins' bedtime,' added Archie, pulling a comical face. 'You haven't got a drink.'

'It's all right, I'll wait till dinner.'

Archie poured himself a glass of wine. 'So tell me where you've been. I could do with a bit of vicarious glamour. At some glittering show-business do? A champagne reception for the great and the good?'

'Not at all. I've been in a flat off the Finchley Road visiting the horsy daughter of old friends.'

'And vetting the bloke she shares with,' added Richard, 'whom her father suspects is after the family silver.'

Archie shook his head. 'It's another world.'

'Don't trouble your pretty little head about it, Archie,' suggested Richard. 'And behold the lady wife, hot from the battle.'

'Archie!' protested Alison between kisses. 'You never turned the veg on!'

It was a jolly enough evening: the chicken chasseur was reasonable and the charlotte russe exemplary, having been bought from the frozen-food specialists who called door-to-door. Accompanied by Richard's stylish claret it was a nice dinner, and Archie and Alison were always droll company. At eleven thirty Amanda Stainforth returned.

'Come in, darling,' called Alison, 'and say hello to Richard and Isla.'

Footsteps trudged across the hall and Amanda appeared. She was a well-built girl of fifteen wearing jeans and a checked shirt. Her expression of contemptuous impatience cracked into a smile when she saw Isla.

'Oh, hi.'

'Where have you been?' asked Isla. 'Anywhere interesting?'

'Just hanging out with friends.'

'It's the best thing, isn't it?' agreed Isla, including Archie and Alison in the remark. 'You do look nice, by the way.'

Amanda glanced down at herself. 'I do?'

'Yes. You can't beat 501s on a smashing young figure.'

'Can I have a drink, Dad?' asked Amanda, now completely won over.

'Um, well—'

'No,' said Alison. 'Off you go, school in the morning.'

The thunder threatened to return. 'I wish you wouldn't say that as if I was ten or something.'

'I'm not, darling, I'm saying it as if you were fifteen.'

Isla caught Amanda's eye and smiled. 'You'll be glad one day.'

'I'll take your word for it!' Only partly mollified, Amanda stumped off.

Archie leaned to watch her go. 'Night, petal!'

'Night.'

'She's not a bad kid,' he said, addressing Isla and Richard, 'but I wish I knew what "hanging out" involved.'

'Nothing half as sinister as your worst imaginings, I'm sure,' said Isla. 'You only have to look at her to see she's not doing drugs or OD-ing on alcopops. The odd ciggy perhaps, but then who didn't at that age? She's an absolutely lovely girl.'

'She is, she is . . .' Archie agreed. 'But that doesn't stop us worrying.'

Alison's brow furrowed. 'We think—what if she has a secret life?'

'On that score,' said Archie, 'I draw some comfort from the fact that Amanda's like the rest of her ilk, pretty lazy, and conducting a secret life would be far too much like work!'

They agreed amid laughter, and moved on to another subject.

Richard didn't consider that he had a secret, or even a double life. He thought himself honest, open and truthful, on a need-to-know basis. That this entailed a great deal of day-to-day concealment was a fact he chose to overlook. His ability to rationalise, justify and validate the behaviour of his clients stood him in good stead when it came to the salving of his conscience.

His relationship with Jen predated his marriage to Isla by fully two years. He had met her during the period of his divorce from Caroline. She had been nothing short of a lifesaver. By the time they had known each other for a week, it was impossible for Richard to imagine what it had been like before. In her company he relaxed, and in doing so realised that he had not relaxed properly in years. Here, at last, was a woman who accepted him absolutely as he was—who was neither resentful of his strengths nor waiting to pounce rapaciously on his weaknesses. He had never known whether she loved him in any romantic way, but oddly that didn't seem to matter. She was always pleased to see him, and there was a calmness about her pleasure, as though he had only gone out a short while ago and she was happily surprised to see him back so soon. Her life did not change because of him.

Physically, Jen was not a woman to induce an awed quake of desire, like Isla, but one to melt into. What he experienced with her was an animal warmth and cuddliness, an infinitely comforting closeness. What their lovemaking lacked in grandeur it made up for in a snuggling intimacy that Richard had never known, even in childhood.

On those rare occasions when he attempted to analyse the relationship, that was what it was all about. All that bracing fortitude, the firm grip of so much parental aspiration, steering him towards his destiny. It had worked, of course. Without a trace of vanity he could say that he was one of the smartest lawyers of his generation. He could name his price. But he hadn't chosen this. It had been chosen for him.

He was an only child, the focus of much expectation but very little attention. His mother, Sylvia, was a widely respected and admired scientist—quiet, clever, soberly dressed, self-sufficient. She had died before she was sixty. Now that there was only him and his father left, he realised how little his mother had needed either of them. Unusually for her generation she had lived for her work. She had not been an unkind woman, but she had been utterly preoccupied.

Alec Wakefield had been an orthopaedic consultant at Tommy's. In those days he was a tall, corpulent, florid man with bright blue eyes and a mane of wavy hair. He was not preoccupied in the way that Sylvia was, his manner was extrovert and unfettered, but he was no more accessible to Richard. Noisy, genial and a poor listener, he crashed about the Wakefields' domestic life as little as he could, itching to escape back to a larger stage.

But different though his parents were, they were united in one thing—their only son should want for nothing and get to the top. It was fortunate for all of them—especially Richard—that he was bright, good-looking and socially adept. Like a well-flighted arrow in the hands of a skilful marksman, he shot towards his starred first at Oxford and then pupillage at the most distinguished chambers in London. When he encountered Donatella they were both tearing headlong along the fast track.

Donatella Sperenza was a divorce lawyer. Richard's dealings with her had finally convinced him of what he had always suspected—that when it came to blood and guts, divorce law left the criminal courts for dead. She was a small, short-waisted, big-breasted woman with a shock of black hair and hot, dark eyes that could melt hearts of stone or scorch the unworthy depending on her mood. She was in her early thirties when she met Richard, five years older than him, but, in spite of twenty years' residency in England, her grasp of the language remained erratic and her accent, gestures, and mind-set irretrievably Italian. This, combined with a razor-sharp mind and a deadly grasp of the law, made her terrifying, not just to the unfortunate opposition but also to her clients.

Richard had been bowled over from the moment she was introduced to him at a party and said, in her husky, resonant voice, fruity with red wine and tobacco, 'I have been looking at you for some time across the room. You are a very sexy Englishman of a particular kind. You have beautiful hands. I believe we shall make love soon.'

Richard had laughed nervously, but it was clearly not a joke. Her eyes rested on him like a couple of hot coals. He experienced a shockingly vivid premonition of what it would be like to have her blunt, beringed hand holding his cock in its commanding grasp.

'What makes you believe that?' he enquired caustically.

'You don't wish to go to bed with me?'

The burning look, the flaring nostrils, the haughtily raised eyebrows . . . Richard hesitated. Fatally as it proved. She gave a short, grunting laugh and turned away, tossing over her shoulder as she did so, 'QED.'

From that moment Richard was ensnared. Being propositioned by a renowned older woman, as well as the focus of half-admiring, half-appalled general speculation, would have turned older and wiser heads than his. The affair with Donatella was intoxicating: the subsequent marriage an unmitigated disaster.

With hindsight and greater experience he could see that it was Donatella, not he, who had been trapped into marriage. Her Latin heart entertained a fantasy of hearth, home, sex and well-nourished *bambini*. But her lawyer's brain could not, in the event, cope with any of it. Well before the *bambini* stage, hearth and home had become a howling wilderness and sex had shrivelled and died in the atomic blast of Donatella's discontent. It wasn't until post-Caroline that Richard was able, in some small way, to sympathise with his first wife and what she must have gone through. For Donatella was not cut out for domestic intimacy.

Now, when he saw her, as he often did, cruising the room at legal gatherings, swooping on the unsuspecting objects of her predatory fancy, he felt a perverse tenderness for Donatella, who had been, without doubt, his first grand passion.

Caroline followed as night follows day. Cool, fair, moon-faced Caroline, conventional and in control, a woman to rely upon and take for granted, a woman with high standards and a low sex-drive, a soothing tepid bath after the white-water ride of Donatella. Richard mistook relief for true love. This was how it was supposed to be: he would be free to scale the legal heights and Caroline would always be there, behaving impeccably and oiling the domestic wheels.

To be fair to Caroline, she did not suddenly begin to behave out of character. It was simply that Richard had never envisaged the way in which life would change when the children came along. With the birth of Giles he felt a slight, unsettling shift in the centre of gravity; within weeks of the arrival of Marcus he realised he had been marginalised. Caroline was not cruel or cold; she was a good wife in every way, except that she did not love him half as much as she loved the children. Their house in Muswell Hill, though it continued to be impeccably run, was completely dominated by the demands of these two, small, pampered tyrants. The qualities in his wife, which Richard had perceived as perfectly complementary, suddenly began to rush the two of them in opposite directions. Caroline and her Home Counties mother were the undisputed experts in all things connected with the nurture and upbringing of children. Their calm, unshakable assurance sapped Richard's confidence. Not caring to risk being wrong, he left them to it, and, without really meaning to, he set about becoming the kind of distant, work-obsessed father that Alec had been.

When the break came it was more or less a case of formalising a situation that already existed. They accepted the inevitable with a gentle mutual understanding. And it had been for the best, because now Richard was able to be a better father. With distance his hopes and fears for his sons were clearer. He talked to Caroline for the first time about how he didn't want them processed, pushed through a particular system, and why, and to his surprise she was understanding and agreed with him.

'Why didn't we have this conversation before?' he'd asked.

'Because we were married, perhaps.'

'But surely that's a reason to talk, not the other way round.'

'Yes, it should be . . . if you're happy.'

He looked at her in astonishment. 'You weren't happy?'

She shook her head. 'I was always much too dull for you, Richard. It's awfully sad not being able to make someone else happy.'

Caroline had not remarried, but they had remained friends. And he had Jen.

He had met her when his car—a Merc back then—broke down in the Archway Road on the way to Marcus's primary-school nativity play. He had stood in a biting east wind gazing at the car's intransigent engine in a fury of ignorance. Jen had come to stand next to him. Shrouded in a huge black duffle coat with a hood, he hadn't even been sure whether it was a man or a woman till she spoke.

'Has it simply packed up?'

'Yes . . . blasted engine died on me at those last lights.'

'What a lousy thing to happen—and in this car, too.'

'It happens to the best of us.' He leaned forward, as if a halo of flashing lights might suddenly advertise the problem. She too leaned slightly forward, pushing back the duffle hood and releasing a shaggy chrysanthemum of fair hair.

'Is there anything I can do?'

He glanced at her. 'Why, do you know about engines?'

'No.' She sounded rather surprised. 'But I'm sure someone does.' Before he could prevent her she'd turned and addressed the hurrying throng on the pavement. 'Does anyone know about cars? We're at our wits' end—can anyone help? Please?'

'I am a member of the AA . . .' muttered Richard, mortified. But already two men, with Jen in between them, were competing vociferously under the Merc's raised bonnet. In less than five minutes a petrol-feed problem had been diagnosed, some mechanical sleight of hand performed, and advice given to top up with petrol at the first opportunity to avoid 'recycling the gunk'.

'I can't thank you enough,' said Richard, gratitude outweighing embarrassment as the men went their separate ways. 'Or you,' he added. 'Look, I've got to dash. I'm going to Highgate—can I give you a lift?'

'Thanks.'

He went into the nearest filling station and topped up with four-star. When he got back in, he asked, 'Where would you like to be dropped?'

'Where did you say you were going?'

'St Mark's in Highgate West Hill—it's my son's school—'

'Near there'll be fine.'

During the short drive he found out her name, that she was a painter, and that she herself drove a VW Beetle. It was a small amount of information, but she delivered it in such an unselfconsciously droll, circuitous way that Richard was sorry to say goodbye.

'Where are you going now?' he asked as her hand was already on the door handle.

'Back home. Crouch End.'

He frowned. 'But that's miles away.'

'Sorry. I'm afraid I only wanted a ride in your car.'

Laughing, not at him but at herself, she climbed out. He leaned across to stop her from closing the door.

'May I buy you dinner some time?'

'You certainly may,' said Jen.

**A**nd then there was Isla. Isla whom he worshipped and wooed, and who finally came his way. Isla, with the luminous glow of popular fame which somehow set her apart from the ordinary messy travails of human relationships. Isla who, against all the odds, loved him in return.

Richard often wondered if she knew about Jen, and usually concluded that she didn't. After all, there had been no sudden changes in his behaviour, no differences that she would notice, no cooling in his behaviour. Jen had always been there.

## chapter three

'**E**VERYTHING'S FINE,' Isla told Barbara over the phone. 'Trust me.'

'Oh, I do,' said Barbara. 'And Bill does, too, in so far as he trusts any woman. Unfortunately he believes we're all easily led. I tell him he flatters himself, but it makes not a blind bit of difference. I think he thought you'd take his side.'

'Easily led . . .?'

'Precisely.'

'Well, anyway, I'm not just going to leave it there,' said Isla. 'I thought I'd invite the two of them to dinner, to see how they perform in company. I'd be amazed if something wasn't going on. And if there is, you should encourage it. He's an absolute charmer.'

'Yes, but Nell isn't,' said Barbara with bracing frankness. 'So if he's bedding her it's got to be for some ulterior motive, surely?'

'Bar, I despair of you—did you never hear of beauty being only skin-deep?'

Barbara grunted. 'There, if I may say, speaks a woman who's always been able to take the top layer for granted.'

After that Isla called Ned Braden. 'I wonder if you'd come and have supper in a couple of weeks' time—we could make it a Sunday if you're working.'

'Do what?' Ned gave his fruity Welsh chuckle. 'I'll come any bloody night you like, my lovely.'

'Friday fortnight then?'

'You're on. Any particular pretext? Anything I should know?'

'No, a mixed bag of people . . . nothing grand.'

'That's just as well, girl, because I don't do grand. As you know.' Another choice chuckle, ripe with cigarette smoke. There were times when she missed her *Lady in Charge* days.

'I'm really looking forward to seeing you, Ned.'

'Me too, petal. Can't wait.'

**R**ichard couldn't believe it. 'You're here! And no one else is?'

'Only the cats.' Jen grinned. 'Make the most of it. Drink?'

'I think I will.' Richard rolled his eyes to the ceiling. 'So where's he?'

'School trip to Amsterdam, he was telling me all about it.'

'And that,' Richard reminded her, pulling off his tie and undoing his collar, 'was *before* he went. Imagine what it will be like when he comes back with several rolls of film and a host of colourful memories.'

Jen handed him a whisky. 'Poor Keith . . .'

They began to laugh. She flopped down next to him, slopping wine on her shirt and wiping at it with her hand. He wiped too, his hand strayed, they were laughing helplessly now. She undid her shirt and hugged him to her, hands in his hair, her toes pushing at the waistband of his trousers. One-handed, he helped her. The rhythm of the laughter became the rhythm of sex. It was broad daylight and the living-room window was open onto the street, but they neither of them thought of that.

**W**hile Richard and Jen lay together in Crouch End, Isla was attending a photocall at the Hawkes Road City Farm in Bethnal Green for the animal charity Gain Without Pain. It was not one of the causes on whose letterheads she regularly appeared, but they had told her that a mere hour of her time, being photographed in jeans and T-shirt surrounded by lambs, rabbits and children from the local playgroup, would give their campaign an incredible boost. She'd been happy to oblige and was enjoying herself. By midday three rolls of film had been taken, the children were piled back into their minibus, and the animals were herded away to be fed and watered.

'We can't thank you enough,' said the press officer from Gain Without Pain, 'you were a star in every sense.'

'Don't thank me, I had fun.'

'Well, you say that, but . . .'

'She means it,' said another voice. 'Believe it or not.'

It was Robert Scott-Chatham. 'Scotch? What are you doing here?'

'PR, don't you know.' The press officer absented herself with a discreet smile. 'And no one calls me Scotch except Nell, though I give you permission.'

'Well, thanks.' She smiled up at him. 'So whose image are you burnishing today?'

'City Farm's. It's actually a mutual image-booster for our firm—shows we're on the side of the angels, but no bucks in it, as you might imagine. Fancy a drink?'

It took Isla less than a second to decide, and when she declined it was because she wanted to go. 'I'd have loved to, but I have a home to go to and a husband to feed.'

They were now out in the road. 'What does he do, your husband?'

'He's a QC.'

'Ah, so an actor *manqué*.'

'Not at all. Richard's a star in his own firmament—a much more important one than mine, and a much bigger star.'

'There you go, selling yourself short again.' Her limo slid alongside.

'Can we offer you a lift?'

He held up his hands. 'Er—no. People might talk.'

The driver opened the door. 'I'll see you soon, I hope,' she said. 'I'm going to ask you and Nell to dinner.'

'Sounds a blast, we'd like that.'

Isla noted the 'we'.

The driver from the limo firm she used often was experienced enough not to make conversation. Isla thought about her husband, making his way back to their house from wherever he'd been. Not in court that afternoon, that much she knew.

She had always felt, instinctively, that there was someone else. Or a series of someones, she wasn't sure which. It had not been a case of accepting it tamely so much as realising that this other life was an integral part of Richard, something that had been there long before she was, and which was not going to go away. From time to time she despised herself for putting up with these fears and suspicions, but she simply could not bring herself to confront Richard with them. It was not just that she could not summon up the right lines, but that she did not want to see Richard, whom she loved and admired, compromised; and if that meant she was a tacit collaborator in whatever was going on, so be it. Besides, she never for a moment doubted the strength and passion of Richard's love for her. From the moment he had come after her she had seen it in his eyes and felt it in his touch—she was adored. Isla was used to being desired, but this had made her more, rather than less, sensitive to the real thing; with Richard she had found pure gold.

And yet . . . there was this secret which ran through their life together like an underground stream. She tried not to think about it. She was happy, she was loved, she had many friends, and she enjoyed great comfort and security. What was the point of digging beneath the surface in order to uncover something she was better off not knowing about?

When Isla first got to know Richard's friends and colleagues, they had never portrayed him as a womaniser, but rather as a man who had been through the mill of two disastrous marriages and to whom she, they assured her, represented likely salvation. His fearsome professional reputation seemed at odds with his notably unsuccessful private life, a tension which struck a chord with her, and which she found attractive. After years of actors who resorted to everything from gyms to make-up to alter their appearance, she appreciated a man upon whom an embarrassment of physical gifts were left to go hang. Richard was six foot four with dark, greying hair worn, through idleness, a little overlong, and brown eyes with a sardonic droop at the outer corners. His attachment to good food and wine and his aversion to exercise for its own sake had resulted in a distinct bulge above the waistband of his trousers. If Isla teasingly grabbed it, he would frown anxiously. 'Does it disgust you?'

'No.'

'You,' he would add, also teasingly, 'who could have any man you wanted?'

'Do I seem disgusted?'

The exchange usually ended in a kiss, at least. Isla's only real concern was for Richard's health. She did her best to lower fat and raise fibre, but there was nothing she could do about the wine and the weed.

Isla was sure that if she had not met Richard she would never have married. It was only after she had accepted Richard's proposal—his fifth? or was it sixth?—that she realised no one else had asked her. Those men—mostly actors—with whom she had had relationships of any duration had all professed to worship her more than life itself, but none had proposed. Richard, against all the odds, believed in wedded bliss. She had been touched by his faith in an institution which had so signally let him down. Her pride was challenged—having accepted him, she wanted very much to be the wife of his dreams.

And that, she supposed, as the limo began the climb up towards Hampstead Heath, was what she was being. The perfect wife.

On the way home, Richard, having pulled up at a red light on the corner of Archway Road, stared at a flower stall and debated whether to buy flowers for Isla. He could see the white trumpet lilies and creamy stocks that she adored, and he would like to have given her some. If they could have reached her at this very moment by other means—by fax, say, or delivery—he would have given in to the impulse. But to arrive with the bouquet in his arms would inevitably prompt the question, full of delight, 'What are these for?' And the message might not accord with something in his eyes . . .

Just before he reached the round pond, Richard pulled over and got out of the car. He retrieved his jacket off the back seat and shrugged it on, then locked up and strolled a little way down the broad, sandy track, an expedition he often made when travelling direct from Selwyn Street to Hampstead. There was a seat a couple of hundred yards from the road where he sat down and lit a cigar. As he lifted the lighter he inhaled briefly, to detect what of Jen remained on his sleeve.

The sun beat down. For the past couple of weeks the weather had continued relentlessly perfect. Sitting high on the wooded hill overlooking London, waiting for the heat and the cigar smoke to burn off the traces of Selwyn Street, and anticipating the shady seclusion of his garden at home, Richard was happy.

Now that he'd gone, Jen, too, was out in the sun. She lay on her back, eyes closed, Abel crouched sphinxlike on her solar plexus. Her patch of luxuriant, uncut grass grew smaller as the summer progressed and the surrounding vegetation encroached. The drone of distant traffic, the buzz of wasps over fallen greengages and Abel's rattling purr created a kind of aural whiteout. Added to which was the deep peace of Keith's absence.

She thought, tranquilly, about Richard, and the wife to whom he had returned. Even if Jen had been a devotee of newspaper and magazine gossip columns, she was unlikely to have known the identity of Mrs Richard Wakefield. This was because Isla had made a point of keeping her marriage as private as possible. Only her closest friends had known about the wedding, and many others only came to hear of it months later. There had been no press at the ceremony and when attending legal functions with Richard she remained scrupulously in the background.

Jen considered her ignorance a positive advantage where it concerned Richard's present wife. She knew he had been married twice before—he was not long divorced when she first met him—and it had been more than two years before she realised he had married again. A 'we' had slipped back into his discourse and there were references to an unmistakably shared social life—friends for dinner, Sunday lunches . . . a holiday in St Lucia. Jen should have been shocked and outraged, but she wasn't. She had never wanted or expected marriage, and she felt herself to be secure in whatever part of Richard's affections she, uniquely, held sway.

But lying in the sun this late afternoon, her thoughts did drift in that direction. The last thing she had ever wanted was to hurt another woman, but what was a woman supposed to do when she found she was the other woman by default?

She also knew that Richard loved his wife, and she was glad of it. Jen realised how much worse it would be to be having sex with a man who had entered into some kind of marriage of convenience, but who still needed her to spill his seed into a couple of times a week. As it was, she gleaned a certain self-respect in knowing that she was the mistress of a happy man. But that didn't stop her from indulging, from time to time, in idle curiosity.

A shadow came between her and the sun and she opened her eyes and squinted up from under cupped hands.

'Sorry, can't see a thing—who goes there?'

'It's me.'

'Red, sweetheart—' Jen sat up and patted the ground next to her. 'Come and sit down.'

'No, Mum, you've got a visitor,' said Claudia.

'Oh God. Who?'

'How on earth should I know? We just met by the gate.'

'Oh God,' said Jen again, scrabbling to her feet and dusting herself off distractedly.

Claudia followed her mother, at a distance, back into the house. She remained in the kitchen, while Jen went to meet the visitor.

'I'm awfully sorry to descend on you like this without so much as a phone call, only I've been carrying around your leaflet for weeks, and when I found myself in the environs I thought I might as well drop in.'

'That's OK.' Jen shook the proffered hand. 'Come on in.' She led her visitor into the living room. 'Excuse the mess.'

'Home from home. How do you do? Petronella Fyler.'

Claudia went upstairs. She had come home this afternoon to rummage through the clothes which she'd left in her room, in the hope of finding something suitable to wear.

The bedroom had always been spartan—the only room in the house that was—even when she'd been living in it. The wooden bed, made by her father, was covered with a dhurrie striped in shades of red and yellow. A threadbare woven rug lay on the floor, which was otherwise bare boards. There was a long mirror propped against one wall and two Indian prints stuck on another.

The wardrobe was an old-fashioned, freestanding one with a speckled mirror on the front and slightly uneven legs. The door was stiff, and as it jerked open the wardrobe teetered threateningly. Some of the clothes were still on their hangers, but most, having been haphazardly arranged in the first place, had fallen to the floor to join a collection of dusty boots, flattened espadrilles, odd trainers and chewed-looking belts. Having riffled through and discounted what was hanging up, she scooped up a large armful of the rest and dumped it on the bed.

She spent very little on clothes, and most of what she did buy was secondhand. She liked odd, broken-in things that did not speak of sex—a look that was interesting, occasionally picturesque, often challenging rather than alluring.

In the pile she saw a flash of something green and glimmering, shot with blue. It was a dress, vaguely ethnic, a market buy from a couple of years ago, now creased and crumpled beyond recognition. She gave it a few vigorous shakes and held it out at arm's length. It was a good colour and seemed to have some beading round the neck, which quivered and caught the light. She kicked off her boots, removed her overalls and tugged the dress over her head.

The speckled mirror revealed a tall streak of brilliant green like a reed. The dress wasn't lined and it clung to Claudia's legs almost to the ankle. She tugged at the creases, some of which were stuck together with damp, revealing weals of discoloration when separated, but she quite liked those. She pulled her boots back on. The pleasing incongruity was what decided her. This would do for going to see the designer. Standing sideways on to the mirror, she held a pose for a split second before yanking off the dress in a hot rush of embarrassment.

'She's a lovely old thing,' said Jen, looking at the photograph that had been handed to her. 'I can see why you'd want her portrait done.'

'Well, as I say, it's for my mother. She's a very practical, hard-hearted countrywoman in most ways, but she's terribly soppy about her dogs.'

'She's got more than one?'

'Oh, there are scads about the place, but just the two indoor dogs—Portia and Pepe. Poor old Portia's on the last lap.'

Jen handed the photo back. 'I'll need some more of those. Quite a lot if you want it to be a surprise. Normally I work from photographs that I've taken myself, so I have seen the sitter in the flesh at least once.'

'I've got a whole film in the car—of course they may not be good enough—hang on—'

In a moment she was back, clutching a paper folder. 'There you are.'

Jen took them out and leafed through them. 'These should be fine.' She replaced the photos. 'How quickly do you want it?'

'Well, my mother's birthday's actually the end of next week . . .' Nell grimaced, half-grin, half-scowl. 'Sorry!'

'I'm not busy,' said Jen disingenuously. 'I can do it by the end of this, if you can sort out framing—my chap's snowed under.'

Nell clasped her hand. 'Thank you so much. You are a sport. I'm so glad I decided to drop in.'

Claudia waited till she heard the front door close before coming down, the green dress scrunched up in one hand.

'Fancy a glass of wine?' called Jen from the kitchen.

'No, thanks, I'm off.'

Jen appeared, glass in one hand, bottle in the other. 'So soon? I thought you'd be staying for supper?'

'No, I want to get back, I've got an essay to write . . .'

'Oh, you found that dress.' Jen put down the bottle and came over to her. 'I always loved you in that.'

'Yes, well . . . it needs a wash, but it'll do . . .'

'Got a date?' Jen touched her daughter's cheek.

'Sorry to disappoint you.'

'No! Hold it right there!' Jen ran back into the kitchen, returning with a scrap of paper which she waggled at her daughter.

Claudia took the paper. 'What's this?'

'He called to speak to you, but I was very discreet and said I'd pass a message so you weren't caught on the hop—he's a bit old for you, but I'm not bitter.'

'Who, for heaven's sake?'

Jen flipped the edge of the paper. 'Red—Anthony Saxby.'

'Who?' asked Claudia again, loudly, to disguise the thunder of her heart.

'You know,' protested Jen. 'Your fellow bastard.'

**R**ichard enjoyed artistic spats, professionally speaking. Though not always as profitable, a good dirty fight between creative types was infinitely more satisfying than the self-righteous whinging of pompous politicians, more edifying than pop stars spitting tacks. As he parked the Jag behind chambers, he felt his usual enthusiasm for his work edged with a keen, bright happiness at the thought of the award-winning author whose damaged reputation it was in his power to restore.

He paused as Archie's red Nissan Frontera lurched round the corner and stopped next to the Jag. Archie got out of the car and advanced towards him, an overstuffed briefcase clutched in his arms like a baby.

'Morning, old man.'

'Richard . . . Christ—' Archie lost his grip on the briefcase and grabbed it as it slid down his chest. 'You know—I sometimes think about you as I'm getting ready to leave home.'

'Do you?' asked Richard. 'Why's that?'

The two men began the ascent of the narrow stairs, made narrower and extremely dusty by plywood partitions masking the refurbishments which were currently in progress. 'I bet it's paradise compared with Casa Stainforth of an early morning.'

Richard didn't counter this speculation. 'We're seeing you tonight, aren't we?'

'Yes!' exclaimed Archie, his face lighting up as he remembered. 'Oh, excellent! I can't tell you what a difference knowing that has made to my day already.'

Archie's enthusiasm finally caused him to drop the briefcase in the reception area. Richard left him to pick up the drift of loose paper with the assistance of Mrs Colley from behind the desk, and went into the clerks' room. All were present and at their desks with cups of coffee. The senior clerk, Terry Goldman—a slick, bright thirty-year-old from Basildon—made Richard think of some palmier era when gentlemen had gentlemen. Theirs was an entirely harmonious relationship based on an underlying agreement to differ on everything that did not pertain to these chambers and the running of Richard's professional affairs.

'Good morning,' said Richard.

'Morning,' replied Goldman, who cultivated a drily democratic air with his superiors.

Richard put down his case and riffled through his pigeonhole with a slight frown. He relished the prospect of his day, but didn't wish to betray that relish to Goldman. 'What time's our first?'

'Ten.' Goldman added, 'Literary lions—perlease.'

Richard enjoyed the morning's conference with the senior of two Booker-winning brothers. It was clear to him that this was a straightforward case of sibling rivalry—this older and more academically brilliant brother being rapidly overtaken by the younger and more popular one, coming up on the inside. Richard's client took the deepest exception to remarks quoted in a Sunday paper to the effect that his work was 'stuffy, self-serving and derivative'. There had been other, more personal insults, but it was these about his work which had caused blood to heat and tempers to flare.

'**W**ho else will be there?' asked Alison, licking her finger and scrubbing at a mark on her lapel. 'Do we know?'

'No. Richard didn't say, and I didn't think to ask.'

'But it's not just us, or they'd have said.'

'Presumably.'

Alison held her arms away from her sides. 'Do I look all right?'

Archie detected the tremor of genuine anxiety in his wife's voice and hastened to reassure her. 'You look absolutely wonderful.'

She gave a rueful smile. 'With all due respect, love, I never look absolutely wonderful.'

'To me you do.'

'But I have to be the very least presentable in that company.' She brushed briskly at her skirt, a snip from the mid-season sale in her favourite catalogue.

'You'll be far more than that,' said Archie stoutly, sensing that the moment's vulnerability was at an end. 'I'll go and turn the car round.'

**U**nusually for her, Isla couldn't decide what note to strike. She firmly believed that the job of a hostess was to provide a background against which others could shine, particularly on an occasion when a young couple were among the guests. She wanted to be able to sit back and observe, knowing that everyone round her table was happy and confident. On the other hand, if she was completely honest with herself, she hoped to deserve another compliment from Robert Scott-Chatham.

Changing her mind, she removed the blue shantung shirtwaister, threw it on the bed, and put on a short, sleek grey silk shift from Ghost. It was a dress of perfect minimalist beauty. She added minute pearl drop-earrings and silver sandals.

'I say,' exclaimed Richard, dropping the *Evening Standard* over the side of his chair. 'Have some pity, woman.'

'Too much?'

'Quite the reverse.'

'That's what I thought.'

'Don't change!' called Richard, as she crossed the hall. 'Why change?'

Ned Braden took the bus to South End Green, for both social and economic reasons. He wanted to be able to have a drink, and he couldn't afford a cab. His professional status at the moment was ill-defined—he had a name, certainly, though increasingly it rang bells only with an older audience, but it was a name based on past successes, notably *Lady in Charge* and his will-they-won't-they on-screen relationship with Isla. After *Lady in Charge*, they'd given him his own comedy drama series, entitled *Sparrow in the Treetops*, following the future fortunes of the character he'd made his own. When it failed to take, they came up with something else—*Lockwood*—based on a character who was just Jake Sparrow by another name and in another job, the CID. But by now roguish charm was giving way to gritty reality, and coppers were more or less indistinguishable from villains, so it was inevitable that after one series *Lockwood* left the screens never to reappear. Since then he'd done guest spots in other people's series and appeared from to time on celebrity panel shows. But he wasn't downhearted. He loved the business, he still had his looks, more or less, and a trickle of work.

He wondered who else Isla would have over tonight. As he paused at the entrance to the Wakefields' drive a car came up behind him. He stood aside for it to pass, but it stopped next to him and the passenger window hummed down at eye level—it was one of those family four-wheel drives. A homely sort beamed out at him.

'Sorry, was that a bit close for comfort?'

'Not at all, you weren't to know.'

'Going in for dinner?'

'I do hope so, or it's the homeless men's shelter for me.'

She gave a cheerful, honking laugh. 'See you in there.' The driver—her husband presumably—was a large, dim, background presence. As husbands so often were. The car moved on.

Of course they all fetched up on the doorstep together and the woman saw to the introductions. The husband, Archie, was one of those distrait owl-of-the-remove types with a hot handshake and a high shine. But when Richard opened the door in his no-contest toff's kit of cream jacket and flannels, it was Archie who got the shoulder slap.

'Hello, hello! Archie old man . . . Ali, mm . . . and Ned, it's been far too long. Come in and have a Pimms without further ado.'

They went through to the wonderful tangled orangery, where the doors stood open and Isla—with impeccable grace and timing—was walking towards them across the grass with a tangled wreath of uprooted pink and white convolvulus trailing from one hand. Had she, Ned wondered, actually stage-managed that—nipped down to the end of the garden when she heard the doorbell in order to present this picture of exquisite, artless informality? She wore a brilliant blue dress with a crisp shirt neck, some green beads, flat green pumps. What a pro . . .

'Look who I found,' said Richard. 'I take it everyone will have one of these . . . ?'

This time Alison got the first greeting, Archie the second, himself last, but he was confident her kisses had been meted out in ascending order of importance.

'You look absolutely stunning,' he said.

'Doesn't she always?' asked Alison, and Ned thought he detected a moment's embarrassment in the husband.

'Your garden is amazing,' said Archie, walking past them and out onto the mossy terrace. 'How do you do it?'

'Don't look at me,' said Richard. He hung back slightly as Archie, Alison and Isla ranged themselves overlooking the garden. 'How are you, Ned? Plenty of work?'

Ned always suspected that Richard took a fairly dim view of what he probably called 'theatricals'—his wife excepted, of course—so it took a considerable effort not to feel patronised.

'Plenty, no. Enough—just about.'

'It's a cruel profession you're in.'

'And you.'

'Not really—ah, I see what you mean.'

'Nothing personal,' explained Ned. 'But wielding so much power . . . it would frighten the living daylights out of me.'

Richard smiled and said something self-deprecating, but he was irritated by Ned. There was an unmistakable streak of bitchiness which wasn't helped by Ned's past association with Isla. Underpinning any exchange was the playing of the shared-history card, as if the acting profession were a mystical brotherhood the roots of whose allegiances went deeper than mere marital ties. To his relief the doorbell rang.

'Will you excuse me?'

'Ned,' called Isla. 'Alison suddenly realised why you look familiar. Come and meet another of your fans.'

Richard's reaction on opening the door, bearing in mind his wife's assessment of the situation, was that if these two were a couple they were an exceptionally odd one. Nell Fyler, though handsome, had if anything even less idea about self-presentation than Alison, and was done up in sprigged Laura Ashley, which clashed with her crunching handshake. Robert Scott-Chatham was self-possessed and stylish in the unshaven manner of the times. Richard tried to remember what he did for a living. Media, he supposed, in that suit.

'Come on through,' he said, 'and meet the others. We're a small, select group this evening—only the best people invited.'

'For goodness' sake don't tell him that,' boomed Nell. 'His head's quite big enough already!'

Ned looked across at Robert Scott-Chatham. This, by God, was a horse of an altogether different colour. Things were looking up.

When the second round of introductions had been completed, and Richard was circulating once more with the Pimms, Isla withdrew to the kitchen. She was not a natural cook, but she did like to entertain. She got round this by a means only available to the affluent, which was to use the very best ingredients. She aspired to a simple, unadorned lavishness, perfectly presented.

Tonight the dining room was lit by tall ivory church candles which gave off a faint scent of honey. Flowers were white and cream, blooming among wayward greenery. There was polished oak, softly gleaming silver, and white china edged in red and gold: a decor mellow and traditional, but also sleek and spare. Isla and Danielle—a sophisticated Belgian help of the kind only to be found in Hampstead—set out heaped black pearls of caviar in a silver bowl, and placed Melba toast and lemon wedges on green Wedgwood. In the kitchen there waited saddle of lamb, tiny new potatoes shining with butter, starred with parsley and mint, *al dente* sugar peas and baby carrots; blackcurrant fool in tall, fluted glasses; a gold-crusted half-moon of brie, oozing ripeness; spears of pale celery; misty black and green grapes. The sensuous beauty of such food delighted Isla.

'I hope you have the nicest guests,' said Danielle, 'who are going to appreciate all this.'

'Don't worry,' replied Isla. 'They are. They will.'

She was happy because things seemed to be going well. The only worry she had was that Ned might drink too much. She had invited him out of genuine affection and because she had faith in his judgment of other people, but she was the first to admit he was a loose cannon. Another reason for inviting him was that a spare man introduced a note of informality, a tacit assumption that this was not a couples-only event.

Ned's role tonight was that of single male. The table was a long oval, and Isla had arranged the places elliptically, with no head. She didn't have a seating plan either, preferring to see how people arranged themselves.

In the event Scotch and Nell separated, which she took to be an indication that they were close enough to be comfortable apart. It had become surprisingly important to her that these two *should* be an item. She found herself between Ned and Alison, which demanded a high level of sympathetic diplomacy. Alison hadn't a mean bone in her body, but she was as tactless as Ned was touchy.

'Why didn't they go on with that police thing?' asked Alison. 'We loved it.'

'A lot of people did. But not, unfortunately, the powers that be.'

'Still, presumably you don't need to worry.'

'Sorry?'

'You made your pile with Isla here, surely, in *Lady St George*. I mean, everyone watched—you were stars.'

'*Lady In Charge*. And there was no pile involved, I do assure you.'

'Really? How's she done it then?' Alison jerked her head at Isla.

Ned's complexion darkened ominously. 'Clever management?'

'I married money,' said Isla. 'It's the only way.'

As Alison laughed, Ned thanked God for true friends.

Scotch addressed Richard. 'This is the most beautiful house. Would you consider leaving it to a total stranger?'

'There's a waiting list,' replied Richard drily.

'I can believe it. It's wonderful. Don't you reckon, Nell?'

'Yes, indeed.' Nell gazed round. 'Very grown-up, I always think.'

Archie laid a confiding hand on the table next to her. 'You make a good point there. We have a perfectly good house, but it's stuffed to capacity with kids and their effects.'

'My parents' place is like that,' said Nell. 'My mother will allow her dogs to do more or less what they like, as Richard well knows.'

'Your parents are among our dearest friends,' responded Richard with ambiguous gallantry.

'I want to meet them,' declared Scotch. 'But she won't invite me.'

Nell speared a potato from the dish. 'You'd hate each other on sight.'

'I bet you're wrong,' put in Archie. 'Opposites agree and all that.'

'Listen to the man,' said Scotch. 'I want to be shown round the gun room. I've even got the waxed jacket.'

Nell rolled her eyes in horror. 'It's brand-new, from Simpson.'

'I'll take the darn thing to Wimbledon Common and distress it comprehensively before I come.'

Ned leaned across. 'I beg your pardon. Am I missing something interesting here?'

'He's referring to his Barbour,' explained Archie, 'and the fact that it's too pristine to pass muster in an authentically rural environment.'

Isla got up to clear and Nell pushed her chair back. 'I'll help.'

'No need. Danielle's out there.'

'But I'd like to.'

As she took the fool from the fridge, Isla scrutinised Nell from the corner of her eye. Beneath the ill-chosen sprigs she had a nice figure, and her eyes were bright with enjoyment.

'I'm so pleased you could both come,' she said, decanting some cream. 'It's nice to have an evening in really relaxing company.'

'Ditto,' replied Nell. 'You have no idea.'

'Scotch is a dear.' She chose her words to convey an older woman's indulgent approval.

'Isn't he?' Nell picked at the leftover sugar peas with her finger and thumb. 'He was an absolute find. He and I are thick as thieves.'

'Anyone can see that.'

'There's nothing whatever in it, Isla. We're just pals, really.'

'Well, that's even better,' said Isla imperturbably, holding the door for Danielle with the tray. 'Loving don't last—liking do.'

She was rewarded by an incandescent grin which only confirmed her in her view that there was Something Going On, and that whatever it was could be the making of Nell Fyler.

They all went out into the garden for coffee. Generally Isla preferred to keep everyone round the table so that the delicate spider's web of connections, which had formed during dinner, should not be broken. But this time the moonlit summer's night was too good to miss. She had put two iron lanterns on the stone wall at the edge of the terrace, and left a lamp lit in the orangery. She watched the way people lifted their faces slightly as they walked out, as if they were subject to the benign tidal pull of the moon and its far-flung net of stars. Alison sat near Richard on the wall. Nell, Scotch and Ned wandered down the shallow mossy steps and across the lawn. Archie came to stand by her.

'We're like Shakespeare alfresco,' he murmured.

'Isn't it lovely?'

'You did that,' he added solemnly. 'Aren't you clever?'

'In the library,' murmured Danielle discreetly over the coffeepot.

Danielle glided away. Isla walked slowly to the door of the orangery, and more quickly once through it. She almost ran across the hall, pushed open the library door and whisked it to behind her.

Marcus stood with his back to her.

'Marcus . . . ?'

'Yeah?'

'What are you doing here?'

He turned round and she was shocked by the whiteness of his face, burning with a kind of angry exhaustion. 'Nothing. I'll go if you like.'

'No! No, please don't.' Boldly she went over and took him by the shoulders, kissing him on the cheek. He didn't respond, but neither did he resist. 'Are you all right?'

He shrugged. 'Sure.'

'Does the school know where you are?'

'I left a note. I told them I'd get back in touch.'

'What about your mother? She'll be worried sick if the school rings.'

'Maybe . . .'

'Of course! We'll contact her—Richard will.'

He mumbled something. It sounded like 'suit yourself'. His expression became wary again as Richard appeared.

'Look who's here,' said Isla.

'I can see. What's up?'

'I was pissed off. I had to get out of that place!'

'He's left them a note,' explained Isla. 'But we should call Caroline.'

'Yes, we will in a minute.' Richard went over to his son and stood before him. Only the fact that he kept his hands in his pockets prevented him looking threatening. 'Fancy something to eat?' he asked. Marcus shook his head. 'Want to come through and join us?'

'I don't mind.'

'Come on, then.'

Richard placed a light hand on the boy's shoulder and accompanied him from the room.

'Darling,' he said to Isla, 'could you give Caro a call? Tell her everything's under control and I'll speak to her properly in the morning.'

'And Hawtrey's . . . ?' she said.

'Let's leave it till morning unless they contact us.'

A few minutes later, having phoned Caroline, Isla returned to the garden. Everyone was on the terrace, sitting together, some on the wall, others on chairs of different heights. Nell and Ned were smoking. Richard, cigar in hand, was circulating with a bottle. Marcus had been absorbed into the group; the soft glow of the lanterns showed his face to have quietened as he listened to the others.

The scent of Richard's cigar reminded Isla how much she loved him.

# *chapter four*

**H**AWTREY'S WAS characteristically understanding about Marcus. He shouldn't have gone AWOL, of course, and that much would have to be acknowledged on his return; but they appreciated it hadn't been an easy term, and the academic year was nearly at an end. They'd expect him back on Sunday night.

Richard didn't worry about it too much, either. His younger son was given to these sudden urges to escape and they all, school included, had learned to live with them. Marcus slept for most of Saturday and Caroline came over in the evening to run the rule over him, bristling with a disturbing mixture of maternal anxiety and suspicion.

'But there must be something the matter!' she insisted over supper. 'And you must tell either me or your father about it, or what can we do to help?'

Marcus was predictably tightlipped. 'There's nothing the matter.'

'Come on, darling, we weren't born yesterday—'

'Then get off my case, why don't you?'

'There's no need to bite my head off! Richard . . . ?'

Richard said, 'I'm sure he'd let us know if it was anything important.'

Marcus pushed his chair back. 'I'm going for a walk.'

'I wonder, if you're going out,' said Isla, also rising, 'would you do me a favour and pick up a pint of milk? I've miscalculated.'

She went with him into the hall, gave him some money, closed the door after him, returned.

'Well done,' said Richard.

Isla cast an apologetic look at Caroline. 'I thought the milk might be a hostage to fortune.'

'What if he doesn't come back?' Caroline's voice wobbled. 'I feel as though I do everything wrong at the moment. Everything.'

'I think you're wonderful,' said Isla. 'He'll come back. I'm going to make coffee.' As she left the room Richard rose and went round to sit by Caroline, who had covered her face with her hands.

Out in the kitchen Isla found she was trembling.

**M**arcus was back inside an hour and went to bed. He even managed a 'Night, Mum' from the hall, which went some way towards mollifying Caroline. The next day Richard drove him back to Hawtrey's. Little by little but discernibly, in the privacy of his father's car, Marcus unbent.

'Will Mum be OK?'

'Of course. You saw for yourself. She's already OK.'

'I didn't mean to have a pop at her.'

'Yes, you did,' said Richard.

Marcus pushed his fist against the walnut facia of the glove compartment. 'All right, I did. I couldn't help it.'

'Yes, you could.' Richard glanced at him with a reproving half-smile. 'But she couldn't help worrying, however annoying you may find that.'

'She goes on and on, she wants to get everything organised, she's not happy unless someone gives her an answer,' protested Marcus. 'It does my head in.'

'Yes. Well, it does your mother's head in not being able to help,' said Richard. 'And I must say I'm with her on that score. We're on your side, we want to be made use of.'

'I came to your house, didn't I?'

'I'm pleased you did.'

'Yours was the closest,' added Marcus, to wipe out any hint of favouritism. 'My ride had to drop me at Platts Lane.'

'I'm sure Mum understands about that, don't worry.'

'I'm not worrying.'

'Glad to hear it.'

Richard let the silence expand and wash round them, covering the tracks of the last exchange, before asking, 'How's Giles?'

'How should I know?'

'I assume since you attend the same boarding school,' said Richard, unable to entirely curb his impatience, 'that you might run into each other from time to time.'

'Not if I can help it. He's an idiot,' muttered Marcus venomously. 'Reckons he's the dog's bollocks . . . screwing Fay Gadney . . . Idiot!'

Something clicked inside Richard. The tension eased. Just occasionally life wasn't complicated. Like the warring authors, it was as simple as sibling rivalry.

'Giles won't be there much longer,' he pointed out.

Marcus muttered something which ended in the words '. . . too soon for me', but though his brow was thunderous Richard recognised a moment of truth.

It was this sense of 'crisis over' which persuaded him, after returning

Marcus, calling on Giles, and having a brief bloke-to-bloke with the headmaster, to go and call on his father at The Hayes, Lettaford. But first he rang Caroline to assure her that the panic was over.

'Thank God,' she said. 'But why must he be such a drama queen?'

'It gets it out of his system,' suggested Richard. 'I believe drama's quite healthy, psychologically speaking.'

'Healthy for him, maybe. I feel about a hundred and fifty and completely shot to pieces.'

'Well, if it's any consolation, you don't look it. You're looking marvellous at the moment.'

'Oh, get on with you,' said Caroline, mollified. 'Anyway, thanks for doing the honours, I appreciate it. I'm quite sure if it'd been me neither of us would've kept our tempers.'

Richard then called Isla. 'They feed them disgustingly early in that place,' he said, 'so I'll have something to eat with the old boy and be back about ten.'

Richard's father, now ninety, had lived at The Hayes for the past six years without passing comment on either the Georgian architecture or the beautiful surroundings. This studied lack of interest was the most scathing criticism available to a man hitherto famous for having an opinion on everything. When Richard and Isla had first presided over Alec's move from the flat in St John's Wood, where he'd lived since his wife's death, they had tried to draw his attention to The Hayes's many outstanding features, from its imaginative cuisine to its classical music club, but to no effect. He had acknowledged the necessity of the move, but he didn't have to like the place, and he was buggered if he was going to. That was the message, and they'd received it loud and clear.

Richard had the chance of a quick word with Karen, the matron, whom he encountered in the hall.

'How is he?'

'Physically, doing well. He loves his food,' said Karen. 'But like all of us he has his good days and his bad days.'

'And which is this?' asked Richard.

'I can't tell a lie—not so good,' admitted Karen, but added, on seeing Richard's alarmed expression, 'I'm sure all that will change now you're here.'

He wished he could be so sure. He followed Karen's neatly belted waist and bobbing ponytail up the staircase.

'Will you be having dinner with your father?' asked Karen on the landing outside Alec's room.

'Would that be possible?'

'Vegetable curry or haddock mornay?'

'Haddock sounds nice.'

'Haddock. Apple and peach crumble or chocolate surprise?'

'I think I should enjoy the element of surprise . . .' It was like one of those childhood games offering endless options.

'Where does he usually eat at the moment?'

Karen sighed regretfully. 'We can't dig him out of his room—but you might be able to.'

'I'll do my best.'

Karen tapped on the door and opened it. 'Alec! You've got a visitor.'

'Oh God! Who . . .?'

'And I do hope you're going to offer him a drink.' Karen withdrew, closing the door.

'Hello, Father.'

'It's you. Excuse my not getting up, I don't get up much these days.'

'Don't even think of it.'

Richard went over and patted his father awkwardly on the arm. Alec was sitting in his armchair before the bay window, a tumbler of whisky in his hand, legs planted firmly apart, feet in corduroy slippers. Because of his girth, he still conveyed an impression of bulk, but Richard knew that one of the reasons he refused to struggle to his feet was that age and arthritis had shortened his bones. He still had a fine head of hair, though—thick, wavy and iron-grey, worn a little long out of vanity, so that it curled on the collar of his checked shirt. The room was large and well proportioned. Many of Alec's own things were here, they'd insisted he have them, though Richard knew he was probably being truthful when he said it was a matter of indifference to him—he wasn't sentimental about things any more than he was about people.

'Take a pew,' said Alec. 'Get the weight off your feet.'

'Thanks, but I've been driving. I'll stand for a bit.'

'Suit yourself. Help yourself to a drink, by the way.'

Richard went over to the drinks tray. It was the salver presented to his father on his retirement, engraved with the signatures of other doctors; kept brilliantly polished, he was pleased to note. He poured himself a small whisky and topped it up with water from the basin tap.

'There are some monkey nuts in the cupboard,' said Alec, 'if you can be bothered.'

Richard got out the nuts, opened the packet with his teeth and put it on top of the *Daily Telegraph* on the table next to his father.

'They've offered me dinner,' he said casually, 'which was nice of them. Shall we go down to the dining room?'

'I wasn't planning on it.'

'No—but as I'm here. You won't have to sit with anyone else, because you'll be entertaining me.'

They went down to the dining room at six thirty. It was high-ceilinged and elegant, with hot plates on an oak sideboard, respectable watercolours, George Stubbs table mats and linen napkins.

'How nice to see you, Alec,' said Karen, showing them to a table in the window. 'Are you going to have some wine?'

'Why not?' said Richard.

Alec brightened up considerably over the haddock mornay, and downed the wine thirstily.

'How's Isla?' he asked.

'She's fine.'

'Bring her next time, she's extraordinarily decorative. And a sweetie, to boot.'

'She is both of those things, you're right.'

'And my grandsons?'

Richard had anticipated this question, and how to pitch his reply. 'Chasing women, smoking, drinking—business as usual.'

Alec gave a wheezy, bellows-like laugh. 'Glad to hear it. Any chance of getting a look at them some time?'

'Come and have Sunday lunch next time we're at the cottage. You ought to get out, and they'd like to see you.'

'I take leave to doubt that, but we'll see . . .'

Pudding arrived. The chocolate surprise was, not surprisingly, a slab of gâteau.

Alec poured custard over his crumble with a self-satisfied air.

'Bad choice. There's always one out of a packet, and you got it. It'll be like cotton wool and shaving cream,' said Alec, a prediction which turned out to be wholly accurate.

They went back upstairs for coffee, brought by a pale auxiliary.

'Shall I be mother?' said Richard.

'Yes, and there's some chocolate. Same cupboard as the nuts.'

Richard fetched it and handed it to his father who broke off a generous chunk. 'No? You realise you can't smoke in here? It's not a wonder I'm getting so damn fat.' He looked at Richard. 'And how about you?' He tapped the *Telegraph* with his forefinger. 'Saw the piece about your case. Congratulations.'

'Thank you. Yes, it was very pleasing.'

'And very remunerative.'

'That too, although—' Richard was about to make some point about money, which he always felt compelled to do with his father, when the phone rang. Alec got up quite spryly to answer it.

'Isla, my darling, we were just talking about you! Saying what a wicked, sour-faced dragon you were . . . Ha-ha! Yes! Do you want to speak to the old man? I suppose I'd better not keep you.' He held out the receiver. 'Your wife.'

He sat down heavily as Richard took the phone. 'Hello.'

'I was thinking about the two of you, and felt the urge to ring. How is your father?'

'Excellent. We had a nice dinner and we're just having some coffee upstairs before I have to push off.'

'Give him a kiss from me.'

'I'll convey it somehow or other, never fear.'

'See you later.'

Alec was consulting the television page and didn't look up as he spoke. 'See she's checking up on you, then.'

'Isla? Hardly. Why on earth would she do that?'

Alec peered down at the listings. 'Don't know, old boy. You tell me.'

On Tuesday morning Claudia skipped a lecture and presented herself at the London address of David D. She told herself she had nothing to lose. She was perfectly happy with her degree course and the way things were. These people were interested? They'd have to make the running.

She wore the green dress, the sprucing up of which had proved rather trickier than she'd anticipated. But the overall effect, with the boots, was pleasing, and she borrowed some earrings off a friend—twin blizzards of small brass stars that chinked confidingly when she moved her head.

David D was on the first floor. In the reception area a middle-aged woman sat at a large wooden table which had nothing on it except a computer and a bonsai tree. She wore a white shirtwaister with epaulettes which made her look like a nurse. She gave Claudia a penetrating look over half-moon glasses.

'Yes?'

'I rang—I made an appointment with—' Claudia couldn't remember who with, rummaged in her fishing-bag and found the card. 'It was Olivier Marc who gave me the card, and my appointment's with Jane Porter.'

'Wait one moment.' She rose. 'Do sit down.'

Claudia now saw that there was a row of spindly steel and plastic chairs against the wall behind the door. Like a doctor's waiting room. Her hackles rose. 'No, thanks.'

The woman glanced at her for a nanosecond before disappearing. It was fully five minutes before she returned, accompanied by another, younger woman, in black leggings and a white shirt.

'Hello, Claudia, I'm Jane Porter. Come on through.'

The contrast with the receptionist could not have been more marked. Claudia strode past the receptionist's table with her head held high and followed Jane Porter into a cavernous room, half full of clothes on rails, with an office space at one end.

'Would you like some coffee?'

'No, thanks.'

'Bun?' Jane Porter offered a cardboard carton containing three jam doughnuts. They looked delicious. Claudia wasn't sure whether this might be some sort of test to see whether she was really model material, or the sort of girl who stuffed her face between meals.

'Don't worry.' Jane gave the box a little shake. 'Models eat like pigs.'

'Well—thanks.'

She took one and bit into it. Jane Porter did the same, and put on horn-rimmed specs before speaking through sugar-coated lips.

'Olivier is one of our Paris PRs, and he acts as a kind of *ad hoc* scout. I expect you thought he was in a prostitution racket. I've told him before about sidling up to strangers and slipping them our card.'

'I did wonder,' said Claudia, 'but I have heard of David D, so I thought why not?'

'Absolutely. And I'm so glad you did. I'm sure you don't need me to tell you that you're absolutely stunning.'

Claudia could think of no appropriate response.

'We're always on the lookout for unusual girls to model at our rail sales. They're informal fashion shows for favoured regular customers. Do you know anything about it?'

'I'm afraid not.'

'No, that's fine.' Jane rubbed her mouth with a Kleenex and pushed the box across the desk in Claudia's direction. 'Now, you said you knew about David D . . . ?'

'I've heard of him.'

'Them. Jean David and Dieter Gras. The look is classic—a sort of continental view of Englishness, really. Englishness with attitude. What the English country lady would wear if she didn't have a big backside and too many dogs.'

Jane reached behind her for something and slapped it down on top of the Kleenex box. 'That was our autumn/winter collection. Don't bother to look at it now, take it with you. The point is that we like to cast our models against the role. Have the strongest, wildest, most individual girls to show just how wonderful the clothes can look. I mean, for instance, I can see you in our cream twill breeches and green hacking jacket—perhaps with those earrings and a really mean-looking whip!'

She laughed. Claudia laughed too. Jane said, 'I hate to ask you to do this, but would you mind standing up and walking away from me as far as the door, then turning and walking back. Just walk normally.'

Claudia got up and walked to the door. Turned and walked back.

'Fine, that's great . . . I do like what you're wearing.'

'It's all ancient.'

'I can see that. But it suits you. And the boots are magic.'

'Yes, they're good boots.' Claudia looked down at them.

'So—by the way, what do you do?'

'I'm a student. Last year of my degree, here in London.'

'Could you manage to do a couple of shows in the early autumn? They'd both be here. We'd want you in for a rehearsal before that. Then afterwards, we'll see.'

'Yes.'

'We'll sort out your travel and expenses and I'll get someone to send you a contract. Linda Evangelista wouldn't turn over in bed for it.' Jane gave a wry little smile. 'But you never know.'

On the tube on the way back to her flat Claudia studied the David D catalogue. She got the picture instantly. There were tweed micro-kilts, massive caped overcoats, sleek velvet breeches and tailored satin shirts with moleskin waistcoats, all modelled by ethereal teenagers with big, black, exhausted eyes and spiky hair. Interesting.

She raced up the steps from the tube station two at a time and the side seam of the green dress finally gave up the ghost, revealing a length of pale, slender leg that nearly caused a seizure in two elderly vagrants sitting on the pavement outside.

An invitation to Barbara Fyler's birthday celebration on Sunday arrived, written in Bill's large shambolic handwriting. 'The old dutch will have notched up three score, so drink will flow. B.'

'Sounds jolly,' said Richard. 'But you know their do's—we'd better stay the night.'

'Let's go on Saturday and the boys can join us.'

'I've been parental only recently,' Richard pretended to grumble, 'and even filial. Couldn't I be let off for once?'

'That's not how it works,' said Isla, 'and you know it.'

Isla had an idealistic approach to the family, and a desire, almost a need, to do right by her stepsons and their mother. She put this down to her own extremely happy childhood as a daughter of the regiment. She was a team player from a long line of team players, and her whole experience of acting—especially in a long-running TV series—had underlined for her the importance of teamwork. The whole was only as strong as its component parts.

Both her parents had died some years ago, her father from peritonitis, her mother not long afterwards from a sort of starvation of the heart. They had lived in Malaya, in Singapore, in Hong Kong, Muscat and Germany. If their marriage had been through rocky patches (her mother had occasionally referred in passing to 'ups and downs') then Isla had been completely protected from them. She never had the slightest doubt, throughout a childhood spent in a succession of charmless married quarters and in the most trying of climates, that she was secure in their affections, and they in each other's.

She had had a younger brother, Ewan, born when she was two, and killed in a swimming accident at the Tanglin Club in Singapore. She must have been about seven when it happened. She could remember, with sickening clarity, Ewan being brought out and laid on the grass, and the peculiar quietness, in spite of all the people, as first her father, and then the army doctor, had tried to bring him back to life.

She had missed Ewan, but she was too young to feel the loss acutely or for long. It was the experience of her parents' devastation that cast a deep shadow over her life in the months following the accident. There was a funeral at the Anglican cathedral, but she didn't attend. Afterwards a few of her parents' friends came back and she sat on her father's knee in the steamy garden while they drank, and talked in quiet voices. That night she woke, startled and sweating, in the dim cocoon of her mosquito net, and lay listening to her mother's awful gut-wrenching, uncontrolled sobs rising and falling in the room across the landing.

Isla had gone to army schools and then, at eleven, to a boarding school in Berkshire. Her parents had come back to England, first to Catterick and then to Wiltshire. At first she'd had unsuitable boyfriends (always made welcome), then a spell of suitable ones, then had gone to the Central School of Speech and Drama and found the men and women she liked best. Her parents regarded her success as both proper and predictable, a cause for wonder, not for surprise.

They had, however, wanted her to marry. They wished for her happiness and in their book marriage was a prerequisite. Not that they would ever have dreamed of mentioning it, but when Isla reached thirty her sensitive antennae picked up a wistfulness in her mother's manner and a certain tender confidentiality in her father's.

Perversely, when fate stepped in in the large, eligible and distinguished form of Richard Wakefield, her parents were the tiniest bit wrong-footed. This urbane and twice-wed QC wasn't quite what they'd expected. They'd become used to her louche, lovable acting friends. It had been a rite of passage—the moment when she grew up and ceased to dance, however discreetly, to her parents' tune. Once she was Richard's wife, she was never quite so close to them again. Their deaths within eighteen months of each other had hit her hard, but not as hard as they would have done before her marriage. She had cut the cord.

Isla was in a mellow mood when she drove out to Bradenham to attend Barbara's birthday party. The only pity was that Richard was under the weather with a fluey cold and so had opted not to come. In consequence, they'd abandoned the idea of going for the whole weekend and she went bearing his apologies and the *Ultimate Gardening Book*.

Having dozed through Isla's departure, Richard was roused by the sound of the Sunday papers arriving. On the way downstairs in his pyjamas he noted a dull, heavy day outside. He collected the papers, made himself a mug of tea and trudged back up to the bedroom. He was perspiring slightly by the time he got there, and pushed the window open, but still pulled the quilt over himself when he got into bed.

He leaned his head back on the pillows. He hadn't got much of a cold, though that was his pretext. He just felt tired 'unto death'—a melodramatic expression of which he now appreciated the meaning. He hoped he would feel better tomorrow. He was due to be in court and it was a dry, difficult case that would require a clear head and a sharp mind.

He sighed and picked up the paper. In the gossip column there was a small piece about the war between the two literary brothers, which cheered him up. He snorted mirthfully to himself as he read it. All good sport, and it would probably be a last-ditch, out-of-court settlement without loss of face on either side. He read on, scanning and discarding supplements, but there was nothing else half as interesting. War, famine and the resulting harvest of desperate refugees made him turn the page quickly. Richard told himself that it was a sign of advancing years to long for good news.

It started to rain—a muffled summer drizzle that drew a sharp mouth-watering scent from the parched grass and trees outside. He dozed again, the papers sliding off the quilt onto the floor as he curled on his side. But his sleep churned with garbled dreams of anxiety and confusion and he woke up sweating and aching. There was a jug of lime juice by the bed and he poured himself some, his quaking hand making the lip of the jug clink against the glass. Childishly, he wished he wasn't alone in the house. He took a long drink, held the glass against his forehead for a minute, then put it down and picked up the phone.

Cain and Abel lay on the sofa. They had come in from Selwyn Street through the open living-room window. When the phone rang—for the third time that morning—their eyes widened in well-bred surprise as Keith's keys clattered in the front door and his slightly breathless voice answered the call.

'Hello? . . . Oh, hello there, how are you? . . . No, as luck would have it she's visiting clients, somewhere countrified . . . yes. Shall I give her a message? . . . Are you sure? . . . Okey-dokey, then. Bye.'

Having got only Keith, Richard turned on the answering machine, pulled on last night's clothes and went to sit in the orangery with some court papers. He wished now that he had gone with Isla, if only to remain at Brook End while she attended the party. Sundays were depressing enough on one's own without feeling as rough as this. Inside half an hour he had fallen asleep, slewed uncomfortably round in the wicker chair, his head sagging to one side, the papers drifting, one or two at a time, to the floor.

Isla had a good journey. It rained for a while as she toiled through the outermost reaches of north London, but by the time she put her foot down on the motorway the sun was coming out. She arrived in Bradenham with half an hour to spare and headed for Brook End, planning to park there, freshen up and air the cottage.

Before walking round to The Bury, Isla rang Richard. Rather to her surprise, the line was engaged. She rang off and pressed 'Redial' a couple of times, but it was still engaged. The third time she got her own voice explaining that no one was available to take her call. She closed the door behind her with an easier mind—if he was up and about, she concluded, he must be feeling better.

Among the thirty or so guests gathered in the drawing room and garden of The Bury, Isla noted a number of what might be termed political invitees. Norman Brake, chairman of the parish council; the ambitious rector, Brendan Mather, and his loyally smiling wife, Joyce; and—more surprisingly—the Scott-Chathams. Whether this last denoted a cunning attempt on Bill Fyler's part to wrong-foot the younger Scott-Chatham, who she could see by the French windows, Isla couldn't begin to guess.

She left the gardening book and its accompanying card with other presents on a table near the door, and took a glass of champagne from a passing tray. Barbara was at her side immediately.

'Isla, how lovely of you to come all this way!'

'Happy birthday, Bar.' Isla kissed her friend's weather-beaten cheek which smelt incongruously of Joy. 'You smell gorgeous.'

'Oh God, yes!' Barbara snuffed noisily at her own wrists. 'The old man bought it for me. Where's your other half?'

'Not well, I'm afraid. Took to his bed. He's devastated not to be here.'

'I should think so indeed! Doesn't he know the best way to see off bacteria is to hose them down with alcohol?'

'He sent his love, and asked you to have one for him.'

'I shall—several, probably. Now, who don't you know . . .?'

'Don't worry, I'll fend for myself.'

'Well, your face is your fortune, dear, so that will probably be less trouble for you than the rest of us.'

It was true that a well-known face helped. Isla was more likely to find herself with an embarrassment of company than with no one to talk to.

'Afternoon, neighbour!' Norman Brake was grinning at her over a bowl of cashew nuts.

'Hello, Norman. How are you?'

'Up to my eyes in harvest, shouldn't be here at all.'

'It's been a good year then,' opined Isla.

This was altogether too optimistic a slant for Norman, whose grin was now replaced by an expression of grim foreboding. 'We'll see. Got the family with you?'

'As a matter of fact, no. Richard's ill and the boys have gone to their mother.'

'Tell your husband from me he shouldn't go letting you out to parties on your own. Anything could happen.' He grinned again.

'I think I'm pretty safe here, don't you?'

'Don't bet on it.'

She sensed Scotch was at her side before he spoke. 'Isn't this terrifically jolly?'

'Hello, Scotch—yes, isn't it nice! Do you two know each other?' She introduced them. 'Norman's our neighbour.'

'And a conscientious one, I bet,' said Scotch. 'But then who wouldn't be under the circumstances?'

Norman's eyes grew flinty. 'They know they can call on me. So how long have you known Barbara, then?'

'Not long at all. My parents know them both quite well—my connection is that I share a flat with their daughter.'

Norman looked scandalised. 'Petronella's a lovely young lady,' he asserted pugnaciously. 'Champion horsewoman, did you know that?'

'I did as a matter of fact. I hope to see her in action some time.'

'She can outride any man,' insisted Norman as though in an argument, 'and sort out any horse.' He looked over his shoulder. 'If you'll excuse me, I'll go and have a word with her before I go.'

'Not staying for lunch, Norman?' asked Isla.

'Not me.' His expression changed to one of smug secrecy. 'I got my dinner being cooked for me later on back home . . .'

Isla was trying to unravel this as Scotch stepped in front of her with an unrepentant air. 'Is he always like that or was it something I said?'

'You didn't have to say anything,' she told him. 'But the flat-sharing didn't help.'

'I was only filling in the background.'

'*I* know that. So how are you, Scotch?'

'Terribly well. By the way, Ned Braden called me up after your dinner party to see if there was anything I could do for him.'

'And was there?' Isla's tone was cool but her heart skipped a beat.

'I don't know. Most of our stuff is corporate, but you never know. We agreed to keep in touch. Nice guy.'

'Yes, he is,' she agreed. 'He and I go back a long way.'

'He said. He thinks the world of you. But he worries you're not happy.'

'Ned likes a bit of drama, and if it's not his it might as well be someone else's.'

'So he's wrong?'

For some reason she said, 'No one's happy all the time.'

'Underlying happiness is the thing, though, don't you reckon?'

'Isla, my dear!' She was rescued and engulfed by Bill Fyler's smothering embrace. When she emerged, Scotch had gone. 'What's he been saying to you? He's only here on your recommendation, you realise that?'

'Yes,' said Isla. 'Thank you.'

'Now, come along with me,' said Bill, gripping her round the shoulders. 'There are no end of people dying to meet you.'

Isla, being near the drawing-room door at the time, heard the bell, walked across the hall and opened the front door. The late arrival held out her arms in an embracing gesture and threw her head back.

'I'm here! I made it! I'm so sorry, my organised daughter would kill me for this, but I missed my turning on the motorway listening to *Desert Island Discs*'. She stepped over the threshold. 'Is the car all right where it is? I didn't want to spend even more time parking it out in the lane when I was late already.'

A small white car decorated with purple flowers was parked facing the front door. Isla was reminded of a dog tied to a railing, patiently looking in the direction from which its owner would return.

'I'm sure that's fine.'

The woman beamed at Isla as she closed the door. 'And anyway,' she held out her hand, 'Jen Delaney. It's so lovely to meet you at long last.'

Isla shook the proffered hand. 'Well, thank you.'

'And *happy birthday*.'

'Oh!' Realisation dawned. 'It's not *my* birthday.'

'Not?'

'I'm Isla Munro. You want Barbara Fyler.'

Jen struck her forehead. 'I do, I do. I'm so sorry. Late *and* barmy. Sorry.'

'Jen!'

Nell rushed into the hall and Isla watched as the two of them exchanged an untidy embrace. 'I thought you'd never get here!'

'Join the club. I took a wrong turning, *and* I mistook this lady for your mother, so a great start all round!'

'You thought Isla was Mummy?' Nell boomed. 'You are about to find out what a totally hilarious mistake that is!'

'You do look a bit young for the job,' Jen allowed apologetically. 'But that doesn't mean a thing these days when absolutely everyone is fit and glamorous.'

'Come and take a sneak preview at your handiwork,' said Nell. 'The great unveiling can take place now you're here. Isla, you come too.'

Isla allowed herself to be led into the dining room. In the bay window stood an easel, draped with a sheet. Nell went over to it and removed the sheet with a flourish, revealing a painting of Portia, looking suitably baronial but recognisable.

'Ta-da!'

'Oh, yes . . .' Jen went over to the picture, peered at it, touched the gilt frame. Isla detected a sea change in her manner, from daffiness to focused professionalism. 'It's quite some frame.'

'I expect you think it's too much,' said Nell, 'but Mummy will go for it.' She turned to Isla. 'Jen did the painting.'

'Did you really?' Isla drew closer. 'You are clever. You've really captured something.'

'That is what I'm paid for.' Isla felt that she had been gently rebuked.
'Of course.'

'The Aged Ps will be completely bowled over,' declared Nell. 'And I
invited Jen so she could accept the glory that's due to her.'

'I don't know about glory.' Jen straightened up. 'That left eye is distinctly dodgy.'

'For goodness' sake,' said Nell, replacing the sheet, 'wait till you see
Portia—the whole thing's dodgy.'

Everyone was summoned to the dining room. Nell clapped her hands
for silence and made a little speech. Bill brought Portia in, towing her by
the collar, and sat her by the easel. The painting was unveiled to a burst
of applause. Barbara's delight was a joy to behold. Jen was dragged forward to be thanked in person. Portia and Jen were introduced.

Throughout this little ceremony Isla stood at the back, with Angela
Scott-Chatham next to her. Angela was a smart, highlighted, Alexon-
clad matron. When the speeches were finished she turned to Isla.

'A portrait of a dog! Quite a nice portrait, but just the same—'

'I thought it was a very good idea of Nell's.'

Angela sipped and bridled. 'Well, animals are her *thing*, aren't they?'

'She's a very kindhearted girl.'

'You know . . .' Angela took another sip. 'There are certain English-
women who contrive to go on being "girls" till they're old and grey, and
Petronella is one of them.'

'Yes,' said Isla, who could feel dislike for Angela filtering like iced
water through her veins. 'I know what you're implying. But I assure you
that Nell is no such thing.'

Angela raised an amused eyebrow. 'I wasn't implying anything. We're
devoted to the whole Fyler family,' she continued in a more conciliatory
tone. 'And Scotch thinks the world of Petronella—he shares a flat with
her, you know.'

'Yes, I did know that. He's a lucky man.'

Angela looked as if she might be about to take issue with this, but was
fortunately prevented from doing so by the arrival of Nell herself,
sparkling with the success of her present.

'I'm so pleased I got that organised—hello, Angela—it's gone down a
storm with Mummy.'

'I can see I must go and take a closer look,' Angela murmured, drifting away.

'You did very well,' said Isla. 'And the artist is nice.'

'Isn't she? Because I didn't give her any time, you know, and she'd
never met Portia—she did it all from snapshots.'

'So a real pro . . .'

'Exactly. That's why I asked her to be here. But I'm so sorry to hear about Richard. What a shame!'

'He's much better off where he is,' said Isla. 'He'll live.'

**R**ichard woke from a deep, troubled sleep in the chair in the orangery, aching in every joint and with his neck so painfully stiff that he actually had to support his head with one hand as he straightened up. He sat staring blankly at the papers which were now strewn around his feet in disarray. Then he rose heavily, and at once stooped to steady himself on the arm of the chair as a wave of giddiness overtook him. When his balance returned, he walked slowly and carefully into the kitchen and ran himself three successive glasses of cold water from the tap, draining them greedily. As he put the glass on the draining board, his own hands looked huge to him—huge and separate, like great fish. He pressed them to his face, wishing he were anywhere but here, on his own.

As he lowered them, he blacked out. It was for no more than a couple of seconds, simply a long blink of unconsciousness, but when he came to he found himself slumped sideways against the leg of the table. Shocked and shaking he hauled himself up and onto a chair.

After about three minutes, he rose, carefully, keeping one hand on the table, and took the cordless phone from the wall. He sat down again heavily and began to dial the Fylers' number, but then thought better of it. The place would be packed with people, his excuses would be made, and anyway, what was he going to say? 'May I speak to Isla, I need to hear her voice.' It was too pathetic. She'd be back in a few hours.

He rang Jen again, just in case, and when Keith answered, he hung up. Almost at once the phone rang, startling him so that he broke out in a sweat.

'Hello?'

'Oh, it's you—this is Keith—you called just now.'

Not for the first time, Richard cursed the call-tracing facility. 'Foolish of me, yes. I suddenly realised I'd dialled your number by mistake.'

'Yes, it happens, doesn't it,' agreed Keith, 'with numbers you dial a lot. Anyway, as you probably gathered, she's still out in the sticks.'

'That's all right.' Richard was tight-jawed. 'It wasn't her I wanted to speak to.'

'She'll be back some time this evening, is my guess.'

'It's not a problem. I'm sorry to have disturbed you.' Richard rang off, breathing heavily. He fetched another glass of water and called Caroline. Giles answered the phone.

'How's it going?'

'Not too good—I've got some bloody bug or other.'

'Do you want to speak to Mum?'

'If she's within hailing distance.'

'She's doing something strenuous to a button-back chair. Hang on.'

Richard listened to the distant voices, Caroline's approach to the phone.

'Richard!'

'How's the chair going?'

'Terrifically hard work but I *hope* it's going to turn out beautiful.'

'I'm sure it will,' said Richard humbly. He had a deep respect for his former wife's competence in the field of home improvements. 'Giles sounded cheerful.'

'He's not long back from the pub. Marcus has staggered out of bed— shall I get him?'

'No, don't bother. How is he?'

'Seems all right. He's eating.'

There was a brief pause, then Caroline asked brightly, 'So what are you two doing today?'

'Isla's gone to an old friend's party up in Bradenham. I'm nursing germs here feeling a bit sorry for myself.'

'Well, of course, one does . . . How's work? Anything I should be watching out for in the papers?'

'One or two colourful ones in the pipeline. I've been attempting to acquaint myself with the papers, but it's a bit like wading through treacle.'

'There's no earthly use in trying to concentrate when you're below par. Make a hot toddy and look at an old film or something.'

'I may well do.'

There was another pause. 'Are you sure you're OK, Richard? You sound terribly depressed.'

'No, no, no . . . I'm going to take your advice. Bye, Caro.'

Richard replaced the phone, turned on the answering machine and went back upstairs. Lying in bed he shivered with pure terror.

'This is so pretty,' said Jen. 'How can you ever bear to leave it?'

'With the greatest difficulty. Not quite so much for my husband.'

They were sitting in the garden of Brook End drinking tea, having both left The Bury at the same time. Jen put her mug down on the grass.

'Do you mind if I smoke?'

'Please. I live with a smoker.'

'Crikey, I wish I did. I live with a man whose idea of a vice is to cycle without clips and a helmet.'

Isla laughed. 'Really?'

'But he's my lodger, so I suppose I should be grateful.'

'Yes,' agreed Isla. 'I imagine what one looks for in a lodger is a complete absence of those things that would be a prerequisite in a lover.'

'Except in bathrooms.' Jen lit a cigarette.

'So how does your lodger score on the bathroom scale?'

'A near-perfect nine point nine.'

'That,' said Isla, 'sounds like "ninety-nine per cent of all household germs"—it leaves a person wondering about the other one per cent.'

'Yes, but the perfect ten doesn't exist. Thank heavens. I mean—who wants perfection? How wearing it would be to share one's life with a paragon.'

'True.'

'Pardon my asking, but where's your other half?'

'He stayed at home. He wasn't well.'

'What a shame. But you came anyway. I mean, you didn't feel you ought to be at home administering cold compresses or anything? Forgive me, but I'm interested in marriages, never having had one myself.'

'Not at all.' Isla realised she could not only very easily forgive this person, but that it was a positive pleasure to talk to her. 'It obviously wasn't anything dire, and the Fylers are very dear friends.'

'Don't get me wrong,' said Jen, 'I'm not implying you're heartless or anything, I just don't feel terribly *au fait* with the norm.'

'I don't think there is one. And if there is, it's not us. We make it up as we go along.'

'What a terribly good idea. So what does he do, your husband?'

'He's a barrister.'

'Oh my God, not another word. I know one of those and the whole thing's a closed book to me. I feel ashamed of my ignorance but completely powerless to overcome it. Do you have things like that?'

'Lots, far too many.'

'Such as?

'Computers make me nervous. Fancy cooking. Changing tyres—'

'For heaven's sake, you try to change tyres?'

'Well, if you get a flat on some country road—'

'You wait till a well-built farm labourer happens by and burst into tears!' Jen watched Isla's face, joined in with her laugh, then asked, 'And do you and your husband have children?'

'He does, from a previous marriage. They're more or less grown-up.'

'Like the rest of us—more or less grown-up. I've got a daughter. She's more grown-up than me. A foot taller, a stone thinner, and able to read maps and run to time. I haven't a clue where she gets it from because her father's a disorganised sod as well.' Isla's almost too serene composure must have prompted her to add, 'Yes, I did say I'd never been married. I wish I could say I regretted it, but I honestly don't. And Red is the most together young person one could wish to meet—she scares the living daylights out of me sometimes, so it hasn't done her any harm.'

'It must be lovely to have a daughter.'

'Do you know, it is?' said Jen. 'It's not how much alike you are, it's how different. Fascinating.'

'I can imagine.'

Their first small, but not awkward, silence intervened, before Jen asked, 'And now I'm going to have to admit it. I recognise your face from somewhere, but I don't know where. Have we met before?'

'No, not that I know of. Although . . .' Isla frowned. There was something familiar, some sense of *déjà vu* . . . 'No, I'm sure we haven't.'

'So where do I know you from? I have this ghastly feeling you're going to tell me you're a cabinet minister or something and I shall be completely humiliated, not for the first time—'

'I'm an actress,' said Isla, 'so it's just possible you may have seen me on the box.'

'That'll be it then!' Jen snapped her fingers in the air, apparently perfectly satisfied with this explanation. She could only think that she had never known the meaning of charm until she had met Isla Munro. She could not remember liking someone so instinctively and immediately, so much. She found that the other woman's beauty and style, instead of making her feel like an unmade bed, pleased and soothed her. They were restful. It was easy to be with Isla—easy to talk, easy to listen, easy to look. Her gentle good manners and natural reserve were like a gift. Jen wanted, hoped, to be liked by her in return.

Isla tried to picture Jen's tall, stern girl. 'Does your daughter have a boyfriend?'

'Red? Not that I know of. No one would dare.'

'You make her sound frightfully intimidating.'

'Yes, I do, and she is slightly, but she's adorable. You'd love her. I bet you and she would get on like a house on fire.'

'And her father . . . ?' asked Isla cautiously. 'Are you in touch at all?'

'Sort of.' Jen frowned. 'He and she are. She's the one who makes the effort, invites herself for weekends. Usually winds up baby-sitting for them on Saturday night. The only reason I don't is sheer idleness, not animosity. He's a decent enough bloke, but history . . .'

'He's married since?'

'Isla, you never saw anyone so married. If you think you're married, you should see Mo and Julie. It makes me realise what a lucky escape I had. Sorry.'

'That's quite all right, I know what you're saying.' Isla thought of the Stainforths. 'We know a couple like that and they make us feel complete amateurs.'

Jen said, 'Tell me about these children. How old are they?'

'Eighteen and sixteen.'

'They must think they've died and gone to heaven with you for a stepmother. Do you like them?'

'I do, yes. And I find them interesting.'

'Like I find marriage?'

'I suppose so, yes.'

'Do you wish they were yours?'

The bluntness of this question took Isla back, but not as much as it would have done coming from anyone else. She absorbed the small shock and looked aside, thinking.

'No, I don't wish they were mine. If they were they'd probably drive me to drink. But if you meant did I wish I'd had children of my own, the answer is yes. But I don't spend time feeling miserable about it.'

'What about the mother of his children?'

'She's amiable . . . busy . . . and—this is going to sound unkind—'

'I doubt it.'

'Peculiarly sexless. I like her, I believe we're friends, but there it is.'

'Maybe that's why. Why you're friends. Because she's sexless. A sexless ex, what could be better?' She caught Isla's doubtful look.

Isla felt she had been tempted into indiscretion, something she sought strenuously to avoid.

'Have you seen the time?' she said. 'If you don't start to head into London soon the traffic will be appalling.'

'You too,' said Jen. 'And you've got that sick husband to attend to.'

'As a matter of fact I'm going to give him a ring before I leave . . .' Isla rose. 'Can I get you anything before the long haul home? Another cup of tea? Coffee? Or something to eat?'

Jen threw her head back, hand to brow. 'Please, no more! I shall never eat again—your friends know a thing or two about carbo-loading.'

Isla, laughing, went into the house. Jen watched her go and sat for a moment. She was reluctant to leave, although she knew it was true about the traffic.

This time Richard answered the phone.

'Darling,' said Isla, 'you sound utterly miserable.'

'I am. I've had the creeps all day.'

'I've tried to ring, but first you were engaged, then the machine was on.'

'I'm sorry. I called Archie about something, but then found I couldn't work anyway so I crawled back into bed. I should have come with you—all that's happened is I've got more and more morose.'

'Well, I'm on my way any minute now.'

'I can't wait. Hurry back.'

'I'll do my best.' Isla put the phone down. Jen stood with her bag over her shoulder near the front door.

'How's the patient?'

'Depressed.'

'So you must fly. And I'm off. Thanks for the tea.'

'Not at all . . .' Isla opened the door and they moved outside. 'I enjoyed talking. We must do it again some time. It's not as if we live that far away from each other.'

'I already thought of that. Here—' Jen handed Isla a dogeared business card. 'That's me. Give a ring and we can have lunch or something.'

'I will,' said Isla. 'I definitely will.'

Jen raised an arm through the car's sun roof as she turned into the lane. Isla studied the card and slipped it into her jacket pocket. Feeling ridiculously cheerful she went round the cottage, locking up.

**R**ichard felt slightly ashamed of himself. Now that Isla was on her way back, he felt better. He supposed it was something to do with help being at hand. He roused himself, sorted through his scattered papers and, acting on instinct, made a call to Archie.

'Archie, I'm sorry to disturb the peace of your Sunday afternoon.'

'The what? Come on.'

'Well—whatever. I tried to get you earlier but you were out.'

'In the park. Fergal's first go with stabilisers.'

'That would be it. I just wanted to check a couple of points before the conference tomorrow.'

'My pleasure,' said Archie. 'Excuse me one moment while I bar the door . . .'

Following a brief conversation, during which he asked several questions to which he already knew the answers, Richard took a bottle of Australian Burra Valley sauvignon from the fridge and two green glasses from the cabinet. He placed them on a salver which he carried carefully into the orangery. With a good deal of effort, he also opened a jar of large black olives: he had always been a bit cack-handed and when the lid jerked open he slopped a good deal of the dark liquor over his hand

and wrist. Upstairs in the bathroom he washed his hands and slooshed cold water over his face and the back of his neck, then folded the duvet back and straightened the bed. He put on a clean striped shirt and grey trousers and, sweating slightly, went back down to wait.

**B**y the time Jen got back, Keith was preparing the next day's packed lunch in the kitchen. He took sunflower spread to the edge of the bread and then scraped off the excess and placed it on the next slice.

'Good day?' he enquired, taking square ham from a packet.

'Yes, thanks. Keith—have you heard of an actress called Isla Munro?'

'Certainly have.'

'How? I mean, what's she famous for?'

Keith licked his fingers. 'She did one of those comedy detective things ages ago, but now she's mostly photographed with endangered species and children in need, that sort of thing.'

'Would you say she was a big star?'

'She's very popular with all age groups. And she always seemed like a nice person, even dressed in those kinky costumes.'

Jen uncorked the half-full bottle of Spanish red on the side table and sniffed it before pouring herself a glass. 'I met her today.'

'You never,' said Keith. 'I don't know, you do see life.'

'You're right, she is nice.'

Keith put the sandwiches in his lunch box, shut the lid and placed the box in the fridge. Washing his hands at the sink he said over his shoulder, 'By the bye, Rumple of the Bailey rang, twice. The second time he claimed he'd dialled this number by mistake, but I wasn't born yesterday.'

'OK.' Jen moved towards the living room, but paused. 'I wish you wouldn't call him that.'

'Oh dear, is it rude?'

'Not particularly. But it's not very funny either.'

'Oh dear,' he said again, and slapped his own wrist. 'Sorry.'

Jen pushed the living-room door to, and put on an old but favourite tape. She sipped the vinegary Spanish red and thought back to her afternoon with Isla. The cottage in Bradenham, with its textured whites and creams and Wedgwood blues, its deal table and rush-bottom chairs, its modern watercolours and sweet peas in a stoneware jug, was like a memory of water at the end of this hot day. When the phone rang she was slow to respond, and Keith was already halfway down the stairs.

'There you are,' he said. 'I thought you must have dropped off.'

'No.' He retreated as she picked it up. 'Hello?'

'It's me.'

'Hello.'

'Something tells me that you're not alone.'

'No, but I shall be shortly.'

She followed Keith with her eyes as he reached the top of the stairs.

'I tried earlier, did he tell you?'

'Yes.'

'He got on my nerves so much the second time I told him I'd dialled the number by mistake.'

'So I understand.' Keith's bedroom door closed. She continued to speak as she trailed the phone into the living room and heeled the door to behind her.

'I've got nothing to say,' he said. 'I just felt like hearing your voice.'

'That's nice.'

'Good day?'

'Yes—yes, lovely. I'll tell you all about it.'

'You must.'

'You sound a bit down,' she said. 'Are you all right?'

'No, I've been here all day feeling crummy—look, I've got to go.'

'Bye.' She put the phone down at once, used to these sudden endings. And as she did so a small, cold thought made her shiver.

As Isla opened the front door, Richard was walking across the hall towards her, his arms outstretched.

'Darling . . .' She walked into his embrace. 'You look tired.'

'Better for seeing you though,' he said into her hair.

But Isla's experienced eye had seen the film of secrecy over his face before his smile dispelled it. Perhaps it was time, she told herself sadly, that she too had secrets.

# chapter five

DURING THE LAST FORTNIGHT in July, Isla and Richard began to freewheel downhill towards their month off. They didn't generally go abroad in August. When the boys had been younger—and even, to some extent, now—August had been a month when, with the courts closed, they made themselves available to Caroline, either in Hampstead or Bradenham, so that she could go away without her sons. This year Giles and Chris Beales had gone to discuss their business plans for an unspecified period in Ibiza where, apparently, everything worth having in a holiday could still be got plentifully and at rock-bottom prices. Marcus was working in an electrical-goods warehouse on the North Circular. Caroline, who liked project-driven holidays, had opted for two weeks of archaeology in Wiltshire, so Marcus's base would be at the Hampstead house. Isla told herself that these few weeks would be quiet, her own to do with as she wished. There would be few if any outside calls on her time. Richard intended putting in some ground-work on what he called his literary scrap and otherwise taking it easy apart from a couple of golf breaks with cronies.

What she most wanted to do was invite Jen Delaney round, but when it came to it she couldn't find her card. So in the interests of killing two birds with one stone she rang Nell's number in Swiss Cottage. In response to standard enquiries Nell sounded rather flat.

'Is everything quite all right?' asked Isla. 'How's Scotch?'

'Away. It's like a mausoleum around here without him.'

Isla was pleased to hear this. 'So where's he gone off to?'

Nell sighed. 'He's gone on location with that Ned friend of yours, doing a car commercial up in Scotland. Scotch has agreed to do some PR for Ned, so this is what the politicians call a fact-finding tour.'

Isla's pleasure faded as quickly as it had come. 'But a brief one,' she suggested hopefully.

'I think they're having a week's jolly at some country club in the bor-ders, all boys together,' said Nell, with unconscious irony. 'And when he gets back I'm booked to go to Bordeaux with a girlfriend, so see if I care.'

Which would give Ned ample time to follow through, thought Isla. She changed the subject to something less unwelcome.

'I wonder if you could let me have Jen's telephone number. The artist? Only we promised ourselves a lunch and I've lost the card she gave me.'

'Absolutely, toot sweet. Hang on a mo.' When Nell had passed on the number, she added, 'Could we do the same?'

'What a good idea—lunch?'

'Well, or anything—the pictures, a drink, even just a walk. There are things I want to talk about and you're such a brilliant listener.'

'It beats talking,' said Isla. 'Yes, I'd like to.'

'Perhaps—while Scotch is still away?'

She's mad about the boy, thought Isla, and who could blame her? And he's up in the Highlands a-chasing the queer . . . They agreed that Nell would take a half-day off from the gallery on Thursday, so they could meet at the Royal Academy Summer Exhibition.

Isla then called Jen Delaney. There was no immediate reply . . . it would be frustrating if she'd taken off somewhere. She let it ring—Jen was probably working. Isla was going to suggest that her new friend come to the house in Hampstead for lunch in the garden one of the days when Richard was off golfing.

She listened with a sense of happy anticipation as the phone continued to ring, just across the hills and valleys of north London.

At two o'clock Jen was surveying the almost finished portrait of Horace, Lady Saxby's basset, while eating a slice of pitta bread filled with lettuce and peanut butter. She waited till the phone stopped ringing, before approaching it rather as if it were a venomous spider. As she lifted the receiver and dialled one-four-seven-one she told herself that she must do herself a favour and invest, as Richard had so often suggested, in an answering machine.

She listened to the bland female voice deliver its information, and advise that she 'press three to return the call', but hesitated for a full minute before doing so. It was Richard's number for heaven's sake, Richard, who rang her all the time, and she had nothing but the vaguest and most ill-founded suspicions . . .

When she did, and Isla answered, Jen was stunned—as much by the awesome accuracy of her intuition as by the voice itself.

'Hello? Eight-o-three-o?'

Jen sat there with the phone in her hand, unable either to speak or make a decision. Even to put the phone down would be a waste of time, since her call could be traced as easily as she had traced this one.

'Hello?' Isla asked again. 'Who is this?'

'I think I may have the wrong number . . .' Jen said faintly.

'Perhaps—Jen? Is that you?'

'Yes.'

'It's Isla, I just rang you. You must have pressed three.'

'Yes. But I didn't—I don't know—'

'Are you all right?'

'Well'—Jen saw an escape route—'actually no. I'm feeling very rough.'

'Oh, I'm sorry . . .' Isla's sympathy was more chastening than the sharpest reproach. 'It's probably this thing my husband Richard's had, it's going round.'

Of course the remark meant nothing, but Jen rushed to deny it. 'It'll be Keith—he brings all the latest bugs home from school.'

'Were you in bed?'

'No, but I was thinking about going.'

'Go. Now, at once. I'll call you back another time.'

'It's all right,' said Jen. 'I'm here now.' A near-suicidal curiosity pulled her irresistibly along like an underwater current.

'I was going to ask if you'd like to come over here for lunch, say a fortnight today? Richard will be on the links in north Devon, and I'll be rattling around here. But anyway . . . don't worry about it now. Concentrate on getting better.'

Jen thought that until that moment she hadn't known the meaning of shame. Her face burned and her eyes smarted. She felt as if she were bulging to bursting point with the infected mass of her deceit. She was only glad that Isla couldn't see her.

'Jen . . .?'

'Yes.'

'Oh, you're still there. I thought perhaps you'd keeled over on me.'

'No.'

'You don't sound right. Please go and climb into bed—we'll talk another time.'

'No,' said Jen. 'There's no need for that. It'd be nice to meet.'

'That's marvellous!' Isla's pleasure was painfully genuine. 'No standing on ceremony, we can kick our shoes off good and proper. And tell you what I'll do, so that you don't have to stand there a moment longer, I'll send you our address, and directions of how to find us.'

Us, thought Jen. Us, us, us . . .

'You can give me a ring if there's any problem.'

'Fine.'

'So I'll see you then. Acts of God apart.'

'I'll look forward to it.'

'*Au revoir*. Get well soon.'

Jen had, naturally, from time to time speculated on what manner of woman Richard's wife was. Although he didn't talk about her, she had occasionally caught a whiff of her over the telephone line, like an evocative scent that lingers in a lift or on a staircase. Snatches of music, a light step in the background, a half-heard voice in the hall . . . From these tiny clues and trace elements she had built up a picture, as romantic and unfocused as a photograph taken through gauze. This was a woman serenely confident, of coolly assured taste and elegance—someone who listened to Debussy, who wore clothes by Jean Muir, who had her own bathroom . . . This was a woman admirable in every respect—competent, talented and exquisitely decorative but (Jen always told herself) perhaps just the tiniest bit bloodless.

But now there was Isla, of whom she was sure only the good things were true. Jen wondered why she had ever supposed that Richard, of whom she was so inordinately fond, and to whose warm, weighty body, redolent of good living, she so often and so willingly succumbed, would marry anyone who wasn't—well—lovely. It was a simple enough realisation, but devastating. And Isla was so exceptionally nice. Jen recalled their conversation at the cottage with the wistful pleasure reserved for never-to-be-replaced happiness. Because now that the arrangement had been made she knew, of course, that she could never go. And that this marked the end of one relationship before it had even begun, and another after more years than she cared to remember.

**R**ichard walked down to the Embankment for a breath of air. He could hardly wait for the pleasant, sultry tedium of August to begin. It would be nice to see the back of chambers for a bit. Also, he had to admit he was by no means A1. He had said as much to Archie that morning.

'Ah well,' Archie had said, in a stab at irreverent humour, 'all those years of unclean living are bound to catch up with you sooner or later.' He slapped his own midriff apologetically. 'Not that I can talk.'

On the Embankment, Richard sat down heavily on a bench. It was stuffy and he felt tired. He wondered, though, if there wasn't reason in what Archie had said. Sitting with his arms folded, he could feel the solid swell of his stomach and the stretch of his jacket across his shoulders. Maybe he should lose weight. Perhaps his heart, his whole system, was beginning to labour under the strain of carrying such a load. He went hot and cold at the memory of his lonely, ignominious collapse at the weekend. But the world of diet and weight loss was a dreadful mystery to him. Gravy lunches and custard puddings with chums in Middle Temple Hall were one of the small but utterly reliable pleasures of his chosen profession, as were drinks with cronies at El Vino's and the Athenaeum, and entertaining at home. Though Isla, of course, was sweetly chary of his health and attempted with utter tact and discretion to regulate his intake of what was not good for him.

Sitting there in the dusty, polluted sunshine, Richard for the first time experienced his body as no more than a sort of packaging, and one which was deteriorating with time and usage. He had never been especially introspective, nor a great worrier about anything much, especially his health, which he had always taken for granted. He was one of those who tended to joke about the muesli police and fitness fascists, and who reckoned that the pleasure and well-being that came from good living was infinitely preferable to the grey complacency of virtue. And until now he'd had no cause to change his tune.

Abruptly he got up and began to walk along the Embankment in the direction of Waterloo Bridge. He half heard a name called twice before he realised it was his, by which time a cab had pulled in alongside him at the kerb and Donatella was leaning out of the window.

'Ricardo! Don't do it, I beg you!'

'I'm sorry . . .?'

She opened the door of the cab and got out. She was wearing Levis and a red shirt, cowboy boots, gold hoop earrings. He saw the laughing faces of two younger men behind her. She kissed him with her usual gusto.

'You looked so sad and grim, my darling, we were quite sure you were planning to end it all.'

'I'm fine, thank you. I was just taking a walk.'

She pulled a stern face in mockery of his own. 'Then we must let you get on with it, I suppose.'

'Well, anyway'—Richard was a little ashamed of his curmudgeonliness—'you're running up a huge fare on my account.'

'Pah—!' Donatella's soaring hand poured contempt on money. 'I have earned it with the sweat of my brow, and now I'm on holiday. Tomorrow I am flying to stay with my family in Fiesole. You go!' she cried to her companions in the cab, one of whom, Richard noticed, was carrying a bottle. 'I shall pick up another one.' She slammed the door and tapped smartly on the roof with her knuckles.

Richard felt trapped. He glanced at his watch. 'I have to be back in chambers in fifteen minutes.'

'I know, I know.' She linked her arm purposefully through his. 'You are walking and I shall accompany you. Where shall we walk to?'

'Along to the bridge and back.'

'*Andiamo!*'

They set off. Despite the disparity in their heights there was no need for Richard to adjust his stride because Donatella lengthened hers amply.

'What is all this walking?' she asked.

'I feel I need the exercise.'

'Poor old thing!' She squeezed his arm against the side of her breast. 'Is your wife not looking after you?'

'I decline to dignify that with an answer. I've been a bit below par, that's all. Working hard—'

'That's good for you! Stress is healthy. An intelligent being like yourself needs stress if he is not to become a jellyfish.'

'You may be right. At any rate, it's nothing serious.' They had reached the bridge and Richard extricated his arm. He glanced at his watch. 'I must get back.'

'I'll walk with you.'

'By all means.'

They crossed the road at speed. Though they were side by side he felt he was being led, and was slightly embarrassed when they met Archie emerging from Goodies to Go with a bulging paper bag.

'Caught in the act,' he said sheepishly. 'And Donatella, good gracious, what a lovely surprise . . .'

'Archie, Archie, Archie—' Donatella placed an explosive kiss on both Archie's pink cheeks, then placed a commanding hand on his arm and leaned confidently towards him. 'What in the wild world is the matter with Richard?'

Wondering why in the wild—or even wide—world he allowed it, Richard submitted to their combined inspections, Archie's baffled, Donatella's searching.

'I don't know,' said Archie at last. 'What is the matter with you?'

'Nothing.'

'Pah—' Donatella stepped forward and gave Richard's left cheek a tap. Then the right, a little harder. 'Pah!' and the left again, still harder.

'Um—I get the distinct impression she doesn't believe you,' said Archie, conscious of a discreet, fleeting audience of passers-by.

'I don't,' Donatella affirmed. 'I do not!'

Richard, also aware of the audience, decided enough was enough. It was always too easy to fall beneath Donatella's spell and relinquish all initiative.

'I'm under the weather and I am going to see the doctor,' he said firmly. 'And now I really must get back to chambers.'

'As you wish. Goodbye.' Donatella began to walk away, the search-light, as it were, switched off as abruptly as it had been switched on.

'Have a good holiday!' Richard called after her, but she only raised a hand, Führer-like, palm uppermost, and strode on.

'Phew!' exclaimed Archie as they walked together in the direction of chambers. 'What a woman!'

'She can be quite insufferably meddlesome.'

'But you must be a bit flattered, surely. I mean she obviously still cares about you.'

'Hm.' Richard was disposed to admit nothing. 'I think she may be what my sons would call a control freak.'

'Well, I don't know . . .' Archie puffed slightly on the stairs behind

Richard, who was trying to disguise his own heaving lungs. 'She seems a great girl to me . . . your trouble is you've got an embarrassment of riches. First Donatella—shit-hot legal brain and every junior's fantasy lay—and now the sainted Isla.'

'And Caroline. Don't forget the mother of my children,' Richard reminded him as they entered the reception area. 'How would you rate her on the desirability scale?'

'She was lovely too,' said Archie. 'But she was more the sort of woman we could all aspire to, if you know what I mean.'

'Like Alison?' Richard took a bunch of papers from his pigeonhole.

'Um, absolutely,' said Archie.

**R**ichard was pleased to find that he had no messages. He sat down and rang his doctor, Jim Furmston.

'Wondered if you could run the rule over me, Jim,' he said. 'It's donkey's years since I paid you a visit, so I thought perhaps . . . the complete MOT and oil change.'

'And what's made you jumpy all of a sudden?' Jim Furmston made a living at least as good as Richard's with this uncompromising cold-showers and wire-wool style of patient management.

'I'm not in the least jumpy,' said Richard in a tone which demonstrated exactly how jumpy he was. 'But as the end of one's fifth decade hoves in view it would seem judicious to get the all clear.'

'And if it's not?'

'You mean not judicious?'

'Not all clear. Same difference, some might say,' rasped Jim. 'You have taken that into account?'

'Of course.'

'Fine. I'll look forward to seeing you on Monday, then.'

Richard, his hand still on the phone, gazed through the window at the green trees and stately rooftops. He did not look forward to Monday.

**J**en was packaging the Saxby basset for delivery when Richard arrived. She was so attuned to his approach that she did not actually need to see his car reverse smoothly into a space on the other side of the road to know it was there.

Her heart galloping, she stuck down the last of the bubble-wrap and propped the picture against the wall beneath the window. As she did so she saw Richard get out of the car, lock it with a snap of his magic key, smooth the buttons of his waistcoat and cross the road towards Number 65 with a preoccupied air.

For a split second she debated with herself whether to answer the door . . . but then he would only let himself in anyway, and Keith was upstairs and would be sure to give the game away. She had no alternative but to go to the front door and let him in.

Leaving the door open, she walked back into the living room and waited for him there. Her pleasure in seeing him was intensified by her feeling that the doomsday clock must surely now be ticking. When his arms enfolded her from behind, and his head rested on top of her own, they carried for the first time the poignancy of an experience whose days were numbered . . . She closed her eyes, letting his warmth flow through her and considered, also for the first time, the frightening possibility of love. When she hadn't needed to worry, she hadn't bothered to analyse. Now it seemed important to evaluate what she was almost certainly about to lose.

'That's nice,' he said, on the back of a gusty sigh. 'That's nice.'

For a second she found herself unable to reply, but she put her arms round his encircling ones and held on tight. It was the sound of Keith's door opening which helped restore her composure.

'Wait . . .' She went to the living-room door and pushed it to. 'I'm seriously thinking of getting rid of him,' she said, thinking seriously of it for the first time.

Richard sat down on the window seat and held out his hand to her, drawing her to him. 'Why . . .?' he asked, putting his arms round her and his head on her breasts.

She dared to touch his hair, to stroke, soothing this time not him but herself. 'I don't know. Loss of privacy. Naff music. Cycle helmet.'

Still without lifting his head he said, 'He's a pretty decent bloke.'

'He is. That's the trouble.'

He gave a grunt of laughter. 'I don't know how you stick it.'

'Neither do I.'

Now he looked up, and directly into her face for the first time. 'I do hope it's got nothing to do with money.'

She laughed and ruffled his hair. 'Of course it's got *something* to do with money . . . That's why he's here in the first place. But I'm no longer so desperate that I have to have him living in my house and subjecting me to death by terrible jokes . . .'

'Mmm.' He pulled her head down for a kiss, and when he released her added, 'As long as you're sure. Because if it is money—'

'No, I'm sure.' She stepped away. 'Look, I'm going to fetch us a drink.'

She felt him watch her as she left the room quickly, smiling as she closed the door. But in the hall she paused to catch her breath. Money had never before been an issue between them. Richard had never, ever suggested that he help to finance the least part of her life. His sure instinct in this area, in response to what was a feminine and emotional, rather than a feminist and political, sensibility, was one of the planks of their relationship. But now—she dragged her hands down over her face—the unmentionable had been mentioned. Suggested, already. In such small, deadly ways did everything change.

Keith was at the stove poking at a saucepan with a wooden spoon.

'Hi there! I'll be out from under your feet in two ticks.'

'That's all right.' Jen fetched the Scotch, the supermarket sauvignon and the glasses. 'I'm not cooking.'

They sat together on the sofa with their drinks. Richard sat at one end, his legs stretched out; Jen was curled up next to him. His arm was round her shoulders, the hand down the front of her shirt.

'How's your wife?' she asked.

He'd mentioned money, she would mention this. The amorousness ebbed, and as it did so sadness, tinged with a bitterness she had never before felt, claimed Jen.

'Why do you ask?' he said.

'No reason.'

'Don't be coy, it doesn't suit you.'

'Don't tell me how to behave.'

He withdrew his hand, then his arm, pulled himself up on the sofa. 'I'm sorry if that's how it seemed, it wasn't intentional. I just can't imagine why you want to know.'

'Can't you?' She took a sip of wine to steady her mouth as well as her nerves. 'Tell me about her.'

He set his glass down. Covered his eyes with his hand. There was a long, painful silence. Jen controlled her urge to embrace him and tell him to forget it.

Massaging his eyes with fingers and thumb, he shook his head. 'No.'

'Why?'

He looked at her, his expression bleak. 'I thought you understood why.'

She did. It was the money, only worse. But she wasn't quite ready to let go of it yet. There was something she needed to hear him say, no matter how much it hurt.

He looked away briefly, and when he looked back she could see he'd gathered his forces. 'I don't want to discuss her with you, because I love her.'

'All right,' she said. Her turn now to tough it out. 'Fair enough.'

'Jen—' He reached for her hand but she moved it lightly away. 'What did you expect me to say?'

'Exactly that.'

'Well, then. What are you trying to do?'

She shrugged again, but this time it was a mere inarticulate twitch of the shoulders, because she did not trust her voice.

'Can we leave it alone?' he asked gently.

'How much do you love her?' Her voice sounded small and colourless, crushed by the weight of what she was saying.

'Jen—'

'No, I do want to know. It's important to me.'

He sighed. She felt his clear, clever, well-stocked lawyer's brain getting into gear, and when he spoke it was in precisely the way she expected.

'Well. If I'm forced to define it . . . I'd have to say that I couldn't contemplate life without her.'

'And what about me?' She tried to sound not plaintive and petulant but coolly, seriously enquiring. 'Could you live without me?'

She only had to wait a moment for his answer. But in waiting at all she knew, whatever he eventually said, what the answer must be.

August slouched on. At the warehouse on the North Circular, Marcus toted microwaves and tumble driers with a furious, scowling energy which belied his wasted appearance and impressed even his (initially sceptical) workmates. In the evenings he returned to Hampstead and ate supper with his father and stepmother, hoovering up whatever was placed in front of him in a silence occasionally punctuated by curt monosyllables.

After supper he would submit with a poor grace to a phone call from his mother, who rang for her own peace of mind, but whose regular interrogations left her none the wiser. Duty done, he went out, only he knew where. But since he was always back by midnight, they tried not to worry. His ability to sustain a physically demanding job and an equally punishing social life, in spite of the absolute consistency of his morose humour and unhealthy habits, persuaded Richard and Isla that all was as well as could be expected.

Occasionally Richard tried to open up a fatherly discussion on Broader Issues.

'Have you,' he would ask over supper on the terrace, 'given any thought to what you'd like to do when you leave school?'

'No.'

'Any ideas at all?'

'Uh-uh.'

At this point Isla, agonised, would absent herself to commune with the dishwasher, clashing plates so she couldn't hear them in their pointless, bloodless locking of conversational horns. The worst of it was she knew that Richard only conducted these interrogations because he thought he ought to. It seemed to her that Marcus, though uncommunicative, had an agenda at least as serious as anything his father envisaged and, what was more, sufficient resolve to see it through. But there was no telling either of them, nor would she have dreamed of trying.

If she were to confront her husband, now or ever, there were more profound matters on which to do so than his behaviour towards his son.

Claudia, now installed in a vacation job at Pleasurelands, was interested to discover that she didn't love children. The curious thing was that the children seemed to like her, or at least to attach themselves to her. As she walked or biked about her area of the compound each day, she was invariably accompanied, Pied-Piper-like, by a squad of children who seemed simply to want to be with her. Perhaps, in this fun-led environment on the edge of the Cotswolds—where most of the staff were hellbent on fulfilling their every need—the children found something calming in her tranquil indifference.

Claudia had opted for site ranger, a roving brief that involved patrolling her given quadrant and checking that all was as it should be in this artificial world. This could entail anything from removing the overflow from litter bins to restoring lost children to their cabins, and to providing the answers to any number of random queries and demands pertaining to laundry, ten-pin bowling, lost bicycles and the opening hours of the John Peel Wine Bar. On Tuesdays and Thursdays she had to cover, on foot, that area of Ramblers Wood designated for dog walking, armed with a pooper-scooper and a black binbag. On these occasions Claudia would concentrate her mind on the green dress, the card from David D and the glossy catalogue of drop-dead clothes.

As to clothes at Pleasurelands, there was a uniform. Claudia loathed all of it. The clothes, with their much-vaunted 'stylish comfort', felt as alien and restrictive as a spacesuit. Though she felt a complete idiot she was assured she looked a knockout in the black cycling shorts, which she topped with an XXL regulation white T-shirt, tied on the hip. Fortunately the weather was good throughout August, so she didn't bother with the black brushed-cotton bomber jacket, and never touched the black nylon bumbag. She wore her own wire-framed sunglasses and kept her hair as short as the site supervisor would allow.

But children, animals and uniform notwithstanding, Claudia enjoyed her work. She liked being out-of-doors, she enjoyed the sensation of others being—in the main—happy around her. She liked the mobility and the problem-solving. She made no close friends, but she was accepted.

Towards the end of her second week, she was patrolling Ramblers Wood with her pooper-scooper when she heard cries of anguish coming from near the perimeter fence. On the far side was the rolling open farmland typical of the county, with sheep grazing between dry-stone walls, and occasional islands of woodland. It was made clear to both staff and holidaymakers that any unauthorised incursions onto this land by either dogs or people would be viewed with the gravest displeasure by the local farmers.

Claudia rushed to the scene. The source of the shrieks was an elderly woman whose beribboned Yorkshire terrier—showing considerable stamina and initiative—had tunnelled out, and was careering across the field, scattering before it a highly satisfactory number of alarmed sheep.

'Oh Lord!' exclaimed Claudia. 'Damn!'

'Don't let him do it!' the woman cried, clutching the chain-link fence. 'Stop him!'

For a split second Claudia thought the woman's distress was for the sheep, but then she saw a man in a cap and a green pullover standing by the bonnet of a Land-Rover, levelling a gun at the dog.

Appalled, Claudia took a deep breath and bellowed at the top of her lungs, 'STOP!'

She heard the click of the gun being cocked. The dog, yap-yapping, wheeled and headed excitedly towards the instrument of death, driving a couple of fat-bottomed ewes before it.

'STOP!' she shouted again, her voice breaking crazily in her effort to be heard above the dog's barking and the woman's wails. She was rewarded by a small movement of the man's head as he looked her way.

'Stop! Don't! I'm coming! Wait there!' she said to the woman. She raced to the nearest gate, fought with the padlock with her emergency skeleton key, and was through, closing the gate behind her.

She ran faster than she had done in years, and was fighting for breath by the time she reached the man. He had collared the terrier and was holding it roughly, at arm's length. Without their tormentor the baaing sheep were regrouping fussily in the middle of the field. The man's face was flinty with rage.

'Give me one good reason why I shouldn't wring this bloody animal's neck here and now!'

'I'm sorry . . . I'm sorry . . . He dug out . . . Sorry . . .' She put her hands on her knees and bent over to catch her breath.

'You *should* be bloody sorry, sheep-worrying's a criminal offence.'

Claudia straightened up, her legs trembling. 'I've said I'm sorry.'

'Yes, well—' Still holding the squirming and yelping dog, the man laid his gun in the back of the Land-Rover and took out a piece of rope, which he looped through the dog's collar. He handed the end of the rope to Claudia. Their hands touched briefly. Their eyes met. 'Hang on. I've just realised you're—who you are.'

'Yes. And you're—' She frowned, not about to betray a better memory than him.

He gazed at her. 'Anthony Saxby. Well, I'll be buggered . . .'

'Oh, I do hope not,' said Claudia, with a coolness she savoured for hours afterwards. 'Not on top of everything else.'

She returned the dog, Tiny, to her tearful owner and went straight to Admin to report the incident before Anthony could.

'The dog dug its way out,' she explained.

'Never mind,' said Sean, the supervisor, who was chubby and camp and in love with his work. 'We've got the maintenance team on the job, and I've sent some show tickets to Mrs Wilbram.'

'It's not her I'm worried about,' said Claudia.

'Sir Anthony?' Sean bridled. 'You leave him to me.'

Whatever masterful action was taken by Sean, it resulted in a call from Admin to the girls' block at about ten that evening: would Claudia please go to the office at once?

Sean was all smiles when she arrived, and Anthony Saxby was standing there with his hands in his pockets.

'Hello,' he said.

'Hello.'

'Sir Anthony wanted a word,' explained Sean with a twinkle.

'Perhaps I might'—Anthony turned his head slightly in Sean's direction while keeping his eyes on Claudia—'take the young lady out for a drink, or is that completely *verboten*?'

'No—but back by midnight,' said Sean, 'with both shoes, preferably!'

'Speaking of shoes,' said Claudia, as they made their way across the car park to the Land-Rover. 'I'm not exactly dressed for a date.'

'Who said it was a date?' He opened the door for her. 'It's just by way of apology for behaving like a pig this morning.'

They went to the sort of country pub which only the natives know about, where her cycling shorts, extreme height and funny hair attracted not a flicker of interest from the other customers.

She had a Malibu, he a pint of flat, cloudy draught cider. Conversation was not particularly easy. They circled and sparred. His unreturned phone call lay at the edge of their discourse like unattended baggage. He asked after Jen.

'She's fine.'

'My mother's cock-a-hoop with the painting.'

There was a short, deep silence, broken only by the slither and click of two youths playing shove-halfpenny at the bar. Claudia watched the shove-halfpenny; Anthony Saxby watched Claudia. She practised remaining completely composed under his scrutiny—she'd have to get used to that in the modelling game—but inside she burned.

'So,' he said, setting down his tankard with an air of finality. 'I'd better get you back before the jeep reverts to a pumpkin.'

She didn't smile. As they barrelled along the lanes, he glanced at her and asked, 'Shall we do this again? What do you think?' He was musing on the future rather than extending an invitation.

'I've no idea,' she replied in a detached tone, though she did not feel detached.

'Speaking personally, I'd like it if we did.'

'It's up to you.'

There was a brief silence during which she didn't look at him, but thought that he was smiling. 'Is it? All right, I say we do it again.'

'Fine.'

'Tomorrow?'

'I can't tomorrow.' She felt she was being hurried.

'I tell you what, you ring me.'

'OK.'

She was trapped. In the reception car park he got out a cracked and dogeared wallet and handed her his card.

'I think you may already have it, but just in case.'

'Thanks.'

'It was nice seeing you again.' He swung back into the driver's seat. 'And I'll look forward to hearing from you.'

Claudia opened her mouth to say something, but the Land-Rover's engine starting up stifled her remark at birth. She made her way back to the staff quarters.

On this August morning Isla and Nell found the Royal Academy Summer Exhibition packed with a cheerful crowd composed mainly of women, pensioners and tourists, all three categories frequently overlapping. The two of them moved from room to room with the throng.

Collapsing onto the first free seat they'd seen in an hour and a half, they agreed it was all a bit much. 'Let's go and eat,' Isla said. 'And, more importantly, drink!'

The dining room of the Ritz had never seemed more delightful, nor Isla's fame more welcome. A corner table with a view of the room was theirs, unrequested and without question, and the management's recognition and approval was evident in every discreet gesture.

They had buck's fizz. Isla raised her glass. 'Escape!'

'Freedom!'

They clinked, smiled, drank.

'Well now,' said Isla. 'I got the impression over the phone that you wanted to get something off your chest.'

Nell reddened. 'It's about Scotch.'

'I thought it might be.'

The blush faded into a more accustomed sternness. 'He's an absolute gem, you know. A bloody good sort.'

'I can believe it.'

'So why can't the parents? What exactly is their problem?'

Isla hesitated while collecting her thoughts. A pearly trout was placed in front of her, and ravioli with fresh basil before Nell.

When the waiter had gone, she said, 'They're old-fashioned in the best sort of way. They think he may be taking advantage of you.'

'Oh, please! Do I look the sort to be taken advantage of?'

'Anyone's that sort in the hands of an expert,' suggested Isla gently. 'And you said how much you cared for him.'

'Er—no, I didn't actually.'

'Forgive me, but you—'

'I called him a good sort. I don't "care for" Scotch in the way you mean,' went on Nell.

'But in some way you do?'

'As a chum. A pal.'

'Well,' said Isla, trying not to feel a fool, 'your parents will be pleased.'

'He's *terribly* attractive,' insisted Nell almost angrily. 'And I'm desperately fond of Scotch, but I'm not in love with him.'

'I'm beginning to understand that.'

'You should—because I'm in love with you.'

Isla didn't think she imagined it . . . the wineglass grew soft in her hand so that it bent and fell, splashing and splintering onto the floor.

The debris was removed instantly. 'Please don't worry, madam, another one is on its way.'

'Isla? Did you hear me?'

Perhaps she hadn't. Or perhaps she had misheard.

'No, I'm sure that I did.'

'I said,' repeated Nell, freeze-framing as the waiter brought another glass and filled it for Isla, then continuing in a fierce whisper, 'I said that I'm in love with you.'

This time Isla gripped the glass before it could turn soft, and took a long pull at her wine. She was utterly confounded.

'I don't know what to say.' Her voice was a dry thread.

'Oh, Christ!' Nell bowed her head and clasped her large, strong hands against her forehead. 'I knew I'd make a pig's ear of this!'

Her companion's embarrassment had the effect of restoring a little of Isla's composure. 'You haven't made a pig's ear of anything,' she said. 'You've just told me something for which I was completely unprepared.'

Nell peered up from under her clasped hands. 'But you can't have been! Not completely. *Surely*.'

'Completely.'

'Christ!' groaned Nell again. 'This is all so unbelievably horrendous!'

Isla drew more strength from the role of comforter. 'No, it isn't.'

'What on earth must you think?'

'Well,' said Isla, 'now I do think, I feel flattered and privileged.'

Nell shielded one side of her face with her hand, grimacing. 'I hope no one's listening!'

'At the Ritz?' Isla shook her head. 'They won't be. And if anything's overheard, it will be by the most sophisticated eavesdroppers in the world. Our secret is safe.'

# *chapter six*

'So THERE YOU HAVE IT,' declared Jim Furmston, on Richard's second visit. He switched the light off behind Richard's X-rays. 'Either you check in somewhere and get that carotid hoovered out, smartish, or you're going to have the granddaddy of a stroke any day now.'

Jim sat down. 'I'll get things moving, shall I?' he asked.

'Um—yes, sorry.' Richard, more shaken than he cared to admit, strove to seem preoccupied with other matters. 'What exactly would that involve?'

'Get you referred asap to see Martin Wheatcroft at the Brodrick, and then in to get the job done. You could be out of harm's way by this time next week.'

'It's such a ruddy nuisance, Jim. I've got a big case coming up—'

'Time for your understudy to have his fifteen seconds of fame, then.'

Richard pushed his chair back and rose. 'I'd like to talk to Isla.'

'That's allowed. But don't hang about—there is a degree of urgency.'

'It's hard to cultivate a sense of urgency from a standing start when none existed'—Richard looked at his watch—'ten minutes ago.'

Jim stood up. 'You rang me, not the other way round,' he reminded him, and at once held up a hand to silence argument. 'Men of your age who suddenly decide to have the full medical are without exception scared shitless.'

With a sense of urgency, Richard left.

Isla pulled into one of the unmade car parks on the edge of the heath before going home. She and Nell had got through lunch acknowledging that something untoward had occurred, but nonetheless trying discreetly to put clear water between them and this bit of local difficulty. At least, that was what she tried to do. Nell, after her first fine frenzy, became almost tongue-tied. Isla had made some of the right noises about a 'dear, dear friend' and 'affection and respect' and Nell having her 'whole life before her' (whatever that had got to do with it), but she knew in her heart of hearts that it was guff, dishonest guff at that.

And Nell had known too. On the pavement in Piccadilly, as a cab thrummed beside them, she made that clear.

'I did mean it, you know. I meant it, and it's true, and it's not going simply to disappear now it's been mentioned.'

'I realise that,' said Isla, who had been hoping that was exactly what would happen. 'We shall have to talk some more.'

With a glum expression Nell said something like 'I suppose so'. Isla had waved her off and fled, exhausted, to the car.

When Richard got home he thought at first that the house was empty. He poured himself a beer and considered ringing Jen. There had been something slightly out of kilter in her manner last time . . . a kind of self-consciousness which he sincerely hoped wouldn't last.

He carried the beer into the orangery, loosened his tie and shrugged off his jacket. Seeing the shadowed and dappled green of the garden, he sat down and unlaced his shoes and discarded them, then his socks.

The pleasure of the different textures beneath his soles—the smooth floor of the orangery, the licheny stone of the terrace, the mossy ridges of the steps and oh, yes! the delicious, unmown coolness of the grass— was exquisite. He sat down on the bottom step with his beer clasped in both hands, clenching and unclenching his toes, feeling the strands of grass thread between them . . .

'What are you doing?'

It was Marcus, standing behind his right shoulder.

'Cooling off,' said Richard. 'Do you want a beer?'

'No thanks, I got a Coke on the way from the bus.'

To Richard's utter astonishment, Marcus sat down, if not exactly next to him then at least nearby, on the flat top of the pillar that flanked the foot of the steps.

'You're home early, aren't you?'

'Probably.'

'Any particular reason?'

'I asked them.'

Just in time Richard stopped himself from putting the obvious supplementary question, and was rewarded.

'I'm totally knackered.'

Richard looked his son full in the face, and noticed that even by his own exacting standards he did indeed look knackered. The yellowish pallor of his face emphasised the grey-blue scoops beneath his eye sockets, and a couple of angry pustules decorated his chin.

'You do look pretty rough. Any symptoms?'

Marcus coughed. 'Not really. Just knackered.'

'You'd better get to bed.'

'No . . . I'd rather chill out down here.'

'Fair enough.'

They sat in silence for a couple of minutes.

'So, what's up?'

Richard recognised this query as indicating a modicum of real interest. It required an answer. 'I was knackered too.'

'You've been looking like shit for weeks,' agreed Marcus equably. 'You ought to see a doctor.'

'As a matter of fact, I've been to see my doctor this afternoon.'

'Oh yeah?' Marcus made no attempt to disguise his scepticism.

'Yeah—yes. He says I'm in pretty good shape for a man of my age.'

'Yeah? So what made you go then?' This brutal logic, so similar to Jim Furmston's, pricked Richard's conscience. He had to come clean some time . . . On the other hand he hadn't spoken to Isla about it yet.

'I may have to have a small operation—a preventative measure.'

'Heart?' asked Marcus matter-of-factly.

'Er—no.'

'You can tell me, you know. I can take it.'

'I realise that, that's not the point. It's nothing of any importance, and anyway there's other people I need to tell first.'

'Have you told Mum?'

This was yet another new departure—an awareness of connections and relationships and their relative weights. Richard was astonished.

'No, but I will, of course.'

'And it's no big deal.' There wasn't a hint of sarcasm in Marcus's voice. There followed another silence, broken by the sound of the front door. Marcus got up. 'Maybe I will crash for a bit.'

'Yes, you do that. A good kip does wonders.'

As Isla came out onto the terrace she passed Marcus going the other way, and said hello, to which he responded with his usual nasal grunt. She went down the steps and bent to kiss Richard on the top of his head.

'Everyone's home,' she remarked, sitting down by him. 'And I thought I'd find an empty house.'

'Would you rather have done?'

'Of course not. What brought Marcus back from the coalface?'

'He's tired.'

'And you? What did Jim say?'

He hesitated. 'Not much.' He realised he had expected her to notice the hesitation, and was disappointed when she appeared not to.

'Look at your bare feet. I think I'll do the same,' she said, and slipped out of her thick-soled white deck-shoes. She seemed to be bubbling over with something of her own, and her next remark confirmed this.

'If I tell you something, will you promise not to mention it to anyone else? To behave, in fact, as if you never heard it?'

'Depends what it is.'

'All right. I've just been having lunch with Nell.'

'Oh yes—how was the RA?'

'The usual curate's egg. Afterwards I bore her off to the Ritz—which was probably my big mistake.'

'You're going to tell me she ate enough for an entire Sumo team.'

'Actually, she hardly ate a thing. She says she's in love with me.'

'Well, I must say it doesn't surprise me.'

Isla, who had been pulling at the grass between her feet, head bowed, glanced up at him. 'It doesn't?'

'No.' Richard put his arm round her and drew her into an embrace, a little awkwardly since they were both sitting on such a shallow step. 'Just about everyone I know is in love with you. As I've told you before, you have absolutely no idea of the effect you have on people.'

'Yes, I do. I'm not an innocent. I'm a professional. But this was a shock. And now that she's told me, what am I supposed to do?'

'Do you have to do anything?'

'I think so, if it's only to find a way to say no. I owe it to her to come up with some sort of considered response.' She felt Richard laughing. 'What's so funny?'

'I was thinking about poor old Bill and Barbara. Have they ever been barking up the wrong tree!'

Isla smiled in spite of herself. 'I know. Delicious.'

'All that outrage and suspicion squandered on the innocent Scott-Chatham.'

'I'm not sure innocent is how I'd describe him. He's in Scotland with Ned as we speak.'

Richard sighed heavily. 'Let them all get on with it, that's what I say.'

'But it's not only them, is it?' said Isla. 'It's me too, now.' Richard didn't comment. She stood up. 'I think I'll get myself a drink. Do you want another?' He shook his head.

Passing through the hall she heard Marcus on the telephone. 'OK,' he said. 'Bye.' He emerged.

'How are you doing?' she asked.

'I was talking to Mum. She's back.'

'Did she have a good time?'

'I reckon. I forgot to ask.' Isla was on her way when he added, 'I think I might go home.'

She paused, turned. 'Of course—when are you off?'

'I'll get my stuff together and . . .'

'Do you want a lift?'

'No, thanks.'

Isla thought that, unlike the rest of them, he was a self-sufficient person, who made his own decisions without reference to anyone else and did not either seek their approval or fear their condemnation. She found that she admired that more and more, and she envied Caroline the sudden upsurge of filial feeling which was sending him home.

She returned with a glass of wine to find Richard, shoes back on, sitting in a chair on the terrace. She sat down next to him, tucking her feet up on the seat.

'I'm sorry if I seemed dismissive about Nell,' he said. 'I agree it's a facer. But I still think you should do nothing.'

'Will I seem to acquiesce, though?'

'Yes. Why not? She can be in love with you whenever she wants. Doesn't mean you have to be in love with her.'

'I thought you'd be shocked.' Isla decided to let it go. Jen would understand how she felt. 'You're right. It's nothing to get worked up about. By the way, Marcus is going home.'

'You mean to his mother?'

'Yes. He was talking to her on the phone just now. A sudden pang of homesickness, I suppose.'

Richard held out his hand to Isla and she took it, grasping it firmly to establish contact.

'There are days,' he said, 'and this is one of them, when I feel that marrying you is the only thing I've got halfway right.'

'Don't be silly. But I'm glad you think that. We'll have to stick together, won't we?'

He didn't answer.

**N**ext day, on the phone to Jim Furmston, he took an assertive line. It was his problem, after all, and his embolism. He was the customer.

'I've decided to wait till my case is over. In the meantime, I'll clean up my act. Isla will be delighted.'

'Have you discussed it with her?'

'Not yet, a suitable moment hasn't presented itself.'

'Sod a suitable moment, Dick, I told you it was urgent.'

'If it was urgent yesterday it was urgent weeks ago, only we didn't know.'

'So when will this case be completed—in your opinion?' Jim's voice was thin with disapproval.

'Shouldn't be more than a few weeks—hearing's set for the second week in September. I'll get back to you when I can give a firm date.'

'No. I'll get you an appointment with Martin Wheatcroft four weeks from now. You'll be in an opt-out situation, Dick. And I want to make it quite clear once again that this delay is against my express advice.'

'Don't worry,' said Richard. 'If the balloon goes up, I shan't sue.'

'Too right you won't, old boy. You'll be dead.'

**J**en was in uproar. What, oh what, was she going to do? She raged at herself for allowing things to reach this point. And yet it was because they had gone on for so long, undisturbed and uneventful, that she had come to accept the situation as part of her life. She had told herself she was hurting no one because Richard so obviously loved his wife. But the off-stage wife had become a centre-stage player now—Isla, whom she had liked on first meeting and felt to be a soul mate. A state of affairs which she had never before thought of as deceitful, she now plainly saw for what it was: shoddy, underhand, despicable.

She was by nature sanguine. She placed no burden of expectation on those she cared for, including Richard, and in return they placed none on her. Red disapproved, of course, but not vociferously, and at the moment she was too preoccupied with her own life to spare a thought for Jen's travails.

Jen didn't know what to think about Claudia's new liaison. One of the qualities she most admired in her daughter—and there were many—was her emotional self-sufficiency, her ability to behave not according to the expectations or wishes of others, but according to her own intentions. The part of herself which Jen recognised as conventionally maternal had worried slightly over recent years about Red's lack of a boyfriend. So she couldn't help being pleased that some sort of relationship appeared to be getting off the ground. But Sir Anthony Saxby? Not for the first time she wondered what was going on inside her daughter's head, not to mention her heart. Not that he wasn't attractive, or nice, or—thank God—unattached, but he was old enough to be her own lover, let alone her daughter's. What was a man of his age and social status doing pursuing a student? She couldn't get a handle on it. But Cupid was a notorious practical joker, and one thing Red had proved was that she could take care of herself.

Richard came round—something else that she felt powerless to prevent—and behaved as if everything was exactly the same. She had to remind herself that to him, perhaps, it was. She'd hoped and believed that something of her own perturbation had communicated itself on his last visit, but he was at his most maddening and attractive—brainy, dishevelled, preoccupied. This was the Richard she found hardest to resist, and she failed completely to do so. After making love she was dismayingly weepy, unable to distinguish between love and the fear of losing it.

'Hey,' he said. 'Come on, chin up. Do you want to talk about it?'

Dumbly, she'd shaken her head.

After he'd gone, heading west for a few days' golf in the country, she picked up the phone to cancel her lunch with Isla. With his voice and his touch uppermost in her mind she was utterly determined. But she'd underestimated the effect Isla's voice would have on her.

'Hello? Jen, how lovely! I was just thinking how much I was looking forward to our lunch.'

'That was what I rang about,' said Jen.

'You're not going to cry off?'

'I'm afraid I must.'

'Oh, no . . .' Isla sounded genuinely downcast. 'You have no idea how much I've been looking forward to it.'

'I know. Me too.' Already Jen felt herself losing her footing, slipping back, and every moment the exchange lasted she could only lose more ground. 'I have to be somewhere else—work, I'm afraid.'

'Never mind. Let's pick another day.'

'I'm likely to be pretty tied up for the foreseeable future.'

There was a short silence. Jen, holding her breath, had the impression that Isla was weighing up this remark, which had undeniably been one of those open-ended excuses bordering on rudeness.

When Isla did answer her voice was gently teasing. 'All work and no play. You have to eat.'

Jen knew she'd lost. 'Yes. You're right.'

'Here's a suggestion—my diary's empty, so you say where you're going to be and I'll meet you there.'

So the meeting remained, but relocated to South Kensington, where Jen was, indeed, due to arrange a photo session with a Dalmatian. As she put the phone down she felt both exasperation at her weakness, her susceptibility, her fatal hesitation and relief that she would be seeing Isla after all, in what would be relative safety.

The day after Isla had spoken to Jen on the phone there was quite a sheaf of envelopes to be opened. There were two postcards, one from Giles, addressed to them both, and another to Richard from Donatella in Fiesole. She read this one first, without guilt—they agreed postcards were fair game.

> *I am having a simply heavenly time, and there is a young man here who is after me like anybody's business. My family all send their love. I am fat and brown and sexy. I hope you are better than you were by the river. Love to you, Ricardo, Donatella*

Isla shook her head. Better than by the river? But Donatella—whom she liked—had an idiosyncratic way of expressing herself and that could mean anything. She picked up Giles's card.

> *Hi folks. This is a blast and the mix of people is the best. There are some really wild German lads. Jealous? Cash running out so back end of the month and all systems go on the party circuit. Ciao, Giles*

In addition to these, there was an invitation to the David D rail sale at the Great Titchfield Street showroom, which she set aside to enter in the diary. There was also that rarest of communications, a letter from her agent, Lori, at Prize Performers. Though Isla read to the end of the letter, she did not need to consider the offer to appear as a regular panellist on *Over the Parrot*—a crazy quiz programme with Adrian Coote and some abrasive young alternative comedians. She had already made up her mind. Lori was astute, and her own interests coincided unerringly with her favourite client's. The quiz show was the right thing at the right time. She was going to ring Lori and accept.

The next letter she picked up was from Nell.

*My dear Isla,*

*I'm just about to leave for France. I'd say what must you think of me? Only I'm pretty sure of the answer. What a prize idiot I must have seemed, ruining a nice lunch like that. I do apologise for being so ham-fisted, and thanks for handling it all so elegantly. But having grovelled, I can't pretend I didn't mean everything I said. I love you dearly, that's the way it is. If when you've read this you think there is the remotest chance you could care for me, please get in touch. Otherwise I faithfully promise not to bother you.*

*All my love, my dear, dear Isla,*
*Nell*

Isla sat down and wept as though her heart would break.

**N**ot long afterwards, Isla went out to Bradenham for the day. It was on impulse. She craved the uncaring, unchanging quality of village life, the tractors doggedly dragging the fields towards autumn, the parish newsletter dropping hints about the best-kept village competition and begging produce for the Harvest Festival. It had been a desperately dry year, but good for the roses, and even the most desiccated gardens sprouted heavy swags of blooms. Norman Brake was mowing the recreation ground on a small tractor, describing ever-decreasing circles on the smooth green.

Marjory's bike was propped by the front door of Brook End, and Marjory herself was pulling up weeds in the garden. She sat back red-faced as Isla appeared in the kitchen doorway.

'Oh, my dear, I had no idea you were coming—I'm so sorry you had to find yours truly grubbing about in your border.'

'Not at all, Marjory. Bless you.'

'I love it . . .' She got heavily to her feet. 'Golly gosh, anno Domini is playing havoc with my knees . . .'

'Cold drink?'

'A squash or something would be lovely.' She followed Isla into the kitchen and sat down at the table. 'Isla, I do hope you don't mind my coming and going like this.'

'Of course not.' Isla snapped ice cubes into tumblers and ran cold water onto lime juice. 'There. It's nice to know the cottage has a friend when we're not here.'

'Yes, a friend, that's certainly how I like to be thought of.'

'And you must always say if it's getting to be a bind. I mean the bike, in all weathers . . .' Isla tailed off.

'It's my trusty bike that keeps me going! I'd be a complete crock without it. Besides, I come down here most days to cook lunch for Norman.'

'Norman?' Isla couldn't disguise her astonishment.

'Well,' went on Marjory hurriedly, 'he prefers his main meal in the middle of the day and so do I, and I enjoy cooking for two. On Sundays he comes to me,' she added. 'And I do a proper roast.'

'Lucky Norman. I saw him,' said Isla, 'up at the rec. Mowing.'

'He does such a lot around the village that people don't know about. I tell him he needs a PR person.'

'Yes, he's not the easiest man to get on with. He's a good neighbour, but pretty crusty.'

'He adores you,' said Marjory. 'Simply adores.'

'But you and he get on well?' asked Isla.

'Awfully well. We're both plain-speaking types, we've lived in Bradenham all our lives, always lived alone—we're quite a pair, really!'

'Good on the both of you! Just you make sure he helps with the washing-up.'

'That's what I got the dishwasher for,' replied Marjory, spiritedly.

**R**ound at The Bury the portrait of Portia was in pride of place over the drawing-room mantelpiece.

'Portia's dead,' declared Barbara.

'Oh, Bar,' said Isla. 'I am sorry.'

'Can't be helped. And I have that to remind me. Now I must away, committees call. Bill knows where the cold lamb is. Bye, ducky.'

'Sod cold lamb,' said Bill as the door closed behind his wife. 'Let's go to the pub.'

But there was no hot food there either, the landlord of The Diggings informed them, because of the Live Music Night. 'You can have the Essential Ploughman's,' he offered.

'What do you think?' asked Bill.

'Sounds fine.'

'Will that be outside?' enquired the landlord hopefully.

'Not on your nelly, in here in the cool and away from the fumes.'

His choice of words reminded Isla of what she had come to say. As they sat at a corner table with their drinks—a pint for Bill and a spritzer for her—she said, 'Let me give you an update on Nell.'

'Hell, yes. What goes on?'

'She's in France with a chum at the moment, as you probably know.'

'That's right. Now you come to mention it she did say something on the phone. So what about Scott-Chatham?'

'He's delightful, but you have absolutely no need to worry. He's certainly not after Nell.'

'Thank the Lord for that.' He cast her a sharp, scowling look. 'She's not fallen for him or anything bloody silly like that?'

'No. They're just firm friends, devoted to one another.'

'I see. So long as she's free to form an alliance with some decent, dependable bloke.' Twin ploughmans were set down before them. 'What, no pickled onions?'

It had been Isla's intention to spend a lazy afternoon at Brook End, reading her book in the garden, but in the event she couldn't settle. So at about three o'clock she locked up the cottage and headed north to The Hayes, Lettaford, to visit her father-in-law.

'A visitor for you,' said Karen, adding coyly, 'a lady visitor.'

Alec leaned forward heavily and peered round the side of his chair. 'I don't know any ladies—'

'Yes, you do.' Smiling broadly Isla went over and bent to kiss his upturned face as Karen closed the door.

He grabbed her hands and held them tight in both his. 'Isla, my darling, is it really you?'

'Yes, and you're quite right to be taken aback. It's been a shamefully long time since I was last here.'

'It has, it has, but never mind that, this more than compensates, in fact it's made my day. Not,' he added in case she should think him too cheerful, 'that that's saying much.'

'Give over, Alec . . .' She left one of her hands in his and with the other pulled up a stool and sat on it. 'You're looking awfully well.'

'Hm.' He shot a look at her beneath beetling brows. 'You and your leading lady's flannel . . . You're as beautiful as ever. He doesn't deserve you.'

'He doesn't have to deserve anything. I know you find this impossible to believe, but I love him.'

'The trouble with you, my darling—' began Alec, but was interrupted by the arrival of an auxiliary with a tea tray. 'Ah, good, what sort of bickies have we got?'

'Garibaldis,' said the auxiliary.

'I like squashed flies. Just stick it over there and my lady friend will see that I'm saucered and blown.'

The auxiliary withdrew. Alec, who had picked up the expression 'saucered and blown' from a patient decades before, and whose own forebears had, to a man, sipped Darjeeling with the utmost propriety, consumed his tea and squashed flies with gusto, blowing, stirring, slurping and dunking with noisy relish.

'Tell me,' he asked, 'are you going to stay for dinner?'

'I'd like to, but I can't. I didn't even tell Richard I was coming.'

'So you need his say-so for a day out?'

'No, but he's away and he likes to ring in the evening. Still, it's only three thirty,' she pointed out. 'I needn't go for another hour.'

'In that case'—Alec hauled himself to his feet—'I want to show you something.' Isla replaced their cups on the tray and abandoned the stool in favour of the other armchair. She watched as with painful, jerky steps Alec went to the chest of drawers, and opened the top drawer. He breathed heavily as he stirred the contents with a slow hand.

'Here we are . . .' He took out a letter, closed the drawer and returned with his jerky robot's gait to the chair, collapsing with an explosive exhalation. 'Must you sit over there?'

'The stool's a bit hard.'

'You're getting old, like me.'

'That's right.' Isla was an expert on not allowing Alec to rile her.

He unfolded the letter. Isla recognised Richard's handwriting, but said nothing. Alec scanned the pages thoughtfully for a moment.

'He wrote me the funniest letter . . . what do you make of this? "I've not been feeling too jolly and may have to go in for an op in the foreseeable future." Did you know that? No you didn't, but then why should you?—you're only his wife. At any rate it's of no account, he goes on, let's see, "but not till after my present case is completed, and the prognosis is good—just a little tidying-up to ensure my future well-being . . ." I was a bloody doctor, I know a classic coronary presentation when I see it!'

Isla was shocked, and it must have showed, for Alec wagged a hand at her. 'Sorry, my darling, didn't mean to put the wind up you.'

'I just wish he had confided in me. He has been feeling poorly.'

'There you are then. In that case he probably thinks he'll drop down dead if he speaks the word "operation" out loud.'

Isla could think of nothing else to say in the face of this abrasive dismissal, and more than anything she did not want to weaken in front of Alec, who did not approve of weakening.

'But that's all by the bye,' he went on, turning the page. 'It's when he starts getting all metaphysical on me that I can't make head nor tail . . . For instance . . . yes . . . here we go . . . "I would be interested to know, if you are prepared to tell me, whether you and my mother enjoyed a happy marriage. The reason I write to ask, rather than doing so in person, is because I wish to make it clear what I mean. Dad, I want to know if you made each other happy, in every way, and if there were areas in which the answer is no, then why not? What went wrong? And if you never really stopped to consider whether you were happy, what is to be inferred from that? I dare say you'll regard all this as the apotheosis of impertinence, and you're perfectly entitled to bin the whole thing and never return to it again, but I'm anxious to know." There's a bit more in the same vein. What the devil do you think he's on about?'

'He makes it crystal clear,' said Isla. 'But does he say why he wants to know?'

'In a stew about his op, I imagine,' said Alec callously. 'I'll have another cuppa.'

In her attempt to seem perfectly unruffled, Isla moved with exaggerated care and slowness. 'Poor Richard.' She handed Alec his tea, keeping a hold on the saucer for a second until his hand steadied on the other side. 'He's doing so much thinking.'

'Candidly, I don't know whether to dignify the whole barmy litany with an answer.'

'Of course you must. He's your son. Your only child. How you answer is another matter and none of my business.'

'True.' Alec rolled his eyes at the letter, now on the arm of the chair. 'Care to look at it yourself?'

Isla was tempted, but also repelled, her fearful curiosity shrivelled by the taboo of reading a private letter intended for someone else.

'No, thank you. It wouldn't be right.'

'You want to know if you're mentioned.' It wasn't a question, and Isla did not answer. Alec smacked his lips. 'You're not.'

Jen drove to Pleasurelands to visit Claudia, and met her at reception.

'Is that what they make you wear?' She hadn't seen Claudia in uniform before.

'Mum—' Claudia took her elbow in a grip of steel. 'Don't.' She turned to the receptionist. 'This is my mother.'

'Hello, there!' said the girl, flashing a big professional grin.
Jen smiled back.

'Mum, I've got an hour and a half. What do you want to do?'

'You could show me round. If I park inside somewhere—'

'Cars aren't allowed in the compound. We walk or cycle.'

'Whatever. Although I'd be a bit of a liability on a bike.'

Claudia's expression indicated that she'd be a liability in any case.

'I'll take you to the boating lake—there's a fairly bearable café there.'

It was a much longer walk than Jen had anticipated. She was quite light-headed, and the soles of her feet, in well-worn espadrilles, were beginning to blister by the time they got there. On the other hand, the exercise seemed to have restored Claudia's mood, and she thawed still further over a cheese and mushroom toastie, as they sat overlooking the gliding boats and scudding ducks on the lake.

'Sorry I was a moody cow.'

'Were you? I didn't notice.' Jen tapped her half-finished Spanish omelette with her fork. 'This isn't bad. Sorry I can't do justice to it.'

'No, the grub's quite reasonable. Though the burger bar's to be avoided. Mad cow heaven.'

Jen had to laugh. 'My darling Red, what are you doing here?'

Claudia cracked a dark, sheepish smile. 'Funnily enough I enjoy the bit I do. I'm out on my bike most of the day, not stuck inside, and the punters are a good-natured lot on the whole.'

'And how's the social life?' Jen left Claudia to interpret the question as she would.

'You mean Anthony? He's OK.'

'Seeing much of him?'

'No, because I don't get much time off.'

'But you really like him?'

'Yes. I'm slightly surprised to find I do. I really do.'

'How old is he?'

'Forty-two, shock horror.'

'Age isn't important.'

'Good old Mum.' Claudia gave Jen an affectionate look over her milk shake. 'So how's things in your camp?'

'Oh, jogging along.' Having come all this way to tell her daughter her plan, she now felt compelled to make light of it. 'I'm going to finish with Richard.'

'I'm sorry,' said Claudia.

'It's got to be done.'

'What brought this on?'

'A combination of things. I knew you'd be pleased.'

'That's an awful thing to say, as if I wanted you to be unhappy.'

'But you never liked my arrangement with Richard. I'm not complaining, Red, just stating a fact.'

'I don't like to think of you being used.'

'I never was. Richard isn't like that.'

'Mum! Get real! It's a classic—he has exactly what he wants, with everything neatly compartmentalised, and you—and presumably his poor wretched wife as well—know your places and stay in them! It beggars belief!'

Jen lowered her voice, pushing the anger back down her throat. 'I'm important to him.'

'You're not important at all! You're a non-bloody-person.'

'That's not true.'

'Not you, I don't mean the real you. I mean this put-upon, obliging bit of stuff that he visits a couple of times a week and who meekly puts up with it. It's not like you, Mum, it's not the you I know.'

'But it *is*!' Jen leaned forward to look into her daughter's face, but Claudia turned away. 'It is, this *is* me. Has it ever occurred to you that the arrangement suits me? That I'm not equipped to deal with anything more committed? You may not like it, love, but that's the truth.'

Claudia kept her face averted.

'Red?'

There was a small sniff. Claudia put up a hand and swiped away a tear.

'Anyway,' she said. 'You're going to finish with him.'

'Yes.'

'Well—I'm sorry, really sorry, Mum, if it makes you unhappy. But thank God is all I can say.'

## *chapter seven*

THEY MET AT THE ENTRANCE to the V&A. Jen, concerned that they might be going somewhere smart for lunch, had accordingly worn a skirt for the Dalmatian's photo session, where normally she'd have worn jeans. The skirt was ankle-length Indian cotton in reds and

112

ochres, with a drawstring waist to which were attached a carillon of tiny brass bells. She'd teamed the skirt with a plain cream scoop-necked T-shirt, flat plaited sandals, a chunky coral necklace and brass earrings and bangles. Unfortunately there was no escaping the baggage she had to carry for a morning's dog-watching: camera, folder, satchel. She could never aspire to elegance, but she was a person with her own style.

Isla, wearing lean jeans and a faded chambray shirt with the sleeves rolled up, was standing on the steps of the V&A, talking to a handsome old man whose face Jen recognised. There was a long-handled rush basket over her shoulder.

'Hello,' she said, 'don't you look nice? This is my old mate Percy, Percy, this is the artist Jen Delaney.'

'Madam,' said Percy. 'My pleasure.'

Isla patted his cheek. 'We're going to Alma's.'

Percy gave a little bow. 'That, if I may say so, is no place to take an artist.' He turned to Jen. 'But leave your sensibilities at the door, my dear, and you will have fun.'

Alma's, Isla explained *en route*, was no more nor less than an old-fashioned drinking club and Alma herself was an old-fashioned drinker.

'In other words a hard one. She started the club just after the war so that she could surround herself with all the theatricals she liked so much without setting foot outside her own front door.'

Jen thought Alma's quite wonderful. It was really no more than two large basement sitting rooms, one of which contained the bar. There were sagging sofas, freckled mirrors, hundreds of paintings and photographs, and a piano. A French window gave onto a small paved yard.

Alma, from diamanté hairslide to ebony cigarette holder, was quite perfect. A comely black girl was introduced as 'Rosie, my main squeeze'.

'We'd like to eat,' said Isla. 'What are you poisoning us with today?'

'Poison no longer,' rasped Alma. 'Rosie does the cooking these days. Get to the kitchen, woman, and be about your duties.'

Isla bought a bottle of wine and they sat down in chairs near the French window. There was no one else there. The sweet smell of louche-living permeated the atmosphere.

'I love it here,' said Isla. She glanced invitingly at Jen over her glass. 'The perfect place for a serious exchange of confidences.'

Jen managed to keep the confidences at bay for some time. She had come out today with the intention of behaving like someone in retreat, and there would never be another such invitation. But the moment she had seen Isla in her frayed and faded denim, Jen was reminded again of exactly why she had given in. She liked Isla—deeply and instinctively—and delighted in her company. It was hard to be cool and withdrawn when so much was forthcoming that was exactly right. The place, the ambiance, everything had been chosen to please and amuse her, with an ease of manner that demanded no litany of gratitude, but which said: your being here is enough.

They talked about her work, and pets generally—dogs, and owners, and dogs versus cats. From there, however, she was unable to prevent a progression to families—specifically Isla's stepsons, Richard's former wives, and his father . . . Jen had to keep reminding herself that this was Richard, her Richard, Isla was talking about. She'd heard this cast of characters mentioned before, but this woman knew them intimately, and had a stake in their lives, whereas she—well—perhaps it was true, as Claudia had said, that she was a non-person . . . Rosie's arrival with the food—conch, and fresh fish cooked with okra and served with dumplings of cornmeal, banana and plantains, sufficient for half a dozen people—created the opportunity for a change of subject.

'My daughter's going out with a man twice her age,' said Jen, digging in. Isla suspected that this particular confidence had been preying on her mind for some time and had finally found its moment.

'What's he like?' she asked.

'Nice enough. And loaded. He's landed gentry. A Sir, at any rate.'

'But do you like him? You have met him . . .?'

'A couple of times. I did his mother's basset. And yes, I did like him. But it's funny to meet a man who is the right sort of age to go out with oneself, and then to discover he's pursuing your student daughter.'

She sighed and began to eat ravenously. Isla helped herself as she considered the scenario. 'Do you think she's in love with him?'

'I couldn't possibly say. She's never been in the least interested in having a boyfriend. And now this. I only pray he's not some sort of father figure, and that it won't end in tears and be all my fault.'

'Why should it be your fault?'

'How long have you got?' said Jen.

'Who is this man, anyway?'

'He's Sir Anthony Saxby. The seat's near Oxford, and very pretty it is.'

'Actually,' said Isla, 'I've met him. We were on the same table at a dull do and he more or less saved my sanity.'

'But what does he see in her?' persisted Jen. 'I mean of course I *know* what he sees in her, she's twenty-one and six foot, outrageously beautiful and sharp as a tack. But all that aside, what's he after?'

'Maybe she's a lovely, lovable girl,' suggested Isla. 'And different from the sort he usually encounters.'

'Maybe. Probably. But still the whole thing confuses me.'

Isla leaned back, one arm behind her head, the other hand balancing her wineglass on the arm of her threadbare armchair. 'It shouldn't. Simplify, that's the thing. Your daughter sounds wonderful, and she and her aristocrat have got a real love affair going on. Lucky, lucky them . . .' She closed her eyes for a moment and thought of Richard. What would make her, and her alone, indispensable to his life and his heart . . .?

'Anyway,' she said at last, 'let me tell you the extraordinary thing that's happened to me.'

To Jen, the most extraordinary thing about what Isla told her was Richard's reaction.

'I can't believe he was so unconcerned,' she said. 'After all, you'd just told him you have a lover.'

'Someone who's in love with me. Not quite the same thing. But he was almost—not interested.'

Jen tried to imagine Richard hearing the news and found it was quite beyond her. In that exchange he was another person, one she didn't know. 'Maybe,' she said, 'he had other things on his mind.'

'Yes, possibly. He's incredibly busy, and he hasn't been all that well recently, and then there's the boys . . . yes. That's probably it.'

'You could do much worse than be loved by Petronella,' said Jen.

Isla sat up. 'I realise that. And of course I'm only telling you this in the strictest confidence.'

'Telling me what?'

'Thank you.' So much for the confidence she had promised to respect. Twice already she had breached it. 'I don't like myself very much,' she remarked matter-of-factly, trying not to invite sympathy.

'Join the club,' replied Jen, just as evenly.

That, thought Jen, was my cue—and I missed it. But then, if she intended to see neither Isla nor Richard again, what point would there be in delivering herself of the appalling truth? The trouble was she knew, exactly, what the point was—so that in the far distant future, Isla, who had been honest with her, would know that her honesty had been reciprocated. And then they might—but no, it wasn't going to happen.

At about three thirty they left Alma having her temples massaged with essential oils by Rosie, and walked back to South Kensington tube.

Isla said, 'I have enjoyed this. It was exactly what I needed.'

Jen agreed that it had been lovely.

'So shall we do it again?' Isla didn't need to look at Jen to know that she was fumbling for an excuse, just as she had on the phone. What was the matter, when they got on so well, when they enjoyed each other's company, when they were able to be so frank with one another—when they had the makings of the perfect honest friendship?

The silence was uncomfortable. And when Jen broke it, it was to say, 'I'm absolutely snowed under with work at the moment.'

As soon as she'd said it she realised how affected it sounded—it was a phrase which set her teeth on edge even had it been true.

'I know,' said Isla. 'I'm going to be busy when the silly season's over, but we all need time off for good behaviour.'

Now Jen felt even more foolish—this woman was a famous actress, for crying out loud, with more calls on her time than she could possibly lay claim to. A change of tack presented itself and, with it, an escape route. 'Have you got something exciting coming up?'

'Yes, as a matter of fact. I've got a telly offer for a very modish quiz show with a tribe of off-the-wall young comics.'

'I'd be scared shitless.'

'I will be. But it will be fun, it will be different—it will be much harder than it looks, which is very good for me at my age.'

'I suppose,' said Jen humbly, 'that money doesn't come into it?'

'Yes it does.' Isla was firm. 'I was an independent woman for much longer than Richard was a single man. He's three times married, but I had to be dragged kicking and screaming to the altar.' There was a pause, which Isla broke by adding suddenly, 'And what about you?'

'Me?'

Isla laughed. 'Yes, you. You have your beautiful daughter and your independence. But what about love?'

What about it? thought Jen. 'I'm not really looking,' she said. 'In my experience it has to creep up on you.'

'You're so right.'

They arrived at the station and stopped, having reached the parting of the ways—Isla was going by cab to Church Street. 'But if I had my wish, someone wonderful would be waiting in the wings for you as we speak. Maybe you should take a fresh look at your lodger . . . ?'

Jen shook her head, covered her eyes. 'I can see I shall have to introduce you.'

'I'd like that.'

Jen realised she had been led into the gentlest of traps. 'Look,' she said, 'for heaven's sake, I didn't mean it.'

Lori was waiting for Isla in the Greek coffee shop next to Lalage's Art Nouveau. She was what men call a pretty woman and women recognise as a smart operator. This afternoon she wore a bright red suit with a long tight jacket and flirty pleated skirt. On seeing Isla she rose with a broad smile and leaned across the table to deliver a kiss.

'Great to see you. Did you have a nice lunch?'

'We went to Alma's.'

'Say no more. Can I get you a nice glass of Andrews Liver Salts?'

'Turkish coffee, please. It was good as a matter of fact.'

Over coffee Lori ran through the TV offer, and produced the draft contract. Isla didn't need persuading but Lori pitched anyway. When the waiter brought over a white rose for Isla, Lori touched the velvety petals admiringly.

'You see,' she said, 'this is it. The whole world loves you. That's why these comics need you on board; they're no different to anyone else, underneath the crap they just want to be loved too.' She leaned forward happily, tapping Isla's saucer with her spoon. 'Let me tell you, you're about to conquer new worlds.'

**R**ichard wondered what Isla had made of the postcard from Fiesole. Donatella was naughty to write the sort of thing that was calculated to irritate . . . He was a little surprised to find his wife out. He poured himself a mineral water, put on John Williams, and went upstairs to change, with the tumbling chords rippling all round like water over stones. He was making an effort, and Jim Furmston's grim prognostications notwithstanding, he believed he felt a little better for it. His waistband felt easier, his step lighter, and his head clearer than it had in ages. And with his physical improvement there was an accompanying lift in his spirits. He slightly regretted having written that letter to his father. At the time the need to find out was strong upon him, but he had always been the first to advise his clients to say, do, or write nothing in the heat of the moment, and he had gone against his own advice. The fact that Alec had not replied indicated the extent of his embarrassment.

The phone rang. It was Caroline, in exuberant form.

'I had a wonderful holiday—we didn't actually find anything, but the people were all absolutely super, and the chap in charge was a genius, an absolute genius—Daniel Hetherington. Have you heard of him?'

'No, but that doesn't mean anything.'

'He's one of the top men in the field. He spent literally hours one evening in the bar just talking about his work . . . I haven't enjoyed myself so much in ages.'

'That's terrific. How's Marcus, by the way?'

'Oh, fine . . .' She dropped her voice to an intense whisper. 'He seems to be changing, for the better . . . stringing whole sentences together, that kind of thing . . . I do hope it's not a false dawn.'

'I'm sure it's not,' said Richard. 'Isla's always maintained he had the right stuff.' At once he could have bitten his tongue off.

'And so have I, always, so have I.' Caroline was predictably quick to rise. 'It's just that you long for the day it finally shines through.'

'What about Giles? We had a postcard.'

'Giles is back, and gone again, looking ghastly beneath his tan. He and the Beales boy have got themselves into a horrible flat in Earls Court. They're working in a wine bar while they build up what they call their client base for the party thing.'

'I see. What's the name of the wine bar, do we know?'

'Yes, and to my eternal shame I've already checked up on it. They're the lowest form of kitchen life.'

'The perfect milieu in which to build up a client base . . .'

Caroline giggled. 'I should so love to be a fly on the wall.'

**O**ver dinner, Isla realised that for the first time in weeks she and Richard were both completely happy—happy in small ways, about what they'd been doing and who they'd seen, but truly happy nonetheless. She felt ridiculously elated. Was this all it took to make the future rosy—lunch with a new friend, the promise of work, relaxed conversation? She hadn't mentioned the letter Alec had shown her, and she knew now she would not, at least for the time being. Why spoil a good thing?

'Let's go away for Christmas,' she said. 'Let's fly to the sun.'

'You always said you liked a log-fire-and-pine-needles Christmas.'

'I do, but change is good. We mustn't get stuck in a rut.'

'So what'll it be—St Lucia?'

'Something like that. Perhaps more remote. The Maldives—we'll go native.'

Richard pushed his chair back and rose, slowly. He dropped his napkin on the table, walked to her chair and stood behind her, his hands on her shoulders. She put her right hand up to his, and waited.

He said, 'It must be all this talk of sun, sea and sand . . .'

She lifted his hand, the palm close against her face. 'And going native.'

**A**fterwards he went downstairs to fetch their unfinished bottle of wine. Isla dared to think, This is almost perfect. The bedroom was bathed in a soft, reflective light. It was the end of August and the beginning of a new season. A quiet assurance claimed her. The troubled uncertainty of the past few weeks seemed to be receding.

Richard came back and sat down on her side of the bed to pour wine.

When he'd given her her glass he didn't immediately pick up his, but put out a hand and stroked the hair back off her face.

'I love you, my darling.'

She smiled. 'I know.'

He leaned forward to kiss her. 'But I want you to know I mean it. And I want you to believe me.'

'Richard . . .!' She began to laugh, but his face was anxious: she was reminded of the letter to Alec and stifled the laugh. 'Richard, I do believe you. And it's the most important thing in the world to me.'

He gave a sigh of relief, and raised his glass in a toast. 'That's that, then. Here's to happiness. And Christmas in the sun.'

For Jen, there was a certain rhythm to the long, hot journey back, a rhythm dictated by what she would do when she got home. She would close the front door, remove her sandals, drink a pint of cold Evian water as the cats wove silkily round her bare ankles . . . and then lie down on the sofa, and try, for a mere fifteen minutes, not to think.

And to begin with it looked as though she would succeed. The cats materialised by the front door to welcome her and the house was quiet. Keith was at a staff meeting and she expected no visitors.

But when she went into the kitchen she saw them—Claudia, Anthony Saxby and Keith, sitting in the back garden. She took a quick step back, but not quick enough.

'Mum—!' Claudia appeared at the back door. 'Mum?'

'Red—how lovely.' They embraced.

'Sorry to surprise you. It's my evening off so Ant suggested we come up and say hi. We did actually ring on the mobile, but you were out.'

*Ant?* thought Jen. *Ant?* 'Yes, I had a job and a lunch down in Kensington.'

Claudia tilted her head, quizzically. 'Are you OK?'

'Fine.'

'Come on and join us then, we made a jug of Pimms.'

She followed Claudia out into the garden. Anthony and Keith were deep in conversation, but Anthony got to his feet as she appeared.

'I do hope this is all right,' he said pleasantly. 'There are few things worse than being wrong-footed in your own home. Especially after a long hot day in town.'

And what would he know about that? thought Jen, demurring, but a tad frostily. She accepted a Pimms and sat down.

'I thought you had a meeting,' she said to Keith.

'I do, but not until eight.'

'Keith's been talking about the Lakes,' said Claudia, 'and we've decided we've got to go there for a weekend.'

'I was dragged up various fells and escarpments in torrential rain as a child,' remarked Anthony, 'but I don't remember much and those memories I do have are rather negative. Have you ever been?'

'Years ago.'

'Not with me,' put in Claudia.

'Can you blame her?' joshed Keith. To Jen's amazement something like a smile flickered on Claudia's face.

Anthony laughed agreeably. If this strange little gathering was anything to go by he was certainly the Fitters'-in Fitter-in. 'I wondered,' he said, 'since we've turned up out of the blue like this whether we could compensate by inviting you out for something to eat?'

'Oh, I don't think . . . It's kind of you but it's been a long day—'

'Mum,' said Claudia. 'Supper? Somewhere local? Come on.'

Suddenly, Jen thought she might be going to cry. She pressed her lips together and hoped that no one would demand a response. Help came from an unlikely quarter.

'No, no, I'm with your mother,' said Anthony. 'I'd feel just the same in her shoes.' He smiled briefly, understandingly at Jen. 'There's always another time.'

'Yes,' she said, hot with gratitude. 'There is, and I'd like that.'

With easy politeness Anthony turned to Keith. 'I don't suppose you've got time to keep us company over a curry?'

Jen stared at him. He couldn't surely? He *wouldn't,* would he . . .? Her stare became a glare.

But Keith rose to his feet, dusting the seat of his trousers fussily. 'No, no, no, thanks a million but I mustn't. Someone's got to have something thought through to say on the new guidelines, and no prizes for guessing who that will be. But thanks for asking just the same.'

Jen exhaled with relief. Keith did possess some rudimentary social sensibilities. And thinking this reminded Jen that she'd been rather less than civil herself, when even the Pimms she was drinking wasn't hers.

'I do apologise,' she said, 'if I was brusque when I arrived. It's been a long day, but it *is* lovely to see you.'

'Says she,' said Claudia, with a touchy smile.

'No, really, Red.'

Anthony dropped his eyes for a moment in discreet acknowledgment of this small mother/daughter thing. When he lifted them again it was to remark, with an equally discreetly lowered voice, 'You're fortunate with your lodger. He seems a nice sort of bloke.'

'He is,' said Jen. 'And you're right, I'm extremely lucky.'

Anthony got up. 'And now we must clear off and leave you to some well-earned peace and quiet.'

'Steady on,' said Claudia, 'I live here, remember? I'll say when it's time to go.'

'You're right, how rude of me.' He meant it. He's the genuine article, Jen thought. No wonder she loves him.

'Only joking.' Claudia scrambled to her feet. She was wearing long, crumpled khaki shorts and a black cheesecloth shirt, now covered in bits of grass. 'Cheers, Mum, don't get up.'

'Of course I'll get up. But give us a hand.'

Claudia yanked her to her feet and she went with them into the hall and opened the door. Now, of course, she saw the Land-Rover parked opposite—an outsider in this street of clapped-out saloons.

She stood in the doorway, watching them cross the road as though they were a couple of teenagers. Claudia cavorted round him with her long strides, galloping alongside and walking backwards in front of him.

Jen closed the door. On her way home she had stopped off at Boots. Now she carried her shopping into the sitting room, leaving the door open, and took out the bag containing the pregnancy tester.

It was years since she'd held one in her hand. Since coming off the pill three years ago she'd kept condoms in the house, and Richard had been conscientious. But you were never too old to be careless. As she stared at the label, then unfolded the sheet of instructions, the enormity of it all rolled down over her like an avalanche.

Was there any feeling, Richard asked himself, as he shook hands outside Court Number 12 with the author and the author's family, like that of having won? And the best of it was, thought Richard, as he basked in the gratitude, no lives would be ruined because of it. His client had been awarded costs, which his brother was well able to pay, but damages of only £1,000—not enough to disgrace the loser, or to prevent normal family relations being resumed in due course.

Archie was red in the face with pleasure. When they finally left the author and his supporters, and were on their way to the robing room, he asked, 'Drink, Richard? We must celebrate.'

'I'll pass, thanks.'

'Come on, you must. It's a famous victory.'

'I don't know about that. But an extremely pleasing one.'

'Damn right! You were in top form, played an absolute blinder.'

Richard smiled. 'We had right on our side.'

'Well,' said Archie, 'you were the very devil in there. It was a pleasure to watch you work, eh, Dilip?'

'It was,' his pupil agreed. 'It will be in all the papers.'

'You betcher it will!' Archie was irrepressible. 'Dilip, you'll come for a celebratory snort, won't you?'

'I'd like to.'

'Good!' Archie turned to Richard. 'Come on, won't you reconsider?'

'The very last thing I want is to cast a blight,' said Richard, 'but I'm going to go home.'

'Yes, yes . . .' Archie opened the door of the robing room and stood aside for Richard. 'Can't argue with that. This man,' he said to Dilip as they went in together, 'has the most enchanting wife in England.'

Isla's voice was on the answering machine.

'Congratulations, darling! I rang chambers and Terry gave me the news. Look, I'm at Television Centre with Lori, surrounded by unbelievably clever people aged about fourteen, and we're running late. *So* sorry not to be there. I've got a driver outside and the minute we're done we'll head home at speed. See you then. Bye . . . Bye.'

Richard reached Selwyn Street in the late afternoon. Cain and Abel were sitting in the living-room window like Staffordshire pots, more perfectly, contentedly feline than any real cats deserved to be. He even managed a small surge of affection for them.

He locked the car and walked over to the house. The cats, biding their time, betrayed not a flicker of interest. He let himself in and stood for a moment with his hand on the door.

'Jen?'

There was no reply, and no sound from upstairs. Cautiously he went as far as the kitchen door and looked across the kitchen and into the garden: no one there. Well, to hell with it. He took the bottle of Scotch from the cupboard and poured himself a generous shot, topping it up with tap water. When he turned round the cats had come into the kitchen and were posing, tails raised, on either side of the door. With a drink in his hand, Richard's brief change of heart did not extend to opening tins of cat food.

'Sorry, chums,' he said. 'I'm not the man you want.'

In the living room he sat down in the armchair facing the window and breathed in the familiar scent. With the conclusion of the case he felt he had proved something to himself. Both physically and mentally, he'd held up well—*more* than held up. He felt a great surge of positive health and energy. Even so he'd humour Jim Furmston, go and see the head honcho, get things moving there. There was nothing now in the pipeline at chambers that Archie couldn't handle, and he'd be able to cruise into the new year a new man.

He ran his wrist over his forehead, then undid his cuffs and rolled up his sleeves. The heat was terrific. The country was crawling through a punishing Indian summer. Loosening his collar, Richard returned to the kitchen to look for ice. He was happy to be alive.

Jen was photographing a parrot in Muswell Hill. At least, she would have called it a parrot, but the owners, a retired couple in their early seventies in an immaculate mansion-block flat, were keen to impress upon her that Chipper was a sulphur-crested cockatoo.

'He's extremely handsome,' said Jen as she packed up her stuff. 'And he'll be my first bird.'

By the lifts, Mrs Hastings addressed Jen with careful, near-silent enunciation—the flat door was open.

'When do you think you might finish?'

'I don't know . . . two or three weeks.'

'Only'—she drew Jen closer—'he hasn't got long.'

'Oh, I'm sorry. So you want this as a memento?'

'No. Doug. My husband. A few months, he's been told.'

'No—oh dear.' Jen was overcome with remorse and a terrible compulsion to laugh hysterically. 'That's awful.'

'He worships Chipper.'

'I'll be as quick as I can,' Jen promised.

Down in the road she put her things in the boot of the car and locked it. The afternoon was fiercely hot and she felt limp and exhausted as she climbed into the car. She remembered this feeling: low blood sugar. She unpeeled the chocolate bar she'd brought with her, and bit into it in the sort of ecstasy only available to a person on their own and not being watched. She thought about Mr Hastings and his beloved Chipper. She herself didn't care for birds, but she would do a good job on this one. And by the time she finished, she would have reached her decision and have done what needed to be done. She had life, she told herself grimly, an embarrassment of it at present.

Richard wondered how long to wait. After the adrenalin high of the last few days the pressure was beginning to catch up with him and the whisky, after a period of relative abstinence, had made him rather muzzy. He wasn't sure now that it had been such a good idea coming over to Selwyn Street. He'd been disappointed to find Isla not at home, and had wanted to share his victory with someone. Now he was confronting a drive home in heavy traffic in the stifling heat.

He massaged his temples fretfully. He wished that he hadn't had the whisky, it had given him a headache. It was time to go. In the kitchen, washing his glass—he didn't want to advertise his abortive visit to the returning Keith—he actually felt unwell.

He was in the hall when the floor rose up at him with a sickening rush. There was a boom in his head, no pain, but a shock that eddied through him. Nauseous and disorientated, his vision blurred, he realised he was lying on his side. One arm was flung out in front of him but it seemed detached from him. He thought he might be bleeding and tried to drag the hand towards his head, but couldn't. His other arm was trapped beneath him. He was icy cold. There was a bitter smell and he realised he'd brought up a small amount of vomit; its grainy wetness was a dark halo round his field of vision.

He had never been more helpless, nor more terrified. When he tried to make a sound he could hear something inside his head, a vibration that rattled round like distant thunder, but no sound emerged. Tears trickled sideways across his face, over the bridge of his nose, his cheekbone, his temple, to join the mess on the floor.

In the eternity that was the next five minutes his consciousness shrank to a wavering pinprick, his senses shut down softly, one by one.

By the time the front door was opened, and the phone picked up, he didn't know where he was nor who was with him.

When Isla got back she was not entirely surprised to find that the Jag wasn't in the drive. Richard would probably be celebrating with the team. She, too, was on a high—her afternoon had been the greatest fun and she positively hummed with pleasurable anticipation at the prospect of the recordings.

She went into the library. Before picking up the phone she saw that two messages were registered, one of them, as she knew, her own.

'Alison?'

'Isla! How are you?'

'Terribly cheerful. I rang to say great news about the case—Richard's not back yet, and I needed to go "whoopee!" with someone.'

Alison made a sound of irritable dismay. 'Do you know I didn't even know? You shame me.'

'No, no. Richard's been a bit low, so I especially wanted this one to go right for him. I rang chambers while I was still in town.'

'That would explain why Archie's so late,' said Alison. 'They must be carousing together. So much for—hang on, here he is—'

Alison half covered the mouthpiece and Isla heard a door bang and a muffled exchange before Alison returned in full force.

'—would you like a word with the returning hero?'

'Yes, please.'

'Isla, hello.'

'Archie—well done. Is himself absolutely cock-a-hoop?'

'Quietly satisfied was more the sort of thing, and with some justification. He was in dazzling form.'

'He has a great team behind him, Archie, we all know it. Anyway, I imagine if you're back he can't be far behind so I'd better look out a bottle of something jolly.'

'No,' said Archie, 'actually he wasn't with us.'

'Not?' Isla was baffled. 'Where did he go?'

'Home, he said. He specifically said he wanted to get back to you.'

'I see.'

There was a silence, which Isla was too preoccupied and Archie too awkward to fill. Alison spoke in the background and Archie said, 'It looks as if everyone's just missed everyone else.'

'Yes,' said Isla, 'I suppose it does.'

When she'd put the phone down she stood still for a moment, letting her mind quieten. Her mood had travelled on a queasy switchback from exhilaration to trepidation. She pressed the button on the answering machine and listened to her own voice. Then the next beep. Then the voice of a strange man. 'Hello—hello? My name's Keith Burgess. This is a message for whoever is there, concerning Richard Wakefield. I got back to find he'd had a fall and was unconscious. He seems very poorly. I've called an ambulance and we should be at the Royal Free very soon after this. The time's five fifty-five—ambulance is here. Bye.'

The tape whirred, bleeped, whirred, bleeped again and restored the status quo. The red nought stared up at Isla.

She leaned slightly forward on the edge of the desk. A wave of panic reared up, fanned her, made her face cold, but she got a grip. A fall was a fall. It happened. She must get to the hospital.

When she was in the car and driving down the hill the questions started to hit her like dive-bombing birds. Who was Keith Burgess? And what had he meant by 'I came back'—back where? What was his connection with Richard? And what in God's name did he mean by 'very poorly'? Her mind was in turmoil, and her heart thundering, but she drove with particular care and precision.

The note was Sellotaped to the newel post at the foot of the stairs. It was written in capitals in thick black marker pen, so Jen could read it the moment she opened the door. RICHARD COLLAPSED. CALLED AMBULANCE AND GONE WITH HIM. WE'LL BE AT THE ROYAL FREE. KEITH. She didn't stop to think, but turned and went straight back out.

She'd got as far as Bishop's Avenue when full awareness struck, and she pulled up at the side of the road. Her heart was pounding and she was shaking. Should she go? Was Isla likely to be there? Knowing Keith he would go through all the necessary procedures in the correct order, and do what needed to be done. His concern would be for Richard, and information—she could almost hear him saying it—would be on a need-to-know basis. There was no doubt she had needed to know. But now that she did, what was the right thing to do?

Gripping the steering wheel, she banged her forehead down onto her clasped hands. The horn blared, and the shock made her eyes prickle with tears. Get a grip, she thought. What's the worst that can happen?

Isla found a parking space on her second circuit of the one-way system. She'd allowed herself five minutes to park legally before resigning herself to the possibility of being clamped. Her coolness was a learned skill, one she had never been so grateful for.

At the reception desk in the hospital foyer, Isla spoke quickly, to stifle the delighted recognition in the woman's eyes before it found expression in words. 'I believe my husband's here—Richard Wakefield? I had a message. He was brought in by ambulance about an hour ago.'

The receptionist consulted a screen. 'Yes, here he is, Richard Wakefield. Hang on please.' She dialled a number on an internal phone and, as she waited for an answer, glanced up at Isla. 'Are you who I think you are?'

'I don't know,' said Isla.

'I think—hello? I believe you have a patient admitted about an hour ago, Richard Wakefield? Mrs Wakefield is here—could someone come down?' She replaced the receiver. There were two more people waiting behind Isla, so she contented herself with a let-it-be-our-secret look. 'Take a seat.'

Isla sat. Back against the back of the chair, shoulders down, legs together, hands loosely on her lap. When she saw a tall, red-haired doctor approaching, accompanied by a man in a track suit whom she didn't recognise, she knew they were for her, but did not rise, leaving it to the receptionist to point her out. The doctor came over.

'Mrs Wakefield?'

'Yes.'

'I'm Dr Vulliamy, I've been looking after your husband.' He extended a solicitous hand. 'Shall we find somewhere more private to talk?'

Jen rationalised it like this. If Richard had been in the house then the chances were Isla was not at home. If Keith had accompanied him then it was also likely that Richard's whereabouts at the time of his fall would sooner or later be known. Apart from anything else the Jag was parked in Selwyn Street. If the balloon was going to go up, then better that she should go up with it, with all flags flying, rather than compounding her deceit by flight and concealment. The truth was she wanted to see Richard, to know that he was all right. That was all. When she had her answer, she'd go.

Having parked in a loading bay behind Europa Foods, the first person she saw as she entered the hospital was Keith. He was sitting on a chair in the reception area and his face was turned towards the door so that their eyes met the second she came in.

When he stood up, there was something deliberate and dignified in his manner; it was immensely reassuring. As she walked towards him she realised that she had never in her life been more glad to see anyone.

Isla sat down on a tweedy chair with wooden arms. Dr Vulliamy sat down in an identical chair on the other side of a squat wooden table. 'I'm so very sorry to have to tell you,' he said, 'that your husband died shortly after arrival.'

'What happened?' asked Jen. 'Where is he?'

'There's no easy way to say this, Jen,' said Keith, and the use of her Christian name alerted her to the enormity of the news. 'He's gone.'

'Your husband had had a massive stroke, and he had another as we were taking him up to resuscitation. He will have suffered very little.'

'I understand.'

'I'm so sorry.' He rose. 'Please stay as long as you like.' He went to the door. 'Can I get one of the nurses to bring you some tea?'

'Yes, please.'

'I am so very, very sorry.'

As he was about to close the door, she said, 'I wonder—if Mr Burgess is still here—do you think I could speak to him?'

'Of course. I'll see. And I'll be back myself shortly.'

Dr Vulliamy went back into the reception area, and deputed a nurse to organise tea and go in to Mrs Wakefield, who he now realised, of course, was the actress Isla Munro. There was no sign of Burgess. He went over to the desk.

'The chap who came in with Mr Wakefield, stroke victim—Mr Burgess, in a track suit. Any idea where he is?'

**K**eith said nothing directly to Jen as he drove them both home in the Renault. Before getting in, he'd had to make their peace with the manager of Europa Foods while she sat dumbly waiting to be taken away. She couldn't stop crying, but he didn't offer a hanky, nor say it was a good thing, for which untypical restraint she knew she would, in time, be truly grateful.

In Selwyn Street she tried not to look at the Jag. In the hall of Number 65 the note was still attached to the banister post and—something she hadn't had time to notice before—there was a faint smell of disinfectant. She went into the living room and plumped down on the edge of the sofa, her head on her knees. Her body, if not her mind, feared that if it leaned back and relaxed it would leave itself open to a body blow of grief with which it was not yet ready to deal. The cats, repelled by the atmosphere, were nowhere about.

Keith came back with a mug of tea in one hand and a glass and whisky bottle in the other. He crouched down in front of her.

'Which would you prefer? Or shall I add this—to this?'

She nodded blindly. He put down the glass, splashed some whisky into the tea and tapped her on the shoulder before handing it to her.

Messily, through her crying, she gulped some of the tea. Keith sat down on the other end of the sofa, holding the bottle in both hands.

When she could, she said, 'Keith—tell me what happened.'

Jen listened intently as Keith described what he had found.

'He'd been here for a little while. This'—he raised the bottle—'was on the table. And this'—the glass—'is his. He'd washed it up.'

'I can't believe it,' she said. 'Why can't I believe it?'

'You won't for a bit. Or that's what I read.'

'It's the thought of him being alone . . .' The tears oozed forth again.

'Um—just so you know. In the ambulance I stayed right out of it. Let the professionals get on with their job. He seemed . . . pretty peaceful.'

**I**sla felt sorry for the little nurse, who looked about Marcus's age. 'Is there someone you'd like to call? Your family?' the girl asked.

'I'll make some calls later. From home.'

'Yes, of course. Only I was wondering about you getting back to your house.'

'I have the car.'

'I'm not sure you should drive,' said the nurse, more confident with practicalities to address.

'Well—whatever. I can walk.'

'If you're sure.' There followed a long, screaming silence.

Is that it? Isla wondered. Do I just finish my tea and go? The cool composure she'd striven for earlier had set round her like plaster of Paris. She couldn't find her stride, locate her feelings, achieve spontaneity. She was numb.

Dr Vulliamy returned. 'Mrs Wakefield . . . Would you like to see your husband?'

'Yes, please.'

The nurse shot to her feet, took Isla's cup and opened the door. Isla emerged into the corridor. She felt the doctor's large, firm hand momentarily cupping her elbow, steering her to where she had to go.

'This way.'

She followed him, the Woman Who Has Just Lost Her Husband. But of course this was a busy hospital—how would people know? And if they did, she was an everyday phenomenon.

They went up in a lift in which, mercifully, there was no one else. She was ambushed by what she knew to be a foolish and irrelevant fear. She wanted to see Richard in order to acknowledge his departure; to play the final scene. Except that she didn't know how to play it. Her inadequacy was pitiful.

'Are you all right?' Dr Vulliamy's finger hovered over the 'Doors Open' button. 'I mean, do you feel strong enough for this?'

'Yes, thank you.'

He led her through heavy swing doors with glass portholes and into a room that seemed to Isla to be crowded with equipment, presently pushed to the sides in her honour. A very young man in a green overall hovered. Richard lay on a table with a thick, clean white sheet pulled up to his chin and folded neatly back.

'This is Mrs Wakefield.' Vulliamy gave the young man a nod and he withdrew.

He cupped her elbow again. 'Take your time. I'll be right outside.'

Isla approached the table. She looked down carefully, beginning with the sheet and moving up towards his face. That was all it was, she told herself—just his face. Nothing behind it, any more. When she finally allowed her gaze to rest on it she did not see the fabled peace of the dear departed. This wasn't peace, it was blankness, absence.

When she stretched out her hand and touched him it was both a farewell and an acceptance of her own utter loneliness.

**I**t was the second time Keith had described, in painstaking detail, what had happened.

'And his wife came to the hospital. I had to look in his wallet—call someone.'

'You did the right thing.'

'This is a horrible situation for you.'

'Keith'—she looked him straight in the eye for the first time, her face gross with grief, his pinched and earnest—'Keith, it is horrible, yes. But it's my situation. I made it. And now I'd better learn to live with it.'

**D**r Vulliamy accompanied Isla back to reception.

'Shall I walk with you to your car?'

'No, thank you. I'll be fine.'

'I'll see you out anyway.'

Outside the main entrance Isla walked the hundred yards or so to the car with a fierce concentration which shielded her from interest and intrusion. She drove back to the house with the same concentration.

In the empty drive, the mellow sun now barred with evening shadows, she dwelt on the fact that Richard's car was not there. And realised that wherever the car was, there was another woman whose life, from this moment, was never going to be the same.

**I**'m going to put a hottie in your bed,' said Keith. 'And then I'll make us some supper.'

'Thanks.' She looked up at him. 'Thanks, Keith.'

'No, please. You stay there.'

She caught his sleeve and reached for the whisky bottle. 'Give me that.'

'Do you think it's wise?'

'I don't want to drink it.'

Reluctantly he released the bottle. When he'd left the room she drew up her knees and hugged it close. It was the only thing, in the whole of this house that he had visited for twelve years, which belonged to him.

**I**sla crossed the hall and sat on the bottom step of the stairs. The house lay quietly around her. It seemed neither desolate nor expectant. Like Richard at the hospital, it was simply empty. No one there.

For half an hour she did not move. She couldn't face any other room but this when they were all full of what he'd left behind.

When she did at last stand up she went to the bedroom Marcus had slept in. The bed was neat, made up with clean sheets since Marcus's departure. She stretched out on top of it and lay there wide-eyed as the phone rang, every hour or so, below.

# chapter eight

IN THE DAYS between Richard's death and his funeral, Isla, with Archie's stalwart help, organised those things which had to be done. The funeral was to be private, in Bradenham. She wanted as far as possible to maintain the tenor of their marriage, which had been something separate and secluded, a life set deliberately apart from that which they led in public. Her determination to achieve this helped her to stay calm.

The letters that arrived overwhelmed her with their expressions of love, admiration and solidarity. No one failed to mention the strength and joy Richard had derived from his marriage to her. 'He was a private man where you were concerned,' wrote one QC whom she had never met, 'but also the one man whose most sacred bond was never doubted.'

That had made her cry—'sacred bond'.

Caroline rang, but had to hang up after three minutes, unable to continue. Her letter, which arrived the next day, was dignified and generous. At the end she wrote:

> We both loved him, but you were better at it than me, and I could see how happy he was since marrying you. I was pleased, in a way, not to have the responsibility for his well-being—a responsibility I could no longer discharge. But he is the father of my sons, and we feel his loss dreadfully. The boys have been wonderful, both of them. I can only imagine what it must be like for you. Sorry I was such a wet dishcloth on the telephone, it's the last thing you need.
>     All our love and good thoughts,
>     Caroline

Isla herself wrote to Donatella, to let her know that she would be welcome at the funeral. She received no reply.

Three days after Richard's death Isla locked up the house and went with Giles to Bradenham. She had two purposes: one, to discuss the funeral arrangements with the rector; the other, a task she did not relish—seeing Alec. She had had an almost monosyllabic conversation with him on the phone when she had felt like someone performing an amputation without anaesthetic. Her distress, kept in check for the occasion, made her cool. His, new and raw, made him brusque. It had been awful.

Giles was her driver for the day. 'He wants to help,' Caroline assured her, though Isla thought that it was probably Caroline who needed to be of assistance, and Giles who was subject to a three-line whip. He arrived in Hampstead at eight thirty. They set off at nine, in Isla's car.

Giles drove with exaggerated care as if she were very old or very ill. Several times, at traffic lights and junctions, he gazed out of the window and she knew he was struggling with tears. When they reached Bradenham, and the cottage, she said, 'Giles, this is so good of you. I want you to know how much I appreciate it. I'd have hated to come all this way on my own.'

Then, at last, he had a big cry, sitting with his head in his hands and sobbing noisily. She put her arm round his shoulders but said nothing, because she was crying too. When he regained his composure with the aid of several squares of kitchen towel, she said, 'Giles. Do you think you could read something at the service?'

'I'll try.' He blew his nose to cover the small bloom of vanity of which he was ashamed, but which pleased Isla.

'I'd like that. And I think your mother would, too. And your father would be tickled pink.'

'I'll give it a go.'

'Good.' She kissed his cheek. 'Look, why don't you go and call on the Fylers. When I've seen the rector I'm going to visit your grandfather. You can come or not as you like.'

'I'll come.'

'Good. I'll see you later.'

She tried hard, when discussing the funeral, to imagine what Richard would have liked. Though not a regular churchgoer he was a tradition-alist and would, she was sure, want something staunchly celebratory. She chose 'For all the saints', 'He who would valiant be' and 'Lead us, heavenly Father, lead us'. She herself would read from *Cymbeline*: 'Fear no more the heat o' the sun, Nor the furious winter's rages . . .'

For Giles, subject to his approval, she chose Robert Louis Stevenson, the passage that opened with: 'That man is a success who has lived well, laughed often and loved much . . .'

The rector was impressed. 'I don't often meet a widow quite so sure of what she wants.'

'It's a case of what suits Richard,' said Isla.

After she had seen him out she rang the Fylers.

'May I have my chauffeur back?'

Barbara was gruff. 'Isla, dear, won't you come and have some lunch?'

'It's sweet of you, but no. We'll grab a sandwich. I'm a zombie at the moment and I need to see Alec while I'm still holding myself together, and then get back to town.'

'It's only four days to the funeral. Can't you come and just be at the cottage—or with us?'

'I shall come to the cottage, but not tonight. There are still some things I have to see to. Don't worry about me, Bar, I've got masses of support.'

'Very well. Giles is going out of the door now—he's been walking Pepe. Anyway, you know where we are.'

'Dear Bar—of course I do.'

They stopped at a pub on the edge of Lettaford and ordered a large portion of chips, a salad for Isla and scampi provençale for Giles. Isla ate three chips and picked at the salad as Giles shovelled down everything else.

'Sorry to be such a pig.'

'You're not. I like to see you tucking in.' She phrased her words carefully. 'Caro said you were too thin when you got back from Ibiza.'

'Yes, well . . .' He grimaced. 'You know how it is. We had a great time, but you have to decide what to spend your money on.'

'I shan't ask.'

'I wish Mum wouldn't.'

'That's what she's there for. How is she?'

'She's still crying a helluva lot.'

'And Marcus?'

'Not speaking, so what's new? But he's been good with Mum. He just sits there and lets her run on.'

'That is good.'

Giles scrunched and unscrunched his paper napkin. Not looking up, he said, 'You haven't got anyone to run on to, have you?'

'Yes, plenty of people.'

'Like who?' He was almost truculent.

'Friends, good friends. You.'

He blushed scarlet. 'You haven't even mentioned Dad to me.'

'But I know I could if I wanted to,' she said, adding, 'I think about him all the time, you know.'

He didn't answer.

Back in the car, she asked to drive as far as The Hayes. It helped, made her feel more in control. When they pulled up outside the door, Giles peered out.

'Christ, it's ages since I was here.'

'He'll be enormously chuffed to see you.'

'You think?'

'I know.'

Karen said how very, very sorry she was.

'How is Alec?' asked Isla, as they followed her up the stairs.

'Taken it hard, but not letting on,' replied Karen. From the corner of her eye Isla saw her touch Giles's shoulder, lightly but reassuringly, as he followed Isla into Alec's room.

'Good God,' said Alec. 'Who's this you've brought with you?'

'It's Giles, as you well know.'

Isla watched as Giles, uncertain what his greeting should be, inclined slightly for an embrace, then thought better of it and stuck out a hand. Alec took the hand and slapped his grandson awkwardly on the shoulder.

'Hello, fella-me-lad. Pity we have to meet under such wretched circumstances.'

'Yes.'

Alec plumped down wheezily. Isla took the other chair and Giles perched on the windowsill.

'Anything I can get you?'

'Nothing at all, we stopped at a pub.' Isla decided, for all their sakes, to be swift and direct. 'Alec, we shan't stay all that long, but I did want to come and see you. We've both lost Richard, and . . .' She wavered. Giles folded his arms and stared with interest out of the window. She drew a breath. 'I wanted to say that we're all thinking of you, a lot.'

Alec grumphed. 'I've done a lot of thinking. I was a pretty terrible father.' He put up a hand to silence her protest. 'No, I was. I harbour no illusions about it. But I believe Richard and I understood each other. We established a *modus vivendi*. Which is as good as many and a great deal better than some. Eh, Giles?'

'Absolutely. He talked about you a lot.' Isla had no way of knowing if this assertion were true. Richard had not talked about his parents that much with her, but perhaps it was different with his sons. 'He admired you,' added Giles. 'He said you bestrode his life like a colossus.'

This went down a storm. Alec's spluttering laughter was its stamp of approval. 'A lawyer's comment *par excellence*! Good old Richard!'

'No, it's a compliment,' said Giles. 'I know that, because I feel the same way about him. Both of us do.'

'He was a clever chap,' agreed Alec.

'A hard act to follow.'

'You'll be bloody hard put. But that's what a young man needs.'

Watching Alec's change in mood Isla wondered whether Giles should not, after all, consider a career in advocacy. She said, 'Alec, would you like to come to the funeral? It will be in Bradenham, and lifts can easily be arranged.'

'No, no, no, you're better off without me. I'm a frightful old wreck.'

Giles stood up. 'Anyone fancy a walk?'

They spent almost twenty minutes walking in the garden and sitting on a seat in the shade of a chestnut tree. Isla found she couldn't talk, but Giles made up for it, asking questions about The Hayes and making Alec chuckle by describing his recent holiday as a dope-fiend's paradise.

When they returned to the house, grandfather and grandson said goodbye and Giles went to the car as Isla saw Alec up to his room. He was obviously tired, his steps heavy and uncertain, but back in the room he gestured her to wait while he went to his chest of drawers.

He returned with a letter, addressed to Richard. 'I wrote this in reply to that strange one he wrote to me,' he explained. 'But I have this senile notion that you might like to read it, on his behalf.'

'I would. Thank you.'

He took her hand and planted the letter in it. 'There.'

She kissed him, and saw a tear trembling in the creases at the corner of his eye, although his mouth was firm. 'Forgive me for not coming to the bakemeats?'

'Nothing to forgive.'

'I couldn't stand it,' he said, and turned away. As he stumped back to his chair Isla closed the door.

They got back to London before six, and had a drink together in the orangery—white wine for Isla, Coke for Giles.

'Do you want me to stay the night?' he asked.

'No, thank you.' She recognised at once the wording of an offer which had been put into his mouth by Caroline. But all she wanted was to be alone, to mourn, and adjust, and think of Richard.

'It's so kind of you, Giles,' she added, easing his carefully concealed relief. 'But I have things to do, and to think about. You're not hurt, are you?' He shook his head. 'I knew you'd understand. But before you go,' she went on more briskly, 'let me show you the reading I had in mind.'

She watched him as he took the book and scanned the passage with a frown of concentration.

'It's OK,' he said, with the surprised, upward inflection that denoted unconditional approval. 'I can handle that.'

When Giles had gone, she locked up and went upstairs to the bedroom: hers and Richard's. She undressed, had a bath and got into bed. She opened Alec's letter carefully, prising open the flap without tearing it, conscious of her privilege. Paragraphs, written in thick blue ink, started well and became less legible as they went on. Isla read carefully and systematically, wanting to be sure of the sense first time round, deciphering one sentence to her satisfaction before moving on to the next.

*My dear Richard,*

*How are you? I understand from Isla, who was good enough to drop by recently, that your health's giving cause for concern. Be sensible, won't you? Prevention is better than cure.*

*I was a bit put out about your letter, I must admit. To begin with my inclination was not to reply, but on reflection I see that's churlish, so here's my answer for what it's worth.*

*Yes, your mother and I were happy. We were an extremely successful and contented partnership for over forty years. But you ask were we really happy, as if you automatically suspect me of evasion. And again I say yes, I believe we really were.*

*If on the other hand this insistence is your way of asking about fidelity, then the answer is no, or not in the generally accepted sense. Both your mother and I had other encounters at various times. None of them affected our loyalty to each other or placed our marriage in any sort of jeopardy. Everyone concerned knew this. We lived as husband and wife to the end, and since your mother's death I have felt the world to be an empty place and myself a poor thing in it.*

*That is all I have to say. Except perhaps this. There is marriage, and there is falling in love. The first cannot exist without the second but the second can, and does, exist without the first. Marriage, if that is what you choose, is nothing if not for life. And falling in love is part of life.*

*All this has left me completely buggered! I very much look forward to your next visit, dear boy, so don't leave it too long.*

*Your ancient but ever-loving,*

*Dad*

Isla put the letter back in its envelope and sealed it. It was a long time before she slept.

# FLOWERS WON'T FAX

**T**he main reason she had returned to London was to discharge the responsibility which she dreaded most: that of contacting Keith Burgess and organising the retrieval of Richard's car.

The hospital had handed her a piece of paper with Burgess's name and address on it as she left the hospital, but she had not yet even taken it out of her handbag. None of her friends could understand why it was taking her so long to establish where Richard had been taken ill, and the exact circumstances, although everyone, like her, assumed it had happened in the street and that the admirable Mr Burgess had been first on the scene and to the phone. But it was so unlike Isla, they said, not to have been in touch with this Good Samaritan earlier.

It *was* unlike her. But, then, she was not herself. It was not only the past that was another country, thought Isla; this terrible, unrecognisable present was just as foreign. There were things which would have to be learned if life was to go on, and she dreaded learning them.

Dully, she sat down by the phone with her piece of paper, but then saw that there was no telephone number written on it. At the foot of the piece of paper she noticed a PTO. On the other side was written: *Working hours c/o Gunner Grove Primary School* and a phone number. She dialled the school's number and a harassed female voice answered.

'I wonder,' said Isla, 'if I could speak to a Mr Keith Burgess?'

'He's with his class at present.'

'I'm sorry, I won't keep him a moment.'

'Are you a parent?'

'No—my name's Isla Wakefield. Mr Burgess was kind enough to accompany my husband to hospital recently when he—when he—' She was suddenly, hideously ambushed by emotion, but the woman's attitude had changed in an instant.

'Mrs Wakefield—yes, of course. I do apologise. Hang on and I'll get him at once.'

Isla struggled to take control of herself.

'Keith Burgess.'

The sound of his voice brought her round. 'Mr Burgess, it's Isla Wakefield. I apologise for calling you at school, but I wanted to thank you properly for what you did for my husband.'

'There's no need at all.'

'And to ask you—you know, how—and when—'

'I understand.'

'And then there's Richard's car. I wondered . . .'

'Yes, it's in my road. Safe and sound. You just say when it would be convenient and I can see you there.'

'Perhaps this evening—say at about eight? I have to call a friend to come with me so that I can drive the Jag back.'

'Eight o'clock's fine. Turn into Selwyn Street at the Crouch Hill end and the car's a hundred yards on the right.'

How, she wondered as she put the phone down, did he know?

**A**rchie drove Isla to Selwyn Street. They didn't talk. It was a perfect late summer evening: even the lowly terrace-covered hills and littered pavements of this part of north London were placid and romantic in the slanting sun. But for Isla it was a haunted journey. Why had Richard come all this way? What part did these streets and shops play in his life, that she had known nothing about? She sat paralysed with fear and grief in the passenger seat as Archie finally located Selwyn Street.

She consulted her piece of paper for the house number, but Archie said, 'There it is—is that your man?'

'Yes, that's him.'

Keith stood by the bonnet of the Jag and waved them down. 'Let me out, can you?' said Isla. She got out and Archie went on to find a space.

She held out her hand. 'I do hope you haven't been hanging about for ages—I had your address.'

'No, no,' he said, nodding. 'It's a nice evening, anyway.'

'Look,' she said, 'I must ask you what happened. In your message you said you got back from somewhere—'

'I'd been at a meeting in school,' said Burgess. 'I live just along there.' He pointed in the direction Archie had driven. 'When I arrived your husband was collapsed near the door.'

'But why was he here?' She looked round.

Burgess went on. 'He must have been taken badly and tried to get help for himself. But not made it. I went straight in and called the ambulance.'

'I'm so grateful for what you did.'

She looked at the Jag, touched the roof. It was warm from the sun.

'So then,' said Keith, 'I got his wallet out of his jacket pocket and left a message with you. That was it, really. He was conscious at that stage,' he added, 'I think.'

Isla couldn't bear that. She could think of nothing else to say. She simply wanted to be away from this place, away from this man—this stranger—who had been with Richard as he died.

Archie appeared, driving back from the opposite side of the road. 'Can't find anywhere here.'

'Let's go,' said Isla. 'I think we should go anyway. Archie, if you drive to the corner and wait, I'll follow you.'

She took the key of the Jag from her handbag and stared at it.

'It's a remote-control lock,' said Burgess.

'Yes, of course.'

She got in. 'Goodbye, then, Mr Burgess.'

'Goodbye,' he said. 'God bless.'

She had almost reached the corner when she saw Jen Delaney walking down the pavement on the other side. In her attempt to wind the window down she pressed the wrong button and started the windscreen wipers. The small flurry, and the impatient toot of a car behind her, caught Jen's attention. Isla waved, but Jen looked blank and walked on.

In her rearview mirror, as she turned the corner, she saw Jen and Burgess meet, speak, and go into a house together.

And she knew then what she had instinctively sensed a moment earlier—that Jen had seen her, but pretended not to. She could not deny what she'd seen. But oh! she thought, oh Jen! Did it have to be you?

'You have to speak to her,' said Claudia.

'I think about it all the time. And then I think—and say what?'

'I don't know, but it's been too long already. It makes me feel sick to think of it. It's making you sick—you look awful.'

'I'm tired,' admitted Jen. They were sitting in the Jollyboys Arms. Jen sensed that Claudia, although sympathetic, was angry with her. Compassion fatigue had set in. Red was happy and wanted to see her own happiness reflected back from the faces of other people, not to be confronted by someone beset by sorrow and intransigent dilemmas.

Jen sat up straighter, settled her shoulders, forced a smile. 'It'll pass. Time will do its stuff.'

'So are you going to tell her then?'

Jen's nerves jangled. 'Tell her what?'

'How about . . .' Claudia shrugged eloquently, 'everything?'

No, thought Jen, not everything. And if not everything, better nothing.

'I think she knows anyway. We saw each other. We both knew. It doesn't get much worse, Red.'

'You like her a lot.'

'I did, yes.'

'Well, if you're going to be enemies now you could at least try and be honest ones who've levelled with each other.' She paused, but went on when Jen didn't respond, 'And Richard meant a lot to you. You should square the circle. Why throw the baby out with the bath water?' The choice of metaphor made Jen wince—it would have been funny if it wasn't so terrible. Claudia sighed with exasperation. 'You could at least *try* to make it right. *And*'— she leaned forward to lend emphasis to her next remark—'I bet you anything she's thinking the same thing.'

'Maybe.'

'I'm going to get us the other half.'

Jen had been ready to do the sensible, independent, single woman's thing, and have a termination. She'd screwed up her courage and fixed the date. But then Richard had died, and that changed everything. Because the tiny tadpole of life in her womb was part of him, his legacy, and she guarded it jealously. What she wanted was to keep this life inside her, all hers. Or hers and Richard's. She knew it was sad, and unhealthy, and wrong; that it was not a sensible, mature way to reach a decision. That it was *not* a decision, but a kind of stubborn drifting. But she couldn't help herself. And the result was that she was now eighteen weeks pregnant.

Claudia returned with their drinks.

'What do I owe you?'

'Forget it. I've been earning for the past six weeks. And I've got this modelling job coming up.'

'Will it fit in with college?'

'I wouldn't be doing it otherwise.'

'What does Anthony think?'

Claudia bristled. 'Does it matter what he thinks?'

'I suppose not, except that you're obviously keen on him.'

'I don't actually know what he thinks. Except that he regards my life as my own. He's the least controlling person I know. He has such an incredibly open mind.'

Jen began to feel better. The drink and her daughter's happiness were finally having their effect.

'He's very attractive,' she allowed.

'Yes,' agreed Claudia, 'that doesn't hurt.'

'Are you serious about him?'

'That's such an old-fashioned expression. I've never felt less serious in my life. But he's the business, Mum. We get on so well it's ridiculous.'

For the first time in days—weeks—Jen felt a smile begin inside her before it showed on her face. She leaned forward and planted a kiss on her daughter's cheek.

'Be happy, Red,' she said. 'That's all that matters.'

The next day her spirits inched up a little more. The morning was fine, but with a first nip of autumn. She awoke feeling refreshed and—she noted with surprise as she spread Marmite on toast—not in the least sick.

The usual routines had been re-established. Keith had left for school, and the Dalmatian required its finishing touches. She'd been dissatisfied with it but this morning it looked fresh and alive. She felt enthused by it and by the prospect of finishing the parrot for Mr and Mrs Hastings.

She threw open the windows, changed the sheets on the bed and cleaned the house with such enthusiasm that the cats left at speed and took up positions on the pavement, looking huffy.

People warned Isla that after the funeral would be the hardest time. It might well hit her then and she was going to have to give in to her grief a little, having been so marvellous throughout. Up till now there'd been a million things to think about, but with the organisational escape route out of the way, the permanence of her loss would become real.

However, Isla had a great deal to occupy her beyond the funeral. Lori had contacted her to say that there was no pressure whatever for her to fulfil her contract with the quiz show provided she could let them know within reasonable time. She had assured Lori that she intended to honour her commitment and was looking forward to it. Work was therapy; work was identity—another of the incontrovertible assertions of grief management. And thinking about work helped her to postpone what she least wanted to do . . .

It was almost a relief when Ned, who had been unable to attend the funeral, turned up on the doorstep with a bottle of malt whisky.

Having clasped her in his arms for over a minute, he said, 'I know you don't drink this stuff, but I do.'

'I might well join you today.'

He poured them both a generous slug and they drank it at the kitchen table with a packet of tortilla chips between them.

'I'm sorry I couldn't make the observances,' he said. 'Work, for once. And I'm bloody sorry about Richard,' he added. 'He was the best. Tops. I shan't ask how you are.'

'Thanks.'

'But word is, my lovely, you're going to be the toast of the airwaves with all those toothsome young men in baggy trousers.'

'I don't know about that.' She smiled. 'How's Scotch?'

Ned lit a cigarette, buying time. 'You heard, then.'

'Nothing concrete. But Nell implied that he and she were just good pals. And when she told me the two of you were in Scotland . . . Well, I've known you a long time, Ned.'

'And you drew the obvious conclusion.'

'Am I right?'

He shook his head, blowing a long stream of smoke. 'I did my best, can't deny it. He's a genius with publicity—got me my first halfway decent job in ten years, the reason I couldn't come to the funeral.'

'Proper acting?' It was a joke between them.

'Better than that—improper. I play a middle-class wife-beater who gets to snog the leading lady before beating shit out of her.'

'When shall we see this?'

'February. So you see young Scotch is the architect of my professional renaissance. But sorry to disappoint—there is no "thang" going on.'

'Not?' Isla was surprised.

'I gave it my best shot, but no. His heart wasn't in it.' He studied her face for a moment. 'Meanwhile—is gossip appropriate or inappropriate?'

'Gossip's comforting.'

Ned leered. 'You may already know this—Scotch and the redoubtable Petronella have an understanding. He goes his way, she goes hers.'

Isla trod carefully. 'I see.'

'Her parents aren't aware of this, of course, and they've been getting a bit exercised about his intentions. Wonderful, wonderful—!' He threw his head back in delight. 'Anyway, Scotch likes Petronella, they confide in each other, and he tells me that she is about to fling wide the closet door.'

Isla digested this information with a large mouthful of malt. 'Oh?'

'Isla, petal, can you imagine? I know you've met these people and I haven't, but Scotch has described them to me, and the comic possibilities of this scene are rich indeed! Ah—I've overstepped the mark.'

'Don't be silly. I was just thinking about it.' She tried to lighten her voice. 'It's brave of Nell anyway. Do we know if there's anyone special?'

'She went to France with a solicitor named Frances Acourt. We think the bold Frances may be the cause of this *glasnost*.'

## chapter nine

*I*SLA TOOK THE JAG. The night before she had decided she would go and see her husband's mistress. She wanted to re-create this journey that Richard must have made so many times, in the way that he would have done it. It was strange to realise that this car—his car—was exactly as it had been on the evening he died. There was an *Evening*

*Standard* from the day before on the back seat. A parking docket on the dash. The radio tuned to Radio Four. A CD on the player.

She had made a deal with herself. If there was no one in, then it wasn't meant to be, and she would come away and never go back. The deal at least gave her a predetermined structure which meant there were no more decisions.

**J**en reached that moment when she knew she was finished. For the best part of an hour she'd been refining and retouching the parrot painting—then the switch was thrown that said: 'That'll do'. She put down her brush. Each painting was a small triumph. At worst it represented a victory over sloth, at best a decent piece of work, honestly completed.

She had been up early and lost all sense of time, since Keith had brought her a cup of tea on his way out at eight fifteen. It was for this reason that she had just consulted her watch, and knew that it was eleven forty-three precisely when she looked out of the window and saw, with a queasy lurch of disorientation, Richard's Jag drawing up.

**I**sla had assumed there would be nowhere to park. She remembered how crowded Selwyn Street had been on her last visit. But now it was midmorning and most people were at work. There was space to spare. She wouldn't have chosen to park immediately opposite, but she was tense and flustered and misjudged the numbering.

She didn't dare change her mind—she had to keep moving forward or her resolve would falter. Without looking about her she got out, locked the car, and walked across the road and in through the gate of Number 65. A cat, two cats, scampered across her line of vision, running ahead of her, and disappeared. At the front doorstep, which was covered in sunken red and black tiles, she raised her eyes.

The door was wide open, and Jen Delaney sat on the stairs, waiting for her.

'It was you, wasn't it?' said Isla.

'Yes.'

Jen watched as she closed the front door. It became darker, the source of light shifting from the street to the living room. Jen had put on weight in the last few weeks, but Isla had lost it. She wore the same blue shirt and jeans she had worn that day at Alma's. But now she was pale, pin-thin, frighteningly stressed out.

She walked into the living room. She had no handbag with her, just a bunch of keys in one hand. When Jen followed her she found her standing in the window next to the easel, her back to the light.

'Can I get you anything?' asked Jen.

'You can tell me how long it was going on for.'

For ever, thought Jen. 'Some years.'

'Which years? How many?'

'I think—twelve.'

A minute delay as Isla absorbed the shock. Jen told herself, Soon this will be over. It will be the worst thing that ever happened, but it will be in the past.

'How often . . . ?' Isla cleared her throat. 'How often was he here?'

'Once or twice a week.'

'What time of day?'

'Lunchtime or late afternoon, usually. Weekdays.' It sounded so tacky, and she knew it had not been tacky. And yet to deny or assert anything would be to inflict further damage.

There was another pause, during which Isla turned her back on Jen and stood, arms folded, looking out into the street, where the Jag gleamed in the early autumn sun.

'Why?'

Jen was taken aback. 'I'm sorry . . .'

'Why did he come here, when he loved me? When we were so happy?'

'We were friends,' said Jen. 'We were close, relaxed together, we made no demands—'

Now Isla whipped round. 'And you suppose that I did?'

'No—I don't know—'

'Do you have any idea'—Isla's voice dropped as she came towards Jen—'what I'm trying to say? Can you begin to understand?' Her voice was thin and bitter, compressed by pain. 'Why do you think I'm here?'

'We needed to see each other. If you hadn't come here I should have come to you.'

'You knew, didn't you? You knew who I was.'

'Not to begin with.'

'But you found out. You knew and you still carried on.'

'Isla, I'd found a friend. It meant a lot to me—I was terribly shocked when I discovered who you were. Shocked and ashamed, not of me and Richard, but that I was deceiving you. You will never, ever know how sorry I am.'

Isla gave a small, sharp cry of anguish and dropped onto a chair. The keys fell to the ground with a chink as she pressed her hands to her face.

'I am so sorry,' said Jen again. 'I know how you must hate me.'

Isla shook her head. Sobbed, or laughed, Jen couldn't tell which, then looked up. 'No, I don't hate you. I'm too tired to hate you. But I despise you. Which is sad, Jen. It's so sad, but that's how it is.'

She looked round the room. Jen felt her gaze move over her possessions, her home—her life—like a spider walking over her skin.

'He must have known this place so well. As well as his own home.'

Jen didn't answer. She endured the torture of Isla's scrutiny. The long, scraping silence.

'How long did you say?'

'About twelve years.'

'Longer than we were married . . .' Isla looked at her. 'You knew Richard longer than I did.'

'Perhaps . . .'

'You must have known when he married me—did you?'

'I was aware of a change . . .' Her eyes met Isla's. 'Yes, I did know.'

'So, you could justify it. Because I was the intruder. I was the interloper, is that what you told yourself?'

'No.'

'Well, what did you bloody tell yourself?' Isla had not, until now, raised her voice. The shock of it made Jen flinch. 'What did you say to yourself in the late afternoon or early evening'—she gave the words a cudgelling emphasis—'when my husband had gone back to his wife?'

'I didn't think about it.' This was the literal truth, but Jen could hear herself how it sounded—dismissive, callous, insulting. 'I mean that I accepted Richard as he was here. When he left to go back to his life, I went back to mine. We never made any claims on each other—'

'That was generous of you.'

'I never wanted any more than I had, than he gave me. And if he had suddenly stopped coming here I wouldn't have gone looking for him.'

'What am I supposed to do—be grateful?'

'Of course not.'

'When I said those things—all those things'—Isla shook her head to dislodge the memory—'you just listened and answered. Knowing what you knew. How could you do that? Did it make you feel superior? Powerful? Is that the only reason you pretended to be friendly, so you could sit there smugly and watch me humiliate myself?'

'No.' Nothing could be further from the truth, or harder to explain. Jen was defeated. 'Look, I think you ought to go.'

'I bet you do. All I can say is, my dear, that this hurts me a hundred times—a thousand times—more than it hurts you!'

It was the 'my dear' that freed Jen. The part of her that had been shrinking like a whipped pup, beaten down by shame, stirred itself and bit back.

'Don't dare to tell me how much I hurt!'

'Your feelings don't interest me,' said Isla. It was the exact opposite of the truth.

'I've been through hell!' shouted Jen, red-faced, tears coursing down her cheeks. 'Hell, these past few weeks! Because of Richard *and* because of you! I agreed to see you the other day because I didn't know what else to do—I liked you, for God's sake! Because of you I'd decided to finish with Richard. But then it was all done for us, wasn't it? It was fucking well finished for us . . .!'

Her voice broke. There she stood, the woman whom Isla could not hate: her forearms over her face, fists clenched, sobbing. Isla, who had barely cried, envied her. The contrast between Jen—passionate and demonstrative, and herself as she must seem to be—jealous, resentful, sarcastic—was not one she found comforting.

'I'll go now,' she said, and picked up her keys.

'No, you don't!' Jen crouched down in front of her, clutching her wrist. Her hands were strong, there was paint on the fingers. 'You came here to act this stuff out, so let me do my acting!'

'Acting?'

'Yes—something you know all about! Let me say my piece!' Jen grabbed her other wrist, gave them both a shake.

'Let go of me.'

She let go, but knelt there right in front of her, barring her way. 'One of the reasons I cared so much for Richard was because he loved you. I knew nothing about you, I never asked about you, but the only time I did he said he couldn't live without you. I was a part of his life which he'd become used to, and attached to, but you were completely indispensable to him. You made him happy, you made him what he was. He was fond of me but he never loved me. If I did love him I never stopped to think about it, and, now it's too late, I try not to. But please, please, please'—the fists again, this time held up between herself and Isla in a gesture something between a plea and a threat—'please believe that I wasn't wicked. I was stupid and weak, but I didn't mean to cause all this damage. It horrifies me, and I'm more sorry than I can say. But it was you Richard loved. You, you, you! Lucky you,' she added exhaustedly, sitting back on her heels, head bowed.

Isla was moved. She wondered if Richard, who knew this room so well, was standing near them, hands in pockets, collar curling, looking on. Richard, who had lived these two lives, made this journey repeatedly, gone from that room to this, from her to Jen. Richard who had lit the blue touch paper and retreated into the perfect, sanctified safety of death, while their lives blew up in their faces.

'I believe you,' she whispered. 'I do believe you.'

'Thank God.' Jen went on all fours to the sofa and dragged herself up onto it, thrusting her hands into her hair, closing her eyes. 'You must believe me, Isla,' she said fiercely. 'Because I'm pregnant.'

When Jen said that she was pregnant Isla had been able to do nothing but walk away. She left the front door open behind her, crossed the road without looking—not hearing the scream and blare of a terrifying nearmiss—and drove away. Somehow, she got home. She supposed she must have negotiated other vehicles, T-junctions, traffic lights and roundabouts, but she was not aware of doing so.

She was in shock. Back at the house, delayed reaction sent her swooping into shivering nausea. She took Richard's Black Watch plaid dressing gown—one she had bought him from Simpson—out of the bedroom wardrobe and wrapped herself in it. Then she climbed into bed, her hands, feet and face still icy, and lay with her teeth chattering for almost an hour before she started to relax.

Of all her confused feelings, the one that thrust its way forward, not to be denied, was her anger at Richard. All her love, her sorrow, her unswerving loyalty, seemed thrown into question by that small accumulation of cells in another woman's body, in another part of London. That he could not have known about this legacy of his seemed all the more wounding. It was so casual, so easy, the most natural thing in the world—but something she herself had not been able to do. Even the dignity of her widow's grief had been corroded by this bitter, bitter jealousy.

She raged against Richard, weeping, moaning, tossing and turning, wishing, like a child, that none of it was true, or that it was just a dream. Eventually, she fell asleep. When she woke it was late afternoon and for a split second everything seemed normal, before the enormity of what had happened hit her with the force of an express train.

A bell was ringing: the front doorbell. She got unsteadily out of bed and discarded the dressing gown. The sudden exposure made her start shivering again. She caught sight of herself in the dressing-table mirror and was shocked to see how old she looked—old, thin and pinched. She snatched up a brush and dragged it roughly through her hair.

It was Archie. He was already moving away from the door, or pretending to, and turned round with an anxious look when he heard her open it.

'Oh—Isla. Have I disturbed you? Were you resting?'

'I was, but you haven't disturbed me. Come in.'

'Are you sure? Well, OK. I just thought I'd drop by to see how you were doing.'

'That's nice of you, Archie. Come in.'

Archie selected tea in preference to a drink—he'd had a lunch, he explained, and also had to drive home, but she mustn't let that stop her if . . . He seemed to believe that she must be desperate to drown her sorrows. She made a pot for them both and Archie carried the tray into the drawing room. Whether or not it was her imagination, their footsteps seemed to echo slightly as if the house were only partly furnished.

'The house seems so empty,' she said as they sat down.

'It would do . . . of course it would.' Archie took his tea.

She raked her fingers through her hair. 'I'm sorry, I look like death.'

'Not at all you don't. You look a little tired and stressed, but who wouldn't? Ali and I just wish there was more we could do.'

She made herself smile. 'You've both been absolute bricks, and I know I haven't been easy to help. You don't know how you'll react to— to this—until it happens to you.'

Archie shifted in his seat, put his cup down with a jingle on the piecrust table. Isla thought, I'm losing it, I'm losing my ability to put people at their ease.

'Archie, I want you to know I'm not going to pieces.'

'Of course you're not!' The promptness and emphasis with which he agreed betrayed him utterly.

'I don't want you going away from here thinking I'm a wreck. I shall miss Richard to the day I die, but I can face my own life. I can look into the future. I have plans.'

'I'm sure you do. It's what we've all come to expect of you,' said Archie, as if he were the elected spokesman for all who knew her. 'But— you have to recognise—I don't want to sound like one of these frightful self-help books, but you must allow yourself time, not rush things—'

'Archie, please!'

'Sorry.'

'Don't be sorry. I didn't mean to bite your head off. I've had a bad day, that's all.' She took a deep breath, brought her voice back down. 'And since you're here, I want to ask you something.'

'Please, I wish you would.' Poor Archie. 'Anything.'

'Did you know Richard had a mistress?'

He was incapable of dissembling, the most transparently honest person she knew. His appalled disbelief was painfully genuine.

'No . . . ! No, absolutely not, I didn't. In fact, Isla, I must say—'

'Well, he did, Archie. For years. This isn't some kind of deranged, grief-stricken fantasy. I've met her and talked to her. Are you quite sure you didn't know?'

'Isla, I swear to you. I'm certain that no one—' He shook his head. 'I don't believe it.'

'You have to. It's true. But it's not the end of the world,' she added, as Archie continued to shake his head like a wounded animal. 'And it's nothing new.' She was being cruel, because Archie's new, fresh pain was a comfort to her; it showed her she was past that.

'But Richard,' he mumbled, 'of all people!'

'He wasn't a saint.'

'No, but—' Archie raised anguished eyes to hers. 'He loved you so much!'

It was Archie now who broke down, and she went and knelt in front of him and pulled his head onto her shoulder. She was ashamed for having exacted the words which above all she needed to hear, at such a cost, from such a willing victim.

On the way out, Archie said, 'I don't really know how to say this, and it will probably sound even more stupid than usual, but—um—'

'Archie.'

'If it's true'—he held up a hand, apologising for doubting her—'and if you say it is then I'll take your word for it. If it's true, I honestly believe that it made no difference. You were Richard's, um, one true love. He was never completely happy till he married you. And then he was one of the happiest men one could wish to meet. If there was someone else, he must have had his reasons, but it was you he loved. Oh God, what a speech—!'

'It was a nice speech, Archie. One of your best.' She kept her distance, but smiled at him. She had used him shamelessly and yet he saw it as his privilege. He was a good, dear man.

'Oh yes, I nearly forgot what with—Ali wondered if you could stand supper next week?'

'I could do more than stand it. I'd love it.'

'Splendid!' His face lit up. 'A bientôt, then.'

'Thank you for coming, Archie.'

She played back her messages. The first, from Lori, was congratulatory: 'You were brilliant, a real pro. I'm so proud of you.'

Barbara, who didn't like machines, was brusque: 'Are we going to see you? Brook End's looking a bit sad since Marjory took up with Norman Brake. Ring me back.'

She played the last message three times. 'Isla . . . ? It's Scotch. I'm thinking about you every moment. You and Richard were the business. What can I say? I wish I knew you better so I could help you more. Fare thee well, not goodbye.'

Isla went out into the garden. The garden in Hampstead they had always kept as a low-maintenance green space, with two or three statues, and a pool and waterfall among the trees at the end. In the summer, Isla filled the terrace with pelargoniums, lobelia, trailing fuchsias and petunias, but the secretive, changing green shade was what she and Richard had liked. The Brook End garden was where Isla indulged her enthusiasm for scented, old-fashioned flowers.

She walked down to the end and sat on the seat among the trees, looking back towards the house. She found herself thinking of Selwyn Street, of Jen's small, busy, untidy house, and of the life she led there. Had sometimes led with Richard. She tried to quieten her heart, to let her mind drift, and settle. It was difficult, the control of pain by surrender, and she only partially managed it. But when, about twenty minutes later, she rose and walked back up the lawn to the house, she was aware of the faint, tremulous dawn of something that was not despair.

Jen could no longer fight her pregnancy. Quietly, relentlessly, it was taking her over. How could she have forgotten how it felt, this sea change? Now that the daily battle with sickness had gone, she was reduced—or elevated—to the role of support system for what was inside her. Her waistbands, those with fastenings, would no longer do up. She sewed panels of elastic into the sides of her dungarees. In the Wednesday market she found a couple of loose Indian tops that came down well over her seat. She bought some leggings two sizes larger than usual. That would have to do. Her hair became an unmanageable fuzz: she had it cut very short. Her bust burgeoned, she was voluptuous. When she was nudged by the notion that Richard would have liked her like this, she slapped it away and fastened her mind, penitentially, on Isla: reed-slim, fine-boned, long-limbed . . . It was a bad joke. If Richard had wanted more children, he would have had them with Isla.

That this baby was going to be born was no longer in doubt. She told Claudia because she didn't feel she could leave it any longer. The response was diametrically different from that which she'd expected.

'Mum—that's brilliant!'

They were in the supermarket, but Claudia embraced her mightily by the petfoods.

'You're pleased . . . ?'

'Of course I'm pleased—what did you expect?'

'I don't know.' Jen was dazed. 'Not this. You approve, do you?'

'No, I don't *approve*, in fact I disapprove strongly—you ought to have known better at your age, but a little baby! I'll help out, you know that, and since you've obviously decided to go ahead—well—enjoy!'

Out in the car park as they loaded the boot, she said, 'Red—I'm not trying to put a dampener on the proceedings, but I can't honestly say that I decided to go ahead, as you put it.'

Claudia looked at her over the top of the car. 'Of course you didn't— you've never made a decision in your life.'

'Oh.' Jen gulped this down and got in. She leaned across to unlock the passenger door and Claudia got in next to her.

'Sorry, that wasn't meant to sound so rude.'

'No offence taken.'

'You do well, Mum. You're like Ant, you keep an open mind. Go with the flow.'

'This is hardly what I saw myself doing in my forties.'

'But you are pleased about it, aren't you? You must be.'

Jen started the engine. 'I'm resigned to it.'

'Hang on.' Claudia leaned across her and switched the ignition off again. 'I do hope you're going to be a bit more positive than that. Resigned is no way to embark on a new chapter.'

'I dare say I'll be positive in due course. But the truth is, right now I'm shell-shocked.'

'Yes . . .' Claudia pursed her lips thoughtfully. 'How far gone are you?'

'Eighteen . . . twenty weeks.'

Claudia glanced briefly downwards. 'You don't show.'

'That's because I'm working on it. I may not show, but I feel.'

'It's so exciting!' burst out Claudia again. 'I'll shut up now.'

They let it lie there for a while as they drove back to the house. Anthony was due to collect Claudia there at about six. Jen had got used to these early-evening exchanges, and she liked Anthony. He allowed his demeanour to speak for him, always putting Claudia first, according equal deference to both her and Jen, and slotting himself modestly into the pecking order at Selwyn Street like a suitor half his age. His manners were part of him, never faltering but never conspicuous, either. In what could have been a vexed situation, Anthony's humility was the sincerest proof of his love for Claudia.

Which was why she dreaded him knowing about her pregnancy. She cared what he thought, and feared that no matter how he concealed it, secretly he would be appalled. This in turn might have some subtly destructive effect on the relationship between him and Claudia.

Claudia's enthusiastic reaction did nothing to set her mind at rest. This was her pregnancy, her responsibility: it would be awful if it were to reflect on Claudia in any way.

This evening, Anthony arrived in his silver Mercedes. They were going to the Royal National Theatre to see a new play which had caused a certain amount of outrage among the self-appointed guardians of the nation's morals. Jen, watching him from an upstairs window (she had deliberately contrived to be out of the way at this moment), reflected that nothing displayed the generation gap more clearly than what he and Claudia had chosen to wear for the theatre. He was immaculately suited, Claudia was in loose, baggy striped trousers which looked like— and may well have been—men's pyjama bottoms, whose frayed ends flapped just above her ankles. She'd teamed these with a navy-surplus jumper and baseball boots: she looked extraordinary. They made an arresting couple who might very easily have been taken for well-to-do uncle and wayward niece.

Standing in front of the mirror tweaking at her bits of hair, and putting on bigger earrings—anything to detract from her waistline—she listened to the sounds of his arrival. Claudia's verbal greeting was laconic, but punctuated by what Jen thought of as kissing intervals. She heard Anthony say 'Hello, my darling' and 'Mm—mm.' The front door closed and they went through to the kitchen. There was a chink of glasses, and Claudia's voice again, rattling on nineteen to the dozen now they were out of earshot. Jen's heart sank.

When she went into the kitchen, Anthony was leaning against the worktop, with Cain in his arms. He let the cat slither to the ground when she came in, and kissed her lightly on the cheek—they had progressed to that.

'Jen, good evening. I say, you're different.'

She touched her head. 'I needed a change . . . Oh look, he's covered your suit in hair.'

'That's nothing. By the way, congratulations, what wonderful news.'

'Thank you.' She was guarded.

'Everything they say must be true—you look absolutely tremendous.'

'Do I?'

'See?' said Claudia. 'Have a drink.'

She poured a glass of white wine. Anthony said, 'I'd have brought a bottle of champagne if I'd known.'

Jen took a sip. 'Perhaps we should reserve that for wetting the baby's head.' It was the first time she'd mentioned 'the baby' as a separate entity, something apart from her current condition. It felt strange but not unpleasant.

'Good idea.'

Keith came in at the front door. 'Good evening!'

'Come on in and have a glass of something,' said Jen.

'Oh, I don't know, should I?' He stood in the hall, removing his cycle helmet. It left his hair flattened and a red mark across his forehead.

Anthony poured a glass and held it out. 'This do?'

'Go on then, you twisted my arm.' Keith glanced round at the three of them. 'Everyone's terribly smart—are we celebrating something?'

There was a split-second pause before Claudia said, 'I'm going to be a big sister.'

Keith's face was a study as he grappled with his disbelief and then sought an appropriate response. He looked at Jen. 'Well!' He was blushing. 'You could knock me down with the proverbial! Congratulations.'

'Thanks.'

'So, my goodness, there'll be a few changes made round here, I'll be bound.'

'Not too many, I hope,' said Jen. 'Anyway, it's a long way off . . .' She changed the subject without drawing breath. 'These two are off to see That Play at the National, Keith. Do you think it's likely to deprave and corrupt them?'

'I can't say I care if it does,' replied Keith spiritedly. 'I'm against censorship myself.'

Anthony laughed and put his arm round Claudia. 'Jolly well spoken. We few, we happy few, are well on the way to being the last outpost of civilised values.'

We are? thought Jen. *We are?*

Isla invited Barbara to go to the David D rail sale with her. She needed friends about her who were solid and unsentimental. Barbara could be relied upon to take such an outing at its face value.

The sale was on a Monday, and she spent the Saturday and Sunday nights at Brook End, so that they could drive into London together. She knew at once what Barbara had meant about the cottage seeming 'a bit sad'. It was clear Marjory had been in and done her stuff—it was tidy, there was milk in the fridge and the immersion heater was on—but the windows were filmy and the affectionate little touches were missing. There was no posy of flowers on the dining-room table, no scrawled note bristling with exclamation marks.

And yet Isla felt more at ease in Brook End. This had always been her place more than Richard's. It was less haunted. She left the doors open front and back and flung open the windows. Then she put on some music—Ella singing Gershwin—and went out into the garden. It was six o'clock; hovering, in late September, on the edge of dusk. She could hear the secretive chuckle of the shallow brook, and the idle, intermittent barking of a dog up in the village. She took comfort from the sense of the wide, warm fields all around, of the birds roosting snugly in the trees and beams of The Bury, of the churchyard where Richard lay, his headstone not yet weathered but already a part of that kindly, dignified gathering. She felt at home.

Norman Brake appeared at the five-bar gate onto the lane as she inspected what would be her last parade of flowers before winter.

'Evening.'

'Hello, Norman. Isn't it a lovely evening?'

'It'll do.'

'I'll have to get busy on these borders tomorrow.'

'Keep busy, that's the thing,' he agreed. And then, on a pugnacious note, 'It doesn't do to leave a place empty all the time.'

'We don't—I don't. We've always come as much as we can. I dare say I'll be coming more often, now.'

'Dare say you will.'

'Come in, why don't you?' said Isla, safe in the knowledge that he'd never once accepted such an invitation.

'Could do.' To her astonishment he opened the gate and entered, testing the latch fiercely as he closed it again. 'Can't stop, though.'

Having conceded this much to neighbourly sociability, it was clearly as far as he was prepared to go. He wouldn't even sit down, still less come into the house or have anything to eat or drink. He and Isla stood, a little awkwardly, just inside the gate.

'Good service the other day,' Norman commented, by which Isla knew he meant Richard's funeral.

'It was, wasn't it? I think Richard would have approved.'

'Old boy did well.' This might have referred to Richard, the rector or any one of half a dozen others, so she confined herself to agreeing.

'You doin' all right then?' asked Norman.

'Not bad—you know.'

'You look all right.'

'I feel better for being here.'

'Working?'

'I've got some television work coming up.'

'They need someone halfway decent on the telly, it's mostly bloody rubbish,' he opined. Isla was sure that *Over the Parrot* would fill Norman with fear and loathing, and changed tack.

'How is Marjory?'

'Tearing about all over. This place don't deserve her.'

In Norman's admittedly limited lexicon of praise, this constituted honours of the very highest order. 'She is absolutely wonderful,' agreed Isla. 'Every village needs a Marjory.'

'She won't be able to do so much around the place once she's a married woman,' said Norman, testing the gate latch again. 'She'll want to stop at home a bit more. With 'er 'usband.'

'Of course . . .' Isla nodded thoughtfully. Put out a probe: 'Lucky man.'

'I am,' declared Norman. 'But I got work to do.'

'I feared as much!' cried Barbara on the way into London on Monday. 'I told Bill I reckoned it was on the cards but he laughed me to scorn.'

'So long as they're happy,' reflected Isla.

'But Marjory hasn't a clue! The woman's a complete innocent.'

'We don't know that, Bar. She may not have a lot of worldly experience as we'd recognise it,' said Isla, 'but she's not daft. A lot of people with strings of relationships behind them are as foolish as the day they started out—that's why they keep on making the same mistakes. Marjory's sensible and pragmatic, she feels she'd like to be in partnership with someone in the last quarter of her life—' She faltered slightly. 'And this is her chance.'

'But Norman Brake? For goodness' sake.'

'Maybe she'll change him.' This provoked a snort of scorn. 'You never know.'

'Yes, you do. Still, you're quite right,' conceded Barbara. 'There's nothing to do but wish them well.'

It was some time later, when they were coming into London, that Barbara said, 'Bill and I have got to tell people some time, so I may as well start with you.'

'Yes?'

'Hold on to your hat—this is a bit of a shaker. Nell's a lesbian.'

Isla, travelling at under thirty, cruised through a red light. 'Is she?'

'Bill's completely poleaxed. Completely. We both are, but women are a million times tougher than men.'

Isla pulled into the inside lane, in the comforting shelter of a container lorry. 'Did she tell you herself?'

'She jolly well did.' Barbara ran big square fingers round the string of pearls that lay on her bottle-green Pringle jumper. 'Took more guts to do that than to take a novice round Burghley, I can imagine.'

'Yes,' said Isla, 'I can imagine it would. Is she happy?'

'Well, do you know, I think she is.' Barbara sounded mystified. 'After a fashion. I don't suppose anyone outside the norm like that can be really happy, but she certainly looked bright-eyed and bushy-tailed. And not wearing a collar and tie, or anything, thank God.'

Isla had to smile. 'She hasn't changed, remember. She's still your daughter.'

'Don't I know it! Pig-headed as ever. God in heaven.' Barbara shook her head. 'There's a girlfriend, of course.'

Isla fixed her eyes on the back of the container lorry, counting slats. 'Is there?'

'Oh yes. We haven't met her, but apparently it's some young lawyer woman that Nell went to France with last month.'

'Really?'

'Not the first. There was some tragic unrequited thing going on before this—it makes you look at your friends, I can tell you. And don't we feel ninnies for getting so worked up about the Scott-Chatham boy!'

'I told you not to worry about that.'

'You did'—Barbara gave her an astute look—'but not, I think, with this in mind.'

'No,' Isla admitted. 'Anyway, this new relationship—it's mutual?'

'Big thing, we gather, though Lord knows what we're supposed to do about it. I mean, what's the protocol? I'm not sure,' said Barbara gruffly, but quite equably, 'that the old man and I are ever going to feel comfortable again.'

'Yes, you will,' said Isla. 'You will, because Nell's happy.'

At the rail sale there was one model you couldn't help looking at. She was inches taller than the rest, with the swan neck and small, imperiously tilted close-cropped head of a Masai *moran*. The clothes she displayed might have been blown onto her astonishing frame by some freak wind, so oblivious did she seem to them. She had a long stride and a natural aloofness quite unlike the affected blank stares of the other girls. She was, thought Isla, a girl who in any context you cared to name would draw the eye and the attention.

'Call me old-fashioned,' growled Barbara without irony, 'but none of these girls is what you'd call pretty.'

The MC referred to the tall model as 'Red'. Isla found a list of the models' full names in tiny print at the back of the catalogue. No Red, but Claudia Delaney. She was quite sure it must be her, the daughter Jen had mentioned that day in Alma's.

'If this is the type of girl they pay good money to, I reckon our Nell would be in with a chance,' stage-whispered Barbara. 'And look at these prices, my dear, for the sort of stuff you can buy at the county show!'

'Not really, Bar. This is the designer version.'

After the show they toured the rails. Isla was an instant focus for the *vendeuse*, but for once she could summon no serious interest in the clothes. In the end she bought a long tunic in cream shantung with a mandarin collar. As her Gold Card was processed, she said, 'You have one very remarkable model here today.'

'You mean Red—isn't she exquisite?'

'I'm not sure about that,' said Isla. 'She's too individual to be exquisite, and too emphatic, somehow, to be a model.'

'It's her first time,' said the *vendeuse* apologetically. 'She's a little rough round the edges.'

'No, it's a compliment, you mustn't change her—Claudia, is it?'

'Claudia Delaney.'

'She's perfect as she is.'

The *vendeuse* smiled thinly and returned Isla's Gold Card.

Barbara hrumphed to Isla as they walked away. 'There's not a lot here for an elderly size sixteen with animals to attend to.'

As they walked down a side road towards their meter, Isla saw someone she knew coming towards them.

'Oh look—hello!'

'Isla, how nice to see you,' said Anthony, clasping her hand in his.

'This is Barbara Fyler—Bar, meet Anthony Saxby. He and I met at an insufferably boring charity lunch.'

'How do you do?'

'We consoled each other by playing hangman during the speeches,' explained Anthony, 'but very discreetly.'

'Good works can be heavy going,' agreed Bar.

'Is that what you're doing today?'

'No,' said Isla. 'Today we're frivolous—we've been at a fashion show.'

'David D?'

'How on earth did you know that?'

'Because I'm here myself to meet a friend from there,' said Anthony, glancing beyond them up the road. His face broke into a broad smile. 'And there she is.'

They turned to see the tall model striding towards them. As she drew level, Isla felt her glance whisk over them. Anthony stepped forward—he was fractionally shorter—and planted a light kiss on the girl's mouth.

'Claudia, I want you to meet Isla Munro—and Barbara Fyler. They've been at your show.'

'Yes, I saw you there. Hello.' It was clear Claudia wouldn't have shaken hands, but Barbara thrust out a paw, and it would then have seemed rude to exclude Isla. The girl's hand was very cool.

'How do you do, my dear?' said Barbara. 'Jolly good show, but horribly overpriced.'

'I bought something,' said Isla. 'And it was a good show. Well done.'

'This is pocket money for her,' explained Anthony with a touch of pride. 'She takes her finals next summer.'

'I'm quite sure,' said Isla truthfully, 'that you could make thousands at this game if you wanted to.' With difficulty she looked into, and held, the girl's eyes. Be direct. Be open. Face value. She was perfectly certain that Claudia knew.

The next remark confirmed it. 'I'm really sorry about your husband.'

'How sweet of you . . . I miss him.'

Isla caught Anthony's aghast expression. 'I'm most frightfully sorry, I had no—'

'Of course you didn't.' She gave him a quick, reassuring smile.

Claudia's gaze hadn't shifted. 'We all miss him,' she said.

'I'm hopelessly muddled,' said Barbara as they headed for King's Cross and her train home. 'What's the connection?'

'She's the daughter of your painter lady—the one who did Portia.'

'Good grief, you don't say! I should never have guessed. There isn't a hint of a family resemblance.'

'I suppose not.'

'The fairies must have brought her,' said Barbara.

Jen delivered the parrot to Mr and Mrs Hastings. And not a moment too soon, it seemed to her. Doug Hastings's decline since Jen's last visit was shockingly marked. Mindful of its importance, she unveiled the portrait with a certain amount of trepidation, but their reaction was one of unfeigned, unreserved delight.

'It's beautiful, it's absolutely perfect,' declared Mrs Hastings. 'Hasn't she done a wonderful job, Doug? Look at him, dear,' she whispered to Jen, 'he's quite overcome.'

And indeed he was. His eyes were shining with tears, and one gaunt, freckled hand covered his mouth.

'You've done for him,' said his wife cheerfully. 'Will you have a drink with us, to celebrate?'

There was no point in demurring: the sherry decanter and three glasses stood on a lacquered tray on the side. 'I'd love to.'

She sat down. Mrs Hastings—she implored Jen to call her Avis—brought over the sherry and a little basket full of cheese footballs.

'Where will you hang the painting?' Jen asked.

'Over the sideboard,' said Doug, strong on the practicalities. 'We'll put the mirror opposite.'

'Good thinking,' said Jen. 'That way you get two for the price of one.'

When she eventually rose to leave, Doug tried to struggle to his feet. She didn't like to stop him, but fortunately Avis stepped in, with a firm but gentle 'No you don't.'

Jen held out her hand. His was very cold and dry, the thin bones rubbing against one another in their sheath of papery skin.

'Thank you my dear.' He was tearful again, but in command. 'It means a lot to me. I can't thank you enough.'

In the hall Avis took an envelope off a side table and pressed it into her hand. 'I wish it could be more.'

Jen pointed out gently, 'It's my usual rate.'

'But it's worth ever so much more to us.'

'I'm so pleased. I really am.'

Avis opened the door, put it on the latch and accompanied Jen to the lift. When it arrived, she patted Jen's shoulder. 'You get along. But do come back to see us, dear. It does us good to see people.'

'I will, definitely.'

She got into the lift, pressed the button. Avis waved—a small wave, because it was only a short distance.

'Bye, dear. Don't leave it too long.'

Jen felt tired on the way home—dead tired, emotionally and physically. The oasis of calm which had been the Hastingses' flat seemed to have left her more vulnerable to the churning uncertainties of her own life. She promised herself some serious self-indulgence when she reached home—a stiff drink, a hot, scented bath, and an early night with the radio and her book. The picture of herself tucked up in bed, glowing from the bath, with the cats purring on the quilt, was so vivid and seductive that it was a rude shock to discover on arrival that there was a power cut in Selwyn Street.

Keith met her in the hall with a rapidly dwindling candle on a saucer. 'I found this, but remind me where the others are.'

Together, in the small, wavering light, they shuffled into the kitchen and located the carrier bag, among other carrier bags in the bottom drawer, where Jen's assortment of candles were kept.

'I don't believe this,' she moaned. 'How long have they been off for?'

'Three-quarters of an hour. I rang them, and it's this whole part of the grid apparently. They're on the case.'

'You don't happen to know if the immersion heater was on?'

'No—yes. I mean, I do know and it isn't. I turned it off when I came in.'

'Keith!'

'I'm sorry, but you generally like it off during the day, and since you seemed to have forgotten—'

'I had, but—oh, to hell with it. Maybe the water's still hot.'

'You could try,' said Keith.

She did, and it wasn't. Because the bath was now definitely out of the question she began to crave it quite desperately. She felt heavy and drained—the small of her back ached and her stomach was tight. She went and lay down on the sofa in the living room, put on a Clannad tape, and tried to relax, but couldn't. There was a sensation of pressure that she couldn't relieve.

Keith came in. 'I tell you what, I've got my camping Gaz burner upstairs. What say I make us a cup of tea?'

'Thanks. That'd be nice.'

He peered at her in the flickering twilight. 'Are you all right?'

'I'm just so tired . . . I've no reason to be so knackered . . .'

'Who needs a reason in your condition? I'll make tea.' He went to the door, then returned. 'Better yet, why not go and get into bed? I could do you a hot-water bottle.'

She knew that it was a good idea, but the thought of moving, of going up the stairs, was too much.

'I'll have the tea first, and then see . . .'

'Okey-dokey.'

She almost dozed off lying there, but it was an uncomfortable state of semiconsciousness rather than the welcome surrender of sleep. In the background she could hear Keith pottering about, up and down the stairs, clanking around with the Gaz burner, assembling mugs, tum-te-tumming away to himself.

When it happened, it took a few seconds for her to realise that the tiredness and discomfort had become something more urgent.

Keith put a nightlight in a saucer on the tray and carried it through into the living room. As he came round the end of the sofa he saw Jen's hand stretched up towards him.

'The cup that cheers,' he said. He put the tray down and proffered the mug. 'There we go . . .' He peered at her in the dim light. 'Hey there, anyone at home?'

**D**inner with the Stainforths was a mixed blessing. So many things reminded Isla of being here with Richard. In this robustly domestic context he had always been quieter than usual, and less confident, aware of his own shortcomings. She found this awkwardness touching, and loved him for it. And Archie, of course, was—both literally and metaphorically—at home, his body language relaxed, his manner freer, in a way that was nice to see.

Almost unconsciously they tried to compensate for Richard's absence. They spoke a little louder, and moved and ate a little quicker. Where they had never even thought of it before, they each feared a silence and were concerned about what to say next. It was something of a mercy when, as they sat round the kitchen table over coffee, Amanda appeared.

'Hi,' she said from the doorway, to all of them. And then again, specifically to Isla, 'Hi.'

'Hi yourself.'

Amanda came in and took a carton of yoghurt out of the fridge, and a teaspoon off the draining board. She peeled back the lid and began eating.

'Pull up a chair,' said Archie. 'Join us.'

'I'm OK, thanks.'

Alison got up to make more coffee. A faint wail came from upstairs. 'Archie, get that, would you . . . ?' Archie went obediently and Amanda sat down in his place. She scraped the last of the yoghurt from the carton and set it on the table, where the weight of the spoon caused it to tip over. She licked the fine rim of white from her upper lip and glanced briefly at Isla.

'I was going to write to you. I'm sorry about—you know . . .'

'Yes.'

Alison stood the cafetière, plunger protruding, on the table. 'Do you want coffee, Mandy?'

'Yes, thanks.'

She put another mug with theirs, and sat down. Isla studied her own hands closely. She wished someone could take the pain away. It lay like a sleeping beast inside her, occasionally leaping up to slash her and make the tears spring to her eyes. She smoothed the fingers of one hand between the fingers of the other, as though pulling on gloves.

'Isla—your coffee.'

'Thank you.'

'Mandy . . .'

Amanda put three spoonfuls of sugar in her mug and stirred. 'Will you still be doing that television show?'

'Amanda!'

'Mum—I wasn't talking to you.'

'No, it's fine.' Isla felt relieved. The beast subsided. 'Yes, it's all going ahead. I'm going to try to get tickets for you.'

Amanda dropped the spoon with a clatter. 'Brilliant! That is so cool.'

'And you'll be able to meet Adrian Coote.'

'Wicked. Thanks a lot, really.'

'My pleasure.'

Amanda abandoned the coffee, stood up and leaned across to kiss Isla warmly on the cheek. She smelt of cigarettes and strawberry yoghurt.

'Thanks!'

As she disappeared, Alison grimaced. 'Gone to phone the coven. I'm sorry—she's not a bad kid, but sometimes they have absolutely no sense of what's appropriate . . .'

'She was perfectly appropriate,' said Isla. 'She cheered me up.'

On the way home Isla reflected on the fact that other people's offspring were a constant source of fascination. What was so intriguing was not their similarity to their parents, but their striking separateness. Amanda Stainforth's chameleon changes from brusque reserve to charming effusiveness were not mere teenage caprice, and certainly nothing to do with Archie and Alison; they were her own. And Giles and Marcus bore no discernible resemblance to either parent. One of the things she'd loved about Richard was his capacity to allow these differences, and to let them be themselves and go their own way. His sons' individuality was their greatest tribute to him.

When Barbara had spoken of Claudia Delaney's looks being brought 'by the fairies' it seemed not a whimsical but a perfectly reasonable suggestion. How else, on earth, could one explain the startling magic of the unknown factor?

Isla went to sleep with these reflections running through her mind, and woke next morning refreshed, for the first time since Richard's death. She knew, now, what she would do.

It took some time for the phone to be answered, and the voice on the other end sounded wary.

'Hello . . . ?'

'Is that Mr Burgess?'

'It is.'

'It's Isla Wakefield.' There was a short intake of breath, a hiatus. 'Isla Wakefield? You helped my husband.'

'Yes, I remember.'

'I wonder if I could speak to Jen?'

'I'm afraid she's not here.'

She sensed that the choice of words was a careful one. No indication of where Jen was, nor for how long; no offer to take a message.

Isla was equally careful. 'When do you think I might be able to talk to her?' Non-intrusive, open-ended, unthreatening.

'Ummm . . . that's a bit hard for me to say, really.' She could almost hear the sound of matters being weighed up. She hoped Jen appreciated all this diplomacy.

She decided to take a risk. 'Look, this is obviously difficult. I didn't mean to put you on the spot. I'll call back.'

She was actually lowering the receiver when she heard him say, 'No, don't. Look, Mrs Wakefield, she's in hospital.'

There was one of those dizzying shifts of equilibrium which accompany a new perspective. Isla had been full of her own resolve, her intentions, her positive thoughts. Now, in an instant, they were relegated to second place. Rebuffed, she clutched at professionalism, acted concern for all it was worth.

'I'm so sorry! What's the trouble—nothing serious?'

'Umm. I don't know if you were aware of this, but she's expecting a baby . . . ?'

'I did know, yes.' She no longer needed to act. Her voice was flat as she asked, 'Is everything all right?'

'She had a threatened miscarriage. I had to get an ambulance. Night before last.'

'And—the baby?'

'She was still bleeding when I called this morning.' Isla heard, now, his relief at being able to talk about it.

'Where is she?'

'The Royal Free.'

'Do you think I'd be able to see her?'

'Umm.' The caution crept back. 'Possibly. I couldn't say.'

She saw his difficulty. 'Let me put it this way. Is she allowed visitors?'

'One at a time. I've been. Her daughter. You know.'

'I'll give the hospital a ring.'

'Mrs Wakefield—'

'Yes?'

'It's none of my business, but do you think it's a good idea?'

He was a patently decent man. Now was the time, thought Isla grimly, to put that decency to the test.

'Actually, Mr Burgess,' she said. 'I think it's a very good idea.'

To be returning to the hospital after such a short interval, and for such a different reason, was unnerving. This time, although she found a place in the hospital car park, she sat in the car for a full ten minutes before she felt composed enough to go in.

Until this moment, with only a hiccup during her conversation with Keith Burgess, she had managed to hang on to the clarity of this morning's feelings. But now, as she followed the signs along endless corridors, her confidence wavered. The feelings might be clear, but how was she going to put them into words? And, if she managed that, how would they be received?

She asked the nurse at the desk which room Jen was in.

'End on the right, nearest the window.'

'Is there anyone else with her?'

'Not at the moment. If another visitor does turn up we'll pop along and tell you—she gets rather tired if there's more than one at a time.'

'Of course—I understand.' Isla was about to go, and then paused. 'How is she?'

'Very down.'

'But the baby . . . ?'

'Baby's still there, just. And the bleeding's under control. But it could be a long haul if she's going to hang on to it.'

'Thank you. I shan't stay long.'

It was a six-bedded room, and all were occupied. Six stories, thought Isla: six disordered lives. Of the two window beds, one was occupied by a stout teenager reading a magazine. The other had the curtain pulled two-thirds of the way round.

Jen was asleep. Isla was shocked at how pale and drained she looked—but also younger, almost like a child herself. She lay on her side, facing the window, with her arms flung up onto the pillow before her face, in rather the same attitude she had used when kneeling in front of Isla at their last meeting, except that now the fingers weren't bunched into fists. It was too warm in the ward, and airless, and her bedclothes were round her waist. She wore a large T-shirt with a panda logo on the front, but the slight swell of her pregnancy was clearly visible.

Isla laid some freesias on top of the locker. It was strange to be an unseen watcher—Isla felt at once privileged and a little ashamed to be intruding on Jen's privacy. She sat down on the upholstered leatherette chair between the bed and the window. It was three thirty. She sat there, quietly and at peace, for nearly an hour. Once, like an anxious mother, she felt compelled to get up and bend over the bed to hear Jen's breathing. But a nurse, popping in to check, smiled approvingly.

'Let her sleep. Best thing for her.'

Shortly after that, the nurse from the desk appeared.

'Excuse me—'

'Yes?'

'Mrs Delaney's daughter's here . . .'

'It's quite all right, I'll leave now.'

The nurse withdrew. Isla took from her bag the card she'd brought with her, and laid it beside the freesias. Then, without hesitation, she took Jen's hand in both of hers and held it for a moment, before replacing it gently on the counterpane and walking quickly away.

Jen woke to find Claudia sitting on the windowsill, her long frame silhouetted against the westering sun.

'Red . . . ?'

'Hello, Mum.'

'How long have you been there?'

'About—fifteen seconds. Sorry, did I wake you?'

'Don't be silly . . . it's lovely to see you.' She stretched out a hand and Claudia took and clasped it before bending to kiss her. The gesture reminded her of something. 'Have you done that once already?'

Claudia pulled the pillows up behind her. 'What?'

'I don't know . . . This is embarrassing. Squeezed my hand?'

'No.'

'I must have dreamed it. I had such a strong impression, some time when I was asleep, that someone was holding my hand . . . That I was actually being led, very firmly, by the hand . . .' She pulled a shamefaced smile. 'Talk about sick fancies.'

'I don't know.' Claudia sat down on the chair and leaned forward, elbows on knees. 'As a matter of fact, Isla Wakefield was here.'

'When?'

'Just now. She left when I arrived.'

Jen dragged a hand over her face. 'Oh God. How long was she here for?'

'I've no idea. She did say that you'd been asleep the whole time.'

'Oh God—Red—how did she seem?'

Claudia looked down at her hands, spreading her long fingers which were so thin the light seemed to shine through them. When she looked up she was very serious.

'She seemed—really nice. Lovely, actually. I was glad she'd been.'

'Oh God,' said Jen again. The helpless tears began to course down her cheeks. She seemed full to the brim with tears at the moment; the least little jolt and they spilled over. 'How could she bear it?'

'Very easily, I had the impression.' Claudia leaned over and took the envelope from the top of the locker. 'She brought the flowers. And I imagine this is from her.'

'You open it.'

'No, Mum. You.'

Claudia laid the card on her lap. It was addressed formally, though not correctly: *Mrs J. Delaney.*

Claudia, in a burst of embarrassed tact, opened the locker, got out a carton of apple juice and poured some into her mother's glass. Then helped herself to one.

Jen slid the card out of the envelope. It was a photograph. A big, rumpled man, disordered hair, a beaming smile, eyes that stared with infectious delight into the camera lens . . .

Richard.

Slowly, she turned the photograph over. On the back, in black ink in a smoothly rounded hand, Isla had written: *Jen—You can do it, and you must, for all of us. I thought you might like this to put with any of your own. Isn't it good of him? With my love—Isla W.*

**R**eturning to the Hampstead house that evening, Isla found a bouquet propped against the front door—stocks, delphiniums and white roses, sweetly scented. The accompanying note, scribbled on a torn-out diary page, read: *I brought these with my own fair hand. Haven't been able to stop thinking about you. I'll be back. Scotch.*

For the first time in weeks, as she opened the door and went into the house, she found it free of ghosts. And made up her mind, at that moment, to leave it.

**I**t was a fine Sunday in June, in Bradenham, and the sun shone impartially on the just and the unjust. Isla was in the garden of Brook End. She sat at the wooden picnic table washing new potatoes for lunch. In the middle of the lawn was a plaid rug with her book lying on it, open and face down. Upstairs in the bedroom her wedding outfit of cream and navy hung on the wardrobe door, with her broad-brimmed hat on the shelf above, and her matching spike heels standing trimly to attention beneath. Marjory and Norman's wedding had been a delight, but even more delightful was to sit out here in shorts, shirt and sneakers, without make-up, and feel the first really hot sun of the year on her bare skin. Marjory and Norman would be in Corfu now, but though she wished them every happiness, Isla didn't envy them. At this moment she did not wish to be anywhere but here.

She plopped the last of the potatoes into the saucepan of cold water at her elbow, and stretched her arms above her head. Then she left the picnic table and lay down full-length on the rug. Her head nudged the book and she felt for it with one hand and closed it.

From next door came the intermittent plop and ping of tennis on the Fylers' court. Marcus and Giles— who had both attended the wedding—were playing with Nell and her friend Frances. She was impressed by how easily they'd accepted this relationship, and even seemed to admire and respect it. Running counter to this was the fact that she'd had to cajole, then order them to visit their grandfather that afternoon. But they had agreed, and were going—whether in deference, still, to her widow's weeds, or respect for their father's memory, or because they wanted to get it over with, she couldn't say. She preferred to think that a sea change was taking place.

They'd travelled mostly in silence, but it was a peaceful one. In his baby seat in the back ten-week-old Harry slept, his mouth slightly pursed as though turning weighty decisions in his dreams.

As they came into Bradenham, he began to stir. Jen looked over her shoulder.

'Perfect timing. He knows when refreshments are due.'

'He's my kind of people.' The driver slowed to turn right. 'By the way, where did you get the name Harry from?'

'It's the second name of the friend who helped deliver him.'

'First name no good?'

She shook her head. 'Keith.'

'No good.'

'But his other name was Harold, so I compromised.'

'Nice idea.'

'Nice man.'

Isla took the saucepan of potatoes into the kitchen and put them on the stove. She had put up a notice board on the wall, because this was her home now, and she had a life here, and things to do. Prominent on the board were invitations. One was to a fork supper with Caroline, to meet (as Caroline confided at the bottom) *Daniel Hetherington—my chap!*

The second was a fax: *Would you like to see a play? Or a film? Or have dinner? Or would you be content just to sit there and let me gaze at you? Let me know what suits you best. S.*

The Renault turned in and stopped. 'Journey's end, everyone,' said Jen.

Isla opened the cottage door and stepped out into the sunshine. There was a burst of laughter and a shriek of protest from the tennis court on the other side of the lane, waves and smiles as the car doors opened.

Scotch got out and released Harry from his seat. He handed the baby to Jen and let her go first.

Isla opened her arms wide, and walked forward to greet the three people who embodied, for her, the possibility of happiness in an otherwise uncertain future.

# SARAH HARRISON

Best-selling author Sarah Harrison achieved fame and fortune with her first novel, *Flowers of the Field*, which became an international best seller. She proved to be one of a very select band of would-be authors who have their first attempts at novel-writing accepted on the strength of a mere synopsis. Apparently, she heard that a publisher was looking for a historical saga so she dashed off an outline of a story that she had in mind—and the letter of acceptance, together with an offer, followed almost by return of post.

The sequel, *A Flower that's Free,* also became a best seller. Between finishing that and finishing her latest novel, which appears in this volume, she was not surprisingly invited to put together a practical guide called *How to Write a Blockbuster*. A glimpse through its pages reveals the secrets of her success. In a nutshell, her four hot tips on how to write a saleable novel are: 1) good characters 2) emotional pull 3) a good story and 4) manageable targets.

Of course, it is a lot easier said than done for an aspiring novelist to achieve these ideal objectives. For instance, where does Sarah Harrison, living in a sleepy village in Cambridgeshire, get the inspiration for her sophisticated urban characters?

The original idea for *Flowers won't Fax* was inspired by two newspaper stories she had read: the death of footballer manager, Matthew Harding, whose funeral was attended by his wife and his long-term mistress, and President François Mitterrand's funeral, during which both his mistress and wife actually walked side by side in the funeral cortege. The inspiration for the professional side of Sarah Harrison's heroine—and indeed the looks!—was none other than the TV celebrity, Joanna Lumley. 'She is a successful actress and also a much-loved national institution.'

In writing *Flowers won't Fax* Sarah Harrison wanted to investigate 'the eternal triangle' and 'explore the idea of whether somebody can genuinely love two people.' She says that she still doesn't know the answer but has no doubt that many people are wrestling with the dilemma.

As well as being a full-time novelist, Sarah Harrison is the president of her local writers' circle and also very involved in the local amateur dramatic society. She has a son, Laurence, who is twenty-seven and two daughters, Thea, who is seventeen and studying for her A-levels and, Fran, who is expecting her second baby. The youthful-looking Sarah Harrison thoroughly enjoys combining the roles of being a best-selling author and a grandmother.

Grianan is a charming country-house
hotel in the heart of Scotland.
It is also Sally Buchanan's much-loved
childhood home, run by her stalwart
Aunt Janey, to which she returns after
a broken love affair in the hope that
the house's spirit will work its healing
magic. It does so, but in strange
and unsettling ways.

# CHAPTER ONE

I T WAS A LONG TIME since Sally had been to the Edalmere cottage. The road looping up onto the eastern Lakeland fells was still single track but dark now with new tarmac, litter bins at every passing place. She even met cars coming down, glimpsing faces red from a day in the sun of early May. Edal village had spread to at least twice the size she remembered, lines of new houses straggling out along each of its arms. She was glad Aunt Janey had arranged for the key to be left in the door. She could not have faced calling to collect it from Ann Jackson, who used to clean the cottage for Aunt Ursula and still kept an eye on it, and who would have exacted her due of gossipy nothings about the family, and about Sally's own long-ago visits here.

At the southern end of the lake the tarmac ended in a car park, with a map in a glass-fronted case, fire warnings, the green-and-white pointing arms of signposts. There was a row of bungalows beyond it.

Sally nearly turned back. She didn't want it to be like this, didn't want change, didn't want people. It had been disconcerting to find today, with decisions behind her and the break finally made, that the whole wretched fiasco with Julian had filled her mind with renewed agony. Humiliation and anger eating into her, she had registered little of the journey and felt exhausted now. But there was nothing to go back to, and as she wasn't ready yet to meet Aunt Janey's searching eyes and stringent comments, the cottage would have to do as a staging post. At the very least it would provide solitude and freedom from demands.

Once past the bungalows, the track following the lake shore was more familiar. The old whitewashed farmhouse on the bend looked the same but was clearly occupied now, chimney smoking, a muddy estate car at the door, a child's bike propped against the wall. It was now called, Sally saw, Edal Bank. She was filled with swift irrational resentment. When she had come here for childhood holidays with her parents and later with Janey, this house had always been shut up and deserted.

Bars of sunlight flickered maddeningly across her face as the track swung closer to the lake and the trees thinned, then she was driving blind in dense shade as it turned away again. She was too tired, too empty of interest to feel anything but exasperation—at the unexpected intrusion of people into this once secluded place, at the minor irritations of the sun in her eyes, the ache in her shoulders after the unbroken spell of driving, the sweatiness of her thighs clamped together for long hours without moving.

She didn't even like the cottage much, she remembered wearily. Well, it was only intended as a steppingstone between the disaster her well-adjusted life in the south had turned into and the hard work and challenges ahead. She turned into the steep-pitched driveway and came out onto the grassy ledge where the little house faced west into the eye of the sun. As she stepped stiffly out, shaking her skirt free of her legs, lifting her heavy hay-coloured hair out of her collar, sweet air met her, smoothing across her face, filling her nostrils with the tang of resin mingled with the scents from Aunt Ursula's once-loved garden. With a long sigh of relief she leaned against the warm wing of the car and, tilting back her head, closed her eyes. The sunset light, spreading its last brilliance along the dramatic skyline, glowed through her eyelids, warmed her face. Tension seeped away. A few days alone here, with nothing to do, nothing expected of her, then Grianan, and no need to look further for the whole of the summer.

After a moment, she reached into the car for the keys and went to open the boot, noting the grass which now grew where gravel had been. Aunt Janey came here when she could get away from Grianan, which wasn't often, but no one else ever used the cottage as far as Sally knew.

The fancy little wrought-iron gate whined at her touch, the fleshy cables of buttercups reached across the path, dandelions had rooted in the cracks of the steps. A sudden rush of loneliness took her by the throat; a mixture of a nostalgia she hadn't expected to feel and dread of the empty future.

Nothing had been changed in the kitchen. Carved pine rioted everywhere; Beatrix Potter china crowded the dresser shelves. Gaudy tulips rammed into a too-small vase were deciding whether to turn up or down. The cuckoo clock had been wound. Damn Ann Jackson.

Sally dumped down the bags and duvet she'd brought from the car and went through to the hall. The door to Aunt Ursula's room was open. Shrouding the bed was the familiar beige silk counterpane with its faded satin-stitch bamboos. Aunt Ursula had died in this bed; Uncle Teddy too for all she knew. Sally would rather sleep on the kitchen table with the Pigling Bland condiment set.

She tried the small room she had always been given as a child and was met by the smell of cold unstirred air. Dead flies lay on the peeling paint of the windowsill. She could live with that.

Settling in didn't take long. She hadn't brought much with her and basic food supplies had been left in the fridge as promised. The boiler was switched on, the house warm. Too warm, too cluttered. Every surface was busy with objects. Everything possible was ruched, gathered and flounced. Net curtains hid the view down the shining length of Windermere. This single piece of elaboration suddenly loosed in Sally all the suppressed anger of the day. She felt stifled, desperate with the need to be outside, to have space around her, breathe cool air.

The two main choices for walks had always been to take the steep path up through the trees behind the house and come out onto the fell, or to go along the lakeside track to reach the open southern shore. Sally had no energy tonight to face a climb and took the lower track. She had forgotten already that the house down the lake was now inhabited and was taken by surprise to meet two children playing in the lane on their bicycles, a brown-haired boy of perhaps ten, a younger sister with red-gold curls. They both answered politely when she spoke to them, pausing as she passed.

Sally found she couldn't wind down. She sat on a rock and watched a pair of mallard with nine dots of ducklings bob on the glinting ripples beyond the sandy beach; on the island a hundred yards away the cormorants were drying their wings; in the shadows under the farther shore she caught the white gleam of the swans. None of it meant a thing.

She had come here to be free, however briefly, of time and people, past and future. To sleep, eat, walk, idle. It sounded simple, but how first to subdue the churning thoughts?

Shivering as a small wind came off the water, she pushed herself up off the rock and turned to go back. Food, bath, bed. Sleep? That she could not be sure of.

The lane was empty, the children gone. A battered pick-up had joined the estate car outside the house. Its bonnet was up and a man was standing beside it turning something over in his hands, holding it up to the light, too intent on what he was doing to notice Sally passing. He was tall and lean, with curly red hair darker than his daughter's, big oat-mealy sweater sagging as he leaned forward and replaced whatever part he'd taken out. That was all she saw, but in one of those waves of long-ing that swept Sally still she felt an acute envy for the woman in the neat white house, with her husband, her children, her home in this lovely place, secure, looked after. These people had their life together, as a family, whatever it was like, while she was about to return alone to an alien little dwelling, ill-suited to her mood, feeling uprooted, dispos-sessed and without armour of any kind.

She woke late, still feeling tired. She dawdled about, but the brilliance of the spring morning, the clean lines of the hills, the emptiness and silence woke a spark of enthusiasm. Idleness and introspection would do no good. She would walk down to the village for bread as they always used to, look in and thank Ann Jackson for getting the cottage ready—and make sure that she understood she wouldn't be needed again while Sally was here.

As she walked, gradually sounds impinged: birdsong, lambs' cries from the fell high above, a tractor working somewhere down towards the village. And a nearer engine, coming along behind her. She stepped up onto the bank to let the vehicle pass. It was the pick-up from Edal Bank. She lifted a hand to acknowledge the raised hand of the driver but didn't look at him, not ready for encounters yet. But you're going to shop in the village, you fool, you're going to have to speak to someone.

'It was so sad about your auntie, and going so soon after your uncle too. One week she seemed just the same as ever, the next . . . and how is Miss Buchanan these days? It's a while since we've seen her but of course she's a busy person with the hotel to look after and it is quite a drive down here.'

It was always a surprise to hear Grianan called a hotel. It was more like a house where Aunt Janey allowed friends to stay, gave them a rough time if they didn't behave and then made them pay for the privilege.

'And you're staying with Miss Buchanan for the summer, she tells me,' Ann Jackson ran on. 'That'll be grand for you both.'

Be bloody hard work, more like, Sally inwardly retorted, but even that prospect held a certain comfort. Janey's letter asking her to help, an unprecedented request, had jolted her at last out of the futile existence she had found herself in after Julian—but thoughts of him had made yesterday a harried nightmare. She wouldn't think about all that today.

There were several cars in the car park at the lake foot, and as she started along the track she saw groups of walkers ahead of her, the crude colours of their weatherproof clothing intrusive against the light spring colours of the broad-leaved trees along this part of the shore and the darker mass of plantations.

Where were these purposeful groups heading? The lane, as Sally recalled, petered out in mud and bramble thickets after a quarter of a mile. She had enjoyed 'exploring' round the shore as a child, though probably she hadn't gone as far as she imagined, but once she had grown too big to duck under the branches of the tight-packed conifers it hadn't been much fun. Had a path been opened right round the lake now? She felt outraged at the idea, then laughed at herself. She hardly qualified as an inhabitant.

She scraped together a lazy lunch and, when she had finished it, decided to follow the walkers and see what had happened to this quiet place where no one came.

A lot of work had been done along the track north of the cottage; trees and bushes trimmed back, a ditch dug, stone bottoming laid in the muddy patches. A view had been opened up to High Rigg. After half a mile a new footpath branched off, logs set across it to make steps, a split-log railing curving above the drop. A signpost read 'Harter Fell and Haweswater Reservoir'.

Steps, handrails, signposts—no wonder the place was crawling with people, Sally thought angrily, then realised there wasn't a soul in sight. She kept to the lower track, soon coming to the point where a small beck came down, now crossed by a wooden bridge. A favourite route had been to climb the narrow ghyll to a tiny waterfall. Surely that wouldn't have changed—but could she get up to it still? With an impulse to recapture some fragment of a past long jettisoned she turned off among the bushes, thinly clad with early foliage, and began to thread her way up the bank. Hidden, secret, sparkling in sunlight filtered through leaves, the fall splashed down into its rocky cup. The fallen branch that used to form a rudimentary bridge had long ago rotted away.

Determined to reach the same boulder from which she used to sit and watch the fall safe from grown-up eyes, Sally saw that above her head a solid-looking branch would let her swing across. She eyed the rush of water with new respect, jumped for the branch, letting go at the top of the swing and arching out towards a flat stone. She barely made it, and there was a scrambling moment before she got her weight forward and her fingers round a rock. As she clutched it, a voice above her commented, 'Most people find it easier to use the bridge I've built for them.'

A few feet away, camouflaged against the trees in a rust-brown sweater and worn cords faded to a yellowish olive green, regarding her with amusement, stood the man she had seen last night outside the old farmhouse.

Laughter seized her. A responsible, competent, career woman of thirty-one swinging from the trees. 'Recapturing my childhood,' she explained, looking for a way up the bank. 'Never a good idea.'

He came forward and, smiling, reached down to pull her up. 'Can be fun though. And if this was a childhood haunt of yours then you must be Ursula's niece.'

How had he worked that out? Ann Jackson, of course. 'Sally Mayn—' But suddenly, in this place, in transition between two phases of her life, Sally came to a decision she had been circling round for weeks. It was time to leave behind her English surname, her father's name. 'Sally Buchanan,' she said firmly.

'Mike Danaher.' If he had noticed the amendment he gave no sign. 'I live in the house along the lane.'

'I saw you there as I passed yesterday evening. Doing something to the pick-up.'

'Distributor cap.' He was still looking at her with enjoyment, as though welcoming the entertainment she provided on an uneventful afternoon. 'And I passed you in the lane this morning.'

'Oh, yes, of course.' Had he noticed that she had not looked at him, evading contact?

'You'll see some changes here if you haven't been back for a while,' he went on easily.

'Don't tell me you're responsible for them?' she demanded.

'One or two. Though you can't say I've done much tampering up here,' he observed, looking round at the sequestered little place.

'So what were you doing up here?' she asked.

'I was working just below. Hearing some strange creature blundering about in the bushes I thought I'd better investigate.'

'Elephant or bear, I suppose.'

'I didn't expect something in the simian line, certainly.'

They laughed and the thought flicked across Sally's mind that it was the laughter of friends. Mike Danaher's lean face, made longer by the fact that his dark red springy hair was already receding above the temples, the all-year-round tan of the outdoor man, his hazel eyes alive with amusement, already seemed strangely familiar.

'A simian lunatic,' said Sally resignedly.

'I wouldn't have missed it,' he assured her, his grin widening.

# GRIANAN

The Danahers had owned the house at the lake foot for years, Sally recalled, and quite a lot of ground with it. 'Are you living here all the time now?' she asked. 'I always remember the house being empty.'

'We came back after the children were born. Michael's ten now.'

That long since I've been here, she thought, with a pang of renewed guilt. 'And do you farm here? Do you own all this? I don't remember.'

'Most of the land up here belongs to the North West Water Authority. Used to be the Manchester Corporation. The lake was one of their reservoirs back in the 1880s. Then when they made the big new reservoirs like Thirlmere they sold off some of their ground up here. My grandfather came over from Ireland in the twenties and bought the farmhouse and some land at the southern end of the lake and cleared the trees. He farmed it, but it was too small to be economical.'

'Were there trees right round the lake at one time?'

'Corporation policy. Dense planting right to the water's edge helped to prevent evaporation and increased water extraction. You still see it elsewhere, and it's currently the subject of a major conservation battle.'

'So why do you work on their footpaths?'

They had fallen, oblivious now of their surroundings, into this conversation, settling without discussion on the big, flat-topped rock where Sally always used to sit.

'These days they're very keen on opening up the land to walkers and so on,' Mike went on. 'And I wanted a means to live here full-time. I was brought up in Kendal after my father gave up farming and leased the land, but I'd always wanted to come back here one day. At the time when my father died I didn't have the knowledge or the interest to try to start up the farm again. I'd trained as a civil engineer and done a pretty mixed lot of jobs in different parts of the world. So now I'm a sort of warden, pottering round clearing ditches and building bridges and counting birds for people like the RSPB—and keeping an eye on vandals who don't keep to the paths.'

Sally turned her head to smile at him, a smile of pure pleasure. Every separate element of this moment was good. The shining ribbon of water spilling down the rock face with the white churn of foam at its feet, the skittery sunlight that came and went through the branches, the absolute sense of peaceful seclusion and the strange and equally strong sense that time had ceased to matter, that this moment could be held and savoured—and that for this man beside her, unknown half an hour ago, the feeling was exactly the same. His full attention was turned to her; those clear hazel eyes which were so striking and alive were very intent.

She made a serious effort to keep the conversation on a normal, unexceptionable, level. 'So you knew Aunt Ursula and Uncle Teddy?'

'Not terribly well.' A small reserve there? 'I saw more of your aunt after your uncle died. I used to look in to make sure she was all right.'

'That was good of you.' Sally paused. 'I never came to see her. When she was alone. When she was ill.' She had not voiced that guilt before.

'You were living in the south?' It was a question; he wasn't offering her an excuse.

'In Reading.' Suddenly it all seemed too remote, too painful and petty and exhausted for this place and this moment.

'And you're going up to see Janey?' He had this easy way of carrying her forward over difficult moments. And his familiar use of her aunts' Christian names was agreeable and somehow comforting.

'Yes. I'm going to Grianan.' She caught the quick turn of his head and knew that, in spite of all the years of absence, the selfish absorption in the life she had created for herself, she was still unable to say that name without love. 'Just for the summer,' she added, as though needing to make her independence clear.

'That was Ursula's home—and your mother's?'

'Yes, my mother was the youngest sister. Rose. She married a doctor.' Her tone was so dismissive that only as she went on did Mike realise this was not some earlier marriage, as he had assumed, but that she was referring to her own father. 'He's a consultant haematologist now, very successful and very busy . . .' She said this with a terse bitterness she could not suppress. Mike made a small movement as though he wanted to protest, then checked it.

Sally took a steadying breath. 'Sorry. I don't talk about him usually.'

'And you don't use his name.'

So he hadn't missed that. 'As of today. As of just now, actually. I'd always wanted to be a Buchanan.' What would Janey think? Would it please her or would it jar on her peculiar sense of absolute honesty?

'Go on about your family.'

'Well, my mother decided she'd had enough of blood when I was eight and left.' Again Mike looked as if he would like to soften the harsh offhandedness of her words, but he didn't interrupt. 'My father established her very definitely in my mind as the one at fault, abandoning us for no reason and so on. I adored him at that stage and never saw enough of him, so I was thrilled to get so much attention from him all of a sudden. In theory I was given the choice of who I wanted to live with and I chose to stay with him. I can't tell you how callous I was to my mother.' She dropped her head into her hands for a moment, closing her eyes against the uncomfortable memory. 'Then I discovered—only it took me a long time to realise it—that I had just been a weapon for my father to wound her with. He took no notice of me at all after that.'

'Did you keep in touch with your mother?'

Had he divined in some way that this was the part that mattered?

'Not very successfully,' she told him, trying hard to be matter-of-fact. 'She went off to Australia and married a mechanic in a town called Orford, a tiny place outside Goulburn in New South Wales. She's now called Rouse. Rouse Brumby, that is.'

Mike laughed, but his eyes watched her attentively. 'Go on,' he said.

Sally found that suddenly she wanted to put it all into words, the long-ago disillusionment which she had grown so used to burying. For this unknown man seated beside her in the secluded windless corner, where she felt quite separate from the train of everyday events and carried back to childhood simplicity, would listen, would hear what she was saying.

'Oh, it was my own fault, I suppose. I had this dream all the time I was growing up of one day going out to Australia to find her—big reconciliation scene. When I finally went, taking a year out before university, it was a complete non-event. To start with, there were four little Brumbys. Not so little either—the eldest was ten. They were a big, noisy, close-knit mob, enjoying life, very laid-back. I was critical, bored and intolerant. I couldn't accept that my mother really wanted to be part of it. God, I can't believe how crass I was.' She shook her head, her mouth tight, carried back even after all this time to that misery of separateness and arrogance and baffled need.

'How long were you there?'

'Three months. I hated every moment of it. I know I was too ready to find fault but it was a pretty one-horse place. I kept hoping that there'd be some point of contact with my mother, but in the end I came to the obvious conclusion—she didn't actually like me and couldn't wait for me to take myself off again.'

'You would remind her too much of your father. Do you still live with him?' Mike asked.

'I hardly ever see him now. Even when I was growing up I went mainly to Grianan—I was mad about the place in those days. Sometimes I came here after Teddy had retired and he and Aunt Ursula were living here all the time, but Grianan was my great love.'

'Has the family owned it for long?'

'It was built by my great-grandfather. Janey inherited it because she was the eldest and unmarried and because she had looked after my grandfather when he became crippled with arthritis.'

'And now she runs it as a hotel?'

'After a fashion.' Sally grinned fleetingly to think of Janey's highly individual style of doing things. 'I'm going to help her for the season.' Beyond that she could not look, and perhaps her tone said so for Mike asked no more questions.

They sat and talked, comparing childhood visits here, finding that much ground each had thought private had in fact been shared. They talked about their travels. Mike had been in Australia too, for a couple of years, and they had both stopped off in Malaysia on the way home, following the same track down the eastern side of the peninsula. Sally, doing sums, decided that he must be in his early forties.

As they talked, the sun moved round till the high screen of Sitkas at their backs left them in chilly shade. Mike had made no reference to time, work or having to get back, and Sally had been content to leave that to him. Now he said, 'Come on, you're shivering,' and rose to his feet, half offering a hand to pull her up. She smiled her thanks but didn't take it. He hates this extraordinary little interlude being over as much as I do, she thought with certainty as in silence she followed him down the slope, ducking under the bushes, catching the springy branches he held back for her, jumping the drainage channel onto the track where the pick-up was waiting.

'Like a lift home?' Mike offered formally.

Sally hesitated. She wanted, most simply, to go on being with him. But sitting beside him in the pick-up, heading towards his home, perhaps meeting his children in the lane . . . It wouldn't really matter and yet that was his life. This meeting, the amazing simplicity of being with him and talking to him had been perfect in itself. It had been good. She counted herself lucky to have shared those quiet hours with him.

'No, I'll walk back, thanks.'

His hand on the open door of the van, Mike turned and said, 'I'm going out after foxes this evening. Would you like to come?'

Sally was conscious of the beat of her heart. Mike was not going to allow this good thing they had found to vanish.

She hadn't answered but he said, 'I'll come by at about half eight.'

She walked home in a mood of lightness and simplicity. No questions presented themselves. She would just let things be. Which didn't prevent her from singing in the shower, or from putting on her favourite sea-green shirt which matched her eyes.

She had just begun to cook supper when she heard the creak of the gate. Mike stood grinning on the step, in combat jacket and boots, rifle slung over his shoulder. It was less than an hour since they had parted.

'Thought I'd watch you eat your supper.'

Laughter, delight, a feeling of certainty which reason couldn't shake, rose in Sally giddily. 'You idiot. Come in.'

'I knew you'd be pleased,' he said complacently, propping his gun beside the corner cupboard and looking around him. 'Nothing much has changed in here, I see.'

'Isn't it a nightmare?' But in this mood of carefree happiness the words were tolerant, benevolent even. 'Ursula really did go over the top. Look at this Jemima Puddle-Duck kitchen timer.'

'Dear old Ursula, how she loved all this kitsch. I've always thought it was good of Janey not to sweep it all away.'

Probably didn't have time, Sally thought. 'Would you like some supper? I was just about to make an omelette.'

'Thanks, but I've had something.'

'Then would you like coffee, or a drink?'

'A beer?'

'Now that I didn't bring.'

'Coffee then, thanks. Is that all you're proposing to eat?'

Oh, man, do you think I can concentrate on food?

'Is shooting foxes part of your conservation role?' Sally enquired, as they sat at Ursula's tricky table where unwary thighs tended to jam painfully under pine scrolls and twirls.

'Don't give me a hard time. It's a question of choosing which predators you want to encourage. Or balancing the numbers of predators so that they all get their share. If the foxes take all the food there'll be nothing left for the kestrels or peregrines. And keeping the numbers down stops the farmers muttering about losing lambs. It's part of the job for me. Does the idea bother you?'

'No, I was brought up on all that in Glen Ellig.'

The Edalmere foxes were safe enough that night. Though Mike led the way to a bank where he knew a vixen had cubs and they dutifully lay waiting in silence for signs of activity, Sally thought that if Mike's mind was as far as hers from the job in hand his reactions would be too slow for even the most unwary target to be in danger.

When the light had finally gone under the trees they made a move, going down to sit in the dusk on one of the cleared rocky points above the lake. They talked compulsively, luxuriously. Once or twice Sally found herself wanting to move so that her shoulder was against Mike's; a simple instinct, part of the deep closeness of their mood. But each time she checked the impulse. She wanted to change nothing, initiate nothing.

It was hours before they stirred and headed slowly back along the lane. They came to a halt at the bottom of the cottage drive.

'Smell that hawthorn,' Mike said. Letting the heady scent wash over her, Sally knew she would never be free of the associations of this moment.

Apart from pulling her up from the beck's edge this afternoon Mike hadn't touched her yet. She didn't know if he would touch her now and found that she was ready to accept whatever choice he made. None of the usual questions which are part of any new encounter, especially one charged with such powerful mutual attraction as this one, seemed to exist. There was only acceptance and a great contentment.

'I'd better walk you to your door.'

A few more moments together in the cool early darkness, standing by the little iron gate—and suddenly the conventions came pushing in.

'I shouldn't really ask you in for coffee, should I?' she said, intending the words to be light and matter-of-fact but merely sounding awkward. 'Your home territory.' She had wanted him to know that she respected it but was afraid she had struck a clumsy and false note.

But Mike understood. 'Thanks for that,' he said and bent his head to give her two or three swift little kisses down cheek and jaw. The minutest pause, a similar light kiss on her lips, and he had turned, going down the slope with his rapid long-legged stride, leaving Sally—mature, experienced, almost married—as vividly conscious of the touch of his lips as if no one had ever kissed her in her life before. The tingle of it spread through her veins, unquestionably delicious and glorious.

# CHAPTER TWO

A HIGH FLUTING SOUND penetrated Sally's uneasy dawn sleep. Some wretched bird. White light glared through the unlined curtains. The insistent sound came again. Whistling. In one leap she was out of bed, yanking aside the curtain. Standing against the tree across the roughly mown grass, gun slung on shoulder, grinning at her cheerfully was Mike.

There was a brief fierce tussle with the sticking window. 'What *do* you think you're doing, you madman?'

'Get the kettle on, woman, stop wasting time.' He was gone, heading round to the door.

Sally swore to herself, banging a brush at her rough hair, grabbing up a frilly dressing gown she'd only packed because it was so light. Trousseau gear, she remembered, and for the first time there was no pain in the reminder.

'Where's the coffee then?' Mike demanded, coming in larger than life, bringing with him a waft of crisp dawn air and a male smell of hill clothes and gun oil which was headily evocative to Sally. Below the immediate pleasure of seeing him she felt the stir of a new eagerness for the life she was returning to. With an effort she made herself turn away to fill the kettle.

'Are you going out after that vixen again?'

'Been up there already. No sign of her.'

'Good.'

He laughed. 'Yes, I can't say I'm in killing mode myself this morning. I only went out because I was having trouble sleeping. The cat was a bit startled to meet me as he was coming in.'

'I'm not surprised.'

In the fussy kitchen they sat leaning forward across the table, drinking each other in with eyes, words and nerve ends. Once when Sally got up to give him more coffee Mike put his arm round her, comfortably, naturally, not drawing her towards him. That feels so normal, she thought, leaning lightly back against his arm for a few moments as they talked. In the instant that her muscles began to take her weight again she felt his arm start to withdraw as though their brains were one. The need for touch had been acknowledged, but they had agreed they were not yet committed to it. Perhaps would not be. Sally was almost sure Mike had made his decision on that.

Ursula's maddening cuckoo burst from his little door and yelled at them. 'He might end up sorry I brought my gun,' Mike said. It was his only reference to time. When he got up to go Sally made no protest or comment. But when he stood below her on the steps to say goodbye, their faces level, she felt small and cold.

'I'll come this evening,' he said. The warmth of the relief which swept her shook her. It was a long time since physical reactions had been so emphatic.

In memory the day was a blur of peace and brightness. Sally took her breakfast through to the sitting room where the sun was warm at the big window. Then with a new urge for space and simplicity, which she knew went a lot deeper than improving the view, she began to strip away the swathing loops of net. It was a satisfying exercise, freeing every window from its shroud. Then, enjoying the new feeling of space and light, she made fresh coffee and went back to the sitting-room window.

The marvellous view from it tempted her to drive down to Windermere. She didn't want to explore round the lake where Mike might be working. If she had not been in such an addled state she would have known perfectly well what she would find in the little town, plastered with signs and choked with visitors.

In her mood of large goodwill, however, she was prepared to accept it all, ambling and shopping with a mindless indifference to the commercialism and the crowds, and she drove home contentedly with the car filled with the smell of new bread, planning to have lunch and then catch up on some sleep.

She had just tipped her shopping out onto the kitchen table when she heard the gate screech. Her heart leapt into her throat. It can't be, you fool.

The door opened and Mike's head came round it. 'That looks promising. I was about to make myself a sandwich when it occurred to me I might do better here.'

Where was his wife? Sally didn't ask. The children presumably were at school. 'What a chancer. Still, it'll stretch to two, I suppose.'

She carried the tray into the sitting room. His reaction didn't disappoint her. 'You've let in the light. What a difference. Poor old Ursula and her frills. I could never work out who she thought could see in. This house can't be overlooked from anywhere.'

'Not overrun with neighbours, certainly. Apart from you, nothing nearer than those new bungalows at the foot of the lake. Wasn't that ground part of the farm?'

'It was. I sold the plots a couple of years ago. Needed some cash.'

'And who lives there?'

'One young family, but the rest are retired couples.'

He didn't stay long—he said he had to meet someone from the National Trust that afternoon—but as he left he told her, 'Nine o'clock.' Sally felt so high on the promise of those brief words that she threw the dishes into the sink and took off up the path to the fell.

She was less fit than she'd thought and her thighs were aching and her knees trembling when she reached the ridge. But it was worth it. She had been in the south too long, she thought, gazing with delight at the high ramparts of Helvellyn away beyond the pass. And soon she'd be in Glen Ellig, the landscape that truly moved her.

She had barely got back to the cottage and was running water to wash up, missing the sound of the gate, when a rap at the door made her heartbeat accelerate. It couldn't possibly be Mike this time—could it?

A tall, white-haired female stood there, tubular in baggy tweed skirt with a bulge at each knee and a dated quilted jacket.

'Elsa Callander,' she announced in those ringing tones which imply that no further introduction can be needed. 'Heard in the village you were here. Old friend of Teddy and Ursula's.'

'How do you do? Won't you come in?' Sally asked, wondering as she spoke what sort of inexorable conditioning makes us incapable of saying, 'I don't care who you are—go away.'

Elsa Callander was not a kitchen-table sort of visitor. In the sitting room she lowered herself without enthusiasm into one of the rocking chairs which flanked the fireplace.

Sally went back to the kitchen to scrounge round crossly for something to offer by way of afternoon tea and realised she was going to have to sacrifice her breakfast croissants.

They conversed: 'Of course Ursula was so thankful to have me on hand for company. Someone she could *talk* to, you know. It makes all the difference, doesn't it? There are so few people of our sort here.'

Sally felt a fierce resistance to the prospect of her referring to the Danahers. To Mike's wife. It was vital to learn nothing. They passed safely on to Aunt Janey.

'Naturally, one can't blame her for wanting to do absolutely *nothing* when she's here. Hotel life must be so demanding.' Good for Aunt Janey.

'And I gather you have some frightfully high-powered job. I do admire all you girls so much. And I do understand that you must have found it very difficult to get away . . .' To visit your aunt, ill and suffering, widowed and alone.

'So sad this delightful little house should lie empty. All the Beatrix Potter memorabilia, an amazing collection. It must be quite valuable.' She clearly hated it. 'Our dining circle gets ever smaller, alas. Do come and see us, won't you, while you're here? The second bungalow from this end. Now, how long will you be staying?'

Christ, she's getting her diary out, Sally realised with horror. The thought of missing Mike if he found time to come made her ruthless. 'I'm really not sure but I'm afraid I'm here to escape rather.' Automatically wrapping it up in her guest's language. 'Things have been rather difficult lately'—a pretty piece of understatement—'and I was just planning to be thoroughly lazy. It's very kind of you but I'm sure you'll understand . . .'

Sally was pottering about doing her make-up, not impressed by the effect the wind this afternoon had had on her unquellable hair, when a tiny sound penetrated her happy anticipation. A sound she didn't want to recognise or accept. She turned, brush in hand, to stare at the window, every atom of her rebelling at the sight of the first needle-fine streaks. But rain had been threatening all day; she had just been too besotted to relate it to herself and Mike.

He wouldn't come. He couldn't come. No one went out to shoot foxes in the rain. How could such an improbable excuse be offered or accepted? The branch of an unpruned japonica tapped the pane against a sky much darker than it had been this time yesterday evening. Yesterday, when she had first met Mike. That couldn't be only yesterday.

It was nearly ten when he came and this time she couldn't resist asking, 'But what are you meant to be doing?'

'Oh, I come and go, you know. It's a pretty flexible job.' But he didn't enlarge on it, and Sally asked no more.

For the first time the ease between them was not complete. Perhaps it was because that doubt still hung between them, perhaps because questions were beginning to nudge closer. It was Sally who asked, 'Would you hate walking in the rain?'

'I could stand it,' was all Mike said, but she sensed his relief as they went out into the soft air, rich with garden scents against the ever-present background of spruce and pine. The thin rain barely reached them as they went in silence along the track.

Then Mike stopped and with one firm sweep of his arm drew Sally against him, and she responded as readily as a dancer, as though at that exact moment her body too had shared the same need. They stood close and still, their bodies fitting against each other with an aptness that seemed utterly familiar; stood for long, silent moments of intense awareness and strange peace.

He didn't kiss her, simply held her for unmeasured moments. Then, by a decision transmitted from each to the other, but coming from whom neither of them could have said, they moved on—but this time Mike's arm stayed round her.

When they reached the cottage again Sally knew he would come in. They went through to the sitting room, taking a bottle of wine and a couple of cans of beer.

'Good, I'd hoped you'd remember those,' Mike said, a remark Sally thought would repay examination later.

When they lit the mock-coal fire the room seemed suddenly normal, welcoming, theirs. And when Sally was about to sit down Mike said,

'Not near enough,' and reaching a long arm pulled her chair close to his.

'So what was wrong with Reading?'

The question cut across their easy inconsequential talk and Sally felt her head jerk round and knew she had given herself away.

'We've talked about big chunks of our lives but that's one that's been left out.'

'Reading, well, how shall I put it?—a settled, conventional, achieving existence with excellent prospects which came to pieces in my hands.' She did her best to speak lightly but heard the effort in her voice, as though she was having trouble with her breathing. She had not talked of this to anyone. 'The best-laid plans . . .' She could not go on.

Mike's hand, long and brown, with darker freckles across the back, its palm leathery smooth with manual work, took hers, folded it in his. 'Your job was there?'

'Yes, with Sieber Research, just outside Reading.'

'How long were you there?'

'Six years. I went in as a junior administrative officer—did business studies at university, nothing intellectual—then a couple of years ago I landed the senior admin post. Glorified PA, really.'

'Only a lot better paid.'

'Indeed.' Perhaps it was easier after all to keep to the mundane for a while. 'It was like belonging to a big club. Everything's laid on—swimming pool, squash, badminton, tennis, gym. Very good food, and nowhere else near enough to go for lunch anyway. It all tended to get a bit incestuous, I suppose. You could have an entire social life without ever moving outside the Sieber net.'

Mike said nothing, stretching out his long legs to the fire.

'I met someone. Well, I'd known him vaguely for some time. He was a research chemist, one of a very elite crew. He was involved in a major presentation I was doing; we had to work together quite a lot . . .' Her voice trailed away. This was so far from what she wanted to say, what she needed Mike to know.

'What happened, Sally?' His keen narrow face looked compassionate, his striking, clear hazel eyes intent and perceptive. 'What went wrong?'

'He was divorced.' She spoke rapidly now. 'That all happened three years ago—well in the past. We started going out together about a year ago, more now. It all seemed so good, lots of things we liked doing together. We got engaged last summer. We were going to be married in February, then somehow—I can't describe it—the glow seemed to fade. Julian was suddenly busier, had less time to spend with me and it all just fell flat. There was nothing more tangible to it than that.'

Mike put an arm round her shoulders. Sally felt reassurance and comfort flow into her. 'The thing was,' she said baldly, 'he'd started seeing his ex-wife again. He'd had to go and look at some problem with the house—and they'd just—well, he'd gone on going to see her—and then he—'

'Decided he wanted to go back to her?'

Sally nodded unaware that she was clutching his hand tightly.

'You poor girl.'

'The worst part was,' she said, having difficulty with her voice again, but determined to get this into the open at last, 'he was so good about it. He even waited to tell me, when it was perfectly clear that he couldn't live without Mandy, until after Christmas, so that he wouldn't spoil the holiday for me. Can you imagine anything more ludicrous? How decent can you get?'

'He must have been a bit out of touch with reality.' A note of anger in Mike's voice was welcome balm.

'Oh, completely. He was a well-meaning dreamer. He genuinely considered sticking to me and trying to make things work. Only, when he finally saw that wasn't a good idea—presumably Mandy was able to help him there—I decided that for once I'd put up a fight and not be turned down. Only, you see, Julian was an essentially honest person, and when I demanded to know why he was going back to Mandy and what was wrong with me, he told me. He preferred her in bed. There's not a great deal you can say to that.'

'Oh, Sally.' Mike's arm tightened round her.

'Well, that was it. Nothing to fight about.' Her voice wavered and she closed her eyes tightly. 'Anyway, I decided it would all be too difficult staying on at Sieber and of course he couldn't leave. I thought I could find another job in the area. All my friends were there. But they weren't, really. They were all tied up with Sieber and basically I'd left the club. It all just fizzled out naturally. My fault as much as anyone's, because I wanted to be on my own. What a pathetic tale.'

She lifted their linked hands and pressed her forehead against them, closing her eyes, letting the present seep back.

'And you're going back to Scotland to live?'

'I'm not sure that I'd have managed to haul myself out of that mess on my own initiative,' she confessed. 'But just when it was beginning to dawn on me that I was in trouble Aunt Janey wrote and asked if I'd consider helping her this summer. It seemed the obvious answer; a summer at Grianan won't leave me much time to feel sorry for myself. After that—well, to be honest, I don't have the faintest idea.'

'You don't have to yet, do you? Isn't that the point? You'll have the breathing space you need.'

If life with Aunt Janey could ever be called a breathing space. And then there were the other questions she had been pushing away. How to tell Janey what had happened? She had never explained and her aunt had never asked. Would Janey think she had been blind and naive about Julian, cowardly about throwing up her job so readily? Whenever she thought of Janey, Sally found she was measuring herself once more against the standards Janey had set, and it felt as though she was returning to Grianan with remarkably little to show for the years she had been away.

No whistling outside the window the next morning. Sally slept on undisturbed. It had been very late when Mike left, with one comprehensive hug and not even the light little kisses of the previous evening.

Sally lay relaxed and peaceful. She felt as though the dark nightmare of helpless rejection, the humiliation and acute sense of isolation had stopped pressing in upon her and could be dealt with.

Just talking to someone. That was all it had taken. Or just talking to Mike. Beneath the tough exterior, the fitness and energy, there was a capacity for understanding and sympathy which she trusted implicitly. How incredible this meeting had been; the instant pleasure and confidence in each other, then the tacit shared instinct to let it be simple, unstated, perfect in its own right.

She was still drifting round eating muesli and banana when the sound of a hoarsely protesting engine grinding up the short drive shattered the silence and her mood of contentment. Going frowning to the door, Sally was in time to retrieve a note from under a stone on the doormat before the squat, glowering bulk of Garth Jackson came rolling towards the steps.

'The wife said were you wanting anything?'

'No, everything's fine, thank you,' Sally assured him with the best smile she could manage, burning to read her note.

'I'd best be doing that grass round the back then. Been waiting for a while, has that.'

'Oh, no, please don't bother. I'm sure it's fine. I really wanted—' Peace and quiet, you moronic troglodyte.

Garth Jackson, a man unshakably convinced that no one else knew anything about anything, had already gone to drag a Flymo out of his sagging rust-eaten van.

You pig-headed creature, Sally fumed, recognising defeat and going back into the house. Outside the Flymo coughed and roared into life. The quality of life at the cottage had suddenly deteriorated. She pulled the note from her pocket.

'Come and build bridges.' Did that have any particular meaning? Whether or not, she would go.

Leaving everything as it was, and not bothering to mention to a deafened and engrossed Garth that she was going, Sally fled down the drive with a lovely feeling of irresponsibility and escape.

Mike was not working below the waterfall where she had expected to find him, but she knew all she had to do was go on. He was working on a footbridge a few yards up a beck which the track crossed by a shallow ford. Where the stream ran out into the lake there was a tiny triangular sandy beach, on either side of which the conifers had been felled, leaving grassy banks. Seeing Sally, Mike came to meet her, lively open pleasure on his face.

'So you finally woke up?' He scooped her into a rough, one-armed hug, turning to walk with her, and it struck Sally that it was the sort of welcome a man would give to someone who was part of his life. That felt very good.

'I certainly did a bit more sleeping than the night before.'

Mike turned to face her, took her hands and held them wide as he studied her, smiling. 'It's been a long, slow morning.'

He was just finishing the rail of the bridge, and when that was done they turned their attention to the beck above it, its narrow, deep-cut course clogged in several places by mats of tangled branches, twigs and surface rubbish which winter spates had carried down. They worked away unhurriedly, talking or not as they felt like it. It was peaceful, wet, messy work with satisfying visible results, cool at first in the leafy shade, then surprisingly warm as the sun reached round into their sheltered bay. She felt as though she'd known Mike for ever.

'How about some lunch, or is breakfast still too near for you?'

'Cheek. Come back to the cottage—oh no, don't. Garth is scowling and tearing at the grass.'

'Jackson? Oh, to hell with that.' He turned to the pick-up as he spoke, and produced sausage rolls and apples and a pile of ham sandwiches. Sally saw a sudden unwanted picture of hands making them for him, his wife's hands, the wife they never mentioned and whom it was important to keep shadowy and unreal.

'Hope you like mustard. I'd slapped it on before I thought about it.' Mike was propping up the flask against a rock as he spoke and Sally was glad he wouldn't see the absurd relief on her face. There was masses of stuff here, she now realised. He had made this lunch for them both. They were safe for a little longer in their fragile private enclave.

In all Mike told her on that quiet afternoon she understood his love for the place. He was fascinated by its history and geology, its wildlife and ecology and she saw his passion for this patch of ground and his profound sense of belonging to it. In boyhood he had never been able to spend enough time here but no one else in his family had shared his feelings. When his father died there had been no contest about ownership of the farm. His younger brother had gone back to Ireland, and their mother had gone with him.

'They used to come over fairly regularly, but they could never find much to do here.' His face was sombre. 'Anyway,' he went on, 'my mother has a fairly serious heart condition these days and probably won't leave home again. We'll have to go and see her in future.'

'We'. The word he had never used. The word Sally knew could only be ignored for a brief respite.

Waking knowing that someone was in the room, yet knowing in the same moment that there was no reason to be afraid. Dimmest of grey light, the tall shape of Mike beside the bed.

'Thought you'd be sure to hear me in the kitchen.' A clink as mugs went down on glass-covered pine. 'Here, prop yourself up on this.' He shoved a cushion behind the pillows, laughing at her joyful surprise.

He settled comfortably on the bed, propping an arm across her, very much at ease. But in spite of her delight at seeing him there, she took it for granted that as before they would only talk, intimate and absorbed and close.

After the perfect hours yesterday, the peaceful work and leisurely talk, she had let Mike go home without her and had sat on for a while alone, savouring the contentment of the day in a mood of tranquil acquiescence. Mike had been booked to give a talk to a Saga holiday group in Keswick, and knowing she wouldn't see him that evening she had wandered home as the warmth died from the day, at peace as she had not been for many months.

So now she was breathless with surprise when Mike slid his hands behind her shoulders and began to kiss her as though he meant it.

He laid her back eventually against the pillows, keeping his arms round her and smiled at her in the growing light.

Sally gazed up at him. Nothing had ever felt so right. He bent his head to hers again. He was so sure, so much at ease, that it seemed at once incredibly exciting and the most natural thing in the world to be held and caressed by him. She felt her unsure, tight-clamped body melt and clamour as it had not done for far too long.

Mike knew. He knew, precisely, everything she was feeling. And he understood her sharp involuntary exclamation of loss as he withdrew his arms and stood up.

'It's all right, I'm here. I'm here. Damned boots, not the gear in which to go a-wooing. And I think we'll have those mugs out of the danger zone.'

She waited, this trivia, which she knew was meant to reassure her, hardly reaching her, trying to hold onto the sensations he had aroused, dreading the return of doubt and tension. She wanted this to be so good for him—but Julian hadn't found it good enough.

'I've forgotten how,' she gasped absurdly, out of her distress, panic tightening her stomach like cramp.

'Well, I haven't,' Mike said cheerfully, sliding in beside her and wrapping her up against him with a sort of robust matter-of-factness that did her a lot of good. 'We'll get rid of this for a start.' And he stripped away her nightdress deftly, making her feel as light as a doll when he lifted her with one arm.

'There that's better.' And then he said no more, his hands beginning to move over her body, gently exploring or, as it seemed to Sally as she gradually relaxed, rediscovering what he had always known.

'Beautiful,' he breathed, 'God, so beautiful,' as he slid into her.

And later, 'That bastard Justin, Julian, whatever he was called, must have been out of his mind . . .'

Words to lock away. But Sally knew she didn't need them. Her body had not forgotten what to do, but at the same time it had discovered a satisfaction she had never imagined.

'I'll never be able to think of this house in the same way again, that's for sure,' Mike remarked as he swiftly dressed, sounding exuberant and looking remarkably full of energy.

'You look a very relaxed lady,' he commented with amusement, gazing down at her. Then he stooped to take her face in his hands and kiss her lightly. 'Stay there, have a little kip. And don't forget, you are a lovely, lovely woman.'

The day was warm, warm enough to take a rug and lie out on the sweet-smelling pale mown grass. In a glow of indolent euphoria Sally dozed and dreamed the hours away. Her body felt light, renewed, coordinated. More importantly, she felt sure of herself in some deep fundamental way that was new to her.

There could be no relationship. By his restraint, by what he very gently wasn't saying, Mike had made that clear and Sally respected him for it. She closed her mind to the first bite of anguish that something like this should exist, all of it—Mike, this place, the chemistry between them—and not be for her. Yet part of her wanted it to be this way. She knew she wasn't ready for serious involvement with anyone; she felt too vulnerable and fearful. Instantaneous and powerful though the feeling between them had been, there had all along been a strong sense of boundaries which would not be crossed. Mike wasn't free. The very absence of discussion about what they were doing, and of any attempt to justify it, was revealing in itself. They had simply found something marvellous, each sure of the other's reaction, and they wanted to keep it happy and uncomplicated if they could. Mike would not hurt her; instead he had given her a delight she had thought might never be there for her again. What more could she ask?

And how she shrank from doing harm in his life. She had asked no questions about it, been careful to make no references that would even touch upon it. She did not pretend she had not taken something which didn't belong to her, but she had allowed that to be Mike's decision and felt no regret. This was something outside real life, outside time.

The hours, the days and the sequence of Mike's snatched visits blurred, never later to be disentangled in her mind. There was an early morning walk which took them right round the western shore of the lake; there was a rainy afternoon when she had not expected him and they made love with the squalls pelting and drumming against the window, and Mike said, 'It won't be quite so easy to see you for the next day or two. Weekend and all that.'

His voice was brusque. Time was no longer theirs.

'I'll go,' she said, leaping over all the implications and options.

'I won't let you,' he said instantly and fiercely, gripping her tightly, and she needed no clearer statement of how he felt. But when he released her, turning on his back and throwing an arm up behind his head, she knew he was quite aware that his instinctive reaction could mean nothing.

'You understand, don't you?' he said, in a tight voice after a pause. It wasn't a question. 'I don't need to spell it out.'

'We've both always known.'

'I don't want to spoil this place for you. I'd hate to think you felt you couldn't come back because of what's happened between us. This is part of your life, a place you care about.'

'I'll come back.' Impossible to imagine.

'I'll look out for a red Renault coming along the lane.'

Sally nodded, smiling, unable to speak.

'You've always been so discreet. You've never asked a single question. I'm so grateful to you for that.' His voice was thick, emotion almost getting the better of him. 'And I can't give you a damn thing.'

'You know what you've given me,' she said steadily.

'Is that what you feel? Is that what you'll take away with you?' She knew that he had accepted that she must go, but that made it very near and real.

'Yes. You've put me together again.'

He turned to her, seizing her roughly, crushing her to him. 'You know what this has meant to me, don't you? I don't want you wondering later. I want you to be sure that it's been really important.'

But when after a quick hug he released her, tossing back the duvet, leaping out of bed resolutely, all her good sense and discipline fled.

'Mike—' She sat up, arms out, heard the threat of tears in her voice.

He leaned down to her, his face tight with pain. 'Sally, come on, we mustn't get—we must be—' He couldn't find the words, but already his urgent appeal had reached her. She hunted through her anguish for some words that would do no damage.

'You've even reconciled me to Aunt Ursula's silly house.'

Banal, but he accepted it, letting it return them to ordinary things. 'And what would she think if she could see you now?'

Before he went he took her hands for one silent moment, vibrant with all the things they mustn't say, things foregone, things never claimed. It was too late now. Sally looked up at him. His eyes thanked her, read the ache of loss in hers and winced at it.

Then his steps going away. The house an empty drum again.

# CHAPTER THREE

A T FIVE THIRTY Sally gave up trying to sleep and, feeling numb and hollow, got up and went mechanically through the chores of packing and tidying, refusing to let pain penetrate as she walked out of the cottage which had become such a different place for her now. Would she ever be able to come back? He had been adamant that she must not lose this place because of him. But come and do what? Sit in the cottage, walk the fells, avoiding their shared places, alone, remembering?

The remorseless traffic of the A74, pelting the slush of a grey rainy day across her windscreen, pushing along too fast for the visibility, focused her mind, however disagreeably. Then it was just numb miles, automatic actions.

Only as she ran into Muirend some time midmorning did practical considerations re-emerge. God, she hadn't even let them know she was coming today. Aunt Janey was not a person you just landed on to suit your own timetable. And what excuse was there not to have done so? She shook her head angrily, as if to dislodge the guilty reminders, feeling Grianan reaching forward with its expected standards, its work ethic, its paramount law of guests first, no matter what.

The road was climbing. This was a wider, higher landscape than the Lakeland one, its lines more sweeping, its beauty spare and challenging. Sally felt the old excitement rise in response, yet at the same time a resistance build to the moment of arriving. It was four years since she had last visited Grianan. In this mood of raw loneliness, the immediate loss of what she had found with Mike sharper now than the misery of Julian's rejection and the debacle of unravelling wedding plans and returning presents and facing the world as a single (unwanted) person again, Grianan seemed suddenly the last place she wanted to be. There would be Janey's discerning eyes to face, not only with all that fiasco still to explain, but knowing that yesterday she, Sally, had been in bed with the husband of their Edalmere neighbour, whom Janey undoubtedly knew. Put like that, the magical happiness with Mike, kept till now so carefully separate and intact, was abruptly brought into the light of everyday social reality.

Sally drove grimly on.

Then an unexpected thing happened. She turned into the climbing drive onto the wide shelf where the square, stone house stared out across the glen. Leaving everything in the car, she crossed the gravel to the two semicircular stone steps which her feet took with an automatic hop and jump. The weight of the heavy door as she twisted the square brass handle was utterly accustomed. And in that instant the harried vulnerable present fell away. The smell of childhood met and engulfed her. Boots and washed stone, fires of birch and fir, beeswax mixed with turpentine, tweed, fifty-year-old carpet, Aunt Janey's horrible cat.

And Sally knew that this was the only place where she could possibly have come, to deal with the new pain and the old. She stood in the quiet, feeling her tense muscles relax. For this moment, before anyone knew she was here, she could luxuriate in the sensation of absolute belonging.

The door from the dining room opened. 'Sally! *What* a lovely surprise! Maureen insisted she'd heard a car but of course I thought she just wanted me out of the kitchen as usual—'

Aunt Janey, brown face creased into her big grin, thick grey hair curling as bouncily as Sally's own, denim skirt stretched over solid hips, bare legs already tanned, broad feet in basket-like sandals. Sally felt an impulse to hug her, saw her aunt check her own impulse to do the same, and understood that hesitation with a piercing new clarity. She had rebuffed such gestures in the years when she had turned her back on the family, and Janey had been careful to respect her wishes.

'Hello, Aunt Janey.' She felt wooden, uncertain, caught unexpectedly in a storm of conflicting emotions and associations.

'Darling, darling Sally. How wonderful it is to see you again.'

'I should have phoned. I'm sorry.'

'You're here, that's all that matters. I've been so looking forward to it.' Her pleasure was warm and open, her eyes smiling, drinking in every detail of Sally's appearance. 'Coffee before we bring in your things? You must have set off very early.'

Dawn light in the little room. Remembering the dawn when Mike had first come in . . .

'Pretty early.' Sally found she had to clear her throat. 'Yes, coffee would be good, thanks.' And on a long sigh, 'It's lovely to be back.'

She meant it. This was refuge; this was home.

Janey beamed at her in pleasure. 'How good to hear you say that.'

'I mean it,' Sally said, and, with a loving instinct too long buried, stepped forward quickly to wrap her arms round that sturdy body and kiss the cheek soft as an overwintered apple. Janey responded with a vigour that squeezed the breath out of her niece.

'Oh, dear Sally,' she said, and Sally was astonished to hear a huskiness in her voice. 'Now, come along and we'll organise that coffee.'

In the dining room a small dark woman was banging down a tray of silver. 'I knew fine I'd heard a car,' she said by way of greeting.

'Yes, how very clever of you. Bring some coffee to the sitting room for us, would you, Maureen?'

'Well, Sally, and how are you? Are the phones not working down in England then?'

'Mellowing with the years, I see,' Sally remarked, laughing at her.

'Am I to make this coffee before I get my silver away?' Maureen demanded pettishly of Janey.

'Oh, don't be such a pain,' Janey replied equably. 'And fresh coffee, please, not what's left over from filling the flasks.'

'Would I do that?' asked Maureen affrontedly, winking at Sally.

Sally laughed, her spirits lifting. Aunt Janey and Maureen locked in combat was part of the very air of Grianan. All absolutely normal, yet she sensed something special about her welcome today. Not least because there was Janey stopping in the middle of the morning to drink coffee, *sitting down*, in her private sanctum, a small study with French windows opening onto a paved, sheltered angle where there were always cuttings taking root and pot plants hardening off.

The room itself, ferociously guarded from guests, was a cavern of piled clutter, redolent of Janey's thin black cigars, woodsmoke and the huge grey Persian cat which rose in wrath to puff itself out to twice its size at the sight of an old enemy before bounding away over a row of budding geraniums. Here Janey read Dickens and Trollope, drank gin and mixed and listened to Mahler and Wagner, watched rugby, wrote acid letters to tradesmen and kept her collection of Victorian cookery and household books.

'Now, is this coffee going to be drinkable?' she asked before Maureen was well out of the room, adding with her gruff laugh when the door had banged, 'I'm surprised she didn't tell me to make it myself. She must be pleased to see you, Sally.'

'I don't know how she puts up with you.'

'Can't think what you mean. No cook was ever better treated. Now'—all of Sally's early life in that 'now' of her Aunt Janey—'about your room. Your old one is so tiny that I wondered if you would prefer a more grown-up one now. Then I thought how chilling it might be to find yourself moved without being asked. I simply didn't know what you'd like, so Connie got two rooms ready.'

Sally felt touched and grateful to think of her aunt anxiously tossing the decision back and forth. It was so unlike her to hesitate over such considerations. And Sally was even more startled to realise that Janey was actually prepared to give up a letting bedroom. Her return must have mattered to Janey, she thought with genuine surprise.

'Come and see what you think.'

Janey had chosen for her the old west dressing room, a very popular room. White-panelled, with windows on two sides, with its elegant curved French bed and the kingwood bureau inlaid with olive and satinwood which was one of the special pieces in the house, it was indeed a grown-up room.

'Don't say anything yet,' Janey ordered as Sally turned to her helplessly.

Back they went to the door on the main landing which opened onto a narrow staircase.

At the top of the stairs long attic rooms on either side held the usual miscellany of broken lamps, rejected furniture, old files and cashbooks, trunks, cardboard boxes and Christmas decorations. Straight ahead opened a slit of a room high above the front door, its casement window wide, Janey style, to the cool damp morning. The view clear across Drumveyn to Ben Breac framed by that long window still made Sally catch her breath in delight. The pink cream-sprigged wallpaper was faded, the pattern of the counterpane almost invisible, but the Pooh-sticks rug was still there, washed almost white, the collection of carved animals on the shelf, the well-read books. Memories poured back—first evenings of school holidays, the dread that any detail would be changed, the relief when everything was exactly the same, the joy of gulping in the sweet glen air after the hours in the train, the wild, choking, almost unbearable thankfulness to be here again, safe.

'I don't think I feel very grown-up after all,' Sally said unsteadily, and Janey gave her a quick look then patted her arm with her hard-working, dirt-ingrained hand.

'Then we'll fetch your things,' was all her aunt said, but Sally knew she was pleased.

'I'll fetch them.' Janey hadn't charged up the stairs in quite her remembered style, Sally had noted. 'And then would you mind very much if I had a sleep?'

Sleep, at Grianan, in the *daytime*? But either Janey had grown more tolerant or Sally looked worse than she knew, for Janey only said, 'Come down whenever you like. Just do whatever you want to do, little Sally—I mean it.'

Sounds woke her. Car wheels on the gravel, car doors slamming, feet scrunching. Around her the house itself felt different, peopled, living.

Mike. Instant waking happiness to think of him, followed by the hammerblow of fact. For a moment she lay folded in on herself, not ready yet to grapple with Grianan. Easy as it had been to persuade herself when she was with Mike that because there had been no false hopes there would be no pain, the reality of knowing she would never see him again, that he would never make love to her again, was going to take time to accept. But those few light-filled, floating days without doubt or reserve had been worth it; God, they had been worth it.

Presently she turned on her back and pulled herself up on her pillows, letting her eyes rove from one well-loved object to the next, consciously trying to divert her thoughts. How far she had come from that passionate child's love for this place. What a wedge she had deliberately driven between Janey and herself over the years. That naively eager journey to Australia had done the damage. After that disaster she had been bitterly determined to establish her own independent life, to achieve a security which no one else's failure in love or understanding could damage. She had worked hard at university, got a good degree and landed the excellent job at Sieber Research with a defiant, almost vengeful satisfaction, then had set about establishing for herself a settled, comfortable lifestyle which would have suited a fifty-year-old. Julian had been part of that world. She had thought that with him she would be safe, that nothing would ever change.

Groaning, she threw back the duvet. No good lying here and letting those well-worn thoughts take over. Better to go down, face people.

Half past four. Guests coming in from their invigorating outdoor activities, changing their shoes, washing their hands, tidying their hair, hurrying down to sit round the table in the library and help themselves with polite greed to a huge tea of scones, pancakes, homemade jam, heather honey and Maureen's cakes.

Only Connie was about in the kitchen regions, big, slow-moving Connie who did the rooms in the mornings and sometimes stayed on for the afternoon to clean brass and silver.

'Well, it's grand to see you back,' she said comfortably, 'but whatever in the world have you been doing to yourself? You're thin as a rake, lass. I can see that we'll have to feed you up.'

Bless you, Janey, for not saying it. But it occurred to Sally to wonder with a new perception what it cost her blunt, outspoken aunt to refrain from such natural expressions of concern.

'How are you, Connie? And the family?'

'Ach, we're all pretty much the same as we were, I suppose,' Connie said peacefully. 'There's treacle scones over there. I didn't put them all out for their tea. We've only ten in tonight and they've enough to be going on with. You put the kettle on, love, my hands are black.'

Janey's kitchen was not at all the cosy gathering place one might have expected. It had an Aga, certainly, because much of Janey's French-style country cooking demanded long hours in slow ovens, but the rest of it was strictly functional. Even Marchmain the cat was banned.

Sally made tea and buttered the still-warm scones, relishing the comfort of reaching for familiar things in familiar places, then perched in her old spot on the dresser while Connie's podgy grey fingers worked on unhurriedly through the pile of polish-smeared rat-tail spoons.

'So you're to be up for the whole summer. Quite like old times. Miss Buchanan'll be fine and pleased to have you here. She's not as young as she used to be—and that goes for the rest of us, too.'

'Well, we'll see how it goes,' Sally said temperately, conscious of a reluctance to be committed, a resistance to assumptions being made.

'Then back to England, will it be?' Connie asked with an automatic disparagement in her tone of which she was quite unconscious.

'Probably.' But Sally couldn't imagine it. Already her life in Reading seemed utterly unreal. Except that Mike was in England. Oh, for God's sake, she warned herself angrily, don't start thinking like that.

She had opened her jaws to take a bite of fat scone slathered with bramble jelly when the door from the passage opened and a stranger walked quietly in.

He was slightly built, Sally's age or perhaps older, with a thin brown face and smooth dark hair to his collar. He was wearing a faded shirt and well-washed jeans which had been beautifully ironed but showed signs of rough usage. Lowering the scone Sally said hastily, 'Were you looking for tea? It's put out in the library.'

'Not for me, I'm afraid,' he said in a gentle and markedly upper-class English voice, a friendly smile twisting his well-shaped mouth.

'Oh my, that's a good one,' crowed Connie. 'Piers is the gardener, have you no' met him yet?'

'How do you do?' He offered a slim hand, his dark eyes smiling without embarrassment. His lashes were long and soft and sooty black, his teeth very white and even. Wherever had he come from? As he turned to take the mug Connie had quickly filled for him, dirty hands or not, Sally was aware of the contained grace of his movements.

'Any tea in the pot?' Janey came stumping in. 'Sally, you're up. Had a good sleep? I think we've got a rabbit in, Piers, a baby one, by the look of the nibbles on the lettuce. We'll have to check the whole fence again, fearful waste of time. Oh, thanks, that's lovely. Goodness, Connie, you have got on. Are all the punters back?'

Janey had mud on the worn hem of her skirt, a dark ring round her thick calves where the earthy tops of her gumboots had rubbed, and the bright green feathery tips of early fennel in her hand sent out a potent wave of aniseed.

'All except the Ormondes,' Connie replied. 'The rest are at tea.'

Marshalled. Counted. In the right place at the right time. Sally grinned privately.

Janey's stubby hands swiftly buttering a scone for herself, the sight of Connie rubbing away at her spoons, Piers's intriguing and somehow unthreatening presence—all these added up to something Sally knew suddenly she could face after all. She felt calmed, sanguine. It would all lap round her and gradually the destructive threadbare anger over Julian would dissipate and be forgotten, and the newer, simpler pain of missing Mike would be easier to bear, and only the happiness he'd given her would remain.

Connie was bundling up her grimy cloths and carrying a tray of gleaming silver to the sink.

'We'll do those, Connie. You've stayed quite late enough and I'm very grateful. But your family will be clamouring to be fed.'

'Do you want a hand with them, Aunt Janey?' Sally asked as Connie departed.

'Absolutely not, everything's under control. You're not to do a thing tonight, or until you want to. I mean it, no argument—'

The telephone began to ring and Janey broke off to answer it. 'Wretched child!' Aunt Janey exclaimed as she listened to the voice at the other end. Sally noticed Piers's face soften in a sort of resigned affection, though she observed that he carefully did not share his amusement with her. She liked him for that.

'You're not feeling too well? And what precisely am I to understand by that?' Aunt Janey was demanding heatedly. 'I suppose something more attractive than washing my pots has offered itself. Oh, now you're feeling like death? Then do by all means die, but first I should be grateful if you would deliver the cream which you promised to bring up with you. You're not feeling up to that? Naturally not, but please remember, if I hear that you have moved one step outside that house tonight . . .'

Janey and her light touch with her minions. The surprising thing was that they were rash enough to phone in the first place, Sally thought, laughter rising freely for the first time that day.

'These frightful people,' growled Janey, banging down the receiver.

'Do we need the cream for tonight?' Piers asked.

Sally noted the 'we' with interest. Support, involvement?

'Apricot pancakes are fairly meaningless without it. And I've made the compote already. It's shrimp soup too—that needs a good dollop. Damn. Well, nothing for it, I shall have to go down and fetch it. Oh, *miserable* girl, she knows perfectly well it's Maureen's night off.'

'Aunt Janey, I'll go.' Solidarity or not, Sally noticed that Piers wasn't offering. He finished work at five, presumably. She wondered where he was living.

'No, Sally, I won't hear of it. You've only just arrived. You're not to do a thing this evening, I'm quite adamant about that. I shall have plenty of time to get everything done if I go straight away.'

Inevitably, when dinnertime came Sally did the pot-wash. More surprisingly, Piers not only appeared to help her but, in a formal wordless ballet that looked pretty accustomed to Sally, he fed Janey the necessary back-up throughout the meal. No one waited in the dining room. In her unsavoury butcher's apron Janey crashed in and out from time to time, slapping dishes of delectable food on the sideboard. She considered producing good food an everyday skill, not an art form. This could be a delicate tightrope to walk for those guests who came year after year to gourmandise.

The guests helped themselves and cleared the plates with a 'we're family' zeal. If something had to be carved, Janey would sharpen her knife *in situ* with flashing steel and masculine showmanship and, spattered spectacles on the end of her nose, would perform with the skill taught her by Sally's grandfather.

Tonight the haunch of roe with juniper berries required no blade wielding. It was followed by hot cheese soufflé and then coffee and homemade peppermints in the drawing room, the washing machine churning in the kitchen. When all the tidying-up was done, Janey only ever wanted a plate of anything she could shovel in with a fork and tonight Sally felt the same. Two plates of roe, creamed potato and baby beans appeared from the bottom oven of the Aga.

'Doesn't Piers get food?' Sally asked, looking round for him.

'Not mine,' Janey said with one of her snorts of laughter that made you forget she was well into her sixties. 'He's welcome to it, of course, but he's a vegetarian. It must be quite loathsome for him to help dish up cooked creatures. He's so good to help as he does.'

'So who is he?' Sally asked as they carried their plates through to the chilly sitting room. 'Where does he live? How did he turn up here?'

'He's Piers Hinchcliffe.' A slight warning note there that Sally's questions, or her manner of asking them, had not been wholly acceptable.

'And?' Sally persisted nevertheless.

'And he lives in the garden cottage. He came here looking for peace.'

'There must be more to tell than that,' she protested.

'Oh dear, labels,' said Aunt Janey, sounding quite cross. 'Well, he's an organic gardener, and he doesn't like noise or anger or machines. He doesn't accept frameworks of time either, which means I live in a permanent state of guilt because I can't possibly repay him for all the hours he puts in.'

'He doesn't drive?'

'It is a pest up here,' Janey acknowledged.

'And I suppose he hates money too?' Sally immediately regretted the cynicism when Janey fixed her with a cold eye.

'You disappoint me.'

Sally felt a flush come to her cheeks at that long-remembered tart rebuke. Her standards and attitudes would need some overhauling here. How Janey would hate what had happened with Mike. She would feel Sally had abused the freedom to use the cottage. Without realising she was going to do it, Sally reached out a hand to touch Janey's muscular forearm, noticing as she did so how crepy the brown skin had become.

It was an unprecedented form of apology between them, but if Janey was surprised she didn't show it. 'He's naive about money,' she amended, and Sally knew she was making the effort to meet her halfway.

In the pearl-clean early morning the garden cottage looked as simple and neat as a piece of cross-stitch, with its blue slate roof, its central door and two white-painted windows. A strip of gravel along its front wall separated it from mown grass dredged with dew, flanked by symmetrical mounds of rhododendrons covered with fat buds. That was all, and it satisfied Sally as deeply as it always had.

It wasn't like her to be out in the garden at this hour—but she had been harried by restless dreams. Waking to find it was first light, thoughts of that other early morning when Mike had first made love to her, and then of yesterday's bleak departure, had flooded unbearably back. She had felt she needed time to work through them before the day engulfed her.

She had gone to one of her favourite places, climbing the high stile over the deer fence which formed the outer boundary of Grianan and heading up the hill to a high jut of rock overhanging a small cliff. The varied greens of the trees reaching away down the line of the river had become gradually distinguishable as the light grew and warmed. The white froth of wild-cherry blossom, mixed with the pinky fawn of copper beeches in new leaf, dominated the landscape below her.

Thoughts of Mike consumed her. To find something so incredible and know that it was not for her was going to take some getting used to. If he had been free. The vision tortured her with its unattainable simplicity. But men like Mike were never free. They were the natural family men, the providers and protectors.

Coming back slowly to the fence, she had reminded herself that she was grateful for what he had given her. He had made her feel wanted again, whole, normal. Couldn't she just learn to accept it on that level, as some wonderful therapy given to her when the time was right?

'Would you like to come in for coffee?'

Sally jumped. The early morning had seemed so completely hers.

'I startled you, I'm sorry. I've been out seeing if I could spot marauding baby rabbits.'

Piers, smiling, calm, kind, with that freshly laundered look of his in clean jeans and another soft pale shirt. 'Come in. Talk a little.' Was there a sympathetic perceptiveness in his smile or did she just want to see that? Silently Sally followed him.

The cottage was an enormous surprise. Much as she had always loved its simple exterior, she remembered the inside as dark, dingy and ugly, forever connected in her mind with a bad-tempered old gardener who used to shout at his wife.

Now it was bare, clean, light and beautiful, the internal walls removed, the shell taken back to the stone and newly repointed, the wood of doors, window frames, floor and fireplace stripped. There was a futon on the floor, Navajo rugs, stone jars of dried grasses, a long row of books against the wall and what looked like a flute case on the mantelpiece. The fire had been converted to a wood-burning stove.

'How beautiful,' Sally exclaimed, transfixed with delight. 'I used to hate coming in here. How long have you been living in it?'

'Since last summer.'

Almost a year. Had Janey told her about him? Perhaps in one of those letters she had barely had time to read in the preparations for the wedding. The non-wedding.

They sat side by side on the futon with freshly brewed coffee in fine china mugs.

'Will Grianan help you?' Piers asked.

For a moment Sally floundered. The question leapt so many facts which he couldn't know and she couldn't explain. Then she saw that there was no need to explain. He had understood enough to ask the question, and Sally was absolutely sure that Aunt Janey would not have discussed her with him. He simply knew there had been hurt.

'I don't know,' she answered him equally simply.

'It's a good place,' was all he said.

'Has it helped you?'

'More than any place I've ever known.'

'Janey didn't say why I'm here?' she asked.

'No. But she's delighted that you are.'

'She said so?' Sally asked in surprise.

'No,' he repeated, amused.

The room accepted their silence and their thoughts.

'Give it time,' he said gently after a while.

'Yes, I know.' It didn't matter what he knew or guessed; he was right. Walking back to the house Sally felt as though some of his quietness had transferred itself to her.

## CHAPTER FOUR

D ID YOU RUN into the Danahers at all while you were at Edalmere?'
Sally was sitting with Janey on the low stone wall beside the compost heap, trimming a pile of rhubarb. A bright stem landing on the green fans revealed that she was not as ready for the question as she believed. Reaching down to retrieve it she was careful not to let Janey see her face.

'I saw the children in the lane once or twice. And I ran into him working on the new path round the lake.' She had no idea of how impossible she would find it to say his name.

'Oh, good. I'd hoped you would meet.' Janey didn't seem to have noticed anything odd in her voice. 'Mike was so good to Ursula after Teddy died and when she was ill herself. He looked in every day. She was determined to stay there but it would have been impossible without someone nearby prepared to keep an eye on her.'

'But didn't she have a nurse?' Sally was ashamed of how little she knew of the details of that swiftly ravening cancer. She saw that she had been allowed to be ignorant of its horror like a child, and like a child had accepted that. Even now, most of her mind had locked onto the thought of Mike, imagining him there in the house with minute clarity—his loose-limbed stride as he crossed the kitchen, the freckles on the back of the tanned hand he reached to the door handle, his voice calling a reassuring greeting . . . He had taken trouble over maddening, chattering Ursula. Sally felt the blood in her veins pulse at the vividness of these images.

'That was only when she came back from hospital the last time,' Janey was saying, and Sally dragged her mind back with a wrenching effort. 'Before that she really could manage.' Reassuring herself. 'But I should have gone down more often, made the time.' Janey too.

'It was good of her neighbours to do it.' Clumsy, and creakingly obvious to revert to him, but Sally couldn't help herself.

'It was always Mike. I don't think Isobel ever went along. Her preference is generally to head the other way along the lane.' With a little huff of sardonic amusement.

Isobel. It had to come. The shadowy person whom Sally had permitted no name, no face, no form, had to take on an identity some time. A first, base, sickening jealousy gripped her.

What had Janey said? There had been some implication there. Sally was too shaken to pin it down.

'. . . he found her on a beach, it seems. In Malaysia. They were both travelling, wandering down the coast. She'd been with some chap who'd dumped her, leaving her with no cash and no ticket home. Mike of course stepped in. And that was that.'

She was heading down the path ahead of Sally, speaking half over her shoulder. Sally longed for more, dreaded it like the drill swinging in towards a tooth.

'Mike Danaher's one of the world's great looker-afterers, of course. Such a competent person, such wide interests. Did he tell you about his painting? His stuff goes really well in the gallery in the old village school and at the Grisedale theatre and so on. It's hard to imagine that side of him when you see him out there heaving boulders and swinging his axe. His son Michael loves the place, fortunately. He's always out and about with his father whenever he gets the chance . . . Now, we'll get this lot straight into the freezer—so good when it's young, far too nice to waste on jam. We'll keep back enough to make a crumble for tonight, though. The first of the season's always a treat.'

Sally had been greedy for any detail connected with Mike and she had paid the price. With piercing regret she knew that the perfect bubble of their loving privacy had burst.

Keeping occupied was the only thing that helped, and that at least was easy at Grianan, however mundane the activities. She deliberately avoided the long solitary walks she used to indulge in because she knew she would not be able to keep her mind off fantasies of Mike writing, Mike telephoning, Mike even miraculously appearing. She knew she mustn't fool herself. Their meeting, inevitably, had meant different things to each of them. For her there had been a stronger attraction than she had felt for any other man, reassurance and tenderness after the time alone, and delight and confidence in her own sexuality restored. For Mike it could be nothing more than a brief and finite affair, however genuine his feelings had been. What would please him best would be to know he'd left her happier than he found her. Well, I am, I am, she cried to him, but it had been such a little time to have together.

She threw herself into the scrum of Grianan life: helping in the kitchen where Aunt Janey unswervingly pursued perfection and Maureen hissed and muttered as her short cuts were circumvented one by one; hurtling up and down the glen fetching eggs from here, honey from there, lending the fish kettle, delivering plants; or being trusted with some piece of garden drudgery where she could do no harm.

Anything was better, she would remind herself, weeding gravel or ironing pillowslips or scraping the scrambled-egg pan, than torturing herself over happiness glimpsed and gone.

'I suppose I really ought to sell the Edalmere cottage.'

Shattering comment lightly tossed out by Janey one wet afternoon when she could find no further excuse for avoiding the bills and was sitting glumly at her desk with her hair on end and her feet twisted round the legs of her chair like a rebellious child.

'Sell it?' Sally felt literally winded, not only by the unexpected suggestion but by discovering how far she had been from accepting that she would never be there with Mike again.

'Well, I hardly use it and to tell you the truth I find the drive down a bit daunting these days. A little capital would come in handy. We keep sticking on the Elastoplast when what this place needs is the knife.'

'But Janey, Edalmere—isn't it a good thing to keep money in property?' She grabbed at the first practical thought that surfaced. 'Unless you urgently need a big injection of cash?'

Janey peered at her over the slipping spectacles. 'I suppose so. And when you're here I may manage to get down more often. It's a perfect place to hole up and God knows I could do with a rest now and then.' Sally couldn't ever remember her admitting it before. 'But in the long term . . . I can't believe this man—he's saying I haven't paid him since March. What does he think cheques are, junk mail . . .?'

Sally sank back into her chair, feeling as though she had swum a mile. Why, she asked herself, did she feel so shaken? Did she seriously think that one day, when enough time had passed, she would be able to go back? Go coolly along the lane without listening for the sound of the pick-up coming, pass the house without a flicker of feeling, walk the lake path without looking, longing, remembering?

'Janey, how would you like me to sort that lot out for you?'

'Oh, darling, would you? Honestly, would you? I hardly liked to ask, you do so much already.'

'I'll be better at that than at making meringues.' Yesterday's disaster.

'I certainly hope so. Come along then, start now.' Janey sounded relieved, moving her chair to one side, sweeping a clear space on the desk with her forearm. Sally drew up a chair beside her. Engage the brain.

**B**lended scents rose around Sally as she cut tough stems of thyme from the overgrown bushes at the end of the herb bed.

'Are you going to dry them or freeze them?' Piers stood in the sunlight on the mossy path, a bundle of stakes under his arm.

'Ho, that's decision-making. Outside my job spec,' she told him, snipping industriously.

Piers laid down the stakes and, taking a knife from his back pocket, bent to help her. 'Want some marjoram too?'

'Everything. I've been waiting for days to get all this no-rain, post-dew, pre-sun stuff just right.'

'Not hankering yet for a bit of decision-making?'

'Nope.'

'Do you ever miss your old job?'

Pause. Piers worked quietly on. Sally knew he wouldn't repeat the question. He respected everyone's right to reserve.

'It could be satisfying on occasion. Demanding even.'

He waited patiently for a more informative answer, if she felt ready to give one.

'Demanding in the wrong way, though,' she went on slowly, after an interval of snipping away companionably in the aromatic sunny warmth. 'More stress and frustration than a sense of achievement, in general. I seemed to be forever pushing to get things organised against the clock. But I was good at my job. I'd have gone on thinking it all mattered, I suppose, being promoted, getting pay rises. I didn't see how artificial it was. I was leading a life considered normal, acceptable, praiseworthy even. Yet now—' She straightened, her hand crushing the purple-leaved sage she held, her eyes turned to the lifting swells of the Drumveyn moor and the great curving ridge of Ben Breac. 'Sometimes, now, I find I do miss the thought of a career stretching ahead of me,' she said. 'I shall have to start thinking about what to do next, I suppose.'

She realised that a month ago, less, she had been shutting her mind to it in terror, her self-confidence in tatters. Now the thought was there, ready to be turned over without urgency or threat.

'This is a good place for thinking,' Piers said, laying their plunder in effortless order on the weathered grey trug. 'Establishing values.'

'I think you've established yours?' Sally suggested, smiling at him, ready to turn to another subject.

'You don't read much, do you?' he asked.

What did that have to do with anything? Sally wondered. 'I'm out of the habit, I suppose.'

'It might help.' She felt, as she had felt before with him, that he somehow comprehended everything. He knew about rawness and need, and that was enough.

'There are thoughts one comes across,' Piers went on in his understated way. 'Meeting one's own feelings brilliantly phrased—and therefore shared. Come and look whenever you feel like it. You may find things that are right for you.'

The garden cottage on midsummer nights, moths dashing themselves against the glowing apricot shade of the single lamp, Piers cross-legged on the futon playing Andean folk songs on his flute, Sally stretched out beside him, dreaming, pain held at bay. Once he read poetry to her, but it was too soon, too apposite. She had fled from Piers's voice, which understood too clearly what it read.

The tendrils of this life, of the glen itself, were reaching out to her, as she was aware. On her lending and borrowing expeditions Sally met newcomers drawn willy-nilly into Janey's trading network, and renewed acquaintance with families who had known the Buchanans for three generations. (Janey had, after all, been moved and delighted that Sally had decided to use the Buchanan name herself.)

There were changes among them too. At Baldarroch, droopy spineless Margot Thorne had been replaced by Julie, a rough-cut product of the London School of Economics who had little time for glen socialising, but whom Sally rather liked. And at Drumveyn, across the glen, there was a new young Lady Napier who, according to Janey, had been hitchhiking up the glen and been given a lift by her future mother-in-law. Now she was married to Archie and they had adopted two small girls. Pauly was a friendly creature, always up to her eyes in some activity, but always with time to chat. Sally was completely won over. She felt that possibilities for renewed contacts were waiting in the wings, when she was ready to face them.

Meanwhile, the usual emergencies rolled over Grianan: blocked drains, a jackdaw coming down the chimney and flying about the dining room during dinner, shedding droppings and soot, a herd of Glen Ellig stirks getting into the garden.

As the skin of the place began to grow over her; her sense of rootlessness faded. No decisions need be made yet. Julian had dropped out of her mind and recent wounds were clean.

Then a letter came with a Kendal postmark. Not a letter, as it proved, when her shaking hands had ripped the envelope open, but a plain postcard which said, *I'm still looking out for that red Renault.*

# CHAPTER FIVE

FOR ONE AWFUL MOMENT of doubt Sally stood rooted, not knowing how to greet him. She gazed at him helplessly, her body trembling with uncertainty. No uncertainty for Mike. He plunged forward, beaming, to seize her, lifting her off her feet, swinging her round exuberantly, head back to laugh into her face, then crushing her tightly in his arms.

'Hey, little anxious face, aren't you pleased to see me?'

'Oh, Mike.' She tried to hide the surprising giveaway tears against his shoulder.

'I couldn't not see you again. You do understand that, don't you?' he asked later, his voice very quiet, almost constrained, his arm gathering her close against him, her head in the hollow of his shoulder. He meant, Sally knew, that he wanted her to understand on what terms, warning her that nothing in their situation had changed.

'It's all right. I know.'

He gave a low exclamation which was close to a groan. 'God knows, Sally, the last thing in the world I want to do is hurt you.'

She reached up to run her hands through the springy dark red hair, pressed closer to him. 'I won't be hurt by you. Hoping is what hurts.'

The sort of hurt he meant, anyway. The rest she would have to cope with as best she could. It was her choice.

But they both knew where they stood. They needed more; their discovery of each other had mattered too much to be given up so soon. They both felt incapable of relinquishing something so marvellous with so many things still to say, so much loving still to share. The outcome would not change and after this brief exchange they didn't discuss it.

Edalmere. The very name took on a different meaning on the snatched days of early summer when Sally would take off down the glen at dawn or as soon as dinner was over, turning thankfully off the motorway to take the roundabout route which climbed to Edal village, to come at last along the lane with hammering heart, wondering how soon Mike would be able to get away.

Once or twice he took time off and they had a whole day on the fells together, going over to Haweswater or along High Rigg, but preferring the less frequented if less interesting ground to the east. They both wanted solitude, being together in the landscape Mike loved. And in the evenings the lake was theirs, the walkers and birders and environmental-study groups gone, the car park empty. Even the pretentious little cottage became a treasured place because it was theirs.

'It's so good to *talk*,' Mike would say with satisfaction, in the languid contentment after loving. 'I never really talk to anyone these days.' It was the nearest he ever came to a comment on his relationship with Isobel. A crumb. Though Sally supposed it could not be perfect if he was here with her.

Little by little facts filtered in. Learning more of Mike's life brought with it other less desirable knowledge. The 'we' of marriage could not be eliminated entirely. His son, she knew, was Michael; now his daughter had become Kirsty. Sally wanted to hear about the children because they were part of him and he loved them—and also, with a grim honesty, because references to them kept matters in true perspective. Whatever fantasies might creep in, in spite of her most determined efforts, about Mike one day leaving Isobel, she could never for one moment pretend that he would leave his children. He was a responsible, loving man who would do all he could to protect and look after his family. That was part of his attraction.

She was also obliged to accept that he was a lively, talented and gregarious person and with that went the reluctant awareness that she was not going to be the only female who would find him attractive or whose company he would enjoy. The only small consolation was that Isobel rarely seemed to go anywhere with him. He went alone to conservation meetings, spoke to various groups on environmental subjects, but was also part of a wide circle of Lakeland painters, writers and musicians and it was here, Sally knew, that he found the stimulus and friendship closest to his heart.

The drive back to Grianan became something to be dreaded. Once there, no matter how doggedly she tried to fill her mind and time with work, images of Mike—at home, with his family, somewhere around the lake shore with Michael at weekends sharing the jobs she had done with him, spending his evenings in some intelligent, articulate, relaxed, like-minded group—were not easy to deal with.

These thoughts mostly attacked her when she was exhausted after the drive home, the emotional high of the few greedily hoarded hours, too much loving and too little sleep. It was then that she would wish that 'something would happen' to Isobel, something unspecified but final, simply and painlessly removing her from the face of the earth.

The next worst thing to missing Mike was deceiving Janey. If she noticed that Sally returned from these 'days off' at Edalmere more exhausted than when she left, her aunt made no comment, but that didn't help the guilt. But Sally knew it was something she could never discuss with Janey.

Piers, perhaps, Sally could have told, but she realised that in some curious way there was no need to. He simply understood that she was in need of help and comfort, and gently he offered it, the impersonal solace of beauty, music and peace, sometimes allowing Sally some small insights into his own life, realising that at present it would be impossible for her to talk about hers.

Bit by bit she pieced together a background for him, a conventional—and rather grand—home, an existence at public school made tolerable by remaining largely underground, the absolute refusal to go up to university or to conform in any way to the life expected of him, then the solitary journeys to offbeat places, the dabblings with the more mystic forms of religion, the jobs on organic farms in California, Kerry and New Zealand. He didn't care for direct questions and Sally didn't ask them, each allowing the other their essential privacy.

She never enquired either how Mike managed to spend as much time as he did with her when she was at Edalmere. It was from a disapproving comment of Janey's that she learned Isobel was always running up and down to see her mother, who lived alone near Jedburgh.

'One of those mothers who simply can't let go,' Janey said. 'I met her once. She used to come and visit Ursula to tell her what a frightful backwater Edalmere was and how she wished her daughter was living somewhere more civilised.'

Sally dreaded meeting Isobel in the lane or the village. Once she saw the estate car parked outside the shop and went on to Windermere, startled to find herself literally trembling as she drove.

Pain was unavoidable. But there was great happiness in their brief times together that summer. Sally had never imagined she could feel so close to anyone, so effortlessly in touch with feeling and intention and reaction, so sure. And certainly she had never experienced such physical awareness, nerve ends alive to his lightest touch, senses floundering at the mere smell of his skin, her body flowing and opening to him.

'You're incredible,' he would say, staring into her eyes to read there what his hands were doing to her. 'It really is like touching a live wire.'

It's love, she wanted to say, submerging with a gasp under the waves of sensation. But love was not a word they allowed themselves.

As the season built up and Grianan grew busier it grew harder to make the time to go down to see him. And the crowded summer roads made the journey longer and more frustrating. Janey was willing to let Sally take time off whenever she wanted it, delighted that she used Edalmere as a refuge, but once school holidays had started Connie and Maureen both wanted more time at home.

The retired couples of early summer gave way to families, often second-generation Grianan guests, whose needs were far more varied and demanding. Many of them Sally knew, and they welcomed her warmly, so that inevitably she found herself drawn more and more closely into the life of the house.

Janey always pretended that she couldn't bear the guests but the truth was that they had become her friends and she loved their company. One of the shared interests, as well as food, birds and gardens, was music, and one of Sally's most abiding images of Grianan in the years she had stayed away had been of summer evenings in the big drawing room, level golden light pouring in through the three long sash windows, her eyes on the outline of Ben Breac, as a pure voice sang *lieder*, a violin drew out its sweetness, or Aunt Janey thundered away on the piano at the more dramatic music she favoured.

It was all so dated but innocent, *safe*. The lady who had sung *lieder* was dead, but now Piers was here with his flute. The mood remained unchanged, and Sally could dream under its nostalgic sentimentality.

She knew that she was lucky to be in such a place, where not only could every moment be filled, but where, when the chance to vanish presented itself, it could be seized.

For Mike it was not so easy. Sally couldn't warn him when she was free and sometimes her visits were hopelessly mistimed. Later than in Scotland, but all too soon, the children were on holiday and Michael spent every moment he could with his father. Cousins of Isobel's came to stay, Mike's brother was over from Ireland. Mike was as loving and tender as ever but she was aware of the subtle pull away from her, and she felt for the first time an intruder in his life, and ashamed.

She told him how she felt, and that she would stay away till the holidays were over. He said little, his face grim, holding her tightly, but he didn't attempt to make her change her mind.

In September she went back, and they had three days of intense, aware happiness. When they talked it was of immediate inconsequential things. The last evening they made no move to go to Sally's little room but sat on at the kitchen table with the dusk gathering about them.

'Have you decided what you want to do when the season's over at Grianan?'

Simple, normal question, but opening the doors wide to real life, which they had so carefully held at bay for these three days.

'No. Though it's time to think about it, I suppose.' Sally had some vague ideas, but even to sketch them out would have distanced her from him, from this shared secret place, this precious time which already she could feel slipping away from them.

'You wouldn't consider staying on there?'

'I'd probably go mad with boredom in the winter.' Then Sally saw that Mike's hands were clamped round his glass as though they would crush it by main force. She knew that he was forcing himself to ask these questions, forcing himself to face the fact that she would move on, make a new life for herself, in which he would have no part. After that second of icy realisation nothing really needed to be said. She made herself look up and met Mike's eyes; she saw that he could not speak.

'Mike, it's all right. I know.'

He shook his head once, his face clamped shut against the over-whelming feelings, then, said tightly, 'It's just that sometimes when I go back I wonder what the hell I'm doing. To you as well.'

In those two short sentences he had taken them from the vague and unstated to the specific heart of the problem. A terrible chill washed through Sally—it was over. They had reached the end. She felt wild inner protest rising in her but she knew there was no going back from the words that had been spoken.

She summoned up all her resolution. 'It's all right,' she said.

'I don't want to—cause any waves.' Banal response, but she understood that he couldn't bear to discuss this, and that it would be the only apology and self-justification he could bring himself to offer. The muscles of his face were rigid with pain, his eyes full of appeal.

'I know,' she said again. 'Nor do I.'

'Christ, you're even making this easy for me,' he protested with a spurt of shamed anger.

'We mustn't spoil what we've had.' Sally heard her own voice sounding brisk, but she knew he would not misread her tone.

'You've got some guts,' Mike exclaimed, pulling her towards him so that she shouldn't see how much this had moved him. That last embrace was almost clumsy, without tenderness. There suddenly seemed to Sally a thousand things she hadn't said to him, needed to say, couldn't remember, would never be able to say now.

'Look at me,' he said abruptly, urgently, holding her away from him. 'We feel exactly the same,' he went on fiercely, giving her a slight rough shake as though to insist on her comprehension. 'Remember that.'

She nodded, mouth trembling, praying that the tears he would hate wouldn't overtake her yet.

The whine of the gate sounded behind him for the last time. Sally sank down at the table, letting her forehead rest on the cool surface, wrapped her arms round her head and held herself together as best she could.

# CHAPTER SIX

SALLY TOOK A LAST LOOK round the little office before locking up. A proprietorial satisfied look. The white shelves against the blue-grey walls, the orderly stock, were still new enough to give her a buzz.

It was just after seven but scarcely dark yet. The eternal winter of blizzards and floods and blocked roads must surely be over at last.

Sally crossed the almost deserted Muirend square, crammed with parked cars during the day, and dived down a narrow cobbled vennel leading to the river. This was the old part of the town, until the early years of the century a bustling centre of mills and warehouses. Several of the old stone buildings had been converted into flats, and the area was now considered rather desirable.

Sally had been lucky, as she had been lucky to snap up the office premises on the square at just the right moment, to find the flat in the ex-boathouse loft, with its big window across the end wall overlooking the weir. It still pleased her to run up the stone outside steps—must get something into those tubs as soon as the weather's warmer, Janey will find something—and open the blue door into the long room which was kitchen and living area in one.

It had been easier in a way to drive away from Edalmere and Mike the last time than it had been the first. Then, too, many questions had been left unanswered; they had quite simply needed more of each other. The hardest thing Sally had had to face had been the lack of words when the end came. When she had gone quietly away for good, she had needed, illogically but passionately, his assurance that he understood and was pleased with her. She wanted to be able to tell him that she had almost at once taken a grip on her life. A grim resolution, whether inherent or dinned into her by Janey (always it was her influence that counted for Sally, not her father's), had enabled her to get herself moving and make this new start.

Once she had captured Janey to talk to her about it, not giving her undivided attention of course, but tidying and cutting back the first victims to autumn in the herbaceous border, she had been startled at the enthusiasm of her aunt's response.

'Of course you must do it. I'm delighted you want to. This was never meant to be more than a stopgap, though I've loved every minute of having you here and you've been the most tremendous help. Unskilled, admittedly, but devoted,' she added, protecting a hypericum from Sally's secateurs. 'Spring for those, as I'm sure you must know.'

'It may take some time to get organised, though,' Sally went on, snipping away more cautiously. 'Premises to find, all the legwork to do of leasing or buying. And someone else may get in first.'

'In Muirend? Not a chance. To be honest, I shall be thrilled to have you so near, but it's not what I'd have foreseen.'

'I suppose being up here again I've discovered it's where I want to live.' The only place that gave her any sense of belonging.

'That's good.' But Janey darted her a sharp look. 'Are you truly over it all? I haven't liked to ask—always too damned busy for one thing.'

For one blank astounded moment Sally misunderstood, then hastily called her face to order, wondering what it had betrayed. 'Well, Grianan in the summer is hardly the place for soul-baring chats,' she managed to say easily—she hoped. 'But yes, I'm over it.'

Over Julian and her damaged pride. It all seemed so far away now, and from this perspective she could see how unsuited to each other they had been. Her quite different feelings for Mike had taught her that.

'I'm glad. It was a hard knock to take and you've been so good about it. I know you haven't even started looking for anywhere to live yet, but do regard this as base, won't you, Sally, for as long as you need to? Goodness, how silly of me—I don't really have to say it, do I?'

'Well, I'm glad you did,' Sally said firmly, reaching out to pat the scratched hand wielding the pruning knife. 'Anyway, it will probably all take ages. You won't be getting rid of me yet, Aunt J.'

Piers had not approved. 'You've got a job here,' was all he would say when Sally outlined her plan.

'A job? Running up and down the glen with a bootful of laundry or loo rolls? Getting my head bitten off in the kitchen when Aunt Janey's had another fallout with Maureen? Making beds and dusting because Connie's child is off school again?'

'There are few human activities which can't be reduced to similar terms,' Piers pointed out calmly. 'Certainly not persuading every innumerate small-business owner that his simple cashbook would be better replaced by a system that will oblige him to pay someone to run it and bury him in print-outs.'

'You know nothing whatsoever about it. That is a truly retrogressive attitude. A computer will take his books up to audit level, do his wages at a touch, and his end-of-year returns, tell him exactly what his cash level is, work out his projections.'

'Jargon,' Piers snapped. 'I thought you had more innate intelligence.' He sounded really angry and more contemptuous than Sally had ever heard him, and she didn't like it. 'And have you considered Janey's position?'

'Of course I have. I'll be less than twenty miles away.'

'She would prefer to have you here.'

Sally was astonished. 'Janey? Are you serious? She thought I needed somewhere to lie low for a while, that's all. She knows I can't look on working at Grianan as permanent or fulfilling—'

Piers, the gentle and tolerant, threw his fork on the ground, kicked it for good measure, and walked away.

The hectic weeks of finding the office and flat had meant examining freezing-cold office premises, had meant grappling with dry rot, wet rot, woodworm, prohibiting clauses in leases, too many stairs, being too near the piggery, too far from the main drag. There was the interminable sequence of solicitor, bank, valuation, offer, closing date, failure. Then when it all began to come together at last the appalling winter had added its quota of problems.

Grianan had closed at the end of October. Sally had never known it in its dormant phase. She had always been there during school holidays, and even at Christmas Janey had always opened up for a house party. Not so now, it seemed.

'Haven't opened at Christmas for about five years,' Janey said. That long? 'To be honest, I can't face the hassle these days. It used to be fun, though.' She sounded almost wistful and, looking at her face set for once in heavy lines, Sally realised how she depended on her aunt's energy and ebullience. It occurred to her that most women of Janey's age would have stopped working years ago.

Their world at Grianan during those autumn weeks shrank to the small sitting room and the kitchen, which temporarily took on a more human face. Meals became simpler and fairly arbitrary as they worked their way through surpluses. Piers almost always joined them. During the day he and Janey attacked together the heavy work in the garden; in the evenings they listened to music, read or played chess. Seeing their quiet accustomed sharing of this time—they would go for hours without exchanging a word—it struck Sally that they had spent last winter here together, in this contented quietness. Did they mind her presence? Nothing in their manner or behaviour gave the slightest hint that she wasn't wanted.

On the contrary, Janey often openly expressed her pleasure that Sally would be living in Muirend, and Sally realised with surprise how much her aunt had been dreading the possibility that she would return south. Only once did she ask about Sally's father.

'Does he mind your being here?'

'I doubt if he knows where I am,' Sally retorted, automatically resorting to glib antagonism as soon as he was mentioned.

Janey checked her with a quick grip on her arm. 'You are not a child any more, Sally.'

Sally looked away from her, ashamed but still mutinous.

'Sally darling, I know that in terms of human relationships he did everything wrong, but do you suppose he isn't intelligent enough to realise that?'

Sally made an effort to reply without emphasis. 'I did tell him that I'd be here for the summer. And I shall let him know my new address as soon as I move.'

'Good. And Rose—are you—do you write to her?'

This was clearly harder to ask, and as Sally turned to look at her she saw how afraid Janey was of intruding, and how much she cared about the answer. It was like a new facet of her suddenly catching the light. Janey, the eldest sister, who, it had always been taken for granted, loved this house, this place, and was happy to spend her life here, but who after all had never been given much choice, particularly as both her sisters had fled. Neither of them, Sally realised, looking at it in a new adult context, had given Janey much in the way of support, contact or love.

'Oh, Janey, I should have talked to you about all that long ago,' she exclaimed, contrite. 'I shouldn't have left you wondering.'

'I realised it had been a disaster when you came back from Australia, but I saw so little of you afterwards. It's always been impossible to talk properly in this wretched place and you were always up here when we were at our busiest. Can you tell me now what happened with Rose?'

'I was just in the way.' It was suddenly obvious and terribly simple.

Janey's face tightened in pain, but her voice was carefully neutral. 'She would have found it hard, you know, to meet you on such different terms, separate from your father. He'd made her so miserable.'

Mike had said something of the sort.

'I was too young to handle it, too brash. I went there wanting far too much, expecting far too much.'

'Tell me about it.'

'She never wrote and told you herself?' Sally asked curiously. The sisters had been close when they were younger, she knew, and to the others Janey had been a protective mother figure for most of their lives.

'She said so little I knew there was more to tell,' Janey replied drily. 'Not the best of correspondents, my sister Rose. Tell me about the house, Orford, the family . . .'

So now the move from Grianan had been made. Sally was settled in the boathouse flat, spring was finally on the way and business looked promising. Certainly all the small stuff in the shop, the copying, faxing and typing services, as well as the sale of stationery, was building up with reassuring steadiness. By a great stroke of good fortune, she had secured the franchise for the software package. She already had two consultancy jobs in the bag, setting up office systems for a motel and a plumbing firm—and tonight she had some work to do on both. She had been surprised to find how much pleasure and satisfaction she was deriving from her new enterprise, which she had embarked on more out of a resolve to find independent occupation than in any expectation of actually enjoying it.

She had just shoved a lasagne into the microwave, looking forward to a peaceful evening's work at home, when the telephone rang. Janey.

'Darling, I just thought I'd let you know in case you were thinking of going up to Grianan this weekend—I'm down at Edalmere, having a little break before we open again.'

She sounded terse and Sally's conscience stirred uncomfortably. She hadn't been up to Grianan very often in the rush to open the shop. 'Janey, are you all right?'

'I'm fine, Sally, but I've just heard some appalling news—' Sally could hear her gathering control. 'I'm sorry, it's rather shaken me. The poor Danahers, such a dreadful thing has happened . . .'

For an icy, heart-stopping moment Sally remembered how she used to wish that something would happen to Isobel. Horrified guilt held her rigid with shock. 'Janey, what's happened?' she whispered.

'Poor Isobel, it really is the most terrible thing. Mike collapsed a few weeks ago, an aneurysm of the brain. He was rushed to Newcastle and they managed to save him, but he's in a total coma . . .'

Sally had sunk to the floor, clutching the receiver in both hands, shaking, tears spilling down her face. 'Janey, that's so awful . . .' she whispered. 'So awful,' she repeated desperately, more loudly, feeling it was vital to make some response that would sound normal.

'Yes, it's a frightful tragedy. Everyone here is so distressed about it. Of course they've had time by now to get accustomed to it but I must admit it was a great shock to me.' She sounded deeply upset; old, Sally thought in a sudden flash of fear. 'Such a strong, fit young man, absolutely in the prime of his life. It just doesn't seem possible.'

That active, well-muscled body, so intimately known, the long limbs and lean back, the rangy stride. The keen perceptive eyes and teasing smile. The competence, the caring and protectiveness. It could not all be destroyed like this, in an instant. 'Janey, it's dreadful . . .'

'I'm sorry to tell you such sad news. I think rather selfishly I wanted to share it with someone. Isobel has been wonderful, everyone says. Such a nightmare for her, the children to look after and having to go back and forth to Newcastle all the time . . .'

I can't go to him, Sally thought blankly. I can't help him or care for him or even see him. I can't find out how he is. I can't talk about him or share this numbing shock with anyone. I am shut off from him. Whatever wrong she and Mike had done this was too terrible a price to pay. She stayed there huddled on the floor for a long time, weeping, as though to move would bring more pain.

**S**ally moved through the days in a blur of shock and disbelief. Driving, she would be blinded by tears and have to pull up; or would arrive somewhere without any recollection of how she had got there. She did her best to deal coherently with Cheryl, her assistant, the shop, reps, suppliers and customers. She forced her brain to concentrate on explaining accounts packages and spread sheets to computer-illiterate clients and often drove away quite unable to gauge how much she had managed to make clear to them. Twice she had to go back and deal with queries, and knew it was her own fault.

Small shreds of comfort gradually surfaced in her thoughts. Janey had told her the news on the phone and not face to face, so nothing had been given away to her. And she was living alone, so did not have to go through the continual torture of pretence. Also, no one need ever know.

At first she was desperate to see Mike. She wanted to forget good sense and civilised behaviour, cut through all the problems of finding him, getting access to him, simply to be with him for a few seconds and touch his hand. Then, as she learned more about his condition from Janey, she realised how pointless and destructive that would be. Mike knew nothing and no one. He didn't know where he was or who he was or what had happened to him. In all probability he never would. How could she contemplate for a second saying or doing anything that would bring more pain on his family? On Isobel. Sally's thoughts turned to her constantly in those first days, appalled at what she must be going through, and it put her own situation into perspective.

Work was the only thing that helped and the pace was already demanding.

Sally now had a computer in the flat and regularly took work home, pushing on into the small hours almost every night, shutting out the unendurable. She rarely went to Grianan, knowing she couldn't talk about Mike but not sure she could be with Janey without revealing too much. She knew Janey was hurt at her almost complete disappearance, and Piers disappointed in her on Janey's behalf. The affection and sense of homecoming of last summer seemed far away now. The reassuring discovery that Aunt Janey's love, rock-solid, had survived the years of neglect and non-communication had helped then, but was impossible to tap into as a source of comfort for her present pain. And Piers's eyes were too discerning, his gentle patience too liable to draw out unwary confidences.

All she could manage was to go doggedly on from day to day, schooling herself to separate thoughts of Mike from the rest of her life. Brutal as it was to put it into words, the total destruction of Mike's world could have no effect whatsoever on hers. Her life had not altered in real terms.

But no matter how hard she tried there was, behind everything she thought and did, the image of him lying white and still, recognising nothing, understanding nothing, strength and vigour stripped away. Now he was helpless, fed and cleaned and bundled about by busy hands—he who had been essentially one of those who make the world work, who construct, invent, repair and control. And one of those who look after others.

'Sally? Hi!' An unknown female voice on the phone, young, warm and eager. A hint of 'Selly' rather than 'Sally'.

'Hello? Is that Sally Buchanan?'

'Speaking.' Someone who knew she had dropped Maynard.

'Oh, great! This is Nona.' The voice sounded excited. 'D'you remember me?'

Nona—offhand, independent-minded ten-year-old glowering at Sally from under an untidy flop of dark hair, patronisingly fit, skinny, brown. The eldest of Sally's mother's second brood, the one who had never for one moment relented.

'Nona! Where are you?' An infusion of telephone warmth as Sally's brain raced, half intrigued and half apprehensive.

A laugh. 'In Perth. Perth, Scotland, that is.' No mistaking how much she had enjoyed saying that.

'Goodness,' Sally said blankly. Less than an hour away.

'Thought I'd give you a surprise,' the voice rattled on. 'I came across with a couple of friends and we've been touring round England, but they've gone over to Europe for a while and so I came on up to Scotland to see if I could see you. I phoned Aunt Janey and she gave me your number.'

Aunt Janey! What a cheek! Then Sally pulled herself together hastily. Nona had just as much right to call Janey aunt as she had herself, though the thought had never struck her before.

'Nona, I can't believe it. I had no idea you were coming over.'

'Oh, well, I told Mum not to say anything in her letters. See how everything worked out, you know.'

The voice was definitely more hesitant now, a little rising inflection in the last words making them a question which Sally couldn't miss.

'But you're going to come and stay, aren't you?'

'Well, I don't want to mess you about. I can stay at the hostel here, but it'd be cool to have a chat.'

'Of course you can't stay at the hostel. I'll come and fetch you. Where are you phoning from?'

'The bus station. The next bus to Muirend leaves in seven minutes.' They both laughed at what this said, a tiny first step towards each other.

'I'll come straight away.'

'I can be there in the time it would take you to get here. So where do I get off?'

'Where the bus ends up. I'll be waiting.'

'Right, see you.'

Finishing off what she was doing on the computer, reducing to order the paperwork which was spread all over the flat, then walking up to the square, Sally found she was not resentful but interested.

Her eyebrows climbed into her hair as Nona appeared on the steps of the bus. The skinny scowling child had turned into a beauty. Dark hair sleeked smoothly back, white shirt knotted across brown midriff, slim thighs encased in brilliantly patterned shorts, wide smile flashing in a deeply tanned face—she looked stunning.

'Hey, isn't this fantastic?' Nona cried, beaming.

'Yes, it is,' Sally said, laughing involuntarily, and she meant it.

'This is neat.' Nona was fascinated by the echoing alleyways down which Sally led her and the secluded little courtyard by the river.

'Ex-boathouse,' Sally explained. 'The dock below has been covered over to make a garage. The flat's up these steps.'

Nona loved it all. 'What a *place*,' she exclaimed, roaming the long room, standing at the window to gaze down at the pool below the weir where the first yellow leaves drifted against the bank.

'I was lucky to find it.' And had hardly given herself time to enjoy it, Sally realised as she spoke. All summer she had used it as a mere shell in which to work, sleep and eat. She had done nothing to it since she moved in, and in spite of her tidying today it had more the air of a workroom than a home.

'OK if I look?' Nona nodded at the doors which led to the tiny bathroom and bedroom at the back.

'Help yourself.'

'It's a really great place,' she pronounced, coming back. 'But listen, you don't have to put me up, you know.'

'You're staying,' Sally said. Part of her was still tempted to let Nona go—her arrival was so sudden, the flat really not big enough for two— but at a deeper level she knew there was no evading this. It mattered; and she and this startling new Nona had things to say to each other.

'Well, I'll have the couch.'

'We'll argue later. Food first—though the pickings may be a bit thin. We'll have to stock up properly tomorrow.' As in much else, Sally had been subsisting on the minimum.

'I'll stand you a pub supper.'

About to object, Sally realised how out of the habit she was of doing something so obvious and normal. She had never been in a pub or restaurant the whole time she had been living in Muirend. They tried a hotel half a mile down the river and enjoyed the garden even if Janey would have snorted at the food. They ate scampi and chips and drank chardonnay, and Sally tried to relate the resentful child she remembered to this cheerful, laid-back girl.

Nona must be twenty-three or twenty-four now. Sally knew from her mother's letters that Nona had qualified as a physiotherapist, had worked briefly in a hospital in Melbourne and then moved to a private practice.

'You can make a bomb going private,' Nona explained. 'That's why I was able to come over. I'd always wanted to see England, well, Scotland, mainly because of Mum. And I wanted to get to know Aunt Janey.'

'You must have given her a surprise when you phoned.'

'She took it pretty well.' Nona laughed at the memory.

'You weren't sure you'd contact me, though?' It was better said, and surprisingly easy to be direct with her.

Nona's dark eyes met Sally's honestly. 'Oh, I was sure I wanted to come, all right. I just didn't know how you'd react.'

I did that, Sally thought with shame, I with my patronising arrogance and open criticism. Sally had behaved that way because she felt uncertain and unwanted, but that wasn't how it would have seemed to them.

'I'm so glad you phoned,' she told Nona. A second chance—and a reprieve from loneliness. 'Tomorrow we'll go and see Janey.'

'To tell you the truth she sounds a bit alarming.' The word gained power from her unfamiliar accent. 'Wasn't she a bit on the heavy side with Mum and Aunt Ursula? When they were growing up, I mean? Vetting their boyfriends and all that?'

It was unexpected and fascinating to find this new angle opening up, discovering her mother via Nona. They opened another bottle of wine when they got back to the flat and talked for hours.

When Sally was finally stretched out on the sofa—which she had insisted on taking because she was the shorter by three inches, but really preferred since a night never passed without the dark weight of sadness breaking her sleep and she knew she would need her resources of work, coffee and pacing—she realised that she hadn't thought about Mike all evening. It was good, but agonising too.

Their time together now had no existence outside her own brain and memory. She had made herself get used to that fact. Even if he recovered, though she knew from Janey that a total recovery could never be hoped for, Mike would never know that they had met. He had been in hospital for eight months now and had undergone eleven operations. He still didn't know who he was or who Isobel was. By this stage Sally had reached the limit of her capacity to suffer for him. It didn't hurt any less, but there were no new thoughts to think. The real and continuing nightmare was Isobel's. Sally could only be thankful that Isobel had never known of her existence.

Sally took Nona up to Grianan the next morning. It was a mellow September day, the heather just turning to its first glowing rust. Nona wound down her window and breathed in the clean air, thrilled to be seeing at last this glen where her mother had been born, and making

Sally realise that for months she had been closing her eyes to its beauty. And Nona's gasp of delight as they pulled up at the door of Grianan reminded her that the well-proportioned stone house, with its huge sash windows staring across the tree-sheltered lawn to the shapely mass of Ben Breac, was after all rather splendid.

Nona had no problems with Aunt Janey's forthright manner. She had a good deal of that directness herself, less the gruffness. What did startle Sally was Janey's warm delight in the appearance of this new niece. She felt a small sting of jealousy, followed by a most salutory new idea. Was it possible that independent, busy, positive Janey could sometimes be lonely?

Piers also, to Sally's secret indignation, was visibly bowled over by Nona. Sally was uncomfortably reminded that she had not mended fences with him after he had spoken his mind about her leaving Janey, nearly a year ago now. He knew nothing about Mike and as far as he was concerned she had simply gone off to do her own thing when Janey needed help, and had buried herself determinedly in her own concerns ever since.

Today, Sally, Nona and Janey set off to tour the house and, presently, Sally was aware of an odd feeling of being excluded as her mother's girlhood memories were recounted by Nona and added to by Janey with obvious enjoyment. Well, Sally reminded herself, she had been too young to be told any of this before her mother left. These were things you chatted and laughed about with a grown-up daughter. She minded quite surprisingly for a few minutes till she took hold of herself and began to listen. No point in missing out a second time—and Janey's frank pleasure in a youth suddenly returned to her and shared was irresistible.

They had lunch, Piers joining them, in the little paved corner outside the sitting room, basking in the yellow sunlight which had burned off the early haze. They strolled afterwards in the garden, blazing with great clumps of montbretia and Michaelmas daisies and potentillas of every shade in full flower. But was it really Aunt Janey setting this lazy pace? Sally found herself wondering more than once.

She left them quite soon, carrying a handful of herbs to get her canard en daube started, which she said would need at least four hours in the slow oven. Sally led Nona through the wild end of the garden and took her up the hill to her favourite rocky viewpoint.

'God, you were lucky, growing up here,' Nona sighed, letting her eyes follow the soaring bare skyline of the hills to the head of the glen. 'This air, so soft, and smelling so gorgeous. And the colours, that amazing velvety green. No wonder you couldn't stand Orford.'

'Did it show?' Sally asked guiltily, knowing the answer.

'Oh, well, it was a bit of a disaster, wasn't it?'

'Did you all hate me for turning up like that?'

'Hate you?' Nona turned in surprised protest. 'Oh no, it wasn't like that at all. We were dying to meet you, big sister and all that, but then when you arrived we were scared to death of you. You seemed so grown-up, and so ultra pommy, you know.' Again that rising inflection which made the words sound almost an appeal.

'So snooty, you mean?'

'Well, we could see you thought it was all pretty crude. And Mum always seemed to be ratty while you were there. I don't think she's ever forgiven herself.'

Perceptions, Sally thought, with a wry sense of defeat and loss. Did one never learn that everyone looks at everything from his or her own angle?

'I was looking for all the wrong things.' It was good, and surprisingly easy, to talk about it at last, perched there on the rock slab with the light wind bringing the sound of a tractor working far below them and the sun warm on their faces.

'I was so envious,' Nona confessed.

'Of me?' They had seemed so invincibly secure, so united.

'Of the way you looked. That incredible hair, and your clothes. You made me feel such a mess.'

'I don't think you have too much to worry about now,' Sally commented with a little spurt of laughter, looking at the shining hair, the evenly tanned skin that made her look so exotic.

'Oh, well, I suppose I can pass in a crowd,' Nona acknowledged, grinning, and Sally was astonished at how close she felt to her after less than one day.

'You could stay up here, you know, if you wanted to,' she suggested, as they paused on the way down to cram their mouths with blueberries. 'Janey would love to have you.' The house would be full, but there was her own little room.

'That's an idea.' Nona said. 'I felt guilty about moving you out last night.'

'Nona, you're perfectly welcome to stay at the flat.'

Nona hesitated, then said shyly, 'I'd really love to be with you—sort of get to know you, if you really don't mind.'

Sally stood up to face her, frowning, wanting there to be no doubt about this. 'There's room for us both.' Twenty-four hours ago the thought of someone intruding on her busy space would have been unthinkable. Now Sally wanted to give Nona the best she could offer.

And deep down she knew that Nona had something to give in her turn which she most desperately needed.

She was right. Having Nona around lifted her out of her trough of lonely grief. And it was time. She had come to terms with the fact that Mike had gone. She knew that she must make the best of her own life and not go on clinging to something that couldn't exist, had never existed in reality. Now she had help.

# CHAPTER SEVEN

H AVING NONA AROUND was like being plugged into a powerful regenerative current. In a matter of days Nona seemed to know half the population of Muirend and be involved in a dozen different activities and endless new interests.

She went to play squash and volleyball and work out in the gym at the new leisure centre, which Sally had never so much as seen. She bought a mountain bike and disappeared helmeted and Lycra-clad to explore Glen Maraich and Glen Ellig. At six in the morning when Sally was rattling away at the computer, having been unable to sleep and on her fifth cup of coffee, Nona would be pushing up the hill above the town and taking a ten-mile run round the farms and lanes.

Bodies in sleeping-bags appeared regularly on the floor of the flat, and other multinational birds of passage who couldn't be accommodated there were dispatched to Grianan and welcomed by Janey with a warmth Sally found surprising but which Nona took for granted.

Not only did the flat silt up with the most stupendous mess but Sally's time was encroached upon just as thoroughly. At first she tolerated it, because she knew it was good for her to be hauled out of absorption in her own affairs and because she felt she owed Nona something, but soon she began to like it.

She saw, with gratitude, that she had been given the chance to make amends for past failures. The easy, warm, two-way relationship with Nona brought her not only nearer to her mother but to the whole family, including Nona's father, that silent background figure she had always so sweepingly discounted. How insufferable she must have seemed to him. At nineteen she had been quite old enough and intelligent enough to have been fairer to him. Now Nona's chatter of home revealed him as generous, hard-working, easy-going and above all devoted to their mother. Sally saw that in her desperate insecurity she had closed her mind to their happiness together as though willing the relationship not to exist, far less be successful where that of her mother and her own father had failed.

The paperwork went back to the office. Apart from the fact that there was no longer room for it in the flat, Sally didn't need the work as a prop, and didn't need to spend her time out of shop hours on it anyway. She had efficient help at last. Nona came to work for her.

'Are you quite sure it's your scene?'

'You mean I'm not capable of doing it and that dozy Cheryl is?' (Cheryl had decided to 'have a year out'—euphemism for failing her Highers and loafing round Muirend for the foreseeable future.)

'I meant you'd find it boring.'

'Oh, what? I'm never bored. And it's not all running the copier—you do have the odd customer coming in and out, don't you? That should keep me awake.'

Most weekends found them heading for Grianan, often with extra passengers in the car. Nona couldn't get enough of the place and Sally had to deal with a most unworthy reaction of possessiveness on seeing Nona simply dive in, eager to learn everything, laughing at her mistakes, full of energy, dauntingly fit, capable and adaptable. No problems in that extrovert, confident life.

Sally was to find that she was wrong again.

There wasn't a great deal of time for serious conversation as they rushed headlong through the days, though there was plenty of the companionable chat and laughter which she had been missing so badly. But occasionally they would find themselves with the flat to themselves for the evening and would open a bottle of wine and cook up something special. Then they would sit talking for hours.

Sally told Nona that there had been a married man in her life a year ago, and that they had stopped seeing each other because of his wife and family. She could not, *could not*, put into words what had happened to him. And she didn't say she had met him at Edalmere, which of course Janey often talked about to Nona.

One evening, when a gusty wind battered rain against the big panes and they had drawn the curtains for the first time, with that mixed enjoyment in the sense of cosiness it gave and reluctance to admit that winter was near, Nona told Sally about the married man in her own life.

'It's one of the reasons I came over. The main reason really. It's got to be his decision.'

'Oh, Nona, that's so hard. I do know. But I had no idea, I'd really never guessed. What's he like, what does he do?'

'Oh, he's a great guy. Really great.' Her voice softened and Sally caught her breath. Lovely as Nona was, she had never seen that gentleness in her face before and she found it moving and somehow precious, as though she had gained more of her in that glimpse of tenderness.

'Tell me about him—if it would help.'

'Sometimes I feel quite desperate to. I feel as though if I can't talk about him he doesn't exist.'

The knife turning.

'Well, let's see,' Nona said, settling herself more comfortably on the cushioned window seat and sounding more cheerful already. 'He's called Ray, Ray Tamerlaine, and he's forty-two, and you can bet Mum's going mad about that for starters.' Sally recognised that the affectionate exasperation was a step back from more difficult revelations and let her take her time. 'But when I'm with him it feels *right*, I never even think about the age thing, it just doesn't exist.'

'Well, I'm not sure that "Mum" can complain.' The inverted commas couldn't quite be eradicated. Sally thought of her still as 'Mummy', which was absurd, and 'my mother' was impossibly possessive. 'After all, my father's about that much older than she is.'

'Straight up?' Nona looked at her in amazement. 'She kept that quiet.'

'Mind you, that didn't work out, did it? Perhaps that's what she's worrying about?'

It was good to giggle together, and easier afterwards for Nona to go on. 'Things have been pretty bad with his wife for quite a while, rowing and that. She likes doing different things—you know—but there are these great kids, two boys, and Ray's mad about them—'

Oh, little sister, I know, I know . . .

Janey delighted in Nona. 'It's so *good* to see you together,' she would say to Sally with some of her old vigour. 'Knits back together something that has been horribly unravelled over the years.'

Sally was glad she had this new pleasure, for Janey had grown noticeably more impatient and short-tempered lately. She had lost weight and her skin no longer had that healthy outdoor look. She did less work in the garden, which probably explained it. She moved more slowly, had more trouble hauling herself out of a deep chair, snapped with less humour at her underlings and had even begun to allow things like baker's bread and frozen prawns into the house.

When Grianan closed Janey went to Edalmere for a couple of weeks, an unheard-of length of time for her to be away.

Walking with Nona into the kitchen at Grianan on the evening her aunt returned, Sally felt a sick churning inside, knowing Janey would certainly have heard news of Mike. She was totally unprepared for what came, once the greetings were over.

'By the way, Sally, I heard some wonderful news at Edalmere. Mike Danaher's out of hospital at last.'

Sally stared at her in shock, delight mixed with the feeling of having received a dizzying blow.

'The family are absolutely overjoyed, of course,' Janey was saying. 'Now come and sit down, all of you, and don't let this food get cold.'

Dazed, Sally found herself in her chair. Why did the queasy knot in her stomach feel as though it had received a kick from a heavy boot?

'Is this your neighbour at the cottage?' Nona was asking. 'The one with the subarachnoid haemorrhage?'

Thank God for Nona with her brisk professional interest, Sally thought. She knew why the sensation of being winded had followed instantly on her joy at knowing Mike was at home. He belonged once more, completely and irrevocably, to Isobel and his family. As he clawed his way back to normal life he would learn everything in his world again, but he would never learn that Sally had been in it.

'Subarachnoid?' Piers was asking. 'Spiders?'

'The membrane is so fine it's like a spider's web. If a clot forms it presses on it and breaks through. One of my friend's father had one. He'd had headaches for ages and he began to vomit a lot, then he suddenly collapsed.'

'I'm not sure what symptoms there had been beforehand,' Janey said. 'They operated I don't know how many times. They think he'll be nearly normal again eventually.'

Nearly normal. Mike. 'How long would it take someone to recover?' Sally asked Nona. Her voice sounded quavery, but all their voices were subdued, concerned, and no one noticed.

'It varies a lot,' Nona replied. 'One of the problems seems to be how well they cope with fitting back into ordinary life. My friend's father did all kinds of bizarre things.'

'Yes, apparently Isobel is going through all that, poor girl.' Janey looked distressed and suddenly much older, Sally thought. 'Mike goes to wash in the middle of the night and gets back into the wrong bed. Shouts and swears.'

Sally was shaking, knotting her hands under the table, fighting to hide her horror.

'But they wouldn't have let your friend go home if he was still too dis-inhibited,' Nona was saying. 'Especially not with children there. He'll be back in the family to relearn social controls. In fact children help a lot because they take things for granted and offer normal interaction.'

'Isobel says that every day he has to be told where he is all over again, and her name and the children's names. Yet he remembered how to use the telephone—only the poor soul doesn't know who he's phoning.'

Poor soul. The hard body, the long hands with all their technical skill and strength which could also produce those delicate paintings, the tough exterior cloaking humour, tenderness and the essential goodness which she had respected enough to walk out of his life. Poor soul.

'—often patients can recall things they learned in childhood but all recent memory has gone. Or certain areas of memory will come back intact and not others,' Nona was saying.

Worse almost than the images which tortured Sally after this conversation was the report Janey brought back after a later visit to Edalmere. It seemed that the aggressive, uncontrolled phase had lapsed into apathy and inertia. Mike now slept for most of the time, and sat in a chair in his studio for every waking hour. She could not check her tears at this desolate picture.

'Darling, I know, isn't it the saddest thing you ever heard? It breaks my heart to think of him in there as I pass. And he's so often on his own, that's the awful thing.'

'On his own? How can he possibly be left alone?' she made herself ask on a note of more practical concern.

'Well, I'm quite sure he shouldn't be.' Janey looked tightlipped. 'Isobel goes to see her mother a lot.'

'She always did, didn't she?' Sally ventured after a tiny pause.

'Yes, well.' Janey's face wore a look of grim disapproval as she stirred her vegetables, Sally asked no more.

Later she went out alone, going past her favourite rocky lookout, away up the steep face of the hill through the drab drenched heather and up to the sparse grass and rock of the ridge. She went fast, oblivious of the sullen clouds, trying to assimilate this new picture which hurt so much. Mike sitting hour by hour, unmoving, alone. Mike who no longer knew they had ever met.

There came sudden, disturbing realisation. She could go back. The thought spun her to a startled halt. She had for so long thought of Edalmere as barred to her; first because she and Mike couldn't go on seeing each other without doing harm, then because she couldn't bear to be there and shut off from him.

Now she saw that it wouldn't matter if she went there or not; no one knew or guessed that she had any interest in him. She could be near him, perhaps glimpse him. If memories hurt too much then she could come away. No one would know about that either.

For the saddest of reasons she could go back with complete impunity.

Edal Bank looked deserted, no vehicles outside, no lights. Did she imagine its air of dereliction or was it just the dead clumps which needed cutting back in the flowerbeds, the shaggy lawn. In the equally lifeless studio, was Mike sitting alone, trapped and lost in helpless confusion?

She drove steadily past, her mouth dry, her jaw clenched. Not till she reached the cottage did the terrible trembling overtake her. She had expected, did expect, nothing. She had only wanted to be near him, know that he was still there. If she could stand it. She wasn't sure now that she could.

The squawk of the unoiled gate was louder than ever, bringing memories surging. It was a year since she had been here. She made herself walk through the house, into every room, braving whatever associations they would face her with. And anyway, she reminded herself sharply, what was this sort of pain compared with the tragedy which had torn Mike's life apart?

Though there was a perpetual gnawing unease somewhere in her stomach which she identified as fear, fear of this hurting so much that she wouldn't be able to handle it, she did eventually find a certain relief and even comfort to be back.

She could walk in the familiar places, could close her eyes and breathe in again the scent of those lost marvellous days, listen to the voices. But she couldn't turn into the ready arms, her hand would never again be taken in that firm warm grasp, nor her body be aroused and satisfied in their perfect loving. There were a lot of tears. But she accepted them, knowing that she had been right to come. She was no longer shut off from the happiness she had found here, and more importantly she didn't feel so utterly excluded from what was happening to Mike.

For the first time she saw Isobel. The sound of the car coming along the track behind her as she walked to the village. The woman at the wheel acknowledged her with a lift of her hand, but to Sally's relief didn't stop. In that brief glimpse an image had been stamped into her brain which she knew she would never be free of—a small-featured face with clear pale skin and light eyes, and a soft mass of curling, red-gold hair. Anonymity gone; the shadowy figure suddenly real and sharp—and pretty. Thank God I hadn't known that, Sally thought, stepping back into the track and walking on oppressed by fresh guilt. The cold white light of reality had abruptly replaced the golden glow of memory. She, Sally, had had an affair with this woman's husband, tenuous and temporary as it had been. And now it was not even a memory for Mike. It was between him and this woman that permanence existed, and commitment, a commitment all the greater because he was disabled. Their marriage was impregnable now and, walking blindly on, Sally made herself face that fact.

She discovered that the need which had brought her here, to assure herself of Mike's existence and to learn all she could of his present state, was easily satisfied. What had happened to the Danaher family was a topic of great interest and sympathy locally.

'Gets out into the garden now. Doesn't do anything, like, just stands and stares, but it's better than nothing, isn't it?'

Ann Jackson, overturning Sally's image of Mike imprisoned all day long in his chair in the studio. Just to think of him outside, looking about him at the lake and woods and fells he loved so much, was intensely moving.

More unsettling was Elsa Callander's version when she invited herself for coffee and held forth on the subject with complacent authority. 'He's perfectly capable of carrying on a conversation. Nothing complicated, naturally, but that doesn't matter. Of course he'll never be normal again, you can't expect that, can you? But sometimes you'd hardly think there's anything wrong with him at all. Isobel is ridiculously overprotective. When I called, Mike was pathetically pleased to see me. He should meet people, that's what I say, do him good, get back to normal. He's supposed to relearn everything, Isobel said so herself, and what better way to do that than with supportive friends, especially as Isobel leaves him such a lot.'

'What do you mean?' Sally asked, frowning.

'Oh, well!' The slightly bulging eyes swung back to her, a look of eager satisfaction lighting them. 'It's hardly right, is it? I mean, it can't be safe for *him*, being left alone like that. She hates the place, always has. And now with him in that state, well, I suppose you can hardly blame her. Up and down to Jedburgh all the time. That's where her mother lives, you know. Spends more time there than here, I sometimes think.'

'But where are the children?'

'Oh, packed off to boarding school. She'd always insisted on that, though Mike wasn't keen, put it off as long as he could. Young Michael loves the place, of course, but there's nothing for them here, is there? And nothing for Isobel—no one could call her a country girl.'

This self-satisfied speech left Sally with such a welter of helpless resentment and disturbing new information to sort out that she took off up the path through the wood as soon as her unwelcome visitor left. How desperately jealous she had felt that Elsa Callander could call on the Danahers, could see Mike, had, as it seemed, some stake in him simply because she was a neighbour, while she, Sally, was forever shut out and obliged to deal alone with her grief.

Why had that conversation about Isobel filled her with such foreboding? Certainly the news that the children were now away at school had made her sad on Mike's behalf, but that was assuming he would miss them. She didn't know that. Nor did she know what life in that house was now like, the day-to-day actuality of it. Perhaps it had been necessary to protect the children from things too hard for them to bear.

She was deep in these thoughts as she came level with Edal Bank when a movement caught her eye. She felt her limbs, her breath, the blood in her veins, check for one dizzy moment. Across the garden a tall pale figure was just going in at the studio door.

Ghost-pale; that was the prevailing impression. Bony skull with cropped grey hair; grey-blue shirt and pale jeans hanging off clothes-hanger shoulders and skeleton frame. His movements were laborious and slow, or was it just that time for Sally had gone into a lower gear as she tried to take a step forward and felt her feet rooted to the ground, as she tried to call out and could make no sound?

But should she call? Would Mike know her? Would it startle him to see her, harm him? But he was there, he was there.

The moment vanished, the one precious chance snatched away. Mike, who was inaccessible to her, only to her, had gone with shuffling feet and sagging shoulders through the door of the studio. Sally sank down where she was on the bank, wound her arms tightly round her knees and dropped her head on them, fighting one more desperate lonely battle for control.

Unbearable as it was at the time, this incident did put things finally into perspective for her. Now she knew that beyond all doubt or hope Mike was cut off from her, not only by his condition but by family, friends, neighbours. He would be cared for, would make a recovery of sorts, adjust to a new level of living. Nothing would ever put Sally or their brief shared happiness back into his memory or knowledge as he struggled back to some kind of normality. Even longing to see him had been an intrusion on her part, and she would not intrude any further on this sad family.

'Hey, Sally, how would you like the flat to yourself again?' Nona came bounding up the stone steps and burst in dramatically.

'I wouldn't,' Sally said blankly, arrested with one hand on the tap, the other holding the kettle under it to be filled.

'Ah, that's nice. I thought you'd be over the moon.' Nona let an armful of shopping slither onto the worktop, and gave Sally a quick hug. 'But listen to this, it's great—'

She couldn't guess at Sally's hollow feeling of apprehension as she asked, 'Are you going home? Have you heard from Ray?'

The glow faded momentarily. 'I wish. No, no point in going home yet, worse luck. Just listen, this is really cool. You're going to love it.'

Am I? Sally wondered bleakly.

'I've found this great flat, in that new block behind the hospital. There's a couple of us going to share. How d'you like that for a plan? You won't have to trip over my junk any more, or my friends—'

'Here in town?' The relief was enormous. 'But, Nona, isn't it mad to pay rent when you can stay here? You know I love having you.'

Nona laughed affectionately. 'Come on, Sally, we've had a great time and I'm going to miss it as well, but this place was never meant for two unless they're married to each other, you know that.'

'And you need your own space?'

'Oh, well, you know, party once in a while, have mates round for a few tinnies, give the blokes a chance . . .'

'Well, put like that.' Sally knew Nona often hammed the accent to cloak something serious.

'It's been terrific, though. You know I've loved it here, don't you?— being with you, I mean.'

Getting to know a sister. Yes, it had been terrific.

'Well, at least you'll still be in Muirend. I thought for one horrible moment you were buzzing off again.'

'No, I won't be buzzing off yet.' Nona gave her an odd quick look, frowning, then evidently decided not to say whatever it was. 'Come on,' she said briskly. 'I've got the key. Want to come and have a look?'

The flat was a series of tiny rectangles with neutral emulsion slapped on thin walls and synthetic rubber-backed speckled carpet everywhere. Its only attractive feature was a balcony looking south down the course of the river. Nona appeared to be entirely satisfied with it.

'So who are you sharing with?'

'One of the nurses from the hospital, Kerri. We saw her in the pub the other night.' Sally remembered a long-legged smiling Jamaican girl with a lucrative bent for liar dice. 'And Pat, he'll be instructing at the dry ski slope from the beginning of the month.'

'Any ideas for furniture?'

'Aunt Janey?'

Janey rose to the challenge with a zest Sally was glad to see. She had been so much less energetic lately, starting jobs in the garden and abandoning them impatiently. She was definitely looking her age, and perhaps it was hardly surprising that she wanted to spend more time indoors, tucked up in her sitting room, reading or leaning back, eyes closed, to be borne away on tumultuous waves of German grand opera.

But for Nona she roused herself to stump about the house waving the stick she now used at dreadful old servants' cupboards and listing lamps, exclaiming, 'Take it, take it, for God's sake, save me burning it.'

The friendship Sally had tentatively envisaged for herself with Pauly Napier had become a reality for Nona, and Drumveyn also proved a rich source of plunder, including a battered but handsome wing chair which Sally wouldn't have minded having in the boathouse flat.

The flat. Walking into its silence was chilling indeed for the first couple of evenings on her own. Of course she missed the superficial things, the easy gossip, the laughter, the chatting over a glass of wine as they got supper ready, the mild squabbling over their different music, the off-loading of the day's events. But at a deeper level Sally knew she didn't really like living alone, and that was now the long-term prospect ahead of her. And there was nothing to shield her from thoughts of Mike. Every so often some association or reminder would stir a sharp impotent grief, but for the most part it was just something that had to be lived with, like the necessity of coming to terms with a death.

Though she missed Nona acutely, Sally eventually accepted her departure. She had come closer to Nona than to any member of the family since Janey in childhood, and that wasn't going to vanish. Nona would always be there, her sister, loved and valued.

And, to Sally's relief, she was still very much in evidence.

'I thought you'd be very involved in the new set-up,' Sally admitted one evening when Nona had come round bringing with her a Drumveyn pheasant which she then braised with celery and cream.

'Waste all this effort on that mob?' But Nona knew what Sally meant.

'I've missed you,' Sally told her.

'Me too. If you had more room I'd still be here, believe me. Mind you, when I first came I didn't think I'd stay all that long.'

'Nor did I, I must admit.'

Again Sally caught that quick glance, the check, and had the odd feeling there was something she was missing. This time she was going to pursue it but the phone rang and the moment passed.

'There's even a chance it may be for me these days,' she remarked as she reached for it, and Nona laughed.

One evening a few months later, when they were together in the shop putting through a backlog of copying and sending faxes, Sally had been talking idly about going down to Edinburgh to do some decent shopping, throwing out dates in a halfhearted way because she couldn't get up much enthusiasm for the plan, when Nona cut across her ramblings, saying sharply, 'Never mind Edinburgh, isn't it about time you went up to Grianan? You haven't been there for weeks.'

'What are you talking about?' Sally said crossly. 'When were you last there?'

'Two days ago.'

Something in her tone arrested Sally. She turned quickly with a block of paper upright in her hands to find Nona watching her, the faxes abandoned.

'I didn't know that,' she said less truculently, wondering with a strange little quiver of unease what was coming.

'Aunt Janey misses you.'

'Did she say so?'

'Bloody hell, Sally,' Nona exploded. 'Don't nit-pick. That's not the point and you know it.'

'Sorry,' Sally mumbled. 'I do keep meaning to go.'

'Then go.'

Sally stared at her in surprise. Nona's tone was uncompromising.

The shock of seeing her was a moment that stayed with Sally for ever, with its violent jumble of disbelief, compassion and guilt, and beneath them the first glimpse of a fearful emptiness ahead. It's only been six weeks, seven at the most, her brain computed desperately, as though to deny what she saw. Janey's skin seemed to sag from the diminished flesh, her eyes looked out from dark hollows, her hair was thin and flat.

'Janey, darling Janey.' Sally clung to her, shaking with realisation, torn with shame for her blindness, her absence, and terrified of what the answers must be to any questions she could ask.

'I didn't want to worry you. You've had enough unhappiness, enough to cope with.'

No denial. That shook Sally to the depths.

'I should have known. I should have seen—'

'Nonsense, why should you?'

Nona had. And so, it came to Sally suddenly, had Piers.

Later, she went to find him. Gardens and greenhouse were deserted, but she finally ran him to earth stripped to the waist in the biting March air, his arm thrust down the drain outside the old laundry.

'You've despised me for staying away.'

'Yes.' A handful of dank blackened beech leaves, silted grey and stinking foully, landed at her boot toe.

'I truly didn't know.'

'I don't see how you couldn't have.' His voice was unforgiving.

She squatted down beside him, tears stinging her eyes. 'I don't see either. But it's true. Janey's always been—' She couldn't find the words. A grown-up, invincible, invulnerable. My rock, my strength. So utterly familiar that I never properly looked at her, never saw her.

Piers strained further down the pipe, his face concentrated, shutting her out. There was a gurgle far below and he withdrew his filthy stinking arm, shivering as he pushed himself to his feet. With his other hand he plucked his sweater and jacket from where he had tossed them over a bush. 'Better get cleaned up,' he said, and walked away.

Sally turned slowly after him as though weighted down by this new appalling sadness, aching at least for his tolerance even if she had forfeited his sympathy.

Nona too said, though more kindly, 'I just don't see how you didn't realise. Janey wouldn't let us say a word to you till they decided to operate, but if everyone else knew why didn't you?'

'Absorbed in my own affairs,' Sally said with the flatness of guilt. She'd thought she was learning not to be, thought she'd behaved well over parting from Mike, been generous in accepting Nona. Pitiful. Nugatory. She had learned nothing and had failed the person who mattered most in the world.

It was such a short time to be given. As the first days of sun and thaw released the grip of winter in liquid sound and dazzling brilliance, all their hearts and minds concentrated on Janey. Not to the neglect of all else; that was not part of her ethic, and very sharp and clear the rules returned to Sally now, humbling her by their validity. Her mind was wholly directed to what was happening at Grianan.

In only one matter did Janey directly ask for help. 'I'm not one of those sifting sorting people,' she remarked one day, looking round her cluttered sitting room. 'Can you bear to have this lot to deal with when

I've gone? I don't care what happens to it, just do whatever's easiest, but I'd rather like everything to go on looking the same meanwhile.'

'Janey, of course you mustn't touch a thing,' Sally cried, horrified at the idea for her aunt's sake but at the same time filled with a cowardly dread of having to live with visible reminders of what was coming.

'Hoped you'd say that,' Janey grunted. 'But there is one thing on my mind which I should see to myself. I ought to go to Edalmere and sort out what's left of Ursula's belongings. I've put it off and put it off but I really can't do that any more. But I wondered, would you come with me?'

'Of course I will.' Rush of piercing, stinging associations.

'Dreadful bore, I know, but I'm not sure I can tackle it alone. Guilt chiefly, I suppose, not liking her as much as I should have done. But God, she was silly, the silliest person I ever knew.' It was good to see the glint of sardonic humour. 'And Sally, no planning now. Just do whatever you like with the cottage afterwards. It will be yours.'

Strange circumstances in which to return to the place where Mike lived out his shadowy existence. Two seas of grief meeting.

## CHAPTER EIGHT

APPREHENSION, SHOT through with an irresistible nostalgia, clutched at Sally as she drove south, and she felt the tremble of nervous dread in her hands as she passed through Edal village and the road climbed to the lake. Once in the lane each yard seemed to crawl by, each stone and blade of grass separately visible. Yet when she pulled up outside the cottage it seemed to have been over in seconds, meeting no one, seeing no one; emptiness, normality.

With what felt like a physical effort she wrenched her mind back to Janey. What must this feel like for her, coming back to this place which was so tied up with family memories, knowing she was here to tick off last-time things?

Janey clumped stiffly into the kitchen, surveying it with a resigned chuck of her head. 'Poor old Ursula. She really was perfectly potty. Perhaps we could give this lot to the Beatrix Potter Society, or whatever it calls itself. Some of the china stuff is quite valuable. But you must do exactly as you like—change it, keep it, sell it. Same with Grianan.' She swung round on Sally with a sudden fierceness that betrayed how much more that mattered. 'Do you hear me? No idiotic business of trying to work out what Janey would have liked or minded.'

Sally nodded, the muscles of her face tightening. 'Except that to think what Janey would like can be a useful yardstick.'

'Oh ho, pretty speech. Useful when it suits you,' Janey mocked. But Sally knew she was pleased. 'Come on, let's settle in and do something about food. Do you know, I'm quite looking forward to this. When were we last on our own together? Must be years.'

It was a time that would always be precious to Sally. She felt that only by the merest chance had she salvaged it. The terror that Janey could have slipped away while she was obliviously unaware was enough to wake her sweating in the night. Yet the happiness of being with her, the feeling of closeness was scored through by the poignancy of the job they had come here to do, the sifting and sorting which Janey could not face in her own life. Sally was all too aware that soon she would be doing this for Janey. Their minds open to memories, their hands momentarily caressed objects which led their thoughts back to other people, other days, the life that Ursula and Teddy had shared in this house. And beneath the immediate sadness of these visual and tactile associations lay her own private pain at being back in this landscape which other memories made so significant for her.

Sometimes she would feel frantic to get away from the claustrophobic cottage, from a too relentless consciousness of farewell and endings. Sometimes, too, she felt that Janey might prefer to be alone. Then, walking on the fell or wandering round the lake path, Sally would be seized with a sense of wasting irreplaceable time with Janey and would race back, pushing her own memories aside to wait their turn.

It was impossible to shut them out entirely. There was always milk to fetch, shopping to do. On a gusty morning of flittering sunlight and colours that deepened and faded as the clouds bowled along before a crisp wind, on her way back from the village she saw Mike. She didn't realise it was Mike at first, just catching sight of a tall figure standing across the lane from Edal Bank, on the edge of the cleared space between the trees that gave a view across the lake. But then, as though her brain had recognised him before her eyes gave it the message, she felt her knees begin to quiver, her feet stumble on stones that suddenly seemed larger and rougher, as with her eyes fixed on that still figure she walked automatically on.

Would he move? Would he turn to go in before she reached him?

Would someone come out, call him in? It did not seem possible that she might be about to speak to him. Must she nod and pass with a greeting, a stranger to him?

He had seen her now, was watching her approach, peering at her intently and curiously, and it was odd how striking this small absence of customary adult good manners was.

'Hello, Mike.' Sally found that her voice sounded unused, creaky.

'Hello there.' He sounded friendly, pleased, utterly normal, and for one heart-stopping moment Sally thought that he knew her. Then she looked into his face and saw only a sort of general willing affability there. He was not so pitifully gaunt as when she had last glimpsed him. In fact his face was unexpectedly fleshy. The shape of his head, the strong cheekbones, the hazel eyes, the thick curly hair, though grey now, still made him good-looking, but the keenness, the humour, the look of easy authority had gone. His eyes looked bland, blank and vulnerable in their naive friendliness.

'Mike—' Words stuck like marbles in her throat. 'Mike, it's Sally.'

He was looking even more intently into her face, social niceties lost in the urgent struggle to piece things together in his brain.

'Yes . . .' he was saying, 'yes . . . I know who you are. *Wait* a minute now . . .' He spoke differently, slowly, in a sort of relaxed singsong as though there were all the time in the world. As for him there was, time stretching empty, unmeasured. 'You used to help with the bridges. Yes, that's right. You built the bridges.'

Stunned, Sally gazed at him, her face tight, hardly believing what she had heard and terrified of rushing in and destroying this fragile link. 'That's right,' she said quietly, her voice unsteady. 'I stayed at the cottage.' She gestured along the lane.

'*That's* right,' he said again, still in that slow voice, but this time with evident satisfaction. 'I remember you. The cottage along the lake. I haven't been in the place for years.'

'We used to go out to shoot foxes,' Sally offered carefully.

'Foxes, that's right, I remember that.' She knew instantly that he didn't. He was using the line she had fed him. 'And you stayed at the cottage.'

She had said that too, but here she was certain that, however confusedly, he had made the connection. She gained a tiny insight into how, gropingly, he patched together fragments of memory.

'So where are you living now?' he asked.

'At Grianan, in Glen Ellig, with Aunt Janey.'

'Oh yes, Glen Ellig, that's right.' Nothing. Then, amazingly, 'You were in Australia.'

'That's right, I was.' Sally could hardly get the words out. She held herself rigid, hands twined in the plastic loops of the carrier bag with the milk and bread. She wanted to throw her arms round him, hold him safe from the appalling thing that had overtaken him. 'We used to swap travellers' tales.'

'That's right, we did.' He laughed a little, apparently pleased that he was getting things right, but obviously not remembering. 'So you were in Australia? Where did we meet?'

'We met here,' Sally said gently, her voice only just under control. 'I was staying at the cottage along the lake.' Using his own phrase.

'The cottage, that's right.' He nodded, but he was frowning a little now. 'So where are you living now?'

'In Glen Ellig.'

He nodded again, but looked troubled. 'I've been ill, you know,' he said. 'Gone a bit cuckoo, they tell me. Can't remember anything.'

'Mike.' It was a whisper. The crude phrase was not one he would ever have used. Anguish engulfed Sally. She got her voice under control. 'You're getting better all the time, though, aren't you?'

'Oh, I'm a lot better than I was,' he said instantly. 'Couldn't remember this place at all, you know, when I first came out of hospital. Didn't know where I was. Didn't know Isobel or the children.'

'You'll keep getting better,' Sally said, more pleading than reassuring.

'Oh, I'll be just about back to normal. Almost completely normal.' Words he had been taught. 'So where are you living now?'

This seemed to be something he needed to establish to place her, if he could, in some context to which he could relate. Glen Ellig meant nothing, so his brain returned again and again to the question, struggling to make a connection.

'I'm staying just now at the cottage,' Sally said, again pointing along the track through the trees.

'You must come and see us,' he said warmly. A social reflex back in place. 'Isobel would love to see you.'

Sally walked on, torn to pieces by the fluctuating promise and checks of this exchange. Beyond her wildest hope had been the moment when Mike had volunteered the remark that she had helped him with the bridges. He had volunteered it at once, perhaps before his brain became clogged with conscious effort to remember more about her. Perhaps his brain tired.

Harried by pity, a searing sense of loss, yet a hope more vivid than she had allowed herself for months, Sally knew she couldn't face Janey yet. Leaving the shopping bag at the bottom of the drive she went on along the lake, past the path to the fell, and ducked and wove her way to the secret place below the waterfall, a place so intimately connected with that first meeting with Mike that she had not had the courage to go back to it since they had parted. There she crouched for a long time, letting the emotions come as they would, and the tears.

'It's hard to believe, isn't it, that any woman could even think of being unfaithful, with her husband in such a state, poor man? But Isobel's always had a hard streak in her, I've said so often enough, and this just goes to show.'

They hadn't been able to stop her this time, Elsa Callander, her eyes gleaming with satisfaction, her eager voice gobbling out the gossip like some self-righteous turkey cock.

'Of course she still looks after him, he's always clean and so on, and frankly he doesn't know which day of the week it is and probably never will, so in a way I suppose it doesn't matter, but it's the principle of the thing, isn't it? I mean, all this pretence of going to see her mother, up and down to Jedburgh two and three times a week, the children kept away from him, left for hours and hours on his own.'

An outraged instinct to protect Mike made Sally want to leap up and shout her into silence. How dared she write him off so callously, how dared she invade his privacy in such a way? Yet in spite of her furious anger, her brain seized on the implications of this gossip. Had Isobel really found someone else? Was she truly abandoning Mike, not just for hours alone, which surely was not only callous but potentially danger-ous, but for good?

'It's none of our business,' Janey was protesting, but her voice so lacked its usual firmness that Sally's attention was caught. She saw how this visit had drained her and was annoyed with herself for allowing it. Janey should have been resting now, not pinned down under the bom-bardment of Elsa Callander's uncharitable innuendoes.

'Well, we're all neighbours,' Elsa was pointing out affrontedly. 'The poor man ought to be having therapy, companionship. I offered, natu-rally, but Isobel was quite rude about it. But—'

'I'm sorry,' Sally broke in, trying to keep her voice polite and ordinary. 'I think Aunt Janey's rather tired. We had a busy morning.'

'Oh, don't mind me,' Elsa cried gaily, not moving. 'I can see you've been packing up. Could give you a hand, you know?' Her eyes raked the boxes, the bare shelves. 'I hope you don't mind my asking, only natu-rally it would affect everyone here, but are you by any chance thinking of selling? Only one never knows quite who might—'

Aunt Janey gave her one look of unconcealed loathing, leaned back in her chair and shut her eyes.

'I really must ask you to go,' Sally said to Elsa, getting up quickly, not prepared to wrap up the request in conciliatory phrases. After she had left Sally knelt beside Janey's chair, conscious of the little flutter of fear, which was becoming all too familiar, to see her slumped there so wearily.

Janey opened one eye. 'Dreadful woman. How about some fresh tea to wash the taste of her out of our mouths?'

It was so good to hear her evil chuckle that Sally leaned to wrap her arms round her and crush her close.

'Terribly sad though,' Janey remarked, when the tea was made, 'this business of the Danahers. One wonders what the outcome will be. It's easy to condemn Isobel, but what must it have been like for her, the whole fabric of her marriage torn apart in a few moments? And who can judge what harm is being done to Mike? How can any of us know how something like that would affect him?'

She sounded thoughtful, concerned, not asking for comment, and Sally offered none.

Back at Grianan, where Sally now spent almost as much time as at the flat, she did her best to accept that Mike was finally gone. At no point would their lives ever touch. No one, including Mike himself, knew that any relationship had ever existed between them. This had to be faced, accepted, then set aside. Janey now occupied all their thoughts. For Nona and Sally the shop had become a mere job, confined strictly to opening hours. It was no longer their first priority.

Janey underwent a second operation at the end of May, and though they all knew it could only be a temporary remission, she did seem better once she had recovered from the immediate trauma, and her humour and mental liveliness were soon back in place.

It was now that Sally received a great shock and a great lesson, the last that Janey was to give her. She had been up the hill behind the house one evening and was coming down into the garden from the high grassy 'drying green' when she saw the light in Janey's room was on, the curtains open and she could see right into the room. In a way it was very un-Janey, since she had simply lifted everything straight out of her mother's old room and transferred it there without changing anything. It was all very feminine, pale peach and cream, but of course it was completely Janey not to have bothered about colours so long as things were still usable. Sally looked in now with pleasure at the soft lamplight, the big bed with its high tattered satin headboard, its plump pillows, its ragged flounces and faded pink eiderdown quilt. She looked in expecting a comforting familiar picture of Janey with her spectacles on the end of her nose devouring her ninth or tenth Sharpe novel—hurrying to finish them, Sally thought, with the unbearable stab of foreboding which was never far away in these fleeting days.

Instead she saw two lovers, entwined, close, at peace. With a shock that drove the breath out of her lungs in an incredulous gasp, she saw Janey, head back, eyes closed, her arm about Piers, whose dark head was curved down, quiet on her breast. Sally saw in that one stunned second the darkness of his skin against Janey's, the accustomed ease of their bodies, the unmistakable serene containment in the softly lit scene.

Astounded, floundering, she found there came a sense of the fitness of what she had seen, followed by an amused, tender delight. She turned away and went along the face of the slope and down into the vegetable garden where the long beds had been dug over but, except for one small corner, not planted this year.

Janey and Piers. So simple, so astounding but so obvious. Many things fell neatly into place and, with the satisfying sense of things made clear, a great delight filled Sally that Janey had had this, had had her lover to bring her happiness. It thrilled her to realise that the contented accord she had so often observed between Janey and Piers had had its roots in this wonderful intimacy.

No wonder Piers had been so protective of Janey, so angered by Sally's neglect and blindness. But how marvellous for her, Sally thought, wandering on with an instinctive wish not to intrude upon them by so much as entering the house, how marvellous to have Piers's gentleness and perceptiveness lavished upon her. Lucky Janey, she thought, between laughter and tears. Oh, lucky Janey.

There was no question of Grianan opening in the spring and Sally found that her mind blanked out in cowardly fear any thoughts of its future beyond that point. She and Janey had written to tell the guests. The closest friends among them Janey insisted on telling herself. Sally dealt with the rest, a task that left her drained. To write over and over again, 'as Aunt Janey has terminal cancer', which was what Janey wanted her to say, was like a blow descending repeatedly on the same spot.

The replies poured in, nearly all of them, after distressed and shocked reactions to Janey's illness, going on to say what Grianan had meant to them through the years. For the first time Sally saw Janey's prosaic acceptance of what was coming rocked as she read those loving testimonials to her care and hard work.

'How can I not see them all again?' she demanded passionately, crushing a handful of pages untidily to her bosom.

'All those boring old nuisances?' Sally teased her, but very affectionately, going to her and folding her aunt's rough, much whiter head against her while Janey sniffed noisily.

'I know what I'll do, I'll have a party for the nuisances,' she announced with resolution, pushing Sally away.

The project grew at breathless speed and ran away with them. Piers, Nona and Sally began to panic about a houseful of guests who clearly had every intention of staying the night if not the weekend, and were all equally confident of right of tenure to 'their' rooms.

But that wasn't all. It was becoming obvious that Janey's trading network could not be ignored. Its members were the friends of her girlhood. Janey had done little socialising outside Grianan for many years, but such friendships were solid and unchanging.

One thing was plain: everyone who intended to come intended to help. 'We're not short of resources anyway,' Sally remarked after a tricky conversation with Lady Hay of Sillerton, who had made up her mind that they should have her frightful old butler Dewes to 'run things' for them.

'If we've got all these ex-ambassadors and judges and generals' wives and things fighting about who's going to clean the loos, then let them get on with it, I say,' was Nona's reaction.

It was clearly the answer and suddenly it all became as Janey had intended, the reason for the whole enterprise tacitly and thankfully ignored in shared activity.

It was a weekend in mid-June, with feelings treacherously near the surface. There was the tremendously buoyant mood, almost tangible throughout the house, of a group gathered in a place they cared about because of their love for one valued person, a love they were ready to show and share. And beneath that there was the unbelieving grief, publicly hidden, which would pluck at people unawares, sending them abruptly out of rooms in the middle of a conversation, or driving them to the garden to stand with their backs to the house gazing out over the patterned midsummer greens of the glen to Ben Breac's shapely peak, remembering.

The weather was mostly kind to them. It must have been, for afterwards Sally could scarcely remember what it had been like. What she did remember was the extreme efficiency of her elderly male shirt-sleeved pot-washing team; the mountains of wonderful food which appeared on the long tables which Piers had set up in the library and dining room and the extraordinary sensation of being part of what every person in the room was feeling as they sat in the absolute stillness of the drawing room and listened for the last time to the sentimental familiar music in the long-drawn-out summer dusk.

Even more poignant was the image of Aunt Janey, the still centre to whom all turned, on whom everything revolved; Janey passive, allowing herself to be looked after. Sally knew she was not alone to make the comparison with the days when her aunt was the driving force behind the whole show, stumping rapidly about house and garden, ordering, bullying, reprimanding, giving, making, laughing, doing.

There was a terrible gaiety about the thanks and goodbyes, an abruptness about the way one car after another took off down the drive.

Janey went into hospital again in July. This time they didn't operate. She came home after a couple of days and two weeks later she died.

Piers left, mute, rigid, his thin face taut and twisted with pain. Gazing into that hurting face, the eyes guarding their grief so tenaciously, Sally knew she couldn't ask if he would come back. To her he had never relented. He felt that she had failed in her love for Janey. She longed to say something to let him see that she knew the truth of his relationship with Janey and was glad of it, but of course it was impossible to refer to it in any way. Equally impossible at this point to attempt to break through to some understanding between the two of them. Janey had left Nona and the others respectable sums and had given Piers the garden cottage and Sally didn't want any disapproval he felt for her personally to interfere with what her aunt had wanted.

'Piers, you do know that if you want to use the cottage—' A clumsy beginning since it was now his. She tried again. 'I mean, please don't feel that if you live in it you have to be involved here—' Worse still, hopelessly open to misinterpretation.

The deeds had been carefully drawn up, giving separate access and rights to water, leaving Sally's options open to sell Grianan if she wished. That hadn't been discussed, but she knew that realistically Janey had expected it to happen.

Piers hadn't answered, had simply shaken his head. He looked beaten and stunned, withdrawn deep into that ferocious reserve of his. Sally wanted to ask where he would go, what he would do, but knew such questions would not be acceptable.

Then Nona, her arms tight round Sally, her cheek wet against hers. 'I hate leaving you, I feel pulled apart, but I've got to go back. I can't wait any longer, but I just couldn't go till . . .'

'I know.' Sally hugged her. 'I'm only thankful that you stayed this long. I couldn't have got through it without you, you know that. And it meant so much to Janey too, having you here. Not just for yourself but because you were her link with Mother.'

Janey had refused to let them tell Rose in time for her to come. They both understood that she had known she didn't have the reserves of strength left to deal with such a reunion. But she had come very close to Nona in those last weeks.

'You'll write, won't you?' Nona didn't mean write to her when she had gone.

'I've already written.' In the raw aching time after Janey's death Sally had found it surprisingly easy to express many things to her mother which had long needed to be said. 'I wrote to Father, too. I thought he'd like to know about Janey.' But she hadn't written in time for him to come to the funeral.

'Hey, that's *good*,' Nona said warmly. She had worried about Sally being alone but she didn't want to delay going home any longer. She had at last confessed that Ray Tamerlaine had written to her over two months ago, telling her that he and his wife were filing for divorce, and asking Nona to go back. Sally wished so much that Janey could have known about this loving sacrifice which filled her with gratitude and respect for Nona every time she thought of it.

'It's only miles, remember,' Nona said now, 'only hours. We'll never be really separate again.' It was true, and it made a big difference.

The desolation of Janey's going had to be got through and there were no short cuts to that. Sally missed Nona very much and minded about Piers's departure more even than she had expected, yet she found in herself a strength which surprised her, an absence of desperation, even an absence of loneliness. It was as though Janey's courage, Nona's selflessness, the depths of Piers's grief all helped her.

Grianan must wait. She didn't strip it or shroud it in dustsheets. It looked as it always had, as though it was waiting only for the gruff laugh, the heavy tread, the rich smell of glorious food, the pounding piano, to spring back to busy life. Marchmain waited too, poor cat. He had refused to stay with Connie and Maureen and had come obstinately home each time he was taken away. In spite of their dire prophecies of pining, starvation or death in battle the pampered creature fended for himself admirably. Sally wasn't altogether surprised; Marchmain was a ruthless survivor if ever there was one.

It took her a while to find someone to replace Nona in the shop and she was very busy, which helped. Small businesses seemed to be starting up everywhere. Most collapsed and premises stood empty with ominous regularity, but nothing could deter fresh optimists from leaping in in their turn. It was profitable for Sally, though there was a ghoulish feel to it sometimes and she often found herself giving warnings against her own interests. No one ever took any notice of them.

She was discovering that something else had changed since Janey's death, becoming subtly aware of a new attitude from the friends in the glen who had poured to the party and the funeral. Sally, as the only Buchanan left at Grianan, had inherited them, as it were, and in their different ways they let her know that they were there for her when she was ready to turn to them. She didn't need them yet. Like the decision about Grianan itself, she had to have time. But knowing that this easy, undemanding friendship was on offer was consoling.

As the weeks slipped by and the awful emptiness at waking gradually became less frightening, Sally realised that she had another new source of strength to tap into. Through Nona she had regained a family. She had turned her back on it so determinedly after the disastrous visit to Australia that for years she had had no sense of it existing for her. Now they were suddenly there, part of her life. Not only Nona's frequent glowing postcards but letters from their mother brought them all close.

Writing first about Janey and Grianan, free in her grief to allow herself at last nostalgia without apology, Rose had moved on with growing ease to talk of the matters which lay unresolved between them—how she had felt about leaving Sally's father, about leaving Sally, how she had blamed herself for her inability to welcome her when she had come to Orford. For Sally it was like being released from an emotional straitjacket and she let her mother know it.

Less easy, much less warm, was the letter Sally's father eventually wrote, but he too used Janey's death to open doors between them. It was strange to find him remembering Grianan with affection. Somehow Sally had shut him out of all memories there, but of course he had been there often with Rose in the early days of their marriage, and with Sally when she was small. He didn't bare his soul to Sally in his careful letter, didn't refer to her mother, but he did say:

*Although we have drifted apart in recent years, never, never feel that you cannot turn to me for anything you need. I suppose I've always taken it for granted that you would know that, but thinking over what I should say to you in this letter it occurred to me that perhaps it has to be stated. I often feel a need to know more of your life than the bare bones of major events or new addresses. But work, as you will recall, can always protect me from doing anything even slightly difficult . . .*

251

The wry twist of self-mockery dispelled the chill of his words and Sally understood, with her first adult appreciation of her father, how hard it was for him to make contact with another human being.

So although from day to day she was terribly alone, there was none of the sensation of her life being on hold which she had experienced when Julian, behaving so well, had gone back to his ex-wife. She knew she could cope better now. Love, friendship and support were on offer. She had a base.

# CHAPTER NINE

A FIERCE NORTHWESTERLY drove down the lake, funnelled by the hills, whipping up white crests on the waves, breaking in douches of spray against the jetty where Sally sat with her arms wrapped round her knees, her face up to the wind and the wet. It was exhilarating, and gave her a strange sense of solitary defiance.

She had come often to Edalmere in the months since Janey died and the others had gone away. She had never expected to be able to do so, but weekends in the flat were restless and long and Grianan was a house peopled by ghosts.

Coming here tentatively, needing a different scene but not ready to face people, she had wondered if Mike, having once recognised her, would remember more. But from Ann Jackson and Elsa, from comments made in the village and her own observation, Sally had learned how completely each moment vanished for Mike as it passed. Each time he saw Sally he had no idea they had met since his illness and the conversation was always precisely the same. She knew she was gone from his brain the moment she walked away.

It was a miracle to be able to speak to him, be close enough to touch him, though she never did so, and let her eyes drink in those physical details which hadn't changed. Mike was often out-of-doors now, sitting in the garden or standing at the edge of the lake, and he looked fitter, his skin brown and freckled, more flesh on the long bones. Eagerly as she noted each tiny sign of progress, he was still far from the Mike she had known. His face had a strange new blandness, his movements were heavy, his humour and energy and natural authority gone. All his powers were concentrated on meeting the demands of each moment as it came, trying to find ways to evade the constant admission, 'I don't remember . . .'

Sally found it hard to accept that every conversation began at the beginning again. He was gentle, smiling, and gave no indication that he minded his present condition. Sally found that incredibly sad.

Sometimes he referred to Isobel. 'She's never here,' he would say naturally. 'Always shopping or at her mother's, or taking the children out from school.'

Sally asked how the children were; they never seemed to be at Edal Bank.

'Oh, they've been great,' Mike said instantly, proudly. 'I've been ill, you know, didn't know who the hell I was when I came out of hospital. Didn't know who the children were. But they've been great. Michael often helps me—' but a look of anxiety crossed his face as past and present failed to mesh in his brain. He peered at Sally uneasily, examining her face, then asked again, 'So where are you living now?'

She knew he had lost track and that he was worried about it, so she chatted quietly for a few more moments and then walked on.

From Ann Jackson she learned that Mike was often alone at the house, even at night.

'It doesn't seem to bother him, though. Well, poor lad, he doesn't know what's going on, does he? And he'll never be any different, by all accounts. Every day's just starting all over again.'

Sally knew she would have to come to a decision about the cottage soon. Sell, let? She couldn't keep three properties going indefinitely and Janey's solicitor was beginning to make noises. But now that she had begun to come here she dreaded breaking the link with Mike. She needed to be able to see him, however fleetingly, and assure herself that he was safe and, in his own limited way, contented. She was beginning to understand a little of his condition, and that was important to her.

He had no practical worries or responsibilities, and was secure in a familiar place with a simple, known routine and material needs met. As the children were at boarding school, it would appear that finances weren't a problem.

Then Sally would remember what Nona had said about the need to reacquire social skills. Shouldn't that be happening for Mike? Had the task been abandoned as too much trouble or was he not capable of learning and readapting? Sally hadn't enough knowledge to be able to judge, but the question gnawed at her.

ALEXANDRA RAIFE

At Christmas a letter arrived from Nona. There were just enough words among the exclamation marks and dashes to tell Sally she was pregnant. After the first delight Sally felt a pang of loss; with Nona so far away she would miss the excitement when the baby was born. But it was more than that. It was the instant comparison, Nona's life and hers. The knife twisting because her lover was lost to her, altered and maimed, beyond the reach of words.

Her mother also wrote, 'thrilled to pieces' as she put it, and rereading her excited letter Sally was amused and touched to find how easily it flowed, how much her mother had to share with her. They would be able to find a meeting place now, she was sure of it. I could go out there, she thought, as though it was a new discovery, meet Ray, see the baby. The doors were open.

Sally went to Drumveyn for Christmas lunch. She had already begun to get cross with questions about her plans, hating her solitariness being underlined, when Pauly Napier turned up in the shop.

Pauly was impulsive, scatty, chaotic, but warmly generous and out-going and Janey had been very fond of her. She stood there smiling, her toffee-coloured hair wildly untidy under a broad-brimmed hat, wearing jeans and boots and some sort of poncho. 'I don't want to butt in,' she said in her direct way, 'and you've probably got more exciting plans, but if not we'd love to have you for as much of Christmas Day as you could stand us for. Though we're quite a mob, as you know.'

Sally knew Christmas alone at the flat or at Grianan would be pretty desolate and she was glad she had accepted when she found herself warmly welcomed by the large family. Many changes had overtaken the strait-laced household Sally had known. Reserved Lady Napier, Archie's mother, had become a different person after her husband's death a few years ago. She had married the factor and lived with him in a converted barn, happier than she had ever been to judge from her relaxed air and smiling eyes.

Her daughter Lisa, a contemporary Sally remembered, had returned to Drumveyn after her husband had mysteriously vanished, and was now living in one of the estate cottages with an illustrator of children's books whose ex-wife lived next door and ran a kennels. They were all there, plus Archie and Pauly's two small daughters and the sons of Archie's first wife.

Andrew and Penny Forsyth and the Blaikies from Torglas were there for drinks before lunch and Sally felt tension unwind as the familiar conversation flowed around her. Lunch in the big beautiful kitchen wound on splendidly for hours, followed by a brisk walk round the loch.

Kind Archie Napier, worried as they all were about Sally's isolation, took the chance to talk to her, as he had wanted to do for some time.

After some general enquiries about the business he said, 'It must be worrying for you, knowing Grianan's standing empty. These big old houses are a nightmare to keep up. I just wanted to say—don't forget there are plenty of hands here to do any maintenance that's needed. You only have to ask.'

'Oh, Archie, that's so good of you. I know I ought to do something about the place, but I've been putting off making a decision.'

'Take your time. Just think about it when you're ready. We can keep an eye on things for you meantime. Janey was one of the great characters of the glen and we miss her.'

Warmed by his kindness and grateful for Pauly's generous hospitality, Sally drove home after tea, refusing all offers of a bed for the night, feeling comforted and ready to face silent Grianan and its memories.

The next morning was brilliant. There had been a light fall of snow and a hard frost, and a huge red sun hung in the eastern sky. She suddenly felt a need to be at Edalmere; she had never seen it on such a day.

The Lakeland hills were a rich tawny shade in the sun, their tops frosted white. When she reached the cottage (no sign of life at the Danahers'—hadn't they been together for Christmas?) she turned up the heating, put on boots and went up through the wood.

Unforgettable afternoon, here in the landscape she had shared with Mike, the rich blue of the lake vivid against dense green plantations and white ridges reaching away westwards, turning every shade of pink and peach before metallic-blue spread as the light died.

Coming down with the cold air biting her cheekbones, toes and fingers warm with exercise, Sally felt an unexpected happiness. It had been a year of tragedy and grief. No one could replace Janey, nothing could bring back Mike as he had been, but she felt part of the fabric of life again, and that was good.

**H**earing the car behind her, the next morning, Sally moved aside but didn't stop. Where was Isobel off to? Surely not going to Jedburgh today? As the car pulled up Sally felt reluctant to turn; Isobel would talk about Janey.

Kirsty was in the passenger seat, smiling shyly, winding down her window. In the driving seat, leaning to see Sally, was Mike, also smiling.

'Nice to see you. What are you doing here?'

Simple question, so like the questions he always asked when he saw her, but this time utterly different. He knew who she was. There was no doubt of it. His eyes, his face, his voice, all told her that. He was back.

'Mike.' Sally clutched the edge of the window, her brain reeling. 'How did you know—I mean, do you really remember me?' Impossible to avoid the word.

'Of course I remember you. It's a while, though, isn't it? Are you at the cottage?'

He does know me. She felt a sting behind her eyes, a constriction in her throat. 'Just for a day or two.' She managed to get the words out normally, even managed a smile for Kirsty.

'Good. I'll come and say hello later on. It's great to see you again.'

'I'll look forward to it.' Absurd, banal, yet what else was there to say? Sally stepped back from the car and smiled as it drew away, then sank down shaking on the crisscross pattern of rimed grass on the bank.

Mike was driving again. He had known her. He had said he would come to the cottage. Blindly she walked on to the village, bought things there, though unable to think of anything she needed beyond milk and eggs. For the rest of the day she waited, never going out-of-doors, shuttled between expectation and the anguished conviction that by now Mike wouldn't even know they had met.

The squawk of the gate jerked her out of her chair. She was so sick with apprehension that she actually hoped for a moment it wasn't Mike. Then she heard his tread on the steps, his knock. It was an extraordinary moment—incredulous joy and agonising uncertainty mingled. He looked so much the same, yet not the same. He opened his arms and she went into them, but his smile looked wrong, artificial and nervous.

His hug felt as though someone had explained the action to him and he was trying it out for the first time. Sally felt herself pressed for a moment against his now more fleshy frame but not received into his embrace. Stepping back as he released her, she caught that strange smile again. She realised he was uncomfortable. Perhaps anxious as to what was expected of him?

But for Sally in that moment none of that mattered. Mike had come, had remembered for eleven hours that he had promised to come, taking a giant step out of the engulfing darkness of lost memory. The moment of true contact this morning had not been imagined. They were together again, she had felt his arms round her. But was it all right for him to be here? There was a new significance in that question now.

'Are the children at the farm?' she asked him.

'Yes, they're in bed. Michael was reading—reads till all hours.'

'Is Isobel there?' So odd to use her name at last in this simple query.

Mike saw nothing strange in it. 'No, she's never there. Can't blame her really—it's not much fun for her, with me in this state.' He said it without bitterness, without any discernible feeling at all.

'You're sure the children are all right?'

'They're fine. They look after me half the time. But I'll go and check on them presently, when you've made the coffee.'

'Two sugars.'

'You remember that, do you?' He looked pleased.

'I remember you finding the sugar the first time you came in.' Could he possibly remember? Sally held her breath.

'Ah well, you have to know your way round all these damned cupboards of Ursula's,' he said complacently. 'You've tidied away a few things, though,' he added. Sally found her hands unsteady as she took down the mugs. She had never imagined for one second that they would be together again in this room, laughing over however tiny a shred of shared memory.

When she suggested going to the sitting room Mike said, 'Oh, God, no, I hate that room,' and the sheer ordinariness of it made her feel for a moment that everything was back to normal.

She found his recollection was moving forward through the years. The period of their own meeting was still patchy, though what he did recall moved and astonished her—that her wedding had been called off and she had come north to stay with Janey; that he had found her by the waterfall and she had helped him with jobs like clearing the beck; and that she had come to Edalmere often that first summer.

'Some nights we had, didn't we?' he said, watching her closely, and the uncharacteristic phrase and tone told Sally he was guessing. It was as though this area, sex, loving, was something his brain refused, perhaps because physical responses had not reawakened, or because such feelings would take too heavy a toll. When he referred to it he seemed dimly aware of something important but beyond his present powers.

'It was wonderful,' she said gently. 'Always. And do you remember how we used to talk, for hours and hours on end?'

'God, yes.' He seized on that gratefully. 'We did, didn't we? About our travels . . .'

He was safe again, early memory sharp and clear. He could recall effortlessly jobs and journeys, people he'd worked with, place names, which year he was where. He would repeat the same story over and over again, with no idea he had told it a few minutes earlier.

'I was impressed to see you driving this morning,' she said, breaking across the cycle as she got up to make more coffee.

'Oh, I'm good at that,' he boasted. 'That came back right away. I'm supposed to keep to the track, but I could drive anywhere.'

He talked differently in some subtle way. Then it hit her. The voice he used was the voice of his youth, with the faint Irish accent that the years of travelling had smoothed away. It added to Sally's feeling of having to get to know a new person, while at the same time he was still overwhelmingly the Mike she loved.

As he talked, going over the same ground exhaustively, she realised he was getting increasingly rambly. She saw him frown once or twice and wondered if he had forgotten where he was. Perhaps exerting his memory so much was bad for him.

'I've no one to talk to, you know,' he said more than once. 'Not the way I can talk to you. Isobel and I didn't talk. She's never been happy here, hates the place, always rushing off somewhere.'

'Well, if she's not there now, do you think we should walk along and check on the children?' Sally suggested. Mike had forgotten his coffee and she observed with concern a faint sheen of sweat on his skin. If he got too confused she might have trouble getting him home, and once there it might upset the children to see him like this.

'They're fine,' he said dismissively, making a curious gesture with his shoulders as though shutting out a problem that was too difficult.

'Why don't we wander along the lane? It's getting fairly late.'

He looked up at the wall. 'You got rid of that damned cuckoo,' he said, with a glint of his old smile.

The small joke, remembered even through the fogs that were visibly gathering, reminding her that the inner self could never change, nearly destroyed Sally.

As they went slowly down the drive in the starlight he leaned heavily on her, yet gave the impression that he hardly knew she was there. He was newly docile in a way that she found unbearably sad.

He didn't hug or kiss her when she left him at his gate. He had forgotten one did that and felt no natural instinct for contact.

'I'll come and see you tomorrow,' he promised muzzily as he turned to go in. She watched him go up the steps and fumble his way inside. She waited, listening for any sign that all was not well. A light went on. He'd be all right.

Along the dark track in the icy night she went, in the grip of a maelstrom of feelings. Her strong passionate lover, with his humour and tenderness and perceptiveness—how could this have happened to him? And yet against all odds they had been together again, had spent an evening in the cottage as they used to, sitting at the same table, talking of the same things. It was incredibly the same; it was agonisingly not the same.

He had said he would come back. All the next day Sally hugged this promise to herself, turning over every fragment of evidence that he had remembered their time together, longing to see him again. But she was obliged to accept that still, for Mike, a new day wiped the slate clean. He didn't come.

Sally thought at first that the Edal Bank number was engaged. It was only when she tried for the second time that she realised the sound was wrong. She checked with the operator. The line had been disconnected.

Even in the warm flat she felt chill fear flurry across her skin. Had something happened to Mike? She couldn't quell the instinct that there was something ominous here.

Since that Boxing Day impulse to drive down, and the heart-stopping moment when she had seen that Mike truly knew who she was, she had phoned him quite often. The first time had been a strange experience. It was termtime so the children wouldn't be there. Isobel might or might not; she would never be able to work that out. Mike might not bother to answer the telephone, might have been told not to, might be afraid of it. But he had answered at last and Sally had been thrown into panic. They had never talked on the phone—how could he remember her without seeing her, how could she identify herself so that he would make the connection?

She had said in a nervous gabble, 'Mike, hello. Do you remember someone called Sally, Sally Buchanan?'

Mike had laughed and Sally had felt her limbs loosen in relief as she let out the breath she hadn't known she was holding. He had said easily, in that new slow voice of his, 'Sally? Of course I remember you. Good to hear you. Where are you?'

He chatted as though talking to her on the phone was entirely normal, saying every so often, 'This is nice, isn't it? It's been a long time.'

He had no recollection of her recent visit or of going to the cottage, or of anything they had talked about that evening. 'So when are you coming over?' he had asked, but in a casual social way which suggested that he remembered her as friend not lover. It was odd how the sexual element in him seemed to have been suppressed, or perhaps put on hold until his body was ready for its demands.

'I'm stuck here on my own a lot,' he had explained, adding shatteringly, 'Isobel's always up at Jedburgh seeing her mother and there's some bloke up there as well, she tells me. The children aren't here much. You should come over some time—it would be good to catch up.'

It had all been so breathtakingly simple and matter-of-fact. 'I'll come down to the cottage soon,' Sally had managed to reply on the same note.

'*Tha-at's* right, the cottage.' He had this way now of drawing a word out as though facts were filtering back slowly. 'You used to stay there, didn't you? Yes, come on over, we'll have a good long talk.'

'I'll phone again, shall I?'

'You do that.'

Whenever she did, the conversation was much the same, but once or twice there had been some small sign that she was becoming an accepted constant in the slow journey back to normality. Once he had said, 'Jesus, I need this. You can't think how good it is just to *talk*. Don't ever let go of the rope, will you?' and Sally had wept after putting down the phone in a passion of grief for what had befallen him, and for his immense patience and tolerance for the existence he now had.

Now this dead phone frightened her, as though the rope had broken in fact, and he was bobbing away from her on some dangerous sea. Could he have collapsed again, had a relapse, harmed himself in some way? There were so many terrifying possibilities for someone in his condition who was left so much alone.

Who could she ask? She winced at the thought of the gossiping tongues. It would have to be Ann Jackson. God knows what she would make of such a question.

'Edal Bank? Oh, that's a downright shame, isn't it?' Ann was so eager to plunge into the details that she didn't even stop to wonder why Sally had phoned. 'The Danahers have had that place for three generations, and young Michael loves it, wants to do just what his dad did. Of course the job's gone now, well, it had to, didn't it, with Mike the way he is, and who knows whether he'll ever be right again. But selling up when he still doesn't know whether he's coming or going, well, I said to Garth, That can't be right, can it . . .?'

Shaking, Sally let the spate pour over her, setting her face grimly. Eventually she was able to ask, 'Do you know where they've gone?'

'She's taken him back to Scotland. Of course, she never wanted to live down here, she made that plain enough. And the children are at school in Scotland, so I suppose it makes sense.'

'They're at Isobel's mother's in Jedburgh?' Ann Jackson clearly wasn't switched to receive; it hardly mattered how direct the questions were.

'Oh, no—well, Isobel is, of course. She's been more or less living there these last months. But she's put Mike into a home, poor lad, somewhere near—oh, my head's like a sieve these days, what was the name now? I was talking to Mrs Callander about it in the shop only the other day—she'd know right away. Let me see now . . .'

Sally would have phoned even Elsa just then. A home, Mike, the tough, fit, active outdoor man in a *home*. What kind of home, where? She had to know.

'Oh, I remember, some name like Gilsborough, Gisborough, something like that. Not far from that place where Kirsty's going to school, St Andrews. I do recall that because Kirsty was telling me about it herself last time she was here . . .'

Sally prowled the flat, unable to settle to anything. It felt shut in and dark. She found herself longing for Janey, wishing she had told her about Mike. It was quite irrational; she couldn't have approved and it would have made no difference now, but there was a strong need to share this.

She went down to the car, fetched her road map and located Gilsburgh on the south shore of the Tay estuary. After that it didn't take long. Balmenie House. With a strange cold sense of simplicity she realised she could go there. By breaking up their home and abandoning Mike, Isobel had announced to the world that she no longer wanted him. Who was there to question it if Sally went to see him now?

Dull and grey, the main street of the little ex-mining town stretched away in the toneless afternoon light. Sally knew that her own dread was colouring her view of it, her longing to see Mike overlaid with a much stronger reluctance which she could do nothing about, but few places had ever given her such immediate and powerful feelings of distaste. She wanted to turn round and drive away. This was an unforgivable intrusion into Mike's life. He was virtually a stranger now. He hardly knew who she was. Who was she to have a view on what should or shouldn't happen to him when her ignorance of his condition was almost total? Perhaps Isobel was looking after him in the way that best suited his needs. She, after all, was the one who knew the limits of his present capability, and the prognosis for the future.

Balmenie House lay down to the left off the High Street, a square granite building with big bay windows, its sloping front garden one obliterating stretch of concrete with a few straggling bushes on either side. Stark as it looked, at least there was no sense of enclosure.

As Sally rang the bell she felt her stomach clench with nervous apprehension. A sound of yapping approached, then a woman opened the inner door of the porch and squeezed herself through a foot-wide gap while trying to prevent a couple of shrieking, scrabbling terriers from coming with her. 'Come in, come in.'

'We're so pleased for Mr Danaher that he has a visitor,' Mrs Lucas said once they were in her messy office, waving Sally to an armchair covered in dog hairs. Her manner was cosily fawning; her accent didn't sound like the one she would use in the kitchen.

'How is he?' What kind of answer can I expect from her? Sally thought helplessly.

'Oh, he's settled in extremely well, extremely well. Such an easy man, so pleased with everything.' Why did such an ordinary statement make her sound so bogus?

'And it's all right to take him out? There's nothing I should be careful about?' Sally didn't know what she should ask.

'My goodness, he's not subnormal, you know, just suffering a temporary memory dysfunction. People often don't understand the difference.' Sally had asked to be patronised, she supposed. 'He has to adapt,' Mrs Lucas went on brightly, 'get used to everything again. That's all there is to it. Otherwise he's just like you or me.'

So trite. What qualifications did she have, if any, for running this place? What right to pronounce on Mike and his state of mind?

'Then we'll go,' Sally said crisply, needing this gratuitous delay to be over. The dogs let loose skirls of shrill rage as she stood up.

'Oh, he won't be far away, rest assured,' Mrs Lucas cried gaily as the racket subsided into a froth of sub-growls. 'He can't wait to see you. All done up in his best bib and tucker. If he's asked me the time once this afternoon he's asked a hundred times. Come along.'

Sally's throat closed with nervous tension spiked with rage at the woman's fatuous smile as she followed her across the hall. Mike was waiting in a big, sparsely furnished lounge. Sally felt pure joy at the sight of him, never failing, then the small check of adjustment that was becoming familiar to see him as he was now, hair grey, face fleshy and smooth-skinned, body thickened. It was disconcerting too to see him standing passive, as though instructed like a child or a dog, 'Wait there.'

For an aching instant the pain of finding Mike here in this incongruous place, so meekly acquiescent, stopped her in her tracks, and her own appearance here seemed outrageous and unjustifiable. They were nothing to do with each other any more; she should never have come.

Then Mike smiled at her, grinned, his eyes lighting up, and took a step towards her, shattering the unreality of the scene. As he moved, one of the smelly little dogs threw itself at him with teeth bared.

'Bloody animals,' he said calmly, and lifted it aside with a well-timed swing of his foot.

The terrier yelled, more in surprise than anything else. Sally laughed. Mike was Mike again.

'Mr Danaher!' gasped Mrs Lucas. 'How could you? Poor little Gretchen, come to Mummy then—'

Mike winked at Sally. 'She'll live. Are we off then? Where are we going?'

'Anywhere you like,' she said, high on soaring happiness as he took her arm and steered her past a reproachful Mrs Lucas, busy cradling Gretchen and trying to pin her affability back in place.

'Not too late back, please,' she fluted after them, attempting to re-establish control.

Mike didn't bother to answer and for a moment the illusion was there that nothing had ever happened to him. His unruffled air, his contempt for the horrible little dogs, his tall figure beside her and the way he smiled down at Sally with a fervent 'God, it's good to see you' as they walked away made it seem that he was himself again.

It wasn't so. Sally had thought she might take him to Cupar or St Andrews and find somewhere quiet and comfortable where they could have tea and talk, but Mike resisted the idea instantly, looking worried. He wanted to follow a routine he knew and Sally hastily agreed. It seemed that every day—though she found he had no idea how many of them there had been—he walked into the town to fetch a newspaper, went back to Balmenie House to read it, then walked up the High Street on one side, down it on the other, had coffee at a grim little café, then went back to the house. After lunch there he went for a walk, sat for a while in the same café, and so back for supper, television and bed.

The walk he took her depressed Sally quite unreasonably. They went down to the river and along a muddy path where they couldn't walk abreast. There was a smell of sewage and rot; the tide was low and channels of pewter-coloured water threaded the mud flats of the estuary under a threatening sky.

They turned up a road through some council houses and in no time were back in the town. That was Mike's walk, to Sally a mere dim bad-dream background to the turmoil of feelings at being here, with him but separated from him because their minds could no longer find each other.

Sally felt hollow, shivery, anxious, unable to accept the moment for itself. She wanted to establish some basis for future meetings, be reassured that Mike wouldn't forget her, but on the other hand she longed, with an awful sense of guilt, to escape.

Mike's world was now Balmenie, the trivia of daily events there, the other residents, the food—a lot about the food. He asked her more than once how they had met but hardly listened to the answer, as though he found such facts difficult to relate to this new environment. He was more interested in hearing how she had found him here and seemed impressed that she had managed it.

She saw how relentless the struggle was to keep a grasp on the simplest outline of his life. He would ask over and over again what day it was, attempting to place himself in a framework which no longer meant anything to him. He asked Sally several times when she had arrived and if she had been there for lunch. He went obsessively over the ground of where she lived, her job, Grianan, doing his best to pin down facts which were not part of his experience. When that grew too frustrating or tiring he would return to the known present and tell her again how he passed each day.

One thing was certain: he was pleased to see her, not because he remembered how they had felt about each other, but because he knew they had been friends.

'I never see anyone else, you know, from before,' he said once. 'And you can't talk to that lot, they live in a world of their own.' He meant the other Balmenie residents. When Sally asked if the children came to see him he answered too quickly, 'Oh, they're here all the time,' and Sally knew from the anxious look that crossed his face that he was lying. She didn't ask about Isobel.

In spite of his dismissal of the people around him she was struck by his general tolerance. He seemed to have cultivated a new easy-going attitude and a way of shrugging off minor irritations, perhaps because he knew they were beyond his power to alter.

'Who *are* the other people at Balmenie House?' Sally asked him.

'Oh, a bunch of has-beens,' he answered indifferently. 'Dumped, like me.'

'Mostly old people?' she went on, to gloss over the pain of that, though he hadn't spoken bitterly.

'Oh God, yes, one foot in the grave.' Sally was beginning to recognise this facile agreement as a trick he had learned to save himself the trouble of a more specific reply.

Then abruptly he became restless, asking her the time every couple of minutes, and she suggested that they should walk back.

'No, you're all right,' he said quickly, but almost immediately asked the time again, and she saw the faint sweat that she remembered sheening his skin, and knew that anxiety was gripping him. She guessed that part of his brain was telling him that he liked being with her and didn't want it to end, but a deeper instinct was telling him that he had been out longer than usual and it was disturbing him.

'I'd like to see your room before I go,' Sally suggested. 'Would Mrs Lucas twitter about that?'

'Nothing to do with her,' Mike said at once, visibly relieved to realise he could go back to the house but not have to lose sight of Sally yet.

She wished she hadn't asked when she saw the room. It was reasonably big and well decorated, with a decent-sized window. But it looked out onto the blank back wall of the bus station and the furniture was miserably skimpy for a man of Mike's size, crammed in to make a bedroom do duty as a sitting room too.

Two details made her feel choky with misery as she drove away. While Mike was looking in a drawer for something he wanted to show her, she had picked up his pillow and pressed it for a moment to her face. It smelt unclean, distasteful in a way that deeply distressed her. Nothing of him was there. And when Mike turned triumphantly he was holding his sketchbook in his hand, full of soft pencil drawings of scenes she had been in with him and which had now been taken summarily from him. There were pages of birds, minutely observed, delicately drawn, coal tits, goldcrests, a tree-creeper at work. Mike appeared to find pleasure in the drawings but seemed to admire them as something which had nothing to do with him.

'Couldn't leave this behind, could I?' he said with a spurious brightness he had learned to use when there was nothing behind the smile.

## CHAPTER TEN

HOW COULD I HAVE AGREED to Mike coming by bus? Sally reproached herself in guilty exasperation. She could so easily have gone to fetch him, but Mrs Lucas had insisted on the plan, saying the doctor recommended it as part of Mr Danaher's social rehabilitation, and Sally had felt she had to accept that. The Balmenie minibus would take him to Perth and from there he was to come on alone.

The moment Sally saw him she knew it had been a disaster. His face was glistening, his hands making little dabbing movements, his eyes bright with a self-conscious look.

'Thank God you're here,' he said, not touching her but stooping to look closely into her face in trembling need for reassurance. 'I don't know what the hell I'd have done if you hadn't been. Tried to get off too early like a fool. They wouldn't let me, of course—they all knew I was round the twist. Thanks,' he called, raising a hand to the driver who nodded in return, looking at them curiously.

In spite of the brave effort to make light of it Sally could see how much Mike had minded this exposure, and she put her arms round him quickly, hiding against him the distress she knew her face must show.

'That's nice,' he said, pleased in a detached way, as though he found the gesture natural and agreeable but wouldn't have thought of hugging her himself.

He was carrying a holdall, with a small florist's package clutched in the same hand. 'Brought you some flowers,' he said proudly, sure he had done the right thing. Mrs Lucas, it had to be, Sally thought. A dozen freesias, their cellophane wrapping tied with a shiny purple bow and crushed from being gripped against the handle of the holdall, which Sally guessed he had held onto anxiously for the entire journey. An image of him in ex-army combat jacket, rifle slung on shoulder, came back to her. Her eyes stung.

His relief to be safely there was almost tangible as they walked side by side down the winding vennel. Sally decided the question of the holdall had better be dealt with at once. 'What's all the luggage about then?' she demanded mock severely. 'I thought you were invited for lunch.'

'You didn't think I'd come all this way just for lunch, did you?' he parried scornfully, jokingly, but his grin and the look he darted at her were unsure.

'The flat has one bedroom, I'd have you know.' She kept to the repressive tone as she led the way up the stone steps.

'Sounds fine to me,' he replied jauntily, with a sudden genuine glimmer of the old Mike. He was clearly putting the ordeal of the journey behind him.

'And one bed,' Sally said even more sternly, wondering what on earth she was going to do about this development.

'Better still,' Mike replied, and she wondered what memories prompted the cheerfully suggestive tone. Not of her, she was fairly sure.

Mike was full of admiration for the flat and, listening to his comments, Sally found she no longer knew what his standards and tastes were based on now. 'So you really think you're going to stay?' she asked, amused in spite of herself by his complacent confidence. She and Nona had managed, after all.

'What do you think? Anything to get out of that damned place.'

Mike's tone was joking too, but Sally sensed that a decision had been made in his mind and that though he wasn't quite comfortable with it he wasn't going to relinquish it. He wanted to stay, and couldn't afford to let any doubt creep in. Sally wished forlornly that he would say something to show that he remembered they had been lovers, but knew she couldn't seriously hope for that. This was primarily about not going back to Balmenie, and after that perhaps about the idea of sharing a bed with a woman. She, as herself, didn't come into it, she knew.

'What about Mrs Lucas? When does she expect you back?'

'None of her business.' The instant flat rejection which he employed when something he wanted was threatened but he knew he couldn't cope with reasoned argument.

'Well, it is rather,' Sally said mildly, not wanting this to turn into an issue which might upset him. 'Seriously, isn't she meeting you in Perth?'

'No chance,' Mike said swiftly.

Why was she arguing anyway? She had been closer to this man than to any other person on earth. If this mattered so much to him then surely she wasn't going to refuse? It occurred to her wryly that less than three years ago this situation would have been the peak of unattainable bliss.

As she talked to Mrs Lucas Mike watched her, smiling now, sure of the outcome. She would take him back tomorrow evening. As she put down the phone Sally was conscious of a great simplicity calming her. It was just Mike; just the two of them; it would be all right.

He was so happy that day. He didn't have to worry now about the journey back, and he was openly and endearingly cock-a-hoop to be back in everyday life in his own right. When Sally said apologetically that she would have to do some shopping he was perfectly content. In fact it had been noticeable on Sally's visits to Gilsburgh during the last couple of months that he had developed an unexpected taste for urban surroundings. He liked window-shopping, and today he stood for minutes at a time gazing with fascination at the wares of gunsmith, ironmonger and wine merchant.

He ambled round the supermarket, intrigued by everything, patient with the comprehensive patience of someone for whom time had no meaning, and when they left he took the shopping from Sally as though rather pleased with himself that long-buried social behaviour was coming back to him.

He liked frequent coffee stops, loved just sitting and watching people. Sally wasn't sure if he needed to pause and be passive for a while or if it was just a habit he had acquired in Gilsburgh. Mike studied this new scene intently, with a naive readiness to like all he saw, and she realised that any worries she had had about filling the time could be forgotten.

What meant most to him, however, was taking her out to dinner. It moved her to see the evident buzz he got from the simple act of phoning to book a table, going carefully through the small ritual, throwing her a look of disingenuous triumph when he had accomplished it.

He showered and changed still with that air of 'this is what we do', apparently taking for granted the intimacy of their getting ready together. Occasionally he would grin and exclaim, 'God, it's good to be out of that place,' but that was all the acknowledgment he made of a situation which Sally found unsettling in the extreme.

He was touchingly anxious about whether he looked all right and she saw how important all this was for him. She couldn't imagine the Mike she remembered ever caring for a second what he looked like. She had recently persuaded him to get his thick curly hair properly cut and it was good to see the shape of the long head again. He was smiling, a bit hyped up but tremendously happy, and tenderness for him flooded her.

She asked him to drive and was rewarded by his huge grin, and by the smooth competence with which he took the car out of the tight yard and up the narrow streets into the town. There was a thrill in that for Sally too; a feeling of being looked after which she had missed.

It was so good to watch his pride and pleasure that evening. He loved it all—the candlelit crowded restaurant, the high-gloss menu, but above all taking charge, making sure Sally chose just what she wanted, relaying her order to the waiter, choosing the wine, paying. She was not sure Mike would have any idea of how much money he would need, but his wallet was well filled and she was glad there was no need to spoil the moment for him. She understood that for him, this evening, putting down those notes was profoundly significant.

Equally important was the fact that for the first time since his illness no one knew he was disabled; there was no need for explanations or apologies. Sally's heart melted as she looked at him across the table, so proud of himself, so handsome, in spite of the physical changes that had overtaken him, in his new confidence and happiness.

'I enjoyed that,' Mike said with satisfaction as he drove relaxedly through the quiet town. He had drunk very little and Sally had been relieved, not sure if he was supposed to or how much it would affect him. Probably he shouldn't have driven, but then nor should she, and she decided it was a risk worth taking. She knew it would matter to him, driving her home.

He delighted in all the small business of putting the car away, going in together, locking the door, putting on the lamps, making coffee. For him it was resurrecting familiar actions associated with home, family, real life. Sally didn't figure except as the essential other, female half. She didn't let herself mind that. This was his evening.

There was no discussion, no decision about who would sleep where. She saw that Mike expected to share her bed and she simply let it happen. It clearly hadn't crossed his mind that he wouldn't. He knew that they had slept together, though it was impossible to tell in what terms he remembered it. To suggest now that she slept on the sofa would puzzle and disappoint him. And why should she? What reason was there for denying him this?

Part of her brain was reeling with disbelief that, here with her in her room, the man she had so passionately loved and had given up with such pain was sitting on the edge of her bed, loosening the knot of his tie with chin stretched up, unbuttoning his shirt, stripping off his socks—his wife gone, his home sold, his children kept from him.

So matter-of-factly that it was ludicrous—only there was no one to share the joke—they got into bed side by side and propped themselves on their separate pillows. Sally reached out to take Mike's hand.

Blessedly reassuring, it closed round hers at once, a hand now soft and pale, but still long, shapely and warm. 'Isn't this beautiful?' he said softly, and his choice of word, his intimate lover's tone, steadied her.

'It's wonderful,' she agreed, her lips trembling, and turned to lean close and press her face against his shoulder. He moved at once, naturally, easily, to lift his arm and put it round her, drawing her comfortably against him.

His filled-out, unfit body was different, arousing none of the powerful feelings she had once had for him, but after all he was the same person; there had been love between them, and compassion filled Sally, a compassion charged with admiration for his courage and endurance. He had never let his essential self be destroyed by what had happened to him. And now, at this moment, how could she gauge what was going through his mind, what confused memories, doubt or apprehension, what crippling uncertainty as to what he should do? His patience, his quiet acceptance of what had become of his life, overwhelmed her.

She reached up to stroke his face, to kiss him gently, and felt his hands move in tentative exploration and rediscovery. 'Skin,' he said. 'Nothing like it, is there? Smooth, warm, wonderful skin.'

He had put on pyjamas bottoms; old habit or new? She didn't know. She had put on a nightdress and now at these words, spoken in delighted dreamy wonder, she slipped out of his arms, sat up and pulled it over her head. 'There's more skin for you,' she said, sliding down beside him again. She heard him draw in his breath sharply and then his hand moved to smooth over her breast and cup it gently.

'It's been years, hasn't it?' he asked. She had no way of knowing if he was remembering making love to Isobel or to her, and that should have mattered but somehow it didn't; this meant too much to him.

'Far too long,' she said softly, giving herself up to the feel of his hands. It was an experience of such tenderness, such poignant sweetness, this breathless rediscovery of his physical pleasure, that her own needs simply ceased to exist. Slowly, with an awareness so acute that she could feel it with him, he explored her body. For Sally as well as for him it was like being re-endowed with the ability to experience these sensations for the first time, exciting and amazing all over again. And for Sally there was the added pleasure of being able to offer him this delight new-minted, in this quiet room, in the tucked-away absolute privacy of this place, and of knowing that he trusted her. She was seized by a passionate determination to take care of him.

When she felt his emphatic erection she was first and foremost pleased for him. She had feared his distress if he couldn't achieve it. Then she felt her own body melt in response and warned herself fiercely not to expect too much. She had never before known such a desire to be receptive, totally and reassuringly, offering herself without any part of her awareness turned to her own sensations. Her body opened to him, giving, most tenderly welcoming. It was, as he had said, beautiful.

For Mike it was a brief, intent struggle, and there was no room in his mind to remember that Sally was even there. This was an act he desperately wanted to perform. When he achieved it he trembled and shook; in fact, Sally thought he wept. She held him close, stroking the curly grey head, smoothing her hands down the shaking shoulders, drawing the duvet gently up his back, enfolding and comforting him.

'I never thought that would happen again,' he mumbled after a while, his breathing still uneven against her neck. 'Christ, I never thought that would happen again.'

'Darling Mike, it was so good.' It had been; not in the usual sense, for there had been no climax for Sally, or any approach to it, but no loving she had ever known had been more sweet or more intensely aware.

'Thought I was all washed up, you know. They'd written me off.'

Sally's arms tightened round him. She couldn't speak.

'Just to hold a woman again,' he said. 'Just to lie like this . . .'

Sally could feel the tears running down the sides of her face. Would he feel them on his cheek? His slack weight crushed her; she made no move to shift it from her.

# GRIANAN

The next day Mike hardly spoke. He had woken late, couldn't be bothered with breakfast and didn't reply to proposals about what they should do with their day or to Sally's increasingly perturbed questions about how he felt. He did nothing, just stood at the window and gazed at the river. He was there for hours, never so much as turning his head when she spoke.

Frightened and helpless, Sally thought of phoning Mrs Lucas, but what was there to ask? Mike was coming to no harm, he wasn't aggressive or obstructive. If he objected to going back she would have a problem, and the prospect loomed before her all day. But when the time came, after crawling silent hours when all Sally's bright suggestions finally died on her lips and she could only sit anxiously watching him, he accepted it obediently. She had packed his bag for him but he didn't even ask about it. He said nothing on the drive down to Gilsburgh. Sally asked him once if he remembered the house where he was living but he just shrugged. What have I done to him? she thought in panic. She was even tempted, in her dread and ignorance, to tell Mrs Lucas that she had let him do too much, see too many new places, stay out late, drink, eat rich food, make love . . . The catalogue, listed like that, horrified her with her own irresponsibility.

Mrs Lucas didn't give her the chance to say any of it. Oh, he just has these days. Gets a bit down in the dumps, don't you, Mr Danaher?' (Did she call him that when no one was there?) 'Perfectly normal—or perhaps I should say nothing to worry about. One good day, when he's just like anyone else, then off we go again, hardly knows where he is.'

Sally drove home in a turmoil of remorse and anxiety. Would Mike be better off if she never saw him again, if she left him to the repetitive round he had adapted to and now accepted? His brain, as he had explained to her himself as though reciting a well-rehearsed lesson, would never function fully again. The damaged cells couldn't regenerate. Was it wiser and kinder to do as Isobel had done, give him a stable background without responsibility or demands, and leave him there in peace? Then Sally thought of his pride as he sat across the table from her at dinner last night, and how alive his face had looked. She remembered the rapt tone of his voice, tinged with the little touch of humour that was so much his, as he murmured, 'Skin . . . I'd forgotten . . .'

How could she abandon him?

Mike phoned late on Thursday evening asking, 'What time are you coming to pick me up tomorrow?'

It was a huge thrill to hear that ordinary question, to think that he

271

had reached the point of being able to make his own plans. Sally was in tearing spirits as she got up at six the following morning to wash her hair, put clean sheets on the bed, shove in a load of washing, then race round hoovering and tidying away the strewn work which she had intended to get through this weekend.

She also had to do some horse-trading about the shop being looked after on a Saturday. She now employed Tessa who did everything she was told and nothing she wasn't. She was very punctual, arriving and leaving. Sally was sure that one day she would shut the shop with some-one in it.

It took over an hour to get to Gilsburgh and Mike seemed to think she was late. She knew it only meant that he had been watching for the car all afternoon, but still felt piqued after the scramble she had had.

Mike settled in at the flat with every appearance of being at home, putting his belongings exactly where they had been the previous week, openly exultant to be back. His pleasure was infectious and Sally felt herself unwinding as she cooked dinner and he watched *High Road* with a child's absorption. It didn't occur to him to offer to help, but when Sally asked him to open a bottle of wine he was clearly gratified, as though knowing this was the man's job. Otherwise he expected food to be put in front of him, plates taken away. Sally would never know if this was what he had been used to with Isobel or if it was the result of being helpless after his illness and now looked after in the residential home.

There was no doubt that he revelled in the feeling of ordinary home life which being in the flat gave him. He talked about it later when they were lying close in the big bed. He hadn't attempted to make love— Sally thought he had forgotten to—and there had been a bleak moment when she had realised that it wasn't going to happen, a disappointment made sharper by knowing they wouldn't be able to discuss it. But she pushed that aside. Mike's satisfaction to be there with her, to have his arms round her, was unmistakable.

'This was always one of the best things, wasn't it?' he said with a sigh of pleasure. 'Just lying like this, talking.'

'It was,' she agreed. She hoped he meant with her but there was never any way of knowing and that was something she was just going to have to get used to.

'God, it's good to be here and out of that awful place,' he added more forcefully than he usually let himself speak, crushing her to him with a little shudder.

'Do you really hate it?' Sally asked with surprised concern. He always insisted that Balmenie suited him, but she knew by now that this could be part of the protective mechanism he had developed to keep any form of stress at bay.

She felt him shrug. 'Oh, it's not that bad, I suppose. And let's face it, I'll never be good for much again,' he said with the lucidity she had noticed was always most in evidence late at night. 'Can't work, can't look after myself, can't look after the children.'

'Don't.' She crushed her face into the hollow of his shoulder, shivering.

'Hey, come on, we never thought I'd get this far, did we? I nearly didn't make it at all, don't forget. I'm just glad to be alive. No, that place is all right, it suits me very well in fact. I can walk up into the town on my own, fetch a newspaper, have coffee . . .' As he settled into the well-worn account of his daily routine Sally knew he had to be satisfied with the hand fate had dealt him. To allow himself not to be posed too many unanswerable and threatening questions.

Sally had to go into the shop on Saturday morning as Tessa, asked to help at short notice, had only been able to do the afternoon, but Mike went along too and seemed quite content to hang around chatting to customers, carrying the odd box out to a car.

Once Tessa had arrived to take over, not looking too amenable, Mike wanted to 'go out'. All the things they had done together last weekend, at least on the first day when he had been so happy, were evidently still clear in his mind and he wanted to repeat them.

It was a pattern that established itself, with his urgent need for recognised patterns, with each weekend that he came to stay. Though he loved the flat, prowling round every morning when he got up to pick up objects and ask the same questions about them again and again, he nevertheless found it confining and would soon grow restless and eager to be off in search of movement and people.

At least it wasn't necessary to find new things to entertain him. His short-term memory, though improving, was still poor and the same sequence repeated over and over again satisfied and reassured him. A bar lunch in Aberfeldy or Pitlochry, slow-paced shopping, going out for dinner—all that he loved. He particularly liked going into Perth and would wander up and down the High Street for hours, looking in the same shop windows time after time with inexhaustible fascination. Sally would get bored, hating the repetitiveness, the clogging drift of Saturday shoppers, and then be horribly ashamed of herself.

That shame was to grow, swiftly deepening to a guilt that dogged every waking moment. Mike took it for granted that these weekends were now a regular part of his life and that she would turn up every Friday to collect him.

How could she tell him that he couldn't come? He was so vulnerable, but she knew he would instantly hide his hurt under that easy-going acceptance he had been forced to learn. And she *wanted* him to come. All the same, a sense of being trapped in this situation grew in her with a speed that shook her. Her normal week had to be crammed into four and a half hectic days while the rest of the time went into slow motion, geared to Mike's pace and capacity. Hurrying through work that couldn't be done in the shop, and keeping up with all the ordinary household chores, became increasingly hard to manage. And she was getting tired. Mike was at his best late at night and liked nothing better than to talk well into the small hours. It was beginning to take its toll on Sally.

She knew that this driven sense of never quite keeping up had a lot to do with Grianan. She hadn't been there for weeks and the question of what should be done with the place loomed more and more worryingly at the back of her mind. It was shortsighted and irresponsible to let neglect overtake it, and Janey would have hated to see the present state of the garden. So would Piers.

She had suggested more than once to Mike that they should go up to Grianan together, but to her surprise he had developed a deep resistance to the idea.

Whenever Sally mentioned Grianan he would need to be told again that she had lived there as a child, that it had belonged to Aunt Janey (whom he remembered as Ursula's sister visiting the Edalmere cottage) and was now hers, and he would nod, pretending to take the information in but, Sally knew, rejecting it for some reason.

Puzzling over this resistance to Grianan she wondered if he was afraid that it would remind him of Edal Bank. She knew he would never go back there and for her too the place had taken on a different aspect, the magic overlaid by tragedy. She had already put the cottage on the market. She didn't tell Mike. That sort of practical decision had no relevance for him.

One weekend he didn't come to the flat and she hated herself for seeing it as a respite. His brother had come over from Ireland and he took Mike away for a few nights. Sally took the chance of the weekend on her own to accept a standing invitation for dinner at Drumveyn. She hadn't had the chance to see much of Pauly lately, but it was good to sit for hours round the big table in the kitchen talking after dinner with Archie's mother and Tom, her husband.

It was good to see other faces, but afterwards Sally felt deeply guilty at the sensation of release and freedom the occasion had produced, especially as Mike revealed a most unexpected sense of rejection.

'I haven't been here for weeks, have I?' he asked, frowning as he looked round the flat.

'Two weeks,' Sally said lightly, holding his hand in both hers, minding his confusion. 'You only missed last weekend. You were with your brother.'

'Colin. I hardly see him nowadays, you know.'

'Have you ever thought of going to stay with him? Or living with him?' Sally asked tentatively when he had chatted for a while, not about the days spent with Colin last week but about growing up in Kendal and about Colin's house and business in Carlow.

'God, no,' he said at once. 'He hasn't got room anyway. He's just made a separate flat for my mother.'

'Wouldn't you like to see your mother?'

It had frequently occurred to Sally that Mike's family showed remarkably little interest in his circumstances. Perhaps Isobel had convinced them that she had made the best possible arrangements for him 'in his condition'.

Mike shrugged. 'Probably just upset her. She's pretty frail, hardly gets out at all these days.'

It wasn't always easy to know what 'these days' meant to him.

'Colin says she's had to have full-time care for years now due to her heart condition. Live-in.' He often repeated phrases as though he had recently heard them without knowing what they meant.

She couldn't detect much feeling for his family there, but she knew she must take into account the fact that Mike would automatically reject anything that looked too daunting or taxing.

For the same reason, she knew, he rarely referred to the children. He was convinced that they were better off without him (had almost certainly been told that by Isobel), and because this was painful he avoided talking about them at all. When he spoke of the past with Isobel it was always of the time before the children were born.

It was something Sally had to learn to deal with, hearing his memories of those early days. He was incapable of the discretion a man would normally employ when talking about one woman in his life to another.

'She's grown so hard,' he would say. 'She used to be such a gentle, shy girl. Very quiet, with a lovely little private smile. And that glorious hair, like fire in the sunlight. That's how I first saw her, you know, on that beach. She looked amazing. She'd been dumped by the boyfriend she was travelling with, left without any money or anything, poor girl. She badly needed someone to look after her . . .'

Oddly enough, in spite of the tender reminiscent tone, Sally found it didn't really hurt. It was too honest. Instead it filled her with a piercing sadness for all this man had lost.

'She never could cope with much really,' Mike went on once, on a more matter-of-fact note. 'She certainly never reconciled herself to living at Edalmere. Hated the isolation. In fact, mentally she never left home. Now she's got this new man there. Well, not so new, it's all been going on since before I was ill.'

'Since before you were ill?' This must be part of his usual problem with sorting out an accurate time scale.

'Oh, sure. She told me when she came to talk about getting married again. Edward, that's it.' His tone was full of satisfaction that he had pinned down the name that had been evading him.

Sally felt the breath rush out of her body. 'Married? Mike, how could she get married?'

'Why not? I'm no good to her. She'll be far better off with somebody else, anybody else come to that,' he amended with a rare bitterness.

'But Isobel's married to you.' Sally still felt breathless, shaken.

'Oh, they've organised a divorce, Isobel's lawyers. Ages ago. They just had to wait till I could sign to say I agreed.'

Sally was gazing at him in shock and struggling incredulity. 'But Mike, was that what you wanted? Did they give you a choice? How was that ever allowed?'

'Seemed a good idea to me,' he said, shrugging. 'I'm all washed up. Isobel doesn't give a damn about me, hasn't for years. She just wanted out. Only put up with Edal Bank and my unambitious job for the sake of the children. Edward's a good bloke. He's been to see me a couple of times at that place. He can give her everything she wants and take care of the children too. Good luck to them.'

Sally could still hardly take in that he had known all this and she hadn't had the least idea of it. Mike sounded unperturbed, indifferent even, but she ached to think of the hours and days of wretchedness that he must have gone through as all this penetrated his awareness and he discovered what his illness had cost him.

This bombshell—though as always there were reservations about the accuracy of what he had told her—made Sally's brain reel as she tried to take in the implications. How long had Edward been on the scene? And her own sacrifice in walking away so that Mike's marriage and family should be unharmed—had that been meaningless after all?

If Mike and Isobel were divorced, what would happen to Mike? He seemed sure that Isobel, and now Edward, would go on looking after him financially. Could that really be their intention?

One thing was clear to Sally however. Mike had not related the fact of his divorce to his relationship with her, and for that she was thankful, needing time to adjust to this new and startling situation. It unquestionably added to the pressure she was under. Everything except Mike seemed to have been pushed to the sidelines of her life. Her need for her own space grew as she felt her responsibility for him increasing. The flat felt too small, or Mike too large for it. He had started leaving things there all the time and Sally despised herself for resenting it. Also, she was increasingly aware that the problem of sharing a bed with him was something she would have to sort out soon.

The truth was that sleeping with him had become a torment. He rarely made love to her and when he did his concentration focused exclusively on himself. Sally knew it was the only way it could be for him, and she wanted to give him this pleasure, but what she found hard to endure was that he had woken her body to its old need for him and didn't satisfy it, could never satisfy it.

She was concerned, too, about his growing dependence on her. She knew she must, for both their sakes, take a long, steady look at where they were heading. How long could she cope with this two-tier life? How did she truly feel about Mike now? Pity, compassion, tenderness, affection, but was he the man she had loved?

Driving to see clients or going up and down to Gilsburgh, she would turn it all over again in her mind, despising her hesitation, her weighing up of day-to-day trivia. But life is made up of trivia, the inner argument would run. And Mike wasn't really, in cold fact, her responsibility. She was racked by her own meanness of spirit but couldn't help feeling that she was being pushed into something for which she was not ready.

How was she to say to Mike, 'I'm sorry, you can't come again'? He would know why. It was unbearable to think of him accepting her disappearance from his life with that shrug which was the only way he had left to deal with things which hurt too much. He had no other weapon available to him.

As she grew more tired, feeling enmeshed in something too big to cope with alone, Sally was shocked to find herself growing impatient with Mike himself. He incessantly asked what time it was, what day it was, what they had done yesterday. Sally understood why he asked, yet sometimes it drove her nearly to tears with frustration.

Then she would look at Mike, so patient, so ready to please. She would see the heavy unfit body, the grey hair, the scars left on his forehead by the terrible sequence of operations, and she would be filled with scalding self-contempt, would go and wrap her arms round him, hide her tears against him. And she would cast about for ways to look after him better.

Mike swung, as she had learned, from good days to bad, with every so often a day so marvellous that it seemed total recovery must be just round the corner. So on good days that summer they turned into tourists, Mike responding with surprising enthusiasm to each new scene. It made Sally reflect that, deeply as they had been in love that first summer, they had shared little beyond the bounds of the lake, the fells, talking and making love. Now they enjoyed visiting castles and art galleries, craft shops, the theatre and the salmon ladder at Pitlochry, and on fine Sundays the splendid gardens of Perthshire's big houses.

When it rained, or when Mike was having one of his down days, it was harder. He would watch any rubbish on television, always at a volume that maddened Sally. He didn't like her getting absorbed in some challenging piece of work, or doing anything which excluded him. He didn't say so, but she would recognise the signs in his increased restlessness and constant interruptions.

On these days of depression and inertia Sally knew that his body was husbanding its resources, his brain refusing an overload of anxiety or information. It was hard at such times to believe the positiveness of the good days, and harder to accept that he couldn't pull himself out of it.

The pressures on Sally's own life were aggravated at this point by two crises. The flat was burgled and Tessa said she was leaving. It was a bad week and Sally couldn't face having Mike at the weekend. She phoned Mrs Lucas and asked her to explain to Mike why he wouldn't be able to come, but to assure him that she would be there to pick him up the following Friday.

# CHAPTER ELEVEN

A LOUD THUMPING at the door shot her heart into her mouth. She was still twitchy after the burglary. Nothing much had been taken except the share of the Buchanan family silver which Janey had given her when she got engaged to Julian and insisted she should keep. But a window had been broken, a mess left behind and she was feeling slightly vulnerable.

But burglars don't knock at doors.

An unexpected figure hung back from the door, one step down, ducking his head and turning a filthy cap in his hands. He was usually to be seen shuffling round the square, drunk, talking and singing to anyone who would listen, but quite harmless. His favourite occupation was watching the buses come in. Sally knew he was called Tam Ritchie but she had never seen him outside the square. There was no threat from this familiar figure.

'Tam, what on earth is it?'

'I seen him. I seen them tak him awa'.'

'Who have you seen?' But she knew. 'Tell me who you saw, Tam.' Sally made a big effort to keep her voice calm and not fluster him.

'Yon pollis laddies, they just tellt me to be on ma way. And where's that, I says to them, where's ma way, tell me that?'

The police. Christ, what had happened? Sally grabbed her bag. 'I'll take you up to the square, Tam, and you can tell me what happened.'

'I kent him the moment I saw him. Yon big lad ye're aye ganging aboot wi'. Getting off the bus, he was. And ye werena' there, were ye, ye werena' there.'

'Did something happen to him? Is he hurt? Look, just tell me what *happened*. Where is Mike now?'

'The pollis have him awa' wi' them. I tellt ye,' he said aggrievedly, sniffing and wiping his nose on a disgusting sleeve.

'Is he hurt?'

'Nah.' He sounded contemptuous. 'How would he get hurt? Dinna' be daft. He was just stravaigin' aboot like he didna' ken where to go.'

Sally dropped him in the square, heaving him out ruthlessly, but pushing enough money into his hand to put a blissful smile on his skinny face as he trotted off to the nearest pub.

Sally raced up to the police station. The duty sergeant had recognised Mike and had just been phoning the flat. Mike was in an alarming state, shaking and muttering. He clutched at Sally, hanging onto her arm tightly, and she nearly buckled beneath his trembling weight.

'Now are you sure you're going to be all right with him?' the sergeant asked. 'Wouldn't you be best letting one of us give you a hand?'

'Just to the car, thanks.'

'How about at the other end? Someone can go down with you, you know, and help get him into the house. He's a big lad.'

'It's very good of you, but truly I'll be fine.' All she wanted was to take him away, have him safe and alone with her, to hold and soothe him.

'Well, mind you give us a ring if you have any trouble. There you go, then, sir, you'll be fine now.' The sergeant gave Mike a friendly pat on the shoulder, uncomprehending.

As Sally drove home Mike leaned forward, peering out of the window, still muttering to himself, evidently baffled by what he saw. She talked to him quietly, telling him where he was and where they were going.

He didn't recognise any of it, shaking his head and frowning as she led him up the steps. Once in the flat he didn't look about him but stood apathetically waiting to be taken to the next place.

'You're safe now, everything's all right. We're home, Mike. Come and sit down and I'll make tea.'

'They were staring at me, you know, all the people.' His voice sounded muffled, uncertain. He put a hand to his head and Sally felt fear plume up in her.

'No one's here now. There's just the two of us. You're quite safe, darling, darling Mike.' She drew his head down to her, wishing she could fold him inside her, protect him utterly.

He wouldn't stay in his chair but followed her about as though on a string, needing her nearness. She made him hot sweet tea which he gratefully gulped down, and she held onto his hand as the Balmenie number rang.

'But Mr Danaher's up in his room,' Mrs Lucas insisted with instant defensive indignation. 'He's been there all evening, I can assure you.'

'He's here, Mrs Lucas, right beside me, sitting on my bloody sofa.'

'There's no need to take that tone,' Mrs Lucas protested. 'His television's been on all evening—I heard it myself.'

How could she argue about it? 'Mr Danaher is *here*, for God's sake. He walked out of your house, where you are paid to look after him, and he got himself to Muirend where he was found wandering about and was picked up by the police—' The iron control Sally had started out with was cracking.

'Well, I can promise you, Miss Buchanan, his absence would have been discovered at once when he didn't come down for his hot drink at ten I make it myself every night. I really don't see how you can possibly hold me responsible for—'

'It's your *job* to be responsible!' Sally longed to get her hands round the woman's throat.

'I will need to know, of course, when you intend to bring him back.' As though Sally had taken him away in the first place.

Take him back? Sally looked at Mike, motionless beside her, eyes shut, the sweat of fear still on his skin. She put the phone down before she began to shout and rave at Mrs Lucas, pouring out on her not only righteous anger but a much deeper sense of guilt and failure.

Mike took ages to pull out of it. He wouldn't eat, wouldn't talk about anything except that horror of being lost and helpless among strangers in a strange place.

'I'm a useless bastard,' he said at last, sitting forward with his head propped on his hands. 'No bloody use to anyone.' Sally knew that some recollection of how he had come to be there was seeping back.

'Come to bed, come and sleep and forget all about it. Tomorrow it will seem as though it had never happened.' Please, please let that be so.

'Where's my room?' he asked in a groping anxious way that filled her with an agony of pity for him.

'Just here. You'll remember when you see it.'

'Don't leave me,' he begged, as she led him to the bedroom.

'I'll be there,' she promised, tears audible in her voice. 'I'll be there with you, don't worry. I won't go away.'

'They were all looking at me, you know. They know I'm crackers.'

He slept quite soon, to Sally's relief, exhausted, but his sleep was restless and broken and often he called out in muddled terror and she held him, stroking and soothing him to sleep again. Towards morning he sank at last into a sounder sleep and she felt more hopeful and slept for a while herself.

When Mike woke he knew at once where he was, and Sally hugged him in passionate thankfulness. He thought this was an ordinary weekend visit, and though he was noticeably silent and subdued he was a long way from yesterday's dark confusion.

All night Sally had worried about what to do with him today. She had at last taken the step of agreeing to have Grianan valued and was due to meet Janey's solicitor—her solicitor—there this morning. What concerned her was that Mike had shown such a reluctance to go there whenever she had suggested it before. Would it be bad for him today to make him do something he would dislike? Then Sally realised that it wouldn't matter to him where he went. So long as he was with her he would be docile and unquestioning. It was hard to get him moving, though. He roamed about, looking intently at everything, picking up objects at random but not seeming sure that he recognised them.

They were late leaving and were well up the glen, Mike passive beside her, before she even noticed what a marvellous day it was. The white froth of the bird cherry was browning now, but gorse and broom spread great swaths of blazing gold, rhododendrons were mounds of colour from palest pink to crimson, and tall purple-blue cranesbill edged the road. When she wound down the window the scent of hawthorn met her in a wave of sweetness.

Her spirits rose. Why on earth didn't she come up here more often? Nowhere in the world was more lovely than Glen Ellig on a sunny morning of early summer. A year since Janey's party, she thought in disbelief. Three years since she had met Mike.

She glanced at him and was glad to see that he was looking about him with awakening interest. She put her hand on his thigh and his came down over it. Sometimes when she did that he took no notice, and this morning she was especially glad that he had responded. She still didn't know what her touch or touching her meant to him.

The solicitor who had looked after Janey's affairs for many years had recently retired and the partner waiting for them on the gravel sweep in front of the house was John Ballantyne, a smooth-skinned, plump and arrogant younger man. There was more than a suggestion that he was doing her a favour by being here on a Saturday morning, though Sally knew he had been fishing in Glen Maraich for the past week. She foresaw that any selling blurb concocted by him would set her teeth on edge.

Mike followed amenably at their heels, looking about him admiringly as they went through the dusty rooms, while John Ballantyne pursed his lips, shook his head from time to time and tapped his teeth with his Biro. His darting eyes assessed and disparaged and even rooms Sally had thought quite presentable turned shabby, faded and ill-cared-for under his calculating gaze.

Sally was glad of Mike's quiet approving presence. His rangy frame, these days so much heavier, looked at home in the big, well-proportioned rooms and she was glad to see that he obviously liked the house now that he was finally here.

'Well, we should be able to get something together,' John Ballantyne said, with a finely tuned edge of doubt in his voice just this side of rudeness. 'Of course major refurbishment would be required and that would naturally affect any offer we could hope for. Difficult size as well, too large for a family home in today's terms, and as a commercial enterprise it has never been properly adapted or equipped.'

Sally had never been more thankful to see any car disappear down the drive.

'If that's all he can say I should get someone else to sell it for you,' Mike recommended, easy and relaxed beside her, his face turned up to the sun which was now getting hot.

'I think you're right,' Sally agreed, laughing and giving his arm a little squeeze. It hardly seemed possible that this was the man who yesterday had wandered helpless and afraid among Muirend's unthreatening shoppers. 'Let's wander round the garden, shall we?'

'It's some place. And you own it?'

'I do.' Though probably not for much longer, she thought with a bleak tug of loss.

'But why haven't you brought me here before?' Mike asked as they went in the sunshine down the ragged grassy paths and she felt peace flowing through her in a warm tide.

'Because you wouldn't come, you obstinate so-and-so,' she told him, laughing.

'I wouldn't?' But a small grin told her he remembered something about it. 'And to think I've been missing all this.'

Everywhere was the richness and profusion of new growth. From a distance it all looked marvellous. White cushions of snow-in-summer lined (or choked) the paths, lupins speared up through the weeds in ranks of colour, poppies splashed vividness and Janey's azaleas were a dream of exotic scent and beauty.

'And this is really yours?' Mike asked again, wonderingly.

'All except that cottage. It was left to a friend of Aunt Janey's. A boyfriend,' Sally amended, smiling through the ache of memories.

'Why doesn't he use it? It's a gem.'

Sally gazed at the neat, contained little house. How could a stone exterior say so plainly that its soul had fled? Would Piers ever come back? Suddenly she realised she could tell Mike about it, could tell him anything. He loved stories, and the tolerance and kindness that had always been part of him were much more in evidence now. And it was his memory that had been damaged, not his powers of understanding. Even so, she found that she had underestimated them. Telling him about Piers, the hurt showed more clearly than she had intended and Mike saw it.

'You should find him,' he said, looking closely into her face, his own showing open sympathy. 'You should tell him how you feel.'

'I wish I could.'

'Poor little Sally, you've had a rough time, haven't you, one way and another? Come here.' His arms went round her, and as she leaned gratefully against him she reflected that it was the first time since his illness that he had comforted her, and it was good. But then perhaps it was the first time she had let him see that she needed comfort. Did it feel good for him too?

'Why didn't we come here before?' Mike asked again and she was so pleased to see him enjoying Grianan that she didn't care how often he said it.

'We could stay, you know,' she suggested with sudden inspiration, a strange excitement quickening at the thought, instantly followed by anxiety that it might confuse Mike to sleep in yet another place.

'Could we do that?' he enquired, sounding eager. 'I wouldn't mind a walk. I used to love being in the hills. I haven't been anywhere like this for ages. Have I?' The familiar little check of doubt.

'Not for a long time,' Sally said gently, then became brisk because that was too sad a thought just now. 'We'll have to go down to the village and get something to eat. And the beds will be damp,' she warned him.

'So? And what do you mean, beds?' His arm came round her and his grin was cocksure. Sally knew in that moment where they would sleep, where it would be right and good to sleep. Nothing about this would offend Janey; she would welcome them.

They went down to the village shop, and because it was Saturday afternoon there was no bread left and no fresh vegetables, so they bought a pile of frozen foods and didn't care. Later they went up the hill in the lazy warmth of late afternoon and Sally was struck by how natural it felt to be here with Mike, after all this time and against such odds.

Maybe because everything was a bit makeshift he seemed to take it for granted this evening that he would do his share. Glancing at him as he flipped over chicken legs sizzling in butter and herbs, or twisted one of Janey's bottles of Niersteiner deeper into the peat-flecked ice he'd battered from ancient metal trays, Sally was moved to see his patent satisfaction at dealing competently with these ordinary tasks.

Only once did grief come like a tiger's spring. They had decided to have dinner in the little sitting room, where it was still warm enough for the French windows to stand open, and unthinkingly Sally had gone to put on some music. She didn't check what tape was in, and solemn and majestic there poured into the room the 'Procession to the Minster' from *Lohengrin*. It was as though Janey had stepped into the room and Sally turned with an inarticulate cry, tears filling her eyes.

Mike was there in an instant, reaching to stop the tape, knowing without being told, hugging her close. 'Your aunt? Oh, Sally, poor love. Music can do that, can't it? Scents and music. Nothing bites so deep.'

For the second time that day she had turned to him and he hadn't failed her. It was good, later, to be with him in the big bed with all its plump enfolding softness, the bed where Janey had slept with her lover, Piers. This night Mike was not Sally's lover, and she didn't mind. He had been too exhausted by last night's harried dreams and fitful sleep, and by all the day's new scenes and thoughts, to think of making love to her. But she smiled in the soft darkness of the summer night, unworried, wanting nothing for herself beyond this closeness and the perfection of the day they had shared.

They breakfasted in the little paved corner outside the sitting room, very late, still drowsy in the sun that was already pouring down into this sheltered nook. Mike seemed to have got brown in one day and looked wonderful.

After a while they wandered down to the azalea garden, Mike taking Sally's hand as they stood with closed eyes to drink in the intoxicating fragrance. On every side Sally saw jobs crying out to be attended to. Along a netting fence a mass of wild sweet peas grew, sprawling forward across the weedy ground. She crouched down and began to lift the tough stems and hook the frail tendrils round the wire.

'You'll be there all day,' Mike protested, but he knelt to help her all the same. 'I've always thought the bloke who designed the grappling iron must have grown sweet peas. Look, perfect.'

The sight of his long fingers so delicately handling the minute green curls, the amused comment, so normal and simple, the sun on her back, the sense of sanctuary that Grianan gave, came together in a moment of blinding clarity and certainty. This was the place for Mike, for them. The flat, the shop, her own trivial concerns simply weren't important. What was important was this man, who needed her, whose life had been torn apart, everything he knew and cared about snatched from him.

Sally stood up, a great calm filling her, her eyes on his long back as he worked patiently at the fiddly task.

'I'm going to keep Grianan,' she said.

'Yes?' Mike turned his head to look up at her, still holding a stem against the wire. Then he nodded. 'Good thinking,' he said.

'I'm going to live here.'

He straightened up, letting the sweet peas fall. He looked at Sally in that new intent way of his, as though he sensed that something was coming that mattered.

'I'm going to sell the flat and the business and move back here.' She felt breathless, shaky, but very very sure; she knew without any doubt that she could give all that up for him.

Mike took her hands, his eyes delighted. 'Sounds good to me,' he said. 'This is the place you really love.'

'Yes it is.' She felt a big beaming smile spread across her face. 'Mike, I've been such a fool.'

How she longed to say there and then, in the peace and sunlight and the swamping relief, 'And you're going to come and live here with me.' But first that had to be arranged.

**A** very villa-ish house for Scotland, incongruous among its sturdy granite neighbours on the outskirts of the town, freshly painted white with a big bow window. A neat short drive the colour of breaded haddock led to a tiled porch. A clean little Fiesta and a clean little Metro were parked outside. Female cars. The garden was very bright and very tidy.

Isobel was wearing a silk dress and high heels. She was painstakingly made-up and the glorious red-gold hair was piled into a careful edifice then tweaked out messily. She was very thin, tense to the point of hostility, and at the sight of her Sally's own nervousness vanished.

She had always been intimidated by Isobel, or by her image of her—the beautiful gentle girl Mike had longed to look after, his wife, the mother of his children. Now Isobel seemed oddly out of her depth, wary and defensive, and hopelessly uptight.

Sally was here chiefly because of the children. The divorce was now final and she had already taken legal responsibility for Mike. His brother had come over from Ireland to see her at Grianan and had admitted that his wife had refused absolutely to let him offer to look after Mike. Having her mother-in-law, now severely incapacitated, living with them in supposedly self-contained quarters was as much as she felt she could cope with. Colin broke down as he said goodbye in mingled guilt and gratitude that Mike would be adrift no longer.

What Sally wanted today was to establish her own contact with Isobel, so that arrangements for the children to see Mike could be made in a spirit of cooperation and, if possible, goodwill.

'Thank you for letting me come,' she said, as they settled in a room full of gleaming repro. 'I thought it would be a good idea for us to meet.'

Isobel's mother was present, very nervous but, Sally suspected, ready to be aggressive.

'Oh, that's all right Mike doesn't mean anything to me any more,' Isobel cut in quickly. 'He's just not the man I married. He'll never be normal, you know that, don't you? He's impossible to live with.'

Her tone was so callously dismissive that Sally felt anger spread through her, realising with disbelief that Isobel's viewpoint was entirely subjective. How she, Sally, might feel about such a comment hadn't entered Isobel's mind.

Sally was about to tell her that she had been to see Mike's doctor and the neurosurgeon who had operated on him, both of whom had made sure she knew Mike would never make a complete recovery but had been equally emphatic about his capacity to achieve an acceptable quality of life. Then she found that she herself didn't want to enter into any discussion with Isobel about it.

'Such an appalling time she had with him,' Isobel's mother was con-
firming, almost to herself, in case an input from her would not be well
received. 'No one knows who hasn't been through it, no one.'

Sally attempted to steer the conversation to the question of the children but Isobel didn't seem to hear. Perched with half a buttock on the
edge of a red-and-cream striped sofa she let it all pour out.

'I had the house to look after, stuck away up those miles of track, and
the whole responsibility for the children, I nearly went mad up there by
myself. And paying for Mike's care—these places cost the earth. I know
his father would have liked Michael to have the house but how was I
supposed to cope till he was old enough? And with Mike's brother living
in Ireland, and his mother needing looking after as well, it was just a
nightmare . . .'

Sally had done her best to imagine what all these problems must have
been like for Isobel, and even now a sort of exasperated fairness took
the edge off her anger.

'. . . and that awful place, no neighbours, miles from anywhere,
impossible to get a thing. And it wasn't a marriage any more that part
was out of the question, of course . . .'

Good.

'. . . I know people think I should have stood by him, but I did, I did
everything for that man when he came out of hospital. Everything. It's
easy to talk if it's not you that's stuck there, day after day. The only thing
I could do was sell up . . .'

Listening as Isobel's querulous voice ran on in what was clearly a
well-worn defence, with supportive murmurs coming from her mother,
Sally waited for some acknowledgment of what Mike had lost and suffered. But gradually it dawned on her that Isobel had agreed to her
coming here to absolve herself from blame.

Before Sally could get round to the practical question of the children's
visits to Grianan, a black Jaguar came scrunching across the gravel and a
moment later a man walked into the glossy room. The boyfriend, Sally
thought, surprised and intrigued by his appearing like this.

He came straight to her, hand outstretched, immaculate blue-and-
white striped cuff emerging from dark grey sleeve. 'Edward Rokeby.' His
warm tone and hearty smile gave no impression of falseness. He was
short, compact, buzzing with a current of power which Sally could
actually feel as he shook her hand, his grip hard and brief.

'I thought you had meetings all day.' Isobel sounded far from welcoming, and the sulky tone suggested they were well into a relationship.

'Change of plan.' A man with no time to waste, a man with shrewd eyes which met Sally's with a message of understanding and reassurance. He had known she was to be here and why. He had intended to turn up at this precise moment, she was convinced. Whatever his degree of involvement was, he had not trusted this interview to Isobel.

Sally's hope for workable solutions over the children reawoke.

'It's a great relief to Isobel, as I'm sure you will appreciate, to know that Mike will be properly looked after,' Edward—now officially tagged as the fiancé—assured her, calmly ignoring Isobel's indignant glare. 'He's had a bad time of it, all in all.'

Isobel opened her mouth but he shot her a look from which his cultivated *bonhomie* was suddenly absent, and she shut it again, wriggling her thin shoulders and allowing herself a pout of defiance.

'I think Grianan will be a good place for him,' Sally said neutrally. 'He seemed to like towns and lots of people about at first, but maybe that was just part of the relearning process. He doesn't seem to miss them now."

'He doesn't know where he is, and that's all there is to it,' Isobel stated flatly, with instant automatic possessiveness. 'You may think he knows, but in actual fact he hasn't the faintest idea.'

Sally kept her eyes down till she had made sure that her voice was going to be under control. She had not been prepared for this utter dismissal of the idea of Mike as a functioning human being. 'Well, Grianan will certainly be ideal for the children, whenever they want to see their father. You will let them come, won't you?' In spite of herself her voice grew urgent, and it was to Edward she turned, not Isobel.

Edward answered, with great firmness. 'They will most certainly come. You needn't ever worry on that score.'

'They loathed going to Gilsburgh,' Isobel leapt in petulantly. 'Half the time Mike didn't even know who they were, you know that. It upset them and there was nothing for them to do and he wouldn't go anywhere else with them . . .'

Edward frowned quickly. Sally wondered at the power of female helplessness combined with glorious red hair. It seemed to her that Isobel, weak and self-centred and, it must be said, not conspicuously intelligent, had cornered two admirable men.

It was Edward who came out to see her off. Isobel hovered for a moment in the porch, waggled her fingers in self-conscious farewell and turned to go in before Sally had reached her car.

'We shall be married in a month's time,' Edward said quietly.

Sally turned to look at him, not sure what he was telling her. Perhaps that he would take charge? 'It will be all right, won't it?' she asked, more urgently than she had intended.

'I guarantee it. The children really miss their father, especially Michael. I shall look after them and make sure they get everything they need in material terms, but it's Mike they love.'

They stood with the car door between them and their eyes, almost on a level, met unsmiling, expressing mutual concern, finding mutual reassurance. 'It was good of you to come back today,' Sally said quietly.

Edward nodded an acknowledgment, making no fudging excuses. 'I think, if you'll allow me to say so, that at the end of the day Mike is a lucky man.'

Sally could find no appropriate answer to that, an extraordinarily generous compliment in the circumstances, but she felt her face light up. There had been no one till now to give her that encouragement.

'Keep in touch,' Edward said, nodding. 'If there's ever anything you need to discuss you can always contact me.' A dye-stamped card.

Sally knew that at last she had an ally. 'I'm so glad we've met.'

He smiled, the kindness in his eyes genuine. 'Drive carefully.'

He had known she would want to put her foot down on the way home. Not only to get back to Grianan and Mike but to get the taste of Isobel's callousness out of her mouth. Yet in a strange way Isobel had become unimportant today, her power finally gone. As Sally headed up the motorway her mind ranged forward contentedly, conscious of a firm base of happiness beneath the flow of thoughts.

The Edalmere cottage had been sold. She had taken the first offer that came for it, ignoring John Ballantyne's protests. The boathouse flat was on the market. Now that she was back at Grianan Sally wondered how she could have been content in it for so long. In retrospect it seemed dark and confined. But it had been a refuge, and it had been the place where she had got to know Nona.

The business she minded giving up more than she had expected. It had been a positive thread which had held her life together. It had been swiftly snapped up and she was glad that after the effort she and Nona had put into it, it looked as though it might survive. But she had no serious or lasting regrets; Mike came first.

From that moment in the sunny sleeping garden at Grianan, watching Mike hooking up the wild sweet peas, when she had known with absolute certainty what she wanted, she had never looked back.

All doubts, all the practical objections had simply fallen away. Who else did she want to be with? She had loved Mike more than she had ever loved anyone and he was Mike still. Deficient in one small function of the brain, the emphasis of his personality altered, but still that person.

She had put off proposing the new plan to Mike, fearful that he would reject it or be worried by it in a way which would retard his progress. Hesitating like this had given Sally plenty of time to discover what it would mean to her if he didn't agree.

They had been at Grianan for the weekend and she had been due to take Mike back to Gilsburgh that evening. She had kept to the pattern he was used to so that no hint of change should unsettle him before it was certain there would be no legal or practical obstacles.

They had just finished watering the small patch of ground which they had planted with lettuce and spring onions and a couple of rows of spinach and broccoli. One of the victims of Sally's neglect had been the garden hose, left out all winter, and they had been going back and forth with watering cans. Mike was very patient about that sort of thing now.

Sally had felt harried, with a sense of time closing in on her, angry with herself for having let the whole weekend slip by again without saying anything, but feeling it would be a bad idea to launch into the subject in the car on the way down to Gilsburgh. At a deeper level, of course, she hated having to take Mike back at all.

The outside tap on the greenhouse wall wouldn't turn off properly. She had seized it with both hands, quite unreasonably infuriated by the petty setback. It went on dripping and she had gone down on one knee to put more beef into her effort. All her churning doubts and fears had focused on this one obstinate object. God, something else that ought to be seen to, she had thought in despair. Her own inadequacy had seemed suddenly too great to bear. She had hit the tap a violent blow with the metal watering can, a gesture of complete futility, jarring her arm. A stronger spatter of water had rewarded her and she had realised to her horror that in a couple of seconds she would be in tears.

'Hey—*hey!*' Mike's voice had protested behind her, amused but concerned. A hand had appeared over her shoulder, shutting off the tap without apparent effort, then both hands had gripped her arms and lifted her to her feet. 'Come on, what's all this about?' He had turned her towards him, smothering her anger in his embrace, bending his head over hers. 'You've been like a lit fuse all day. And do you think you could let go of that damned can?'

Giggling with the slight hysteria of averted tears, she had let it clatter at their feet, butting her head against him.

'You going to tell me what's eating you?'

The moment had come and she had seized it. She had arched away from him to look into his eyes, supported by the circle of his arms. 'Mike, would you like to come and live here, at Grianan, with me?'

He had stared at her for a moment, a curious blankness in his eyes as though he was in shock, and she had had a moment's terror that she had done some irreversible damage, set back his recovery for weeks or even months. Then his eyes had come alive, those arresting green-brown eyes, a joyful light leaping in them followed by a relief so overwhelming that he had tried to hide it from her, pressing his head hard down against hers again, and she had felt the tremor of intense feeling which ran through his big frame. She had heard his breath drawn raggedly, harshly, and had known that he was weeping.

'Mike, darling Mike.' Her own voice had wavered, her throat aching. 'Oh, Mike, don't, it's all right. Everything's all right. You can decide whatever you want, we can talk about it all . . .' She had stroked his bent head, soothed and comforted him, shaken to pieces at his reaction.

After a moment he had lifted his head, his painful grip on her relaxing. 'Damn fool, aren't I?' he had said, with an attempt at a laugh. 'But did you mean it, Sally? Were you serious? Is it what you want yourself?'

'More than I've ever wanted anything.'

'But—live here? What about the flat?'

'Sell it.'

He had stared at her, drawing a long shaky breath. 'Live here with you. Christ, I can't believe this is happening.' He had released her and taken a couple of jerky steps away and back. 'But are you sure it's what you want, Sally?' he had repeated urgently. 'I'm no bloody good to anyone now, you know that. I shouldn't let you lumber yourself with me.'

'Be a darn sight easier living with you here than rushing up and down to Gilsburgh all the time,' she had told him cheerfully, seeing the fear that was overtaking him as he began to think through the realities. 'We want to be together. That's all we have to worry about. We can just take it one day at a time, as you say yourself.'

'Yes, but it's different for me, that's all I can manage,' he had pointed out, with a small rueful smile she had been glad to see. 'It's hardly the same for you.'

'Why not? I'll be here, at home.' And safe, she had thought, in the way only Grianan can make me feel.

'Bloody hell.' He had looked around him and Sally had seen the tension draining from him. 'What a prospect,' he had said softly.

'We probably ought to be on our way now, though. It's getting late. You can think about this during the week and then on Friday—'

'I'm not going back.' The instant panicky flat defiance had sharply reminded her that he was not equipped either to think anything over or to argue his case reasonably.

'It won't be for long—' she had begun, but she should have known better by this time.

'No point in going back there, is there?' A little attempt at jauntiness there that she had recognised; a casualness which could not hide his alarm. 'And anyway, who's going to care?'

Sally had suddenly glimpsed what it would be like for him to be back at Balmenie House alone, not counting off the last few days in relief and anticipation as anyone else could do, but terrified that he had imagined it all, fighting to keep hold of his fragile grip on time.

And what difference did it make, after all? Mike was right. Who was there to care?

She had looked up at him and laughed in relief at the simplicity of it. 'I'll phone Mrs Lucas.'

'Yes?' Mike's skin was glistening faintly in the familiar ominous way. What had she put him through in the last few moments?

'You're right, Mike. Why should you ever go back?'

'Christ, Sally.' His arms reached for her again and he crushed her to him. 'I thought I'd go mad in that place. Sometimes I thought I *was* mad. I wanted to top myself. I used to think, Is this it, for the rest of my life? These doddering old fools around me, this smarmy woman patronising me, this dismal little town, the mud, the smell of the river—sometimes it seemed as though I'd never get it out of my nostrils.'

Sally hugged him, shocked, stunned with guilt. He had suffered it all because he had known there was no alternative that he could demand. What sort of courage was that?

Watching him adapting to his new life Sally couldn't believe that she had waited so long to bring him here. At Grianan, where Mike had felt at ease from the first moment, he was secure and occupied in an environment he enjoyed and understood. He was never alone, which had been a dread Sally hadn't fully grasped but which he now described in terms that made her wince.

She had wondered if he would like to have his own room, but he'd simply laughed at her, picking her up and swinging her round exuberantly. 'Are you joking? Separate rooms? No chance, you're not getting away with that.'

As simple as that. And how much she would have minded, she knew, if he had chosen otherwise. She wanted him there, wanted to sleep with her body against his, to wake and find him beside her. She would have been miserable alone, knowing that he was sleeping somewhere else in the house.

Even if Mike had never made love to her at all she would have wanted to be with him. But the change which moving to Grianan made in him had affected more than his mental stability. He was leading a more active life, eating and sleeping better, and he looked fit again, the incipient paunch gone. Sally had grown used to his hair being grey but now it had more life to it, the flattened dead look gone, and his skin was as brown and freckled as it had ever been.

Occupied, belonging, secure, Mike was at last able to look beyond his own struggle to survive and take more notice of other people again. This new awareness was evident in his lovemaking, bringing a return of tenderness and sensitivity which she had never thought he would be capable of again.

It was good to watch his growing assurance as he found himself in a scene he could deal with, and where he felt he had a role. It was a self-generating cycle of confidence and improvement, and Sally loved those quiet days when they were always together, watching him rediscover lost skills and pleasures, seeing his concentration span increase in leaps and bounds.

One day, as they were working together on making the greenhouse weatherproof once more, she was startled and moved to hear an almost forgotten sound. Mike was whistling as he expertly thumbed putty into place round a new pane. Sally hadn't heard him do that since before he was ill and she stopped work to stand still, filled with joy. It was hard to forgive herself for having made him wait even one extra hour for this, but he was safe now.

# CHAPTER TWELVE

ONCE SALLY HAD MADE the decision to live at Grianan she hadn't looked much beyond establishing Mike there happily. In financial terms there was no immediate worry. The capital she had realised was, hopefully, reasonably well invested. Mike himself had his disability benefit and his share of the proceeds from Edal Bank and its adjoining land, and he was adamant about both going into the kitty. Finding how deeply this mattered to him, Sally had agreed. They could

ALEXANDRA RAIFE

live quietly at Grianan, pottering away at the endless jobs such a place
threw up, establishing a new routine for themselves and a sense of permanence and peace. Sally saw Mike as her job now.

It didn't work out like that.

Michael and Kirsty were the first to come, Michael in particular stiff
and shy with Sally, very grown-up and masculine and, she guessed, terrified of any new development which would take his father still further
away from him. Kirsty, more outgoing and with much of her father's
practical adaptability, relaxed a couple of hours into her first visit and
never looked back.

Sally had been apprehensive too, about occupying them as much as
anything else, so it was a relief to find that they revelled in the place,
glad to be back in the type of environment they were used to and had
badly missed. Another thing she was thankful for was that, in spite of
Isobel's assertions that they had hated going to visit Mike in Gilsburgh,
their father's limitations didn't seem to worry them at all. They simply
took no notice of them, each showing a ready kindness towards him
and truly impressive patience with the way he endlessly repeated himself and wandered off in the middle of doing things.

Sally made no special plans for these visits—other than providing
favourite food. She just went on with whatever she was doing, letting
the children be with Mike or go off on their own, swim in the river, get
out the old croquet set, have the run of house and garden.

Sally loved watching Mike with them. He kept to a light touch but
sometimes she caught in his face an incredulous gratitude that he hadn't
lost them, that the tamped-down feelings which he had not been able to
risk showing could be expressed again. He had missed them deeply, and
his satisfaction at seeing them so much at home at Grianan was one of
the great pleasures of the new life they were establishing.

An even greater joy for Sally was the fact that the old chemistry was
alive between her and Mike again. Time had absorbed the shock of the
changes illness had made in him. The unease with sexual contact was
long forgotten. Now he would hold Sally's hand, slip an arm round her,
show his need for her nearness just as he used to. At night he held her in
the melding ease of lovers, and when he made love to her they were
in tune once more in their own private world of pleasure, not swept up
in the wild need of their early loving but wrapped in a restored mutual
tenderness which meant more to Sally than all the old urgent passion.

Any guilt that beset her these days was for having been so blind to his
needs. He had lived through a nightmare at Gilsburgh, a nightmare
endured with a self-discipline phenomenal in his condition. All he had

needed was to belong and to feel of use again, and those needs Grianan could fulfil, at the same time providing that other essential for him, calm. Because he was no longer trying to fit into a timetable arbitrary to him, he gradually abandoned his obsessive questions about what time and what day it was. When he had bad days, which he still did, and which Sally had learned to see coming from his reluctance to get up and his extreme slowness in dressing, they could be got through quietly. There was no pressure on him to do anything he didn't want to do.

On such days he wouldn't touch jobs he had been engrossed in the day before but would wander and stand at windows, silent and withdrawn but not apparently disturbed. Sally learned that these were recuperative periods, protecting his brain from the threat of overload, and once she had understood this they didn't alarm her.

Far outweighing them, in any case, was the joy of seeing the first flicker of humour return, a link once so important between them. Mike had begun to tease her again, just standard male put-downs about the time it took her to change a plug or the rough-and-ready job she was satisfied with when she slapped some paint on the greenhouse door, and though she defended herself hotly she secretly relished the signs that he was no longer taking her for granted as the competent figure in charge. She had never loved him more.

People were gradually becoming necessary to him again, not to watch and wonder at as if their antics belonged to some existence he could never share, but to be with on equal terms. Mike soon seemed to know half the glen. He would chat to everyone he met and people soon forgot that there was anything wrong with him. Outwardly no one could have told at first meeting that there was. The self-conscious air and the trick of looking closely into people's faces were gone. Only when he was with someone for any length of time did the faulty memory show. When for instance they went to Drumveyn, for a barbecue lunch by the loch so relaxed that no one left till seven, Sally was conscious of him repeating things he had just said and clinging determinedly to anecdotes from the past, where he felt sure of his ground.

She knew no one would mind. As she and Mike drove home, his relief at his own success was boisterous and gloriously conceited and Sally laughed at him, as pleased as he was.

'You're just a huge show-off.'

'I've always been popular. I think I need a wider stage, though. How about opening Grianan up for guests again?'

'Not you, too.' Every person she had talked to today seemed to have asked her about it.

'Have you thought about it?' Mike was serious now.

'It certainly wasn't part of the plan.'

'It's a possibility, isn't it?'

'Not really. I'm no Janey, remember.'

'You don't have to be, do you?'

'But people came to Grianan because of her—and because of the food. You know I'm not in that league. I'm not even interested in cooking.'

'Someone else could cook. And the guests loved the place as well, you told me so yourself.'

'They'll all have found somewhere else to go by this time.'

But later, coming in from a last wander on the hill together before bed, she asked abruptly, 'Mike, do *you* think I should open the place up again?'

'Well,' he said, in that new easy-going way of his, 'it seems a bit of a waste, just the two of us here, doesn't it? This big house in such a perfect setting. And you're used to being busy. Don't you think you'll get bored after a while?'

'You're worried that I've given up a meaningful career selling envelopes for your sake?'

He laughed. 'To the point, as ever.'

'Seriously, do you think something like that?'

'I think eventually you will need more than your present existence to occupy you, and I think this place could be better used. And we know the guests still miss it.'

All through the year there had been a steady trickle of message saying things like, 'How we miss Grianan, we can't find anything remotely like it,' or, 'This place isn't a patch on Grianan—food's frightful and water's always hot . . .' Sally knew it was a reaching out to Janey through her but she knew it was genuine none the less.

'Maureen would come and cook.'

'How do you know that?'

'She said so.' Mike's cheerful grin nearly distracted Sally from the whole conversation.

'You've discussed this with Maureen?'

The grin widened. 'And with Connie.'

'But Mike, listen—' She followed him across the kitchen and clutched his arm in her need for his full attention as he went to draw the kettle onto the Aga hob. 'Wouldn't you hate it? People around all the time, me always having to put them first and work to a timetable? And it never stops, you know, there's no such thing as time off.'

Mike put his hand over hers, smiling at her sudden urgency. 'Sweetheart, I like people, I always have. And you could have as many or as few as you liked. We don't have to make a living out of it, though a place like this ought to bring in some return. And it stops in the winter, doesn't it?'

'Are you trying to persuade me because you feel it would be good for me?' As she spoke, it struck Sally how impossible it would have been to have put such a question to him even a few weeks ago.

He looked down at her hand, clasped in his. She saw his struggle to find words. 'I don't want to be a passenger. Damnation—' She could see the words slipping away from him because this mattered too much. 'Just slow down,' he muttered to himself, then went on with taut effort, 'Sharing. Contributing. Doing this together, where we live.'

That overriding need, to feel that he was making an input again. Suddenly Sally realised that it was all supremely simple. 'Then we'll do it,' she said. 'A new enterprise together.'

'Do you mean it?' Mike looked attentively into her face for a moment, then seized her and they clung together in exultant excitement.

Sally knew she should have brought the washing in long before this. There was more than a hint of autumn in the dusky air and the sheets were probably wetter than they had been an hour ago. That damned scullery tap blowing its top just as Maureen was starting dinner may have been hilarious but dinner would be late. Good job Mike had been on hand to deal with the crisis with his usual calm competence.

As she started down the crooked steps a light caught her eye away to the right. The garden cottage. Had someone broken in? Or—?

Her heart beating fast, she dumped down the laundry basket and began to run. It didn't occur to her to be afraid of what she might find, or to fetch Mike. She slowed as she approached, doubt assailing her. The door wasn't closed and she could hear music. She paused, head cocked. Simon and Garfunkel, 'El Condor Pasa'.

Relief and delight swept her forward. He was standing by the unrolled futon, sorting out a pile of belongings which he had emptied onto it from the backpack at his feet.

'I thought you would never come back.'

She was across the room, shaking him, clutching him. He rocked under the attack and steadied her, gasping. Then, her eyes shut against tears, Sally felt his hand hard behind her head, pulling her cheek to his.

'Oh, Sally, bless you for that,' he said, his voice muffled. 'Let me look at you.' He held her off, smiling, his cheek wet from hers. 'Tears too,' he said softly.

'I thought you'd gone for ever.'

'Time,' he said, 'I just needed time.'

'I thought you hated me—'

He shook her gently, frowning. 'Never. Never in the world. But there were a lot of feelings. We'll talk about it, I promise.'

Sally looked at him, at his sensitive face, his dark eyes which she had last seen stony with pain, and she felt a core of guilt and remorse deep inside her melt away. 'Yes, we must talk.'

'We will,' he said definitely. 'There'll be plenty of time.'

'You're staying?'

'I'm staying.'

'We're open again,' she told him, grabbing at any bit of news, hearing the childish elation in her voice and not caring.

'I know,' he said, eyes smiling.

'How d'you know?' she demanded indignantly. 'Connie? You've been in touch all the time? The miserable wretch—why didn't she tell me?'

'I asked her not to.'

'She could at least have said you were coming.'

'She didn't know, truly. And are you enjoying having guests here again?'

Sally allowed herself to be deflected. The truth was she had never imagined how much fun it would be. Feeling very tentative, she had written round to the guests who usually came in late summer and autumn, hoping that some might not have arranged an alternative holiday yet. The response had been startling, not only in immediate bookings but in enthusiasm and good wishes and plans for next year.

'You thought you'd keep the numbers small?' Mike had mocked. 'I'll be building an extension at this rate.'

Sally didn't ask on what terms Piers had returned, but it seemed that he intended to take up where he had left off. The only thing she insisted on was that he was paid. Janey had let him live in the cottage; that had been their deal. But now the cottage was his property. Sally had Mike to back her on this and Piers had to give in.

She and Piers found their chances to talk in the late autumn days when he began the job of reclaiming the garden, which they hoped to have fully productive again next year.

'I know you think I failed Aunt Janey.' At last it could be said.

'I was too hard on you.'

'Because you loved her.'

Piers straightened up from his digging and looked at her with a sudden penetrating scrutiny.

Sally met it as calmly as she could. She wanted this out in the open and accepted. For a moment the shutters of the intensely private person seemed ready to come down and she regretted what she had said. Piers read that in her eyes and took a deep breath.

'Yes, I loved her.'

Sally touched his arm in quick grateful acknowledgment. 'And you thought I didn't love her enough.'

'No, I thought you were going to realise too late just how much you loved her. And I wanted you to see her pain and understand how deeply she minded leaving you, the most precious person in her life.'

He smiled wryly at Sally's reaction of surprised denial. 'Oh, Sally, of course you were. I just wanted you to look past yourself. That's why when I heard you'd given up everything to look after Mike, and were opening the doors of Grianan again and letting life come back to it, I knew you had learned that and it was time to come back.'

Stark truths, but oddly acceptable to have them put into words by him. There was a feeling of completeness to have him there again, quietly in the background of their lives and for Sally there was a special pleasure to be able to share books and poetry once more, a world largely closed to Mike now.

They got on well, these two so different men. Slow-moving, without urgency, talking or silent for hours as inclination or Mike's mood swings dictated, they gradually worked their way through the maintenance jobs so long neglected, Mike supplying muscle and professional know-how, Piers his craftsman's skills.

They all shared their amusement at the guests, who one and all declared themselves ready to accept any changes but universally longed for everything to be exactly as it had always been. Outwardly it was. Nothing had changed in the rooms, or in the pattern of the days. Packed lunches were put out on the same table in the hall, dog bowls left on the corridor windowsill by the kitchen door, the same boots and tweeds stank out the boiler room. Even the food was almost the same. Maureen felt the mantle of Janey had fallen on her shoulders. All the energy formerly channelled into outwitting and circumventing the boss now went into outdoing her.

Mike was perfect with the guests, who yearned for personal attention and a feeling of involvement. Janey had always muttered about the way they expected her to sit and chat to them, and Sally was discovering just how impossible it was to make the time for such indulgence, but these first arrivals, particularly since they felt they had been specially invited, yearned for personal attention and a feeling of involvement. Mike loved that side of things. He had all the time in the world for wordy old generals and even more for their flirtatious old wives.

Sally knew it was early days and that the pleasure would almost certainly pall under the pressure of sheer hard work, but for the time being it felt so much like having a houseful of friends to stay that it seemed outrageous to accept their cheques.

It was Mike who persuaded her to ask her father to come. He understood her deep-seated reluctance, but knew too that it was a shadowy and unsatisfactory area of her life which should be dealt with.

'You don't have to be on top of each other all the time. In fact you hardly need to see one another if it doesn't work out.'

'But he hates me.' It was a last-minute cry of protest, voicing the old buried fear.

Mike didn't bother to answer it, just pulled her in close, saying, 'I'm here, remember, you're not on your own.'

With her father too, when he came, Sally realised that she had been missing the obvious. As a member of the medical profession, who better to understand Mike's problems and help her to understand them? And his pleasure at being at Grianan again surprised and shamed her. She had held onto it fiercely as her territory after her mother had gone, her place and Janey's, but now she saw that her father would readily have come here with her if she had given him the chance.

They still talked with difficulty. Her father could infect her with his own communication problems in seconds flat. But they did fumble towards a new frankness.

'It's meant a lot to me, you know, being here again,' her father said awkwardly one day, when he had found her madly plucking pheasants which she had forgotten they needed for dinner and had most uncharacteristically started to help her. 'I hope it's been acceptable to you—that is, not upset you in any way?'

'It's been good.' He should not have had to ask such a question.

'This is a pretty special place, Sally. It has a spirit very much its own.'

'Janey's spirit.'

'Yours now.' He studied her, his gaunt face sad. 'I've missed so much of you. My own fault.'

'You needn't miss any more of me.' How crass that sounded. She hurried on. 'I mean, I do want you to come here, whenever you want to, if you'd like to.'

He smiled and she had a startling glimpse of the father who had loved his small girl, and been adored in return. 'I should like to.'

They plucked on, slow and not so slow.

'And Sally—'

She looked up, the urgency of his voice arresting her.

'—about Mike. Don't have any doubts. He's the right man for you, I'm sure of it. And he'll give you every ounce of himself, always. Sorry, that's probably unacceptably intrusive—'

'No, I'm glad you said it.'

He *was* the right man. Her weighing up of the pros and cons of living with him seemed incredible now. Once the pressure of trying to cope with him and her own separate life had been lifted, so all the impatience which would in turn torture her with guilt had evaporated. There was never conflict or even minor arguments between them. No man could have been more generous, loving or tolerant. And, as her father had said, everything Mike was or had was hers.

They were on their way one Friday afternoon to collect Kirsty from school for the weekend when Sally opened a fat letter from Australia which she hadn't had time to look at when Postie came. It contained yet another photograph of Nona's dark-haired son to join the rest that had been winging to Grianan since August. 'Oh, look, isn't he heaven?'

'Would it be all right if I looked later?' Mike asked with mild irony. He liked to drive in the glen though they changed over before Muirend.

'Oh, and goodness, guess what—'

'Tell me.'

'My mother and Bill are thinking of coming over next year. My mother asks if it would be all right if they came to see us. Oh, how *awful* that she thinks she has to ask. How truly awful. Of course they must come.'

'Phone her.'

Two calm words and all the panic went.

'Oh, and listen to this . . .' She read on eagerly.

'Try out loud.'

'Sorry, but this is such a turnup. Danny, my eldest brother'—the word easy now because of Nona—'is having a year's travelling before university and wants to know if he can come and work at Grianan for a few months, do anything . . .'

Her voice trailed away as she looked up from the letter, caught up in amazing new visions reaching forward through the meshes of relationships and friendships, through the unexpected twists of time's plotting.

'It's Grianan,' she said. 'It's Grianan, isn't it?'

Mike pulled into the lay-by where they always changed places. He reached over to pull her into a headlock as he would have done his son Michael.

'What's Grianan?' he asked, giving her a little shake.

'Let go, you big brute.' Breathlessly Sally dragged her head free and shook back her thick hair. 'I mean, making everything possible, drawing everyone together. I used to think it was Janey.'

'It's you, you absurd woman. It *was* Janey and now it's you. You've stopped holding people off.'

'Giving not taking,' she amended grimly.

'That too.' Mike leaned over and dropped a kiss on her temple.

She knew that it was true. As soon as she had opened the doors everything and everyone she cared about had come flocking towards her. She turned her head and pressed her lips to the back of the hand that lay on her shoulder.

# ALEXANDRA RAIFE

'After taking my degree, I decided I wanted to live somewhere in the hills and somewhere beautiful, so I got out a map of Scotland, a country I'd loved for many years, took a pin, shut my eyes and stuck it in, and that's how I came to move from my home in Shropshire to the Highlands,' said Alexandra Raife when I met her in Perthshire.

In her picturesque cottage, a tortoiseshell butterfly fluttered against the window of the room where we were sitting, looking out across the glen to stunning views of the hills beyond. Dressed in comfortable outdoor clothes, Alexandra Raife told me, 'I have had a variety of jobs abroad but I have always returned here.' The jobs have included the post as governess on a Gaucho cattle ranch in southern Brazil, teaching English in Finland and Portugal, looking after a family in a Scottish castle and a six-year commission in the RAF. She has written for her own pleasure all her life, but her first novel, *Drumveyn*, was only published two years ago. She was persuaded by a friend to submit a synopsis to an agent, who agreed to read the script. She was so convinced of its lack of merit that she posted it second class; it found a publisher within two weeks.

'I am not interested in money or material things,' she told me. 'I like living a simple life, in my simple cottage which I have not changed since I came here.' She acquired this philosophy in her thirties, when, co-running a country-house hotel, she lost everything in a fire. She realised then that possessions would never be important to her again.

In fact, her experiences in the country-house hotel are mirrored in some of the events which take place in *Grianan*, her third successful novel.

When writing a book, Alexandra Raife has a strict routine. She wakes every morning at four o'clock—and does her writing in bed. She told me 'when I decided to move from writing on typewriter to word processor, I was worried about the extra weight. I worked out from the specification that it would equal the typewriter plus two kilos, so before buying I wrote for a couple of hours with two bags of sugar balanced on the typewriter.'

Alexandra Raife is very content with her life as a writer. The fact that a growing band of fans enjoy reading what she writes is to her the most exciting bonus of all.

*Marysia Juszczakiewicz*

IMOGEN
PARKER

*These*
*Foolish*
*Things*

In the hottest summer for twenty years
three mothers-to-be meet at an antenatal
class. Over the telling months that follow,
these very different women are to become
inextricably linked.

## Alison

sophisticated, successful, married to the
ideal husband, but still wondering what the
future holds.

## Lia

serene, beautiful and living in blissful
contentment with the man she loves.

## Ginger

chaotic, effervescent, unable to hold down
a relationship for more than a few weeks.

*July*

$\mathcal{I}$T WAS THE HOTTEST summer for almost twenty years.
The tinted windows of her sixth-floor office made the sky a deep, cool blue. Alison gazed out, watching an invisible aeroplane's vapour trail cut a white gash through the pure, even colour. The air inside the building was chill, almost alpine. Alison tried to imagine the wall of hot air that would hit her the moment the revolving door downstairs twirled her from fridge to oven, but she could not. It was difficult to believe that outside the pavements burned like coals. There was no let-up from the heat, even when dusk fell. It was safe up here, sealed in a cold box. The office was like a haven, where she knew what she was doing, and the world outside suddenly seemed a terrifying realm of uncertainty. For a moment, she wished she could stay for ever just as she was, sitting at her desk, insulated from real life.

Alison looked back at her screen. All she needed to do was give the article a title and then her work would be over for four whole months. She was going to come in the next day, but only to tidy up and leave some instructions for her replacement.

'"All Things Nice", how does that sound, Ramona?' She spoke across her desk to the fashion editor. 'It's an article about spices . . . I know it's weak, my brain's scrambled, help me out.'

'"The Wages of Cinnamon"?'

Alison laughed. 'That's worse than my worst effort, "Amazing Mace".'

'How about "Spices: Aniseed to Zafferano"?'

'Perfect.'

As Alison struck the keys her phone buzzed.

'There's a man down here for you,' the receptionist announced.

'OK, I'll see him on my way out,' Alison said, and replaced the receiver with a sigh.

'What's up?' asked Ramona.

'Someone in reception for me. It's probably the photographer who's been plaguing me to look at his portfolio. I can only give him five minutes. I've got the excuse of my antenatal class.'

'Good luck,' said Ramona, adding, 'but a word of advice—Pethidine.'

Alison blew Ramona a kiss across the desk.

In the lift she composed her face into a businesslike frown, which dissolved instantly when the doors opened and she saw who her visitor was.

'Stephen!' She laughed with relief.

Her husband spun round and smiled at her. His smile still had the capacity to surprise her. It transformed his serious expression into one that promised spontaneity, intimacy, and lifted her with a buzz of pride and desire.

'Anything interesting?' she asked wryly, nodding at the staff noticeboard he was reading. There was a memo from the personnel department about the company's new policy on luncheon vouchers.

'A cost-cutting exercise disguised as a bonus,' he pronounced as they wandered to the door.

'Unheard of in your workplace,' Alison teased.

'Oh, for us it's closure of another emergency bed dressed up as an efficiency measure, rather than a reduction in the sandwich levels . . .'

There was always an edge to Stephen's humour. She admired his intelligence, and yet sometimes she wished he would just lighten up.

'What a nice surprise, you coming to meet me,' she said, trying to hold on to the feeling of delight she had experienced at seeing him moments earlier.

He smiled at her and took her hand. It was a public gesture of love and it set off another surge of affection in her body. In their single days, she thought, wistfully, he had often come to meet her from work, or even in the lunch-hour, whisking her into a cab, racing to one of their flats to make love. They didn't do that now that they lived in the suburbs. You couldn't just pop back to Kew for a quick fuck, and since she had been pregnant, the mere thought of sex made her feel sick anyway.

'Tube or taxi?' she asked him as they stepped into the busy street. A film of sweat broke instantly all over her skin.

'Oh, the tube, I think. A taxi would take hours,' Stephen replied.

'Yes, but I just can't stand up all the way,' she said, regretting offering him the choice.

'Surely people give up their seat for you?' Stephen said.

'Well, sometimes, but that's not the point,' she said, impatiently. She didn't want to have a logical discussion, she wanted him to hail a cab.

'OK, we'll get a cab. Of course it's the sensible thing to do,' Stephen agreed, acknowledging her rising distress.

I don't give a damn about the sense of it, she suddenly wanted to scream at him. I'm eight months pregnant and I want to sit down.

'So, what's going to happen at this class of yours?' Stephen asked her. They had both read just about every book on conception, pregnancy and birth.

The taxi was an old one, with no air conditioning. The interior smelt of cigarette smoke. Alison pulled down a window. The traffic was moving slowly, as if the hot air were glue.

'I don't really know,' she said. 'But we're not going in order to learn, we're going in order to meet people,' she told him, adding, gently amused, 'it's what you do when you have a child.'

'Oh, is it?' Stephen sounded reassured by this information.

She smiled. Stephen liked rules, even when it came to the process of making friends. They were each so busy at work there hadn't been any opportunity to meet people who lived in the area. Sometimes she wondered why they had ever bothered to move there, but it had all been part of the plan. Stage one: find a property in a leafy suburb with a garden for future children to play in. They had settled on an Edwardian house in one of those avenues that led away from the Royal Botanic Gardens at Kew. Stage two: conceive. That hadn't gone according to schedule at all, and even after she had finally become pregnant, she somehow always associated the house with failure. Recently, she had found herself filled with nostalgia for her little flat in Islington, now rented out, for the cheap pine furniture she had once saved so hard to buy, the shabby kitchen where she had hosted dozens of informal dinner parties.

The taxi crawled along in the rush-hour traffic. Alison glanced at her watch. They were going to be late. Stephen had been right. It would have been better to take the tube. A lot of men would have pointed this out, but Stephen wasn't like that. He didn't harbour unspoken resentment.

'I booked a table at the River Café for afterwards,' he remarked casually, as they approached Hammersmith.

'Really?' she said, delighted by the reminder that, amid his generally methodical approach to life, Stephen was capable of conjuring up treats.

'Yes, I thought it would be pleasant to have dinner together by the river before I go.'

'Oh!' she said, her mood sinking.

She had forgotten he was flying to a medical convention in America the next day. When the invitation had arrived a couple of months before, she had imagined it would be fun to have time on her own before the birth. Now that he was about to leave, his departure felt like a betrayal.

'What's up?' Stephen asked.

'I just wish you'd told me about the River Café,' she said, trying to think of a reasonable explanation for her sudden feeling of despondence. 'I'll never have time to change.' The sleeves of her black linen jacket were crumpled and she felt damp all over.

'You look lovely. Hot, but lovely . . .' he said, reaching over to smooth her hair back from her face. The gesture irritated her further. She pushed his hand away.

'Perhaps we should just skip the class. I don't know if I can face it,' she said. Suddenly the last thing in the world Alison wanted to do was walk into a room full of people she didn't know. 'I feel too anxious.'

'What are you anxious about?' he asked patiently.

'Everything. I don't know . . .' She shrugged.

Stephen could be so infuriatingly pedantic. He behaved as if there was an answer to everything when for the last few months she had been feeling she did not even know what the question was.

'Darling, you're being a bit irrational . . .'

'Emotions *are* irrational,' she retaliated icily, adding under her breath, 'not that you'd understand.'

As soon as she said it, she wished she hadn't. She saw that the comment had wounded him.

'I'm sorry,' she retracted it immediately, 'that was so unfair . . . It's just so hot, I'm stifled . . .'

'It's OK.' He forgave her instantly.

Blinking back tears, Alison wondered why it was that her relationship with Stephen, which had run perfectly smoothly for five years, had begun to snag. It was a bit like the zip on her shoulder bag, she thought. The two halves always used to slide together, but recently one side had started to catch the lining, making Alison tug at it with a disproportionate impatience that threatened to destroy the fastening altogether.

Lia was lying naked on the bed. The electric fan hummed as it turned lazily, rustling the curtains, then blowing gently on her skin. It was only when she registered Neil's footsteps on the staircase that she opened her eyes and realised that she had been lulled into an afternoon doze.

'Hello, gorgeous.' Neil was beside the bed, leaning over and brushing her mouth with a soft, dry kiss. He put his lips to her belly. 'Dad here,' he whispered. 'Have you been a good baby today?'

He planted a kiss on the dome of Lia's tummy, then turned his face towards hers, smiling bashfully, half embarrassed by his own silliness.

Lia liked it when he talked to the baby. His northern accent was so gentle, and the uncharacteristic soppiness made him seem somehow vulnerable. She loved the sheer physicality of the weight of his head resting next to their baby. They lay staring at each other, joined in a silent cocoon of contentment.

'What's the time?' she asked him eventually.

'Sixish, I should think,' he replied. 'I'm sorry I'm a bit late, but the first team made heavy weather of it at the start.'

Neil was head of sports at a local comprehensive.

'Did you win?' she asked, turning on her side. He loved cricket. Playing it was best, but watching the kids win was pretty good too.

'Thrashed them!' he said, grinning. 'Four wickets to spare in the end.' He looked at her, beaming.

She smiled at him. Neil was a good teacher, and he was going to be a good father. She remembered watching him kicking a football around with the village kids the day after they met. She had been sitting on the porch of the Portuguese beach café drinking beer, feeling dazed, wondering how, after the night they had just spent together, he could find the energy to throw himself into the football match with the unguarded enthusiasm of a boy. She noticed the way that he passed the ball around, ensuring that each of the children, however small, got a fair crack at it. She suddenly knew, with a kind of fated certainty, that she wanted to have his children.

Lia snuggled her head next to his. He turned his face and kissed her slowly. She felt the familiar wave of arousal, like warm syrup suffusing every cell of her body. Their lovemaking had not diminished until recently, when the doctor had advised against penetrative sex, but they had discovered almost the same profound satisfaction in the exquisite tenderness of restraint. She held his face in her hands, looking into his eyes, eyes that were turquoise, so pale she sometimes felt she could see into his soul. Then suddenly a stray thought brought her back to the realm of the mundane, and she remembered why she had wanted Neil to come home early.

'The antenatal class . . . we're going to be late for the class,' she said.

'Oh, do we have to go?' Neil sighed, drawing her closer.

'Now, women on the floor,' their hostess instructed, explaining that it was best for their babies' position if they did not slouch.

To Alison's amazement everyone, including herself, obeyed, lowering themselves onto the dry wood pile, pretending that they were comfortable. The men slipped into chairs behind their partners.

'We've one or two missing, but let's begin anyway,' said the hostess. 'I'm Judith. I've been through what you're going through twice! My children are now five and three. I've been leading antenatal classes for the last two years. Now, which one of you's going to go first—just tell us your name, and anything you think's important about you?'

Her eyes flicked round the faces and came to rest on Alison.

'Alison,' she said. 'I'm editor of the Lifestyle section of a Sunday newspaper . . . er, what else?' She looked at Judith, suddenly at a loss.

'When's the baby due?' Judith asked.

'Oh . . . in four weeks' time.' Alison realised that, as a mother, you defined yourself in terms of your baby, not your job.

'And your husband is . . .' Judith led her on.

'Stephen,' Alison replied, stretching her slim, manicured fingers back over her shoulder to catch his hand, but grasping air. She twisted round and saw that Stephen was staring into space paying no attention.

A murmur of laughter wafted round the room.

'So, it's Stephen, is it?' Judith asked, pointedly at him.

'Yes, it is.' Stephen turned on a smile of such unexpected brilliance Alison forgave him for his distractedness.

'So who's next?'

Tap tap tap.

A pretty, cheeky face was waving at the window. Judith got up and went to answer the door.

'Shit, I'm so sorry I'm late!' The new arrival seemed to tumble into the room. She slipped a small black patent rucksack off her shoulders and sank gratefully into the last available armchair.

'Mums on the floor,' Judith waggled a finger at her, 'for baby's position.'

'Sod that,' said the girl. 'I've given up alcohol and Brie, but I'm buggered if this little sod is going to get me sitting on the floor.'

Alison smiled at her, warming to her irreverence.

'And you are?' Judith asked.

'Ginger, short for Virginia, ironically,' said the girl, pushing a hand through her short peroxide crop.

'Baby due?'

'Yes . . . oh, in August.'

'And your partner's coming separately?'

'Don't they always?' Ginger said, her bright blue eyes registering with dismay that the others were wearing wedding rings. 'Oh, you meant . . . No, I'm doing this on my own, actually. My twin says she'll breathe with me during labour. Perhaps I ought to have brought her along?' she added, making a concession to conformity.

It was clear that Judith had no training in dealing with single mothers with attitude.

'Yes, well,' Judith said. 'We were introducing ourselves.'

The remaining couples gave their names and Judith started handing out pencils and paper.

'Now, I've got a little exercise, just to warm things up, not that we really need it any warmer!' She paused to underline the weak humour. 'Divide into mums and dads and then write down what you like about being pregnant, or your wife being pregnant, and what you don't like. I'll just go and get a jug of water.'

As soon as she left the room, Ginger said, 'Well, one of the things I absolutely hate is those ghastly dungarees that look just like a huge version of what toddlers wear . . . er—' She stopped as she noticed that two women were wearing maternity dungarees. 'Well, you obviously don't need to pee as much as I do,' she added quickly.

'All the clothes are horrible, aren't they?' Alison contributed, eager to rescue someone she sensed was a kindred spirit.

The two women in dungarees eyed her black suit disbelievingly.

This is the only smart thing I could find, Alison wanted to explain, and it's costing me a fortune in dry-cleaning bills. But she said nothing.

'Well, shall we start?' one of the women suggested, pencil in hand. 'I'll write all our answers down,' she added, like a games captain at school, then, as if she were choosing her team, she pointed at her comrade in dungarees: 'You first.'

'I *hate* my ankles swelling; but I *love* wandering round Mothercare, looking at all the little vests and things.'

'They're so tiny, aren't they?'

Ginger and Alison exchanged glances. The exercise had instantly divided the women into two pairs: them and us.

The games captain solemnly noted 'vests'.

In the hall, the doorbell rang again, and they could hear Judith tapping down the corridor to answer it.

Ginger said loudly, 'Well, I *hate* having haemorrhoids and the only thing I *like* is the fact that I'm going to have a baby. Well, sometimes I like it, the rest of the time it scares the shit out of me, or it would if it weren't for the haemorr—!'

Alison felt the nervous giggle she was trying to suppress turn to acid bile in her throat. The heat and the almost palpable confrontation in the air were making her feel nauseous.

A stunningly attractive woman walked into the room. Her face was fresh and lightly tanned, her long wavy hair held back by a pair of Lolita sunglasses with white plastic frames. She was like a Pre-Raphaelite vision of summer, with her meadowy sundress and the mist of light fragrance that seemed to waft in with her.

'Hello,' she said, 'I'm Lia.'

'You?' The games captain was pointing at Alison, with her pencil.

Alison tried to remember what she was being asked. What she liked and what she didn't like. Suddenly she felt very, very sick. Baby. Baby. The words whirred round in her head. The room swam out of her reach and back.

She could hear a man's voice, a soft North Country accent, talking pleasantly in the hall. It was like an echo in her head. Then he walked into the room, smiling.

Baby. Baby. She struggled to maintain her composure, but it was too late, she was going to faint. The last thing she saw before nausea and dizziness overwhelmed her was the man's smile.

'Extra cheese for me, and pepperoni, and olives. Oh God, I'm so hungry I want extra everything on mine!' Ginger grinned at the waiter.

Neil didn't know why he should feel that it was improper for a pregnant woman to be flirting so overtly, but somehow he didn't like it. He tried to catch Lia's eye, but she was entranced by her new friend, laughing at every exaggerated utterance. They had found themselves walking in the same direction after the class, with Ginger pushing her bike beside them. He had issued the invitation to join them for supper on the spur of the moment.

'Lovely bum!' Ginger said, watching the waiter.

Lia laughed. It was a female laugh, half conspiratorial, half knowing. She was very good at passing the time of day with people, moulding herself to the shape of another character straight away, becoming what they wanted her to be. Sometimes it unsettled him and made him wonder whether she was like that with him. But he thought of the intensity in her eyes when they made love, the pure, honest expression of love that seemed to sweep his being like radar, demanding nothing less in return. That, surely, was just for him.

As if she had heard what he was thinking, Lia smiled at him with an intimacy that chased away his momentary doubts.

'That poor woman . . .' Ginger said. 'Do you think it was the heat?'

'I don't know. I barely saw her before she passed out,' Lia replied.

'She seemed quite nice,' Ginger revealed, eager to fill them in on the first part of the meeting they had missed.

'Do you think you'll go again?' Lia asked Ginger.

'I don't think so. I'm not really into all that. I just thought it would be good to meet a few people in the same boat. For the first time in months, I wasn't the fattest person in the room!'

'You're pregnant, not fat,' Lia protested politely.

'Well, at least yours is all where it should be.' Ginger looked at Lia's thin bare arms. 'Mine seems to have laid down fat deposits all over. I've never worn a bra before, and now I need a suspension bridge.'

Neil felt as if he were eavesdropping on a conversation in a changing room. It always amazed him how freely women talked about their bodies when they were alone together. Even though Lia and Ginger had known each other less than three hours, they were already building a rapport. If two men had known each other for this length of time, he thought, we would still be discussing the weather.

'Do you think we'll go again, Neil?' Lia attempted to draw him into the conversation.

'Yes, how was it for you?' Ginger leaned across the table, putting deliberate sexual innuendo into her question and pausing for effect.

Neil shrugged. Ginger was the kind of person, he realised, who always slightly misjudged the boundaries between people. Everyone said that the way to meet other first-time parents was to do antenatal classes. The idea had appealed more to Lia than it had to him. It was the beginning of parental responsibility, Neil had joked, lining up play-mates for your foetus.

'Like you said,' he eventually replied to Ginger's question. 'It's good to know some people in the same boat.'

'Well, at least we've met each other,' Ginger said. 'Oh good, I think this is our order.'

She picked up a slice of pizza, folded it, then opened her bright pink mouth very wide and bit.

'I do hope that woman is OK,' Ginger said, her mouth full.

'If you're so worried about her, why don't you ring?' Neil said impatiently. Judith had issued everyone in the class with a list of telephone numbers and due dates.

The sharpness of his tone seemed to cut through the air.

'Maybe I will,' Ginger replied, slightly defensively. 'Tomorrow, if I have a minute. They're making me work hard for my maternity leave.'

'You said you worked for the BBC,' Lia said, smoothing the atmosphere. 'What do you do, exactly?'

'I'm a secretary. I type letters and get shouted at. Everyone told me that it was the quickest way to get on in television, but they didn't tell me that you had to be a *good* secretary . . . What do you do?'

'Anything that's on offer, really,' Lia said. 'I was waitressing, but my blood pressure's high and the doctor told me to stop.' She was smiling and perfectly at ease.

Alison stood at the bottom of the garden with a cigarette in one hand and a box of matches in the other. On the day the test result came back positive, she had thrown away her lighter but she had never quite managed to quit the smoking.

Stephen watched her from the conservatory as she deliberated whether to light up. He knew she still smoked on occasion, but he never remarked on it. He turned away from the window and sat down at the piano.

The first drag made her feel slightly light-headed. She drew again, inhaling deeply as if the smoke were pure oxygen. She flicked ash onto the ground, then looked at the cigarette, observing that her lips had left a scarlet imprint on the filter.

It made her think of her mother. Margaret's subterfuge had been shopping for groceries she had mysteriously forgotten to buy. 'I'm just slipping out for a tin,' she would call, closing the front door, her pace quickening as she neared the end of their road. One look round to check her husband wasn't following, then cigarette would come out of one pocket, lighter out of the other. Watching from her bedroom window, Alison would see her mother's features changing from pinched to smooth in an instant, the addiction of the nicotine strong enough to overcome even the impropriety of smoking in the street.

I'm turning into my mother, Alison thought with horror, and threw down the butt, grinding it into the grass.

She walked back to the house, where Stephen was playing the 'Moonlight' Sonata.

'I cancelled the River Café. Didn't think you'd want to go out,' he said, taking his hands off the keys for a moment.

'Right,' she said, 'I'll cook something then.'

She walked past him to the kitchen and began to prepare supper.

There was something therapeutic about the sheer monotony of chopping vegetables. She decided to make a ratatouille. She sliced thick rounds of aubergines and salted them, while green olive oil turned clear in the bottom of a heavy pan. She threw in a couple of garlic cloves. The preparation of food gave her mind just enough to think about, to stop it darting forward to the yawning, terrifying unknown, or, worse, backwards, to events she had wrapped in the grey gauze of memory, but which had suddenly become vivid and agonising, all over again.

The scent of garlic brought Stephen into the kitchen. 'Do you need any help?' he said behind her, draping his arms over her shoulders, his hands resting on her bump.

'No, I'm fine,' she said, wishing he would go back to his music.

'Perhaps I should rebook?' Stephen suggested. 'I didn't think you'd be hungry.'

He was trying so hard to be kind, she knew she should be grateful, but she didn't seem to be able to feel anything.

'No, I'm quite enjoying this,' she said.

'As soon as I get back, then. Shall I make a reservation?' he asked.

*Do whatever you want but leave me alone.*

'We ought to make the most of this time,' he said, wandering into the living room and picking up the phone. 'It won't be the same after.'

She could hear Stephen speaking to the restaurant and suddenly she wished they were going out. She desperately needed the distraction.

'Say we'll come this evening, after all,' she shouted to him, but he had already put down the receiver.

'No, I'm sure it's better if we have a quiet time tonight, after your . . . Anyway, what you're making smells delicious.'

'Oh well, next week, then,' she said.

'Yes, next Friday. I said eight. Is that OK?'

'Fine.' She turned back to the kitchen.

'Alison? You *are* all right?'

'Yes,' she said, glad she was facing away from him, and that he could not see her face.


'You hated her, didn't you?' Lia said, as they watched Ginger cycle slowly away.

'Not hated,' Neil replied, cautiously, 'I just thought she was arrogant, and a bit crude.'

Lia laughed. 'I liked her,' she said. 'Under all that shouting, there's quite a scared little rabbit, I think.'

'Shall we get a taxi?' he asked, taking Lia's arm.

'No, let's walk. I like walking in the dark and talking to you,' Lia said.

'Do you want to go to that class again?' he asked.

'I don't know. I thought I wanted to know all that stuff about labour, but I felt a bit funny when that woman passed out as soon as we walked in. It felt like an omen.' She looked sideways at him for reassurance. He pretended not to notice. He felt a seed of anxiety take root in his stomach.

'I don't know,' she continued. 'I think I'd rather have an open mind.'

He breathed a sigh of relief. He most definitely did not want to go again, but he didn't know how to begin to explain why. He didn't want to upset her. And anyway, to mention it would give it a significance it did not deserve, make it seem like a problem. Which it wasn't. Not at all.

Ginger got off her bike at the bottom of the hill and began to push. Away from the busy high street, the air seemed cooler, but as Richmond Hill grew steeper, she could feel her pulse beating against the inside of her skull. As if woken by the slight change in temperature, her baby started kicking. She stopped for breath and watched as a tiny fist, or foot, pummelled inside, rippling across her tummy, like a mouse under a carpet. He (she was sure it was a boy) didn't kick much during the day when she was on the move. But when she let herself stop and rest, he seemed to wake up and demand to be noticed. And it never failed to make her happy when she sensed the vigour of the life inside her.

Ginger smiled and started on her way again. Her flat was in a terrace of houses at the top of the hill. She had only lived there for a few months. Her beloved grandmother, Hermione, had died suddenly in the spring and surprised everyone by leaving her ground-floor flat to Ginger.

As she let herself in, the answerphone on the dining table was blinking like a Christmas-tree light. She pressed PLAY.

Bleep. 'Virginia, it's your mother. Daddy's having his bypass operation on Thursday. He would love to see you, darling . . .'

Ginger sighed. Her mother made it sound so easy. She turned on the kitchen tap and stuck her head under a dribble of water.

Bleep. 'It's just me,' said her twin, Patricia, nicknamed Pic. 'I'm going to see Daddy tomorrow lunchtime and I wondered if you'd like to come with me for moral support.'

Ginger held up her arm and looked at her watch. It was too late to phone. Why did Pic and Ed always go to bed so early?

Bleep. 'Ginger? It's Charlie Prince here. Why don't you give me a bell some time?'

Shit! Her mind raced through all the good reasons he might be ringing: perhaps he'd been abroad for a few months and he had been thinking about her, so as soon as he touched down at Heathrow, he'd called. Very unlikely. Perhaps he and Lucretia had split up for good this time, and . . . No, Charlie and Lucretia were like Hugh Grant and Liz Hurley, together then apart, but they were always really together . . . Maybe he was clearing out his Filofax, and he came across her name, and he remembered the night they had spent together, and picked up the phone? No, that was pure fantasy.

She started to run through the bad reasons why he might be calling. Maybe he had bumped into Robert and Robert had told him, although she had sworn him to secrecy. Oh God, perhaps Charlie had AIDS, and they had told him to contact everyone he had slept with, and he had told them that he always used condoms, but then he remembered that night and . . .

Ginger picked up the phone.

'Pic? You weren't asleep, were you? I'm sorry . . . I've just got in . . . It's just that there was this message . . . Yes, I got yours . . . No, I'm not ringing about that . . . *He* called . . . Charlie Prince . . .'

The next day, as Ginger pedalled up to the entrance of the hospital, she thought how out of place her sister looked amid the dust and cigarette butts, like a fragile orchid growing on a landfill site. From the earliest age, Pic had looked freshly laundered and ironed.

'I've never understood how you work in a laboratory and still manage to look like that,' Ginger said, greeting her with a kiss. She had no idea what her sister actually did, just that it was scientific research.

Pic giggled. 'I do most of my work on computer, and if I'm in the lab I wear an overall.' She took a clean white hanky out of her bag. 'You've got smuts on your face,' she told Ginger. 'Do you really think you ought to be cycling in—'

'My condition?' Ginger interrupted crossly. 'Actually, I mostly push the bike around these days.' She bent to lock her bike to the iron railing. She was wearing black-and-white spotted cycling shorts and a sleeveless shirt that fastened over her bulging front with large white plastic buttons. A bright pink scarf was tied in a bow round her bleached crop. 'Deep breath,' she said, as she straightened up.

'Does that help?' Pic asked, concerned.

'No, silly, I'm just preparing myself for seeing Daddy. It's the first time since I told him.'

'Well, I'm sure he's got over the shock,' Pic said, sounding more confident than she felt.

They found their father dozing in his private room. His face was grey. That is how he'll look when he's dead, Ginger thought, shocked to see how old and ill he had grown since she had seen him last. She felt a rush of fear and affection welling up inside her. Please don't die hating me, she thought, grasping her sister's hand for support.

As if he sensed them there, he opened his eyes. For a second they lit up with undisguised delight, and then narrowed slightly into a frown.

'Well, well, well,' he said. 'My heavenly twins.'

Ginger braced herself for the put-down that was sure to follow, and was surprised when he merely waved his hand at the chairs on each side of the bed. They both sat down.

'I don't know whether to be honoured or alarmed,' he said, 'to have visits from long-lost relatives before I go under the surgeon's knife!'

Ginger bristled, but forced herself to keep quiet.

'Oh, Daddy, don't be silly,' Pic said, quickly. 'The reason you never see us is because you're always away in Brussels or somewhere.'

'I was only joking, my dear Pickles,' he replied, making her blush.

No wonder he is a politician, thought Ginger. He loves control. Usually it was Ginger who walked into his traps because she was far more inclined to fly off the handle and speak without thinking.

'And, Ginger, are you well?' He turned to her.

'I'm fine, thank you, but I certainly picked the wrong summer . . . Now I know why they call it a bun in the oven. It's so bloody hot. I feel like a boiler with the thermostat on high.'

Her father laughed. She was grateful that he had decided to acknowledge her condition. The air in the room seemed to have cleared and she felt able to ask him about the operation. He described the procedure.

'These days it's pretty much routine,' he told her. Even though he sounded confident, she knew he was frightened and that the words were for his reassurance as much as hers.

A nurse came in to monitor his pulse and blood pressure. Pic nodded at her and they got up to leave.

'Good luck!' Pic said, kissing his cheek. 'I love you, Daddy.' She walked out, leaving Ginger alone with him.

Ginger stood awkwardly beside the bed. 'I hope it goes well,' she said.

'Yes,' he replied.

'Right then,' she said, unable to bring herself to kiss him. As she turned to go, his hand, firm and bony, stretched out and grasped hers. She looked at him and saw that his eyes were full of tears. She squeezed his hand and said, 'You take care, I'll see you soon.'

He nodded at her, silently, then let her hand drop.

'Thank you for making me go,' Ginger said later, in an Italian sandwich shop across the road. 'I thought I was quite prepared for him to die without making my peace, but actually that would have been horrible.'

'He's not going to die,' Pic said firmly, then, as if unable to bear any more morbid talk, she asked, 'Now, what are you going to do about Charlie Prince?'

Instinctively, Ginger looked over her shoulder. The name Charlie Prince was one of the few secrets she had ever kept. Only two people in the world knew the identity of the father of her baby. Her best friend, Robert, because it was his party from which they had disappeared together. Who, a few months later, had guessed the reason that she had suddenly stopped drinking. And Pic, because she told Pic absolutely everything.

'I suppose that I'd better find out what he wants.' she said. 'It's probably just something like the direct-line number of someone at the Beeb.'

It had finally occurred to her that Charlie simply wanted something from her, because that was the only reason independent producers ever turned on the charm.

'What if he wants to see you?' Pic pressed on.

'I'm sure he won't,' Ginger said.

'Well, if he does, you will tell me,' Pic said, concerned.

'What, are you thinking of slumming it in some of my clothes, bleaching your hair and playing me?' Ginger asked.

'Now, there's an idea . . .'

When they were little they had sometimes managed to trick people by swapping clothes.

'I knew I shouldn't have told you he was brilliant in bed.'

Now Pic blushed bright red. 'Oh, I didn't mean . . .'

Lia lay on a sunlounger in the dappled shade of the apple tree, drifting in and out of sleep, wondering what it was about the antenatal class that could have upset Neil.

On the way back, an impenetrable cloud of gloom seemed to have settled around him. When he had come to bed, eventually, after pacing the long, narrow garden for an hour, she had seen in his eyes a strange mixture of emotions: distress, fear, and something unfathomable, like loss. Silently, she had opened her arms and drawn him in and held him, until he turned away in sleep.

Perhaps the class had frightened him. Not just labour, but the reality that their lives were about to change irrevocably. Perhaps he had only just experienced the stab of foreboding she had felt months before, suddenly terrified that they were tempting fate by choosing to change something between them that was so perfect.

Lia took a sip of Evian water, then splashed a little over her face. A breeze picked up children's shouts and splashes from the local swimming pool and wafted them into the garden. It was so hot that, if she closed her eyes, she could imagine herself back on the beach by the ocean, the sound of children playing in the waves.

She remembered being in bed with him one evening that first week, lying entwined in a slick of sweat and sex.

'You know that I love you,' he had suddenly said, softly. 'I want to be with you for ever . . .'

'Yes,' she had replied, simply.

She felt the same way as he did. There had been men she thought she loved before, but no one like Neil. It was not just that he was gorgeous, nor that he had a wry smile in his eyes that made her wet whenever she looked at him; it just felt as if they were meant to be together. She had drifted between countries, between men, for ten years, but now she had found the person she wanted to spend the rest of her life with.

She had quit her job that day. They climbed on his motorbike, drove away from the village and roamed along the coast. They had exchanged vows at the far western tip of Europe under a sky brilliant with stars, and then they had come back to England. She had never thought about returning before, but with Neil it had felt like coming home.

'So what was it the editor wanted to say to you so urgently on your last day in the office?' Ramona asked. They were sitting side by side on a park bench in a city park they frequented at lunchtime.

'Not happy with the number of baby items over the past few weeks,' Alison said, dabbing at the corners of her mouth with the napkin. 'I hadn't realised I was so obsessed.'

'Well, at least you've equipped your nursery,' Ramona said drily. 'Does it worry you?' she asked.

'What?' Alison replied. 'Temporary loss of brain cells?'

'No, maternity leave . . . Who knows who'll be sitting at your desk when you come back, that sort of thing . . .'

'I don't have much choice,' Alison said, looking at her bump.

Ramona was a good friend, but she had a way of tapping into insecurities you didn't even know you were feeling. Part of Alison did feel it was odd that today of all days the editor would make his first criticism after three years. But another part had almost wanted him to suggest that she should not return after her leave. What a relief it would be, to be given breathing space, an excuse to decide what she wanted to do with her life. The job had begun to drive her mad. As each month went past, and she planned yet more fatuous features on the style dilemmas

of the middle classes—wallpaper or paint, colours or monochrome—
she became more frustrated with herself, her job, her whole existence.

She had assumed that the prospect of a baby would give meaning to it
all. But it wasn't so. Sometimes she lay awake at night wondering why
she had been so keen to conceive, why it had become an obsession after
three years of failure, and what could have persuaded her to subject herself to *in vitro* fertilisation. She asked herself why it was she was always
desperate to succeed at whatever she did, but never content when she
had achieved it. Her first reaction to the positive pregnancy test had
been pure triumph, her second, utter panic.

As they lay next to one another in the dark that night, Stephen had
asked her why she was trembling, and she had told him, 'I don't think I
want to have a baby.'

'Well, it's too late now, my love.' She had heard the gentle smile in his
voice. He thought she was joking.

'Anyway,' Alison said, scrunching up the waxed paper in which her
sandwich had been wrapped, 'I'd better be getting back.'

There was a small party at six o'clock. The editor opened a couple of
bottles of chardonnay, called the staff into his office and presented her
with a giant teddy bear.

It felt very odd and very final signing off from the computer and
taking the lift down to the ground floor, alone, except for the bear.

Neil watched as Lia turned lamb chops on the barbecue, drops of fat
flaring, making her step back quickly. On the white plastic table beside
her two places were set, a bowl of salad, a basket of cut baguette. He
tried to remember why he had come into the kitchen. Beer. He opened
the fridge and took out a four-pack. Sometimes he found it odd that
someone did his shopping and remembered the things he liked.

Neil smiled, remembering what a bastard he had been to anyone who
tried to get close to him, until the day he had discovered Lia, sitting like
a beached mermaid on the porch of a Portuguese seafront bar. She was
the most beautiful woman he had ever seen. She cast a strange spell on
him, making him feel fierce in his desire for her, and yet gentle towards
the world. He had brought her home, and she had transformed his
house, making it warm and welcoming, not somewhere hard and male.

As Neil closed the fridge door, he saw Judith's list of names of other
couples about to have babies. He stared at the list for several seconds,
wanting to tear it down, but not knowing how to explain if Lia asked
why. Then he checked the garden again. She was still leaning over the
barbecue.

He snatched the phone and dialled the first number on the list. It rang, once, twice; he was about to put it down, then it was answered.

'Hello?' Alison said.

He listened to her breathing for a few seconds, then, unable to believe what he had done, replaced the receiver.

A week after the antenatal class, Lia ran into Alison.

The first thing she noticed was the dress. It was a madras cotton check, purple, turquoise and black. There was something about it that made it look expensive. The woman pulled the last items out of her shopping trolley and straightened up wearily. The second thing Lia noticed was the face. She could not immediately think why it was familiar, but she said, 'Hello.'

Alison looked up. 'Oh . . . hello.'

'I love your dress. Where did you get it? Or is that a rude question?' Lia said, remembering now that it was the woman who had passed out in the antenatal class.

'No, not at all.' Alison's face broke into a smile. 'Harvey Nichols, but I kicked myself because they have some almost the same in Monsoon.'

'It's lovely,' Lia said. 'Are you well?' she added.

'Yes, thank you,' Alison replied, but she looked wary, perhaps not wanting to be reminded of the incident.

The check-out girl swiped Alison's credit card through the till. Lia put her own purchases—a bottle of lemonade and a pound of sausages—onto the conveyor belt.

'Did you come by car?' Lia asked, following her towards the exit.

'Yes, can I give you a lift?'

The invitation was polite rather than meant.

'No, thanks. I haven't got much to carry!' Lia smiled.

They came to a halt beside the lift to the car park.

'Hey, I was just going to go and sit by the river and drink this . . . Would you like to join me?' Lia made one final effort.

Instead of responding, Alison looked at her laden trolley.

'You could put it in the car first.' Lia suggested.

'Oh, well, OK, then,' Alison replied, unable to think of another excuse.

They sat down on a bench. Lia twisted open the seal on the lemonade bottle and offered Alison first sip. For a few minutes they were both silent. By the pier, a riverboat started its engines, making a lot of noise.

'Sometimes I forget how nice it is to be beside water when it's hot,' Alison said. 'It's ridiculous, isn't it? You buy a house in a lovely part of town by the river, and then you're so busy you never even see it.'

'I've been spending a lot of time in our garden,' Lia said. 'But when I get lonely, I come down here.'

The slightly wistful admission of loneliness sent a jolt of guilt through Alison for her earlier reluctance to be friendly. She looked quickly round at her companion.

'You've got a great tan,' Alison said, admiring her arms.

'I've never been this brown before. I think it might have something to do with our "condition",' Lia said, stretching her arms out in front of her. 'Well, at least there are some advantages . . .' she added.

'Name another,' Alison demanded, smiling.

Lia put her chin on her hand and pondered with exaggerated serious-ness. 'No, that's it!' she said, laughing. 'I am so sick of lying around . . . I haven't been able to work for the last six weeks,' she explained.

'You poor thing. I've got itchy feet after less than a week!' Alison laughed.

It was too hot to do anything much, and she felt she was just wasting her time sitting at home in front of a fan. At work, she had longed for time to herself. Now that she was at home, she seemed unable to relax even for a second. She simply did not know what to do.

It was a relief to talk to someone. She found the words bubbling up inside her and tumbling out, and she was surprised by how easily she could articulate what she had been feeling to someone she did not know. Perhaps it was just because she did not know her. Or perhaps, she thought, distrusting herself, she was in fact revealing little of any importance, lulling the girl into a false sense of security, in the hope that when she dared to ask her all the questions she wanted to, Lia would automatically respond. Few could resist a trade of intimacies.

And yet she found that she was deliberately avoiding asking Lia any of these questions. Lia volunteered that she had met her partner in Portugal, and Alison had steered the subject away.

'Have you lived abroad a lot?'

'Since I left home,' Lia said. 'Must have been about ten years, in vari-ous places. I started off in Majorca. I was eighteen and it was my first foreign holiday. Me and my friend just decided to stay.'

'What did your parents think?' Alison asked, mentally calculating Lia's age. Twenty-eight. Almost ten years younger than she was. A stab of jealousy.

'I've no idea,' Lia said.

Alison tried to imagine what it must feel like to be so separate from your parents. She had never been able to shake herself free from her mother's embrace. It was the payoff for the only child—to have the mother's undivided attention as a child, but to continue to have it as an adult. Whenever Margaret took her arm when they were out shopping, and squeezed it in that intimate best-friend kind of way, Alison felt herself shrinking away, not wanting a friend for a mother.

Alison sighed. Margaret would ring this evening, as she did every evening when Stephen was away, demanding to know about her day. Alison would begin by replying cautiously, noncommittally, but somehow, through persistence, her mother would persuade her to part with her thoughts, and Alison would feel as if she had been bled.

Suddenly, she was aware that she had been silent for a long time, lost in thought. 'I *always* know what my mother thinks,' she said, remembering the starting point, and Lia laughed.

The lemonade bottle was empty. Lia stood up. 'I'd better be getting back,' she said.

'Oh.' Alison had enjoyed Lia's company.

'It's just that Neil usually gets in around five,' Lia explained, 'and we eat early.'

'I'll give you a lift home, if you like,' Alison replied.

It was a small terraced house in one of the cheaper areas of the borough, but it stood out from its neighbours. All three windows had window boxes spilling over with red geraniums. Alison began to slow down even before her passenger had told her where to stop.

'It would be lovely to meet up again, some time,' Lia said, opening the car door.

'Yes—' Alison was about to suggest a day when the roar of a motorbike speeding down the road interrupted her.

'Perfect timing!' Lia said, pulling herself out of the car.

'I'll call you,' Alison said, and started the car just as the motorbike came to a halt behind her.

In her mirror, she saw Neil watch as she drove away.

She wondered why he had not told his wife about her. She knew he had not, because she was sure Lia would have mentioned it. She knew he had recognised her because he had phoned her.

She had dialled 1471 after the silent call, suspecting who it was, and checking the caller's number against the list Judith had given them.

Surely he could not still be angry or hurt after twenty years?

'Who was that?' Neil asked as they watched the car pull away.

'Alison,' Lia told him, putting her key in the front door. 'She was the woman who fainted at that class.'

'Oh . . .' He paused, not daring to say anything more.

'I ran into her in Waitrose. She was a bit cold at first, but we ended up having quite a nice chat.'

Alison swerved to avoid a car pulling out in front of her house. She had not seen it. It was lucky there was nothing coming in the opposite direction, or there would have been a crash. Shaking, she pulled into the drive and switched off the engine. Breathing slowly, trying to calm herself, she began to examine possible scenarios.

The first option was to pick up the phone and talk to him. 'Look, this is ridiculous. I'm sorry about breaking your heart, but it was twenty years ago, and can't we just be friends?' What if he silently replaced the receiver again?

If she hadn't fainted, they would probably have said hello quite naturally, introduced their partners, and behaved like grown-up people. But since that had eluded them, it was probably best just to carry on as if they were strangers, which, after all, they were. Now.

Alison got out of the car and opened the boot. She carried the bags of shopping into the kitchen and dumped them on the floor. Taking a bottle of mineral water from the fridge, she wandered into the conservatory. Safely hidden in the cupboards of the sideboard lurked her old LPs. With difficulty, she knelt on the floor and began to rummage through heaps of records: *Ziggy Stardust*, the Beatles *Red* and *Blue* albums, *Transformer*.

Finally, she found the album she was looking for. Bryan Ferry posing on a sky-blue background, his name in red lettering. *These Foolish Things*. She tugged the cover off, then she put the record on the turntable and dropped the stylus onto the last track on side two. Bryan Ferry's plaintive voice and a crescendo of notes played on a distant piano.

> *'Oh! will you never let me be?*
> *Oh! will you never set me free?*
> *The ties that bound us are still around us,*
> *There's no escape that I can see . . .'*

It must have been 1974 that Neil Gardner arrived in the town. It was the year before the town was runner-up in 'Britain in Bloom'. Before the Gardners arrived, no one in the town had even thought of entering the competition.

She had often wondered whether Neil's father had become a professional gardener because of his name.

Her father might even have joked about that the day he came back from the council meeting and announced, 'We've got someone for the park. He's a northerner, grateful for the pay and a roof over his head.'

Pete and Neil Gardner, Mr Gardner's two sons, were both over six foot tall. Pete, the older of the two, was coarser-looking and had greasy hair. Instead of finishing his education at the boys' school, he got a job at a garage, and soon moved out of the keeper's lodge into a caravan, with his newly pregnant girlfriend. Neil, who was quieter, more intelligent, a fine all-round sportsman and heartbreakingly handsome, entered the sixth form and instantly became an idol.

Suddenly the park was the most popular meeting place for teenagers in the town. There was an unseasonal demand for the tennis courts, and mothers were surprised by how often their sulky older daughters volunteered to take their little brothers and sisters to the playground. If Neil was aware of the stir he was creating, it did not show. The park needed a lot of tending. Each weekend, when he couldn't be glimpsed playing cricket at the town club, Neil was to be seen helping his father tidy the flowerbeds. On the odd occasion a giggling adolescent girl dared to speak to him, he replied quietly and laconically, leaning on his spade for a moment or two, sometimes honouring her with a direct look, before going back to his digging. The fact that he never smiled made him seem like the coolest thing on earth.

Like a hundred other girls, Alison watched him from a distance, until her friend Sally's brother threw a party.

> 'You came, you saw, you conquer'd me.
> When you did that to me, I somehow knew that this had to be . . .'

It was her first real party and she was hating it. There were couples everywhere—pressed up against the fridge. sprawled on the sofa, entwined under the dining-room table.

Her father had insisted he would pick her up at eleven. She had protested, but now she wished he had said ten.

She sat on the top step of the stairs, holding a plastic cup of warm cider, pretending she was queuing for the loo, pressing herself to the wall when anyone stepped past her.

'You waiting?'

At school, the girl who had asked the question was a prefect.

'No.' Alison replied cautiously.

'Well, get out of the bloody way, then.' The prefect tossed her loose golden hair over one shoulder.

Obediently, Alison stood up and walked downstairs.

She decided to sit on the floor in the living room. It was dark in there, and the music was so loud no one would even notice her.

'Have you seen Diana?'

Suddenly Neil Gardner was standing in front of her.

She felt a blush shooting to the surface of her skin.

If Woolworths had stocked posters of him, they would have sold out in one Saturday morning. Half the fifth form had his initials engraved on their desk. Girls who had walked home now caught the bus, just for the chance of waiting next to him at the bus stop. It wasn't just his looks, it was his smile, his voice, his black leather jacket. Everything about him spelt total hunk. And now *he* was speaking to *her*!

Diana was the prefect with long fair hair. He had been spotted kissing her in the entrance to Hepworths. Dozens of lovesick fifth-formers wished Diana would get run over by a bus.

'I think I saw her leaving.'

Afterwards, Alison couldn't imagine what had made her tell such a lie. Was the look that crossed his face anger, relief or indifference? She didn't even know whether he had heard her. Suddenly she realised he was actually looking at her. Then, unbelievably, he said, 'Wanna dance?'

No, I'm wearing a dress my mother made me and I'm only in the fifth form. If you knew these things you wouldn't even dream of speaking to me, she thought. She nodded and followed him into the living room.

He swayed about in front of her, and she attempted to mimic his actions, knowing she was in time to the music, but feeling as if she had one joint too many.

'*All the young dudes!*' wailed Mott the Hoople.

The song was really too slow for dancing; it was more for striking poses. She risked a quick glance round the room. Everyone else was too busy snogging to notice.

Then Sally's brother put on the new Bryan Ferry album. The first track was a faster beat. She began to dance, becoming more confident, almost enjoying it. Neil smiled at her. She kept dancing, track after track, until the tempo changed. Sally's brother grabbed his girlfriend and pressed his body into hers. Alison stopped dancing and began to sidle towards the door. But Neil pulled her back.

'Where are you going?' she thought she heard him say, then he raised his eyebrows, just slightly, as if tacitly asking her permission to draw her closer. She froze, terrified that she was reading the signals wrongly. He pulled her gently towards him.

'*I know that this was bound to be . . .*'

As she finally dared to rest her head on Neil's shoulder, she thought, I shall remember this moment for ever.

The song was fading away. Alison got up, walked to the turntable and put the track on again. She closed her eyes and swayed with the music, remembering exactly how it had been the first time she had heard their song. She could almost feel Neil's hands still on her waist, the heat of his skin through his black T-shirt, the exotic smell of his aftershave.

> *'Oh, how the ghost of you clings!*
> *These foolish things . . .*
> *Remind me of you.'*

The song faded away again.

She wondered whether Neil remembered the same things, or different things, or nothing at all. Men didn't remember like women did.

Alison put the track on again, smiling, remembering how it had felt to be sixteen, and wildly, deliriously, in love.

SIA WANTED TO CALL the baby Natalia or Anouska, and she couldn't understand why there was a problem with that. With her damp dark hair and her pinched, delicate face, her tiny daughter looked like a miniature ballet dancer.

Neil said that fancy names led to teasing at school. He wanted something plain. For the first time in their relationship, Lia felt anger.

'No,' she said firmly. 'Anyway, girls don't get teased for having pretty names. I never was.'

'But you were always pretty,' Neil argued. 'If she's ugly or fat, then she'd really suffer if she was called Anouska.'

The way he said the name annoyed her, his voice going up on the second syllable, making it sound pretentious. She looked at the baby in her arms. Couldn't he see that she was beautiful?

'She looks like a little old woman, doesn't she?' Neil said, touching the baby's cheek. The little girl started, as if she had heard and understood.

'I'm going to feed her,' Lia said, turning away from him with the baby resting in the crook of her arm. She wondered if he had wanted a boy.

Neil watched her bare a breast that was round and taut with milk, murmuring quietly, coaxing the tiny creature to suck. He saw the concentration on her face, her total engagement with the baby. It made him feel utterly superfluous.

He did not seem to know what to say to the baby. He realised with shock that he felt no connection whatsoever with the bundle of flesh and bones and vest and nappy. He simply did not recognise her as he had expected to, after all this time imagining the baby and talking to it through the smooth curve of Lia's belly.

It was stifling in the ward. He decided to go outside. Sitting on a bank of brown grass outside the maternity unit, he watched the to-ing and fro-ing of visitors and hospital staff.

The birth, which he had thought would be wondrous, had been darkly terrifying. Seeing his lover's body racked by the force of the contractions, he had wanted to run from the room, but had known that he could not. It was his duty to stay with her and watch her suffer, as he would never suffer. And then, suddenly, it was all over, and she was perfectly calm, gazing at the gore-streaked infant with a beauteous smile on her face. But the fear had stayed with him.

He lay back on the slope, staring at the cloudless blue sky, trying to feel what he ought to feel. But he couldn't feel anything except tired and thirsty, as if he had been crying for a long time. He sat up and took a deep breath, then forced himself to go back inside. He told himself that everything would be fine once Lia and the baby were back home.

In a private room at the end of the ward, a party was going on.

'I've decided that you can be his godfather, Robert,' Ginger said, humming the music from the film, 'as long as you promise to have nothing to do with his moral upbringing.' She took another gulp of champagne.

'Ginger,' Pic interrupted, 'are you sure you should be drinking?'

'I'm not ill, I've just had a baby,' Ginger retorted.

'Yes, but doesn't the alcohol go into your milk?'

'God, I never thought of that. Do you suppose it does? Oh hell, he'll have to get used to it soon enough,' said Ginger, holding out her glass.

Pic looked at her watch. 'Listen, I must go, but I'll be here tomorrow at ten. Bye, little Guy,' she said to the sleeping baby, kissing her finger and touching it against his cheek.

'I suppose I ought to be off, too,' Robert said.

'Oh no, you can't go,' Ginger wailed. 'Pretend you're the father. They're allowed to stay until eight.'

'But would anyone believe me?' Robert responded in his most camp voice. 'Talking of the father,' he added mischievously, 'did he ever call?'

'As a matter of fact he did, a couple of weeks ago,' Ginger replied.

'What are you going to tell him?' Robert said.

'Tell who?' Ginger asked.

'My godson.'

'About Charlie? I've no idea. I'm sure I'll think of something.' Ginger said. 'Goodness me, you're getting horribly responsible-sounding. You can't be his godfather if you're going to be a boring old fart.' Although she masked it with her light tone, she was annoyed.

'What did the father say, then?' Robert asked.

'I do wish you'd stop calling him that,' Ginger said, huffily. 'He just wanted some information.'

'What?'

'Oh, I've forgotten.'

She hadn't forgotten; she remembered every word of the conversation they had had when she returned Charlie's call.

'Ginger!' Suddenly she found all the hours she had spent preparing for the conversation had been a waste of time. She had no idea what to say.

'Yes?' she finally replied.

'So how are you after all this time?' Charlie asked.

'Fine,' she said, circumspectly.

'Work?' he asked.

So he *was* calling about work. She began to relax. 'Work's OK. What can I do for you?' she asked crisply.

'I was wondering whether you've got any lunches free next week?'

It must be a very big favour he was after. Charlie was the sort of person who booked lunches months in advance. Ginger had a sudden attack of dignity.

'I'm sorry, I don't,' she replied, amazed to hear herself.

'Oh, come on!' Charlie was used to getting his own way. 'Can't you cancel something?'

Ginger, whose diary was blank for her last week in the office, was beginning to enjoy herself. 'I'm sorry, no. I'm very busy for the next week, then I'm on leave for a while.'

'Oh, are you going away?'

'No. Anyway, what did you want to ask me?'

'I'd rather not say on the phone,' Charlie said. 'It might be difficult for you.'

'I'll tell you if it's difficult,' she replied angrily, 'and you'll have to smarm your way round someone else for the information.'

'What information?' Charlie asked, and then, as her words sank in. 'Listen, forget it. Bye!'

Ginger had put down her phone feeling pleased with herself. The next time he decided to screw a secretary after a party, maybe he would think twice before slipping out of bed while she was sleeping, using one of her lipsticks to draw a heart on the mirror, and never even calling to see whether she had recovered from her hangover.

'Oh, come on, tell me,' Robert was wheedling. 'What did he say? I just wondered . . .'

'Well, wonder somewhere else,' she snapped. 'This is a maternity ward, remember? You're not meant to upset me.'

'It's just that I had lunch with him a while back, and I had the distinct impression that he was trying to extract information from me about you.' Robert casually threw the bait into the conversation.

'You didn't tell him about—?' Ginger asked, nodding at the Perspex pod in which her child was sleeping.

'Of course not,' said Robert hotly. 'In any case, he seemed rather more interested in your professional performance than your personal one, magnificent though I'm sure the latter is.'

'Oh, do shut up!' Ginger said.

'Temper, temper. You are touchy today.'

'I'm allowed to be. I've just had a bloody baby, haven't I?'

Alison was propped up in bed with silent tears rolling down her cheeks. Her son had eventually been delivered by emergency Caesarean section, after she had spent hours in agony and terror. As she emerged from the anaesthetic, Stephen pointed to the Perspex bowl in which a baby was sleeping, and her first thought had been to wonder whether it was really hers. She still could not quite believe that the well-formed little boy had emerged from inside her.

Her mother visited, and told her that she was proud of her, which was peculiar, because Alison felt she had done nothing except make a fuss. The only positive feeling she was able to experience was a kind of vague pleasure that everyone else was so delighted with the baby. When she did not seem to be able to produce milk, she had become distressed. She looked down at the baby at her breast, rooting around, and felt totally detached, until it clamped its mouth on her nipple, its soft gums like a knife slicing the tender flesh. They told her that her hormones were probably upset and that the milk would come once she settled down. Just relax, the midwives said, as her face contorted in pain each time the increasingly thirsty baby latched on.

Whenever Stephen visited, he insisted she try again. The baby was becoming desperate. On the third morning, when the baby would not stop screaming, and she felt she could not stand the pain any longer, she requested formula. Stephen arrived to find her with the grateful creature slurping contentedly from a bottle. He went white with fury.

'What were the midwives thinking of?' he finally said.

'It was me,' Alison replied. 'I asked. The baby was starving.'

Stephen's mouth pursed with disapproval. 'All the research indicates that breastfeeding is far better . . .'

'Yes, but he was screaming,' she faltered, feeling a complete failure.

She had seen Neil walking past several times, and wondered whether he would look in her direction. She knew that Lia was booked into the same hospital, but not until a couple of weeks after her. Their baby must have been premature, she thought. Fate seemed determined to bring them together, and, in the alien world of the hospital, it didn't seem to matter any more. This time, when he passed, she called out.

He stood in the doorway. They looked at each other for a long time. His face was tense.

Finally, he said, 'Hello, Ally,' in a voice that bore no trace of recrimination, and she sighed with relief.

Nobody had ever called her Ally, except him.

'Hello, Neil.' It felt good to say his name at last.

She pointed at the sleeping baby.

Neil stepped into the room to get a better look.

'It's a boy,' she told him.

'He's big,' Neil replied. 'Ours is only five and a half pounds. How long have you been in here?'

'This is my fourth day. I had a Caesarean. How about Lia?'

'Last night. Four-hour labour. We were lucky. They say we can go tomorrow, although she's very small.'

'You had a little girl! Congratulations!'

'Yes,' he said, then remembering his manners, 'and to you. Well, I'd better get back,' he said awkwardly.

'Yes,' she said, and as he turned she added, hastily, 'I haven't told him and you haven't told her, have you?'

'About us? I couldn't see the point,' he replied.

'Quite,' said Alison.

'Quite.' He imitated her middle-class accent, and for the first time in twenty years they smiled at each other.

'I hear you met Neil at last?'

Alison woke from her doze. Lia was standing in the doorway to her room wearing a cotton robe.

'Hello,' she said, pulling herself up on the sloping rack of the hospital bed. 'Come in!'

Lia pushed a trolley into the room.

'You don't mind if I bring Anouska with me? She's sleeping but I just can't leave her. I'm so frightened someone will steal her.'

'No, of course not, bring her in. What a lovely name!'

'We haven't actually agreed on it yet,' Lia said, perching on the end of Alison's bed, 'but I think that if I say it often enough, Neil will come round . . .'

'We haven't chosen a name yet,' Alison said, glancing at her baby, who appeared to be sleeping contentedly.

Lia peered over the bed to have a good look. 'Oh, he's lovely! So big!' she exclaimed.

'Your little girl arrived a bit early, then?' Alison said, struggling to make conversation.

'Yes, but she was just over five and a half pounds so they didn't make her go to special care, thank heaven! How's the feeding going?' Lia asked.

Lia had been a mother a shorter time than she had, and yet she seemed to know what you were supposed to say and how you were supposed to be. Alison felt that something strange had happened to her, not just to her body, but to her brain, which made her unable to do the things she normally did, like smile or make a joke to mask her unhappiness. Suddenly, she started crying, in great gasping gulps.

Lia's response was instant. She put her arms round Alison, allowing her to weep on her shoulder, and murmuring soothing words into her hair.

'It's just, it's just,' Alison sniffed, 'I don't seem to have any milk, you see, and Stephen's so cross with me . . .'

'It's OK,' Lia said, patting her back gently.

'But it's not . . . if the baby's ill, it'll be my fault . . .'

'Of course he won't be ill!'

She sounded so sure, Alison thought. 'Are you breastfeeding yours?' She sniffed again, blew her nose.

'I am, but I seem to be the only one who is, on the ward.'

'Really?' Alison brightened instantly. 'How are you managing? Does it keep hurting?'

'No, it's all about positioning . . .'

'Is this a private party, or can anyone join in?' a loud voice at the door called out. 'I'm Ginger,' she explained, in case Alison had forgotten. 'We were all at that ghastly class together, until you did what we all wanted to—fainted with the boredom of it.'

Alison smiled and beckoned her in.

Ginger pushed another trolley into the room. It contained a fluffy rabbit, a baby and a bottle of champagne.

'I'm making up for lost time, while there are trained staff around to make sure that this little person doesn't come to any harm,' said Ginger, pulling the wire off the top of the bottle. The cork shot across the room and ricocheted off a window into a basket of forget-me-nots.

Lia's hand shot out instantly to protect her baby's face.

Ginger poured a paper cone of champagne and handed it to Alison, then offered one to Lia. Cautiously, she lowered herself onto the other side of Alison's bed.

'This is what's called sitting down *gingerly*,' she said. 'They don't tell you anything, do they? You think when you've had the baby, your stomach will go back in, but I still look nine months pregnant. I weighed myself, and there's no difference. I'm beginning to wonder whether I actually had a baby, or whether this is all a Pethidine hallucination . . . that's until I try to sit down . . .'

Alison laughed. She was beginning to see why people said that having children was the great leveller. The three of them had very little in common, and yet at that moment they had everything that mattered in common.

'Who'd have thought that something that starts so pleasantly could end in such pain?' The champagne was making Ginger garrulous and she regaled them with her decision to become a single mother.

She had become pregnant by mistake. She had booked herself in for an abortion but changed her mind as she sat reading *Hello!* in the waiting room of the clinic. There was a spread of photos of an ex-model's incredibly ugly baby. For the first time, Ginger had found herself imagining how her own baby would look. She thought about the father's curly black hair and wicked smile. He had been the undoubted star of their year when they had been up at Oxford, and she had fancied him from the minute he walked into their first lecture. She imagined how beautiful their child would be.

'So,' she concluded, 'I walked out of the clinic. Anyway, I was on the shelf.'

'How could you be at your age?' Lia said, laughing.

'Oh, I was, believe me,' Ginger said. 'I may be only twenty-seven, but I've had enough men to know that they never like me for long. They think I'm fun for a night or two and then, when I start showing signs of being human, they take me back under the trades-descriptions act.'

Alison laughed. She was enjoying the performance enormously.

'Does the baby's father know you've had the baby?' Lia said.

'No way! Doesn't even know I got pregnant. I didn't want him trying to change my mind.'

'Perhaps he wouldn't have done,' Lia suggested.

'You must know some very nice men,' Ginger said to Lia. 'Well, of course, your man is to die for.'

A proud smile flashed across Lia's face.

'Have you met Lia's dish of a man?'

The question hung in the air for a few seconds. 'Yes,' Alison said, feeling herself flushing and trying to sound natural. 'Yes.'

'He's gorgeous, isn't he?' Ginger persisted.

'Yes, I suppose he is,' Alison said. The fact that Ginger fancied Neil made things easier to deal with. If Neil had the same effect on everyone, then it wasn't anything special between the two of them.

'Your bloke is pretty tasty too, if I remember,' Ginger went on shamelessly. 'Where did you find him?'

Alison laughed. 'At a New Year's Eve party . . . I literally saw him across a crowded room,' she began, suddenly eager to join in. 'I suppose I was on the shelf too and just when I thought that there were no attractive men left in London, there he was.'

Alison had noticed him as soon as he walked into the gathering. He was very tall and he was wearing a long black coat and a fedora hat. When he took the hat off Alison had been startled to see that he was completely bald. Oddly, it made his violet eyes seem larger and more piercing, increasing his attractiveness.

He had caught her looking at him and smiled. They had spent the evening talking, and then they had swapped telephone numbers.

'He's a cardiac surgeon,' Alison said.

'Really, where?' Ginger asked.

Alison named one of London's big teaching hospitals.

'But that's where Daddy was . . .' Ginger's voice suddenly trailed off.

'What's your father's name? I'll ask Stephen if he saw him. He doesn't do private work, but—'

'No, I'm sure he didn't . . .' Suddenly Ginger looked awkward.

Alison and Lia exchanged looks, then both raised their eyebrows at Ginger, soliciting her response.

'Well, if you must know, my father is Sir James Prospect, the MP, but please don't hold it against me,' she pleaded.

'For heaven's sake, you don't choose your parents,' Alison said, reassuringly. 'I wouldn't have chosen mine.'

'Nor would I,' Lia agreed.

Ginger breathed a sigh of relief, at which point her baby woke and started crying. Then the other two babies woke up and suddenly the room reverberated with the noise of inconsolable infants.

A midwife came in and shooed Lia and Ginger to bed. She handed Alison's baby to her and a ready-made bottle of formula.

The baby drank voraciously. Then she remembered she was supposed to make him burp. She placed him against her shoulder, gently patting his back and wishing that she could feel some connection with the child, as Lia and Ginger so obviously did with theirs.

She lay awake, thinking of those first few weeks with Stephen. In the beginning, the powerful attraction she felt for him was not simply the pure physical high his presence seemed to give her, but the sheer interest she found in his work. It was stimulating to talk to someone with such a different background. They had taken it in turns to educate each other on their first few dates. She taught him about food and media gossip, he took her to concerts and talked to her about music. She had noticed that he never used the verb 'to feel'. In her world, people felt. In his, they reasoned. But when they went to bed with each other, she found that he was an extraordinarily gifted lover, who sensed what she liked and brought her to climaxes on a different plane to anything she had achieved before.

She had not been fair to Stephen in the last few months, she realised. It was she, not he, who had changed. His rational approach to things was the reason she had fallen in love with him. If he had not been as supportive as she would have liked over the business of conception, it was because to him it was just a medical procedure that either worked, or didn't. It was the same with the breastfeeding. He was good at separating statistics from emotions. In his job, he had to be.

Tomorrow, she promised herself, it will be different. We love each other. We have made a beautiful, healthy baby together. This is what we wanted. This is what it has all been about.

The next morning when Stephen popped in she was trying to feed the baby. He rewarded her with a delighted smile.

'Can you bring me some nice food when you come back?' she asked, picking up a triangle of hospital toast with disdain. 'I don't think this is helping.'

'Of course, what would you like?'

'Parma ham and fresh French bread,' she told him.

'Fine,' he said, kissing first her forehead, then the baby's.

As he left the room, she found herself wishing that he would just stay and chat to her. Time passed so slowly in hospital.

'How's your head this morning? Mine feels like a band is playing inside it.' Ginger was standing at the door dressed to go home. Beside her stood a woman so exactly like her it was disturbing, carrying Guy.

'This is my twin sister Pic,' Ginger said. 'And this,' she told Pic, 'is Alison and her son. Did you tell me his name?'

'We haven't decided yet . . . perhaps Benedict . . .' Alison replied. 'Don't you like it?' she added, seeing the look of undisguised horror that flitted across Ginger's face.

'Sounds a bit too much like a saint, but I suppose Ben's all right,' Ginger replied.

'Honestly, Ginger,' her sister scolded. 'It's a lovely name,' she assured Alison.

Alison explained. 'Well, I like the name Ben . . . but then there's the question of Benjamin, or Benedict, and Stephen tells me that Benjamin is traditionally the youngest son. I hope that doesn't mean he wants another one . . .' she added with a short, dry laugh.

'That, at least, is one thing I don't have to worry about,' Ginger said, a frown puckering her impish face.

Ginger was so blasé and confident, it was difficult to envisage her worrying about anything, Alison thought, and yet she must be frightened. She was finding it difficult to imagine how she would cope, even with Stephen there. She began to see Ginger in a new light. She now appeared rather brave.

'Let me know when you're home,' Ginger said, casually landing a kiss on Alison's cheek.

'I will,' Alison said, surprised and rather moved. 'Good luck!' she called, as the twins disappeared.

When Neil's mother first arrived, Lia found it companionable to have another womanly presence in the house. She had also been very helpful with the housework. It had all been fine, until she had begun to offer advice. Now, as Mrs Gardner peered into the carry-cot, Lia was certain she was about to grant yet another pearl of wisdom.

'We used to put them on their front,' Mrs Gardner said.

'Now the advice is to put them on their backs,' Lia replied. 'It's what all the doctors recommend.'

Then Anouska began to cry. Lia picked her out of the carry-cot and put her to her breast.

'She'll get into bad habits if you keep feeding her every time she cries,' Neil's mother opined.

Lia bit back her anger, stroking the top of her baby's head to calm herself down.

'Once every four hours. If she cries, let her. It's a good lesson to learn. You can't always get what you want when you cry.' Mrs Gardner smiled.

Oh, shut up, you old cow, Lia wanted to shout.

'It's a pity your mother can't see you now,' Mrs Gardner remarked.

Lia looked up, surprised. She had always had a nagging suspicion that Mrs Gardner thought it was somehow her fault that she had been brought up in a home. Lia stared at her, trying to see whether she had meant to hurt her, or was just being even more insensitive than usual. Either way, she thought, she was going to have to go.

'I'm not planning to rest any longer. The midwife says I'm fine, so tomorrow I'm going to get up and your mother can go home,' Lia announced to Neil that night.

'But she's really enjoying being here,' Neil protested.

'Maybe she is, but I don't want her here any more,' Lia hissed. 'I've had it with her so-called advice. She seems to think she knows better than the health visitor.'

'She has had two children,' he defended his mother.

'Neil, for God's sake, things have changed,' Lia said angrily, 'and anyway, I'm Anouska's mother. I want to get to know her by myself.'

'But she's only trying to help—'

'No!' Lia began to shout, then stopped abruptly.

It was the nearest they had ever come to a row. In desperation, Lia burst into tears. He had never seen her cry before and she knew he would not be able to bear it.

'I just want us to be a little family of our own,' she sobbed.

'OK, love, it's OK,' Neil said, bewildered, holding her. 'I'll get Dad to collect her first thing tomorrow . . . OK?'

In a tree-lined street just a couple of miles away, in the newly decorated nursery, Alison tried to feed her baby.

'Come on, let's try again,' she said. But he was used to a bottle now, and didn't want to work for his food.

Tears trickled down Alison's face. The pain of his sporadic sucking was almost bearable, but not his bleating rejection. She was so tired she felt her head slump forward, then jerk back out of sleep.

'Oh, don't, please don't,' she pleaded as the baby began to cry again. 'You must try . . . Oh for God's sake, please . . .' she said, returning him to his crib. Nobody told you how awful it was to hear your baby crying, how it sliced right through you leaving your nerves raw and exposed.

'Alison, love . . .' Stephen stood bleary-eyed at the door.

He walked across the room and began to stroke her hunched shoulders, then he picked up the baby and went downstairs. She was too tired to follow him.

A few minutes later he returned with the baby and a bottle of formula. He sat on the floor and put the teat into the baby's mouth.

'I'll do the night feeds from now on,' he said. 'I'm used to less sleep.'

'But . . . formula . . .'

'Oh, plenty of babies grow up perfectly OK with the stuff,' he said as nonchalantly as he could, and his concession made her feel more inadequate than ever.

Ginger was looking at her baby, wondering how many other women in London were awake watching over their children. Probably hundreds, she estimated, and the thought of them made her feel less alone. It was her first night by herself with Guy, and she kept getting up to check that he was breathing.

Pic had stayed the first night, then their mother had come up from the country, but after spending one night on the camp bed she had remarked, 'I don't know what Hermione was thinking of when she left this place to you. It's entirely unsuitable for a baby, so I've decided to hire you a maternity nurse.'

What she meant, Ginger realised, was that the flat was entirely unsuitable for her to stay in, and that she had no idea of what to do with a baby, since she had always employed staff to look after her own twins.

Jeannie had turned out to be really kind, encouraging Ginger through the first tiring days, cooking her nice, wholesome meals like shepherd's pie and milk puddings. She taught Ginger all the rudiments of caring for a newborn with efficiency and good humour, which took the panic out of scary things like bathing him for the first time. Her no-nonsense approach had given Ginger confidence, so that at the end of their week together, Ginger hadn't even thought about whether or not she would cope on her own.

'I think we've done OK, considering,' she said to Guy, evaluating their day. She folded a blanket diagonally, just as Jeannie had taught her, wrapped him, and placed him back in the Moses basket on the bed beside her. Jeannie had warned that if you allowed a baby into your bed you'd never get him out, but it felt nice having him right there next to her. She snuggled down alongside the basket and turned out the light.

'Now, let's see if we can get at least three hours,' she whispered in the darkness to her sleeping son.

# September

On Neil's first morning back at school, Lia watched him unlock his motorbike and put on his helmet. He turned round and waved at them. She held up Anouska's tiny arm and made it wave back. There was a slight chill in the air. The hot summer was finally coming to an end.

Lia went back inside and made a cup of coffee. She told herself she was feeling peculiar because it was the first time she had been alone since the baby was born. But she knew it wasn't that. Neil had been smiling, not at her, but at the road ahead. He had been happy, she realised, to get away from them.

Lia felt that her relationship with Neil had not quite regained its equilibrium since Mrs Gardner's abrupt departure. He was very quiet, and if she asked him if something was wrong he answered no, but his eyes said yes. She had read about new fathers feeling rejected, but she would never have believed that Neil would conform to that stereotype. On occasion she had inadvertently criticised the way he handled Anouska, as he tried to play with her like an older baby, not a newborn. She had seen her child distressed, flailing in his large, strong hands, and she had shouted to him to stop. He had handed the baby back to her and marched silently out of the room.

Lia had been surprised that her love for Anouska had overridden any thought for his feelings. She tried to be sensitive but when he continued to sulk she became impatient, feeling she had quite enough to do without tiptoeing round his sensibilities.

Lia drank her coffee. The day stretched ahead of her and she had no one to worry about except her baby. She felt her shoulders relax as she exhaled a long, pent-up sigh and then she picked up the phone.

From the doorway, Ginger watched the last nanny she was interviewing that morning walk away. She was stout and wore sensible shoes.

'I thought she seemed very good,' her mother said, as Ginger returned to the living room.

'Did you?' Ginger replied. 'I'm afraid I couldn't stand her.'

'Well, what are you looking for?' her mother asked.

'I suppose someone I feel a kind of empathy with,' Ginger said, peering over the edge of the Moses basket. Guy was sleeping. 'Jeannie was fine for a week, but I don't want someone middle-aged all the time.'

'Well, I thought it would be better for you to have someone with experience,' said her mother, giving herself away.

'So you particularly asked the agency for older ones?' Ginger said, outraged. 'Oh, I get it, what you're really trying to do is employ someone to spy on me and report back to you.'

'Don't be ridiculous, Virginia. And if I'm paying for this nanny, it is only reasonable that I have a say in what kind of person I employ to look after my grandson.'

'You sound exactly like Daddy,' Ginger said, staring straight at her mother, who looked away, unable to meet her daughter's challenge.

'Oh, I see. It was Daddy's idea, was it?' Ginger suddenly understood. 'You can tell Daddy to stuff his plan. I've just decided that I won't have a nanny at all.'

'Ginger,' her mother said, 'you are so ungrateful. Daddy's been under such stress—'

'Because of me? Go on, say it. Look, if Daddy didn't have such disgusting views about single mothers, he wouldn't have been caused any embarrassment. Maybe he should change the way he thinks.'

'I've come all this way to help you, but you're obviously not in a mood to be reasonable,' her mother said, picking up her handbag and tying her silk scarf in a knot. 'I'll see myself out.'

Then the phone rang.

'How are you getting on?' Lia said.

'Don't ask,' Ginger replied.

'Well, Anouska and I are about to go for a walk in Kew Gardens and I wondered whether you'd like to meet up?'

The Year to Remember hour on the radio was 1974.

'Alvin Stardust coming up,' shouted the DJ, 'with "My Coo Ca Choo".'

The first jamming notes of bass guitar bounced round the kitchen where Alison was washing up the night bottles. She swayed her hips with the music, staring through the window into the garden. Her mother was pegging out the washing. Alison twirled, enjoying the pounding beat, wondering why it was that every tune from the seventies seemed to carry such a specific memory for her.

The Monday afternoon following the party where she had met Neil, she and Sally were walking down the hill after school listening to Sally's tranny. Sally had spotted Neil before she had.

'Hey up!' she said, nudging Alison hard. 'Your dancing partner is waiting for you.'

'Don't be silly,' Alison replied automatically. She had spent the whole of Sunday assuring herself that there was no chance that he fancied her, deciding that he had taken pity on her. He couldn't be waiting for *her*.

His face lit up when he picked her out from the sea of other girls.

'Hello, Ally,' he said.

'Hi!' Alison replied, her voice croaking with anxiety.

'Where are you going?' he asked them.

'To get the bus,' Alison said.

'I'll come to the bus stop with you then.'

He walked along beside them, saying nothing.

'Good party, wasn't it?' Sally chattered on. 'I was just saying to Alison, it was a pity she had to leave early, wasn't it?'

Alison wished she would go, and yet she didn't know what she would do if left on her own with him.

'Yes, it was,' he said neutrally, and smiled at Alison.

'Oh, well'—Sally conceded defeat—'I think I'll go to Boots,' she said.

They watched Sally saunter across the road.

Then, almost immediately, Alison's bus drew up and she thought it would look really stupid to let it go. Anyway, she had already run out of things to say to him and the fare in her palm was wet with sweat. He walked along slowly next to her as the queue moved up.

'Would you like to see *The Great Gatsby*?' he said finally.

'Yes,' she stated, not sure if it was an invitation or just a question.

'Friday night?' he said, as she stepped onto the bus. 'It starts at eight. I'll meet you outside, OK?'

'OK,' she agreed.

Then he was gone. He just turned and walked away.

'What on earth has happened to you?' her mother asked as Alison tried to get upstairs without giving her a chance to notice her telltale sparkling eyes.

Her mother had a way of extracting information. Within minutes she had heard the whole amazing story.

Their first date had been a huge anticlimax. *The Great Gatsby* was a good film. She knew because she saw every moment of it. When they walked out, Alison remarked that she would love to wear one of those flapper dresses, and he had commented that it would suit her. It was the nearest they had got to intimacy.

He saw her to the bus home, but did not attempt to kiss her or even put his arm round her shoulders. She spent the ride home wondering what she must have done wrong. Neil obviously wasn't interested any more.

But the next Monday, Neil had been waiting at the bottom of the hill again. He had asked her to go with him to the end-of-term disco at the boys' school.

'And now . . .' said the DJ on the radio, attempting to make his voice extra-husky, 'why don't you all stop what you're doing and take a deep breath of "The Air that I Breathe" by the Hollies . . . I bet some of you can remember having a last dance to this one back in 1974.'

Alison emptied the bowl of washing-up water down the sink and sat down at the table, pretending to read the paper, but listening, wallowing in the corniness of the tune.

It was hot and dark at the sixth-form disco. The faint smell of boys' feet and school dinners mingled with the feminine, artificial scents of Aquacitra bubble bath and Silvikrin lemon-'n'-lime shampoo. Neil and Alison sipped non-alcoholic shandy from paper cups, agreeing that it was too embarrassing to dance in front of the teachers.

'Let's get some air.'

When Neil took her hand, she felt the envy of every girl in the room like a cold breeze on her body. Outside they began to run fast across the playing field, into the dark shadows beyond the fall of the light, keeping their bodies low so that no one would witness their escape. At their hiding place beneath the row of poplar trees at the far end of the grounds, the grass smelt of earth.

He lay down, looking up at the sky, pointing out the constellations. She lay next to him, an arm's length away, pretending to see the patterns of stars he was naming. Her heart was racing so fast she was sure he could hear it.

The chorus of 'The Air that I Breathe' drifted across the cricket pitch.

'Do you like this song?' Neil asked, rolling onto one side. He propped himself up on his elbow, and looked down at her.

'Er, I don't know, really,' she replied, nervously, not knowing what he thought, not daring to commit herself.

'It's a bit soppy, isn't it?' he said, plucking a long piece of grass and tickling it under her chin.

'Yes, I suppose it is,' Alison agreed, giggling a little.

'But then, I'm feeling a bit soppy about you,' he said, his face dipping closer.

Oh God, that kiss! She didn't know how to breathe, but she felt she would rather suffocate than stop.

In her 1990s designer kitchen in Kew, Alison scolded herself for behaving exactly like the sentimental housewife the DJ on the radio imagined as his listener, whom he was now patronising over the last wailing echoes of the song.

'Do we have to have this awful rubbish on, darling?' Margaret asked, carrying a basket of washing in.

'No, of course not,' Alison replied, and turned the dial off.

'I'll just fold this lot away,' Margaret said.

Her mother was really helping, Alison was slightly shocked to realise. Instead of roaming round the kitchen as she usually did, running manicured fingertips along surfaces complaining about Alison's cleaning lady, she now rolled up her sleeves and mucked in.

The dynamic of her relationship with Margaret had shifted slightly since Ben's birth. Alison could not have anticipated the transparent joy that the baby would bring to her mother, or the delight that that in turn would give back to her. It was like having chosen the perfect gift—but about a million times better.

'Why don't you take him for a walk today?' Margaret suggested. 'I'm sure it would do you good.'

Alison didn't really feel like going out, but there was no point in refusing. Once her mother had decided something, it was easier to get on with it.

It was a beautiful September day. The sun was warm but there was a crispness in the air that seemed to make the sky a brighter blue than it had been since spring. The leaves on some of the large trees were already fading to yellow after the long, dry summer. As she strolled past the Temperate House towards the lake, she spotted two women sitting on the grass, with prams parked in the shade of a big oak tree. Suddenly one of them started waving at her, beckoning her over to where they were sitting. Alison manoeuvred the pram off the path and pushed it onto the grass.

'I was just saying that you feel like Mary Poppins pushing these things around, don't you?' said Ginger.

Alison parked Ben's pram beside theirs and dropped onto her knees next to Lia.

'And why does everything have a ridiculous name?' Ginger went on, 'Babygros . . .'

'Well, that's just short for baby-grows-out-of-it-so-quickly-you-can't-believe-you-just-spent-fifteen-quid-on-two,' said Alison. 'Ben was too big for the newborn size on day one, and we couldn't take them back because my mother had insisted I wash them before going into hospital.'

'Don't start me on mothers,' said Ginger.

'Mine's been surprisingly OK, actually,' Alison said, with a sudden feeling of loyalty to Margaret, 'apart from knowing best about every-thing. I don't know what I'd do without her.'

'You've got your mother staying with you?' Ginger said, amazed. 'I drove mine out after one night, I'm afraid, and I've just resisted her attempts to impose a nanny on me. What about you?' she asked Lia.

'Neil's mother came up for a few days,' Lia said, lifting her eyebrows. 'Nightmare!'

'What about your own mother?' Alison asked.

'I don't have one. Well, maybe I do, out there somewhere.' Lia plucked grass from the lawn, considering whether or not to reveal her past to the other women. She decided to take the risk. 'My mother couldn't cope, so I grew up in a home.' Her companions reacted exactly as she expected they would.

'You poor thing,' Alison said, her face going through a familiar series of expressions: surprise, pity, embarrassment.

'What was it like?' Ginger asked, with curiosity.

'It wasn't that bad,' Lia said, after a moment's thought. 'Some of the time it was fun. We lived in a cottage with a housemother. They tried to make it as much like a normal family as they could. It wasn't so great when you got a bit older, when you became aware that people thought of you differently, because you were Barnardo's.

'You learn to keep quiet about where you came from,' she continued. 'You listen hard to the other girls at school so you know the sort of things real families do, like eating your tea in front of the telly, going to the shops in the car at weekends, Dad taking you sledging when it snows. I suppose that one of the things that appealed to me about having a baby was being able to do all that properly.'

The three women fell silent for a few moments, reflecting on the enormous change in their lives.

'Does anyone fancy lunch?' Ginger asked, getting to her feet.

'Good idea,' said Alison.

'Yes,' Lia said, glad that she could detect no shift in the companion-able atmosphere between them.

They headed for the restaurant on the other side of Kew Gardens.

'So,' Ginger said as they settled down, 'now that we're all experienced mothers, what's the best thing about it?'

'Not being pregnant,' Alison responded immediately.

'Not working,' Ginger said, with a sigh.

'I think the best thing is just holding her,' Lia said, and Alison noticed that Lia had her baby at her breast. She looked completely at ease, her dark brown eyes smiling.

'Don't you like your job, then?' Alison asked Ginger.

'What's to like?' Ginger said. 'I make coffee and tell lies on behalf of my boss, who can't make up her mind whether she'd rather be powerful or liked.'

When Ginger had gone along for interview, desperate for a career in television, she had naïvely handed over a list of programme ideas. She never saw the list again, but a few months later, when she was filing the minutes of a meeting, she noticed that a number of her suggestions had been discussed without reference to their source. When she raised this, her boss promised they would talk about her promotion prospects. After several months' waiting, Ginger realised that she hadn't a hope of getting any further.

'I was looking for another job when this happened.' Ginger pointed into Guy's pram. 'But there didn't seem much point in losing my maternity leave, and I didn't think anyone would want to take me on if they knew I was pregnant.'

Ironically, the purpose of going to Robert's fateful Christmas party had been to schmooze herself another job. Buoying herself up with champagne, she had made a beeline for Charlie Prince. He had set up as an independent producer and had made his name producing successful youth-orientated programmes. His perpetually expanding company had also produced a low-budget feature film that had been a hit in the States. He was media flavour-of-the-month, and he knew it. Ginger reminded him slightly nervously that they had been at Oxford together, and she was amazed when he volunteered that he had loved her Beatrice in the production of *Much Ado About Nothing* in New College cloisters.

The fact that Charlie had seen Ginger's one moment of acting glory called for more champagne and then more, and somehow she hadn't got round to talking to anyone else at the party.

'You're the only woman I know who slept her way out of a career.' Robert said bitchily three months later.

'All my friends thought I was bonkers.' Ginger told Lia and Alison. 'or that I was just using it as an excuse because I didn't have what it takes to make a career in television. Perhaps I don't.' she said, unusually forlorn. Sitting eating a sandwich in the gardens on a sunny September day, it was difficult to imagine going back to the BBC. But she knew she had to, or she wouldn't qualify for her much-needed maternity pay.

'What about you?' Ginger turned to Lia. 'Are you going to go back to work?'

'I haven't really thought about it.' Lia said. 'But then I don't have a brilliant career. I think I'd prefer to look after Anouska.'

To have no job, no income, no independence, sounded like hell to Alison, and yet, she thought, as she bade the others farewell and pushed the pram down her street, Lia seemed serene and contented. Had she always been like that? Alison wondered, trying to suppress the jealousy in her gut, or was the key to happiness being with Neil?

I could have been with him, Alison thought, remembering.

It was one of those hot evenings two years after they met. They were sitting on the swings in the park. The chains creaked rhythmically as they rocked backwards and forwards.

'You won't laugh at me if I tell you something, will you?' Neil suddenly said.

'Depends what,' she replied, fixing her gaze on the climbing frame in front of them. She sensed it would be something momentous.

'I love you, that's what,' he said.

Her pulse thumped against the hard seat of the swing.

'I want to marry you . . .' He turned and looked at her, realising that she had said nothing.

'No,' she said, looking straight ahead, 'don't say that. That's too far ahead. It's enough to love each other now—'

'Do you?' he interrupted her, desperately disappointed.

She nodded, solemnly.

'Say it, then,' he urged.

'I love you, too,' she said. She turned her eyes to meet his, and they were sparkling with laughter. Then she leapt up and started twirling round and round, arms stretched out horizontally.

They had not been much more than children with their nervous declarations of love, and their hesitant explorations of each other's bodies, which, a few weeks later, had culminated in the loss of her virginity. But who was to say that the love they felt for each other then was any less real than what adults call love later on?

Alison put her key in the door and called out, 'Hello,' to her mother.

'Did you have a nice time?' Margaret asked, picking Ben out of the pram.

'Yes. I saw a couple of people I know,' Alison said.

'How lovely,' Margaret said. 'Now, you've had a couple of phone calls: Ramona says she's dying to see you and Stephen will be home early.'

Later, when Stephen came home, he handed her a bag.

'Present,' he said with a beaming smile.

Mystified, she pulled out a CD of *The Jungle Book*.

'Well, it's for Ben, really,' Stephen said, grabbing it back and racing to the CD player.

Halfway through 'Bare Necessities', she realised with stunned disbelief that Stephen knew every single word to every song and he was singing, performing all the actions, padding round the conservatory like Baloo the Bear with Ben in the crook of his arm.

Fatherhood had unlocked something in him that was childlike and fun. It was wonderful to see him dancing with such abandon, and yet when he beckoned her, encouraging her to join in, she couldn't. Parenthood had chased away Stephen's inhibitions but it had magnified her own. She kept telling herself how lucky she was to have everything she had ever dreamed of, yet all she seemed able to think about was a time when she had nothing. Except the love of a boy called Neil.

A S LIA BECAME fully conscious she realised that the reason she had woken was because Neil's head was between her legs, his tongue very gently licking her.

'I'm just making sure that everything's healed down here,' he whispered, lifting his eyes to look at her.

'But . . .' Lia stammered, trying to sit up.

'It's OK, I've checked,' he told her. 'She's sleeping. She's fine. Now you just relax . . .'

Lia sank back into the pillows with a sigh, trying to let her body find a response to the delicate stimulation of Neil's mouth. She felt a flicker of arousal, like a spark from a bonfire that glows in the air for a second, then dies. He sensed her body tense momentarily then relax. He looked up and she smiled at him, wanting him to believe that she was liking it.

'Hey.' She inched away from him, taking over. 'Hey, come here.'

She kissed his mouth, fervently, drawing him on top of her.

She could feel his penis solid against her stomach.

'Fuck me,' she whispered into his ear.

He drew his head back and looked at her searchingly.

'Please . . .' she commanded.

He couldn't resist. He was trying to enter her gradually, but the pent-up energy of weeks of restraint took over and plunged him into her body. She gasped, and writhed beneath him, using all her energy to thrust back at him.

'Yes,' she whispered in his ear. 'Oh yes, yes, come on.' She was desperate for it to end.

And he exploded inside her.

They lay breathing each other's breath for a few seconds, then he raised his head and said, 'I'm sorry, I should have waited for you.'

'No, it was lovely,' she said, hating herself for lying.

'You are beautiful, did you know?' He stared at her with pure, undisguised love in his eyes. She held his gaze, but it seemed to be asking so many questions she had to look away. Then the baby began to cry.

Later, he came up behind her while she was washing-up the breakfast things and put his arms round her waist.

'Hello, gorgeous,' he said softly.

She could feel his breath on the nape of her neck. Before, when he touched her there, almost unbearable currents of sensual pleasure had shot across her shoulders. Today, she felt repelled by his closeness.

'Let's go into town,' she said, wriggling away from him. She wanted to get out of the house, away from the oppressive atmosphere that unsatisfactory sex left behind. 'There are lots of things we need. You can carry Anouska in the baby sling.'

He pulled a face, then seeing her expression he said, 'OK, OK, it's about time I did my new man act.'

'Oooh, he's grown, he has really grown in the last week,' Pic said, lifting Guy out of his basket. 'Oh look, Ginger, I'm sure he smiled at me.'

'Oh, he smiles all the time now,' Ginger said, slumping into a chair.

Relaxing properly for the first time that week, Ginger watched Pic tackling a whole week's worth of washing-up efficiently as ever, stopping only to turn the rashers of bacon she had put under the grill. Her sister had brought everything for brunch: bagels, cream cheese, smoked salmon, eggs, bacon, even some pancake mix and maple syrup.

Pic draped the cloth over the dining table. She poured two mugs of steaming coffee and called Ginger over, but as soon as she sat down, the baby started crying.

'Don't move,' Pic ordered her. 'I'll deal with him. You eat while it's all still warm.'

Ginger was too tired to protest and began to tuck in. The baby quietened as soon as her sister picked him up.

'There, you see, he's just fine with me, aren't you, darling?' said Pic, putting the baby over her shoulder and patting his back.

'Do you think Daddy is ever going to come to see his grandson?' asked Ginger, shovelling pancake into her mouth.

'He's not very well, you know,' Pic said, diplomatic as ever.

'Oh come on, I know that he voted in the House the other day, I saw him on the telly. If he can make the effort for the government . . .' Ginger's voice trailed off.

She didn't know why it upset her so that her father had yet to acknowledge her baby in person. She had been used to his disapproval as long as she could remember, and it often made her angry, but never sad. Now she was having to fight back tears.

'Have you invited him?' Pic asked her.

'OK, OK.' She held up her hands in defeat. 'Maybe I should do the grown-up thing . . . not because I want him here, of course,' she added, trying to sound serious, 'but because I feel I must allow my son to make up his own mind about his grandfather . . .'

'How noble you are,' Pic said, solemnly, then arched her back to lessen the effect of Ginger whacking her on the bottom with a frying pan.

Alison lit up and inhaled. She had promised herself she would not smoke again. She tried to tell herself that the smell was horrible, but it wasn't. It was quite as delicious as the aroma of freshly ground coffee that wafted over to them from the store's espresso bar. They were grown-up smells that seemed to offer glorious release from the life that smelt of nappies and sickly sweet spilt formula milk.

The hit of nicotine coursed into her bloodstream, making her feel complete again.

'Hmm . . . almost as good as gas and air!' she said, exhaling.

Ramona laughed. 'Did you have Pethidine too?'

'I had everything. But listen, I don't want to talk about all that. I'm not even going to think about motherhood or anything to do with it.'

'Fine by me.' Ramona picked up the card the waiter had handed her and ran her eyes up and down looking for a suitable wine.

'You're looking great, by the way,' she said.

'I'm back to my pre-pregnancy weight,' said Alison proudly.

'My God,' Ramona said. 'I haven't achieved that in fourteen years. Are you up for a bottle, or just a glass?'

'Oh, I think a bottle, don't you?' Alison said recklessly. 'So, what's the gossip?'

Ramona told her there hadn't been any dramatic developments at the newspaper. An affair between the sports editor and the television critic rumbled on.

'Actually, I can't wait to get back,' Alison told her, staring down at the table top as if she could see something incredibly fascinating on the surface, feeling suddenly close to tears. .

'Hey, what's up? Is everything OK?' Ramona asked, as she poured two large glasses of Californian cabernet sauvignon.

'Oh hell,' Alison said. A tear threatened to escape, and she dabbed at it with her napkin. 'Yeah, everything's fine, the baby's fine, he's healthy, he even sleeps through the night sometimes. I know I'm really lucky, but, well . . .' She stopped, then could bear to hold back the truth no longer. 'Sometimes I feel completely miserable, a lot of the time, in fact . . .' She looked up and was hugely relieved to see that Ramona's face was concerned, but not critical.

'I don't know what's wrong with me. It's as if I no longer know who I am . . . I just don't seem to be very good at it—motherhood,' she tried to explain, feeling almost energised by her admission of failure. 'I see all these people enjoying their babies and I think there must be something wrong with me—to have wanted a baby so much, and then to feel, well, nothing . . . I mean I know he's very sweet, but . . . That sounds awful. Listen, you won't tell anyone . . . ?'

Ramona stopped battling with her salad. 'Of course I won't,' she replied. Then, probing cautiously, 'What does Stephen think?'

'Oh, he loves it. He's discovered a whole new dimension to his life.'

'I meant what does he think about the state you're in?'

'Oh, I don't know . . . I don't know if he realises,' Alison said.

'Do you mean you haven't told him how you're feeling?' Ramona said.

'It would only make me feel worse,' Alison said.

'Are you sure? Have you seen your own doctor?'

'I went for my six-week check. Everything's fine.'

'Did you say you were depressed?' Ramona pressed.

'Well, no . . .' Alison admitted, then said, 'Do you think that's what it is—postnatal depression?'

'Sounds like it . . . I had it a bit after Jonty was born. I think I know what you're going through,' Ramona said. 'It all seemed very difficult. Sol and I didn't have sex for months.'

Alison smiled with relief that someone else had shared that experience. At the six-week check her doctor had asked her whether she and Stephen had had sex again, and had seemed surprised when Alison said no.

'What are you doing about child care?' Ramona demanded.

'Well, we're going to get a nanny when I come back to work. At the moment my mother comes up during the week—'

'Oh, for heaven's sake, no wonder you're depressed!' Ramona said, warming to her theme. There was nothing Ramona liked more than the opportunity to prescribe solutions to other people's problems. 'This is what you do. One: get yourself a nanny straight away. Ring up the agency first thing Monday morning, yes?'

Alison nodded.

'Two: ban your mother from the house.'

Alison giggled.

'Three: book a weekend away with that gorgeous man of yours.'

Alison took another Marlboro and lit it thoughtfully. There's just one other thing, she wanted to say. I think I'm in love with someone I went out with when I was sixteen. When I see him, I feel alive. What do I do about that?

After lunch, they wandered round, examining the winter collections, but Alison's heart wasn't really in it. What Ramona had said had thrown a whole new light on her feelings. For some reason, depression had not occurred to her before as an explanation for the weird way that she was feeling. Ramona was holding a £400 Joseph sweater against her and trying to think of a reason she deserved it when Alison kissed her and said she had to go.

Hyde Park was virtually empty. A determined Saturday-afternoon father rowed his two small children in a boat across the Serpentine. Alison sat down on a bench and stared out over the lake, thinking about the last time she had been depressed, not just sad, or unhappy, but that feeling of pure, bleak isolation from which she had not been able to imagine an escape.

It was during her first term at university. It was only when a friend from her hall of residence suggested talking to a counsellor that she began to break through the cloud that seemed to have turned every-thing around her grey. The oppressive hatred she felt for herself began to lift a little each week as she sat sobbing incoherently for her allotted hour to the counsellor.

One day in spring, Alison woke up feeling different. After morning lectures she had slipped away to Regent's Park. She remembered very clearly sitting on a bench, realising that she felt better.

Depression could lift, Alison told herself, sitting in another London park, twenty years later. If postnatal depression was what she had, it would go as soon as her body returned to normal. Just talking about it had made her feel considerably better already. Ramona's advice was sen-sible. Of course she must get a nanny. Of course she and Stephen should spend time together.

She stood up, straightened her jacket and headed home.

'Why do we have to have a brand-new pram that converts into a pushchair?' hissed Neil behind Lia as the shop assistant demonstrated the benefits of the latest model.

'Because we only have your brother's old carry-cot on wheels, and it's old and heavy to push around,' Lia explained in a whisper.

'But it costs almost as much as a small car,' Neil protested.

'We'll think about it,' Lia told the shop assistant. 'Thanks very much.' She started walking towards the lift. 'I don't know why we bothered to come if we can't afford to buy anything.'

'Lia, stop,' he said, chastened. 'Why don't we sit down and work out what we can afford?' He put his hand on her arm. 'Look, there's a café. Let's have a coffee.'

'All right,' she said, taking a deep breath, 'all right.'

She sat at a table by the window, looking back to the counter where Neil was sliding two fresh cream cakes onto his tray. She didn't really notice the woman starting to wipe her table. The woman paused mid-wipe and Lia could feel her staring. Then a familiar voice said, 'It is, isn't it? Hello, Lesley! How're you doing?'

Lia looked up sharply. Before she had a chance to answer Neil was there, holding the laden tray.

'Hello, Trace,' Lia said quietly. 'This is Neil, and Anouska.' She pointed at the baby, who was sleeping tied to Neil's chest.

'Oooh, she's lovely,' the woman squealed.

'Thanks,' Lia replied, noncommittally.

'Well, nice to see you again,' the woman said, and was gone.

'Who was that?' Neil asked, surprised.

'Trace. She's one of the girls from my house,' Lia said.

'She called you Lesley,' Neil said, sitting down.

'Did she?' Lia replied. Suddenly she had no appetite.

Neil said nothing, but the air was charged with the unspoken question.

'It's no big deal,' Lia said. 'I changed my name when I went to Spain. Well, the first person who asked me thought I said Lia, and I liked the sound of it, so it stuck.'

'Oh,' Neil said.

'What's wrong with that?'

'Nothing, I suppose,' he said.

'Well, you seem pretty pissed off,' she said.

'No, I'm not.'

'Oh, this is ridiculous,' she said, getting up to leave.

'I just don't see why you didn't tell me you had changed your name,' Neil said as they left. 'When we were deciding on *her* name,' he added, pointing at the baby as if he hated her, 'you assured me that you had never been teased at school, but you didn't tell me that your name hadn't been Lia then.'

She revealed her guilt in a blush. 'All right, I'm sorry.'

He was silent on the tube home and for the rest of the day. Whenever she tried to talk to him, he walked away. That made her angry. She told him to stop it. He denied he was doing anything. She took Anouska into their bedroom to feed her and slammed the door, fuming.

It wasn't really anything to do with her name, she realised, calming down. It was the combination of weeks of broken sleep, no sex, feeling left out; all these things had been building up like steam inside him, just as she had a list of unspoken resentments: why did he take so little notice of the baby, why was he obsessed with what everything cost? They said that having a baby brought you together, but she and Neil couldn't have been any more together, and it seemed instead as if whatever it was they had shared was somehow irrevocably diminished.

*November*

THE VINE LEAVES had turned a coppery red, and there was a damp smokiness in the air. Dry leaves crackled under the soles of Ginger's Doc Martens like scrunched-up brown paper.

'This restaurant's closing up for winter next week,' Lia remarked, 'so where are we going to meet after that?'

The three women now met regularly in the gardens. 'It'll have to be somewhere they allow three prams,' Ginger said, 'and the only place I can think of is McDonald's.'

'Two prams,' Alison said. 'I'm back at work on Monday.'

'Oh . . . we'll miss you,' Lia said.

'How's your nanny getting on?' Ginger asked Alison.

'Justine? She's an angel. Ben seems to like her and my life is transformed . . . she spends hours puréeing organic vegetables and introducing them into his diet . . . it's marvellous. Honestly, Ginger, I wouldn't be too quick to refuse your parents' offers of help,' Alison enthused.

'Hmm, but I don't want to leave Guy.' Seeing Alison's face, she added quickly, 'Oh, sorry, I didn't mean that to sound . . . I just meant I can't get enthusiastic about going back. Anyway,' she went on, brightening, 'I don't have to think about it quite yet.' Then she asked, out of the blue, 'Do you think I should go on telly?'

'What do you mean?' Alison asked.

'I've been asked to go on telly, you know, one of those awful discussion programmes they have in the mornings. A friend of mine's a researcher, and they're doing one of those "Single Parents—is flogging too good for them?" kind of debates.'

Both Alison and Lia laughed at the deep, serious commentator's voice Ginger put on to make her point.

'You'd be really good on television,' Lia chipped in.

'Of course she would,' Alison said, trying to inject a note of caution into the conversation. 'But what's in it for you, Ginger? They're bound to have some horrible Tory grandee on patronising you, someone like . . .' She thought for a moment.

'Like my father.' Ginger finished the sentence for her.

'Well, yes.'

'That's rather why the idea appealed. It would annoy him.'

Alison laughed. 'Well, I suppose if you could bear to, you'd be a better spokesperson for single people than a lot of the victims they might get on. You made a positive decision to do this and you're enjoying it, aren't you?' she asked.

'Oh yes. I never realised how much fun it would be,' Ginger said, beaming. She stood up, slurping back the rest of her Coke. 'Which reminds me,' she added, banging down her can on the table, 'I've got to run now, I haven't cleaned the flat and my father is coming to lunch.' She spun her pram round and walked off at her usual breakneck pace.

'Are you doing anything for lunch?' Lia asked Alison, as they watched Ginger disappear behind some tall conifers.

'Well, actually my mother's coming this afternoon, so I'd better be getting back,' Alison said. Then, feeling guilty when she saw Lia's face fall, she added, 'Why don't you come back with me and we'll have a bite to eat?'

'Are you sure?' Lia asked.

'Of course, if you don't mind salad,' said Alison.

'It's just that Neil's got a football match tonight, so it's a bit of a long day for me,' said Lia, as they strolled down the road where Alison lived.

When they reached the house, they manoeuvred their prams into the big hall. Both babies were still sleeping so Lia followed Alison into the large room that stretched from the front of the house to a conservatory at the back. It looked like something out of a Sunday magazine, she thought, with its bare polished boards and rugs. The kitchen area was mainly dark green, with a great solid wooden table, on which sat a large blue glass bowl of lemons. Lia watched as Alison began to prepare a salad, tearing lettuce leaves and pink-veined chard over a giant bowl the shape and colour of a cabbage leaf. Even the vegetables went with the colour scheme, she thought.

'Fantastic kitchen,' she said.

'Thank you. Do you cook much?' Alison asked.

'I used to, but there never seems to be the time now. I don't know why. Your life changes, doesn't it, in all sorts of ways that nobody ever tells you about.'

'I think they probably do,' Alison said. 'It's just that you can't imagine what it's like until it happens.'

Lia laughed weakly. 'Is Stephen good with Ben?' she asked, and saw surprise on Alison's face.

None of them ever mentioned their partners, which was odd because when they were together it felt as if they could say anything. Perhaps it was out of respect for Ginger that they didn't mention the men.

'Yes, he is,' Alison replied. 'He's a much better father than I thought he would be, if I'm honest.'

'Really?' Lia said. 'It's just the opposite with Neil . . .'

'Oh?' Alison turned away, rummaging round in a cupboard and pulling out a jar of sun-dried tomatoes. Suddenly she wished she had not invited Lia for lunch.

'I thought he would be brilliant, but, well, perhaps he'll be better when she's a bit older,' Lia went on.

'I believe a lot of men are like that.' Alison breathed a sigh of relief. Subject closed. She dribbled vinegar into the jar.

'Perhaps I'm to blame,' Lia continued. 'So much of me is taken up loving Anouska, I don't have enough time for him—'

'It takes a bit of adjustment,' Alison interrupted.

'I hate having to rely on Neil for money,' Lia went on. 'I'm just not used to not paying my way. I didn't think it would affect our relationship, but it has.'

Why are you telling me all this? Alison wanted to ask Lia. I don't want to know. Don't draw me into your life.

'There's this terrible weight of responsibility that descends on you'— Alison tried to divert the direction of the conversation, as they began to eat—'that you've brought this being into the world and if anything happens it will be your fault.'

'I know that I want to give Anouska the best possible life I can, if that's what you mean,' Lia said, thoughtfully. 'I look at her and I love her so much. I can't imagine how anyone abandons their child . . .'

Suddenly Alison felt a tremendous surge of sympathy for her, remembering the calm way she had told them about her childhood. 'Do you remember your mother?' she asked, gently.

'I think I can remember her,' Lia said quietly. 'But I never know whether I'm just imagining it.'

'Have you ever tried to trace her?' Alison asked.

'I don't think she'd want to be reminded, do you? No, it wouldn't be fair,' Lia replied.

Alison felt chastened by the selflessness of Lia's answer.

They both ate mouthfuls of salad.

'You move on, don't you?' Lia said, eventually. 'You don't always want to be going over the past.'

'No,' Alison agreed, not trusting herself to say more.

**A** black Rolls-Royce drew up at the top of Richmond Hill, and the chauffeur jumped out to open the kerbside back door. Sir James Prospect rose, with some effort, from his seat and stood on the pavement. His driver listened to instructions, walked round the car, got in and drove away.

Ginger watched from the window of her ground-floor living room, hoping that none of the neighbours had witnessed her father's arrival. He was such a hated figure she had wanted to keep her relationship to him a secret. Now he looked at the window and saw her standing there. She waved to him without returning his smile and went to open the door.

'I haven't got very long, I'm afraid,' were his first words.

She felt like slamming the door in his face.

He bent to kiss her, but she stepped back, unwilling to act out the meaningless ritual of greeting.

She marched back into the room, reminding herself she had promised she would be charming and courteous to him. She picked Guy up from his mat, holding him to herself.

'This is Guy,' she said, turning round so her father could see him, but not offering the baby to him to hold.

She watched Guy as he became aware that there was another person in the room. Sometimes he stared at people with such undisguised suspicion it made her want to laugh.

'Hello, young man,' her father said.

He sounded like an uncle visiting his nephew at Eton, not wanting any un-English displays of emotion. She half expected her father to give Guy's hand a good firm shake.

She waited for as long as she could bear for him to say something nice about her baby.

'Well, what do you think?' she finally demanded.

Her father sniffed. 'I think there's something burning.'

'God, the quiche!' Ginger thrust the baby into his stiff, besuited arms and ran to the oven.

The Marks & Spencer broccoli and tomato quiche was a rather darker brown on the top than the colour of the illustration on the box.

'I thought perhaps you were being a little overambitious inviting me to lunch,' her father laughed. 'Come on, let's call Colin up on the mobile and he'll take us somewhere nice.'

Ginger was seething. 'No,' she said, trying not to shout.

'Really, darling, it's no trouble. He's only driving round and round the block until I need him.'

She didn't know whether it was his treatment of the chauffeur, his casual dismissal of her hospitality, or the way he was holding her precious baby like a spare overcoat that made her more furious. She became all the more determined to make him eat the burnt quiche.

'Certainly not,' she said, taking Guy back. 'I haven't got a car seat for Guy and I don't want to take him out again today. It's too cold.'

'But the car's very cosy and surely you can hold him on your lap. We always did.'

'It's illegal actually,' she said to him. 'And we wouldn't want a government minister breaking the law . . .'

His face registered the potential of a reporter snapping him with his single daughter and her brat, and she knew she had won.

Ginger put Guy in a bouncy chair. Then she opened a bag of salad, emptied it onto two plates, cut the quiche in half and slid one piece onto her plate and one onto her father's. While he ate, she spooned a jar of organic vegetable purée into Guy's mouth, feeling cruelly triumphant as she watched her father masticating the unappetising dry food.

Sir James dutifully drank the cup of instant coffee she made him, then took out his mobile phone. 'OK, Colin, if you'd be so kind.' Then he said to Ginger with the false note of regret she had heard him use so much on television, 'So sorry it had to be such a short visit.'

'Aren't you going to say anything about my baby?' she asked him as the car drew up outside.

'Well, I'm sure he's very sweet, darling. I was never good with babies. I'm sure we'll be great friends when he's a little older . . .'

'**W**hat's up then, mate?' Pete asked, as he plonked two straight pint glasses down. He picked up one and tasted it. 'Ugh, that's your one, mate. I don't know how you can drink it with lemonade.'

'I'm on the bike, and it's better than those non-alcoholic lagers,' Neil said.

'Yeah, well, a can of Tango'd be better than that crap,' his brother observed, taking a long draught from his glass. 'Been meaning to tell you, Cheryl's pregnant again.'

'Well, congratulations!' Neil knocked his glass against his brother's.

'What about you? Going to have another one?'

'No way,' Neil said quietly, adding, for the sake of politeness, 'not for a long time, anyway.'

He had found the experience of being a father very difficult to get used to. When he looked at the baby he could only see a tiny creature with a startled face, who had just two ways of expressing herself: a toothless grin, or, more frequently, a roar of discontent.

'Seems so much work,' Neil expanded in the silence that had followed his statement. 'Well, it does for Lia. I don't know, she spends her whole life making pear purée . . .'

'Yeah, well, takes a bit of time getting used to it, you know. For ages you get nothing back, but it's great when they're older.'

'Maybe I'd know what to do if we had a boy.'

'I think men find it pretty scary how small and helpless they are. Women are better at that bit,' his brother, the man of experience, said.

'Yeah, well,' Neil said, looking into his glass.

'That's not it, is it?' Pete asked him.

'What?'

'Come on, mate, you come all the way down here on a cold dark winter's night when you haven't been for months, and you've got a face like a man who's lost his winning lottery ticket.'

Neil smiled. His brother had always been able to sense when something was bothering him. That was why, he supposed, he had needed to come and talk to him.

So he bought him another pint and told him hesitantly that he felt everything had changed since the baby was born.

'It happens, mate,' Pete said. 'What else?'

So Neil told him about the row they'd had after he discovered she'd changed her name.

'So what's the big deal? It's only a few letters.'

'I don't know . . . I just feel like if she's lied to me about that, then how many other things has she lied about?'

'But you just said she never lied, she just never told you. What's wrong with that? I don't blame her for changing it myself, Lia's a much classier name. Perhaps that's it,' Pete said, nudging Neil's arm, trying to jolly him out of his mood. 'You prefer a bird with a classy name. You always had a thing for snooty girls. There was that silly slag, you know, who lived up in the Willows . . . Daddy was an estate agent. What was her name?'

'Alison, and she wasn't a slag,' Neil said defensively, twirling a beer mat around. 'I met her again recently.' He attempted to keep his voice light and casual, but as soon as he'd said it, he wished he hadn't.

'Oh yeah.' Pete put down his pint and stared at him. 'So, finally we get the reason . . .'

'No,' Neil protested. 'No, she's married, she's got a kid.'

'Reasons why you shouldn't, not why you don't want to.'

'Well, I don't want to . . .' Neil said emphatically.

'I hope not, mate,' Pete said, finishing his beer. 'Because I'll tell you something. Lia is class, mate, real class. She's the real thing. That Alison, well . . . anyway, I'd better go.'

Neil drove back on his Kawasaki bike much faster than he should, taking risks on corners of the country lanes where ice was already form-ing, his anger daring him to the limits of danger.

Speeding through a village, he saw a child run into the road. As he braked, he realised he was going to hit the little girl. He swerved and skidded to a halt, miraculously keeping control of the bike and just avoiding her. Her mother ran over and scooped her up, shouting at him.

'You should hold her hand, then,' he shouted and roared off.

A hundred yards up the road, he stopped again, realising he was shaking too much to drive safely. He sat down in the freezing grass on the verge and pulled out a packet of cigarettes.

Pete was right, he thought, taking a long, determined drag. His criti-cism was fair enough. He knew he shouldn't be having the thoughts about Ally that he had been having, but he didn't seem to be able to stop them. He couldn't get out of his mind the memory of the exquisite moment their bodies had joined. It had felt as if he were being sucked into her soul. He had never really left.

Stop it, he thought, throwing down the cigarette. She left you. She didn't even tell you that she wasn't going to come back. You waited, like an idiot, for a long time, but she never even bothered to find out whether you were still alive. Everyone had told him that time healed wounds. It had taken nearly twenty years, but he had eventually found a better woman to love. Go home, he told himself.

Lia couldn't sleep. Sleeplessness had become a habit, and even though she had come to bed early, relishing the prospect of a few hours' oblivion before Anouska woke up, she had not been able to drift off.

Where was Neil? It was after ten and he still wasn't home. She knew that he wasn't at the football match, because Bill, his junior, had rung earlier to tell him that the team had won, and asked her to pass on the message when Neil returned. She had probably misunderstood, Lia thought. He'd probably gone up to his sports club, but it was strange that he hadn't rung to tell her. Perhaps he had gone for a spin on his bike. He often did that. When something was troubling him, his impulse was to work it out on his own.

It was cold out. The weather map of England had three large letters over the whole of the southeast. ICE. Oh God, perhaps he had had an accident! She looked at the clock again. Half past ten. The police would think she was neurotic. Silly cow, perhaps hubby's somewhere he shouldn't be? Lia tried to stop the thought gathering momentum. Surely he couldn't be seeing someone else? Surely things hadn't got that bad between them? And yet it would explain so much.

It was the not knowing she hated. But it was only one evening, the other side of her said. What had happened to them if she didn't trust him just to stay out one night for a few hours without telling her where? It was far more likely that he had had an accident. She shuddered. She would wait until midnight, she decided, then ring the police. The moment she had made the decision, she heard his key in the lock.

The flood of relief that he was safe was quickly replaced by irritation at his lack of consideration for her feelings. Couldn't he have rung? Didn't he realise she would worry? She pulled the duvet up protectively over her ears and closed her eyes.

He leapt onto the bed and lay beside her, still clad in the cold biker's leather. 'Are you asleep?' he whispered.

'Not any more,' she said tightly.

'I'm sorry I'm so late,' he said, then he put his arms round her and whispered, 'I'm sorry about a lot of things . . .'

She felt her resolve melt. 'That's OK,' she said, turning towards him. 'Didn't you go to the match?'

For a second, he hesitated. He had forgotten that he had told her he was taking the football team to an away game. It was such a silly thing to have said, when all he had wanted was a chance to think about things.

'No, I just went for a ride around,' he told her.

'Well, good night then,' she said, turning away from him, knowing that there was something he wasn't telling her.

The morning of Ginger's screen debut, Charlie Prince was early into the office. He had already made half a dozen calls when he chanced to look up through the glass wall that separated his office from the reception area at the television positioned above the receptionist's head.

A girl's face was talking animatedly and rapidly, although he could not hear a word because the glass blocked out the sound. It took him a few moments to realise that he recognised her.

'What's it about?' He pointed at the screen.

'I think it's something about single parents.'

'Turn it up,' Charlie ordered, sitting down on one of the leather chairs. Somebody he recognised as a Tory baroness was looking distastefully at the girl sitting opposite her. The camera followed her gaze back to Ginger.

'Look,' Ginger said, trying to keep her voice reasonable, 'you don't like single mothers, and you object to abortions, right? So what's the alternative?'

There was applause from the audience behind.

'You could control yourself,' the Tory lady suggested.

'Oh, get real!' Ginger said.

The camera zoomed in on the show host who was smiling with pleasure that the discussion was becoming controversial.

'Well, if I may say so, it's all very well for people like you who have money—' the Tory lady began.

'Oh, so it's OK for the rich,' Ginger interrupted her. 'So, next step eugenics and then you'd be happy . . .'

'No, I'm certainly not saying that.' The Tory lady looked flustered. 'All I'm saying is that people with the means to do so can get proper, trained help, whereas those who don't—'

'Are forced to look after their own kids . . . oh dear!' Ginger finished her sentence for her. 'So it's fine to have a well-paid nanny, but if you're a single mother in the poverty trap and have to bring up your child yourself then that's wrong. Look,' she went on, gathering momentum. 'I'll tell you what's wrong: one, poor single mothers don't have the freedom to choose whether to work: two, they don't have the money to buy their children the things they need, like food and shoes. People like you think it's fine, preferable, in fact, to get a stranger to look after your children until they're old enough to be sent away for months to public school . . . and you're the good parents?'

Charlie laughed out loud.

'We're going to have to leave it there,' said the host, as the titles rolled.

'Get me Robert Preston,' Charlie instructed the receptionist.

# THESE FOOLISH THINGS

The room was still dark, but outside the sun was shining. There was a bright sliver of light, white, like a moonbeam, breaking through the gap in the curtains. The room smelt unfamiliar—of potpourri and beeswax—and the covers on the bed were heavy and reminded her of the pre-duvet days of her childhood. Alison felt like Sleeping Beauty waking up in a palace after sleeping for a hundred years.

Stephen was propped up on a bank of white pillows looking down at her. She stretched her arms in a huge, waking-up yawn.

He dipped his head and kissed her lips. She tasted mint and soda. He had already brushed his teeth.

'Did you sleep well?' he asked her.

'Blissfully . . . did you?'

'Oh, you know how I am,' he said. Stephen had trained himself to do without sleep, and now that ability almost amounted to insomnia. 'I watched the video they gave us when we arrived. Their version of a brochure, I suppose. It tells you what you can do.'

'And what can you do?' she queried, amazed at the clinical thoroughness he brought even to an away-from-it-all weekend in one of the most luxurious hotels in the country, where the only rule was to relax.

'Oh, everything—riding, swimming . . . '

'In the pool where Profumo met Christine Keeler?' she asked.

'Another alternative is to make love to the very beautiful woman in your bed,' he said matter-of-factly, putting his hand on her arm very gently.

'That's on the video too, is it?' she asked.

'Well, I suppose they might have hidden cameras'—he looked at the drapery above their heads—'but I don't think they'd give away a film of what we did last night for nothing . . . '

She smiled at him, the memory making her immediately wet.

What a good fit we are, she thought, shivering with the pleasure of his warm skin against hers. She clasped her hands behind his neck, reaching up to kiss him deeply, and felt him harden against her thigh. She rolled over on top of him. He spread-eagled his legs and she lay perfectly still between them. Then she raised her bottom and knelt above him, and he rested his hands on her pelvic bones and guided himself into her.

She still felt tender where last night his fingers had tickled and coaxed and rubbed her hard through soft undulating ripples to sublime torrents of orgasm. Now her flesh seemed to be remembering, retracing again the unfamiliar ascent of sensation to climax.

We can do it, she wanted to scream with joy, we can still do it!

# December

'HE ASKED ME why you had suddenly become a spokesperson for single parents, so I told him that you had a baby,' Robert was saying.

'But that programme was weeks ago,' Ginger said.

'Yes, well, we kept missing each other's calls, you know how it is,' Robert told her, adding sarcastically, 'Perhaps you weren't at the very top of his agenda?'

'Well, thank you for telling me. So, when am I going to see you?'

'Well, you *are* coming to the party?' Robert said.

'If Pic will look after Guy, yes . . . Oh, but Charlie'll be there,' she remembered.

'Well, you're bound to bump into him some day. Better in familiar surroundings,' Robert advised.

'I suppose you're right,' she admitted.

After a perfunctory farewell, she waved at Guy, suspended from the door-frame in a Baby-bouncer and jumping happily up and down. His face lit up with a smile of pure, undiluted joy. It had been a delightful surprise to meet this tiny person, who had been dozing in her tummy for a while, and find that he was exactly the sort of friend she would have chosen.

Guy smiled again. With his mass of dark curls and his determined square face, he was unmistakably Charlie's son.

She had been so sure that not telling Charlie had been the right thing to do, but since Guy's birth she had been having doubts. She caught herself imagining the first conversation she would have with Guy about it, and knew that she would not be able to lie, and yet she did not want to mix him up by being truthful about things he could not understand until he was older. She wasn't even sure that she herself really understood the reason she had decided to go ahead with the pregnancy. It was all very well talking about *Hello!* magazine changing your life, but she wondered whether her motives had been more to do with angering her father.

She bent to pick up her son. 'Come on, let's find the credit cards and spend some more money we don't have. Mummy has to wear something nice for meeting Daddy.'

**A**lison was hurrying past the Early Learning Centre when she noticed a small crowd of toddlers gathered round a bigger child who was prowling on all fours round the play area. It was only when the older child looked up that she saw it was Ginger, who had discovered a display of model zoo animals and was demonstrating to her son the noises they made. Guy sat in his pushchair solemnly watching his mother trumpeting like an elephant and roaring like a lion.

'Now,' Ginger asked herself out loud, picking up a rubber penguin, 'what noise does a penguin make?'

'I don't think they make much noise, do they?' Alison said, as she walked into the shop.

Ginger laughed, and got to her feet.

'I can't wait to go to the real zoo with him,' she said, breathless from her performance. 'How's Ben?' she asked.

'Fine, thanks,' Alison said. 'He's with his father. Stephen was feeling guilty, so he's taken him out.'

'Why?' Ginger asked.

'Why guilty? Oh, because he's got a seminar in New York over New Year. So, shall we have a coffee?' Alison said.

'I'd love to, but . . .' Ginger hesitated. 'Could you do me a favour first? I've got to get something to wear for a party and . . . I just wondered . . .'

'I'd love to,' Alison said enthusiastically. 'What are you looking for?'

'Well . . .' Ginger said tentatively. 'I kind of feel I've grown out of black miniskirts and Doc Martens. I want something kind of . . .'

'. . . more sophisticated?' Alison finished her sentence.

'Yes,' Ginger said, pleased with the word.

In the next hour, she was taken into shops she would never have thought of entering. After some coaxing, she began to enjoy having colours and fabrics picked out for her.

'What do you think about red?' Alison asked her, flipping along a shiny rail of dresses.

'I don't really. I've never worn it,' Ginger said.

Alison held up a short dress in crimson crushed velvet, and laughed as Ginger's eyes widened.

'Go on, try it on, it'll look superb.'

It did. The shape was simple, just two rectangles of fabric joined by the merest stitch at the shoulders, but the cut was so expert that the material fell in softly draping horizontal folds from the neck. The gorgeously rich fabric shimmered as Ginger's frame moved uncertainly beneath it.

'You look like a million dollars,' Alison said.

'That's because that's what it costs, almost,' Ginger said, looking at the price label.

'But I'm sure you'll wear it lots,' Alison said, adding, 'I always divide the cost by the number of times I wear something, and then it doesn't seem so much.'

'On that calculation,' Ginger said, 'I reckon my jeans owe me money, but . . .' She was tempted. 'You see,' she whispered, 'it's Robert's Christmas party, the one where last year . . .'

'Oh heavens!' said Alison, understanding immediately. 'And *he* will be there?' She didn't know how to refer to him.

'Yes . . . Will I do, do you think?' Ginger said.

She looked so very vulnerable standing bashfully, slightly knock-kneed. Alison wanted to hug her.

'You'll be perfect. It's very sexy, but not overt. He won't be able to take his eyes off you, if that's what you want . . .'

'I don't know what I want, really,' Ginger said. 'I suppose I just want to look grown-up.'

'Well, you do.'

'That settles it, then.'

Later, as they sat in Prêt-à-Manger drinking coffee, a pair of new black suede shoes in a carrier bag hanging from Guy's pushchair, Alison issued further instructions.

'Now, I know you're thinking that you should wear black tights, but you absolutely mustn't. That would look tarty. Choose a sheer, natural colour,' she said with a smile, realising that she sounded exactly like the copy she used to write, 'and absolutely no jewellery,' she concluded firmly, 'except possibly some plain earrings. You do not want to look like a Christmas cracker.'

How odd, Ginger thought as she pushed the pushchair up the hill, that Alison should turn out to be such a girlie girl. She had always thought of her as the kind of person who liked to keep her distance. She felt she had made a new friend.

There were at least three football matches in progress on the playing fields. Eventually, Lia picked out Neil's outline. She pushed the pram slowly along the frozen muddy edge of the field.

His face lit up when he recognised that it was her. It was such a spontaneous expression of pleasure that she smiled back, blushing with surprise. The moment made her wonder how she could ever doubt his love.

'Sir, is that your wife, sir?' A short, cheeky-looking boy of about twelve danced round Neil's legs as he strode towards her.

'Yes, Sean,' Neil replied briskly.

'She's ever so pretty, sir.'

'I know that, Sean,' Neil replied, winking at Lia as they approached.

'Your wife's not wearing a wedding ring, sir. Are you sure she's your wife, sir?'

'Don't be cheeky, Sean,' said Neil evenly but firmly, sending Sean running off back to his teammates.

'Hello, gorgeous,' Neil said, leaning forward to kiss Lia on the lips. A few yards behind him a cheer went up. He draped his arm round her shoulders, and she had the definite feeling that he was proud of her and glad she had come to meet him.

'My street cred just went up a few points,' he whispered to her, and laughed.

A pale, lemon-silver sun slipped towards the horizon, and the air was suddenly cold. It was getting very wintry.

'What shall we do for Christmas?' Neil asked her, as if the whiteness of the ground had triggered a Christmas-card snow scene in his mind.

'Well, I'd like to spend it at home . . . a real family Christmas together,' she said, looking at Anouska.

'At our house?' he asked, surprised.

'Yes,' she said.

He was silent for a few minutes.

'Your parents could come for the day,' Lia volunteered.

'It would be a lot of work for you,' Neil said.

'Well, better me than your mother,' Lia replied.

'If you're sure . . .'

'Of course,' she said, then, capitalising on his positive reaction, 'Neil, could we afford a car?'

'A car?'

The surprise in his voice could not have been greater if the question had been, Neil, can we buy an elephant? It obviously hadn't occurred to him that she might need, or want, a car.

'It's just . . . well, I seem to spend my whole life trailing backwards and forwards to the shops with the pram, and I worry about Anouska catching cold after swimming, and I could do things, if we had a car . . .'

'I'll have to have a think,' he said, retreating into gloomy silence for the rest of the walk home.

Lia unwrapped the baby and sat her in a bouncy chair in front of the playgym she had made her.

Neil picked up the phone and dialled his parents. Lia tried to listen in but the noise of the kettle boiling made eavesdropping impossible.

'Well, I think retirement must have gone to my dad's head,' he said, coming into the kitchen after his call.

'Why?' She poured him a cup of tea and handed him a plate of biscuits.

'They've booked a time-share in Lanzarote for two weeks over Christmas. They're taking Pete's boys with them.'

'How lovely,' Lia said, almost unable to contain her smile of relief. This was surely a good omen, to have the credit for offering to 'do' Christmas, but to avoid entertaining the in-laws after all.

'Shall we invite Pete and Cheryl instead?' Neil suggested.

She was pleased that he seemed keen on the idea of making a family Christmas out of it. 'Yeah, ring them now,' she said. 'Let's get a big tree.'

'OK, and I'll maybe string up some lights,' he joined in, walking towards her, and for the first time in weeks she felt herself relax into his embrace rather than stiffen away from it.

'Bad news?' Ramona asked, dumping her bag on the opposite desk.

'Not really, but I can't decide what to do,' Alison explained. The woman who rented her flat in Islington had written to tell her that she was getting married at Christmas, and to ask whether Alison would mind if she gave less notice than the lease required. Alison supposed she would have to agree.

'Sometimes I find the best thing to do when you can't decide is decide to decide some other time,' Ramona suggested. 'At least then you've made a decision of sorts.'

'Like Scarlett O'Hara. You're right,' said Alison, resolving not to do anything until the New Year.

'Hey, at this rate, I'm going to have to start charging for my ideas . . .'

'All right, I'll give you a fiver if you can come up with something original for Valentine's Day,' Alison said, getting back to work.

'And you're the one married to a heart specialist,' Ramona quipped.

Alison made a face.

'Last year, it was Shrove Tuesday at around the same time, so I made pancakes and cut them into heart shapes with a biscuit cutter—sprinkle of cinnamon and lemon, delicious!' Ramona said.

'You old romantic,' Alison said, 'but it's a lovely idea, simple. Do you mind if I use it?'

At lunchtime, Alison hugged her charcoal-grey cashmere coat round her waist and lifted her face to the sun. It was the kind of exhilarating winter's day that feels as if the crisp air is breathing you, rather than the other way round. The sunshine made cubist mirrors of the surfaces of the tall buildings, and the sky was solid blue. Even the roar of the traffic seemed invigorating, like the whoosh of a magnified heartbeat, throbbing through the City's arteries. It was impossible not to feel optimistic.

It was a day like this, she remembered, that she and Neil had come up for the day to Biba. He had encouraged her to try on amazingly clingy purple dresses, even though they hadn't enough money to buy a meal in a Golden Egg. They had spent everything they owned on tickets for Bryan Ferry at the Rainbow.

In his white lounge suit, Bryan Ferry had symbolised everything that London was, and their town was not. Sophisticated, cool, distant. When he sang 'These Foolish Things', they did not dance or kiss, but reached discreetly for each other's fingers in the dark, hoping no one would see them. How satisfied they had been then with so little, she thought.

'Are you sure you'll be all right?'

'Of course we will, won't we, Guy?' said Lia, taking him from Ginger.

Pic had called the night before, with a temperature of over a hundred, saying that Ginger would have to find another baby sitter. Ginger had resigned herself to missing Robert's party, but Lia, who had called shortly after, had insisted that she go. She had offered to take Guy for the whole night so that Ginger could be out as long as she wanted to be.

Lia put Guy on the floor beside Anouska. Ginger divested herself of a number of bags and took off her coat.

'Oh my God, it's the most beautiful thing I've ever seen!' Lia said. 'Neil, come and look at Ginger.'

Neil walked through from the kitchen, an open packet of crisps in his hand. 'Very nice,' he said laconically between crunches, then smiled.

He was extraordinarily good-looking, Ginger thought, blushing as she did an embarrassed twirl, especially when he smiled.

'Alison sent me the tights, can you believe it? She told me not to wear black. Of course I forgot, then this morning a Jiffy bag arrives with two pairs of Christian Dior Nude. She must have guessed that I always put my fingers through the first new pair.'

Lia laughed. 'That's so sweet of her.'

'She's really lovely,' Ginger said, as if she were speaking of a fairy godmother, or a much-favoured aunt. 'Is she coming?'

'Well, I said that we were having a Christmas drink before you went to the party, and she said she would try,' said Lia.

'I've brought a bottle of pop,' Ginger said. 'It's in one of those bags.'

'Oh, you shouldn't have,' Lia said, pulling out a bottle of Veuve Cliquot.

'I should,' Ginger replied. 'It's the least I could do when you're looking after Guy.'

There was a knock at the door. Lia went to open it. In a blast of cold air, Alison came in carrying Ben in his car seat, followed by Stephen, holding another bottle of champagne.

Alison kissed Lia on the cheek. 'I hope you don't mind me bringing Stephen,' she said lightly. 'He hasn't met the other babies, and he's heard so much about them.'

'Of course not,' Lia said, thrilled to be the hostess of an impromptu party. 'Here, give me your coats . . .'

Alison was wearing a black Nicole Farhi woollen dress simply adorned with a large silver brooch. It made her look particularly slim and elegant. Lia suddenly noticed the shapeless blue jumper she was wearing over her jeans and wished that she had changed.

'So, this is the dress,' Stephen said, looking appreciatively at Ginger. 'You were right, darling, it looks fabulous.'

Alison hadn't even been aware that she had told him about the dress. Without thinking, she took his hand and squeezed it, grateful for the grace of the compliment, then released it, noticing that Neil's eyes were fixed on the place, midair, where her fingers had just clasped Stephen's. He shook his gaze away, avoiding eye contact with her, and stepped forward to shake Stephen's hand in a friendly, masculine way.

'Champagne?' said Ginger, who had registered the awkwardness.

There were two sorts of good mothers, Alison decided, the champagne making her feel oddly flat. There were the ones like Ginger, who had many childlike qualities of their own. Ginger didn't have to get down to Guy's level, because in some sense she was already there, with her uninhibited imagination and delight in simple games. Then there were the ones to whom mothering came naturally, like Lia, who seemed to know instinctively what children wanted, and who could transfer a certain calm within themselves onto the child.

And then there were the mothers who didn't really know what to do at all, she thought, taking another slug from her glass. Perched on the arm of Stephen's chair, she watched with envy as Lia took first Guy, then Anouska, upstairs, humming soothing snatches of lullabies, enveloping them in warmth and care.

'That was quick,' she said, as Lia returned.

'Well, Guy was off anyway, and Annie has a thing that lights up and plays a tune and she just drifts off. I sometimes wish they made them for grown-ups,' Lia elaborated. 'It must be nice to fall asleep with all these little pictures going round on the ceiling . . .'

'I can't imagine it,' Stephen said. 'Will you show me when she's asleep?'

Lia smiled. 'Of course. Do you want to come up now?'

'May I?' Stephen stood up. 'I love watching them sleep. They are so exquisitely beautiful and innocent.' He looked lovingly at his son, asleep in his car seat.

Alison exchanged glances with Neil. Neither of them said a word, but she knew that they were thinking the same thing. She glanced at her watch, wondering how much longer she could bear to be there. When she mentioned Lia's invitation, Stephen had been keen to go. She had assumed that he would quickly tire of baby talk and they would make a quick getaway. But Stephen seemed blissfully contented playing with the babies and discussing developmental signs with Lia.

'What are you doing for Christmas?' Neil asked, to fill the silence that gaped between them.

'We're going down to my mother's,' she told him.

'Oh . . . does she still live in . . . ?'

Alison glanced nervously at the staircase. 'Rustington, yes. It's by the sea,' she added, unnecessarily.'

'And your father?'

'Died, a while ago . . . just before I got married.'

'I'm sorry.'

'Thank you.' She realised politeness probably required her to ask about his parents, but she was finding the woodenness of the conversation almost unbearable.

'So, you're a teacher?' she said finally.

'Yes, it's a bit of a long way from opening for England, but it pays the bills, just,' he said.

It was the first reference either had made to things said in the past, and she was thrown off-balance.

'Yes, well, we've all come a long way,' she said, fighting a sudden urge to ask him whether he remembered seeing Bryan Ferry.

Her words sounded trite and patronising, she realised, repeating them in her head, especially since he was talking about being a long way from his ambition and she meant something completely different.

With relief, she heard Stephen and Lia's footfall on the wooden staircase. 'But what's Alison going to do?' she heard Lia say to him.

'Oh dear, you're making me feel guilty,' Stephen replied. 'You'll be all right, darling, won't you?' he said, dipping his head to avoid the beam at the bottom of the staircase.

'Yes, of course,' she replied, assuming they were talking about New Year, and leapt up to hand Stephen his coat before he could settle down once more in the armchair.

Soho was pulsating with people. Ginger couldn't decide whether it had always been like this and she hadn't noticed, or whether there had been a restaurant boom that coincided with her confinement in the suburbs. As she approached the club, she began to feel excited. She was out on the town and she was going to have a good time.

There was a phone in the lobby, but she forced herself to walk past it. The only thing she would achieve by ringing Lia now would be to wake the babies. Guy would be fine, she told herself. She slipped into the ladies, reapplied her lipstick and blew a kiss onto a thoughtfully provided tissue. Then, imagining Alison's horror at the notion of taking her black patent rucksack into the party, she reluctantly checked it into the cloakroom, with her coat, feeling naked without it and not quite knowing what to do with her bare arms. She took a deep breath and walked into the room.

Robert's parties were famous for two things—the unlimited flow of champagne, and the hordes of beautiful single men, who were sadly uninterested in the almost equal number of attractive single women.

'You can look, but you can't touch,' Robert said, handing her a glass and watching her eyes follow a slim Keanu Reeves clone across the room.

'Why do you do this to us?' Ginger asked him.

'Well, I just don't know that many heterosexual men,' Robert told her. 'Anyway, if it means anything from an old poof, I think you look quite lovely tonight.'

'Thank you, Robert,' she said, smiling gratefully at him. Sometimes, when you least expected it, he could make you feel completely wonderful. That was why she was so fond of him.

'He's not here, yet,' he said, seeing her glancing anxiously round the room, 'but there are lots of people dying to see you . . .'

'It's been *ages* . . . What *have* you been doing . . .?' Suddenly she was surrounded by people asking her questions. On the tube, she had rehearsed cool responses, but now she found she couldn't resist announcing, 'I've had a baby!'

She noticed several of the faces set in a kind of false, embarrassed grin, before turning away. They would assume that pregnancy had shrunk her brain. Ironically, it was only Lucretia whose face registered interest in her news.

'Is it absolutely awful?' she drawled, blowing a cloud of smoke from her cheroot into the air.

Ginger was pleased to observe that there were distinct lines around her eyes. Her character, Ginger thought spitefully, was beginning to show in her face. The hardness that had earned her the sobriquet La Borgia at university was creeping into her features.

'No, I love it. It's the best thing I've ever done,' she said.

'Hello, darling!' Charlie Prince's unmistakable voice behind her sent a shiver of panic down Ginger's spine.

She looked around for help. Everyone she knew seemed engrossed in animated conversation. Then she realised that it was Lucretia he had been addressing. He hadn't even noticed that she was there. To add to the humiliation, his hand shoved her gently out of the way as he went to kiss his girlfriend. Ginger sidled off in the direction of the bar, wishing that she had worn black and could pass herself off as a waitress.

'You looked very beautiful this evening,' Stephen said, as Alison removed her make-up in front of her dressing-table mirror.

'No,' she protested modestly, 'I looked exhausted.'

'Well, pale and wan seems to suit you,' he said. 'Your friend's husband couldn't keep his eyes off you.'

'Don't be ridiculous, Stephen,' she said, turning her head away to brush her hair and wondering what made him make such an uncharacteristic remark. Was he testing her? In the mirror's reflection, she saw him pick up a Sunday paper and start to flick through it, absent-mindedly. No, she decided, it must have been a chance remark.

'I feel terribly inadequate beside Ginger and Lia,' she said, suddenly.

He put down the paper. 'What do you mean?'

'They're such good mothers,' she said, climbing into bed next to him, 'and I'm hopeless.'

'Hopeless? Have you seen the look on Ben's face when you come in from work?'

'Yes,' she said, smiling, 'it's like a sunbeam, and it makes me feel terribly guilty for leaving him all day.'

'Well, you mustn't,' Stephen said categorically. 'The most important thing for him is that you are happy. That we are all happy,' he added.

'We are happy, aren't we?' Alison said in a small voice, snuggling down beside him.

'We're very happy,' Stephen assured her, switching off the light.

She felt calm and secure listening in the dark to his even breathing, feeling the strength in his arm around her slacken after a few seconds as he fell asleep. She was in bed with the man she loved, who loved her, she told herself. But she did not seem to be able to wish away the frisson of excitement that had shivered through her when Stephen had implied that Neil still fancied her.

'Why on earth didn't you say something to him?' Robert asked Ginger crossly, when he discovered her sitting on a crate of champagne.

'Like what?' Ginger scowled at him to go away.

'Like, can you give me a job?' Robert said.

'In lieu of child support, you mean?' Ginger asked, the alcohol loosening her tongue. She was finding it suddenly exceptionally difficult to work out the meaning of anything anybody said to her.

'He thinks you're an original and he's looking for a development person, but every time he tries to ask, you're rude to him, or don't return his calls. Honestly!'

'Well, for your information,' Ginger said, with what she thought to be great dignity, 'I don't want to be a development person, so there.'

'Have you eaten anything?' Robert asked her.

'Only a couple of those bits of toast with stuff.'

'Crostini,' he said.

'Crostini,' she echoed, mockingly.

'You are intolerable when you're drunk, but I feel it is my duty to my godson to buy you dinner. I can't send you home to him in this state,' Robert told her.

'Does Charlie really want to give me a job?' she said, in the restaurant, after Robert had made her eat a lot of bread to soak up the alcohol.

'I think so,' Robert said. 'I can't think why else he'd be interested.'

'Thanks a lot.'

'Oh, you know I didn't mean it like that, I meant, well, you know Charlie, he's all work.' He flashed a sudden smile at the waiter. 'Hamburger and chips twice.'

'I thought you invited me for dinner, not bloody fast food.'

'Oh, suddenly she's sober enough to tell the difference . . . actually, hamburger is what you eat here,' Robert snapped at her.

The hamburger was served with a thick, yellow béarnaise sauce.

'Do you have ketchup?' Ginger asked the waiter.

'You are unbelievable,' Robert hissed at her. 'I buy you decent food and you ask for ketchup.'

The waiter returned with a big squeezy bottle of Heinz.

'Oh my God, don't look round,' Ginger said, spotting Charlie Prince eating at the other end of the room. He had been hidden by Lucretia's back, but as she bent to light a cheroot from the candle in the middle of the table, he caught sight of Ginger and smiled at her.

She looked away, knowing that her face had turned red enough to match the smear of ketchup she could feel on her cheek.

'What does he see in that bitch?' she asked Robert.

'She's a wonderful actress,' Robert replied, 'and there is something quite fascinating about her ruthlessness. For someone as ambitious as Charlie, anyway.'

'Oh well,' said Ginger, vaguely remembering their earlier conversation and relieved that Robert had insisted on sobering her up.

'If he ever mentions he is looking for a development person to you again, maybe you could tell him to call me.'

'That's not how it works, Ginger,' said Robert.

'I know,' she said with resignation. 'Actually, I don't think I was destined to have a brilliant media career. I'd like to have more children,' she added, partly because she was enjoying winding him up.

'She doesn't want to be in the media, she wants to be Mia Farrow,' Robert sneered. 'Excuse me while I go for a slash.'

The waiter handed Ginger a dessert menu, and she was so engrossed in deciding she didn't look up when he came back to take her order.

'Would it be too greedy,' she asked, 'to have the chocolate marquise with a bit of the vanilla-scented custard?'

'I expect you could get anything you wanted, wearing that dress,' Charlie Prince told her.

She looked up, startled and embarrassed, but relieved to see that he was on his own.

'Where's Lucretia?' she asked abruptly.

He looked slightly perplexed. 'She's powdering her nose,' he replied.

'Oh.'

'You've changed,' he said. 'I hardly recognised you.'

'Oh?' She wasn't sure whether that was good or bad. Was this his way of saying sorry for pushing her out of the way earlier?

'Great hairstyle,' he went on, looking appreciatively at her head.

'Thank you,' she said, as serenely as she knew how.

'I hear you've had a baby . . . I saw you on the box,' he said.

Her heart had started to beat so loudly she was sure the whole restaurant could hear it. 'Yes,' she said, 'a lot of people seem to have seen me.'

'Not mine, is it?' he joked.

So he did remember they had done it. 'Yes!' she said, finding it impossible to lie, but making it sound as if she was joking.

He threw back his head and laughed.

'How would you feel if it were?' she asked him, marvelling at her wit.

'Alarmed,' he said, grappling with the concept, 'and, I suppose, rather proud.'

What could have possessed her to ask? she immediately wondered, because now she wanted to know more.

'Listen, we must have lunch and catch up,' Charlie told her, aware that Lucretia was standing at the door with her coat on.

'OK,' Ginger said, despondently.

'You hear yourself saying something you had absolutely forbidden yourself to say, and you wish the floor would just open up and swallow you,' Ginger told Alison the next morning when she rang to ask her how the dress had performed.

'Oh dear,' Alison sympathised. 'But these things are never as bad as you think they were.'

'How about this? I told him Guy was his child—'

'But that's good, I'm glad you did that,' Alison interrupted.

'No, wait—then I pretended it was a joke.'

'Oh . . .'

'But the dress was great. He remarked on it, said I'd changed, which must be good, I think, and oh hell, what am I going to do?'

Alison thought for a minute. 'If he calls, I think you should have lunch with him—give him the benefit of the doubt. I know it's hard to believe, but some men are nice, you know.'

'Oh, he won't call,' Ginger said resignedly.

'I think he will,' Alison said, hoping she was right. 'Probably not before Christmas, though, so don't be all miserable,' she added.

'I can't promise that,' Ginger said, surprisingly brightly. 'I'm spending it in the country with the family, and Daddy hasn't spoken to me since the programme.'

'Family Christmas is always awful,' Alison agreed. 'The only Christmas I've ever enjoyed I was away. It was just after I met Stephen and we escaped to the Seychelles.'

'Oh well,' Ginger sighed, 'have a good one, anyway.'

It was Christmas morning and everything was as it should be. The turkey was in the oven, the sprouts were peeled and washed, the potatoes and parsnips had just come to the boil.

Neil had built a log fire in the grate and then fallen asleep in front of it, the new cricket jumper she had bought for him by his side. Lia tidied up around him, taking the present he had bought her upstairs, trying to suppress the vague sense of disappointment she had felt when she opened it. If you had to receive underwear for Christmas, she supposed camiknickers in burgundy silk were about the nicest you could get, but it was such an unimaginative present.

Still, everything else was perfect. The tree was decorated with sparkling white lights and silver balls. There was a sprig of mistletoe suspended above the kitchen door. Anouska looked cute in her Christmas dress and white tights. It was her first-ever real family Christmas.

There was a knock at the door and Lia looked out of the bedroom window to see Cheryl, a poinsettia in one hand and a carrier bag full of gifts in the other. She picked Anouska up and took her downstairs.

'Where's Pete?' Lia asked, giving her a hug.

'He's following later,' Cheryl said, as she pulled parcels out of her bag. 'Let me put this lot under the tree.'

Pete and Cheryl had been known to arrive separately on many occasions. He often had to test-drive a car he had repaired.

'You're pregnant!' Lia said, as she took her coat.

'Yes,' Cheryl said. 'Didn't Neil tell you?'

'No . . . Honestly, Neil,' she scolded him.

'Sorry,' he said, slumping back in his chair after getting up to open the door. 'I forgot.'

'Men!' said Cheryl, following Lia into the kitchen and bending down with difficulty to admire the turkey in the oven.

'Are you drinking?' Lia said, taking out a bottle of sherry.

'Well, just a little bit. How are you all getting on, anyway?' Cheryl was never one to beat about the bush.

'Fine,' Lia said.

'It's just we haven't seen you for ages, and, well,' Cheryl hesitated, 'Pete said Neil seemed a bit down the other day.'

'On the phone?' Lia asked, surprised.

'No, when he came down to have a drink with Pete in that cold spell—you remember?'

So that was where Neil had been that evening when he had come home so full of energy. Why on earth had he lied? Lia wondered.

'I didn't know that Neil had been down, but things are fine,' Lia said, feeling an enormous weight of anxiety lift from her shoulders. 'We have our ups and downs . . . well, we all do, don't we?'

'You're telling me . . .' Cheryl replied, laughing, and then there was another knock at the door. 'That must be Pete.' They both stood up to greet him as his bulk filled the kitchen door-frame, his head squashing the mistletoe against the lintel.

'Happy Christmas!' he said. 'Er, Lia, Neil's got something for you . . .'

As she walked through into the living room, Neil handed her a small twist of red and gold paper. She took it, nervously, and unravelled it.

Inside was a car key. For a moment she did not understand, and then she saw Pete glance at the window. A red Peugeot 205 was parked outside their house.

'It's not new, but it goes . . .' Pete informed the room, but Lia wasn't listening, she was in the street. She opened the door, got in, started the ignition and drove.

The streets were almost empty of traffic. She drove up Richmond Hill, past Ginger's house, then on towards Richmond Park. Suddenly, she pulled the car over to the kerb, slumped against the steering wheel and burst into tears. She had woven Neil's silences and moods into a fabric of deceit and disillusion, but all he had been doing was planning a surprise gift for her! She wiped her eyes, recalling with shame the times she had snapped at him, or turned away from his affection. She would make up for it, she promised silently, turning the car round and driving home.

'Lunch will be ready in about half an hour,' Margaret announced. 'Why don't you two go out for a walk? Give yourselves an appetite? Ben and I will be fine here.'

She looked at her grandson who was sitting on the peach and eau-de-nil Chinese carpet, propped up against a couple of damask cushions. She bent down and put the activity cube she had bought next to him, determined that by the end of the day it would be his favourite present. He looked away and picked up the Fisher Price mobile phone instead.

'His mother's son,' Stephen commented, taking Alison's hand.

Alison was rather enjoying her son's resistance to his grandmother's techniques of persuasion. She smiled at him encouragingly and waved bye-bye as they pulled on their coats and left the house.

There was a stretch of grass between the high garden fences and the shingle beach, and they walked along it, protected from the wind coming off the sea by some scrubby bushes.

'We should do this more often,' Stephen remarked, threading his arm through hers and putting his hand into the pocket of her coat.

'Come to the sea? Yes, we should. I love it.'

'Well, I meant come to see your mother,' he said.

She pulled a face.

'She's getting on,' he argued patiently. 'It's good for her to see her grandson. He's the only one, after all.'

For the first time it occurred to Alison that having just one child was probably a very bad idea. The pressure on an only child could be crushing. When she was young she had wished for sisters to play with. Now she wished there was someone else to share the inevitable burden of her mother's ageing.

'I'm going down onto the beach,' she announced, detaching herself from his arm and running off.

The wind blasted her hair back from her face, numbing her ears. She chased a wave down the beach, then struggled up the shingle as a bigger one crashed about her feet, soaking her jeans and boots. Stephen smiled as he watched her twirling and screaming into the wind.

They always strolled back across the fields after the Christmas morning service in the village church. Ginger walked slowly along the bridlepath arm in arm with Pic, who was pushing the pram. In the distance their father marched ahead briskly.

'At this rate, we're going to have two sittings for lunch,' Ginger told her sister as they paused to look over the ploughed fields, their ridges iced with frost, towards the Palladian house they had grown up in, that shone pale gold in the chilly winter sunlight. 'Daddy hasn't spoken a word to me since we arrived.'

'Has it ever occurred to you,' Pic asked cautiously, 'that you are both very similar?'

'In what sense?' Ginger challenged her, rising immediately to the perceived slight.

'Well, you're both so stubborn and unforgiving . . . You're both so sure you know what's right, and both so proud . . .'

'Well, happy Christmas to you, too.' Ginger started to walk quickly on ahead.

'Oh, don't be like that,' Pic called after her. It was impossible to push the pram at any speed on the unmade path. 'I didn't mean to upset you,' she said as she caught up, putting her arm through Ginger's and looking anxiously at her face which was wet with tears.

'Well, take it back then, say that I'm not like Daddy.'

'In lots of ways you're not . . .'

'But in others I am?' Ginger sighed. 'I suppose you're right . . . You're right about being proud. I was too proud to accept their financial help and now I've got to go back to work and I haven't got a clue what I'm going to do with Guy. My life's a bloody mess.'

'Well, how about if I give you some of the money I got from Hermione?' Pic said. 'I'd really love to.'

'No,' said Ginger, 'that's yours. Anyway, when you have children, they'll need it.'

'Well,' Pic said, knowing there was no point in trying to persuade her, 'how about a childminder?'

'The trouble with that is Lia and I sometimes overhear one when we're out in Kew Gardens, and honestly, if the parents knew the way she spoke to them . . . It's a bit of a risk . . .'

'Lia wouldn't look after him, I suppose?' Pic asked.

Ginger stopped walking. 'My God, that is a brilliant idea!' She picked her sister right off the ground in the enthusiasm of her hug. 'I could afford to pay her what a childminder gets. She needs the money. She loves Guy. She's fantastic with children . . . Why on earth didn't I think of it? I'll ring her and ask.' Ginger started to run towards the house.

Lia had poured brandy on the pudding and struck a match to light it when the phone rang. In her surprise she dropped the match and the dessert was immediately engulfed in a halo of blue flame.

'You blow it out, Neil, or whatever you're meant to do,' she giggled, and went to answer the phone.

He heard her giggling a lot more, and then a long silence, and then she said, 'Yes . . . No. I'm sure, of course. It would be lovely. Are *you* sure, more to the point?' Then she came back to the table.

'Well,' she said, 'I just got myself a job!'

'Congratulations!' Cheryl clinked her glass against Lia's.

'What job's this, then?' Neil asked her.

'Ginger asked me if I would take care of Guy when she goes back to work.' She turned to Cheryl to explain. 'Ginger's a friend I met at antenatal classes. She's really nice and she's got a terrific little boy.'

'Congratulations!' Cheryl clinked her glass against Lia's.

Neil knew he should be pleased, but the overwhelming sensation in his body was like a low grumble of anger.

'And you said yes, of course.' His voice was surly. He noticed Pete and Cheryl exchanged glances.

'Of course I did! I love Guy.'

'I don't suppose you bothered to ask her how much she's paying,' he said, turning to his brother as if to enlist his support. 'She's a poor little rich girl, but she's always telling you how little money she has . . .'

'Actually, that's not true,' Lia said, becoming aware that the atmosphere in the room had changed. 'I know you don't like her, but it's a great way of me earning some money, isn't it?' she argued.

'Actually . . .' Neil mocked the use of Ginger's favourite word.

Pete intervened, attempting to diffuse the tension between them. 'Are you going to save that last bit?' he asked, waving his spoon at the remaining wedge of pudding.

'No, go ahead.' Lia pushed it across the table to him, grateful for the change of subject.

They always played charades in the drawing room after Christmas lunch, dividing into teams.

'You go with Daddy, Ginger,' Pic suggested. 'The two of you must be about equal to Mummy, Ed and me.'

'Come along, Ginger,' their father said, rising from the table. 'We'll knock this lot into a cocked hat . . . Now'—he raised his voice like a teacher—'rules: books, films, plays, songs. How about three of each to start with?'

'You forgot television programmes,' Ginger added.

'Well, none of us watch it, do we?' her father said.

'Only when their wayward daughters are on,' Ginger said.

'As a matter of fact, I didn't see you. I was informed about your appearance by colleagues who had,' her father told her in his most cold, patronising voice. 'I presume you did it to embarrass me. You succeeded. Are you satisfied now, and can we get on with the game?'

'Why do you think that everything I do has something to do with you?' Ginger asked him, trying to keep her voice equally chill, but she didn't have the stomach for a major row, partly because she secretly suspected that, on this occasion, he was probably right about her motives.

'How about *Casablanca*?' said her father, ignoring her question.

'No,' she said, 'we had that last year. How about *Men Behaving Badly*?'

'Well, that's too easy,' her father said. 'All they would have to do is stand there and point at me . . .' He turned to face her, his eyes twinkling with humour.

She saw it was his attempt at a truce. Reluctantly she smiled back at him. She could almost hear Pic's sigh of relief from the other side of the drawing room.

Standing in his baby-walker, the present Ginger had bought him for Christmas, Guy chuckled. He had not yet worked out how to push himself along, but he was enjoying being upright.

'He's a very jolly chap, isn't he?' her father suddenly remarked, watching him with interest. 'Darling,' he called to his wife on the other side of the room, 'doesn't Guy seem advanced? I can't remember the girls doing this at his age.'

'Oh yes, he's very advanced,' their mother agreed absently.

Ginger had not known before where the expression 'swelling with pride' came from, but now she definitely felt bigger as she basked in her parents' praise of her son.

Her father turned back to her and winked. 'Next year, Ginger, we'll have him on our team.' It was as if he had finally welcomed his grandson into their family.

When Pete and Cheryl left to go home, Lia watched Neil hand over his helmet and the keys to his motorbike to his brother. Cheryl got into the car she had driven up that morning and Pete sat astride Neil's bike.

'Why is Pete taking your bike?' Lia asked, waving as they drove away.

'Part exchange for the car,' Neil told her, turning back into the house.

Lia followed him in and burst into tears. 'But I didn't mean you to sell your bike,' she sobbed. 'Why didn't you discuss it with me?'

He said nothing. Didn't she have any idea how much a car cost? He went into the kitchen, got a beer, then came back and sat down in front of the television.

Upstairs Anouska woke up. Lia went to her. When she came back down she had stopped crying and was wearing his dressing gown.

'Are you watching this?' she asked.

'Not really,' Neil said, without taking his eyes from the screen.

She slid into his lap, sitting with one leg at each side of his waist, facing him. Then she untied the dressing gown. She had put on the camiknickers he had given her that morning.

'It was a good day, wasn't it?' she said, smoothing his hair back.

'Yeah.' He peered under her arm to watch the screen. 'Yeah, you cooked a good lunch.'

'Not bad for a first attempt.' She smiled at him, then leaned forward to kiss his neck and began to unbutton his shirt. She traced a wet line down his chest with her tongue, then she knelt on the floor, unzipping his jeans. With his eyes still fixed to the screen, he put his hands on her shoulders and pushed her gently away.

'What's wrong?' she asked, her eyes filling with tears again.

It feels as if you're doing it in return for me giving up the bike, he wanted to say.

'I don't feel like it,' he told her.

'OK.' She joined him on the sofa, trying to look as if it didn't matter. 'I think Anouska liked the wrapping paper better than everything else,' she said, attempting to make neutral conversation.

'Yeah.'

'Are you cross about my job?'

'No.'

'I love you, Neil,' she said, snuggling down beside him.

'Yeah, I love you too,' he said, relaxing a little, planting a kiss in her sweet-smelling hair.

'Will you marry me, then?' she asked.

It was the kind of last-ditch desperation to make everything all right on Christmas Day. He thought of all the times he had asked her the same question, when she had asked why change something perfect. And now it wasn't perfect, but he instinctively knew that getting married would not fix it.

'If that's what you want,' he replied eventually.

'No,' she said, quietly, 'you had to think about it. You wouldn't have done before.'

Then she started crying again, but this time they were sad tears, wrenching her. He let her sob into his chest, stroking her, trying to find the right words to comfort her.

'Let's talk about it in the morning,' he said.

It was New Year's Eve.

The moment Alison carefully withdrew her hand from the cot, inching it away in case he sensed the slightest disturbance, and started to tiptoe towards the door, the phone rang. Ben woke up and began to scream. She picked him up and took him to their bedroom. As soon as he was in her arms he fell back to sleep.

'I'm sorry, were you in the middle of something?' Stephen asked.

'I'd just got him off to sleep,' Alison said, the fury and frustration making her voice flat and cold.

'Oh dear . . . Sorry, my love.'

'How are you getting on?' she asked him, her voice softening a little.

'I'm fine, but how are you?'

'Desperate . . .'

'Oh dear,' he said sadly. 'How are you going to see the New Year in?'

'Oh, I thought I'd go to the ball at the Savoy . . . How do you bloody think?'

'I'm sorry,' he said again. 'Why don't you go over to Lia's?'

'I doubt if they would appreciate Ben's screaming,' she said.

'He'd probably fall asleep in the car. He did before.'

'I love you,' she said, suddenly really missing him.

'I love you too,' he told her. 'Happy New Year!'

She stood up and walked back into the nursery, lowering Ben almost imperceptibly slowly into his cot. The moment his face touched the cold sheet, he woke again.

'Go to sleep, my darling,' she whispered, stroking his head.

His roars sliced through the cocoon of calm the conversation with Stephen had spun round her.

'Go to sleep, please.' Her voice became pleading, then, 'Oh, SHUT UP!' she screamed, as loudly as the baby.

It was no good. She walked out of the nursery, trying to collect herself. Maybe Stephen's idea about the car wasn't so stupid. The only reason against going to Lia's was the sense of panic she experienced whenever she saw Neil, but that was ridiculous. They were both adults with jobs and responsibilities, both in happy relationships with partners who suited them. Without further ado, she picked up the telephone.

'Hello?' Neil answered the phone.

'Oh hi! It's Alison, um . . .'

'I'll get Lia.'

'No, wait,' she said, determined to give him the chance to put her off. 'I've got a baby that won't sleep and I'm going mad. I know it's late, but Lia said—'

'Yeah, come round. She'll be glad of the company. I'm off up to the cricket club for a drink. We tossed for who went out,' he said, sounding unusually cheerful.

'OK then,' she said, putting down the phone.

**N**eil nursed his pint of beer. On the way over to the club he had weighed up the advantages of having two pints of shandy as opposed to one pint of bitter, but decided you couldn't go out on New Year's Eve and not have a proper drink. He was pleased that Alison had rung. Now he could relax and not feel bad about leaving Lia on her own.

He would be glad to see the back of this year. Towards the end, as the days grew shorter and shorter, it had begun to feel as if the world were closing in around him. He had looked at Lia and not recognised her. When he met her, she had been something natural, ethereal, more sprite than human being; now, as he watched her endlessly shopping for Christmas, and cooking, and preparing the house, she seemed solid and materialistic, like a housewife. She always seemed to slop around in leggings and large sweaters. And she was always crying. Neither of them had referred to the conversation they had had on Christmas night, but it was there, unspoken in the air. He had been relieved to escape.

He finished his pint, feeling the scrape of bitterness in his throat. It made him want to smoke. He changed a note for coins at the bar and went to the machine.

His friends were swapping resolutions. Drink less, give up smoking, jog. He realised that he had spent nearly all New Year's Eves in the last twenty-five years in sports clubs like this one, having the same conversations. And this year he would be forty. It was a pretty depressing thought.

Tomorrow it will be different, he promised himself as he drove through the deserted streets. A new year and a new life. Maybe he and Lia had made a mistake having a child so soon. But it had happened. It had seemed right at the time, and now they were stuck with it. They couldn't go back to how it was before so they might as well make the best of after.

Lia and Alison were watching a video of *When Harry Met Sally*. It was a film about two people who meet when they are very young and meet again years later and fall in love. No, it wasn't really, Alison thought, taking a paper handkerchief from the box that Lia offered her; it was really a film about being with the right person and refusing to believe it.

Lia flicked to BBC1 just in time for the last three chimes of Big Ben. A cheer went up in the studio and the presenter started singing 'Auld Lang Syne'. Lia and Alison exchanged embarrassed glances, then got up, held hands and joined in. By the end of the song, they were both laughing.

'Happy New Year!' They kissed each other on the cheek.

Then Lia went up to check on the babies.

Alison settled down into the sofa, half watching the television, and was startled by the sound of Neil's key in the lock.

'Happy New Year!'

'Yeah. Happy New Year!'

Clearly he hadn't expected her still to be there.

He bent forward hesitantly. They both turned their faces at the same moment, making the kiss intended for her cheek land awkwardly against the side of her mouth. He jumped back and her lip felt as if it had been stung by a bee.

'Lia's upstairs,' she told him, determinedly staring at the television.

He took the stairs two by two, and she sat feeling utterly helpless as she tried not to hear them embrace. She decided the best thing to do would be to get the car warmed up and take Ben home as soon as they came downstairs. She went outside, let herself into her car and put the key in the ignition. Nothing.

They were both downstairs again when she went back in, and Neil was about to open a bottle of champagne.

'My battery's flat,' she announced.

'I'll give you a lift,' he offered immediately, clearly as anxious as she was for her to go.

'Oh, right, well, if you're sure . . .' she agreed hastily. 'I'll just get Ben.'

Neil drove fast, as she had known he would.

'Made any resolutions?' he asked politely, as they turned into her road, breaking the silence.

'Yes,' she replied, looking at him, 'to stop thinking about you, and what might have been.' She tried to make it sound as if she were joking.

His face betrayed nothing.

Calmly, he pulled the car into her drive and switched off the engine.

'Ally, don't . . .' he said, staring straight ahead.

In the darkness, she sensed his hand searching for hers, and when their fingers touched, it was as if all the pain and joy she had ever felt gathered into one great wave that broke over her body, drenching her with emotion.

He shifted, just an infinitesimally slight movement towards her, and she fell against his chest, shaking. His fingers tentatively smoothed her hair away from her wet face.

She did not know how long she wept.

Eventually, as her breathing began to quieten, she drew away. But as she lifted her head to say goodbye, his grasp became firmer.

He dipped his head and his lips found hers as easily and naturally as they had ever done. His mouth pushed against hers, his tongue coaxing, finding the softest, most tender place just inside her lips, pausing there, tasting, pressing harder, more urgently.

She opened her eyes and saw that his were closed, concentrating, as if he were searching for memories inside her. Her body turned to liquid.

'Come in,' she whispered.

'No,' he said, sitting up and starting the engine, as if her words had woken him up from a dream.

His eyes were pleading with her to be strong. Go. Now.

She released her door, got out, wrenching her spine in her haste to get Ben in his car seat out of the back.

Then he reversed onto the road and roared away.

## January

THE CALL, WHEN IT CAME, was as she had expected, although she had not expected him to find out her work number.

'We have to talk.'

'Can you meet me tomorrow?'

'Where?'

She told him.

He was sitting on the steps, reading the *Evening Standard*. She was late, but he did not look up as she turned into the street.

'It's the basement,' she said, taking out a set of keys. He followed her down the narrow wrought-iron steps.

'What is this?' he asked, looking round the room.

'It's my flat,' she said. 'My tenant left early.'

'Nice,' he said, taking in the bright pine furniture and Impressionist posters she had once loved.

'Shall I take your coat?'

'Not yet,' he said, clasping the open edges of his leather jacket together. 'It's colder in here than out.'

'I'll make some coffee,' she said.

She opened up her bag and took out a small jar of Nescafé and a tin of dried milk she had bought at lunchtime. She found mugs in the cupboard over the sink.

'Don't!' He was suddenly behind her, so close that she could feel his breathing, though not touching her.

She turned round, and they stared at each other. Suddenly, they were on the floor, wrestling for access to each other's skin, through the layers of winter clothing, on the freezing cold tiles. He was all zips, she laces. He gave up trying to remove her boots, throwing her backwards, her skull cracking hard against the floor, her head swimming with pain and lust. She heard his intake of breath as he found fragile silk underwear that tore with a rasp as he tugged it to one side and plunged himself into her. He felt huge inside her, the top of his penis banging mercilessly against the neck of her womb. She imagined her insides, raw and red, as if every nerve in her body led there, carrying all the pain and pleasure to a single point. Then the hot, soothing wash of his sperm pouring into her and his body sagging onto her, as if he had been gunned down. When he lifted his head, she saw the pale blue irises, that looked as if they had been outlined with brown pencil, and she felt the drip of his tears on her cheek.

'We have to talk,' he said, helplessly.

She put an index finger against his lips.

They stared at each other for a few more seconds, then she wriggled out from under him, stood up and held out her hand. She led him to the bedroom.

'Shouldn't we . . .?' He pulled out a pack of Durex from his pocket. 'I bought them today. I don't make a habit of this.'

'I can't get pregnant,' she told him. 'Not by natural means, anyway, so you don't have to worry.' She enunciated the difficult words staccato, not looking at him as she took off her clothes.

Jumping under the duvet, she watched the methodical way he folded his trousers over the back of a chair, rolled his socks together, hung his shirt on a hanger.

His body was a sportsman's body, firm, with strong muscles in his back and legs. It was bigger than she remembered. The way he stood at the foot of the bed, with no clothes on, was endearingly awkward.

She pulled back the duvet, like a bird offering shelter under her wing. He climbed in beside her. They lay on their backs.

'What did you think when you first saw me?' Alison asked.

'That you'd cut your hair, and you were thin.'

'But I was eight months pregnant!' she exclaimed.

'But you looked like a thin person who was pregnant.'

'So I used to be fat?' she protested.

'No . . . you just weren't what I'd call really thin.'

He had never been able to turn a compliment, she remembered fondly.

'What did you think, then?' he asked her.

'I thought, Of all the antenatal classes, in all the middle-class suburbs, he had to walk into mine . . .'

He laughed. 'Yeah, that's about it,' he said, then turned his face to look at hers, and kissed her slowly.

She climbed onto him, lay still for a moment, sat up, straddling his thighs and bent her head to lick his penis. He writhed under her, almost unable to bear the pleasure until the moment she knelt up hovering over him and he grabbed her bottom and pulled her down onto him, arching his back, thrusting into her as if to break her in half. She screamed. He stopped, alarmed.

'No, it's all right,' she said. 'Please, please go on.'

He smiled, wickedly, taking control, rolling her onto her back again gently, his large hands tracing soft circles on the inner part of her thighs. She squirmed with gloriously sensual pleasure.

'Please . . .' she said, staring at him with wide-open, sex-drugged eyes, but he would not be hurried.

His fingers flicked over her clitoris, almost accidentally, and then settled there and began to rub very slowly.

'Oh, please,' she moaned.

'You really want to come, don't you?'

'Yes,' she whimpered, feeling the flood of juices in her vagina as he spoke to her.

He put his finger there, in the wetness, then went back to her clitoris.

'Oh God!' she said, feeling the rise of orgasm. 'Please!'

She closed her eyes and began to fantasise. She was lying on the grass that hot, dry summer of 1976, and Neil was on top of her, thrusting in and out. She could see his face, the pink determination to come, and suddenly she was coming too, fantasy blending with reality, a perfect sexual alchemy, that left her reeling and shaking with shock.

Afterwards, she could not stop kissing him, wanting to touch every inch of his body and make it hers again, then, suddenly exhausted, she fell back into the pillows, and listened, when her breathing had slowed, to the distant sounds and muffled notes from the piano in the room above their heads.

*A tinkling piano in the next apartment . . .*

'I must go,' he said eventually.

'We didn't talk,' she said.

'No,' he said simply.

**A**s she locked up the flat, Friedrich, the ancient pianist who lived above, was tottering at the top of the steps on his way out

'My dear! How lovely!' His old face lit up as he recognised her, an inquisitive frown playing over his wizened old features. Friedrich was the area's own Neighbourhood Watch scheme.

'My tenant has moved out,' Alison improvised, 'and I'm going to have a bit of work done.'

'So, you had a man to give you—how do you say it?' He searched for the word.

'An estimate.' Alison filled it in for him.

'Yes, an estimate,' he agreed.

Was his English really still so bad, or was it his way of trying to tell her that sounds travelled both ways? She was feeling so happy she felt she could deal with anything.

'Yes,' she said, blithely, 'he may be around a lot. It was lovely to see you,' she added, and she walked off feeling as if she were playing a part in a film. The script was written: she had not read it, but she seemed to know the lines; the cameras were rolling, and she did not know when the director would shout, 'Cut.'

**'T**hat was delicious,' Neil said, eating the last of the lasagne straight from the Pyrex dish. 'Here, I'll do that,' he added, seeing that Lia was starting the washing-up. 'Really, you sit down, you must be tired.'

She was too exhausted to protest.

'It was a long day,' she admitted, pouring out a cup of tea and sitting down with it at the kitchen table.

Was this the prelude to her asking why he had been late? He felt guilt extruding from every pore. He plunged both hands into the hot water, trying to wash away the stain of sin.

'But then it was a long day for Ginger too . . .' she went on. 'She's going to ask whether she could start earlier and finish earlier, which would mean she had more time with Guy in the evening . . .' Lia chattered on, unaware of his anguish.

'Really?' He encouraged her to talk, not trusting himself to.

'Poor Ginger, her boss sounds so horrible, although apparently there's a possibility that Ginger could get a better job, but it involves meeting the man she had the affair with.'

Again, he began to tremble inside. 'What do you think of her screwing someone who was married?'

'Oh, he's not married.'

'Well, attached, then?' he said, bracing himself.

'Do you mean, do I think it was right?' she asked, pleasantly surprised at his interest. 'I don't think it's her problem, morally. He's the one with the girlfriend.'

Had he really hoped that she was going to give him a kind of indirect absolution? he wondered, trying to get a grip on himself, scouring the Pyrex dish vigorously with wire wool.

'It's OK,' Lia said, unable to bear the grating sound of metal on glass. 'Leave it to soak. I'll do it later.'

'No, you relax. Turn on some music or something.'

She began to protest, then stopped. It was no good complaining he didn't help if she wouldn't let him.

Later, as he lay in the bath, he could hear Lia singing to Anouska as she fed her before putting her down for the night.

He closed his eyes and remembered Alison's face lit by joy. She looked so strong and determined, and yet underneath she was as soft as clay. It was a devastatingly attractive combination. He wondered if others saw the vulnerability beneath the hostile expression she had when she was frightened. Did anyone else dare to ruffle her sleek hair? Suddenly he was wrenched by jealousy for every man who had ever touched her.

Alison was lying in the conservatory listening to her LP of *Hotel California* knowing that any minute the euphoria must come to an end and the guilt take hold. She tried to think of Lia. She was a friend, and she could not do this to her. But she was not able to associate Lia with anything that had happened. It felt as if she had reclaimed something that was hers.

The sound of Stephen's key in the lock made her jump up and switch off the turntable. By the time he had hung up his coat she was filling a kettle at the sink.

'You look well,' Stephen said, as she turned to greet him.

'Do I?' She frowned.

'Positively glowing,' he said. 'You look as if you've been for a long country walk in the cold! Making tea?'

She looked at the kettle in her hand, as if surprised by its presence. She had grabbed the nearest thing, so that he wouldn't see how her hands were shaking.

'Would you like some?' she asked.

'I think I'd prefer a gin and tonic,' he said, wandering through into the sitting area.

'I'll make you one. You sit down. Bad day?' She busied herself slicing a lemon, clinking ice into long glasses.

'The usual,' he said.

It was as much as she ever heard about his work. She had come to realise that he needed his own mechanisms to get over the stress of his job, and talking only made it worse for him.

She sat down opposite him and said breezily, 'I decided to go to the flat. I think I'll have some work done on it.'

'Right . . .' He paused, then added encouragingly, 'Good!'

She smiled at him.

'We could always move back into London, you know,' he said, seeing how her excursion had invigorated her.

'After all the work I've done to get this house in order? I don't think so. Not now,' she said.

'I've been wondering,' he went on, 'how you would feel about a much bigger move, actually.'

She looked up, startled.

'In New York the other day, I was offered a visiting chair, with a view to tenure, I think.'

'You've let a week go by without bothering to tell me?' Alison fired back at him, barely able to contain her surprise.

'We haven't really seen much of each other . . .'

'And whose fault is that?'

'I know, I'm sorry. Look, we'll discuss it another time.'

'I'm not a computer, you know, you can't just diarise me so that I pop up when it may be convenient for you to have a conversation,' she said angrily.

'OK, OK.' He was furious with himself for handling things so badly.

He had not understood the extent of the resentment that had been festering like an abscess, ready to discharge its poison when touched.

It had been an indulgence to go to the seminar, he realised, and he should not have succumbed to it. She had needed his support and he had let her down by overloading her. Now, his suggestion that they move back into town, offered with her interests at heart, appeared like a palliative designed to soften her up for the discussion he had wanted to have about his career, her career, the future. He kicked himself for his insensitivity.

'Well, I've got some things to do,' she said, getting up and leaving the room, despising herself for her tantrum, unable to comprehend the way she had manipulated the argument in order to make him the guilty party. Later, she lay in bed, her back to Stephen, pretending to sleep. Her body was so tense she felt it would snap if he touched her, but he seemed to know, and didn't. She closed her eyes, trying to wipe out the memory she had suppressed for twenty years.

'We're going to move,' her mother had told her, the morning after she had returned from the clinic, sitting down on her bed, as she did when she wanted a confidential chat. 'Daddy wants to retire early and we've bought a house in Rutington, near Littlehampton.'

'When?' Alison had asked, feeling as if all her blood had drained away.

'As soon as possible,' her mother replied, staring out of the window. 'You'll be away at college during the term, after all, and it will be nice for you to have holidays by the sea.'

'I don't want to,' Alison said, like a spoilt ten-year-old.

'Yes, but it's not really up to you, is it?' There was a threatening edge to her mother's voice.

'No, I suppose not,' she admitted, defeated.

She knew why they were leaving. Ever since she had started going out with Neil, her mother had made her disapproval transparently clear. She had wheedled and undermined for two years, and in the end she finally had the reason to insist that she no longer see him. Margaret was so determined to make their separation stick she was even prepared to move. Alison turned towards the wall and stared at the wallpaper, until she heard her mother leave. Then tears began to fall.

Now she would not let anyone take Neil away from her. Not now she had found him again.

'It's lovely to see you,' Charlie Prince said, kissing the air near each cheek, and showing his lunch-date where to hand in her jacket.

The girl on the desk held the coat a long way from her, as if it were contaminated, and handed Ginger a ticket.

'Did you cycle?' Charlie asked unnecessarily, as Ginger also handed her back bike wheel over the counter.

'Yeah, sorry about that, but I've had two nicked before.'

'Right,' Charlie said uncertainly, adding, to return to territory he was more used to discussing, 'So why did you want to come here?'

'I've read about it. It's had good write-ups.'

The restaurant was modish and fun, and it was the most expensive place that had sprung to mind when Charlie had surprised her by calling on her first day back at the office.

They sat down and listened patiently as the waitress told them about the specials. Ginger had it in mind to choose the most expensive dish, whatever that was, reasoning—unfairly, she knew—that she was saving Charlie hundreds of pounds each month by not giving his name to the Child Support Agency.

She was finding it difficult to look at his face; there were so many similarities with Guy's that she kept having to stop herself planting a kiss on his cheek.

'So how's the Beeb?' he said, after giving the waitress their order.

'I've only been back a week,' she said, noncommittally.

She had promised herself she would not talk about work or Guy, but now she wondered how she was going to get through the next hour, because there was nothing else in her life. She had not been to the theatre, a film, or even hired a video, for months. She had not had the energy or concentration even to read a book or a newspaper. Her idea of a rewarding weekend had become one where she managed to do all the washing and get it dry by Sunday night. She liked her new life, but, God, was it boring for anyone else to hear about.

She looked up and saw Charlie waiting for her to continue.

'Well, it pays the bills,' Ginger replied.

'Why don't you come and work for me?' Charlie asked, almost plaintively, as if it was something they had been talking about for ages.

'Well, you haven't asked,' Ginger replied cautiously.

'I'm sure I have,' he said. 'I've certainly wanted to, but I have had the strangest sense that you've been avoiding me.'

'Really?'

She wished she had not ordered oysters. It was going to be impossible to maintain dignity and eat them. She squeezed the lemon over them carefully, playing for time.

'Can I try one?' Charlie asked, as if sensing her distress.

'Go ahead,' she said, taking one after him, and tipping it down her throat at the same time as he did.

It was a sweet gesture, like holding her hand to negotiate a tricky step.

'In what capacity would you want me to work for you, anyway?' she asked, trying to pick up the conversation.

'In what *capacity*?' Charlie repeated, clearly hearing the same potential for innuendo as she had.

'Hmm,' Ginger said, 'to put it another way—what have I got that you want? God, that sounds even worse!'

'Listen, Ginger,' Charlie said, his face suddenly serious, 'this isn't an elaborate pick-up. We had sex once. I enjoyed myself. I hope you did, too'—he left no time for her even to nod—'but I'm not interested in your body. I'm interested in what's in your head. You have great ideas, and anyone who can stand up to a professional Tory bitch like you did on television should not be stuck in a rut—'

'Oh well, that was just because I'm a loudmouth,' Ginger interrupted, trying to get some space to understand everything he was saying. She couldn't stop herself thinking, What's wrong with my body?

'No, you have a gift for commercial ideas,' Charlie went on. 'A kind of common touch, if you like, that is very rare. I remember you telling me about a show you had come up with, and I thought no, it'll never work, but we've worked it up, developed it, just had the OK for a pilot. I wanted to thank you.'

'My idea?' Ginger said, putting down her last oyster, feeling that she would choke on it.

'Yeah, that food-quiz game-show thing, *One Man's Meat*, I think was your name for it. We've gone for *If You Can't Stand the Heat*, which sounds hipper, less carnivorous, but the idea was all yours and the broadcasters love it.' He looked triumphant.

'And what do I get out of it?'

'Well, no copyright on ideas, darling, but I'd love to pay you to come up with more.'

'You really are an arrogant shit,' Ginger told him.

'Fish and chips,' said the waitress, lowering a large white plate, 'and the lobster. Anything else you need?'

'No, thank you, we're fine.' Charlie dismissed the waitress.

'Did you really think that I would be so flattered by your stealing my ideas that I would come and work for you?' Ginger said. 'I'm sorry, but I'm not quite as stupid as I look . . . and,' she said, standing up and throwing her napkin down, 'you can stuff your lobster.'

She turned and walked towards the door. The passageway seemed endless and she began to feel as if she was walking in slow motion. She reached the desk and retrieved her jacket and bike wheel with as much insouciance as she could muster, and turned to the revolving door, but, at the last hurdle, she was defeated. The bloody door was stuck. As she swung her hand back to hit it in frustration, she felt him catch her arm.

'I'm prepared to pay for an uneaten lobster,' he said, 'but not for a glass door smashed by a bike wheel. You're pushing the wrong bit.'

Instantly, she saw her mistake. 'Oh, thanks.' Her anger evaporated.

'You are wonderfully primitive,' he told her outside.

'That must be where I get my "common touch",' she said.

'Look, I seem to have made a complete hash of this,' Charlie admitted. 'Could we start again?'

She thought of the lobster sitting on her plate, and the crackers beside it, and she could not face wrestling with it. She had won some kind of battle with Charlie. To re-enter the restaurant with him now would make her completely justified anger look like a tantrum.

'I don't want to work for you, Charlie,' she said. 'So I don't think there's much point.'

'But why?'

'It just wouldn't work. I'm sorry,' she added, rather liking the sense of power his mortified look was giving her.

'Well, call me if you change your mind,' he said.

'**W**ell,' said Robert later that afternoon, 'just don't ever moan to me again about your job.'

'Actually,' Ginger said, the confrontation with Charlie having given her a strange kind of confidence, 'it's you that is always complaining to me about my lack of ambition, how I've ruined my life. Anyway, I've got to go,' she said, putting down the phone as she noticed the woman from reception entering her office. She was holding an enormous bunch of multicoloured balloons. Red, blue, green, purple, gold and silver, shiny round cushions of helium, their long narrow gold ribbons were attached to a miniature straw basket out of which peeped a white envelope.

'They were just delivered, so I brought them up,' the receptionist explained, smiling.

The envelope contained a cheque for £500 and a card. *This is an ex-gratia payment for your help with the programme,* Ginger read. *Take care, Charlie.*

'But why balloons?' Pic asked her later that evening, when Ginger phoned excitedly to tell her the day's events.

'Perhaps he thought I was more a balloons kind of person than a flowers kind of person,' Ginger replied. 'He's right as a matter of fact.'

'How on earth did you get them home?' Pic asked her, ever concerned about the practicalities.

'I tied them under the saddle. I think people thought I was advertising a circus or something,' Ginger said.

'You can't possibly accept the money, of course,' Pic went on.

'I've already banked it.'

'Ginger!'

'I shall spend it exclusively on Guy. I thought about it and I realised it would be quite wrong of me, as a mother, to send the money back,' she added firmly.

'Have you thanked him?' Pic asked.

'No, not yet. I wanted to calm down a bit. I want to sound pleased, but not too pleased, you know.'

'Honestly . . .'

'Anyway,' Ginger said, wanting to change the subject, 'have you thought about our birthday yet?'

'It's not for ages.'

'No, but we ought to organise something special. Why don't we go out, just the two of us? We could go to the ballet, and have supper after.'

'OK. Let's do that. It would be lovely to have an evening, just us.'

These days they hardly ever seemed to talk about Pic, Ginger realised as she put down the phone. It was always Guy, or Ginger's problems with work, or men, and when Ginger remembered to ask Pic how she was getting on, Guy would often start demanding her attention. Next time, she promised herself, she would make sure she gave her sister time to talk.

'I have discovered the reason diets never work,' Ramona said, leaning across the desk, as if she were about to reveal a secret of international importance. 'Apparently, mass always remains constant, so I've worked out that if someone loses two pounds, it has to go somewhere, and it usually decides to go to my thighs.'

Alison laughed a little, unwilling to encourage Ramona, who had obviously finished for the day and was in a chatty mood..

'You've lost weight recently,' Ramona observed.

'Have I?' Alison continued to look at her screen. 'Oh . . .'

Ramona tried another tactic. 'Are you coming to Bill's leaving party?'

'No, look, I've got to finish this, and then I've got to run. I'm having some work done on the flat. I'm meeting someone there.' She had said the words several times now and they didn't sound like a lie any more. 'Will you say I'm really sorry?' she added.

**S**he was late, but he had waited in the pub on the corner of the street. She had only just taken her coat off when he knocked at the door.

He offered no greeting as he stepped forward and pulled her against him. She drank the taste of beer and cigarettes from his mouth.

He pushed her against the dining table, tipping her back from the waist. She lay still, her head in the middle of the table, feet on the floor. He dropped slowly to his knees, pushed up her short skirt and nudged his head between her legs, tracing the tops of her stockings with his tongue, his nose grazing the loose silk of her French knickers. Her feet came off the floor the moment he began to suck her. She began to climax almost immediately, her legs locking themselves around his neck. His hands prised her thighs away from his ears, pushing them so far apart she felt the skin at the top of her legs stretching. Then she heard the rip of his zipper, then the iron-hard mass of his penis splitting her in two, and she could not believe she could bear so much pleasure, and still live.

Afterwards, he lay on top of her, for a long time, until she could bear his weight no longer and she asked him softly to stand up.

'What the hell are we going to do?' he said.

'I don't know,' she replied, standing up and smoothing her skirt down.

'I love you,' he said quietly.

'I've always loved you,' she told him, holding out her arms. 'Always.'

They held on to each other, both terrified of being the first to let go.

'**N**O, WATCH DADDY,' Neil told his daughter, trying to demonstrate crawling. In slow motion he lifted one hand, then a knee, making gradual progress across the carpet. Anouska lay on her stomach watching him with an amazed look on her face. 'Push up with your hands, like this,' he said, as if he were teaching an eleven-year-old pupil to use the gym.

Anouska giggled.

'I thought they were supposed to imitate,' he said to Lia, who was watching.

It was as if he had finally understood that the more you put into

Anouska the more rewarding she became. She could see that he was beginning to enjoy the baby. She wondered if the change had anything to do with selling his motorbike. It was as if he had relinquished the part of him that hankered for the days of freedom before they had the baby, and accepted that his life was different.

It was nice playing happy families, but they didn't get enough time together, she thought, wondering what they could do about that. His school was due for an Ofsted inspection and all the additional work of preparing for that meant he often came home from work very late. Now that she was working too, they were usually both too tired to talk much or relax together on their own.

'Can we afford a holiday this year?' she suddenly asked him.

He looked up, smiling. 'I wondered why there suddenly seemed to be brochures everywhere.'

'Well, they're free, and they've got lovely pictures, so I thought they'd be good for her to tear to shreds . . .'

It made him feel terrible that she felt she had to explain why she had picked up the brochures.

'You don't have to justify everything,' he told her gently. 'We're doing OK now. Thank God for Ginger!'

Lia beamed. It was the first time he had acknowledged that her job had been a good idea. Perhaps things were also getting better because she was contributing to the housekeeping. It must have been a strain for him. She hadn't really considered the extra pressure he was under, having to provide for all three of them.

'So can we?' she asked him, excitedly.

'Go on holiday? Why not?' he said, feeling even more guilty as he saw how happy the simplest of sentences could make her. 'At half-term maybe? For a week?'

'Shall we go to Portugal? Back to the village? We could get a self-catering package.'

'Yeah, all right,' he said, not certain that he wanted to return to the place they had met, but not sure why not.

'I'll make some enquiries then.'

'Book if you find what you want.' He smiled at her, getting up from the floor. 'Look, do you mind if I pop up to the club? There's a bloke there who says he'll restring my tennis racket.'

'Of course not,' Lia replied. 'Do you think you'll want supper?'

'How about if I bring back some fish and chips?' he offered.

'Great!' she said.

He walked towards the door.

'Neil?' she said, just as he was about to open the front door.

He turned round quickly. 'Yes?'

'Your racket.' She pointed at his sports bag.

'Right,' he said, snatching it up.

**H**e could not understand how some people could lie all the time and still carry on as normal. One lie led to another, and before you knew where you were you had created another world. All he wanted to do was make a phone call, but now, even though his racket didn't need string-ing, he thought he'd better get it done. It was ironic, because the phone call he was going out to make would end it. It had to stop. His place was with Lia and the baby. He was not a liar.

The phone was situated in the passage to the toilets. Shaking, he took out a packet of cigarettes, lit one and picked up the phone.

'She's not here at the moment,' a young female voice told him. 'Can I give her a message?'

'No thanks,' he said quickly, and put down the receiver.

**T**he next time they met was a Saturday afternoon. She had put a new cover on the duvet, the folds still stiff.

'Do you like it?' she asked him, tucking herself under the crook of his elbow.

'It's OK,' he said bluntly, an alarm ringing in his head.

There could be no building of nests. There could be no relationship, affair, whatever it was, he reminded himself. But when he looked down at her face and saw that he had hurt her by his abrupt dismissal of the new duvet cover, he knew that it wasn't possible. He could not stop loving her.

'How did you get away?' he asked.

'I offered Justine Valentine's Night in exchange for this afternoon. What about you?'

'They're out with Ginger . . . at the zoo,' he stuttered, unable to say Lia's name. 'I wasn't invited. She knows I can't stand Ginger.'

'Can't you?' She turned over onto her front, as if about to enjoy a good gossip. 'I like her. She's open, direct, really honest . . .' She stopped as she realised what she was saying.

'Qualities you admire?' he asked, sarcasm in his voice.

'Don't . . .'

'We can't do this, you know,' he told her, turning away from her onto his side. It was easier if he couldn't see her.

'Talk about them?'

'Yes. It's wrong.'

'So is ringing me at home,' she said.

'How did you know?'

'Justine said someone had called.'

He had meant that they could not go on seeing each other, but she had twisted the conversation.

'Alison.' He turned back over and gazed at her face.

He never called her Alison. She knew what was coming.

'We can't do this,' he said quietly.

'I know,' she said, her eyes filling with tears.

'Do you believe me?' he asked.

She shook her head, her face scrunched up in an effort not to cry. He wrapped his arms round her and she sobbed against his shoulder.

They made love again, slowly, with exquisite tenderness, as if they were bruised and trying not to cause each other further pain.

Later, Alison lay dazed, with no idea whether they had slept or what the time was.

'Do you remember the youth club?' she said suddenly.

'Which one?' he asked.

'The Catholic one . . . Do you think they were trying to convert us?'

She leaned out of bed to pull her handbag alongside, then extracted a packet of ten Marlboro.

'Didn't work,' he said with a grim chuckle. 'I'd only just gone to the trouble of lapsing. Here, give us one . . .'

She handed one over, lighting it for him. When they first smoked, she remembered, he would always light hers from his, inhaling in small puffs as the tobacco caught and glowed. It was one of those teenage rituals that had been *de rigueur* when you were going out with someone.

'All we seemed to do was take it in turns to snog in that big dilapidated armchair,' she mused, lying back.

'We played a bit of pool too, while we were queuing for the chair,' he laughed.

'You were good at pool. I remember you beating that bloke with the moustache. What was his name? The one who just appeared in town on his motorbike . . .'

'Tim?'

'Yeah, that's it,' she said, delighted. 'His name must have been the second-most-scrawled on desks.'

'Yeah? Who was the first then?' he asked.

'You *are* kidding?' She rolled over onto her tummy again and looked at him, searching his face.

'No.' Clearly, he didn't know.

'You, of course,' she told him.

'You carved my name on a desk?' he asked, astonished.

'I was the envy of the school because I was with you. Nobody could understand how I had got you . . . I couldn't either,' she admitted.

'But you were lovely—'

'Were?' she said instantly.

The insecurity was so close to the smooth surface you could practically touch it, he thought.

'Yes. Now, you are'—he searched for the right word—'beautiful.'

'So, I've improved with age? Like a cheese?'

'No . . . yes . . .' He was confused by the quickness of her retort. He hated it when she turned things round.

They finished their cigarettes in silence. The room was dark now, but she had no desire to switch on a light.

'Do you remember what album was playing the first time we danced?' she asked him softly, snuggling down beside him, shifting one of her legs between his legs.

'Bryan Ferry. "These Foolish Things",' he murmured distractedly, lifting her hips as if she weighed nothing and sliding her vagina over his erection as effortlessly as putting on a glove.

'You remembered!' she said, gasping with delight.

'Well, you told me enough times,' he said, the glitter of mockery in his eyes.

She closed her eyes, trying to commit to her memory all the sensations of this moment now, joined to him, completed by him.

'What are we going to do?' he whispered to her after.

'Pray?' she suggested, trembling.

'I'm lapsed, remember?' he said.

She nodded, but inside she was saying the prayer of the desperate.

*Dear God, if you make it all right, I promise I will truly believe in you and never do anything bad again.*

It was Valentine's Day and there were two envelopes on the doormat. One was yellow. The address was written in spindly capital letters in an unsuccessful attempt to disguise Pic's handwriting. The other was a small white Jiffy bag which had a printed address label. Ginger opened the yellow envelope first. Inside the message was 'I love you' with a G underneath.

'Thank you, my sweetie-pie,' Ginger said, planting a kiss on top of Guy's head. 'Look, it's the Valentine you asked your auntie to send me,' she added, giving him the card.

She tore open the white parcel and withdrew, to her surprise, a handmade card, with a red velvet heart and various bits of dried flowers and lace and stuff stuck on in a kind of collage. A few of the elements were badly glued and fell onto the carpet. It was the kind of card that cost a fortune in an expensive boutique in Covent Garden market. It was pretty, Ginger thought, opening it to find that the inside was blank. She guessed it was from Robert, since he had been known to make the occasional thoughtful gesture, he worked in Covent Garden, and he no doubt assumed that she wouldn't be getting any Valentines this year.

'But he didn't realise that you had already sent me one, did he?' Ginger said, kissing Guy's head again.

A car horn beeped twice outside.

'Come on, mister,' Ginger said, forcing Guy's reluctant arms into his jacket. 'Mummy is going to work and Guy is going to play with Lia and Anouska.'

The bit of the day she found hardest was when Lia waved and pulled away, and she went back inside to get her bike.

The front wheel crunched on something as she pushed the bike to the door. She looked down to see that one of the bits that had fallen from the card had been crushed under it. It looked like a piece of painted shell. She pushed the smithereens around with the toe of her boot so that they blended in with the general debris on the carpet.

Lia had been into several kitchen departments, but nobody had what she was looking for. Eventually she found one, in a packet of Christmas shapes reduced to half-price. She had to buy the whole set, but it was worth it. She wanted to do something special. A card didn't seem enough after the enormous bunch of roses he had hidden in the shed overnight. A dozen, tightly furled velvety red blooms, they were the most beautiful flowers she had ever been given. And it was odd, because she had never been so sure she would only get a card. Neil had been complaining about the commercialisation of Valentine's Day since the first heart motifs appeared in the shops.

Alison knew that she shouldn't be disappointed, but she couldn't help it. Throughout the day flowers had been arriving, and she tried to keep her eyes from glancing up whenever the rustle of cellophane announced another entrance, but it was impossible.

'Perhaps Stephen's bought you something,' Ramona said, seeing the disappointment on her colleague's face.

'Oh, probably, if he's remembered. He usually does,' Alison replied, flicking her eyes back to the computer.

She left the office at five o'clock and stood on the pavement, trying to decide which direction to walk in. She could just pop to the flat, just to see . . . No. She would only be disappointed.

She walked towards the bus stop, hoping a bus would come along straight away and whisk her in the opposite direction. It didn't. Two free taxis went past, before her will let her down. Then, having decided that she would take the next one, there were none. If there isn't one within five minutes, it was not meant to be, she told herself. As she looked up again, a black cab pulled into view and her arm shot in the air.

There was no post in the flat. Serves me right, she thought, making a quick check of the rooms, her eyes lingering wistfully on the bed, the duvet cover thrown back as they had left it. She was going to be late, she realised, pulling herself together and switching off the light. In the darkness, she noticed that the answerphone was blinking.

The loud electronic beep in the stillness of the room made her jump. There was an embarrassed throat clearance, and then his voice whispering, 'Well, here goes,' and he began to sing. '*Oh, will you never let me be?*' A pause, then his voice again, becoming more confident: '*Oh! will you never set me free? The ties that bound us are still around us, there's no escape that I can see . . .*' He sang the whole of the song and then stopped abruptly. 'That's your lot. Bye, now.'

The answerphone clicked and whirred and beeped. Unable to believe what she had heard, she pressed PLAY again. Again his voice.

How curiously memory operated, she thought, lying back on the bed, playing the message again. She grabbed a pillow and hugged it hard. How could she have forgotten his singing and his amazing memory for lyrics?

Eventually, she let the message end. She got up, shook the duvet out. Then she removed the tape and placed it in her handbag.

'This looks too good to eat,' Neil told Lia, admiring the food on his plate—heart-shaped pieces of smoked salmon resting on heart-shaped buttered brown bread.

Lia smiled. 'I got the idea from one of the recipes in that paper Alison works for,' she explained, pleased that he liked it.

'Right,' he said, putting a salmon heart in his mouth. He could barely swallow, and yet it was his favourite food, and he would have to eat every morsel because he had told her that he was starving.

'This is great,' he said, wanting to break the silence that seemed to be ticking on for ever. He searched for a relevant comment, staring at his plate. Two hearts eaten, three to go. He picked up his third, looking at it admiringly.

'Hey!' he said. 'You managed to make both halves symmetrical!'

He looked up at her, pleased with the remembered phrase, but his eyes met blank incomprehension in hers. Then he remembered that they had not been Lia's words.

Ally, Lia, Ally, Lia, their names were shouting in his head, running into one another so that he could not tell which was which. He put down the heart.

'I'm sorry,' he said, 'I think I've got a migraine coming on.' And he bolted from the room, racing upstairs to the bathroom, where he was violently sick.

Alison unpacked the food she had grabbed from a delicatessen in Islington. Fresh pasta, black olives, a tin of anchovies, a jar of sun-dried tomatoes, panettone in a pale blue box. Ben watched fascinated as she named each item as she withdrew it from the tall brown paper bag. She unwrapped the panettone, and handed Ben the box to examine in that serious, curious way he had. The pasta could wait until after Ben's bath, she decided.

Now that Ben could sit up, she wasn't so frightened of touching him. It was like dealing with another human being now, not a tiny dependent little newborn creature who needed her oppressively all the time. She knelt by the side of the bath, one hand supporting his back, the other lathering his chubby, cherubic body with soap. Her favourite bits were his wrists, she decided, taking each in turn, holding it in the palm of her hand and marvelling at the simplicity of the design—just a little fold in the flesh where the arm joined onto the hand, no knobbly bones and protruding veins, like adult wrists had. They were so perfect.

She paused, and looked into her baby's face. He was watching her appreciation of him very seriously, but suddenly he smiled at her, and she had the strangest feeling that she was meeting him for the first time.

'What's this? It's delicious,' Stephen asked.

'Spaghetti alla puttanesca,' she told him.

Whore's spaghetti. She looked at the blood-red sauce and wondered if a kind of subliminal guilt had made her choose to cook that dish for this evening. She pushed her plate aside and helped herself to green salad.

It was the first evening they had spent together for a long time. She had been surprised by the absence of guilt, until now. Most evenings,

Stephen was not home until late, and it was easy to lie in bed reassuring herself that he was clearly having an affair too. It wasn't as if he was a house doctor any more, she would rationalise, and consultants surely didn't have to work such long hours. Even if he wasn't actually screwing someone else, he was obviously more enamoured of his job than of her, and so . . . and so, she would fall asleep, exhausted by the demands of her job, her lover and her son, and her husband would come home and slide in next to her without her even noticing.

'The flowers are gorgeous,' he commented. 'Thank you.'

She had bought him an armful of stargazer lilies which filled the room with their intoxicating perfume.

'This is for you.' He pushed a slim narrow box across the table.

It was the moment she had been dreading. It would have been so much easier if he had picked up some wilted roses from a bucket outside a garage. It was the first time in her life she had not been thrilled to receive something in a Tiffany box. She pulled off the white ribbon, opened the box and gasped, her eyes filling with tears. It was the diamond necklace she had always coveted: a single diamond, not too large, but not small either, set in a plain gold chain just long enough to let the diamond rest in that hollow of bone at the base of the neck.

'I bought it in New York—I don't know why I haven't given it to you before, actually,' he explained, embarrassed by her reaction. 'It's just, well, we don't seem to have seen much of each other.'

'It is absolutely beautiful,' she told him, forcing herself to look at his eyes. 'How did you know?'

'You once said,' he answered, 'when we went to dinner with Sir Giles.'

She recalled the evening with the man who was technically Stephen's boss but who behaved more like a benevolent uncle.

'Lady Cressida,' Stephen explained, 'was wearing a diamond necklace which you considered vulgar. On the way home, you said you thought diamond solitaires were fine, but no diamonds anywhere else, except— and then you described it. I drew a sketch as soon as I got in that night. London jewellers have never understood what I was talking about. But in New York they did.'

'New York's like that,' she said, turning the chain over so that the candlelight caught all the brilliant facets.

'Do you need some help?' Stephen asked her as she fumbled with the safety clasp.

'Please.'

He rose from his chair and walked round to her side of the table. She handed him the necklace and he fastened it.

'You have the most beautiful nape,' he told her.

She giggled at the precision of his vocabulary. It reminded her of the afternoon they had once spent in bed when he had touched every visible part of her body giving its proper Latin name. She had found it intensely erotic, and now the memory was making her wet.

'Shall we go to bed?' she asked him, almost shyly.

'Mmm, yes please,' he said, 'I shall have to bring home diamonds more often.'

The remark jarred. Did that mean that her husband now had to buy her sexual favours? She tried to halt the train of thought, to think of Stephen, only Stephen, and the wonderful sex they had always shared, but the fine gold chain round her neck felt like a garrotte tightening as she followed him up the stairs.

'He's not here yet,' she said, as Pic waved and approached the banquette at the side of the Palm Lounge Ginger had bagged.

'Happy birthday, twin!' Pic said, bending to kiss her.

'Happy birthday,' Ginger replied, adding, 'although it would be a lot happier if you hadn't invited Daddy. Honestly, Pic, I thought the idea of this was that we spent some time alone together for a change.'

'Oh, I'm sorry,' Pic said, as she sat down, 'but he seemed so eager to see us, and he never usually remembers. I just felt sorry for him.'

'And the bloody Savoy, for heaven's sake,' Ginger said. 'He only likes it here because people recognise him. Why didn't you insist on a loud, smoky bar?'

'Well, it is near to Covent Garden, and it's better than putting up with him all evening. He was threatening to get a box. Thank God we chose ballet and not opera.'

Ginger summoned a passing waiter and ordered a vodka on the rocks for herself and a glass of white wine for Pic.

'Shall we do presents now?' she said, changing the subject.

And then their father made his entrance, flanked by two waiters, whom he was addressing in the overloud, jocular voice he employed when he wanted people to notice that he had arrived.

'My daughters are seven today!' he told the older waiter with a familiar wink. 'Work it out . . . Ah, I see you got it straight away, leap year, you see. Do you serve champagne to underage drinkers, ha-ha?'

'Oh, I think we can manage that, sir,' the waiter responded, with a kind of servile mateyness. 'Three glasses?'

'Two,' Ginger interrupted, unable to bear the embarrassment any longer. 'I'm drinking vodka.'

'Three,' her father overruled, rewarding her with an indulgent smile, which she found hideously patronising.

Pic stood up to kiss him, so Ginger felt obliged to follow suit. She noticed there were beads of sweat on his forehead, and when he sat down he took time to get his breath back.

Serves you right for all that showing off, she thought.

She accepted the glass of champagne with good grace, sensing Pic stiffen on the sofa next to her as it was offered, and not wanting to spoil her sister's evening.

'Where's Edward tonight?' their father asked, picking up his glass with one hand and loosening his tie with the other.

'He's playing squash,' Pic replied.

'Good man,' her father replied automatically. It was his stock response to any information about his son-in-law.

He raised his glass for a toast. 'To my heavenly twins,' he pronounced. 'Many happy returns.'

'Thank you,' they both said.

'Now, I didn't get a chance to buy you anything, but I thought you would rather do it yourselves,' he said, producing two envelopes. 'Go on, open them.'

There was a piece of paper inside Ginger's envelope, on which he had scribbled, *Happy Birthday, love from Daddy*, and a cheque for £5,500.

'Thank you very much,' Ginger said, surprised, unable to resist a peek at Pic's cheque. 'Why do I get more than Pic?' she asked, seeing that her sister's was for only £3,000, and suspecting a trick.

'Tax. I can give you three thousand pounds each tax-free if I backdate it. But I also wanted to give Ginger something for my grandson,' their father explained.

'Daddy, you're too generous!' Pic told him.

'Will you be able to get something you want?' he asked, twinkling at her.

'Oh yes.'

'I shall open an account for Guy with his bit,' Ginger found herself saying, staring at the cheque in amazement. It wasn't that it was particularly generous. Her father had so much money he didn't need to worry about gift-tax allowances, but his financial recognition of Guy was enormously symbolic. She couldn't help being moved.

'Good plan,' her father said.

'And the rest will pay my childminder for the next six months,' she worked out. 'That is absolutely fantastic . . .' she added, beaming at him.

'Hmm.' Her father did a quick calculation. 'You complain about our party's policy on wages . . . you wouldn't be able to get away with that if we set a minimum wage, you know.'

'If I got tax relief on child care I would be able to pay her more,' Ginger protested, but her heart wasn't really in it.

Just once, she decided, she would allow him to buy her acquiescence. Because he was trying, she realised, and that was a very difficult thing for him to do.

'I thought you handled that very well,' Pic said to her, as they hurried towards the Opera House.

'It's the new, mature me,' Ginger said, self-mockingly. 'Actually, I think I'll blow the lot on drugs.'

'Ginger!'

'Not really! Thanks for arranging that, by the way. He's not such a bad old thing, is he? God, I must have had a lot of champagne!'

They ordered two more glasses for the interval by which time the alcohol had made them rather giggly.

'I must have a wee,' Ginger said, peering round the Crush Bar, trying to see a sign that said LADIES.

When she returned the lights were going down and they had to climb over people's legs to get to their seats. Ginger couldn't stop giggling. There were several shushes.

'Have you got a pen?' Pic whispered.

'What?'

'Shush.'

'Never mind.'

'SHUSH!'

Terrified of being thrown out, they huddled down in their seats and watched the second half of the ballet in silence.

'What did you say?' Ginger asked when the lights came up.

'I wanted to write you a message,' Pic said, putting on her coat, 'so we wouldn't have to whisper.'

'I know *why*, I meant what message?' said Ginger, following her up the steps to the exit.

'Because somebody came up to me while you were in the loo and said, "Hello, Ginger!" and I think it was—' She turned round and stopped talking as she saw who was on the steps behind her sister.

There was a tap on her shoulder. 'Hello, Ginger.'

Ginger turned round.

'Hello, Charlie,' she said, and then, thinking on her feet, 'I gather you've already met my sister?'

'I thought it was bad enough that there was one of you in the world, let alone two,' Charlie said teasingly.

'Oh, don't worry, Pic's not like me,' Ginger told him.

'Pic?' he said.

'Short for Patricia,' Ginger informed him. 'My father was raised on Beatrix Potter and thought it would be amusing to nickname us Ginger and Pickles, you see.'

'How charmingly English of him,' said Charlie's companion, Aaron—a rather handsome man with an American accent—as they walked down the stairs together to the foyer.

'What are you up to now?' Charlie said, as they stepped into the street.

'We're going to eat,' Ginger told him shortly.

'Come and have supper with us at my club,' Charlie suggested.

'It's our birthday . . .' Ginger protested.

'Well, I'm sure they'll have some sort of cake, if that's what you're worried about.'

Pic laughed. Ginger glowered at her. Pic held her look, making it clear that she wanted to accept. Perhaps she fancied an evening with two rather delectable-looking men, Ginger thought, softening a little. After all, Pic didn't get out much.

'All right, then,' she caved in, hissing as the men strolled off ahead of them, 'you owe me one for this.'

'Oh, don't be such an idiot,' Pic replied, uncharacteristically sharp.

The meal was more fun than Ginger had expected. The American was a financier whom Charlie was trying to entice into backing one of his projects. Ginger guessed that having made the gesture of inviting the twins, Charlie was now slightly anxious in case they began to rock the boat on the deal he was on the point of clinching. It gave Ginger a sense of power, that she resisted exploiting, because she found Charlie's vulnerability in the situation amusingly touching.

As they left the club, Charlie flagged down a cab. Kissing Pic on the cheek, he turned to say goodbye to Ginger. 'I can't believe you didn't tell me you had a twin,' he scolded her. 'Especially such a beautiful one.'

He was only trying to be charming, she decided. They both looked at each other for a second, then he grabbed her hand and kissed it. She and Pic waved as the cab roared off.

'He's nice,' Pic said, facing frontwards again.

'Very charming, yes,' Ginger said, pretending to stare at something interesting just outside her window. 'I couldn't believe the way you were flirting with him, and all his comments about how beautiful you were. Wasn't that a bit over the top?'

'Honestly,' Pic said impatiently, 'you are unbelievably thick at times! He was really flirting with you. For God's sake, we look just the same!'

'You seemed to be enjoying it,' Ginger remarked.

'I was basking in your reflected glory,' Pic said. 'He is rather a dish, so why shouldn't I? Anyway, I think he's smitten.'

'Oh, don't be ridiculous,' Ginger said, hoping that her sister couldn't see in the darkness how red she had gone.

'I'm not. I don't see why you have a problem. He seems perfect for you. He's sparkling and clever and almost as opinionated as you—'

'Yes, but you're forgetting Lucretia,' Ginger interrupted.

'But do you *really* know that they're together? She wasn't there tonight. He didn't mention her, for heaven's sake. You should see the way he looks at you.'

'He was only grateful that we were entertaining Aaron.'

'Don't be such a grouch,' Pic said as the cab pulled up outside her house. 'I bet he'll call you tomorrow.'

'I don't care if he does,' Ginger said, wishing that Pic would shut up.

'I think you do!' Pic replied in a singsong voice, kissing her.

'I must remember never to let you drink champagne again,' Ginger told her affectionately.

*March*

GINGER'S PHONE BUZZED. She jumped, as she had each time it had rung. She said, 'Hello?' out loud a couple of times, practising a bored, slightly indifferent voice, before picking up the receiver. It wouldn't do to have him think she was waiting for his call.

'Hello?' Breezy, busy, I'm-in-the-middle-of-something-actually. She congratulated herself.

'Ginger? It's Alison, how are you?'

'Oh, fine,' Ginger replied, disappointed.

'Listen, I was really calling about work . . . I've had this idea for a regular feature. Here's the pitch: two relatives talk about a favourite family dish and then we have the recipe. I was wondering . . . ?'

'Oh, do you mean me and my father?' Ginger asked. 'Um, I don't really want to ask him any favours right now. There's a delicate kind of cease-fire in operation at the moment,' she explained. 'I do think it's a good idea, though,' she added, trying to be helpful. 'I would call it "Like Momma Used to Make".'

'That's good,' Alison said, scribbling down her suggestion. 'Listen, you don't have any other suggestions for famous parents and children?'

Ginger mused and trotted out the names of famous acting and writing dynasties.

'Hey, that's great,' Alison said. 'Listen, if you ever fancy a job as a researcher . . .'

'Watch it, I might take you up on that,' Ginger said with a laugh. 'How are you, anyway?' she asked.

'I'm fine, thanks,' Alison said.

'And Ben?'

'He's fine. What about Guy? How is the arrangement working?' Alison couldn't bring herself to say Lia's name.

'Very well. Of course, I miss him, but he's in very good hands. Lia is fantastic with children, isn't she? I can see her with a great brood, can't you, like the woman who lived in a shoe?'

'I suppose so,' Alison replied, unable to resist asking. 'Is she thinking of having more, then?'

As soon as she had said it, she realised she did not want to know the answer.

'Oh, I expect so, don't you?' Ginger replied. 'I really envy her being able to have them all at once. The way my life is going, Guy'll be twenty before he gets a brother or sister. What about you?'

There was a pause, then Alison replied, 'Oh God, no, never again . . . Listen, I must run. Let's catch up soon.'

'You're not getting a coke habit, are you?' Ramona asked when Alison returned from the ladies.

Alison stared at her, bewildered.

'It's just that you've been to the loo at least six times this morning, you've got red eyes and you're sniffing.'

'No,' Alison said, 'I'm just a bit under the weather.'

'Is there anything I can do?' Ramona said kindly. She obviously knew that Alison had been crying.

'No,' Alison said. 'Thanks, but I don't want to talk about it.'

'You know where I am if you need me.'

Seeing Ramona's face fall, Alison added, 'You're a good friend . . . I'm sorry, but this is something I have to work out by myself.'

'OK, OK.' Ramona smiled and went back to her work.

'Hey!' she said, after a few minutes' silence. 'Would a weekend in Paris help?'

Alison laughed. 'What do you mean?' she asked.

'I want a piece about the young British designers and how they're taking over the trad old fashion houses. Three thousand words . . . Would you like to do it?'

'I'll think about it,' Alison replied. Ramona loved to solve people's problems so much that it was often difficult to resist getting swept along in her generosity.

'Well, not too long,' Ramona warned.

'No, I'll think about it at lunch,' Alison assured her.

Spring had arrived, suddenly, and it was as if someone had switched on the light after the long, gloomy winter. There was real warmth in the sun, and trees were sprouting lime-green leaves, a colour so bright against the clear blue sky it almost looked artificial.

It was on such a day as this, she thought, that she had married Stephen in St Bride's Church off Fleet Street. The austere church with its plain glass windows had been radiant in the sunlight. Alison had worn a floor-length gown of ivory silk with no decoration except a length of soft chiffon that made a gauzy stole about her bare shoulders and was held in place by a cluster of five pale gold rosebuds. She had carried a small, tight bunch of similar roses as she strode down the aisle with the confidence of a woman who knows she looks her best. Stephen's eyes had sparkled with appreciation as she drew near.

Alison crossed the road to the sunny side of the street, and started walking in the direction of the Thames.

The wedding had been perfect, she remembered, and the honeymoon heavenly. It was only when they walked through the miles of passage-way towards the departure gate at Heathrow that she discovered they were heading for a tiny privately owned island in the Caribbean.

It does not get better than this, she had thought, completely at peace with the regular rhythm of her own breathing, as they were snorkelling one afternoon in crystal-clear water that shimmered with the movement of a million jewelled fish.

In a couple of months, it would be their anniversary. Five years. She wished she could truly think five happy years, the best five years of her life. But they had not been. After the honeymoon, there had been the excitement of buying and decorating a house together, and after that, everything merged into a blur of attempts to get pregnant.

At first, making love without contraception had been gloriously exhilarating. It had made sex more emotional. They were doing something profound together, and the depth of trust it required seemed to take her to the very edge of her being. Then, after the fourth month, she began to worry. After that every month rolled into the next. Sex became something they had to do, whether they felt like it or not, on the right days. If Stephen was working, she went to the hospital in her lunch-hour hoping to catch him between operations so they could fuck quickly on his consulting-room floor, the door locked, the blind pulled down, but everyone outside knowing exactly what they were doing. Before they were married, it might have been a turn-on. Now it was perfunctory and humiliating. But not as humiliating as the injections, the operation to extract her eggs, his masturbation to fertilise them. Conception had become a goal in itself. Talking about sex became a no-go area, so did sex for the sake of sex.

Perhaps, she thought as she reached the riverbank, attempting to make sense of her treachery, that was why she had started an affair. She sat down on some steps that led to the river, hearing the wash of a passing pleasure boat lap against the ancient stone. No, she thought, there was no point in trying to excuse it like that. Although infrequent, sex had been fine with Stephen since the baby was born. She was having an affair because she loved Neil. And he loved her. When he had not called for several weeks, she had almost been glad that he had been brave enough to finish it. But now he had called again, wanting to see her, and she had agreed.

The sound of lapping water brought back a memory of the afternoon she had sat beside the same river, in Richmond, with Lia. That afternoon seemed so long ago; it was almost like another life. A life where things were uncomplicated. From what Ginger had said this morning, at least Lia sounded happy. The affair wasn't affecting her. Stop it, Alison told herself. Just stop it.

She glanced at her watch. There was never any time, never a quiet moment for herself. If she only had time for her brain to rest.

'I will do that piece,' she told Ramona when she returned to the office. 'I'll go alone. I need some time on my own.'

'Fine,' Ramona said. 'Great. You're right, men always get in the way when you're shopping.'

'**D**id you manage to find somewhere to put your bike?' Charlie asked, greeting Ginger with a kiss on each cheek.

By the time Charlie finally rang, not the next day, nor even the day after, Ginger had long since abandoned her pause-and-answer strategy. Her boss had just asked her to make coffee for three and she had her hands full of cups, so she wasn't in the best mood, and had simply grabbed the receiver and shouted, 'Yes?'

'Er, Ginger?' Charlie had asked.

'Yes?' still impatient.

'Bad moment?'

'Yes,' slightly mollified.

'Shall I ring back?'

She didn't want to wait another week. 'No.'

'I was wondering whether you'd like to come to a screening?'

'Sure, when?'

'Next Tuesday?'

'No can do,' Ginger said. 'Pic only does baby-sitting on Fridays.'

'Well, there's one on Friday too,' Charlie said.

'OK, then,' she had said, reaching for a Biro to note down the address. She hadn't even asked what was going to be screened.

'I didn't bring my bike, actually,' Ginger now explained as he indicated the way. 'I thought there might be alcohol, and I don't drink and drive.'

'Very sensible,' Charlie said, ushering her into the screening theatre. There was no one else in the room, only a projectionist in a box behind the back row.

'Oh, am I early?' Ginger asked.

'No,' Charlie said, waving at a table set up with a white cloth, a silver bucket containing a bottle of Bollinger, and two champagne flutes. He opened the bottle and poured her a glass. Then he waved at the rows of seats, indicating that she could sit anywhere she liked. She sat down in the front row. Charlie stood in front of the screen and began to make a speech.

'Ladies and gentlemen, before we begin tonight's screening, I'd like to say a word about its origins,' he began, as if he were the master of cere-monies at the Oscars. 'We're very happy to have here tonight the person without whom this show would never have happened. Miss Ginger Prospect.' From the speakers came a blast of applause.

Ginger couldn't help smiling.

'And now, I hope you'll sit back and enjoy *If You Can't Stand the Heat*.' The lights went down. Charlie came to sit next to her.

Ginger had to admit that Charlie's production company had really brought her idea to life. She could see it would be a big ratings success, and she felt proud of herself and, oddly, grateful to Charlie for realising her idea.

She could feel his eyes watching her face for her reaction, and she could sense him relax beside her as she smiled at the jokes.

'Look, this is the best bit coming up,' he said at the end. As the credits began to roll, came the phrase: *Based on an idea by Ginger Prospect.*

It was the first time she had ever seen her name as it were in lights and she was thrilled.

Afterwards, he took her to his club. They drank more champagne and she began to feel almost euphoric. As they sat down to eat, she told Charlie how much she had enjoyed the screening. He smiled indulgently at her. It was at least the sixth time she had said it.

'I still can't persuade you to work for me?' he said.

'No,' she said, hoping he wouldn't ask her why, since she had temporarily forgotten what her objection was.

'Well, if I can't see more of you during the week, how about one weekend?' Charlie asked.

The champagne whirred her brain round at top speed, like a waltzer in a fairground.

'Oh no, weekends are for my son,' she said.

'Well, I could take you out for the day. I love children.'

'Do you?' She couldn't disguise her surprise.

'Yes, I was the oldest of five boys, so I've had a lot of experience with little fellas.'

The champagne roller coaster tipped over its summit and was plummeting downwards. Whatever Charlie wanted, it certainly wasn't commitment. He wouldn't like children nearly so much if he were to discover that he had a son. Even if they were to start a relationship, and she couldn't think how that could happen with the Lucretia question still out there somewhere, like a sleeping scorpion, with her track record, it was bound to last only a few weeks and she had to protect Guy from disappointment.

'Can I ask what the problem is?' Charlie said, sensing her sudden change of mood.

'There's no problem,' she lied, not very convincingly.

'Why won't you go out with me then?' he demanded.

'Because of Lucretia,' she said.

'What has she got to do with it?' he asked, exasperated.

'You tell me,' Ginger replied, levelly.

'Well, it's true that Lucretia and I had a relationship at Oxford,' Charlie said, 'but that was before she discovered she preferred women and before I discovered I preferred women who didn't smoke cigars in bed. We could never be business partners and sleep together . . .'

417

Was it public knowledge that Lucretia was a lesbian? Ginger wanted to ask. If so, why hadn't Robert told her? Why did she believe Charlie? Surely he wasn't such a rogue that he would lie about something like that?

The roller coaster was cranking upwards again. Charlie was so very handsome, sitting there staring at her with great brown eager eyes. What could be the harm in spending an afternoon with him? Guy was far too young to form an attachment, so what was holding her back? Suddenly she thought of the perfect, natural venue.

'Why don't you come and watch the boat race with us? I need someone who can hoist Guy on his shoulders so that he can see,' she said.

Charlie laughed loudly. 'OK,' he said, 'it's a date.'

Neil took a long draught of his lager. He was going to meet her and finish it once and for all. It sounded simple enough, but as the hour drew nearer, he could feel himself growing weaker.

He had decided on Valentine's Day that he could not go on. The deceit was making him ill. All he had to do was hold out. Just say no. This was the cold turkey bit. Soon, it would get better.

It didn't. He had nightmares about running into her at Waitrose. Then, walking beside the river with Lia one Sunday afternoon, he thought he saw her in front of them, her husband pushing the pram. His legs turned to jelly. It was only when he drew nearer that he saw it wasn't her. He began to stay in at weekends. Lia went out by herself, looking at him anxiously, not quite daring to ask what was wrong, but knowing that there was something. The phone was like a magnet, drawing him across the room. He tried diversionary tactics. Gardening. It had always absorbed him in times of crisis. Like the autumn after Alison went to college, when he had hacked all the roses in the park to the ground, swept up the leaves, daily, hourly even. She had not phoned, not even sent a letter saying they were finished.

He could almost have understood if she had told him she had found another boy. At least he would have known. But it was as if he had ceased to exist. He had written to her, persuading himself when he received no reply that the letters were going astray. When he had tracked down her parents' new phone number her mother had ordered him never to call there again.

Now Alison spoke of their separation as if it had been just as painful for her. And the strange thing was, he believed her. So what had happened? He had to know why he had spent twenty years feeling as if some part of his capacity to love had been amputated. He only wanted it resolved, he told himself. Finished. So that he could get on with his life.

He let himself into the flat. He sat down on the sofa. It was like being in a dentist's waiting room, only minutes away from the drill. Then, before he had time to rehearse the speech in his head again, he saw, through the window, her legs stepping down the steps and her face changing when she caught sight of him to a smile of such innocent joy it made him want to hug and kiss and protect her.

He forced himself to remain seated.

'I'm sorry . . . it's ridiculous when I only have to come a mile or two.' She apologised for her late arrival, kicking off her shoes and jumping onto his lap.

She smoothed his hair back from his face, belatedly noticing his stiff, ungiving posture. 'What's up?'

'Nothing,' he said.

She bent her head and kissed him. He tried not to respond, but it was impossible.

'We have to talk,' he mumbled between kisses.

'Later. I've missed you,' she said firmly, pulling him to his feet, leading him to the bedroom.

Afterwards, they lay beside each other, smoking.

'When I'm here with you, I feel as if I've come home. Do you know what I mean?'

She had put into words exactly what he had been feeling. The flat was a safe place when she was here with him. However much he had prepared himself beforehand, he found that here, lying beside her, all the guilt and anxiety simply evaporated. It was the most natural thing in the world to make love to her, to be together in bed. It felt as if this was what they had been created to do. He tried to remind himself of Lia and Anouska, but they were distant figures and he was numb to their pain.

'How do you deal with the guilt?' he asked her.

She turned to look at him. They did not discuss their partners. They were crossing into new territory.

'I tell myself that I'm not hurting anyone if they don't know,' she said finally. It was weak, she knew, but it sounded so much weaker out loud. She thought of Stephen's face when he saw her walking towards him in St Bride's Church. He had been so sure of her. She had not lived up to his devotion.

'Sometimes, I watch them,' she went on softly, 'playing together, perfectly happy together . . .' She sighed, pulling back her head to look closely at Neil, and taking a deep breath, 'and I wonder what would happen if I had to choose . . .'

She was, he realised, daring to pose the ultimate question, and yet to phrase it so that he could veer away if he wanted to. He didn't want to.

'Lia wants another child,' he said after a pause. 'I'm not sure I do. It doesn't seem fair to let her go on hoping—'

'Were you happy until you met me again?' Alison interrupted.

'Yes, very,' he said, and saw her face fall. She had wanted him to say no, he realised. 'But not as happy as I am here with you,' he added. 'How about you?'

'I wasn't,' she admitted. 'It wasn't anything to do with Stephen. He didn't cause the problem.'

'What caused it, then?' he asked.

'I don't know,' she said, looking at the ceiling. 'Perhaps that awful point when you realise that this is it. I gave up everything I had for a dream of something else, and then I got the something else and I think I would have preferred what I had . . .'

'Me?' he asked, his eyebrows raised.

'Yes, you,' she said fondly, running her forefinger over his sternum.

'Is that why you left me?' He sat up in bed. It was all becoming clear.

'I needed to see what there was for me,' she said, hurrying after the easy opportunity he had given her to justify herself. All of it was true, she told herself. 'I didn't want to settle so young.'

'But why didn't you tell me?' he asked her.

She turned the question back to him. 'Would you have understood?'

'Maybe not,' he said resignedly, 'but you never even gave me a chance, did you?'

'I don't know why I didn't,' she said, hating herself for lying to him.

He sat for a long time with his back to her. Then he leaned forward and picked up a discarded stocking from the end of the bed.

'*Silk stockings thrown aside . . .*' he said. 'That bloody song.' He chuckled. 'You know how once you remember something, you can't think of anything else? . . . It's all about a dirty weekend in Paris, I realised. They're having an affair. I never thought about the words before.'

'I'm going to Paris for a long weekend, the first one in April,' she said.

'Lucky you!' He sounded unimpressed.

'Do you want to come?' she asked him, a solution to everything suddenly occurring to her.

'What do you mean?' he asked suspiciously.

'Come with me,' she said, sitting up. 'Look, we can't keep meeting in this place, trying to give each other up. It's a waste of time and it's never going to work, until one of us gets found out. That's not the right way to do it, is it?' She leaned forward, eager for his support.

'No,' he agreed, still cautious.

'Don't you see? Either we're going to be together, or we're not. If we are, we're going to have to make some horrible decisions about Stephen and Lia and our children, but we're never going to know if we never spend any time together, are we? Anyway, I can't say I'm decorating this place for ever,' she added, as if that sealed the matter.

'Hang on—did you plan this?'

She realised he hated being manipulated. She slowed down.

'No,' she said. 'Actually, I've got to do an article. I planned to go by myself, to sort everything out in my head, but now it seems almost as if it was planned for us . . .'

'Hey, before we get totally carried away, haven't you forgotten something?' But the fact that he had said 'we' gave it away. He wanted to go. 'I'm a teacher, remember? I can't just go off to Paris to "do an article",' he added, mocking the casualness of her remark.

'Well, couldn't you say there was a school trip?' She was thinking on her feet. There must be a way.

'I don't like lying,' he protested, ineffectually.

'Oh God, I'll book us somewhere lovely, and we can make love all day and eat wonderful food and walk by the Seine at twilight . . .' she said, throwing her arms round his neck.

'I've never been to Paris . . .'

'You'll love it,' she told him, suddenly turned on by the thought of a weekend together. She locked her wrists behind his neck and dragged him down on top of her.

'What's sex like when you've had a baby?' Ginger asked Lia, the Friday before the boat race. She had persuaded Lia to stay for a drink when she dropped Guy back.

'Don't ask me,' Lia replied. 'We never seem to do it these days. Either I'm tired, or Neil's tired . . .' She couldn't mask the discomfort she felt. 'Why, are you thinking of having some?' she asked, overbrightly.

'No,' said Ginger. 'Well, there might be a possibility . . .'

She told Lia about her date the next day with Charlie.

'Well, if you want a piece of advice, don't plan on Guy being around,' Lia told her. 'There's nothing more of a turnoff than the baby waking up just as you're getting in the mood, and if he's anything like Anouska, he will. It's as if they know.' She laughed. 'Anyway, I find that I just can't relax and enjoy it properly even if she's asleep, because you've always got a little bit of you that's thinking about them, haven't you?'

'So, what do you do?' Ginger asked, mystified.

'We put her in the shed, of course,' Lia said, deadpan, then burst out laughing. 'What we don't do is have a lot of sex,' she admitted.

'God, how awful,' Ginger said, 'to have someone who looks like Neil lying next to you and not . . .'

'Hmm, looks aren't everything,' Lia said. 'Anyway, it's different from sex before, because it's all wrapped up in having a baby. You don't quite think of it in the same way, I find.'

'The way you're going on, I don't think I'll bother!' Ginger exclaimed. 'It's probably not on the menu anyway.' She tickled Guy under his chin.

'Da da da da da!' Guy said.

'Oh dear,' Lia said. 'You'd better tell Charlie straight away that he says that to everyone.'

'God, I hadn't even thought of that,' said Ginger.

'Come along, love,' Lia said, scooping Anouska up. 'Kiss your boyfriend goodbye and wave.'

Both mothers flopped their babies' hands up and down.

'Bye then,' Lia said. She was almost at the door, when she turned back and said, 'Best of luck tomorrow!'

Ginger stood at the window with Guy, waving at the red Peugeot as it pulled away. Then she turned to look at the baby. 'Well, what are we going to do this evening?' she asked, putting him down on the floor beside the sofa. He immediately started to pull himself up to standing.

'Da da da da da,' Guy replied, triumphantly wobbling.

'Hmm, I think you're right. We'll watch a bit of television, have a bite to eat and then bed,' Ginger interpreted.

The phone rang and Ginger picked it up. 'Hello? Oh hello, Daddy.'

'Are you well?' her father asked.

'Yes, thank you. Tired, as usual, but fine.'

'And that little chap?'

Ginger found great pleasure in the affectionate way her father now referred to Guy.

'He's fine. He's standing right beside me.'

'At his age? My goodness, he is coming along,' her father said. 'Now, I hope I'm going to see you both at Ian's tomorrow to watch the boats.'

Her father's closest friend had a house backing onto the river in Hammersmith where he hosted an annual boat-race party. Ginger and Pic had been every year since they were old enough to carry a bowl of peanuts around. Every year, except the previous year, when she was pregnant and in disgrace, she remembered. That fact alone gave her father's offer added significance. She and her son were being welcomed back into polite society.

'Oh, I'm sorry, Daddy, but we've already arranged to meet a friend,' she said.

'Well, bring her along too,' her father ordered.

'No, I'm sorry, we can't,' Ginger told him, firmly, resisting the temptation to overturn his assumption that her friend was a woman.

'Why ever not?' her father persisted.

'I'm sorry, but that's none of your business,' Ginger told him, bristling. There was no way she was going to have her father interrogating Charlie, as he had every other man she had introduced to him. 'I don't mean to be unkind,' she added, thinking that she had sounded rather rude.

'Unkind?' he echoed, haughtily. 'I just thought my grandson would have a better chance of seeing all the razzmatazz, but if you have other plans . . .'

'Well, maybe next year,' she said, so that he would know that she wasn't refusing his invitation on principle.

'We may not all be here next year,' her father said.

Oh God, emotional blackmail now.

'Don't be ridiculous, Daddy,' she said briskly.

'Very well,' he capitulated.

It was the first time she had ever heard him sounding old. The sad resignation in his voice was the only thing that came close to making her change her mind. No, she decided, if he thought that tactic would be a winner, there would be years of hell to pay.

'Thanks so much for the offer,' she said.

'Goodbye, darling.' He banged down the phone.

'I've brought a podium and a couple of periscopes,' Charlie said the next day as he fixed Guy's car seat in his car. It was one of those ridiculous jeep-type things, with four-wheel drive and a rhino bar. Ginger had never been able to understand who would be stupid enough to drive one in London. Now she knew.

'You've what?' Ginger asked.

'I thought about what you said, about not being able to see over the crowds, and I had one of the carpenters on the set knock me up a podium.' Charlie waved at the back of the car. There was indeed a podium.

'How very practical,' Ginger said, giggling.

Charlie turned round, his face pink with the exertion of fitting the car seat, and smiled at her. 'Come on, little fella,' he said, taking Guy and swinging him into the seat.

'Da da da da da,' Guy replied.

'He says that to everyone, by the way,' Ginger remarked as nonchalantly as she could, climbing into the front seat.

'Is his father around much?' Charlie asked, starting the engine.

'Not much, no,' Ginger replied, truthfully.

'Do you mind?' Charlie dared to probe. Somehow it was easier to ask when driving. You didn't have to look at the other person's face.

'I'm used to it,' Ginger said. 'I decided to have the baby without consulting him, so I didn't expect anything.'

'Right,' Charlie said. 'He's a great little fella,' he added.

'Well, I think so,' Ginger said, swelling with pride. 'You know, I look at him and I think, well, what more creative thing in the world could I have done than bring this little being into the world?'

Charlie took his eyes off the road for a second and smiled at her.

'What I didn't realise was how like himself he would be. He was, from the moment he was born,' Ginger went on, encouraged by Charlie's reaction and unable to stop herself. She hadn't realised what a wonderful feeling it must be to have another parent around, to share all the excitement.

Charlie let her chatter on, unable to resist the occasional glance at her face, which, animated by delight in her baby, was sensationally pretty. Zest and enthusiasm for life seemed to hum around her. She had to be the most truly vital person he had ever met, and he suddenly realised, as they stopped in traffic on Kew Bridge, that he was in love with her. It was a strange sensation, which made him feel simultaneously weaker and stronger than he had ever felt before.

At that moment a police siren started wailing behind them and he had to manoeuvre his vehicle to allow it to pass.

'Look, tell me if this is stupid,' Charlie suddenly said, as they crawled towards the Chiswick roundabout. 'We're right on the M4 here. It's a lovely day. Why don't we dare to break with tradition and get out of London?'

Ginger thought about it for all of two seconds.

'Fine,' she said. 'Where to?'

'It's a secret,' he said, and was delighted to see her impish smile as she wriggled down in her seat.

He would take her for a balloon ride, he decided.

There was a place near Bath. But in a service station, his plans were foiled. The baby, who had slept for over an hour, woke up demanding to be fed. There was also a distinctly unpleasant smell wafting from his region of the car. So they piled into the Little Chef to give Guy a bottle and change him, and then they all got back into the jeep.

He turned the key in the ignition. Nothing happened.

'It won't start,' he said, turning the ignition again. Nothing.

By the time the AA arrived, Ginger had fed Guy again, and used the last nappy in the bag. The AA man could not start the car either, but offered to tow it to a garage. Charlie was mortified but Ginger was secretly finding the whole adventure rather amusing. She was almost disappointed when he insisted on calling a minicab to take her and Guy and all their paraphernalia back to London. Charlie carefully transferred Guy's seat from his car to the minicab, negotiated the fee with the driver and handed him notes in cash. Then he turned to Ginger, who was holding Guy on one hip.

'I am so sorry,' he said, for the umpteenth time.

'No, it's fine. Guy's enjoyed it. Really,' Ginger assured him, adding jokily, 'Can I have my surprise some other time?'

Charlie's face lifted for a second or two. 'Of course . . . if you'll ever trust me again,' he said.

The flat felt strangely empty when she got in. She gave Guy another bottle, then turned on the television to see who had won the boat race. Cambridge. The day seemed unfinished. It was too early to start going through all the bedtime routine, and too late and chilly now to go out for a walk. She picked up the phone and dialled Pic's number. Out. Ginger dialled Lia's number and amused her for half an hour with a description of their unsuccessful trip to the country.

'So, no sex then?' Lia asked finally.

'Well, even *I* draw the line at a busy car park,' Ginger replied. 'But I did actually have a very nice time. Maybe we can be friends.'

Ginger rang off and jumped up, with a sudden determination to tackle the week's washing-up.

Later, she decided it was a kind of prescience that had driven her to clean up the flat and get Guy in his cot early, because the minute his eyes had closed the doorbell rang. Charlie was there, with a bottle of champagne in one hand and a takeaway meal in the other.

'How did you know?' Ginger asked him, 'I was about to order something in.'

'Well, order me in, instead,' he said.

'Get in here!' she shouted at him, forgetting her sleeping son for an instant. Miraculously the baby did not stir.

She stood back to let Charlie into the living room. He walked over to the mantelpiece.

'So you did get it?' he said, picking up the Valentine card.

'What? Oh, that! Did you send it?' she asked, amazed.

'Yes . . . didn't you see?' he said, exasperated. 'I had it made with all the things I associate with you . . . look, there's a bike wheel, and a piece of red velvet, a bit of champagne cork and there was lobster shell . . .'

'Oh, that's what it was!' Ginger said, understanding. 'It fell off. Goodness'—she took the card from him and looked at it in a new light—'why did you do that?'

'Because I wanted you to be my Valentine, I suppose,' Charlie admitted tentatively.

'But what does that mean, exactly?' Ginger asked, suddenly very nervous, and playing for time.

They were standing next to each other, not touching, looking at each other in the mantel mirror.

'I think it means . . . well, I'd like to see more of you . . . What do you think?' Charlie said, suddenly bashful.

'I think,' Ginger said, turning towards him, 'I think you'd have been very good at courtly love. You offer lovely presents: balloons, cards and now an Indian takeaway—' she said.

'It's Thai,' he said.

She giggled.

Charlie looked into her eyes. 'Then will my lady favour me with a kiss?' he asked her softly.

'Oh, all right,' she said, throwing herself into his arms.

The tin trays of food remained untouched in the carrier bag. Lia was wrong, Ginger thought, in the early hours of the morning. Sex was no different after you'd had a baby. It was fantastically, wonderfully, brilliant.

## April

'ARE YOU SURE you'll be all right?' Neil asked as he hoisted his kitbag onto his shoulder.

'We'll be fine,' Lia assured him.

'You've got the hotel's number, in case you need it?'

'Yes, but I won't ring. If there's an emergency, I'll be surrounded by people. Anyway, there won't be.'

'Do you really think you ought to be taking Annie when she's got a temperature?'

'Well, I can hardly leave her, can I?' Lia joked. 'She's only got a virus. A change of scene and some country air will probably do her the world of good . . .'

Anouska had been running a fever for a couple of days. There was nothing visibly wrong with her except that she was grisly and out of sorts. Lia had taken her to the doctor, who had told her how to keep Annie's temperature down, but that there wasn't much else he could do.

When Ginger had discovered that Lia and Anouska would be spending Easter on their own, she had invited them to the country for the whole weekend.

'Mummy and Pic and I will look after Anouska, and you can get some rest for a change,' she had volunteered.

'We're going to a stately home, for heaven's sake, not some damp hovel,' Lia reminded Neil.

'Well, those places are sometimes very draughty,' he said, as if he had long experience of aristocratic dwellings.

She was touched by his concern, but thought he was worrying unnecessarily. She wished he would just go.

'You have a lovely time,' she told him, wondering why he seemed so reluctant to leave. She knew it wasn't really a holiday, because he'd be chaperoning a bunch of schoolkids around, but he was going to Paris, after all.

'Right, then,' he said. He put his arms round her, and held her very tight, then he broke away and walked smartly down the street.

Closing the door, Lia took a deep breath. Four whole days! She smiled, realising how much she had been looking forward to a weekend of girls' talk and conversation that flowed easily and was interspersed with laughter.

Recently, Neil had become increasingly introverted and quiet. The Ofsted inspection was hanging over his school like a rain cloud, the teachers spending most of the longer evenings preparing progress reports and work schedules. When Neil came home early enough for them to have supper together, he was often so tired that it was difficult to have a conversation. As she sat jabbering on, he seemed so preoccupied that she had wondered, on occasion, whether he would even notice if she casually inserted a sentence like 'and then I bonked the milkman' into her account of the day.

When Neil had informed her that one of the staff on the trip to Paris had dropped out, and he had been asked to fill in, she had greeted the idea with such immediate enthusiasm that he had looked hurt. He needed a change of scene, she told him. But she hadn't realised, until he disappeared, how much she had been longing for a break too.

When she woke Anouska up and started to dress her, she found that her neck was swollen on one side and her temperature had risen. She rang the doctor, who was at the end of a night on call. He popped by on his way home, examined Anouska thoroughly and assured Lia that it was still the flu. Anouska had quite a bad case of it, but she would soon be better. Lia showed him out, feeling guilty for bothering him, but when she went back to check Anouska, there was something about the way she looked that made her want to run after him and ask him to look at her again. She went to the window, but his car was pulling away. Don't be so silly, she told herself.

Ginger was lying awake in bed, staring at the ceiling, enjoying a moment of perfectly contented consciousness. Beside her, Charlie slept, his dark curls fanned out on the pillow, his features innocent in sleep. The waking-up-with-him bit was almost more special than the going-to-bed-with-him bit, because it was always a surprise to her that he was still there.

Don't start liking it too much, a voice inside her warned, because one of these days he will be gone, leaving you with a few nice memories. Men like Charlie don't hang around for long. The only reason he is still here is because he is not quite sure how much you like him, but once you let him know, you can forget it. But they had fantastic sex together, and lots of fun, and there was no point in stopping doing something just because you knew it wouldn't last, was there?

The sun was coming up. Bright white light seeped round the edges of the olive-green velvet curtains. Charlie turned over, taking the whole duvet with him.

'Hey!' Ginger tried to grab some of it back.

She snuggled in closer to him. She loved the warmth of his skin in the morning, the way his arms flopped round her sleepily and his eyes scrunched up against the unwelcome glare of daylight. Finally, he opened his eyes and smiled. 'Hello!'

'Hello,' she said. God, he was handsome in the morning, with his hair muzzy, his dark eyes glittering with the prospect of naughtiness.

He kissed her lazily, then pulled away, looked at her for a moment, and came back harder, with real urgency. It got her every time, that pulling away, as if checking to see whether she was real. The idea that you were being kissed more passionately just because you were you was so deliciously, hornily flattering. He does it with everybody, the voice inside her warned.

'Do you have to go away this weekend?' he asked her.

'Yes, 'fraid so,' Ginger told him.

'But I only ever see you at weekends, and the first time we get a four-day stretch, you decide to go home,' he moaned plaintively.

She rationed him to weekends. She had to be careful not to let him become a habit, or a regular presence in their lives.

'I've promised Lia, and anyway, I want to go,' she said.

'Why can't I come too?'

'Because I haven't invited you, that's why,' she told him.

'Can I come round on Monday?'

'Well, as long as you bring something to eat,' she said.

'So what else is new?' he teased her, ducking out of the way of a friendly swat with the pillow. He picked up a pillow himself and retaliated, and they bashed each other long and hard, screaming with laughter, until they were both out of breath and the thin beams of sunlight now streaming into the room danced with dust motes.

Then, simultaneously, Guy woke up and the phone rang.

Ginger pointed at the phone, indicating that he should pick it up, and went to be with Guy.

When she came back with the baby smiling in her arms, Charlie was saying, 'She's right here. Hang on one minute, Pic.'

She knew instantly that something was wrong.

She grabbed the phone.

'What is it? Oh no! I'll come as soon as I can.'

She put down the phone then picked it up, dialled, with Charlie hovering, trying to be helpful, but getting in the way.

'Go and make some coffee,' she told him. 'Oh Lia, hi, listen, my father's had a stroke. I've got to go to the hospital . . . He's in intensive care. I'm so sorry.'

At the other end of the phone, Lia said, 'Don't worry. I was about to ring you and cancel anyway. Anouska's not very well at all. It would be madness . . . Do you want me to have Guy?'

She is an angel, Ginger thought. 'Could you?'

'I'd be glad of the company. But I can't pick him up. I just don't want to take Annie out in the cold.'

'No, it's OK,' Ginger said. 'Charlie'll bring us.'

Charlie called from the kitchen, 'Where do you keep the milk?'

'Sod the bloody milk. Bring it black. Sorry Lia, I'm panicking.' She burst into tears. 'Pic sounded so frightened,' she said between sobs.

'It's OK,' Lia soothed. 'Just get Guy dressed. I'll give him his breakfast. Be strong.'

'OK, sorry.' Ginger put down the phone. She took a deep breath. Soon, Pic had said. *Please wait for me, Daddy.*

'We're here,' Alison said, excitedly, as the lift creaked up to the third floor of the hotel. 'I can't believe we're really here!'

'Nor can I,' he replied, trying to smile back.

The room was small and almost entirely filled with bed. Unless you were squeezed up against the window, looking out, there was no way of avoiding its accusation.

'It's very comfy,' Alison said, sitting down and kicking off her shoes.

He sat down too, bouncing up and down on the bed as if trying it out in a department store.

'Yes,' he said.

'You're nervous, aren't you?' she asked him, stroking his arm.

'I suppose so.'

'I am too.'

'Are you?' He turned to her, and saw fear in her eyes.

'I'm afraid that we won't like each other . . .' she said

'No,' he said, putting his arms round her and rocking her from side to side, 'there's no chance of that.'

'What are you afraid of?' she asked him.

'That we'll like each other too much, maybe, I don't know,' he said, not able to describe the confusion he was feeling.

She held his face between her palms. 'Whatever happens, you do know that I love you?' she said.

'I've always loved you,' he told her.

'Sing the song?' she asked him.

'No,' he said. 'Not any more. It's not a dream any more.'

'Well, let's have lunch, then,' she said, laughing.

'And a lot to drink,' he suggested, feeling a little better.

'Isn't it amazing,' Alison said, spearing a forkful of frisée lettuce, 'how the French can make steak and chips and salad taste absolutely delicious, but you wouldn't dream of ordering it in England?'

'Wouldn't you?' he asked, thinking how much he always liked steak and chips. He poured them more wine.

He was beginning to feel pleasantly, warmly, drunk. They were almost at the bottom of a bottle of red. All the crystals of anxiety that seemed to be stiffening his limbs had melted away. On the second glass, he had decided there was no point in worrying.

He was in Paris, and he was with the woman he had always imagined being here with. There was nothing he could do about it, so he might as well enjoy himself.

Alison was wearing black. Slim trousers and a fine black jumper under a short black jacket. She had tied a brightly coloured silk scarf round her neck and clipped hemispheres of pearl to her ears which made her look as chic as any of the Frenchwomen at nearby tables. She always looked so expensive, he thought, suddenly turned on by the sheer quality of her.

'Come on,' he said, glancing at the tab and throwing a couple of notes on the table. He stood up and took her hand.

'I wanted coffee . . .' she said.

'You can have coffee later,' he told her, wanting to rip her clothes off right there.

He ran his tongue up the centre of her body, under the vulnerable arch of her chin, onto her mouth. Then, crouched over her like an animal, he looked down at her lying beneath him half clad, red lipstick smudged, hair fanned out, staring at him with eyes lazy in submission. He thought, She is my mistress. We are acting out a fantasy. This is not real. Then he plunged himself into her, and the suction of her flesh tight around his felt a hundred times more real than he had ever felt. It was the moment he kept coming back for, that momentary clasping of her flesh around his.

Afterwards they slept, with their heads on the hard, narrow bolster, and when they woke, they were cold and grumpy with muzzy heads. They showered together, slightly embarrassed, as if this act were more intimate than anything else they had ever done together.

When he brushed his teeth, he made a horrible throat-clearing sound, she noticed.

When she brushed hers, she squeezed the toothpaste from the middle of the tube, and failed to rinse out the bowl, he saw.

He threw his wet towel onto the bed and left it there. She walked around dripping wet, leaving damp patches on the carpet.

'Let's go out and do some sightseeing,' he suggested.

'Good idea!' she agreed hastily.

He seemed to be wired up to a dozen different pieces of apparatus. He looked grey and expressionless. When their mother arrived they left her with him and went to the canteen.

'Have you talked to any of the doctors?' Ginger asked her sister, carrying their tray to a clean table.

'Well, yes. They can't tell until he regains consciousness what damage there has been, they say, if any . . .'

'*If* he regains consciousness,' Ginger said, sipping her tea, remembering why she never drank it. She hated tea.

'Yes, if,' Pic said.

'I think he will, don't you?' Ginger said, brightly, trying to suppress the overwhelming sense gathering inside her that he would not.

'I don't know,' Pic said. 'He looks awfully grey and old lying there.'

'Let's go back to Mummy,' Ginger said, abandoning her drink.

When they heard their mother's shrill voice talking as they went into his room, they both thought that he had woken up, but he had not.

'One of the nurses said it might help if I talked to him,' she told them, 'but I didn't know what to say, so I've been telling him about the garden.' She turned to Pic, her lip quivering uncontrollably.

Ginger looked away, knowing that her mother would be embarrassed later. She came from the class that thought it impolite to express emotion. The only time Ginger could remember her crying was when one of the dogs got run over. Ginger realised that she had been fooled for all these years into thinking that her mother didn't feel much for Daddy. She loves him, Ginger thought, shocked.

Every time she glanced at her father, she expected him to open one eye and shout 'Boo!' at her as he used to sometimes in the summer, when she had chased him round the croquet lawn until he pretended to drop down dead with exhaustion.

She wandered out into the corridor, not knowing what to do. How long should she wait? What was going to happen? It was difficult to imagine that outside the hospital life was just going on. Here, she felt that they were all in a state of suspended animation, waiting.

She found a payphone and rang Lia, who sounded anxious. She had just changed Anouska and she couldn't decide whether she had a rash, or whether she was just pink because she was so hot.

'Why don't you get the doctor to come again?' Ginger suggested.

'It's Good Friday . . .' Lia said.

'Don't worry about that,' Ginger said. 'You pay his wages, remember.'

'I suppose so,' Lia said. 'I wish Neil was here.'

'Why don't you ring him and get him to come home?'

'Well, I don't want to worry him . . .'

'Why not? You're worried. Why shouldn't he be worried too?' Ginger asked impatiently, not understanding why Lia always shielded him.

'What good would it do?'

'Well, it might make you feel better,' Ginger told her.

Lia giggled.

'That's better.' Ginger smiled. 'I don't know how long I'm going to be here, but I'll keep calling.'

'OK,' Lia said. 'Good luck!'

Ginger tried to think of other people to ring, but all the numbers she knew off by heart had answerphones on. Charlie had told her to call, but she resisted, thinking that his friendly voice might make her cry. And that wouldn't do any good. He would think she was getting clingy.

The doctor told Lia that babies often had rashes for no reason, but it was possible that it was measles. He suggested she sponge Anouska down with lukewarm water and give her plenty of fluids. Would her husband be home soon? She explained that Neil was away. Well, that's a shame, he said, gently, because when you've not had a lot of sleep, it's easy to start imagining terrible things.

'Patronising bastard!' Ginger said, when she heard all this.

'I'm sort of glad to know it's something, though,' Lia said. 'I'm sorry if Guy gets it . . .' she added quickly.

'Don't be ridiculous,' Ginger told her. She looked in the cot at Anouska. The rash was barely visible on her face but her lips seemed unnaturally red. She didn't want to worry Lia more, but she thought that if it had been Guy, she would have wanted a second opinion.

'I'll tell you what, I'll stay the night,' Ginger said, ''then you can get some sleep.'

Lia was so exhausted by worry she did not object.

'I'll get a cab home, get a change of clothes for me and Guy and pick up a Chinese on the way back, OK?'

'That would be fantastic,' Lia told her, truly grateful for the practical support. 'Are you sure?'

'Course,' Ginger said. 'I didn't want to be on my own tonight, anyway. I'd only lie awake and worry about Daddy.'

She returned with two carrier bags of Chinese food and a bottle of wine.

Lia laid the table in the kitchen and started taking the lids off the foil trays: sweet-and-sour prawns, sweet-and-sour chicken, sweet-and-sour pork, plain boiled rice.

'I hope you like sweet-and-sour,' Ginger said, looking despondently at the containers. How could she have done that? She had simply not been capable of choosing. She had struggled all day to keep the rising tide of panic at bay, but it was beginning to burst through the barriers she had put up.

It didn't matter because neither of them had an appetite.

'Let's get drunk, anyway,' Ginger said, pouring them both a glass of white wine.

'I don't think I'd better,' Lia said. 'I want to have good judgment in case Anouska gets worse . . .'

'Yes, you're right,' Ginger said sombrely, corking the bottle.

It was going to be a long night.

At two thirty in the morning, Ginger looked at her watch. She was twitching with tiredness, but the sofa, which she had truthfully assured Lia was really comfortable, seemed to have shrunk and now sloped so that she felt she was rolling down a hill.

When she looked at her watch about five minutes later, she saw that it was six o'clock, and she had been woken up by the sound of Lia crossing the room upstairs. She went into the kitchen, tiptoeing past Guy, who had slumbered peacefully the whole night in the travel cot where he usually took his afternoon nap.

When Lia came down, Ginger handed her a steaming mug of tea.

'Is she all right?' she asked her.

'Yes, she's sleeping. I think she looks a bit better,' Lia said.

They both blew long sighs of relief.

'I feel as if we're in the war. We've survived a long night during the Blitz, or something,' Ginger remarked.

The clothes were even more stunning up close, when you could see the quality of the material and the details of the decoration. Back in London, when she had watched the video of the great Parisian couturier's collection, there had been one dress she had fallen in love with, and now it hung in front of her.

'Do you want to try it on?' John-Fabrizio Jones asked her, recognising the desire in her eyes.

'No . . . really?' Alison said.

He waved in the direction of a kind of medieval tent that rose out of the thickly carpeted floor of the salon. Which rich and famous women had undressed on this spot? she wondered excitedly, as she stripped to her pants and stockings and slipped the dress over her head. It slid on like a glove.

She admired herself in the gold-framed cheval mirror for a few seconds, wishing that someone she knew were here to witness the moment. She imagined Stephen sitting in the antique armchair, smiling at her as she twirled round in front of him. Then she stopped. Not Stephen, Neil, she remembered. But she could not imagine him sitting there. She smiled at herself in the mirror, then pulled back the heavy curtain to show John-Fabrizio.

'Yes,' he said, making a circle in the air with his finger.

She twirled round obediently.

'You have the height for it,' he said, 'but if I were making it for you, I would choose the gold.' He hung a swatch of fabric next to her face. 'You can't get away with silver with your colouring at your age . . .' he added, sending her high spirits crashing. There were as few frills on him as on the clothes he created. He said exactly what he thought.

As she took the beautiful dress off, she consoled herself with the thought that the whole episode would make good copy.

'We sometimes have a kind of ex-pats brunch on Sundays,' John-Fabrizio told her when she emerged again. 'Would you like to come along?'

'I'd love to,' she said, flattered.

As soon as she was out in the street, she did a little jump for joy, before running all the way to her rendezvous with Neil.

'He's asked me for brunch, tomorrow,' she told him breathlessly, waving a waiter over and ordering coffee. 'You don't mind, do you? I mean, it's quite a coup.'

There were spots of colour on her cheeks, and her eyes sparkled with a look of triumph he had not seen before.

'He let me try on a dress!'

He did not understand how unusual that was.

'It was probably worth about ten grand!' she told him proudly.

'People pay ten thousand pounds for a dress? That's disgusting,' Neil said.

She felt as if he had stuck a pin in her bubble of elation. 'You're right, I suppose,' she said.

'You didn't mention that you were here *with* somebody, then?' Neil asked her.

'No, of course not.' She was beginning to understand why he was looking sulky. 'It's work,' she said, gently. 'You can't just say, "Oh by the way, can I bring a friend?"'

But she realised he had zoomed in on something she already felt uncomfortable about. Why hadn't she asked John-Fabrizio if she could bring a friend? It was a matter of difference, she told herself. Over the last twenty-four hours, she had discovered how different she and Neil were. There wasn't anything wrong with that, she kept assuring herself.

She just wasn't used to being with people whose idea of enjoying a weekend in Paris was to visit Montmartre, the Champs-Elysées and the Eiffel Tower, for heaven's sake. It was so *naff* to be herded along with coachloads of Americans like a tourist.

So, they had different tastes. But you didn't fall out of love with someone because they queued for hours to see the Mona Lisa only to pass the judgment that it was very small. Did you? Now, she admitted to herself, the idea of introducing him to a group of the coolest people in Europe was unthinkable.

'Anyway, you'd hate it,' she told him brightly.

'I'm sure I would,' he said, seeing how tense she had become, and not wanting to argue with her.

Anouska did not seem to be any better, but she didn't seem any worse either, Lia thought, peering into her cot. When she was sleeping she looked more or less the same as she usually did. It was only when she was awake that Lia grew concerned, because she was so miserable. But she had had so little sleep herself over the last couple of days that she was beginning to wonder whether she could judge.

She went downstairs and made herself a cup of tea, spooning sugar in to give herself energy. This kind of tiredness was like a massive hangover, she thought, sipping the hot, sweet liquid as she slumped down on the sofa in the living room.

Only two more days, she told herself, trying to keep her eyes open. Then Neil would be home and everything would be easier. The flash of freedom she had experienced as he disappeared now made her feel guilty.

What would he say if he were here? Would he tell her she was being silly, or would he take one look at Anouska and drive her to hospital? Probably the former, she reasoned. On the other hand, he had never had much respect for their doctor. What if there was something terribly wrong with the baby and Lia had just accepted the doctor's word? Neil would go mad. Anouska was his child too, and yet she was assuming sole responsibility for medical decisions about her. Perhaps she was being too feeble. Panicking, she went into the kitchen and picked up the phone. Then put it down. What would she say to the doctor? That Anouska seemed the same, but she was still worried? He would become impatient. All she wanted was for someone to tell her that she was worrying unnecessarily, that her baby would be all right. She picked up the phone again.

It was such a relief to hear the connection had been made that it didn't occur to Lia, until the receptionist answered, that she did not speak French. She said Neil's name a couple of times.

Silence.

'He is a guest at your hotel,' she said, speaking slowly.

No, there was no one of that name staying at the hotel, the woman responded.

He's a teacher, with students. From London.

No, came the reply, this is a small hotel, only twelve rooms. We do not take schools here.

'So sorry,' Lia said, apologising automatically, and putting down the phone as if she had dialled a wrong number. She checked the piece of paper Neil had left again. No, it was the right hotel. There had to be some mistake.

Then the doorbell rang and Ginger was there looking pale.

'How is he?' Lia asked, worried.

'No change,' Ginger said, despondently. 'The longer he doesn't wake up, the worse it is, apparently. How's Anouska?'

'Asleep, and no real change, I think,' Lia said.

'Do you want me to stay again?' Ginger asked her.

'Would you mind?' Lia asked.

'As long as we don't have to eat last night's leftovers,' Ginger said, animated all of a sudden. 'How's my son?'

'He's just fine. He went off beautifully,' Lia said, with relief that someone else was there.

Now that Ginger was back, it didn't seem to matter so much that she had not been able to speak to Neil.

The Place des Vosges was the perfect place to be on a sunny Sunday morning. He had bought the *Observer* from an international newsstand, and he was sitting on a bench reading the sports pages, relieved to be by himself. The square was oddly quiet, as if the whole of Paris was still in bed and had not yet opened the curtains to see what a glorious spring day it was. The sun's warmth fell kindly on his face and he put the paper down and stretched his arms, still waking up properly from the best sleep he had enjoyed in months.

It was over, and he could almost relax.

He wasn't sure yet whether Alison knew too. The evening before, they had barely exchanged a word over supper, as if they had run out of things to say. Afterwards, as they were walking along the riverbank, she had suggested going to see a movie. He had not objected, although he thought it was an odd way to spend an evening in Paris.

Later, there had been an almost vicious air of tension in the room as they lay side by side in bed, not touching, as if the slightest contact would produce an electric shock. He knew that she wanted to ask him what the problem was, but she didn't quite dare. He knew that it would be kinder to tell her, but she would either argue in that way she had, using language to trick him, and make him say things he didn't mean, or cry—and he hadn't the strength to deal with either. Eventually, he said good night and turned away.

He could pinpoint the exact moment he had known that their relationship could not last.

It was in the Musée d'Orsay the previous afternoon. They had been standing in front of one of Monet's lily pictures.

'We've got that one at home,' he had remarked.

'Really?'

The cool aloofness of her tone was beginning to irritate him. He could tell that she wasn't happy traipsing round galleries or doing the sights, but he could hardly go home and say that he'd spent the weekend hanging about in boutiques with snooty assistants, while she fingered handbags or tried on shoes, could he? He thought she would see that.

'Yeah,' he told her, scrutinising the picture closely, 'I think the colours are better in the poster.'

She hadn't been able to stop a grimace of contempt flashing across her face, and he had seen it. That was the moment he had known for sure. It hadn't even crossed her mind that he might be joking.

They spoke a different language, nowadays, Ally and he. She knew all about fashion and style, not just clothes, but books, films, even what food you were supposed to eat. He knew nothing about all that, and cared less. For her, Sunday lunch was going with a few friends to a new place that combined the best of Japanese and Middle Eastern cuisine and writing a column about it. For him, it was a pub with Lia and a crowd from the club. He doubted whether he would recognise a field of lemongrass if he drove past one, let alone wax lyrical about it.

Back in London, insulated in her Islington flat, she had thought it amusing when he asked her what she was talking about. Out in the real world it wasn't a joke. It mattered to her. He had wanted to tell her that he didn't really want to have brunch with a bunch of pansies who spent their lives designing unwearable dresses for the world's richest women, but it would only have sounded defensive.

But that was just the symptom of their problem. They lived in different worlds. Perhaps they always had.

He stared in front of him, not focusing, recalling her hiss of impatience as a teenager when he had told her his ambition was to play cricket for England. She had wanted him to go to a 'proper' university rather than a sports college. Her dreams were always of money, and nice clothes, and one of those great big stucco-fronted houses in Kensington.

She had all that now, or the equivalent. She wouldn't give it up for him. Why should she? He liked the life he had too, he realised, for the first time in months. He wouldn't want to give it up for her, either.

He would make it up to Lia, he promised himself, as a sudden sharp pang of guilt attacked him. He had betrayed her in the worst possible way, because she had known almost from the first moment he had set eyes on Alison again that something was wrong with him. Yet she had not asked, because she had assumed it must be something she had done wrong. He had exploited and added to her insecurity because it suited him. She had borne his child and he had failed her. At the one moment she was relying on him to be strong, he had been weak. He had lied to her and to himself, pretending to be carried away by the power of something greater than he was, when it had all been a fantasy.

He wanted to go home, now, to take the first train, or plane, or even hitch a lift. But stranded in Paris by his own lies, he would have to wait.

'Hello!' Ginger called to Stephen as he walked past the room where her father lay.

He looked at her, perplexed. His expression said that he recognised her, but he could not think where from.

'It's Ginger,' she helped him. 'I'm a friend of your wife.'

'Ginger, of course . . . sorry, you look rather different out of your red dress!' His face was transformed by a smile. 'How is he?' he asked her, pointing to her father.

'I thought you might be able to tell *me*,' she replied, jokily.

'Oh, I'm sorry,' he said, approaching the bed. 'We have this singsong way of talking to relatives, I'm afraid.' Automatically, he picked up the notes at the end of the bed.

'I would like to know what you think. Seriously. I mean, is he going to die?'

Stephen looked at her steadily for what seemed like a long time, checking, she thought, for indications of mental instability.

'Sometimes miracles do happen,' he said finally. 'But not very often.'

'Oh,' she said.

She stared at her father, then looked out of the window at the rooftops and the sky. It was quiet outside. Easter Sunday in the city. It was impossible to imagine the world without her father's presence. Even lying here silently, he was the focus of everyone's attention.

When she eventually looked round, Stephen had gone.

A couple of minutes later, his head appeared round the door again.

'Come on,' he beckoned to her. 'I don't intend to talk about the patient, but I'm on a break, and you look as if you could do with a cup of tea.'

'I hate tea,' said Ginger grumpily.

'Coffee?' suggested Stephen.

'Yes, coffee,' said Ginger, following him out of the room.

When they reached the canteen, he showed her to a table, then walked over to the counter and bought her a piece of chocolate cake and a cup of coffee.

'Yummy! What a gentleman!' Ginger said gleefully.

He laughed and sat down opposite her with his tea.

Since he had informed her that he wasn't allowed to talk about her father, and he didn't seem eager to take the lead in conversation, she felt it incumbent on her to start chatting.

'How's Alison?' she asked, scooping a fingerful of the gooey chocolate icing into her mouth.

'Fine. Or at least I assume she is,' he replied. 'She's away this weekend, working. I've had the last two days off, just Ben and I, which I must say I've enjoyed.'

'They're great fun at the moment, aren't they?' Ginger said.

'They certainly are. Where's your little boy today?' he asked.

Ginger began to explain.

'Poor Lia. I feel terrible about it, really. Her man's away, and her little girl is very poorly.'

'What's wrong with her?' Stephen asked, more from genuine concern than professional interest, Ginger thought.

'She's got a temperature . . .' Ginger began to list Anouska's symptoms, ending with, 'and this morning, her hands and feet were really red, as if she was sunburnt and beginning to peel . . . What do you think?' she couldn't resist asking him, noticing alarm in his eyes.

She had urged Lia to call the GP again this morning, or get a second opinion. Now there was one in front of her. Damn the ethics. It was too good an opportunity to miss.

'Well, it's impossible to diagnose in absentia, and I'm not a paediatrician . . .' Stephen paused, as if deliberating whether to go on, then he added, 'but it does sound as if someone should have a proper look at Anouska . . . Look, I think you should ring Lia and tell her to take the little girl to the nearest hospital. Does she drive?'

'Well, yes, but she's got Guy too. Maybe I should go home and get a taxi with her?' Ginger asked, hoping that he would tell her to stop being so ridiculous. Something about his tone had made her very frightened.

'Yes, good idea,' Stephen said, standing up. 'As soon as possible. She should tell whoever's on duty she'd like to speak to the paediatric registrar and tell him, or her, that you've spoken to someone who thought it sounded potentially like a case of Kawasaki syndrome. It probably won't be, so don't alarm Lia, but if it is, it is essential to get treatment quickly.'

'What's Kawasaki syndrome?' Ginger asked, horrified, quickening her step to keep up with him as they approached the ward again.

'Mucocutaneous lymphnode syndrome,' Stephen said. 'It's a child-hood illness and most children make a complete recovery, but for a few it's not very nice. I probably know a little more about it than most doctors because it can affect the coronary arteries.'

'Is it catching?' Ginger said, hating herself for immediately thinking of her own child.

'Not that I'm aware. Now, look, keep calm.' He saw her looking at the door of her father's room. 'There's nothing you can do for him at the moment,' he said gently.

'But what if he dies while I'm gone?' Ginger asked, tears catching in her throat.

'There'll be nothing you can do,' Stephen repeated.

In the taxi, she thought Stephen must have thought her father was about to die, otherwise he would have said something like, 'It's unlikely'. She made herself imagine how she would feel if he were to die. Relieved, she thought, that he had gone without suffering too much. Relieved that he hadn't woken up a vegetable.

There's nothing you can do about *him*, but there is something you can do about Anouska. That had been Stephen's implication.

Anouska looked so tiny lying in the hospital bed. They had put up cot sides so she wouldn't fall out, but the tubes, drips and wires would surely hold her in place. They had given her intravenous immunoglobu-lin. When the fluid went into her, Lia had felt an enormous sense of expectation that as soon as the medication reached its target, Anouska would suddenly throw off the illness and be transformed back into the placid and smiling child she usually was. But there was no change.

After many different people examining her, the hospital had agreed on the diagnosis. Kawasaki syndrome, as Stephen had suspected. It was an inflammatory process, the consultant explained to her, that had no cure, but possible complications might be prevented if medication was administered early enough.

When she tried to ask what 'possible complications' meant, she was rebuffed with kindness. Eventually, a female doctor sat down with her and explained that it was too early to tell what Anouska might have suffered. They were arranging for her to have further tests.

They gave Lia a bed in the little room where Anouska was lying, and she sat on it staring at her child, with no idea what to do, paralysed by a depth of fear she had never experienced before.

She found herself praying to a God she did not believe in. *Please let her survive. Please let there be no damage. Please don't let it be my fault.*

As the ward outside filled with evening visitors, Lia began to feel desperately lonely. She could not allow herself to leave the ward to find the payphone, and even if she did, there was no one she could ring. This was a time for family, she realised. Friends paid visits to hospital when the worst was over. For the first time in her adult life, she wanted a mum. She wiped a tear away with the back of her hand, refusing to let herself cry. She must be strong for her daughter. She could not desert her as her own mother had done. Here, in the hospital, sitting waiting at the edge of life or death, she could almost understand how her mother could have done that. It was awful being a mother when your child was suffering. It made you completely responsible and totally useless at the same time. In life, there was always an exit route: you could get away from things you did not like. In motherhood, you were trapped and no amount of railing and screaming could get you out. But freedom was a tiny price to pay for the life of your child.

At that moment, she became aware that someone was standing waiting for her to look up, not wanting to make her jump.

'I've brought you a sandwich, a Coke and a mobile phone,' Ginger said. 'We've found the phone very useful with Daddy. We've even taught Mummy how to use it. See, it's easy . . .' She sat down next to her.

Lia could hold herself together no longer. She put her face against Ginger's shoulder and cried and cried.

'Where's Guy?' she asked, when the sobs finally subsided.

'Don't worry about him. Pic's at my place with him. Now, I can't be long, so you'd better tell me what you want.'

'Nothing, really,' Lia said automatically, 'except company,' she added, smiling weakly.

'You can ring Neil now . . .' Ginger said, handing over the phone.

'I don't know his number.' Lia told her about ringing the hotel in Paris.

'Damn . . .' Ginger said, thinking quickly. 'Ring one of his colleagues and ask them to find out and call him.'

'Oh!' Lia exclaimed. 'I hadn't thought of that.'

'Well, you've had other things on your mind,' Ginger consoled her. She went over and looked into the cot. 'She looks a little better, I think,' she said.

'Do you think so?' Lia said, getting up from the bed.

'I think our little friend is going to be just fine,' Ginger said, putting her arm round Lia and giving her a big squeeze as they stood looking at the sleeping infant.

'There may be damage to her heart,' Lia whispered.

'Well, we'll think about that if and when the time comes,' Ginger responded calmly.

'You sound just like the doctors . . .'

'Yes, I'm getting a taste for it. I think I've got the bedside manner now; all I have to do is learn about anatomy and epidemiology and that stuff.'

'Cinch!' said Lia.

'Quite,' said Ginger, glad she had managed to get her friend to join in the weak joke.

After Ginger left, Lia ate the sandwich she had brought her and swigged at the can of Coke. Feeling better, she picked up the phone.

She called directory enquiries, and then called Neil's junior in the sports department.

'It's Lia, Neil's—'

'Hello, Lia, how are you?' Bill said, very friendly.

'Fine,' she said, automatically. 'Well, not fine . . . um, this sounds silly, but I'm trying to get in touch with Neil in Paris. He gave me the number of the hotel, but I think there's been some mistake . . . I wondered if you knew where they are staying?'

'Where who are staying?' He was clearly mystified by the question.

'The school party.'

'What school party? I didn't know there was one.'

'But you dropped out . . . Neil took your place . . .'

'Er, no . . .' he said.

'Oh,' Lia said, feeling his embarrassment, 'it must have been someone else. I'm sorry.'

'I could ring the school secretary and phone you back, if you want,' he suddenly volunteered, as if he had failed her.

'If you could, thanks so much.' She read out the number of the phone, then pressed the red button to end the call.

There was a simple explanation, Lia told herself. Of course there was.

There were probably several Bills, or maybe she had mistaken the name. Don't start imagining things, she told herself. Things are bad enough. Remember the last time you suspected him and all he was doing was keeping the car a surprise. There was bound to be some simple explanation. She just had too much on her mind to think of it. She called Pete and Cheryl, remembering that she did have family, after all. Cheryl immediately offered to drive up, but somehow, now that they knew, Lia didn't feel quite so isolated.

'No, you don't have to do that,' she told her. 'It's just nice to know you're there.'

'Look, we'll come tomorrow,' Cheryl told her.

'No, you don't have to. Neil'll be home.'

'We'll come and be with you until he gets there.'

'All right,' Lia agreed, pressing the red button.

Alison had already consumed a lot of champagne with John-Fabrizio, and it was such a glorious afternoon the only way to spend it, she told Neil, was in the sun, drinking more. They went on a leisurely café crawl of the Marais and then crossed onto the Île Saint-Louis. She took his hand and he put his arm round her, and kissed the top of her head. They said little, but it felt as if that was because they were relaxed in one another's company, unlike the previous evening.

They bought small cones of sorbet from a *glacerie*, apricot for him, cassis for her. The blackcurrant ice stained her lips purple. As they wandered on she caught a glimpse of herself in a panel of stainless steel that shone like a mirror in the golden evening sunlight. She rubbed at her lips with a tissue.

'God! And to think I used to buy lipstick that colour—do you remember?'

'Yes,' he said. 'You liked purple. You had purple loons, and yellow ones.'

'You're right!' she said, skipping beside him. 'I'd forgotten the yellow ones . . . You didn't wear loons . . .'

'I never liked flared trousers,' he said, resting his elbows on the parapet of the bridge they were crossing. He turned and smiled at her, then looked straight ahead, his eyes watching the *bateau mouche* with its sloping bank of tourists.

'Look, Ally,' he began, 'that was a long time ago—'

'God, you're telling me,' she interrupted him. 'You can tell you're getting old when fashion that you wore comes round again. I even found myself toying with a pair of flared trousers the other day, and I can remember taking a solemn vow never, ever to wear flares again.'

'What shall we do now?' Neil asked her, defeated by her chatter.

She thought she knew what he had been going to say, but she didn't want to hear it, not here, not standing next to him in the sunlight on a bridge over the Seine. In her head, she heard Bryan Ferry: *The Île de France with all the gulls around it, the beauty that is spring's* . . .

'More drink . . .' she said, linking her arm through his as they turned towards the Left Bank. 'Lots more to drink . . .'

He died at nine in the morning, just after Mummy and Pic arrived. It was as if he had waited for them. Ginger and Guy got there a few minutes later.

She had thought that he looked dead when he was lying there in a coma, but now she saw that he had not. Dead people really look dead. The man he had been was not present any longer.

She was the only one of them crying, and it was strange to feel her mother's arms enfold her as Pic took Guy out of the room.

'Could I have a moment by myself with him?' she asked, recovering herself slightly.

Her mother released her and left the room, in silence.

Ginger approached the bed and picked up his hand.

'I love you, Daddy,' she told him now. 'You did know that, didn't you?'

How wrong she had been to think that she would feel relief at his passing. All she felt was total, overwhelming sadness, and her tears came thick and fast. She stood there for a long time.

Her father's body was wheeled off to the morgue and, after a few minutes which they all spent wondering what on earth they were meant to do, Mummy suggested that they repair to the canteen.

After the sadness, a wave of euphoria seemed to settle over the three women. They began to chatter with each other, remembering good things about him.

At one point, Stephen came up to their table to offer his condolences, then politely made his excuses and turned away. But Ginger jumped up and followed him.

'I just wanted to tell you about Anouska,' she said. 'Your diagnosis was right. They're keeping her in. But nobody seems to be able to tell Lia anything about the effects of Kawasaki syndrome.'

'Sometimes it is better for people not to know all the details,' Stephen warned. 'Knowing everything about a disease doesn't mean you can cure it, unfortunately.'

She nodded, heeding what he had said.

'You must look after yourself,' he told her. 'You've had two shocks this weekend, and you're coping well, but there will come a time when you may not be so good at dealing with it, so take care.'

'I will,' she said obediently.

'Well, goodbye,' he said, offering her his hand.

She shook it. 'Goodbye, and thanks!' she said. She went back to join her sister, her mother and her son.

'What do you want to do, Mummy?' Pic was asking their mother. 'You're very welcome to come back with me.'

'No, I think I shall go home,' their mother replied.

'Would you like me to come with you?' both daughters asked.

'No, I think I should like to remember him alone, if you don't mind,' their mother said. 'I shall need to make arrangements. I have the dogs, and there are plenty of people to look after my needs.'

Neither daughter knew what to say. It didn't seem right that she should be returning to the country alone, to find comfort in a spaniel rather than a daughter. But it was her home, and if that was what she wanted why should they stop her?

'Shall I get Tom to come for you with the car?' Pic asked, referring to Mummy's driver.

'No, I shall take the train. You could call and tell him to meet me at the station.'

'Of course I will,' Pic agreed.

'I'll take Mummy to Waterloo, then,' Ginger told Pic.

Neil could remember standing on the bridge in the warm, golden glow of evening sunlight, and then the first bar, but after that, the evening merged into a bleary impression of streetlights and snatches of inane conversation about things they had done twenty years before. She had been insistent that they had gone to Biba on the same day as they went to see Bryan Ferry, but he knew for sure that he had never been to Biba. They had had a long, pointless argument about it, and in the end he had got up and walked out into the street, not knowing where he was going. He had been relieved to hear her footsteps running after him.

It was very late when they arrived back at the hotel. Neil had woken up at dawn fully clothed with Alison snoring beside him. They had cleared the room and checked out without a word.

At the station, she had the presence of mind to buy a bottle of water, which they were taking it in turns to slurp. Now, she pushed a couple of tablets across the table at him.

'Paracetamol,' she said.

'Thanks,' he replied, swallowing them.

The train was speeding through the fields of France.

'What are you thinking about?' he asked her after a while.

She was thinking how little he had changed. The day before, she had thought that he had changed a lot, and that was why it would never work between them, but it wasn't that. She was the one who had changed.

At seventeen, he had everything considered desirable—he was handsome, he had a motorbike, he was the captain of the school football and cricket teams. And now none of these things meant anything to her.

'I was thinking about Ben,' she told him, snatching at a neutral subject. 'I've missed him. I didn't think I would . . . Apparently he said ball, so his vocabulary has increased by fifty per cent,' she added.

'How do you know?'

'Justine told me . . . I called yesterday morning.'

Why hadn't he called home? he asked himself, panicking, then remembering they were at Ginger's. Lia would have called him if there were any problems. He calmed down.

'So, Ben says words now, does he?' Neil said. 'Annie claps and she can wave bye-bye,' he added proudly.

Neil thought how ironic it was that they should have ended their weekend talking about the only thing that they had left in common: their children.

At Waterloo she said, 'I'm getting a taxi. I'd offer you a lift, but . . .'

'No, I'll take the tube,' he said.

They stood looking at each other for a long time. Then he took her in his arms and kissed her. It was a kiss of regret and nostalgia, and when they finally pulled apart, he knew that she was trying hard not to cry.

'Bye now.' He picked up his bag and turned away.

Alison watched him go. Her eyes were so full of tears she didn't notice an elderly lady looking at the departure board, and next to her, Ginger, whose eyes followed her disbelievingly as she walked past them towards the taxis.

Stephen and Ben were sitting at the kitchen table having tea when Alison walked in. She kissed them both and sat down. Then she helped herself to a plateful of pasta that Stephen had prepared and began to cram it into her mouth ravenously.

'I'm completely hungover, I have to admit, and starving!'

Stephen smiled at her. He had always thought that hangovers rather suited her, giving her a slightly dishevelled look. She was clearly tired, but sparkling.

'What have you been up to?' she asked him

'Well, let's just say you picked a good weekend to go away,' he replied, with a slight, dry chuckle.

At the news about Ginger's father and Lia's child her fork dropped from her hand, and her face went white with shock.

Stephen was taken aback. 'It's entirely possible that she will make a complete recovery,' he explained, as Alison sat staring at him, nodding, wanting to hear that it was going to be all right, 'but there is the chance of sudden death . . .' He was attempting to make a balanced, but realistic, assessment of the dangers, but Alison was clearly not hearing anything he said.

She jumped up, rushed to the phone, dialled, then put the receiver down, rushed back to the kitchen table, lifted Ben from his highchair, hugging him tight to her, stroking the back of his head, with his face to her shoulder. When she finally returned him to his chair, her smart black jacket was smeared with baby food.

She began to question Stephen, harshly, as if it was all his fault. How could he be so unsure about the prognosis? Was Anouska receiving the best possible care?

They were the sort of questions that he was used to hearing from close relatives who wanted someone to blame for the tragedy and were desperate to hear the doctor say that it was not their fault. He wished he had found some gentler way of telling her the news. The shock of learning two tragedies so close to home when she had been abroad and powerless to do anything had clearly affected her deeply. He tried to understand the hostility of her behaviour towards him as transferred guilt, because she was imagining what would have happened if Ben had fallen ill and she had not been there.

'The chances are that the baby will be fine,' he told her, again. 'The real danger is when the disease is misdiagnosed. Anouska is one of the lucky ones,' he added, mentally crossing his fingers that the reassurances he was giving her would prove correct.

'No, she won't . . . I know she won't,' Alison kept repeating.

He noticed Ben's face, bewildered by her behaviour.

'Why don't you go and have a lie down?' he suggested, anxious to minimise their son's distress.

She looked up, angrily, on the point of arguing, then saw he was nodding at Ben's frowning face.

'I think I will,' she agreed, leaving the room.

**P**ete was waiting for Neil when he arrived home. 'Where the hell have you been?' he asked.

'Paris.' Neil said, dumping his kitbag by the door and slumping into the armchair. 'School trip.'

'There wasn't a bloody school trip.' Pete sat forward, coldly spitting out the words. 'You stupid bastard!'

'Look,' said Neil, 'it's not what you think—' He stopped mid-sentence, realising it was exactly what his brother was thinking. 'Why are you here, anyway?'

When Pete started talking about Kawasaki syndrome and what had happened, Neil thought, for a few bleary seconds, that it was all an elaborate joke that he did not quite understand. Something to do with his motorbike. But one glance at his brother's face told him that it was not.

In the moment's silence that followed, the phone rang. Neil went to pick it up. Nothing. He knew who it was. He slammed down the receiver, furious that she had ever lured him away.

'Let's go,' he said to his brother.

'No, you go and wash your face,' his brother ordered him contemptuously. 'You've got lipstick round your mouth. Lia's been through enough without that.'

**T**he main emotion Lia felt when she saw him was relief, closely followed by sympathy. He looked so worried and repentant, she wanted to hug him and tell him it would be all right, but she could not. She did not know that it would be. Instead she led him to the cot where Anouska lay sleeping. She could see that he was frightened by the heart monitor and the line going into her foot.

'It's a drip, to give her the medication,' she explained.

'Is she going to die?' Neil whispered.

'I don't think so,' she told him quietly.

With her eyes fixed on Anouska, unable to look at Neil, Lia began to explain the little she knew. They were going to go by ambulance to Great Ormond Street the next day. Anouska was going to have an echo scan which would show up any damage to her arteries. The doctors were all saying that she had a good chance of survival, but nobody seemed to be able to promise more than that.

She felt Neil bristle with impatience by her side, and it made her recognise the cycle of emotions she had gone through the day before. Impatience, anger, impotence. You expected a hospital to *know*. You could deal with a yes or no, live or die, but not with this uncertainty.

She felt Neil's arm round her shoulder and did not attempt to shrug it off. She did not know whether they were lovers, now, or even friends, but they were together as parents of a child. Nothing could alter that. That would bind them for ever.

PIC AND GINGER ambled slowly through the bluebell wood at Kew Gardens, taking it in turns to push the buggy. The canopy of tall trees shaded the fierce sunshine of early summer. The rustle of leaves and the birdsong were like balm to tired spirits. 'Have you seen Charlie much?' Pic asked her sister.

'No. He rings, but I don't want to see him,' Ginger said.

'But why?' Pic asked.

'Oh, I don't know,' Ginger replied, clamming up.

Grief had affected them in different ways. At the funeral, Pic had concentrated on how beautiful the music was, and how much Daddy would have liked it. Ginger stood next to her shaking with uncontrollable sobbing. Pic had noticed the concerned surprise on their relations' faces as they followed the coffin out of the church. It was so unlike Ginger. Ginger was the clown who would laugh through anything, Pic was meant to be the serious one.

As each week passed, Pic could feel her sadness retreating. It was as if Daddy was still around, but just out of reach. Her overwhelming feeling about him was fondness.

Ginger's grief was darker. It hung round her like a mood, closing her to the world. Each time Pic arrived at the flat, she expected Ginger to open the door joking, normal again, but it didn't happen. Her relationship with Daddy had been difficult, and it had been left unresolved.

When the will was read it emerged that her father had not only made a generous provision for Ginger, but included Guy too. 'There, you see, he did love you . . .' Pic had whispered, holding her sister's hand.

'I know that,' Ginger had hissed, 'but he didn't know that I loved him.'

'I'm sure he did,' Pic insisted, but even as she said it, she wasn't quite convinced it was true. Ginger had always done a pretty good job of disguising any affection she felt for her father.

'You both gave him enormous pleasure, in your different ways,' their mother had told them, the day he died. Pic kept reminding Ginger of that. But it seemed to have no impact.

'Don't you think it might help if you saw a few people?' Pic tried again, as they came out of the wood and into the sunny open lawns by the lake.

'No,' Ginger said sulkily.

'What about Lia? How is she?' Pic asked.

'I think she's coping a bit better,' Ginger said, grateful for a change of subject. 'The first week Anouska came out of hospital she was very jittery, but she seems a bit calmer now. She says she's happy to start having Guy again, but I don't know what to do . . .'

Ginger hadn't been into work since their father's death. Ironically, she missed it, and would have welcomed any distraction from the constant guilt, but she had not been able to bring herself to leave Guy with a stranger.

'You don't have to work now,' Pic suggested, making oblique reference to the fortunes they had been left.

'No,' said Ginger, 'but I just don't think I'm in a fit state to make any big decisions right now.'

Pic had to admit that was sensible. She only wished she could find a way of making it better for her.

'I just think that if you allowed yourself to have some fun—' she began to say.

'Oh, just leave me alone!' Ginger shouted at her, then dissolved into tears. Pic put the brake on the buggy and held Ginger tight for several minutes.

'I was screwing Charlie when I should have been seeing Daddy,' Ginger blurted into Pic's shoulder. 'Daddy asked me to that boat-race party, and I refused. There was Daddy trying to make a place for Guy in the family, and it was a really big deal for him to do that, and I couldn't even give him the time of day . . .' All the sentences that had been whirring in her brain, punishing her, began to tumble out. 'I was just so selfish, and I never got the chance to tell him I was sorry . . . I was horrible to him, and he died thinking that I hated him.'

'No, he didn't,' Pic told her. 'We saw him on our birthday, and you were really good. You didn't shout at him once.'

'Didn't I?' Ginger lifted her face from her sister's shoulder for a moment.

'No, you were really gracious.' Pic racked her brain to think of some other examples.

'At Christmas you played charades together, don't you remember, and Daddy fell in love with Guy . . .'

'He did, didn't he?' Ginger said, a glimmer of a smile breaking onto her wet face.

'He certainly did. He used to ring me up and tell *me* all the things that he had heard that Guy had done.'

'Did he?' Ginger asked, surprised.

'Oh, he was really proud of him. Anyway, the boat-race party wasn't such a big deal.'

'It was. Daddy said he might not be here for the next boat race and he was right . . .' She burst into tears again.

'I expect he meant he wouldn't be an MP,' Pic said. 'He was convinced they were going to lose the election.'

'Do you think that was it?' Ginger said, replaying the phone call in her head for the millionth time. All her guilt seemed to have focused on those two minutes.

'You mustn't blame Charlie,' Pic was saying.

'I don't blame Charlie, I blame myself,' Ginger said.

'Well, you mustn't do that either,' Pic said simply. 'Daddy would have been delighted, you know,' she went on, 'about Charlie. He was worried about you. He was old-fashioned. He thought you needed a man to look after you . . .'

She saw Ginger's face flush with anger and was relieved. That was much more like Ginger.

'Charlie doesn't want to look after me,' Ginger said, resignedly, 'he wants to screw me. Anyway, I hate men. They're all bastards.'

'Except Daddy,' Pic chimed in automatically.

'No, Daddy was a bastard too,' Ginger said, giggling suddenly. 'There's no point in making him into a saint, just because he's dead. Forgive me, Daddy, wherever you are . . .' She looked up at the blue sky, taking her sister's hand and walking down towards the lake.

'I thought I might take a few days off, take Ben to the seaside,' Alison suggested.

'I think that's a marvellous idea,' Stephen said encouragingly. 'Will you go to your mother's?'

'I thought I might,' Alison replied.

They were kneeling on the bathroom floor bathing their child. Over the last few weeks, they had developed a habit of doing the bedtime ritual together, when they were both home. Stephen found it a wonderful way to unwind, and he had noticed that, since Easter, Alison had been getting home from work in time to join them. It was as if she had been so frightened by the news about Lia's child that she had started to value every precious moment with Ben.

The fear seemed to have remained with her ever since. He could see constant tension in her facial muscles, creating lines where her skin had been smooth. Any unexpected noise made her jump. He was aware that he was more than averagely inured to death and illness, but he felt her reaction was too extreme and it troubled him.

He picked Ben out of the bath and Alison enfolded him in a large towel, drying and tickling him at the same time.

'When were you thinking of going?' Stephen asked, as they each took an arm and a leg and shoved them into Ben's Babygro.

'This weekend. I'll take the back half of the week off and stay till Sunday. You'll be working?'

'I will.' he sighed. 'Will you take Justine with you?'

'No. I thought I'd ask her to go round and help Lia. It would be one way of doing something to help.'

The idea seemed curiously feudal to him. He saw the potential for offending Lia and the rather chippy man she lived with, but said nothing. He had been surprised that Alison had not wanted to go to the hospital. She had made work an excuse and sent flowers. It was one of the many oddities in her behaviour that had concerned him.

'Good.' he said, as they switched off Ben's light and left the nursery.

Lia lay under the apple tree in the garden on a reclining chair, with Anouska asleep in the pram beside her. It was a beautiful warm day and clean clothes flapped on the line. If someone had told her a year before that there would be a time when the quality of the day was measured by the number of loads of washing completed and dry, she would have laughed. But that was what looking after a baby was all about, and, as long as Anouska continued to thrive, she was happy with it.

The scan had indicated that the disease had not damaged her arteries, but the doctors wanted to do another scan in a few weeks' time. The only medical aftercare they would have to administer was a dose of aspirin every day, which seemed simple enough, but Lia found herself in the grip of panic the moment the Peugeot pulled out of the hospital car park. The hospital had staff and systems to protect Anouska; outside it was up to her.

The first day, she had not been able to see how they would survive. The stress was too much for anyone to bear. Every cough or moan that Anouska made sent her racing to her, and when there was no sound she panicked and ran to check that she was still breathing. At night, Lia had dreadful nightmares that blended in with Anouska's waking, and she would dash to her, shaking with fear.

But each day got a little easier, Lia thought. After one day had passed, you knew at least that you could survive one day, and after one week, you realised that it was possible to survive a week. After three weeks, you could almost allow yourself the optimism that Anouska would live to see her first birthday, and so on. You built confidence day by day.

'I've made you a cup of tea.'

Neil's voice woke her suddenly. She had fallen asleep. She sat up quickly, her eyes shooting to the empty pram.

'It's OK, I've got her here, look . . .'

She held her arm up, shielding her eyes from the sun, and saw that her baby was sitting on Neil's hip, waving at her.

'Hello, my darling,' Lia said to her, and then she picked up the mug of tea and said, 'Thank you' to Neil.

They had found a way of existing together. Neil came home as soon as school ended. It took the pressure off when there was someone else in the house. She had to admit that he had become very good with Anouska, taking her for late-afternoon walks, or just talking to her gently, and reading her books before bed.

The school's long-awaited Ofsted inspection finally happened, and the sports department had been praised, so it had been worth all the evenings he had spent preparing for it. If that's what he had been doing. Lia didn't know, didn't ask, and was surprised how little she cared. Anouska's health seemed to have taken over every cell of her waking brain. An affair was nothing compared with Anouska's life.

Sex was not part of their relationship. Even if he hadn't been having an affair, she didn't see how they could have found the peace of mind for it. The few times he had tried to embrace her, she had turned away from him, determined to avoid feelings getting in the way of her caring for Anouska. Once or twice she had noticed pain in his eyes, and felt guilty. Perhaps he had done nothing. Perhaps there was after all a perfectly innocent explanation for his secret trip to Paris. But his silence only confirmed his guilt.

In her heart, she knew it was impossible for two people to live for any length of time with no real contact, but at the moment it was enough just to get through each day.

'The tickets for our holiday arrived this morning,' she informed Neil's back as she followed him into the house to prepare their supper.

'Are we still going?' he asked eagerly, sensing a glimmer of reprieve.

'She'll have had the second scan by then,' she said. 'If that's OK, I've been thinking, she should be as safe there as she is here, if we're careful about the heat. They have hospitals, don't they?'

It was as if she was trying to talk herself into it. He knew how much she wanted to go back to Portugal.

He attempted to catch her eye and smile. 'Well, let's go then, if the scan's OK.'

'Right then,' she said. There was no excitement in her voice. 'We've got lasagne. Do you want salad with it?'

'Yes,' he said, sadly, 'salad would be great.'

The sea air had tired Ben out and he was peacefully asleep. Alison kissed her fingertips then touched them against his cheek.

'I love you, my angel, sleep tight,' she whispered, tiptoed out of the room and went downstairs.

'I thought I'd go for a walk,' she told her mother, who was loading the dishwasher in the kitchen. 'It's only just after six.'

'Is it really? It seems later.' Margaret straightened up slowly.

'Yes, it's exhausting looking after him all day, isn't it?' Alison said.

The shingle crunched under the soles of her deck shoes as she walked down the beach. The sea was calm, milky turquoise in the evening light. There was no one around, and no sound except the gentle turn of the waves. The sun was slipping down through the cloud turning the sky blue-pink. It was the time of the evening when people reflected for a moment on the transience of life. Alison felt the salty wind blowing the tears from her eyes.

For the thousandth time she asked herself how she could have been so destructive. What was it that had made her reject her own happiness, and ruin someone else's? Destiny might have thrown her and Neil together, but destiny had not cast her into his arms, or enticed him away when his child was in peril. She had. And now she hated herself.

She had spoken to him only once since they had kissed goodbye. They had both known it was over. Late that night, when Stephen had fallen asleep, she had crept downstairs and dialled his number again. He picked up the receiver immediately.

'Hello,' she said.

He did not answer for several seconds. Then he said, 'I thought it might be the hospital.'

'I was thinking of you . . .' she had faltered.

'I don't want you to think of me ever again.'

'I know.' Alison began to sob. 'I feel so terrible.'

'You don't,' Neil told her coldly. 'You don't even begin to feel . . . I didn't even know what feeling was until this afternoon . . .'

And then he had put down the phone.

It was all her fault. If she had been strong enough to resist the pull of indulgence on New Year's Eve, to resist her mother that summer twenty years before, it would never have happened. But she had been weak. And now she had ruined his life and her own.

The tide was coming in. If she were brave, she thought, she would walk into the sea and keep walking, but she was not brave. She thought of Ben, and how much she loved him. He would miss her, and she could not do that to him.

She hadn't really known how much she loved her son until she heard about Anouska's illness. It was only then, feeling so awful on someone else's behalf, that she had begun to imagine how much worse it would feel if she were to lose him. Ben, alive and well, was the greatest gift. She felt constantly grateful for his sturdy little form. He had kept her afloat, when she had felt she was sinking.

The sun glowed gold on the horizon. She sat on the wall across the road from the little row of seaside shops, eating chips out of paper. The smell of fish frying, the chink of the boats in the harbour, made her think of holidays long ago, and she was filled with longing for those innocent times. Life had been simple then.

Maybe life could be simple again if she could stop herself being dragged by the undertow of the past. She remembered the therapist who had helped her twenty years before, saying that to let yourself sink into depression was a way of avoiding the responsibility of living. Alison stood up and took a deep breath. She had a choice to make: either ruin all their lives with her regrets, or throw the past away, grab what was left of her life and try to do something with it.

Margaret was sitting at the dining-room table when she arrived back.

'Do you fancy a drink?' Alison asked, determined to be positive.

'Oooh! What a good idea!' her mother exclaimed enthusiastically. 'You have a look and see what there is.'

Alison poured herself a gin and tonic and a sweet white vermouth with lemonade for Margaret.

'This is nice,' her mother said, tasting her drink and shuddering with pleasure.

Alison found her handbag and took out a cigarette. 'Do you mind? I don't in front of Ben,' she said, excusing herself quickly.

'I don't mind, as long as I can have one,' her mother replied.

Astonished, Alison pulled one out of the packet and handed it over. 'I thought you had given up years ago,' she said.

'I never even knew you knew,' Margaret replied, surprised. 'I never smoked at home.'

'No, but I saw you from my bedroom window.'

Margaret's eyebrows rose. Then she lit up and blew out through her nostrils like a woman in a forties film.

'I was only able to give up because I promised myself I could smoke again when I got to seventy,' she revealed, 'and I had forgotten that until a minute ago.'

'So you haven't had one for some time?'

'About twenty years,' Margaret replied.

Alison laughed. 'If I'd known that I would never have given you one,' she told her.

'I'd love to say that I wasn't enjoying it,' Margaret said. 'But it's just as good as I remembered.'

They giggled like naughty schoolgirls sharing an illicit midnight feast.

'It's like old times,' her mother said, smiling at her.

Instinctively, Alison recoiled. She was supposed to be forgetting the past, not reliving it, especially not in a companionable chat with her mother. But perhaps sometimes you needed to unwrap the past, give it a good shake and look at it again.

'I ran into Neil Gardner the other day.'

The words caught in her throat.

'Really? How is he?' her mother asked through pursed lips, keeping her voice determinedly neutral.

'Fine . . . He has a child the same age as Ben.'

'Does he?' Margaret tried to sound disinterested, but the air hummed with her agitation. 'I expect he's a good-looking man. He was such a handsome boy.'

Handsome? Margaret had hated the ground he walked on.

'Yes, I suppose he still is,' Alison said. 'I wondered, actually, what it was about him that made you hate him so much.'

The 'actually' gave away the fact that the question was not as casual as she wanted it to seem.

Her mother gave her a long, hard look.

'Apart from the obvious, of course,' Alison added quickly. 'I meant before that. You were always against him . . .' She looked round the room, to keep her eyes from catching her mother's.

'I hated the effect he had on you,' Margaret finally replied, sighing. 'If you really want to know, you became very silly when you were with him. He wasn't as intelligent as you were, and you tried to make yourself stupid to make him feel better. I had done it all myself and I didn't want you wasting your life too.'

'Oh, that's not true,' Alison immediately protested, but somewhere inside she knew that it was.

She didn't remember it like that, but over the last weeks she had realised that there were a number of things she hadn't remembered correctly. She had forgotten the way Neil retreated into threatening silence when something didn't suit him. Tell me what it is, she had wanted to shout, but she had not dared, because, as her mother so rightly said, when she was around him she became a nervous, twittering girl. She thought of the time they had spent together. Neil felt more comfortable with her when she was in distress or crying than when she was on a high, saying clever things.

The two women each lit another cigarette. The room filled with smoke and unanswered questions.

Finally, Alison heard herself asking, 'Mum, did we go to Biba together?'

Her mother's face lit up with relief that the strange, pregnant silence had come to an end.

'Of course we did! I bought you that purple dress, don't you remember? We had lunch in the Spaghetti House. Then, where did we go? Harrods, maybe. No wonder you have expensive tastes—I'm afraid it was all my fault!'

She smiled, proud of rearing such a well-dressed daughter.

'Yes, it was, all your fault!' Alison echoed, smiling back.

In the early mornings, the sand was cool enough for them to play on. Anouska liked the sand.

'Not in your mouth, Annie,' he told her gently, and she looked at him with a quivering lip, not liking to be told no.

'Here, grab hold of this.' He handed her a miniature shovel, which she banged up and down like a drumstick.

'That's right, bang, bang!' He smiled at her.

She smiled back. 'Baba!'

'What? Say it again,' he encouraged her, unable to believe that he had heard her speak.

She looked at him, mouth firmly closed, with a look that said, Well, you should have been listening.

'Oh well, please yourself,' he said, smiling and glancing at his watch. Nine o'clock. He gathered the buckets and spades into the beach bag and swung it over his shoulder, then he bent and picked Anouska up, throwing her into the air above his head and catching her. The sound of her laugh sent pleasure bubbling through his veins.

He kissed her cheek.

'Now, cheeky, let's see if Mummy's up,' he said.

Lia was watching them from the balcony. It had been a good idea to come to Portugal, she thought. Life was easier here. In the large, cool apartment, with a warm breeze blowing in off the sea, she had been able to sleep. With rest, everything looked more manageable.

Neil was happy here too. His skin tanned quickly and against it his eyes shone bluer than ever. He loved the sea. Every day, when she was getting Anouska ready for bed, Neil swam widths of the bay and then came running back to the apartment, dripping, to shower. On the second evening, as he towelled himself down, she had caught herself staring at his lean, brown torso. An unexpected twitch at the top of her legs had said, Hello, I'm alive down here, but she had looked away, embarrassed by the unwanted flicker of desire.

It was far too hot for the beach during the day, so they wandered round the cool stone portals of the old fish market in Lagos, where the fish the locals called swordfish lay across the stalls, long, flat and silver like blades. Or they drove away from the coast, stopping to buy great dripping wedges of watermelon from little farmers' trucks parked on the edge of the road.

They discovered a tiny spa village perched on the side of a wooded hill, its stone square offering shade and the cool, trickling sound of running water.

'Life is very simple when you have a child, isn't it?' Neil remarked, when they found themselves there for the third day in a row. He took a corner from a loaf and spread it with sardine paste.

'Yes,' Lia said, uncertainly, 'in some ways . . .'

She pulled the middle out of a piece of bread and handed it to Anouska who was sitting on her lap.

'I just mean the pace.' Neil nervously qualified his generalisation. 'You find a routine that suits and you slot into it. The slowness takes getting used to.'

'Yes,' she agreed.

'I quite like it,' Neil said, stretching back lazily in his chair.

'You sound as if it's the first time you've noticed,' Lia said, smiling.

'Well, being out here gives you a different perspective.'

'Yes.'

They were beginning to talk to each other again. Tentatively and carefully, they were sounding each other out. At times like these, she thought it would be easy enough to slide back to how they had been, but she didn't know if that was what she wanted any more. She didn't think that they could go on as if nothing had happened.

It felt peculiar to drive past places that triggered memories of how besottedly in love they had been. It seemed so long ago. It was as if the shock of life being turned upside-down had anaesthetised her to pain and to pleasure.

That evening, Neil said, 'Why don't we go out to eat tonight? If we feed Annie first, we can walk her round the bay and when she falls asleep we can let down the back of the buggy.'

'All right,' Lia agreed.

In Portugal, children were welcomed in restaurants, and she wondered why they had not thought of going out at night before now. Perhaps because it was more intimate to be locked opposite each other for the duration of a meal. Checking that Anouska was sleeping in the bedroom provided a convenient escape route from any conversation that threatened to get too deep.

They sat drinking vinho verde under a trellis of rambling purple flowers. 'Is that bougainvillea?' Neil asked. 'I never know.'

'I think it's that pink stuff,' Lia replied, pointing at a different type of flower without looking at him.

He tried to initiate a conversation again. 'Are you able to relax a little here?'

'Here, as in the restaurant, or here, as in Portugal?' she asked, inadvertently catching the expression on his face. He looked so sad she felt a pang of guilt that she was making it so difficult for him.

'Yes, I am,' she conceded. 'I've always liked this village.' Then she couldn't resist adding, 'Sometimes I wish I'd never left.'

The statement hung between them for several minutes, then the waiter came up and asked them what they would be eating. They gave their order.

Neil leaned over the table and looked into the buggy to check whether Anouska was sleeping. 'She's a lovely little girl. You've done a fantastic job with her.'

She smiled weakly at him.

'No, I mean it, you're a really great mother—'

'What? Letting her have a temperature for days and not taking her to hospital?' Lia blurted out.

Neil hadn't realised that she was angry with herself as well as him.

'The doctor said—' he began.

'Yes, but I didn't believe him. I knew there was something wrong with her,' Lia interrupted. 'I should have trusted my instincts. They tell you the mother's instinct is the most important thing . . . If I had taken her straight away, they could have given her the medication earlier . . .'

Neil tried to calm her down. 'But the scan said that her heart wasn't damaged, so she did get it in time. You can't feel guilty, you did everything you could.'

'It's just . . . I did everything I could and it wasn't good enough.' Finally she succumbed to tears.

'Lia, Lia, please . . .' He sat wanting to touch her, but terrified that if he reached out she would swipe him away. 'Lia,' he said again, and then he could bear it no longer. He went round to her side of the table and held her shoulders, and she turned her face against his jeans and wept.

Finally, she wiped her face with the napkin he offered her.

'Sorry,' she said, sniffing.

'Don't be,' he said, sitting down again.

'It's the uncertainty I can't bear,' she sniffed, 'the idea that I'll bring her up and then bang, one day—there's no guarantee . . .'

'But no parent has a guarantee. We've had a big shock, but she's alive, she's well, she's a lovely little girl, a real fighter,' he said.

'Yes, she is, isn't she?' Lia smiled, gratified that he seemed to like his daughter so much these days.

'We just have a job to do everything we can to give her as good a life as possible,' he said gently.

'Yes.'

I know all this, she wanted to say to him. Why are you telling me all this? He was leading up to something, she could tell.

'I want to be a part of it, Lia,' he said quietly. 'I mean, whatever you decide to do . . . if you'll let me. I know I did something terrible . . .' Then he was lost for words.

'What did you do?' she asked him.

He looked up at her, with an expression on his face that asked whether she really wanted to know. She continued to hold his eyes. He took a deep breath.

'I met someone I had been in love with a long time ago, and I thought I was in love with her again, but I wasn't,' he said, then, seeing that that wasn't enough, he went on. 'I didn't really expect it to be like this when you had a child. I didn't like it much, if I'm honest, not at first. I like it now . . .'

'So where were you when you said you were in Paris?' Lia asked, not letting him off the hook. She didn't want to hear about his difficulties as a father. As far as she was concerned that was immature indulgence.

'Paris. I had given you the right number. It was just that I hadn't thought it was all in her name . . .'

'But it had been going on for much longer than that?' Lia asked him.

'Yes,' he admitted. 'But not any more. It finished in Paris.'

'Yes, I thought so,' Lia said, looking at the sky. The light was always best at this time of night, the few moments after the sun had gone, before darkness took over.

Their food arrived. It was cold. Lia guessed that the waiter hadn't wanted to barge into their conversation. The fish still tasted fresh and delicate. Either the wine or the crying, or something, had made her feel curiously light-headed and hungry.

'I'm actually feeling relieved,' she said, eventually. 'You've just confirmed what I thought all along. The funny thing is that I don't really care that you fucked someone else, but I hate you for lying to me. You made me feel as if I was going paranoid, or I was just being stupid, but there wasn't anything wrong with me . . . except you.'

As she spoke to him, he felt admiration. She was so strong and brave and honest. When he first met her he had been attracted by exactly that independence of spirit and self-reliance. Over the last year, the aura of integrity she carried around her had faded and she had become more dependent and eager to please. He had begun to despise her displays of weakness. Now, she was telling him that he had been responsible for the change in her and he realised that was true. After you had lied to someone and got away with it, you could easily slip into convincing yourself that they were stupid for believing you. It was the loss of respect that was so insidious.

'I love you,' he told her vehemently. 'I'd do anything to have you forgive me . . .'

She looked at him coolly. 'I may be able to forgive you, but I don't know whether I can trust you again. I thought I knew everything about you that I needed to know, and I found out that I didn't. It's a shock. I don't know what happens now. We'll stay together for the time being, because Anouska needs us both,' Lia told him. 'And then, well, we'll see. I won't punish you with it the whole time,' she added, seeing the dismay on his face. 'We'll just try to get back to normal. I can't promise anything else.'

Ginger had just reached the top of the hill when she spotted the four-wheel-drive-with-rhino-bar safari vehicle that couldn't even make it the length of the M4, let alone overland to Africa. Why had he come, she asked herself, just when she was beginning to get herself together?

Charlie was sitting on her doorstep. He jumped up when he saw them approaching.

'If Mohammed won't come to the mountain . . .' he said.

'I wish that Mohammed had given us a lift up the bloody mountain,' Ginger told him, fumbling for her key.

'Since you won't pick up the phone at home, I called you at work. They said that you'd left,' Charlie said, ignoring her crossness and following her into the flat.

'Yes, I haven't really been back since Daddy died. I thought what the hell, I hated that job, and it was never going to go anywhere. I'll start looking around when I feel a bit better.'

'You can always come to us,' he volunteered immediately.

'Charlie, you're like a record that got stuck,' she said sharply.

'OK!' he said, taking a step back. 'I won't ask you again, all right?'

'All right,' she said, pulling Guy out of his pushchair.

'How is the little fella?' he asked.

'He's fine, thank you. He's about the only thing that keeps me going. Do you want coffee?' she said, wishing he would just go away.

'No, thanks,' Charlie said. 'Actually, I wondered if you'd like to drive somewhere nice for lunch?' he asked, looking up.

'Little Chef?' she said bitchily. 'Or perhaps we could ring the changes and go for a Happy Eater?'

'I was thinking of somewhere nearer.' he bantered back. 'I can never rely on my car over difficult terrain. How about Richmond Park? It's rhododendron time. You say that Guy likes flowers, that Lia takes him for a walk in Kew Gardens every morning. I thought he might like a change.'

'All right,' Ginger said. bewildered. as they got into the car.

He had packed a hamper, or, Ginger thought later, as she unpacked the contents—everything from smoked salmon to strawberries and clotted cream—he had ordered his secretary to go out, buy a hamper, fill it with everything she had ever resisted buying in Marks & Spencer.

'Oh,' said Ginger, feigning disappointment as they reached the packet of napkins stowed at the bottom of the basket, 'no sandwiches, then?'

'So why have you been avoiding me?' Charlie asked her, lounging back in the long grass after they had picked at the food for a while.

'What makes you think that?' Ginger replied, looking at him directly.

'Oh, I think it was something to do with the fact that you haven't returned any of my calls for a while . . .'

'I suppose it never occurred to you that I might be sad and not wanting to talk to anyone?' she asked.

'Yes, it did, that's why I called, to see that you were all right,' he said.
'You're very considerate all of a sudden.'

'God, you're in a foul mood today,' he said.

'Well, fuck off then, I never asked you to come over.'

'What has got into you?' He sat up suddenly.

'My father's died, my friend's child nearly died . . .'

'I know all that, but what's it got to do with me?'

'Some things don't have anything to do with you. I know that will come as a shock to your ego, but—'

'That's not fair,' he said, exasperated.

'All right. It wasn't. I'm sorry.' She pretended to be playing with Guy.

'So what is the problem?' he asked her more gently.

'Look, relationships are risky things and I don't want risks at the moment.' Then she blurted out, 'I saw Lia's husband kissing Alison who is supposed to be our friend. I don't want that to happen to me—' She stopped, wondering why she had told him something she had told no one else, not even Pic.

'But it won't happen to you. Not with me. I promise,' Charlie told her. He tried to put his arm round her shoulder, but she wouldn't let him.

'Oh, no, not with good old Mr Reliability, the man who bonks you stupid then doesn't call for . . . nearly a year.'

He looked shocked that she had brought up the subject.

'Is that what this has all been about?' he asked, incredulous. 'But I didn't even know you then! For God's sake, Ginger, you were after a job! I didn't exactly force you, did I?'

'Piss off, Charlie,' Ginger told him, getting to her feet wearily, then bending to pick Guy up off the ground. She began to walk away.

'I'll give you a lift,' he said, throwing packets into the hamper, then stopping and running after her.

They drove back to her home in silence. She didn't invite him in. With Guy perched on her hip, she watched as he drove away and then sighed and said, 'Well, my darling, I'm afraid that's the last we're going to see of your daddy.'

'You're wearing my necklace!' Stephen observed, as Alison slipped her jacket over the back of her chair. The diamond added a discreet sparkle to the sleeveless black shift she had on.

'Yes,' she said, fingering the diamond nervously and picking up the menu.

The River Café was noisy, open and informal, but that meant that nobody really took any notice of you, which is what she wanted. It would have been impossible to say the things she had to say in the sort of place that had waiters with a cloyingly intimate notion of service.

They gave their order, then smiled at each other, happily anticipating the simple, rustic food in this temple of style. At the next table, a film star sat chatting with his actress wife. Alison nodded her eyes in his direction in case Stephen had not seen.

'What?' he asked, looking at them but showing no sign of recognition.

'Doesn't matter,' she said, trying to suppress a giggle. He hadn't the slightest idea that he was in the company of celebrities. She felt a great wave of fondness for him and she tried to hold on to it, like a mental video, in case it was the last time she would be allowed to feel it.

'I was wondering whether that chair in New York was still open to you . . . ?' Alison began, her nervousness making her brusque.

He couldn't disguise his surprise. 'Well, yes, I should think so,' he said uncertainly.

'Do you still want to go?' she asked.

'Not without you,' he said.

It couldn't wait any longer, not even past the starter. There never was going to be a right moment to say what she had to say.

'Stephen, there's something I have to tell you. Please listen, and don't interrupt, otherwise I may not be able to say it . . .'

He nodded, sensing something momentous. His violet eyes were pools of fear.

'When I was eighteen I had an abortion,' she said quietly.

She looked up at him. There was neither approval nor disapproval in his look. Doctors were good at that.

'I think that's why I seemed to find it so difficult at first to bond with Ben,' she continued. 'You see, when I couldn't get pregnant naturally, a part of me thought it was a punishment, and then when we did manage, I thought I didn't deserve it, or something . . .'

She could see that he was struggling to resist the urge to comfort her, knowing that was not what she wanted.

'Then when I had Ben, I kept thinking of my other baby, and how I wasn't a fit person to be a mother . . . I'm not trying to excuse how I behaved, but it may explain some of it to you . . .'

'Poor Alison—' Stephen began, reaching across the table for her hand.

'No, I haven't finished,' she said hastily. 'The only person who knew was my mother. I left my boyfriend without saying anything. It was just before university. I told myself we would have broken up anyway, I told myself it was better that he didn't know . . .'

She wanted to be completely honest, but to go into the complexities of everything that she felt at the time would take hours. She had to compress it.

'At university, I had a kind of breakdown. I found a therapist to talk to. She saved my sanity, really. She told me that it would damage me to keep it secret. I felt so much better I thought it was enough that I had told her. And it was. Until you and I decided to have a baby, and then it all started to come back . . .' She took a sip of water. 'There's more: everything went a bit peculiar. I couldn't get my head round the idea of having a baby, and then, out of the blue, my old boyfriend suddenly appeared . . . and . . . I had an affair with him,' she finally said.

They sat facing each other for several minutes. His face was grim, disbelieving, and then, as his brain processed what she had told him, so sad.

'Well, aren't you going to say anything?' she asked him, unable to bear the look of utter dejection.

'You told me not to,' Stephen said, evenly.

'I've finished,' she told him.

'No, you haven't told me what happens next.'

She took a deep breath. 'I don't know what happens next,' she said. 'I think that's up to you.'

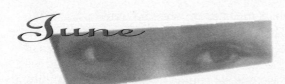

WHEN THE GIRL finds out that the handsome prince is betrothed to another, she goes mad and dies of a broken heart.

Ginger's eyes flitted between the ballerina twirling manically on stage, and the profile of Lia's face, tears streaming down it, just beside her. With one last chord, the ballerina collapsed and the heavy red velvet curtains cascaded down in front of the tragic tableau. *Giselle*, she realised, had perhaps not been the most tactful choice of ballet.

Lia took out a tissue and wiped her eyes, and when the lights came up her face was sparkling with pleasure. 'This is fantastic,' she told Ginger. 'So beautiful and moving. I never thought I would cry in a place like this,' she gestured round the red and gold auditorium, 'but it just got me.'

'I love classical ballet,' Ginger said, breathing a sigh of relief.

They climbed the stairs towards the bar and Ginger recalled the last time she had been there, when Charlie had appeared. She couldn't resist a quick glance behind her, but this time she was being followed by a man with a little girl in a smocked dress.

'It's all so spectacular,' Lia said, looking up at the crystal chandelier as they stood eating ice creams out of paper tubs. She turned to Ginger. 'Not just the ballet itself, but the whole ambiance. It's such a treat, just exactly what I needed, thank you.'

Lia had called Ginger during the week to ask her a favour.

'You know you said if there's anything you could do?' she had asked. 'Well, there is. If you still want to . . .'

'Of course,' Ginger had replied straight away.

'I need to get away for an hour or two. I've got into a neurotic state where I don't feel I can leave Anouska, and it's silly. So Neil's going to look after her on Saturday afternoon, and I'm going to go out, except I know I'll find some excuse to stay in, unless I have a date—so, will you be my date?'

Ginger thought it was a very sensible idea, and was flattered Lia was asking her to help. When she called Pic, who agreed to come over and look after Guy, she had come up with the idea of the ballet.

It felt funny coming out of the grandeur of the Opera House into the thronging streets of Covent Garden when it was still light.

'It's a bit like waking up after having a wonderful dream during your siesta,' Lia said.

'So what do we do now?' Ginger asked, fully expecting her companion to want to go home.

'Well, if we were abroad and it was a siesta, it's now that the fun starts! D'you fancy a drink?' Lia said with a determination to try to relax.

'Brilliant idea!' Ginger said. 'Where shall we go?'

They found an American bar in one of the streets between the Piazza and the Strand. It was cool and dark inside and there were very few customers. Saturday evening had not yet begun. Ginger bought bottles of ice-cold Beck's, and chose Nancy Griffiths on the jukebox.

'It's quite feminist in a way, that ballet,' Lia said thoughtfully. 'I mean those ghosts of women who have been betrayed punishing the men, making them dance themselves to death.'

'Hmm . . . yes, actually, but I don't know why Giselle bothers to save the prince,' Ginger added.

'Well, she still loves him,' Lia told her. 'You don't stop loving someone just because they do something terrible.'

'Don't you? I suppose not.' Ginger said. anxious to move the subject on. 'But I don't see why poor old Hilarion has to die. It's terribly class-ridden, isn't it? I mean, he never did anything but love Giselle. and yet because he's a nobody he cops it. and the prince gets away with it.'

Lia giggled and went to the bar for more beer.

'This is nice.' she said. sitting down a few moments later. 'It's like being single and free again.' She took a swig from the neck of her bottle.

'Do you sometimes wish you were?' Ginger asked her.

'No—well, never for long. How about you?' Lia asked.

'Having Guy is the best thing I've ever done.' Ginger said. 'But I've been lucky so far. He's so robust and cheerful. Maybe I won't be so keen when he turns into a monster at two . . . and I don't know how I'd deal with it if he were ill.' It was her way of saying that she admired the way Lia had coped.

'I don't know how I'd cope on my own.' Lia said, reciprocating the compliment.

'Oh, in some ways I think it's easier for me,' Ginger told her. 'I don't have to bother about all that having-time-for-each-other crap. It's enough getting Guy to sleep without then having to soothe some bloody male ego resenting the time I spend with my baby.'

Lia threw back her head and laughed.

Ginger was warming to her theme. 'Honestly. I think men are more trouble than they're worth at times.'

Lia thought Ginger was probably protesting too much. She had seen how happy she had been when she was spending time with Charlie.

They both drank some more beer. Ginger noticed that Lia was getting slightly fidgety.

'Ring, if you want to,' she said.

'No, I don't want to, really.' Lia said. 'I just wish I didn't feel this constant state of alarm. But it helps to talk to you.'

Ginger smiled. The alcohol was taking the edge off her unaccustomed judiciousness. There were questions she wanted to ask Lia. and she was beginning to forget the reasons why she shouldn't.

'We should do this more often.' she said. 'if Neil wouldn't mind?' She was leading with the subtlety of a bulldozer. she thought.

'At the moment, I don't think he would mind anything I did,' Lia responded with a dry snort of a laugh.

'Oh?' Ginger did her best to appear ingenuous.

'We've been through a difficult patch with our relationship,' Lia admitted, 'but I think we're coming through now, and he's anxious for me to do whatever I want.'

'What sort of difficult patch?' Ginger was unable to stop herself asking.

Lia considered her reply for an agonisingly long time. Ginger was about to change the subject when Lia said, 'He had an affair. You might as well know. It doesn't seem such a big deal now.'

'Do you know who with?' Ginger asked.

'No.' Lia looked up in surprise. 'I don't. It doesn't really matter who, because I could tell it was over.'

'You knew it was going on?' Ginger almost shouted. Were there no limits to Lia's saintliness?

'I did, but I didn't. When he finally told me, it explained everything that had been weird. So, in a way, it was quite a relief. I got my confidence back. It kind of empowered me . . .'

Now it was Ginger's turn to look surprised.

'I know you think I'm too nice sometimes.' Lia went on. 'but I'm not really. It's really important to me that Anouska has a family. I can put up with a lot for that,' she said, 'and I suppose I love Neil,' she added. 'whatever that means.'

Alison was sitting on the floor in the middle of the conservatory surrounded by binliners and the cardboard boxes Stephen had brought down from the loft. There was a binliner just for rubbish, one for Oxfam. and a large box set aside for storage.

The boxes had travelled everywhere with her since she left home. They were full of clothes and ornaments and bits and pieces, lovingly preserved junk that she hadn't been able to part with, talismans of her past. She wondered whether everyone had such a collection, or whether it was because she was an only child. Other people had brothers and sisters to remember special times in their family history. They told each other stories, layering their memories, putting different complexions on events as they grew older. Instead, she had her dolls, and a family of owls made out of shells brought back each year from lonely holidays in Cornwall.

It was like going through a huge photo album, each piece recalling a specific occasion: the little plastic basket with flowers on it she had saved her first pocket money to buy: an empty bottle of Badedas bath foam that had been Neil's first Christmas present to her. Alison dropped them into the rubbish. The clothes were harder to part with, but they went into the Oxfam bag. The tank tops, the jeans with a V at the knee, the purple clinging dress from Biba.

The house was on the market. Several people were interested, and she was expecting another couple to arrive at any moment. Stephen had taken Ben for the afternoon. They were all going to the Big Apple.

They were being as careful with each other as they had been on their first dates, both acknowledging that there was something very special at stake that must not be forced along. Building a relationship took much time and patience, rebuilding it even more. Sometimes she felt overwhelmed by gratitude for Stephen's continuing love. It had been the most difficult thing she had ever had to do, to open her soul and let someone else peer into it, but making herself vulnerable seemed to have made them stronger.

When she thought she had told Stephen everything in the River Café, she found she had only just started, and the intelligence of his questions brought answers that had lain hidden inside her, unexamined, all her life. His reaction had not been what she had expected.

'I thought it would be much worse,' he said.

'What could be worse?' she asked.

'That you were leaving me.'

That had made tears flow, but he had not moved to comfort her. Instead, he had become quietly reflective.

'It was Lia's husband, wasn't it?' he said, eventually.

'They're not married,' she replied immediately. Then, knowing that she owed him complete honesty, 'Yes, it was Neil. How did you know?'

'I just worked it out. There was always a kind of tension between you. I felt it at Christmas. I didn't suspect anything, of course.'

'We weren't, then . . .' she faltered.

'And, of course!' Stephen exclaimed, as if he had just worked out the solution to a crossword clue. 'That weekend you were away in Paris, and now I come to think about it, Ginger said he was away too . . . and your reaction when you heard about their little girl. No wonder you felt so terrible . . . Well,' he said, after digesting the information, 'I suppose he does have a lot more hair than I do.'

She yelped with strangled laughter and pain.

'It never even crossed my mind to compare you, physically . . .' she told him truthfully. It was as if Neil had been part of a different life, completely separate. She tried to explain. 'You know how I compartmentalise my life—work, home, friends—well, I feel that this is what I was doing with him. The affair, kept in its box on the other side of town where it could not hurt anyone . . .'

'And Paris?' he asked, picking up on the flaw in this analysis.

'Paris was because of "These Foolish Things", Bryan Ferry. It was our song,' she said. She saw that he had no idea what she was talking about.

'Our song?' he repeated.

'Like whenever I hear that aria from *Così fan Tutte*, I think of going back to your place for the first time,' she explained.

'*Soave sia il vento?*'

'Yes, you see, you *do* know what it means,' she said.

'Oh yes,' he said, smiling at her. 'Our song, eh?'

He looked pleased, and that was the moment she had known that they were going to be all right.

Alison put the last of the clothes into the Oxfam binliner. Just the records left to do. She wrote a label 'Oxfam' and stuck it on the side of the box she had just emptied. Then she opened the cupboard and started pulling out her albums.

It wasn't a record collection, she thought, more a catalogue of seventies clichés. One by one they went into the box. She was getting almost reckless in her purge when the bell rang. She rose to answer the door, then caught sight of herself in the hall mirror and stopped to push her hair back.

He was wearing a faded denim shirt and looked tanned and relaxed. He had Anouska's buggy in front of him, like a buffer.

'I didn't think you were in,' Neil said, referring to the length of time it had taken her to open the door.

'I was in the conservatory,' she told him. 'I've got some people coming round to see the house.'

'Oh, well, I'll leave you then. We were just passing.'

'No, don't go,' she said, 'come in. It's OK, there's no one else here,' she added.

He hadn't consciously decided to pass the big detached house, but it was en route to the gardens, and he had seen that the car was not there and something had drawn him up the path. He hadn't even considered the risk of finding her husband at home.

'We heard you were leaving.' He followed her through the living room, kitchen and into the conservatory. 'Nice place,' he commented.

'I'm sorting some stuff out,' she told him, explaining away the mess.

He sat down, pulling the buggy up next to him. Anouska was sleeping.

'How is she now?' Alison asked, leaning forward to look at her properly. 'She looks well. So do you.'

'We've been on holiday,' he told her. 'Portugal.'

'Lovely.'

They both fell silent, unwilling to participate any further in stilted small talk.

'I didn't want you to leave without saying goodbye,' he said.

'No,' she responded, 'I'm glad you came.'

Another silence.

Then they both said, simultaneously, 'Look, I'm sorry . . .' And they both laughed, embarrassed.

'You first,' she said, sitting down on the floor, pushing away the strewn albums to make space for herself.

He said, 'I'm sorry I was angry with you on the phone. I needed someone to blame, but it wasn't your fault.'

'That's OK,' she said. 'Did you tell Lia?' she asked him nervously.

'I told her I had an affair. Not who with. She didn't ask,' he added.

'And Stephen?'

'He knows. I didn't tell him who with, but he worked it out. He's very sensitive . . .' Her voice trailed off.

Neil looked horrified. 'Well, I'm glad you're off then,' he said, with a tight little smile. 'America, is it?'

'New York. Stephen's got a job . . .' she said.

'What are you going to do there?' Neil asked her.

'I want to spend some time with Ben . . . I don't know . . . I'd like to do some writing, a book possibly . . .'

'Your turn.' Neil reminded her they had been swapping apologies.

'Yes,' she replied, uncertainly.

Her heart was racing as she tried to decide how much to tell him. There was a choice. Either apologise blandly and hope that the rest was understood, or go further. Which? Unless she explained to Neil now what she should have explained twenty years before, there would always remain the chance that in a few years' time, when resolutions made today had been weakened by time, they would bump into each other again and . . . This way, she thought, summoning her courage, if it ever were to happen, he would look away and pass on.

'There's something I should have told you a long time ago . . . when I ended our relationship,' she began.

He averted his eyes. He was trying so hard to look as if he didn't care, but it was obvious he did.

'I was pregnant and I had an abortion,' she told him. 'I'm very sorry.'

In the past, she had wondered whether the possibility had ever crossed his mind. Clearly it had not.

'But you were on the pill,' he said.

'Yes, but antibiotics affected it, or something . . . I don't know. Anyway, I was.'

'Oh . . .' he said quietly, and then suddenly he shouted at her, 'Why the hell didn't you tell me?'

The words were like blows. She shrank from them.

'Because you would have wanted to marry me.' Her voice began to wobble. 'I didn't want to live like your brother and his girlfriend, struggling to make ends meet in some awful caravan. I wanted a nice life. I wanted pretty things . . .' she said, dissolving into tears.

It sounded so pathetic, so materialistic. It wasn't just that, she wanted to defend herself, but held back.

He sat still, trying to take on board everything she had said. When her sobs began to subside, he said, 'Pete and Cheryl have the best marriage I know. You can overcome anything if you love each other enough.' His voice was no longer angry, only sad and resigned.

'I know . . . I'm sorry.' She could feel the emotion draining from her. Soon, it would be over.

'You didn't love me enough,' he stated bluntly.

'No,' she said, finally accepting responsibility. 'No, I suppose I didn't.'

He fell silent again for several minutes, and then he said, 'You did the right thing.' He rose and turned the buggy towards the front door. 'It never would have worked. We couldn't even last an afternoon in Paris without annoying the hell out of each other.' He smiled ruefully at her.

It would be the last time she saw him, she realised. She suddenly didn't want it to end like this. She bent down, grabbing the sky blue album from the floor.

'Here,' she said, holding it out to him, 'have this.'

He took it from her. '"These Foolish Things",' he read out loud.

With a wry smile, he shook the black disc out of the cover. Then, in one swift movement, he brought his knee to his chest and his hands down hard and snapped the black circle in half.

Then he handed her the broken pieces, and suddenly they were both laughing.

'Bye, Ally,' he said, furling and unfurling his fingers, the way you taught a baby to wave.

'Bye-bye,' she said.

Inside the cool round hall, with its classical statues and marble staircase, Pic and Ginger could hear the ebb and flow of conversation. Exchanging bemused glances, they made their way to the dining room, where their mother rose to greet them. It had been Pic's idea to visit on their parents' wedding anniversary, but their mother had clearly forgotten that they were coming down and had instead decided to host a lunch party.

'Darlings,' she greeted them, wafting them away into the drawing room, a pair of spaniels yapping round her feet. 'It is rather awkward. But I'd love to have tea with you later . . .' she suggested vaguely.

'But—' Ginger began.

'I know!' exclaimed her mother, ignoring her. 'Why don't you drive over to Bath? I believe there's some sort of festival in the gardens near the Royal Crescent.'

'But we've come all this way. Couldn't we have lunch here?' Ginger asked. 'I'm starving, and I know Guy—'

'I'm sure they'll have hot dogs or something there,' her mother replied, anxious to get back to her ladies.

'What a good idea,' Pic said. 'Come on, Ginger, before Guy wakes up.' He was asleep in the car.

'You're getting very bossy,' Ginger told her, hurrying to keep up as she marched back to the entrance.

'Makes a change,' Pic replied equably. 'Anyway, what could be nicer than a lovely drive on a day like this, and the prospect of an afternoon's shopping in Bath?'

'Well, I suppose if you put it like that,' Ginger said, settling down contentedly.

By the time they found somewhere to park, it was past Guy's lunch-time and he was getting irritable.

'We have to stop somewhere and get him something to eat,' Ginger told Pic as they hurried up Milsom Street.

'Oh, can't he wait until we get there?' Pic asked impatiently.

'What's the bloody hurry?' Ginger asked her. 'For heaven's sake, we don't even know there's a festival on. If Mummy's memory is anything to go by, it will have happened last week.'

'Well, let's go to that café in Victoria Park, near the tennis courts.'

Ginger looked at the places to eat around them: the choice was ice-cream, pizza or very expensive French cuisine. Guy had only four teeth.

'All right,' she agreed reluctantly. 'But let's hurry up!'

'You're the one who slowed us down.'

'What has got into you today?' Ginger asked, bewildered by Pic's sudden stroppiness.

'Just come on,' Pic said, heaving an exasperated sigh.

The café was crowded and there were no spare tables, so they bought sandwiches and cans of drink and went back outside to search for a vacant park bench. The flowerbeds seemed to dance with colour and the path was thronging with people dressed in shorts and bikini tops, their exposed flesh turning pink in the hot sun.

'It's like being at the seaside,' Ginger remarked, and then, as they approached the expanse of grass that ran down from the crescent, 'Oh look! Guy! Balloons!'

She ran on ahead like an excited child to get a closer look at the hot-air balloons that were being inflated on the lawns, and then, as if suddenly remembering her responsibilities, she came back.

'It's OK,' Pic told her. 'You go and look. Guy and I are going to sit in the shade under one of those trees and have our picnic.'

'Are you sure?'

'Quite sure,' Pic said.

Ginger scampered up the incline, shielding her eyes from the sun as she looked skywards. There were plain balloons and striped balloons in bold poster colours. She loved hot-air balloons. They were so celebratory, so literally uplifting. She looked back to Pic and Guy. She was about to pull herself away and go back to them when someone a few yards away said, 'Do you want a ride?'

She turned, startled. Charlie was standing in a basket with another man who was inflating the balloon.

'Hello!' she said, walking towards him, gesturing with her arms. 'Isn't this lovely!'

'Yes,' he said, laughing at the expression of wonder on her face. 'Do you want a ride?'

'I'm with Pic,' she said, excusing herself, 'but I've always wanted to go in one,' she confessed.

'We're ready to go,' the man next to Charlie said.

'Are you coming?' Charlie asked again.

Ginger saw that Pic was waving, telling her to go.

'Yes!' she said, taking both his hands, allowing herself to be pulled up into the basket.

The ground dropped away beneath them, and she was suddenly terrified to see Pic and Guy becoming very tiny dots, and then disappearing completely.

'It's OK,' Charlie said, putting his arm round her waist. 'Pic'll look after him.'

It only occurred to her then what an odd coincidence it was that Charlie just happened to be in Bath at the same time as them, and that her normally placid sister was behaving so oddly.

'You planned this, didn't you?' she said to Charlie as they soared out over the valley. 'You and Pic planned this. I don't believe it. My own sister. Get me down at once,' she ordered the pilot.

He looked at Charlie, smiling.

'Charlie, get me down,' she pleaded.

'All right, all right,' he agreed, taking her hands, 'but I just want to ask you something first.'

'What?' she said crossly.

'Will you marry me?'

'Oh, for heaven's sake!' Ginger said, folding her arms and looking heavenwards. It was only then that she saw that the balloon was white and covered with red hearts.

'Oh my God, you mean it!' she cried, jumping in the air, shaking the basket as she landed.

'Will you marry me?' Charlie repeated, putting his arm round her.

'You can't expect me to make up my mind in a balloon!'

'Well, let's go down then.'

'No!' screamed Ginger. 'No, this is a wonderful dream . . . I don't want to wake up just yet . . .' She squeezed Charlie's hand.

'Do you really mean it?' she asked quietly.

'Yes, I do,' he said.

'Guy is your son,' she told him, looking straight into his eyes, pleading with him not to reject them now.

He looked right back at her, his curls blowing in the wind. 'I've been wondering when you would tell me.'

'When did you know?'

'I think in an unconscious way I must have known when I met him, because that was the day I fell in love with you both,' he told her. 'On Kew Bridge.'

'Really?' she said, smiling when she thought of all the time in between she had wasted.

'But I only worked it out consciously after Richmond Park,' Charlie told her. 'I couldn't understand why you were so bothered about our one-night stand, and then I started to think back and calculate the dates and I felt such a fool . . . I want to thank you,' he said, very seriously. 'He's a lovely little boy.'

'He is, isn't he? But you didn't ask me to marry you because you felt you ought to?' she asked, suddenly alarmed.

'I'm afraid I'm not that chivalrous,' he admitted. 'I fell in love with you because of your extraordinary brain . . . and sensational body,' he added quickly, seeing her impish face fall.

'I suppose it's one way of getting me to work for you on the cheap,' she interjected.

'Yes. You could feed me ideas for soap operas over breakfast.'

'Breakfast serials?'

In the distance she could see the Palladian house built of warm yellow stone where her mother was entertaining friends. Had Mummy been dragged into Charlie's plans as well? Suddenly she wanted to be with her family. 'Shall we go back down now?' she asked Charlie, feeling an urgent need to hug Guy.

'Can I take that as a yes? You're not getting out of this balloon until I've had an answer,' Charlie replied.

'Ask me again,' she said, looking down at the green and yellow patchwork of wheat and rapeseed, wanting to remember every detail to tell their children when they asked.

'Will you marry me?' he indulged her, dropping to one knee.

'Well, if you put it like that,' she said, 'yes, yes, YES!'

$\mathcal{T}$HE FOUR ADULTS were sitting in a circle round the remains of a cake baked in the shape of a '1'.

'It's a shame Alison and Stephen and Ben aren't here, isn't it?' Lia remarked, lying back in the grass. 'They went off so quickly I never got a chance to thank them.'

'Thank them?' Ginger said, astonished.

Neil saw the look Ginger shot at him, and knew instantly that she knew. He stared back at her defiantly. They had never overcome their initial hostility.

'For saving Anouska's life. If it hadn't been for Stephen . . .' Lia let the sentence finish itself.

'Do you think Anouska will be able to walk by next month?' Ginger said to Lia, anxious to change the subject, as she watched the little girl trying to push herself up to standing. 'I really want her to be a bridesmaid.'

'I don't know,' Lia said, sitting up again. 'You couldn't leave it a little longer, could you?' she joked.

'Well, not really,' Ginger told her, 'if I want to fit into my dress . . .' She smiled wickedly.

'Oh, for heaven's sake,' Lia said, realising what she meant. 'You didn't hang about, did you?' She turned to Neil. 'We'll have to get on with it now. I want all my children to be the same age as Ginger's.'

At the other side of the world, Alison was watching Ben stumbling about in a sandpit in Central Park.

'Is he yours?' A woman with a pram was sitting beside her on the bench.

'Yes,' Alison said, smiling proudly. 'He's one today!'

'Happy Birthday!' the woman called to him. 'He's cute!' she told Alison.

'Thank you.' The woman was about her age, she judged. 'Your first?' she asked, pointing at the sleeping baby in the pram.

'Yes. We left it a bit late, but we made it,' the woman joked. 'There's a lot of stuff they don't tell you, isn't there?'

'Well, they do, but you don't believe them,' Alison agreed, responding to the overture of friendship.

'A lot of good stuff too . . .'

'Oh really, such as?' Alison asked, joking.

'Well, like you meet people. You start up conversations with people in parks. Children bring you together.'

'Yes,' Alison agreed. Scenes from Ben's first year flashed through her mind. 'Yes,' she said, 'I suppose they do.'


# IMOGEN PARKER

Imogen Parker, dressed in black with an exquisite turquoise velvet-and-organza scarf draped casually round her neck, looked every inch a literary person. She turned all heads as she walked into Orso's, the atmospheric restaurant frequented by theatrical and media people and the place which she had chosen for our lunch. In fact, Imogen Parker has been turning heads in the media world for over ten years, but, until recently, as a literary agent rather than an author. She started work as a secretary at the agent Curtis Brown and moved quickly through the ranks to become a director of one of its rivals, A. P. Watt. She had a natural flair for discovering new talent and when an unsolicited novel arrived on her pile from somebody called Simon Nye, she recalls, 'I spent a whole afternoon laughing and immediately saw it as something for TV.' She was proved to be right: it became the popular TV comedy, *Men Behaving Badly*.

In fact, during her career as an agent, she launched an astounding forty-five first novels and represented numerous new and established authors. At the age of thirty-five, however, she came to a turning point in her life. 'Being an agent had become an all-consuming job. Although I loved the thrill of it, I wanted to see if there was more to life. So I went off to Spain where my husband had got a job working for the British Council. It was there that I decided to try my own hand at writing.' The result was two successful crime novels.

After returning to England she worked briefly for the BBC, spotting writing talent for their Light Entertainment Department. It was during this period that she embarked on her first novel dealing with women's issues. *More Innocent Times* found her a new audience.

It was when Imogen Parker became pregnant that she started to think about writing *These Foolish Things*. 'It wasn't that I was taking notes on my condition,' she told me, 'but I was certainly paying attention and thinking about it very much. Then, shortly after I gave birth to my son, Connor, I realised the blinding truth about the saying that having children is the great leveller—and that's essentially where the idea for the book came from. I have always been interested in writing about people's lives, and an antenatal class seemed to be an ideal place where three completely different women could meet, all of whom would have something profound in common.'

The other reason for her writing the book was Bryan Ferry's recording of the song 'These Foolish Things'. 'It is one of my great favourites and tells such a wonderful romantic story I couldn't wait to explore the lives of two people who shared such a song.'

Imogen Parker lives in London and Connor is now two and a half years old. She finds that being a mother and a writer adds up to a thoroughly fulfilling life.

*Marysia Juszczakiewicz*

Design consultants Vivid
Originations by Rodney Howe Ltd
Printed and bound by Maury Imprimeur SA, Malesherbes, France

601-002-04